Dear Octo and Ali,

thank you for your unwa

support. I hope this book become

cherished read. Best wishes,

J. McEwen"

THE NEXUS - BOOK 1

DEAD DON'T CROSS THE LINE

L. McEWEN

◆ FriesenPress

One Printers Way
Altona, MB R0G 0B0
Canada

www.friesenpress.com

ISBN
978-1-03-830667-8 (Hardcover)
978-1-03-830666-1 (Paperback)
978-1-03-830668-5 (eBook)

1. FICTION, MYSTERY & DETECTIVE, INTERNATIONAL MYSTERY & CRIME

Distributed to the trade by The Ingram Book Company

DEAD DON'T CROSS THE LINE

For my husband Ray McEwen,
My constant guiding light in the chaotic ocean of existence—
my companion, ally, and beloved. Your unwavering persistence,
constant help, and boundless support bring this book to life.
You were the architect of this dream, turning the belief in
me into reality. Not just pages, but every word of this book is
dedicated to expressing my gratitude to you. You made all of
this possible.

To my mother Wilma Thereza Camara, whose support,
encouragement, and belief in me have shaped this journey. This
book is for you, my eternal inspiration.

Prologue

Shanghai, September 11, 2013

Walking fast, almost running, Rachel crosses the busy street and enters the theatre through the first open door she sees. Inside the lobby, she runs toward the sign showing the bathroom and enters without hesitation. During the lunchtime rush, the streets turn into a chaotic maze of honking cars and bustling pedestrians, with everyone converging at once.

On the corner of Huaihai Middle Road in Shanghai, the Cathay Theatre cinema is buzzing with activity as patrons come and go, transitioning between screenings. Filled with shops, banks, shopping malls, and restaurants, the surrounding neighbourhood contributes to the region's bustling energy.

Looking at the clock, Rachel breathes a sigh of relief. She is on schedule. She and Ronaldo rehearsed their route over the weekend, ensuring a seamless transition from the Jiushi Fuxin tower to the bustling cinema. She knows Ronaldo is skilled and will get the car to the side street in a few minutes.

Her trip to the Cathay Theatre was fraught with tension. Upon seeing two men leaving the building, Rachel's senses vibrated with the certainty that they were following her. She spotted them on the twenty-first floor. Their purposeful behaviour marked them as security personnel stationed there for surveillance or protection.

I need to change, and fast, Rachel thinks, her mind racing as she pulls a bag from the pocket of her reversible jacket. With practised efficiency, she takes off her disguise, discards her wig, and discards her leggings. She turns her coat inside out, revealing its light-blue colour before readjusting it to her body. A quick change of sunglasses and a long blouse transforms Rachel's appearance, leaving her unrecognizable. Dark red lipstick applied, hair down, she metamorphosizes into a new persona.

Leaving the bathroom, Rachel stops on the sidewalk and joins a group of tourists guided by their enthusiastic leader. As she examines the movements of cars on the avenue, the lack of Ronaldo's vehicle increases her

1

anxiety. 11:30 came and went, with no sign of him. She assures herself that he is driving to the park in the middle of the congested streets.

She recalls the meticulous preparations of the previous day and ponders the various rehearsals they had carried out, adjusting every detail for today's operation. Ronaldo purchased a white 2013 Ford Focus from the airport rental office, a vehicle now lost in the sea of traffic.

Realizing that standing still will only arouse suspicion, Rachel approaches a family speaking English, her mind racing for an excuse to involve them.

"American?" she risks, getting their attention.

"Yes," comes the collective response from the man, woman, and teenager.

"Hi, I'm Brazilian," Rachel announces, her mind struggling to know her next step.

At that moment, the two shadowy figures reappear, their purposeful steps signalling their pursuit. Frozen in place, Rachel's heart races as she watches their gaze sweep across the crowd.

At that moment, Ronaldo enters the avenue and stops at the corner of the cinema.

"It was great to meet you. My ride has arrived. Bye." She smiles at the family and walks toward the vehicle. The tourists understand nothing. They smile and return the farewell wave.

She enters the back door of the Focus and takes off her clothes without thinking twice. Fortunately, the rear windows are tinted. She grabs a bag from the floor and takes out her prepared outfit. It's all there, just as she left it yesterday.

The small suitcase is still in the back seat. She opens her bag and checks: passport, wallet, car, and apartment keys. Thinking about her well-being, Ronaldo added a bottle of water.

When she sees him looking at her in the rear-view mirror, she says, "What are you looking at?" Until that moment, Rachel continues to feel agony and worry about the two men who followed her. Her heart pounds as she tries not to let her partner notice her nervousness.

As Ronaldo looks at her in the rear-view mirror, Rachel prepares for the interrogation to come.

"Did you get everything? Did he give you the files?" he demands; his tone is worried.

"Better than expected," Rachel replies, as her hands primp her new outfit.

"How so?" Ronaldo continues to press his foot on the accelerator.

"Mr. Chan handed me a flash drive," Rachel reveals, her voice tinged with triumph.

"Is that all the files?" Ronaldo's disbelief is palpable.

"He couldn't print it all, but he said he stored more on the flash drive," Rachel explains, and her deft fingers manipulate the suit onto her body.

"Oh my God! Do you believe him?" he exclaims.

"Of course! Why should I doubt that!? There was no other way," she retorts, and continues to change her clothes.

A silence settles in the car. Rachel continues her narrative. "You know how I act in these situations. When the elevator door opened, I peeked in and saw three men renovating the place. There was nothing connected to the company, just a small sign that said, 'nineteenth floor' in front of the elevator."

He looks at her in the rear-view mirror.

"You can't imagine Mr. Chan's panic when he saw me. He ran to try to hold the elevator door, almost tripping over some pieces of wood that were on the floor. He was in a hurry."

"Did he introduce himself?" Ronaldo asks, eager for details.

"No. He just got into the elevator, pulled me over, and shouted to the workers in Chinese: 'Sorry, this floor is under renovation.'"

Ronaldo shakes his head, a gesture that contains a mixture of reprimand and disbelief, disturbed by the risk of the situation.

"Well, you know I'm not fluent in Chinese. From what little I could understand, that's what he said," explains Rachel, trying to clarify the nuances of the conversation she heard.

"Rachel!" Ronaldo tries to intervene in the story, his voice rising above his usual timbre, but she interrupts him.

"Let me finish, and you focus on driving. You're going too fast. We are on the highway, and the limit here is only seventy kilometres per hour. Do you want to get a fine?!" Rachel's tone expresses concern and irritation.

He grunts in response and remains silent as she continues her story.

"When the elevator door closed, he said to me, 'I didn't have time to print. The documents that bind the companies are on this USB. Later today, I will try to pick up a few more things and deliver them to the hotel.'"

Ronaldo's silence speaks for itself, prompting Rachel to recount the tense conversation with Mr. Chan in the elevator. As she details the secret conversation, Ronaldo's expression hardens with each revelation.

"There were no cameras in the elevator. I took the flash drive; said I would travel today, and you would stay at the hotel. On the fifth floor, the elevator stopped, and about six people came in speaking Mandarin. They positioned themselves between us. When we got to the ground floor, he went left into the crowd while I headed toward the main exit, as planned. That's when I saw those two security guards from the twenty-first floor peeking through the door."

"What was this?" Ronaldo intervenes, his frustration rising.

Rachel searches her bag for her favourite bracelet and doesn't respond.

"We will discuss this later. I want to hear the rest, but before you tell me everything, let's have a meal. You must be hungry. There is an excellent Italian restaurant on the way. We still have time until boarding." His tone has softened.

"Yes, I'm starving," Rachel agrees with a tired smile, relieved that he's stopped questioning her.

1

London, 2019

Sitting in a comfortable armchair, Rachel examines the remaining documents spread out on the table from last week. Her brow furrows in concentration as she scribbles on some of them with a red pen, marking them for further attention. On others, she signs her full name with a blue pen, her thoughts focused on the task at hand.

It's a busy morning, and the secretary, Mary Lai, has just delivered a new batch of files. She mentions there is an important meeting today, and Rachel knows it's essential to understand more deeply about the company seeking her services.

The office itself is a modern oasis, designed with practicality and comfort in mind. Its blue walls and bright white marble floors create an inviting atmosphere. As the morning sun streams in through the large windows, it enhances the feeling of serenity. Rachel notes the discreet surveillance cameras positioned throughout the complex, ensuring security without attracting attention.

Rachel admits to herself that she has never heard of Sandykoni International Logistics Co. This Shanghai-based company has opened a representative office in London. Last week they contacted her for the first time and requested demand-responsive transport (DRT) services. Sandykoni mentioned problems with employees hired through a local agency but did not provide clear details.

What Rachel understands, and is always grateful for, is that a respected company in the city recommended them to Sandykoni. With that, Sandykoni scheduled a meeting for today, September 2, at 11:30 a.m., creating a moment of expectation and also uncertainty in the air.

An almost perceptible smile tugs at the corners of Rachel's lips as she reflects on the company's growth over the years. She places her pen on the stack of documents, allowing her body to relax into the chair. Memories of the challenges and milestones that led the company to its current commendable position flood her mind, making her feel safe for the recognition they now receive.

DRT International Investigations Ltd. may not be among London's biggest companies, even after almost two years in the city, but having no complaints speaks for itself. Success shows itself in all completed services.

Just as Rachel contemplates the future, Mary Lai enters the room, interrupting her reverie. Mary's voice carries a sense of urgency as she announces, "The driver will be here in five minutes. He will wait for you in the garage."

Rachel's gaze changes, noticing the subtle difference in Mary. She has applied makeup and tied her hair in a bun. David Ho, one of DRT's partners, has a long history with Mary Lai's family and was the one who brought her into the company. She is petite and slender, with cascading black hair, and her daily attire consists of a dress paired with high heels. However, today there is an added touch of elegance to her appearance.

Rachel can't help but compliment Mary, a warm smile appearing on her lips as she admits, "You look great. Are you going to an event after work?"

Mary Lai returns the smile and responds by closing the door behind her. "No. I just felt like dressing up a little, that's all."

In no time at all, Rachel jumps up from her chair, grabbing her blazer and bag from the sofa. Just as she heads for the door, her cellphone interrupts her hasty exit. Her response is understandable. "I'm leaving the office. Can we talk later?" Her hand on the doorknob, she hears the response.

Rachel, with a serious expression, asks, her tone rising, "Is it urgent?" She shakes her head and continues listening. "What are you trying to say? I don't understand. We covered this over two years ago. Now there's a new lead, a new investigation going in another direction? You stated that the investigation was closed and filed in both countries!"

Agitated, Rachel closes the door, moving back into her office. She sits in an armchair, listening. "I'm leaving now. I can't be late. Tomorrow morning, come to the office, bring everything, and we'll talk."

She mutters something inaudible under her breath, then gets up from her chair and opens the door. "Okay, I'll see you tomorrow," she says, determination in her voice.

Without hesitation, she heads toward the elevator. As she passes Mary Lai's desk, she adds, "Allan Liu from Interpol will be here early tomorrow. Please locate David and Tyler. Tell them to be here in the office at eight sharp."

Mary nods in acknowledgement, but raises a valid concern: "Okay, but if they don't respond, what should I do?" She knows all too well that contacting David and Tyler on their cellphones is often a challenge.

Rachel either doesn't notice or doesn't care about Mary's response. The elevator doors close, leaving her alone with her thoughts.

Her mind focuses on the contract she is about to sign, but Allan Liu's words echo in her head: "We have new information, and we will have to investigate. I know it has been over two years since the case was closed by both the Chinese and Brazilian police, but you need to know what's reached us. One fact… his death may not have been an accident." The gravity of the accusation weighs on her. The elevator descends and uncertainty looms on the horizon.

Stepping out of the elevator into the bright garage, her high heels on the cold cement floor echo in the silence. The driver, a man named Hassan, looks in her direction, dropping his cigarette on the ground and trying to hide it with his impeccable polished black shoes. Despite his efforts, the lingering smell of mint hangs in the air.

"Good morning." He offers a warm smile as he opens the back door of the car.

Rachel, still carrying the weight of her previous conversation, responds nonchalantly as she enters the vehicle. "Good morning, Hassan. I'm sorry I'm late."

"It's okay," Hassan reassures her, closing the door.

Inside the car, Rachel takes a moment to appreciate the immaculate interior, infused with the gentle scent of lavender. Her gaze meets Hassan's in the rear-view mirror as he speaks.

"Would you like to hear some music?" he offers.

"No thanks. I'm not in the mood today," she declines, reaching for the phone in her purse.

Determined, she makes two calls, one to Tyler and another to David. As expected, neither of them answers, which leads Rachel to leave assertive voice messages.

"Tyler, where are you? Give me some news."

"David, you promised you would be at this meeting with me. I'm on my way now."

Rachel can't help but wonder where her partners are on this rainy Monday morning. Both know their presence is necessary at these negotiations. The weather reflects her mood. Dark clouds appear in the sky, and rain falls in heavy torrents. A strange feeling of discomfort washes over her.

She tries to process this morning's call, dealing with the implications. With a voice tinged with disbelief, Rachel mutters, prompting Hassan to overhear, "I can't believe it… I'm sure this information isn't 'A1'; it's not attested and true."

Hassan notices her discomfort. "Everything okay?"

Rachel looks out into the pouring rain with a thoughtful expression and responds, "Yes." Her thoughts are turbulent, a mixture of uncertainty and apprehension clouding her mind as the car passes through the soaked streets.

As Rachel sits in the car, her thoughts return to her longtime friendship with Allan. He has been more than a friend; he is like a brother to her. Allan has always been a valuable source of information, assisting her in investigations ranging from money laundering to drug trafficking. Both have worked together on various intelligence operations during their time as federal agents. However, in 2015, during a challenging operation, she made the hard decision to leave the Brazilian Federal Police.

"What he suggested… can't be true? It's not possible… I don't want to live through that hell again. We'll see tomorrow what he'll show us," she mutters to herself, contemplating the weight of Allan's revelation.

Looking in the rear-view mirror, Rachel notices the driver watching her. She takes a deep breath, reminding herself to maintain her composure.

Rachel knows that Allan's information has the potential to alter the course of past events. After growing tired of the intelligence world, she accepted David's invitation to join him in creating a private investigation company. Trust and loyalty have always been paramount in their line of work, and partnering with David and Tyler, who both had many years of experience in law enforcement, seemed like the right decision.

Rachel's phone rings, and she reads the message from David: *I'm coming.*

Tyler Scott Hart, one of her partners, is a retired RCMP (Royal Canadian Mounted Police) officer. He brought to the team a wealth of investigative experience and a strong affinity for various types of weaponry. Rachel and Tyler had worked together at "the Firm," and his strong reputation as a team player, known for his loyalty and leadership qualities, made him the ideal choice for this new venture.

The other partner, David Ho, was born in Shanghai but grew up in the US. With two decades of experience as an FBI special agent, he decided to venture into the world of private investigations. David recognizes the value of Rachel and Tyler's experience as former police officers, and together they founded DRT International Investigations Ltd. They headquartered the company at the Gold Gate House building, 10301 Duke Street, London E013A7L, United Kingdom.

She looks out the window, her eyes catching a glimmer of hope that she won't get wet. The rain begins to ease, allowing the sun to peek through the dispersing clouds.

Rachel rests a moment and leans her head back, reflecting on her past. Eight years as an agent in the Brazilian Federal Police, and when she left the police force, she moved to the US and lived with her father. It was a crucial moment in her life, which allowed the chance to redefine her path. What followed was two years at Ponac International Corporation, the Firm, a secretive private international espionage group full of intelligence analysts. The organization operates in over thirty countries, collecting information for various clients and providing specialized services.

A familiar ringtone on Rachel's cellphone alerts her to a new message. She checks.

"Hassan, please let me know three minutes before we arrive at the address." Hassan nods and continues to watch her in the rear-view mirror.

Rachel takes a deep breath and flips her long black hair; it cascades over her left shoulder. She can't help but wonder if Hassan will dream about her tonight, a fleeting thought that brings a smile to her lips.

"We're three minutes away; I'm going to stop at the restaurant's entrance," announces Hassan.

Rachel's eyes scan the cars lining the wet streets, noticing that the rain has now eased to a gentle drizzle. Despite the uncertainty of the day, she is determined to face it with grace and determination, helped by her partners.

2

Friends Forever

Waking up from a cozy sleep to go to work is never easy, but for those passionate about their jobs, early mornings possess a unique charm. As Rachel enters the company's waiting room, she turns on the lights and deactivates the alarm panel, greeted by the gentle scent of lavender from nearby plants. A sudden sound catches her attention, leading her to open the door to the main room. Inside, she finds David engrossed in the papers she had left on the table the day before.

"Did you fall out of bed? It's only 7:30 in the morning," she teases with a smile as she approaches him.

"I'm impressed with the scent. You look great this morning. Any plans for later? Any more meetings scheduled?" David asks.

Rachel laughs. Her tiredness is clear. "No, nothing scheduled. Let's just start planning the investigation we secured yesterday, and thanks for the compliment... you're so kind. Not sure where you got the idea that I look great, considering I didn't sleep at all last night," she says, pointing at the dark circles under her eyes.

"Since 6:30 a.m. I've been here. I didn't sleep well either. Why didn't this company come to the office to sign the contract? I mean, I love that restaurant. The food was fantastic, but it's not economical." David stifles a yawn.

"It doesn't matter if it was there or here. I used our standard contract and added a few specific requirements. After they signed, I photographed the signatures. If we have any additional requirements for this investigation, they have already accepted the condition of signing a new document in the future. I included that addendum in the contract."

David nods, his concern still visible. "I understand, but I couldn't help but think... maybe we should have been more cautious, not accepted all of their terms. Having to share information about our reports? Where is our autonomy in the investigation? I just don't like it. You know me... I prefer a rational process from start to finish."

"Don't worry, the three of us will complete this investigation in no time, and we won't share any details about our progress." Rachel settles onto the couch and opens yesterday's newspaper.

Rachel tries to conceal her tension, her mind filled with thoughts of what Allan had revealed. The possibility of that frightening nightmare resurfacing weighs on her. It seemed they had buried, sealed, and accepted the past, but now, things have taken an unexpected turn. She glances at David Ho, noticing he is engrossed in his notebook.

The office door opens, and Tyler Scott Hart walks in with a wide, care-free smile, holding a box of doughnuts. As always, he's dressed in faded jeans, a white shirt, and a black leather jacket. He is smoking a cigarette.

"Am I late?" Tyler jokes, placing his cigarette in the ashtray on the coffee table.

"As always…" David retorts, his tone teasing.

"You're all marinated in cigarettes," Rachel comments.

Sitting next to her, Tyler seems unfazed by the lingering smell, showing no intention of quitting anytime soon. Rachel returns the newspaper to its place.

"Yesterday was fantastic. I ate like there was no tomorrow. It's been a long time since I've eaten at an excellent restaurant." Tyler picks up the same newspaper his partner was reading.

"A very fancy restaurant. The food is exquisite, but it's quite expensive," Rachel counters, making a playful face at Tyler.

"I'm glad they paid the lunch bill," David interjects, looking up from his notes.

"Rachel! This newspaper's from yesterday." Tyler frowns, placing it back on the table.

She doesn't respond, just mutters something inaudible under her breath.

"Any update from Allan?" Tyler asks, pulling out his phone.

"He should arrive between 8 and 8:30 a.m.," Rachel replies.

Tyler suggests, "Do we have time for a quick coffee?"

"All you think about is food," David retorts.

Rachel lets out a light laugh, easing some of the tension in the room.

Mary Lai enters the room with a friendly smile, greeting everyone with a warm, "Good morning."

"Good morning," the three respond in unison.

With a nod, the secretary acknowledges them. "Could you make me a coffee?" David requests.

"Of course, I'll do it right away," Mary Lai replies before leaving the office.

Rachel checks the clock on the wall, noting it is already 8:00 a.m. Allan has not arrived yet, so they begin to discuss yesterday's meeting while waiting.

"I had trouble sleeping last night. I couldn't stop thinking about the individuals the director introduced as security guards. Did you notice they were sitting at the table next to ours?" David expresses his discomfort. "Something just doesn't sit well with me. What about their offer to pay double our usual rate? I understand the director's urgency and desperation, but I'm not comfortable with that kind of attitude, not to mention their demands."

David paces, voicing his concerns, trying to engage his partners.

Rachel and Tyler, aware of David's tendency to delve into details, focus on their phones, knowing he won't stop his complaints anytime soon.

"I felt he's anxious about what we might discover, perhaps something he doesn't want. That's why he desires to monitor our every move," David concludes, seeking a response from his partners.

Tyler, smiling, tells his partner he needs to check something on his phone.

"This is a serious matter! I'm convinced something isn't right," David repeats.

"Don't worry, if anything seems wrong, I'll look into it. You know I'm the genius among us," Tyler assures, making Rachel laugh.

David is always the most fervent in any situation, demanding meticulous explanations for every detail. Tyler shares something with Rachel on his phone, and the two engage in a hushed conversation about the topic at hand.

Mary Lai opens the door, announcing Allan's arrival. The Interpol agent enters, hugging each member one by one. He gives Rachel kisses on the cheek, saying, "I missed you so much."

"Me too. Leave Interpol and come work here with us," she jokes.

"You know I can't right now. I have a ten-month-old baby, and my wife would kill me if we had to move to London. She would never leave her mom and dad alone in Toronto. Don't worry, I will always find a way to irritate the three of you," Allan explains with a playful wink.

Rachel smiles, nodding in understanding.

The Interpol agent heads to the large conference table, taking out some folders from his backpack and placing them on the table.

David sits at the head of the table, with Rachel to Allan's right and Tyler sitting across from them. Mary Lai enters the room carrying a tray with pitchers of coffee, tea, and milk as well as four cups. The box of doughnuts joins a box of cookies on a nearby table.

"Mary, please, if anyone calls, take a message. We can't be interrupted right now," David instructs without looking up from the folder Allan handed him.

"Don't worry," she assures, closing the door behind her.

Allan begins to reveal the reason for his visit.

"David, Tyler, do you remember Rachel's trip to Shanghai with Ronaldo in 2013? Maybe not all the details, but we all remember one thing: Ronaldo's death."

Everyone at the table nods in acknowledgement, and Rachel responds in a subdued tone.

With a serious expression, Allan continues, "Two weeks ago, there was an international operation conducted by the Portuguese Federal Police in collaboration with the Chinese police in Shanghai. The Portuguese Federal Police detained several individuals in Portugal, and they arrested their major target in Shanghai. Before you ask any questions... we link this operation to money laundering, human, and drug trafficking."

A cough interrupts Allan. He pauses mid-sentence, collecting his thoughts before continuing, "When the police detained the major target... I cannot guarantee the accuracy of what I am about to reveal, as I was not present at the scene. However, the operation report documents this, and I have attached it to the file I brought you. As soon as the Chinese police reported the incident to Interpol, we requested a copy of the process, which you can read in the yellow folder I gave David."

"Please continue, Allan," encourages Tyler.

Rachel maintains her intense focus, attention glued to the agent's every word.

Allan continues his narrative: "At the time of the arrest in Shanghai, they detained the target, along with several accomplices. They resisted arrest until Portuguese and Chinese police subdued them."

Taking a deep breath, Allan continues in a calm tone: "During the arrest, one of the Portuguese police officers, the one who handcuffed the suspect, heard the prisoner making some guttural sounds and approached him. The prisoner said in Mandarin, 'You are going to die. You will die like the policeman in the hotel, but this time your family won't escape.' The Portuguese agents didn't understand the statement in Mandarin, but the Chinese agents did."

As Allan pours tea into a cup, the room fills with the fragrant aroma of jasmine. The partners, absorbed in the story, remain silent, paying attention to every word.

Balancing the porcelain cup in his hand, Allan continues: "Upon arriving at the police station, one of the Chinese police officers reports to the police chief what he has heard. A Brazilian federal police agent's death in a Shanghai hotel in 2013 is the focus of the story. The police chief is familiar with the case and interrogates the suspect. The suspect denies he made any threatening statements at the time of his arrest.

"I want to emphasize that this is all documented," Allan adds, his eyes shifting from one partner to another as he takes two more folders out of his backpack.

David and Tyler grab a folder each, open it, and begin reading, committed to understanding the details of the case.

Rachel looks at the three sitting around the table and states, "I want to talk to that man."

In unison, all three companions respond with a resounding, "No."

Rachel asks, "Why not? No one knows better than me if what he said is true or not."

Allan voices his concerns: "You can't just go in there and question someone without a full understanding of the situation. If what he said is correct, it implies that events could differ from what we believe we know. We still don't understand who may be involved in this."

Rachel and David ask together, "How different?"

Allan stands up from his chair, taking a few steps away from the table before turning to them. "This individual is a Japanese national connected to the Yakuza mafia. The entire operation revolves around expanding the Yakuza in Portugal. He is some high-ranking bigwig, responsible for establishing the mafia in Lisbon and other cities for some time. As you know, his activities include drug trafficking, prostitution, clandestine gambling, human trafficking, money laundering, and much more. Interpol has been cooperating with the Portuguese authorities for some time now, but we were not aware that he had a lover in Shanghai. This only became known when he left and visited her, which caught us off guard and prevented his arrest in Portugal."

Rachel looks at Allan, expressing concern.

Allan continues, now addressing Rachel: "It was Interpol informants who tracked him down in Shanghai. Using all the relevant data in our possession, we negotiated a joint operation with the Chinese police to arrest him. We got the consent and cooperation of the Portuguese and Chinese governments."

Taking another sip of tea and grimacing at the cold temperature, Allan sets the cup back on the table. The room falls silent as the gravity of the situation sinks in and everyone contemplates the implications of Allan's revelation. The agent continues his narrative. "The Japanese government requested a new investigation five days ago, demanding that the prisoner be tried in Japan because of his citizenship. We are no longer involved. We have completed our responsibilities. Interpol will continue its investigation, but considering Ronaldo's case is not a recent incident, we cannot reopen it without concrete evidence."

David rises from his chair, declaring his intention: "I'm going to Shanghai. There's an FBI office there, and I'm confident they'll help me in any way they can."

Allan acknowledges the challenge but warns, "Getting access to this man in a Shanghai prison will be difficult, but you can try."

Rachel asserts herself. "I'm going with you."

Allan sighs, recalling a past operation, and raises a topic: "Do you remember the operation you and Ronaldo led in 2009, which resulted in the arrest of a Yakuza boss?" Rachel confirms, her gaze locked on Allan.

With a solemn expression, Allan recounts: "You, Ronaldo, and two other partners dismantled and disrupted all attempts by the Yakuza organization to establish a presence in São Paulo and other Brazilian states. You didn't allow them any opportunity to prosper and set roots."

The DRT partners note Allan's growing discomfort. "Rachel, let's be clear. The Yakuza suffered enormous losses during that operation. You and

Ronaldo dismantled their operations in São Paulo and beyond, closing restaurants, karaoke bars, brothels, clandestine casinos, and tourist agencies. The flow of 'protection money' from local businesses dried up. They have to sell the baseball and football teams they owned, and the consequences... Do you remember the victims? They know they can't return to Brazil in the same way. You may have opened doors for the Chinese Triad, but you closed them to the Yakuza. Maybe things have changed; I'm not sure. Your operation with Ronaldo became legendary and serves as a 'textbook' for aspiring investigators. So, do you think the Yakuza have forgotten about you?" Allan concludes, wiping his forehead with his handkerchief.

Rachel bites her lip, deep in thought, her friend's words weighing on her. She hasn't considered the full extent of the consequences of that operation. David and Tyler share the same thought-filled silence.

"Allan, is this related to Ronaldo's death?" David asks.

"I'm still uncertain; we are still investigating, but it's a possibility we can't ignore," Allan replies, tired.

The partners remain silent, contemplating the gravity of the situation.

Allan addresses Rachel again, his voice soft but firm. "You didn't answer me, Rachel."

She rises from her chair, slowly walking to the window. Meanwhile, David and Tyler examine the documents.

Allan hesitates, then lets the unspoken words hang in the air.

Rachel, lost in thought, reflects on the profound changes since Ronaldo's death in 2013. He was her first and only love, her partner in every sense of the word. Everyone in the federal police knew about their affection, though they kept it secret.

When Ronaldo's body arrived in Brazil, among his belongings from Shanghai was a box containing a gold ring with diamonds. The receipt revealed he purchased it on September 11, 2013, the day she returned to Brazil. He planned to surprise her with this during their beach date. Maybe, she thinks, he was planning to propose.

Rachel refocuses on the meeting. "I don't care if it relates to Operation Yakuza. Ronaldo is dead, and this situation ended four years ago. I have contacts in the Portuguese Federal Police who knew Ronaldo. They would help me."

"You don't speak Mandarin, and most police in Shanghai don't speak English. I will accompany you; we will both seek the truth," David declares.

"If you go, act before they transfer the prisoner to Japan, which I'm sure will happen soon. Once he leaves, it will be too late," warns Allan.

Tyler, indulging in a doughnut, addresses the partners. "DRT has two investigations underway. The one I'm handling is almost complete; it just requires an address to be closed. Now, I can start the contract we signed yesterday without you two. How long do you plan to stay in Shanghai?"

"I don't know," David responds, devoid of emotion.

"A week at least? Then we can decide our next steps," Rachel adds.

"Alright, I'll handle everything here. Don't worry," Tyler confirms, taking another bite.

Allan offers his support. "We at Interpol will do our best to help uncover new information. I'll keep you updated."

With years of experience, Rachel analyzes the situation. "Everything we discuss here isn't reliable. An almost two-year investigation by the Brazilian and Chinese federal police, conducted with the help of these governments and Interpol, based on forensic analysis, security camera footage, eyewitnesses, body examination, and more, concludes it was an accident. I won't discredit the entire investigation unless we have concrete evidence to support your claims linking it to the Yakuza. I am not undermining your credibility, Allan, but we need solid evidence."

Her partners nod as Rachel continues, maintaining a serene tone with a touch of sadness. "You're right, Allan. We won and they'll never forget it. We dismantled their entire operation, much like what the Portuguese police just did." She lowers her gaze, takes a deep breath, and says, "However, the Portuguese police didn't arrest this man in their territory. He is in the custody of the Chinese authorities, preparing for extradition to Japan. See the problem? There will be no consequences for this man. Therefore, the sooner we contact the prisoner, wherever he is, the sooner we can discover the truth. All this being related to what you said, and if there is any connection with what happened in Brazil, such as the Yakuza, the container operation, and Ronaldo's death, we will need to investigate and establish these links."

"You're right," everyone agrees almost simultaneously.

"Let's get to work; we have a busy day ahead. I'll get back to you later," David says, leaving the office while giving Allan a thumbs-up.

Tyler gives Rachel a quick kiss on the cheek, hugs Allan, and adds, "I'm going to meet with my informant now. I'm counting on everything he brings to help me wrap up the accountant's investigation today." Before leaving, he turns to Allan. "I'll call you later this afternoon. How about we grab dinner together?"

Allan nods and sits with Rachel; the silence is palpable. "Aren't you going to invite me to lunch? It's already 12:30 and I'm starving."

Rachel smiles. "How about an Italian restaurant? I know an authentic one. Yesterday, we ended up at a restaurant David claimed was Italian, but everyone ordered steaks. Today, I want authentic food, something like 'Mom's kitchen.' It's simple, but cozy. And then, if you want, I can show you the flat I bought in Bethnal Green. It'll take me a lifetime to pay for it, but it's worth it… it's all mine."

"Sounds good to me," Allan agrees, returning the smile as he rises from the sofa. He retrieves Rachel's coat and purse, and they both make their way to the door.

"Let's take a taxi to the restaurant. After a leisurely meal, we can stroll to the apartment; it's just a six-minute walk. Then we can catch another taxi back to the office. Is that okay? Sorry, I haven't bought a car yet and I'm not even sure if I want one," Rachel explains, her hands moving as she speaks. She catches Allan looking at her with admiration.

Despite the challenges they face and those that lie ahead, Rachel is determined to ensure that Allan enjoys his brief stay in London, seeking a relaxed, stress-free environment. She holds onto the belief that tomorrow will differ from yesterday, so why not embrace the moment with a smile? Rachel feels happy and at ease in Allan's company.

Allan opens the door, and they step out of the office, embarking on what promises to be a delightful lunch.

3

The Death of Ronaldo

In 2013, Ronaldo and Rachel head to Petra Mio, a splendid restaurant known for its authentic Italian cuisine, just a fifteen-minute drive from the Cathay Theatre. As they walk in, Rachel feels impressed. The atmosphere is perfect, reminiscent of the cozy Italian cantinas she frequented in Brazil. They choose a table in a quiet and strategic corner, away from the bustling conversation of other customers.

"How did you find this restaurant? I love it!" Rachel exclaims, her eyes dancing with excitement.

Ronaldo smiles, delighted with her reaction. "I asked the receptionists at the hotel where there was a typical Italian cantina in Shanghai. They told me about this place. I called ahead and confirmed that we didn't need a reservation for lunch, and here we are. The most important thing is that you like it."

The waiter arrives, presenting them with menus and asking about their drink preferences. As Rachel examines the menu, she notices Ronaldo's thoughtful gaze fixed on her. She meets his gaze and smiles before deciding. "I'll have the lasagna, please."

Ronaldo nods and addresses the waiter: "Bring half a bottle of house red wine, fusilli with polpetone, and for the lady, a lasagna with Bolognese sauce."

The waiter takes the order and nods, leaving. While they wait for the food, Ronaldo, curious, asks about Rachel's activities. "So, what happened in that building?" he asks, leaning closer.

Rachel reaches into her bag and pulls out a flash drive and passes it to him. He takes it from her, their fingers touching. Concern fills his eyes as he gives her gentle advice: "It's best if it stays with you."

Rachel shrugs, puts the flash drive in her purse, and begins her story: "Before talking to Chan, I took the elevator straight to the twenty-first floor. I had about seven or eight minutes to spare. Sunday night at the hotel, I looked for the name 'Konsako' in the yellow pages and found it at the same address we visited today. Forgive me, but I had to confirm that stamp on the packages seized at the 'Operation Container' port. You know, it all seems too coincidental. As they say, there is no such thing as a coincidence."

"You should have mentioned that," he says, concerned.

"I apologize for making assumptions on my own, but for me, it is important," Rachel continues, brushing aside his concern. "When I got out of the elevator, I saw the name 'Konsako Chemistry Lab Enterprises INC' engraved on a glass door. Everything happened so fast, maybe ten seconds. I saw four security guards, four men, bigger than you…" Her voice disappears when she notices the waiter approaching the table.

The waiter serves the wine in crystal glasses. Ronaldo takes a sip, and his nod of approval shows the quality of the wine. Italian music with a lively "tarantella" rhythm begins to play, infusing the place with joy. Other customers enter, creating a lively atmosphere with their conversations and dragging chairs.

"Let's make a toast," suggests Ronaldo.

They both raise their wineglasses, and he proclaims, "To the most wonderful woman, partner, and friend in this world—you, Rachel."

Rachel, looking at him with love, replies, "To the sweetest, most intelligent, best partner—you, Ronaldo."

They clink glasses and look at each other for a moment longer than expected. Rachel shifts her focus back to her story.

"Now, where were we? Ah yes, the elevator. The doors open. I find myself face to face with these four imposing men. The way they are dressed is unbelievable. Remember the Yakuza in that supermarket? They look just like that. I watch one of them heading toward the stairs, while the other two stay inside the office talking in a language that isn't Mandarin. I think it's Japanese, but I can't be sure. The fourth man walks in front of the elevator. It is obvious that he carries a weapon. My best guess is they are company security." Rachel pauses, taking another sip of wine and studying her partner's reaction.

The waiter brings their steaming plates of food, and the generous portions, combined with the tantalizing aroma of the tomato sauce, are impossible to resist. The ambience of the restaurant is impeccable, with the

Italian flag colours on the wallpaper, matching tablecloths and napkins, and a captivating display case at the back. They stock the shelves with a variety of wine bottles while a clothesline displays several types of sausages, salami, and a variety of cheeses. It's the quintessential Italian cantina.

"Continue, tell me the rest," insists Ronaldo, enjoying a forkful of fusilli. He closes his eyes, reveling in the tempting mix of spices, the acidity of the tomato sauce, and the touch of pepper: a pleasant explosion on his palate.

"My God, this food is delicious," he raves.

The delicious aroma of the meal, the busy restaurant full of customers talking and laughing, the ambient music, and the wine combine to make that cold and cloudy day more than perfect.

After lunch, the waiter returns, and Ronaldo orders coffee for both of them before asking for the bill. Rachel looks at her watch; it's already 2:00 p.m. Her concern is apparent, but Ronaldo assures her that the journey to the airport will only take fifty minutes, ensuring she will arrive on time.

After forty minutes of driving, Ronaldo parks the car at one of the airport gates. They kiss, and he regrets not staying in the same hotel as her.

"I'm going to miss you," he confesses, his emotions exposed.

"I love you so much, Ronaldo; you are my world," Rachel replies with a smile and eyes full of affection. "Please take care of yourself. Let's get together on Thursday morning at work and spend the weekend at the beach. I need a tan," she adds with a wink as she grabs her suitcase and heads to the airport.

As she passes through the automated glass door, another world unfolds before her. What she sees, hears, smells, and feels shows her a new adventure that awaits her on the horizon. At least, that's what Rachel believes.

Rachel can hear the names of passengers being called over the intercom in English and Mandarin. Flight arrivals are announced, as are departures and delay announcements. She observes people sitting, others walking in high heels, creating a symphony of sharp clicks on the floor, while the wheels of suitcases roll on the marble. All this sensory information bombards her at the same instant.

She walks through the busy terminal, finding a long open area that leads to several airline check-in counters. She approaches, but the seductive aroma of coffee emanating from a Tim Hortons kiosk tempts her. Rachel decides to give up on buying the tempting nectar, knowing that the airport is crowded, and she doesn't want to risk missing her flight.

Today, her journey takes her from Shanghai to Toronto. Tomorrow she'll board another plane from Toronto to Miami, and on Wednesday morning fly from Miami to São Paulo. The scheduled departure time for her flight from Shanghai to Toronto is 6:15 p.m., leaving her three hours until boarding. However, before that, she needs to go through security and check-in.

Once she locates the departure screen, she confirms she has arrived on time. So, she goes to the counter to get her boarding pass but encounters an intimidating line of about a hundred people in front of her. As she waits in line, she can't help but expect the trip will be tiring, especially since she has decided to visit her father in Miami. She misses him, as well as her stepmother and the twins, whom she hasn't seen in a while. Regret weighs on her. She doesn't have enough time to visit her mother in Toronto, but she takes comfort in knowing that she will plan a trip to Canada for her next vacation.

"I imagine I'll sleep through this entire trip," she comments in a louder tone than usual. A gentleman in front of her in line turns to look at her, wearing a serious expression. Rachel apologizes in Mandarin, but the man remains silent, looking straight ahead. Meanwhile, the flight attendants call passengers from the business class line, and like the others in line, she holds her passport and follows the flight attendant.

Turbulent fights marked Rachel's childhood with her parents, John and Catherine. Life in a military family always has a price, especially when a high rank is involved. Constant upheavals and moves to different cities and states and even countries were normal in her family because of John's profession. Catherine never adapted to this nomadic lifestyle, struggling to understand that for John, the army was everything. Rachel, from a young age, was always on the move, unable to make lasting friendships because of frequent school changes. It was a reality that caused Catherine and Rachel to lose many friends and connections over the years.

Then came the day when her parents took her to the park and informed her that they were getting divorced. They decided Rachel would stay with her mother. It was a devastating blow for her, a ten-year-old girl who witnessed her father leaving the house carrying suitcases. Disillusionment plagued her for several years, but the demands of everyday life strengthened her more than she could have ever imagined.

Four years after their separation, John retired from military service. He used to say that he met "the woman of his life," Milla, who was still serving in the army when they fell in love. John married Milla, and after a few years, they had twins, Bradley and Anthony, who were now nine years old.

Rachel has a deep affection for Milla because she has witnessed her father's transformation. Milla gave him a new life, transforming him into a happier man in the end, which is what matters to Rachel.

Arriving in Miami amid hugs and kisses, the five of them leave the airport and decide to go eat some burgers. The children are overjoyed to see Rachel, but their excitement seems even more pronounced when they realize they are about to devour burgers.

"Ronaldo didn't come with you?" John asks, holding hands with Milla and hugging Rachel, almost suffocating her.

"No, he left Shanghai today and will arrive in São Paulo tomorrow night on a direct flight. It's going to be an endless trip," Rachel replies, laughing with the boys at the table.

"Dad, I just want to get home and sleep. I'm so tired," she adds, her eyelids almost closed with exhaustion.

"I can imagine. What time is your flight tomorrow?"

"At 8 a.m. I need to be at the airport by 6 a.m."

"Why don't you stay another day?"

"There are too many things I need to handle at home. I have to take care of them tomorrow. I promised my boss I'd be at my desk on Thursday the fourteenth."

"Don't worry. When we get home, take a shower, go straight to your room and get some rest. I'll wake you up. You can say goodbye to the boys tonight," suggests her father.

She nods in agreement.

In her room, just before bed, Rachel sends a message to Ronaldo, but gets no response.

The next day, the trip to São Paulo goes well, but she still hasn't received a response to the messages she sent to Ronaldo.

As Rachel had promised her boss, on Thursday at 8:00 a.m., she is in the intelligence office talking to her colleagues. The team shows a lot of respect and admiration for her. In this sector, unity is fundamental, as each person's life, especially during operations or investigations, is often in the hands of their partners. In this police sector, loyalty, trust, and honesty play a crucial role in ensuring the integrity of agents and information.

Everyone in intelligence is eager to hear about Rachel's recent trip to China during the Carnival holiday. Curiosity takes over the office, and her colleagues can't wait to see the photos and hear all the stories. They bombard her with questions, and Rachel obliges, sharing her experiences and handing out the gifts she has bought. She doesn't stop smiling and looking relaxed, having returned from a wonderful vacation, and the atmosphere in the office is nothing short of celebratory.

Rachel, however, becomes worried when she sends another message to Ronaldo and receives no response. This marks the tenth message she has sent, and discomfort begins to plague her.

Her immediate boss calls her by her code name, "Jane." Everyone on the police force knows her by that nickname, but those closest to her only call her by her real name, Rachel.

"Jane, come to my office." Roberto is the subdivision's deputy chief of intelligence.

Rachel walks into his office, greets him with a warm smile, and says, "Good morning. How are you? How was your vacation? Did you party at Carnival?"

"Thank God I had a lot of fun with my family on the farm. Where is Ronaldo?" he asks, rolling up one of the little pieces of paper he always carries, a peculiarity when he is thinking or worried about something.

She explains Ronaldo should have arrived by now but hasn't responded to any of her messages. She doesn't know his whereabouts but suspects he might be at home with his mother.

Ronaldo's mother, Nancy, suffers from Alzheimer's and needs twenty-four-hour care. Ronaldo visits her every day, hoping that his presence will prevent her from forgetting him, although the illness affects her memory.

The phone rings and Roberto answers, muttering some words that Rachel can't understand.

"Hmm, are you sure?" he asks. "You're not sure… It's okay, I'll go up with her." When he hangs up, Roberto stares at the wall in front of him.

Turning to Rachel, Roberto, in a serious tone, announces, "Jane, I don't know what's going on, but they want to talk to you on the twentieth floor in the superintendent's office. I'll go with you. Wait for me in the elevator."

Rachel leaves the room, feeling a sense of unease in the air. She checks her phone again for messages, but there are none.

Paulo Saghantio, a general superintendent of the federal police in the state of São Paulo, is around fifty-five years old, has fair skin, green eyes, and a tall, slender body. He always wears a suit, and his accent reveals his Southern roots whenever he speaks.

"Let's go up; it's some new task," Jane comments as they enter the elevator. She looks at Roberto and notices that his face is a little damp, as if he has just splashed water on it.

Upon reaching the twentieth-floor lobby, the secretary announces their arrival, and they are guided to the superintendent's office. The secretary offers them coffee, but they decline. Jane and Roberto sit on the sofa, waiting while their superior talks to an unknown oriental man. After a while, the man leaves the room.

Paulo Saghantio gestures for the two of them to sit in the armchairs in front of his table. With a heavy heart and a tired expression on his face, he speaks, his tone serious.

"What I have to say is not good... Jane, when was the last time you spoke to Ronaldo?"

Jane looks at the superintendent in surprise and replies in a trembling voice: "It was on Monday the eleventh when he dropped me off at Shanghai airport." Her intuition advises that something is bad. "Did something happen?"

"Why didn't you guys come back together?" the boss asks, his gaze unwavering.

Jane explains that she wanted to visit her father in Miami and arrived a day early to spend time there. Ronaldo didn't change his ticket because it would have cost more. Anxiety plagues her as she begs, "Please, what happened?"

The superintendent stands up and walks toward the two. Roberto, sitting, watches the scene unfold with a heavy heart.

"Ronaldo passed away on Monday night," explains Paulo Saghantio, his voice shaking as he wipes a tear from his eye. "At the hotel in Shanghai where he was staying, he suffered a fall, bumped his head on the pool's corner. There was nobody available to offer help. I'm afraid he drowned."

Dazed, a tight feeling in her chest, Jane looks at the superintendent, panting. "I'm sorry, I don't think I understand what you're talking about."

Roberto reaches out to touch Jane's arm and asks, "Are you okay?"

She looks at Roberto, her voice shaking as she replies, "Yes, I'm fine. I just don't understand." She covers her face with her hands for a moment before looking at Paulo Saghantio with eyes filled with disbelief. "Oh my God. Are you sure about this?"

The superintendent picks up a piece of paper from his desk, his voice soft but heavy with the weight of delivering painful news.

"Jane, I want you to stay calm and try to understand what I'm about to explain," he begins. "Based on information we received from the Chinese embassy, Ronaldo was swimming at night in the hotel pool, as he did every day during his stay there. At 8 p.m., he called the kitchen and placed an order, and a waiter brought him a bottle of whiskey and some poolside snacks."

The superintendent settles into his armchair, his forehead shining with sweat, despite the air conditioning being on full blast. He wipes his forehead with a tissue and continues telling what the director general of the federal police told him.

"On Mondays, the hotel is empty, and most of the employees have the day off. Because of this, there was no one else swimming in the pool. Ronaldo made another call to reception, asking for an extra towel. The towel delivery took a little longer because they needed to find someone to do it. After about fifteen minutes, they placed the order; a laundry employee went in person. When he arrived, he found Ronaldo lying with his head submerged in the water. There was a pool of blood on the pool tiles, confirming the place where he hit his head."

Paulo Saghantio pauses, struggling to maintain his composure, his eyes filling with tears as he continues. "The employee called Ronaldo's name many times, but there was no response. Unfortunately, it was too late to save him. It appears he slipped on the tiles when getting out of the pool. A terrible accident."

Rachel sits there, not crying, in shock, unable to process the tragic news.

In that moving moment, she understands why Paulo feels the urgency to speak now, realizing that failing to communicate everything that needs to be said could make an already distressing situation even worse. She knows this is a conversation that will stay with her for a long time.

Roberto, his voice full of sadness, asks, "And the body? Was there an autopsy? Do you know anything about the investigation?"

"Forensic work began at the accident site on Monday night, including examining the body," Paulo replies, his voice full of sadness. "The police discovered his federal police badge in his hotel room and on the same day informed the Brazilian embassy in China. All investigations and reports will be forwarded to us in a timely manner. The Shanghai Forensic Medical Institute classified it as an accidental death resulting from a fall followed by drowning."

Paulo pauses, lowering his head before continuing. "We have already informed Ronaldo's family, and we are making preparations to transfer the body. It should arrive on either Saturday or Sunday. We will receive further updates."

He looks at Rachel with deep sympathy before speaking again. "Rachel, I understand this is difficult for you to hear, but accidents happen. Accidental falls are the second leading cause of death worldwide among people of all ages. This type of death is sudden and unpredictable. We must accept that."

Roberto, overcome by pain, cannot contain his tears, wiping them away as he fights against despair.

Paulo Saghantio absorbs the gravity of the situation and turns to Rachel, saying, "Life cannot stop, and we have many tasks to complete before the weekend. You are responsible for informing his friends in the armed forces, in the local police ... They will cremate the body on Sunday. I just spoke to his brother on the phone, and he informs me that Ronaldo always expressed his desire to be cremated when he passed away. Make sure you inform everyone you can, and I will take care of the rest."

The superintendent picks up the phone and instructs the secretary that he is ready for the next person.

As Rachel and Roberto are leaving, Paulo calls out to her, "Rachel, I know how much you are suffering right now, but never forget that in this life, everything has a purpose. Nothing happens by coincidence. There is a reason where we cross paths, we share our lives, and in the blink of an eye, everything ends. Understand that, in the end, everything will be fine. Try to have faith in that."

Rachel, with tears streaming down her face as Roberto holds her in a comforting hug, leaves the superintendent's office without saying a word.

4

The Accountant

Meticulous to the extreme, sometimes even obsessive, Tyler has always made it clear that when he accepts a mission, it becomes his unwavering number-one responsibility. DRT's guideline rewards the valuable information it receives from its informants. Tyler not only maintains a network of paid informants but also cultivates relationships with many doormen and hotel staff spread across all corners of London. He boasts a cadre of active and retired law enforcement friends, all serving as a veritable treasure trove of information. However, it is the "girls of the night" who hold a special place in his heart. Their loyalty proves to him they are an invaluable asset. Tyler is the quintessential networking man, always flashing a smile and creating new friendships.

Jonas, one of Tyler's trusted informants, sends a message just before the DRT meeting ends. He works as a delivery boy for a restaurant and carries out his duties every day of the week. His daily mission: deliver lunch boxes to the HH & AM company between 11:00 a.m. and 12:00 p.m.

At just eighteen years old, Jonas is deep within the punk style, wearing several piercings adorning his ears and nose. Jonas always ties back his dishevelled brown hair into a ponytail. He spends his days immersed in music, a constant companion on his headphones.

Tyler generously compensates Jonas, especially when his deliveries produce successful results. In this specific case, his role in Tyler's operation requires him to eavesdrop on the daily conversations that take place during those precious minutes of his lunch deliveries, and today he hears something quite intriguing.

Tyler has dedicated a gruelling forty-five days to this ongoing investigation. His daily routine involves monitoring the accounting office of HH & AM Management Consultancy Ltd., an establishment at One Canada Square in Canary Wharf. Normally, Tyler parks his car or motorcycle beside the company owners' parking space, as they have two spaces, and one is always vacant. Finding a suitable parking space in this busy neighbourhood has never been a simple task.

Jonas and Tyler meet in the busy square, their faces set in anticipation. The delivery man wastes no time relaying his encounter that day.

"When I delivered lunch today," Jonas begins, "I opened the office door and am surprised there's no one at reception, and that's when it happens. The phone on one table rings. The secretary runs out of Mr. Hamim's office and answers the call in a hurry. She can't see me because that service desk is so damn high." Whispering to Tyler, he reveals the secretary's cryptic message: "She says, 'He's not in the office. I will make a copy of the rest of the information you need. Let's meet at the same place.'"

Tyler, interest piqued, asks for more details. "Are you sure about that? When does she realize you're there?"

Jonas nods and replies, "I don't make mistakes, Tyler. Those are her exact words, without a doubt." He straightens his ponytail, a visible sign of his conviction.

Tyler can't contain his excitement; a hint of a smile curves the corner of his lips. Today seems to be a turning point.

Jonas continues; his voice is full of amusement as he acts out the scene. "I jump off the couch. As soon as she hangs up the phone, I smile and say, 'It's time for lunch.' I place the packages on the counter and just look at her. She looks at me as if she has seen a ghost; she just stammers, 'I didn't see you come in.' I don't give her a moment to think. I say, 'Well, I'm here now and the price is the same as yesterday.' The secretary runs to the office and, within seconds, returns with the money. I leave, you know, like a scalded cat, as they say. Soon after, I send the message to you."

Satisfied with the success of the report, Tyler can't help but add, "I think this calls for lunch at the restaurant tomorrow."

Tyler leaves Jonas and goes for a walk around the square. A light drizzle falls from the sky, and the smell of cut grass mixed with the earthy scent of fallen leaves carries on the gentle breeze, evoking memories of the ancient forests of Canada. Seeking refuge from the rain, Tyler spots a sheltered bus stop and sits down on the cold metal bench. The rhythmic patter of drops landing on the ceiling and mixing aromas creates a serene atmosphere, inducing a deep sense of calm and tranquility. Despite the usual urban bustle of traffic, cyclists, and dog walkers nearby, it's as if he's reclining by a peaceful lake.

Tyler takes a small notebook from his coat pocket and examines the written information it contains. Hamim, owner of HH & AM, is a seventy-year-old man with a clean record, having never been involved with the law. Diana, his daughter, and the company's general assistant, studies at an arts college and appears alone, always dressed in jeans, a t-shirt, and a dark-green cardigan. As the rain eases, Tyler puts away his notes and heads to the parking lot, determined to check out Diana's black 2017 Volkswagen Polo.

Jonas said that Diana is getting ready to meet someone, and it's now 4:15 p.m. The timing seems perfect for her to end her workday and head toward the parking lot.

Tyler sits in his car. As the clock passes 4:25 p.m., discomfort consumes him, leading him to wonder if Diana is still in the office. He heads to the payphone across from the parking lot. He dials the number for HH & AM to pose as a curious caller asking about a fictitious company. The phone on the other end rings, and, to his surprise, it's Diana who answers, her voice unbalancing him. He stammers something about a fictitious company. Diana clarifies that he's rung the wrong number. Tyler apologizes and hangs up in relief, rejoicing, knowing that she's still at work.

Five minutes later, Diana enters the parking lot and heads straight to the black Polo. Tyler is using his Jeep today. He left his 'famous' motorcycle at home because he had confirmed it would rain today. Diana drives her car toward the exit, and Tyler follows her. As Diana pulls into the McDonald's parking lot on Payne Road, Tyler reflects and positions himself to observe her encounter with a second vehicle, a sleek, dark blue Audi A8. The driver and Diana embrace. Tyler, perceptive as always, takes some discreet photos of the Audi with his cellphone, then jots down the license plate. The Audi leaves the parking lot and heads toward the A12 motorway.

"This is getting interesting," Tyler mutters out loud as he continues following the car with the couple.

Wasting no time, eager to get information, he dials the number of Anna, one of his girlfriends. She is the daughter of Russian immigrants, forty years old and divorced, the mother of two children, and beautiful. She also works in vehicle control and car licensing in London. Their bond is deep and lasting, and she is well aware of his line of work. Unlike most of his girlfriends, she doesn't mind his smoking habit but insists he drinks vodka whenever they are together.

The urgency in Tyler's voice doesn't go unnoticed, and she sarcastically comments, "I can't believe you remember I exist."

Tyler, panting, hurries to explain. "I need your help, Anna. I'm sorry; I'm overwhelmed with work. You can't imagine."

Concerned about his distress, Anna pushes aside her initial annoyance and asks, "What do you need?"

Tyler's voice cracks as he replies, "I need information about this plate, Z11ZZ1. I need details about the owner, address, any fines, anything you can find. Please send it to my cellphone."

Anna reflects for a moment before stating, "It will come at a price."

"Whatever you want."

"One night, just you and me."

Tyler agrees without hesitation, with a hint of relief in his voice. "Okay, I accept. Let's have dinner and then we'll see which kind we can get into."

Anna can't help but laugh at Tyler's response.

As they end the conversation, Tyler adds, "Guess what? During my trip to Kyiv last month, I found the 'Belomorkanal' cigarettes that you love. I'll bring them for you. I'll get in touch with you to confirm the time and date. Kisses."

Anna, thrilled, forgives Tyler.

Belomorkanal, a Russian brand of cigarettes manufactured in Leningrad, is difficult to find outside Russia. These unfiltered cigarettes, known as "Papirosa" in Russian, hold a special place in Anna's heart, and Tyler's thoughtful gesture brings a smile to her face.

The Audi comes to a gentle stop at an opulent residence on Stradbroke Drive in Chigwell, Essex. As the couple disembarks from the car and head into the luxurious home, Diana carries a bag, her purse slung over her shoulder.

Tyler parks the Jeep about five metres from the garage they have entered, positioning it in front of another house on the other side of the street, taking advantage of the cover provided by the other parked cars.

Chigwell, an upscale neighbourhood, gains its reputation from its wealthy residents, including football stars, politicians, and television entertainers, all of whom live in homes requiring astonishing fortunes.

Tyler looks at the clock, which says 5:30 p.m. Just then, his cellphone chimes, alerting him to a message from Anna. With a smile spreading across his face, he reads the message. He can't believe the name he sees. It is the confirmation he craves, the piece of the puzzle that reinforces his suspicions of the ongoing investigation. Tyler thinks out loud as he readies his camera. "Let's wait and see what else happens." Anticipation and excitement grip him as he prepares for the next phase of the operation, armed with the knowledge he gained that is crucial to his report.

It all started when Sangum Management Solutions, a prestigious financial planning firm in London, made headlines in a financial scandal. This entity is famous for its plans in long-term financing. They can do no wrong with any investment or risk tolerance.

They approached DRT two months ago to investigate who and how someone was stealing financial documents from both the owners and the company and sending them to a famous London newspaper. The front-page news showed that the company's revenues and the owners' annual revenues were not compatible. It was an unprecedented scandal, which demoralized the institution that has existed on the market for years with remarkable success. Now they are responding to a government action, trying to prove that everything is in order in the institution and in the financial lives of the owners. It is a big headache, but the worst is yet to come. At the time of publication, they were taking part in a public competition to manage the financial planning of one of London's major investment banks. After the scandal, Sangum Management received a polite invitation to withdraw from the competition because of the outrage of the bank's associates.

The accountant, Mr. Hamim, manages the finances of this company, as well as those of the owners. He swears to the police when questioned that all documents related to the company are kept in a safe and no one has access. It is impossible to have leaked information at HH & AM. Investigators suggest his daughter might be involved. Mr. Hamim swears she is a saint and never has access to confidential information.

Today, if all goes well, Tyler will confirm who passed on the information to the newspaper and how it was done. Inside the car with his camera positioned at maximum zoom, he gets a clear and stable image. The couple leave the house, walking slowly back to the car. Diana is no longer carrying the bag. In front of the house, the man pulls her by the waist, hugs her, and kisses her on the mouth. Tyler takes a lot of photos, but he wants a perfect one of the man's face, and he gets it. Diana's lover is the son of the owner of the company Mango Financial Planner Ltd., who won the bank's bid.

"Bingo," Tyler exclaims. Tomorrow DRT will have a full report.

The clock displays 7:30 p.m., and Allan, David, and Rachel have already taken their seats in the familiar Polo Bar, expecting Tyler's arrival. This bar has become the usual meeting place for celebrations, and today is no exception, as Allan visits London. As soon as Tyler enters the bar, he exchanges warm hugs with everyone at the table. His arrival appears to brighten the room.

"Why all this happiness?" Rachel asks.

The waitress approaches, placing another beer on the table, and her gaze turns to Tyler as she says, "Hello, my dear. What are we having today?"

Tyler winks at the waitress and replies, "I'll have what David's having."

Eager for an answer, Rachel persists. "What makes you so excited, Tyler?"

Tyler regales them with the story of the day's accomplishments. The attentive group listens to every detail. As he concludes his story, smiles of satisfaction dance across all their faces, and they raise their glasses in a toast, celebrating yet another successful mission. At that exact moment, the waitress returns with plates of food and more beer, and the group enjoys the meal, savouring the victory.

It is another triumph for DRT. David and Rachel are now free and ready to embark on their journey to Shanghai, their confidence boosted by Tyler's unwavering experience.

5

Ikigai—The Secret of a Long and Happy Life

It's 11:30 p.m. and torrential rain covers the city. The persistent rumbles of thunder and occasional flashes of lightning make sleeping difficult for Rachel. She returns home from a celebration full of emotion at the Polo Bar at 10:00 p.m. The day was exhausting for everyone involved, filled with unexpected revelations and the promise of an accumulated workload for the following days. Tyler resolved the problems with the accountant's investigation, as he promised. The night brings moments of genuine happiness.

Pulling back the curtain, Rachel looks out her bedroom window, watching the raindrops run down the glass. She abandons the idea of sleeping, lost in the rhythm of the torrential rain.

"It's raining hard," she murmurs, her eyes wandering to Mozart, the majestic Maine Coon sprawled on the bed.

"I need to get some sleep. Maybe chamomile tea will help." She continues speaking out loud, finding solace in her own voice.

She pads to the apartment's kitchen, the sound of rain following her steps.

"You've had your fill today," she murmurs, noticing Mozart behind her, his empty plate a testament to his feast. "Everything is gone. Want a hug?" She reaches down, lifting him into her arms and stroking his fur.

As she puts the kettle on the stove, waiting for the water to boil, memories float in the air like steam. She thinks about her mother, who sometimes brewed a pot of aromatic jasmine tea. Her mother now lives in Canada with her current husband, while her father enjoys the heat of Miami with his second wife. The pangs of loneliness take over Rachel from time to time, but she knows it's a feeling she has to deal with, especially since leaving her position with the federal government.

After Ronaldo's death, she made a solemn promise not to trust anyone again. His absence plunged her into an emotional abyss, a dark place that took her what seemed like centuries to climb out of. Ronaldo had always been her driving force, the wind beneath her wings, always pushing her forward, defending her causes, and reinforcing her ambitions. He was the one who taught her to differentiate between allies and adversaries, equipping her with survival skills in a predominantly male world. He once confided that, for her to thrive in such a testosterone-driven environment, especially on the police force, she would always need to prove herself twice as much as any man. It was the price she'd have to pay if she wanted respect, admiration, and no unwanted intrusion into her life. She took her lessons to heart and excelled.

After dozens of delicate operations, she felt an urgent need to retreat, to leave behind the frightening shadows of her past, and to embark on a path of peace and stability. Time for a new beginning. She resigned from the government position she held a decade ago and moved to the United States. It wasn't long before she received an offer to join "the Firm," an international investigation agency that she worked with undercover alongside Ronaldo.

However, after a year and a half at the Firm, she accepted David and Tyler's offer to set up their own private investigation agency.

Now, Allan's recent revelations bring the buried secrets from the past back to the surface. Old emotions, which she believed she had tamed long ago, begin stirring within her. She realizes she can no longer ignore them. She has to find out the truth, whether Ronaldo's death is an unfortunate accident or a deliberate act by someone.

Rachel turns off the heat on the stove and goes to the garage, which holds a storage room. Boxes full of documents, reports of previous operations, and investigations house the remnants of her past in this room.

The cool night air greets her as she arrives at the garage. With a quick turn of the key, she unlocks the entrance and begins rummaging through the boxes, looking for one labelled "PF." Locating the box, she takes it back to her apartment for a thorough inspection.

Upon returning to the apartment, she looks at the clock on the microwave. The time shows a little after midnight. Turning the stove back on, the kettle's whistle interrupts her train of thought within minutes. She pours the hot liquid, and soon the comforting scent of chamomile permeates the room.

Outside, the rain continues to fall, hitting the veranda and windows. Thunder rumbles with violence, and occasional flashes of lightning illuminate the room. Rachel walks to the sliding glass door and closes the curtains. She then turns on a nearby lamp and settles on the couch, wrapping herself in a blanket.

Placing her steaming mug of tea on the coffee table in front of her, she digs through the box of files. As she reviews each one, she vocalizes the title written on the cover, stacking them on the table. "Operation Power," she murmurs. "Operation Banking, Operation Port, Operation Lilac Farm…" Her voice trails off as she separates the "Operation Container" folder, setting it aside. With that, she places the still-full document box next to the sofa, ready to delve into the forgotten reports.

Opening the file, Rachel examines the folder, which is organized into two distinct sections: Phase 1 and Phase 2. At the top of the first page of Phase 1, the bold title "Container Report" catches her eye. Her heart skips a beat when she sees Ronaldo's unmistakable signature at the bottom. In contrast, the second file bears her own signature. When she finishes reading Phase 2, the meticulous detail of the information impresses her. She remembers her partner's advice, emphasizing the importance of keeping copies of all the documents she signs. He always emphasized the need to keep a copy with the recipient's signature or stamp, no matter how many years it took to maintain it, as it was impossible to predict future needs.

The memory of a certain pen drive she transported to Brazil then comes to light. This device played a crucial role in the joint mission with the FBI in Operation Container in 2014. The operation covered Mexico and several ports in the United States. This led to a significant confiscation of hundreds of vials of fentanyl originating in China and thousands of fentanyl tablets originating in Japan. The police operation culminated in the arrest of individuals of various nationalities in the United States, Mexico, and Brazil.

Absorbed in the information, Rachel writes down some details. She suspects that the forgotten details may now have great significance. She will take these discoveries with her to Shanghai, reflecting on the unpredictability of life and its events. For Rachel, the notion of mere coincidences does not hold water. However, she also recognizes that life's imperfections mean events do not always turn out as predicted. She examines other documents relating to various operations and concludes that there is no conclusive link between any of them and Ronaldo's tragic death.

Pausing for a moment, Rachel leans back and closes her eyes. Allan's haunting words echo in her mind.

"It makes little sense," she whispers to herself.

Rachel retraces the series of events that led to her partner's fateful trip. Ronaldo had often taken on additional side jobs to supplement his income, but nothing that posed an ethical dilemma with his duties as a police officer. His tasks ranged from private investigations, acting as a courier of confidential documents, capturing evidence of marital infidelity, serving as a personal chauffeur for those needing additional security, and sometimes as a short-term bodyguard. These quick jobs provided decent additional income, which helped a lot given the low salaries of police officers. What police officers lacked in financial rewards, they made up for in an overwhelming workload and immense responsibility.

The day Ronaldo informed her about a job that coincided with her planned vacation comes to mind. He mentioned his upcoming trip to Shanghai during a casual conversation with Alex Hirata, director and chief coordinator of the Firm. Upon learning of Ronaldo's holiday travel plans, Alex proposed an attractive offer. Would Ronaldo be willing to meet a certain Mr. Chan, known for his courier services, while in Shanghai? Alex assured Ronaldo that he would receive all the details, such as the date, time, and location of the meeting, well in advance. All Ronaldo needed to do was collect some documents from Mr. Chan that were important to the Firm associates in Shanghai. Ronaldo accepted, although without knowledge of the content or nature of these documents.

To Ronaldo's delight, the Firm took care of all the travel arrangements. Not only did they take care of his flight and hotel reservations at the luxurious Grand Kempinski Shanghai, but they also provided daily allowances during his stay. They outlined Ronaldo's itinerary: he would leave on February 7th, arriving in Shanghai on the eighth and returning on the twelfth.

However, this arrangement did not please Rachel. She had already spent money on tickets and hotels, hoping they would spend the holidays together. The travel dates were different, with departure on February eighth, arrival in Shanghai on the ninth, and return on the eleventh. This was in stark contrast to the schedule that the Firm coordinated for Ronaldo. The incompatible itineraries left Rachel frustrated.

Rachel remembers the first time she met Alex Hirata through Ronaldo. Alex made a huge impression on her—not for his stature or imposing presence but for his unusual choice of everyday wear: a safari-style hat. For Rachel, it was a fun contrast. Alex embodies the quintessential oriental look with his pale skin, black hair, and round face, often sporting an enigmatic smile that leaves everyone wondering about his genuineness. The pair of black glasses he wears further hides his emotions. A very modest figure, Alex is the type to blend into the crowd without attracting attention. One accessory, however, caught her attention: a worn brown leather briefcase that he always carries in his right hand.

Ronaldo mentioned that much of the communication was done via phone or text message. However, due to Alex's taste for ricotta pie accompanied by coffee from a café in the Consolação neighbourhood in São Paulo, that location was determined to be their meeting place. Ronaldo and Alex shared a unique bond.

In one of these meetings, Alex shared a personal philosophy with Ronaldo. "Ikigai is my reason for living," he proclaimed.

Curious, Ronaldo asked, "What is ikigai?"

"It's the reason you wake up every morning," Alex responds, pausing before adding, "do you know why you get up every day? If you can answer that, then you have discovered your ikigai."

Ronaldo later explained to Rachel that the term *ikigai* was an ancient Japanese concept that many considered to be the key to a fulfilling life. He believed ikigai was the secret not only to a long life but also to a happy life. The essence of ikigai is identifying what you love and what brings you genuine satisfaction. Embracing these elements ensures not only longevity but a life well-lived and enjoyed. It has less to do with the length of life and more to do with its quality and purpose.

Despite understanding the depth of the concept, Ronaldo often expressed uncertainty about his own ikigai. He confided in Rachel, admitting he was still searching for that singular purpose or passion. Until then, he felt he had not yet identified the true reason for his existence.

Rachel stops thinking about Ronaldo and tries to connect with Operation Container. She remembers that when she received the flash drive, there were no specific instructions about who she should give it to. The only thing Ronaldo emphasized was that "perhaps it would be better for her to keep the flash drive." Rachel was aware of Ronaldo's agreement with the director of the Firm. However, after his unexpected death, she felt uncomfortable returning the flash drive to the Firm. Believing it to be the most prudent course of action, she handed it over to the head of federal police intelligence. To protect Ronaldo's integrity and reputation, she said an informant gave it to him, thus ensuring there was no connection to his police work.

A few months after Ronaldo's tragic passing, Rachel received a call from Alex. He clarified that the flash drive's original destination was for the American government. However, as the FBI was planning the next operation in a joint effort with the "PF," the fact that the flash drive did not reach the Firm did not cause any damage. Alex emphasized to Rachel that he would always be there to support her, expressing deep respect and admiration for Ronaldo. This commitment became clear when Alex helped Rachel through her decision to leave the federal police in 2015.

As Rachel flips through the pages of her records, she realizes that, despite her thorough examination, she has been unable to find any connection between what Allan Liu revealed and the details of Operation Container. Operation Portugal is a separate subject, but Allan's statement weighs on Rachel. Maybe the Yakuza hasn't given up.

In a fit of frustration, she throws the folder on the floor, exclaiming, "Everything seems so perfect, but in reality, nothing is!"

Mozart, purring, prowls the room before finding comfort under the coffee table. Feeling cold, Rachel covers herself with a blanket. The storm outside subsides.

Tears glisten in her eyes. Mozart, sensing her anguish, jumps into her lap and licks her face, showing care. It's like he knows how she's feeling. She hugs him, her fingers running through his soft fur.

The alarm clock shakes her. It's 6:00 a.m.

"Oh, shit! I fell asleep on the couch," exclaims Rachel, with a mixture of annoyance and surprise in her voice.

Standing, she waves to the cat. "Come on, Mozart. Breakfast time."

When she looks out the window, the sky is cloudy, but the rain has stopped. She retrieves her notes from the night before and decides it's time to call Alex. After several rings and no response, she leaves a message:

"Alex, it's Rachel. It's been a long time since we talked. I need some information about Operation Container. I'm leaving for Shanghai tomorrow. How can I contact Mr. Chan? Call me." She hangs up, confident that Alex will answer.

As she hurries to get dressed, preparing for another day at the DRT, her cellphone interrupts the silence.

Responding, she jokes, "Did you fall out of bed again?"

On the other side, David responds, "No, I didn't even go to bed. I spent the entire night talking to my contacts. I have our tickets to Shanghai. Pack a suitcase for a week; we leave this afternoon. See you at the office in an hour." Without waiting for her response, he ends the call.

Still a little stunned by the suddenness of the information, she laughs.

Rachel thinks, *David is always on 220V.*

6

Shanghai—Rediscovering the Past

David meets the eyes of his DRT partners and explains his recent actions. "Last night, I spoke to a close friend and contacted the FBI office in Shanghai."

His next words add weight to Allan's previous statements. "I inquired about the operation that the Portuguese police carried out together with the local force. It's in line with what Allan told us." David pauses. "As a private investigator for the DRT, I requested to interview the detainee. Intelligence agents seem receptive. They will try to schedule our conversation for tomorrow morning. Unless they transfer the prisoner to another place, then this will not be possible."

Rachel interjects. "I also asked for help. I contacted Alex. I left a message asking about Mr. Chan, the Firm contact in Shanghai." She pauses, gauging Tyler's and David's reactions. "You never know what information he might have."

In the spacious DRT conference room, the members have gathered around the table to discuss the latest guidance provided by Mary Lay. Tyler, sensing the tension in the room, interrupts with a lighter tone. "By the way, no one needs to worry about dealing with Mozart. This isn't my first rodeo with him."

Allan, with a distant look, gets up. "I hate to interrupt this, but I have to get back to Toronto. Take care, guys." He waves goodbye, and everyone returns the gesture as he leaves the room.

Tyler signals his partners and heads for the door, making sure they get to the airport on time.

* * *

The clock strikes 10:15 a.m. on September 4, and the partners are preparing to board the Air China flight.

Inside the plane, the soft chime of an incoming message accompanies the hum of the engines. David picks up his phone and examines it. Confirmation arrives for their scheduled interview at the Shanghai Police Station for the next day. The message contains additional information: Police are scheduling the prisoner's transfer to Japan within the next forty-eight hours.

"We're lucky," David says, showing the message to Rachel.

She nods, her fingers tightening her seat belt. "We are very lucky."

After a twelve-hour flight, the plane lands at Shanghai Pudong International Airport. Upon arriving at the terminal, around 11:30 a.m., they feel the heat as they walk to collect their bags. The displays confirm the temperature as twenty-seven degrees Celsius.

David smiles, nudging his partner. "I told you there was no need for that coat. It's damn hot here."

Rachel looks at him sideways, a little irritated. "It's okay. I'll leave it at the hotel."

As they come out of the airport's main door, a forty-year-old man greets them. David quickly recognizes him. "Rachel, meet Agent Matthew Elbastar." His eyes widen, exaggerated, attempting some unspoken communication. Rachel, surprised by his strange gesture, just returns a courteous smile.

Matthew holds out his hand, not looking too pleased to meet her. He doesn't look at Rachel, his gaze fixed on the floor.

His indifferent behaviour intrigues her. As their hands separate, she thinks, *In law enforcement, we always maintain eye contact with the person we are speaking to. If the person looks away, it often shows that they are not trustworthy. Effective? Yes.*

As they walk together, Matthew points to a sleek black four-door Hyundai SUV parked nearby. "Our ride."

Rachel sits behind the driver while David sits in the passenger seat next to Matthew. As the car begins its journey, Matthew recites the latest updates in a monotone, as if checking off items on a shopping list.

"The prisoner's name is Yazuo Yorinarie. Intel confirms he is one of the bosses of the Japanese mafia Yakuza. To the public, however, he is just the CEO of a renowned pharmaceutical company in Japan with strong ties to government medical agencies. His arrest caused great turmoil behind the scenes in both governments. Japanese authorities argue that there is no evidence against him and consider his arrest unjustified and illegal. To avoid an international incident, they sanction Yazuo's transfer back to Japan."

Rachel interrupts, her tone empathetic but assertive. "I guarantee you that as soon as he lands, he will go straight to his residence. No jail time."

Matthew doesn't respond.

David's brow furrows as he asks the agent, "Was there concrete evidence of the arrest or not? Why did the Chinese police make the arrest?"

Before the American intel agent can respond, Rachel interrupts again. "Sorry, David. Matthew, do you know the name of this pharmaceutical company? Is he the owner?"

Matthew hesitates. "I'm not sure if he's the owner. I can share the details I have," he offers. Giving no more information, he stops the car on the sidewalk in front of the Shanghai Police Headquarters. "Find Boss Bongwen Zhou. He will help them. Feel free to call him Bo."

They get out of the vehicle, thanking him, and remove their luggage from the trunk.

Looking at his watch, Matthew asks a quick question. "It's almost 11 a.m. and I have a busy day ahead of me. Will you still need my services? If not, I will get back to you tomorrow."

David's response is quick, and his tone is cold. "No need. We'll call a taxi from here to the hotel. We'll talk later." He watches as Matthew leaves.

Rachel's gaze follows the car, a questioning expression on her face. "Who is this agent?"

David sighs, disturbed. "I'll tell you later. For now, let's focus on the task at hand."

Rachel, already feeling the heat and humidity, mutters, "God, this place is suffocating." However, her complaint goes unnoticed.

David and Rachel enter the police station. After exchanging pleasantries and introductions, they leave their bags at reception. The police officer on duty informs them that at the end of the interview, the superintendent will speak to them, as he is not in the building at the moment.

An officer escorts them to an interrogation room. To their surprise, the alleged criminal Yazuo, wearing a modern navy-blue suit with intricate white brocades on the cuffs, looks no older than thirty.

David addresses him in fluent Mandarin. "We represent a private investigation agency in London. I'm David Ho and this is Rachel Barnes. You speak English?"

Yazuo, exuding an air of indifference, lights a cigarette. He takes a deliberate drag, exhaling toward David and Rachel, defiance clear in his eyes. "I know who you two are and yes, I can speak English." He then gestures to the officer standing at the door, signalling service.

Yazuo looks at Rachel and asks, "Do you want tea or coffee?"

The two partners refuse. The officer returns, handing Yazuo a steaming cup.

Rachel opens her notebook with a professional attitude. "Yazuo, I have some questions for you, okay?"

Yazuo stops smoking for a moment, putting out his cigarette in the ashtray before nodding.

Jumping straight into the investigation, Rachel says to the suspect, "You made a comment to a police officer when they were arresting you. Remember? You said, 'You're going to die, just like that federal police officer in the hotel. Only this time his whole family will accompany him.' What do you know about the death of that federal police officer?"

Maintaining eye contact with Rachel, he responds, "I've already discussed this with the Shanghai police chief."

Rachel, holding Yazuo's gaze, pauses for a moment, processing the answer.

Unfazed, Yazuo probes further. "What is your interest in this case?"

Rachel responds with a calm and firm tone, trying to tread the delicate balance between authority and empathy. "This is not an official interrogation, just an interview. We believe you may have information that could shed light on the officer's death."

Displaying a smile tinged with sarcasm, Yazuo replies, "Maybe when I'm free from this place I can help you. After all, I have many contacts. Why don't you leave your number? I'll call you tomorrow."

Refusing to be flustered, Rachel responds with force. "Do you think we're joking? This is an international criminal investigation, and there will be repercussions."

"Did you know that your voice is quite impressive, and you are beautiful?" he comments in English, his gaze fixed on Rachel.

David interrupts in his crisp, precise Mandarin. "We have eyewitnesses who saw you threatening that police officer."

Yazuo, without missing a beat, responds in the same language. "Which witnesses? I believe someone misinformed you." He pauses, allowing the tension to build. "This discussion is taking an unpleasant turn."

With a sudden change in behaviour, Yazuo stands up, turning his attention to Rachel. "This time tomorrow, I will be in Japan. If you wish, we can arrange a meeting. We can exchange some of my intriguing knowledge."

Yazuo leaves with the police officer, and the room becomes heavier. Moments later, the same officer returns, handing Rachel a piece of paper with a phone number scribbled on it.

David and Rachel scan the hallway after leaving the interrogation room. There is no trace of Yazuo, but Police Chief Bo is waiting for them and welcomes them to Shanghai. Boss Bo hands an envelope full of papers to David. His words are uncomplicated and direct: "Count on us for any help needed in Operation Portugal." They say goodbye, certain they will meet again.

As they leave the Shanghai Police Headquarters, David calls a taxi. "Holiday Inn Express Shanghai Tangshan," David tells the driver in Mandarin. Showing signs of stress, David sits back, rests his head, and exhales.

Rachel, feeling David's anguish, tries to understand. "What happened there?"

David grimaces, his lips forming a thin line. "It is all an act, a mere facade. If we want answers, you will have to talk to Yazuo, and I won't allow that." His voice shows his frustration and concern.

Rachel chooses not to respond and turns her attention to the window. Shanghai's bustling cityscape, crowded buses, and speeding vehicles catch her eye.

Arriving at their destination, the pair head to their respective rooms. It's 3:15 p.m., and they agree to meet in the main lobby at 4:30 p.m.

Rachel opens her suitcase and takes out the few pieces of clothing she brought and hangs them next to her coat in the closet. While the oppressive thirty-degree heat is outside, the cool wind from the air conditioning spreads throughout the room. Wanting a momentary break, Rachel opts for a quick shower. After slipping back into her trusty jeans, she chooses a fresh shirt.

While brushing her hair, she sees Ronaldo in the mirror. The sight shakes her for a second. She shakes her head and murmurs to her reflection, "Stay focused, Rachel."

Sitting on the plush armchair in her room, she scrolls through the countless notifications on her phone. A glance at the clock assures her that there is still a quarter of an hour until she needs to reach the hotel lobby.

Tyler's message brings a smile to her face; he claims Mozart is in love with him. He also updates her on the early stages of his new investigation. Next, Mary's succinct message assures Rachel that all is well at the office. Her father's message, however, leaves her thoughtful. His words of longing touch her heart, but they also serve as a poignant reminder of Rachel's estranged relationship with her mother.

A missed call from an unknown number in the US catches Rachel's attention. Checking, she sees there is no voicemail, so she calls back. The call cannot be completed due to weak signal, a common problem with foreign phones in China. The country's tight control over telecommunications often leads visitors to opt for local disposable phones.

Rachel tries to dial the number again. This time, the call connects.

"Hello?" a female voice responds from the other end.

"Did someone from the United States call me?" Rachel asks, trying to mask the anxiety in her voice.

"I missed you a lot, especially those afternoons going for coffee," says Rosemary, with clear joy in her tone.

Rachel, trying to maintain her composure, responds, "It's good to know you're still there for Alex. I was hoping to talk to him."

Rosemary's voice turns dark. "Alex is in the hospital. They found a tumour a few months ago, and he had surgery a few days ago. He is better now but won't be leaving the hospital anytime soon. He received your message and is eager to talk with you."

Shocked by the news, Rachel struggles to find the words. After taking a few deep breaths, she says, "When can I talk to him? It's important. I promise I won't keep him for long. I only have five days left in Shanghai."

"Would an hour from now work for you?" Rosemary suggests.

"Yes, I'll wait for his call," Rachel's voice wavers. Looking at her phone, she sees it is 4:25 p.m. The weight of the news about Alex's health leaves her dismayed. Her mind turns to thoughts of ikigai.

In the hotel lobby, Rachel meets David at the scheduled time. The receptionist calls a taxi, which arrives in a few minutes. As they get into the car, David tells the driver their destination.

Rachel recalls David's previous praise for Shanghai, mentioning this restaurant for its delicious cuisine and affordable prices.

"We need to rent a car tomorrow and pick up some local phones," David says, interrupting her thoughts. His tone shows he's back in command.

Rachel watches David and says, "Is everything okay? Did something happen? Was it the intel agent who bothered you?"

David sighs. "The agent I was counting on is a close friend and long-time associate. He flew to Hong Kong and won't be back until next week." David's gaze remains fixed outside, his eyes clouded with worry and doubt.

Rachel holds her tongue, choosing not to share the news about Alex, as adding news about his friend's health would only add to the stress. She knows David likes Alex. Instead, the conversation turns to the enigmatic agent who greeted them upon arrival in Shanghai. "What's wrong with this agent?"

"He's always been a shit-snitch gossiper who loves sniffing his bosses' asses. You don't know how painful it was for me in Washington. I guarantee that here in Shanghai he is acting the same way. He was always a little bitch." David frowns. It's obvious he hates this guy.

Rachel, surprised by David's candid outburst, can't help but laugh. "Oh! Don't take out your Glock 19, please..."

David looks at her, shocked, and they both start laughing. The driver looks in the rear-view mirror, not understanding, but laughs anyway.

They arrive at the restaurant and ask the taxi driver to wait for them. They enter the place, realizing that it is already packed with customers. As they wait to be led to a table, Rachel's gaze shifts to the busy street outside. Two men get out of a black car parked next to the waiting taxi. Something awakens in her, a vague feeling of discomfort.

"It feels like I'm looking for smoke where there's no fire," she mutters to herself.

David, always attentive, catches her words. "What did you say?"

"It's nothing. Maybe just my imagination."

Once seated, David goes to the buffet and Rachel's phone rings. She gets up and walks away from the table. She answers, and for a moment the line is silent.

"It's your old boss," says a weak voice on the other end.

Hearing Alex's voice again brings a rush of emotions. Rachel, with humour, jokes as she always does. "Hey, Alex, they say you broke both your arms and can no longer enjoy your favourite ricotta pie—oh, and you have a mechanical heart. The wish list you always dreamed of. Oh, I forgot, someone also said… you have a prostate exam every two days."

Alex lets out a tired laugh. "If only it were that simple, Rachel. Anyway, enough about me. What do you need to know? How can I help you?"

"I need to talk to Mr. Chan. I'm in Shanghai. Can you tell me if Mr. Chan is in any way connected to the first container operation?"

There is a pause on the other side. Alex's breathing seems laboured before he responds: "The first Operation Container we carried out was because of illegal activities at the post office and hospitals. The second operation is another story. You are aware of this, right?"

Rachel shakes her head, forgetting that Alex can't see her. "Yes, I remember."

Alex continues. "The tip that started this operation was the one we passed on to American intelligence. The Firm provided the information to the FBI, which relayed it to federal authorities. It all started with sending fentanyl to the USA through the post office. The packages were disguised as dolls, cans, counterfeit books, and so on. Remember? Authorities arrested three Chinese individuals. They admitted to having collected these goods from four hospitals and some laboratories."

"Was everything under the law?" Rachel asks.

"Everything was legal, according to the law. Fentanyl, ampoules, tablets, as well as the chemicals used in the manufacture of this specific medicine acquired from Chinese and Japanese laboratories. No one expected anyone to redirect it like that. Some hospital employees pocketed the medicine in exchange for money and then passed it on to intermediaries. These inter-mediaries distributed fentanyl in multiple states. After the initial seizure, the US intercepted four more shipments of pills from Japanese laboratories in the following months. Can you see how Chan fits into this?" Alex's voice gets tired toward the end.

Rachel understands. "I think I'm putting the pieces together. Alex, maybe we should continue this conversation another time? Your voice sounds exhausted."

Listening to the conversation on speakerphone, Rose interrupts: "Yes."

Rachel looks at her watch. "It's 5:30 p.m. on the fifth here in Shanghai."

Rose's voice, although professional, carries a hint of fatigue. "It's 1:30 a.m. on the fifth here in Washington. Alex will call you around 9 p.m. All good?"

Rachel agrees. "Yes, this is perfect. Call me whenever you want. I will be waiting."

"Thank you, Rachel."

When she joins David at the table, he is already on his second course. He looks up, his eyes full of questions. "All well?"

Rachel recounts her conversation with Alex as succinctly as she can.

As soon as they finish their meal, the two leave the restaurant and get into the taxi. As they settle in, a familiar vehicle passes by at high speed, catching Rachel's attention. She tenses with that uncomfortable feeling again.

That car…

Rachel's instincts tell her it's more than just a coincidence. Now she is on alert.

1

Mr. Chan

Rachel wakes up and sees that the curtain is closed, blocking any glimpse of the sky. She picks up her phone from the bedside table and searches for messages. When she finds nothing, her thoughts turn to Alex, the man who always wears a hat, who personifies strength and intelligence. The phone in her room rings, breaking her thoughts.

She hears David's voice inviting her to have breakfast at the hotel restaurant.

Still drowsy, rubbing her eyes, she asks, "What time is it?"

"It's 7 a.m. Matthew dropped by the hotel earlier and left an envelope for us at reception. I looked at it; it contains a copy of the 2013 report on Ronaldo's death and details about the labs. There is also a note. They transferred the Japanese this morning," David says with firmness in his voice.

"Hmm... okay. I'll meet you at the hotel restaurant in twenty minutes." She adds, "David, what's the weather like outside?"

"It was drizzling in the morning, and now it's cloudy, but still around thirty degrees Celsius. Maybe you should bring your coat," he suggests with a laugh.

Rachel moans playfully. "Ouch!"

Once they're sitting at the breakfast table, Rachel breaks the news about Alex's condition.

David pauses for a moment, setting down his coffee cup before speaking. "It's heartbreaking to hear, but knowing Alex, he's resilient. He'll get through this."

His response catches Rachel off guard, leaving her silent for a moment.

Drinking the rest of her coffee, she focuses her attention on David as he outlines the day's plans. "Look, I won't dwell on this... Our priority now is to stay organized and on track. I'll make a copy of this report before returning it. We'll study the contents and find out if it has relevance to our case. We also need to rent a car and buy two disposable cellphones. Last, and don't get me wrong, but I know your Mandarin is rudimentary, so whenever you're not sure about something that's being said, just ask me … I'll help you."

Rachel nods in agreement.

As they get up from their chairs and head to the elevator, she asks, "Your room or mine?"

David, with a slight smile, replies, "Mine, since that's where the documents are."

At 8:20 a.m., Rachel is already in David's room, and they study the documents given to him. While David rereads the details of Ronaldo's death, Rachel examines her iPad, researching the various laboratory names.

Her phone vibrates with an incoming call. Seeing the same US number on the screen, Rachel answers. "You called early … Of course, Rosemary. Thank you," she says, looking at David.

He raises his left hand, signalling her to continue the conversation. David told her in the café that when they got back to London, he would visit Alex in Washington.

Alex's voice, firm but tired, echoes, "Let's pick up where we left off."

Rachel responds, "Of course. We were discussing the initial phase of Operation Container."

Alex's response is straightforward: "You want details about Mr. Chan, the man who gave you that USB, correct?"

Realizing the seriousness of the conversation, Rachel responds, "As he lives here and has contacts, he can help us." She omits the details of her mission in Shanghai.

A silence ensues before Alex announces, "Mr. Chan passed away a few years ago."

Rachel feels like all the air has been sucked out of the room. Trying to maintain her composure, she asks, "When did he pass away?"

Alex responds, "In 2013, about eight months after his last visit to Shanghai."

This revelation hits Rachel hard. It can't be a mere coincidence. She activates the cellphone's recording feature. She needs to document this conversation.

With a slight tremor in her voice, she asks, "Could you clarify who Mr. Chan was?"

"Now I have all the time in the world." Alex laughs and coughs. "Chan was a Firm informant for five years and helped us with a lot of important information. He had two sons who studied in the engineering department at Seattle University. Today one of them is married, has a son and lives in Vancouver, Canada, the other works for a multinational in Seattle. They are doing very well," he concludes and remains silent.

Rachel is also quiet.

"You heard me, right?" he asks.

"Yes. The connection is perfect," responds Rachel.

"I will continue the story. He worked and lived with his wife and daughter in Lianyungang, Jiangsu, a five-and-a-half-hour drive from Shanghai. He was a manufacturing and production manager at one of the world's largest container construction companies, CTLG, in Lianyungang. Lots of work and little pay. The representative office of Chungnun Transnational Logistics Group, Ltd. is in that building where you met him, remember?

"Ah…"

"The Firm was his contact, you know? Tell me, Rachel… is this phone safe? Are you not using disposable ones?"

"That's my number, Samsung," she responds.

"You are safe… intelligence intercepted Chan on one of his trips when he came to visit his children in Seattle. Despite his complicated finances, he didn't want the boys to drop out of university and return to China. In fact, he sent almost all of his salary to his children to survive here. So, we offered a salary—good value for the information he could give us, which focused on drug smuggling and anything he found that interested us. He accepted and helped us for five years. Today, his children are doing well in their professional careers and have achieved stable finances." Alex coughs, struggling to breathe.

Rachel doesn't say a word.

He chokes up and continues narrating. "His sister lived in Shanghai and a brother lives in Mongolia. At the time, his sister was ill, and he was the one who took care of her monthly expenses when he came to Shanghai.

"His sister was the best excuse we found to receive the information he brought us. The money was always deposited into the children's accounts in Seattle. Mr. Chan and I have never been close. The relationship has always been professional. I'm grateful for everything he did. He saved countless lives."

Rachel, with the little she knows Alex, understands that he is telling the truth.

"About your meeting with him in February 2013..." Alex stops talking and takes a deep breath. "Mr. Chan sent us a message at the end of January. Something different happened, but he didn't say what it was. He wrote a message: '...in the production sector.' What I understood from this message... Mr. Chan inspected a hangar where they were building containers and noticed something different. Our messages were in code."

"I see," Rachel responds.

"My dear, you know that the government monitors all local communication systems. We had to be as careful as possible about what we said to each other. They were short sentences about family and children in which we tried to understand everything we wanted to convey, hence the need for a courier." Alex stops talking and says he needs to drink some water.

Rachel hears Rose say he should stop for today. He responds, "Not yet," and keeps going.

"It was the first time a delivery was made in the place where you met. There were no deliveries or contact previously made there. The usual place to make contact was a park in Shanghai. I don't know why Chan chose that building, that floor, that day, and time. I don't know the purpose of moving from the park to that building. We told Chan that Ronaldo would meet him, with no other premise. You worked at the Firm and did messenger work. You know how this works."

"I know how it works, but it depends on the service," remembers Rachel.

"That day Chan was waiting for Ronaldo, but you went there to get the documents. In the end, thank God, everything went well, but the unexpected happened: Ronaldo's death in the hotel. To this day, when I think about it, I have no words."

"Some losses have no explanation," she says, thinking of Allan.

"You don't know how much I liked Ronaldo. With him, it was never just professional. We had something else, very spiritual," Alex tries to explain to her.

Ikigai, Rachel thinks.

Alex coughs.

"In 2013, after Ronaldo's death, you came to talk to me. Was Mr. Chan's death already known?" Rachel asks.

"I don't know. That was another shock for me that year," Alex responds.

Rachel looks at David, who seems focused on analyzing the documents.

Alex speaks again. "If my memory serves me correctly, I believe we spoke in May. In October, I learned of Chan's passing. I believe we were almost at the end of the year, but I'm not sure. He disappeared after giving you the documents. For me, at the time, I saw nothing unusual because it was normal for him to write every three months. We have couriers who only communicate with us once a year. It was a lesson for us. Today, every person who works with us has to send a check-in message after meetings. We had to change our communication policy."

Rachel remains silent.

Alex ends the conversation as quickly as possible. "We discovered that Chan never returned to the factory. The agent who went to investigate why he didn't communicate with us, or with his children, discovered that he left his job. You know how things are in China. We could not deepen our investigation. The government controls and monitors everything, so it brought the agent back. I don't remember, but I believe it was in October or November 2013 that the FBI alerted us. CTLG officials found the decomposed body inside a freezer container in one of the storage yards in Shanghai. Do you know those gigantic parking lots where they store hundreds of containers? There was no in-depth investigation into Mr. Chan's death because they considered it an accident. If the police did... I guarantee it was insufficient. I know that the record that intelligence sent us was stamped with the word 'investigating,' but we have received no information about what happened."

Rose joins the call and tells Rachel he'd better stop now. "You want to know about Mr. Chan? This is the story." Alex coughs.

"Mr. Chan's death has something to do with Ronaldo's death. What's your opinion?" Rachel asks, ignoring Rose.

"I think about it many times, but we never have a single line, a single piece of information that leads us to investigate Ronaldo's death as a homicide and not an accident," Alex replies.

Silence dominates the conversation.

"Why didn't you ever tell me about Mr. Chan when I worked at the Firm?" she asks, breaking the ice.

"Simple: because you never asked. There is nothing that can be related to Ronaldo's death," declares Alex.

Rachel is incredulous at the words she hears.

"Thank you for answering my question and all this information. I don't want to bother you, especially since you are in recovery. I am saddened by what happened to Mr. Chan. We need someone here in Shanghai to help us. We will try to do the best we can to solve everything we came here to do," says Rachel.

"I do not have anyone in Shanghai at the moment. I cannot help you this time."

"Okay. Next week we will go back to London, and I will do everything I can to visit you in Washington. A big kiss to Rose and you." Rachel controls herself, even though she feels like vomiting.

Alex feels the coldness in Rachel's words and responds in a sweet voice, "We love you so much. Come visit me. I'm waiting for you."

Rose's voice interrupts with maternal warmth. "Rachel, Alex needs to rest right now. It's been a long day for him."

Rachel's mind races, trying to put together the puzzle Alex painted. "I understand. I wish him a speedy recovery."

Alex's voice is tired but remains insistent. "It is important that you know the facts and, yes, although there may not be any direct link to Ronaldo's death, of course there may be more to the story, but there is no proof."

Rachel's voice shakes with mixed emotions. "I can't help but think about that sequence of events," admits Rachel. "I worked with Ronaldo, and his death never seemed certain to me, but without proof, you can't argue."

Alex exhales. "That's an investigator's true intuition, but Rachel, you also need to be cautious. Not all clues will end up where you think they will."

Rachel takes a deep breath, composing herself. "I understand that, Alex. There's a part of me that needs answers."

Alex sighs. "I wish I had more to give you. Stay safe and trust your instincts. As for Chan, he was a good man. The Firm is sorry for your loss."

David watches Rachel as she ends the call. Her eyes remain fixed, a mix of sadness and frustration on her face. "Rachel, it looks like we have a lot more digging to do."

She nods. "Yes, and we will get to the bottom of this, whatever it takes."

"What the hell was that? He thinks we're stupid? That seems like a lot of nonsense," David responds.

Sitting in the armchair, she looks into space.

Her companion approaches, trying to be positive, and says, "Rachel, calm down now. We will find out what happened here, I promise. I'm glad you recorded the conversation."

In her eyes, it seems like she lost something, and she states, "We will. I guarantee it!"

8

A Hot Day

David decides he's going to rent a car. After discussing with Alex, he and Rachel go to the hotel lobby, where they discover a car rental counter in the basement parking lot. David confirms his intention to rent a car, and an attendant calls the company requesting a broker at reception. After some negotiation, they reach a deal.

"We got an excellent rate, six hundred yen, which is ninety dollars a day, and I believe it's a good car, a white 2019 Volkswagen Passat. Renting at the hotel is cheaper than renting from an external company."

"A new car, great," Rachel agrees.

The company parks the car in front of the hotel's main door, and the broker hands the keys to David.

"I'll drive because I know Shanghai," David says, jingling the keys and settling into the driver's seat.

Ignoring David's comment, Rachel gets into the car with a sarcastic smile and exclaims, "Look, whew, it has GPS."

David mumbles something inaudible.

Rachel laughs as David drives the car toward the avenue in front of the hotel. Holding the pad with the notes they made last night, Rachel reads aloud: "The threats made by the Japanese Yazuo to the Portuguese police officer are the only thing that can be related to Ronaldo's death in the police investigation. Correct?"

"That's right. As the Japanese are no longer in Shanghai, we will try to get information through other means. Yazuo is out of the game for now," he replies.

"You know those copies of the investigation into Ronaldo's death that Inspector Bo gave us? I've read each page three times. I tried to find something that could guide us, but what I found was that there was no deep investigation. It contains some statements, photographs, and an autopsy report from the Legal Medical Institute. After so many years... I waited to read these articles... maybe understand what happened better, but I found nothing enlightening. They rushed everything just to finish and send the report and the body, but you can tell that something is not right," she tells her partner.

"Do you remember the superintendent's words when he handed us the envelope with these documents? Chief Bo was clear in his message: 'Preserving social harmony is a large component of Chinese police doctrine. Do nothing you'll regret.' I know there are a lot of holes in this investigation," David declares, looking at her.

She nods. "Did you read about the witnesses? We have a start... that agency that provides temporary employees still operates in Shanghai. The police heard and recorded the statements of only a few employees, only six statements. It turns out the key witness is a temporary employee. The name of the entity is Shanghai Hotel Services Employees Ltd."

"Yes, I read that. It doesn't seem serious. The principal witness was not called to testify once after the incident," Rachel comments with a concerned expression.

"This testimony was fundamental because there was only this one witness," adds David. "He provided the police with the company's address as his home address. Well, it wasn't just him. All the so-called substitute employees, in their statements, gave the same address. I believe this is the company policy. I checked the address this morning while you were talking to Alex. I'm sure finding out the addresses of interviewees was not a priority for the police. The name of this witness is Wang Savin Wei. The address of the establishment is at Xintiandi, about thirty minutes from here. This negligence is because of laziness or incompetence from those who carried out the investigation."

"It's been six years since the accident. What story will we tell when we get to this place?"

"Let's say you are Ronaldo's wife, and you want to meet the people who last had contact with him."

Rachel accepts. "Okay, let's go to that company and see if we can get the actual address of that witness."

It is Friday, and it is 11:30 a.m. David looks at the congested traffic and enters the address into the GPS.

Rachel laughs at his distress.

Her partner ignores her laughter and says, "I'm surprised by what Alex told you. He said this was unrelated to the accident that killed Mr. Chan. Is it?"

"Let's do what we set out to do this morning. Find out this man's address. When we get back to the hotel, if you agree, we will review every sentence Alex said and then break it down," she suggests, touching the back of her head and twirling curls into her hair.

David doesn't respond, focusing on the traffic.

She watches David's driving and agrees that he is the right person to drive. He has a good sense of direction and doesn't get lost on the city streets. She just won't admit it to him.

In front of a fifteen-storey building, they park the car. Getting out, they look for a sign with the company's name. They notice people walking on the sidewalk toward the surrounding restaurants. Looking for the company, they read a sign that says, "Hotel services in Shanghai."

The two exchange glances. As they walk through the door under a bright "Open" sign, a smiling, middle-aged Chinese woman greets them, her jaw moving as she chews gum, with a strong smell of cigarettes lingering in the air. Her red hair is tied up in a bun, and she wears huge round glasses to complete her exaggerated makeup.

Rachel suppresses a laugh.

David speaks in Mandarin, asking for an employee named Wang Savin Wei.

The woman makes a face and says she doesn't know anyone with that name, waving them toward the exit. Then she turns her back, sitting down in a squeaky swivel chair. The table in front of her contains only a telephone and a glass of water. She no longer looks at them.

Rachel covers her face with her hands, walks toward the exit door, and feigns sobbing and crying, wiping her eyes with a tissue.

The woman looks at Rachel and asks David, "What's wrong with her?"

He explains her husband died in an accident inside the Grand Kempinski Hotel. This man named Wang was the one who tried to revive him. He adds they are there to thank him in person.

The receptionist's initial coldness vanishes as she looks at Rachel. She speaks in a much more sociable tone, clarifying she is new to the office, having worked there for only two years, and does not know anyone with that name. She assumed they were police officers. Now she points to a chair and motions for Rachel to sit.

Rachel accepts and continues with the act. Her now weaker lament has no tears.

The woman calls on the intercom at the table, asking if anyone knows where Tony went for lunch. She hangs up and informs the fake spies that there are two employees who have worked at the company for over ten years and maybe they know the history of the hotel and the man named Wang. However, one is off today, and the other has gone to lunch. He should return within the hour.

Rachel and David exchange looks, saying nothing.

The receptionist looks at Rachel with a pitying expression and asks if they want to wait or come back in an hour. She points and explains that there is a good, cheap restaurant on the street in front of the building. The two thank her and head to the exit, saying they are going to eat something and will be back in an hour.

It's 1:00 p.m. when they return, and the same woman greets them with a smile. She shows them to a black sofa, worn with time, in the small reception space. They thank her and sit down.

Rachel and David, observing the place, notice that the entire living room floor has a very worn-out green carpet. The yellow painted walls have faded, and there is not a single framed picture on them. Instead, a 2019 calendar hangs on the wall near a white door behind the chair where the receptionist now sits.

The woman dials a phone number and asks someone to tell Tony that the couple is at reception. She hangs up the phone and, smiling at them both, says he'll be right there.

Rachel and David thank her, returning the smile.

A sixty-year-old man, wearing a mustard uniform with the store's name emblazoned on the chest above his heart, enters the room through the door behind the employee's chair. He is a short, very thin man with black hair cut short, grey at the temples, and in the late stages of baldness. His round face has some wrinkles, revealing carelessness in maintaining his beard and moustache.

Tony approaches Rachel and David and bows in a social gesture, speaking condolences in Mandarin.

The partners repeat the movement.

After some introductions, Tony looks at David and says he remembers the case because he worked that night, replacing a worker in the kitchen. "Who's the person you're looking for?" Tony asks.

David replies, "Wang Savin."

Tony keeps trying to remember. After a few minutes, he says, "I don't know his full name. I remember calling him Wang, and I don't know where he lives. He was not an employee with a contract; he collaborated with the company when someone was needed. If there is a need to replace an employee, we call an acquaintance who needs money or a family member or friend. The company manager accepts this policy, as employees endorse the person. I remember that guy because when he changed his clothes in the dorm, everyone saw the tattoos he had on his body. Each hotel has a specific uniform, and we are required to wear the clothes they send to the company. The tattoos he had on his body were horrible," Tony recalls, grimacing.

David asks, "How many people from the company worked at the hotel that night?"

Tony responds that ten people replaced the off-duty employees. The hotel operated that night with around twenty employees, ten from the company and ten from the hotel.

Rachel, sitting on the sofa, observes the conversation between the two.

"Do you remember who guaranteed Wang?" David asks.

The employee responds that it was a cousin and explains, "Li, the cousin, was a contract employee of the company. A good boy. He died in a motorcycle accident."

"So, there is no way to locate Wang?" David asks.

Tony, looking sad, says, "I liked Li. I'll look in the archives. Surely the administration has the address."

He heads through the same door and disappears. After five minutes, he returns and hands over a piece of paper with the address written on it.

David thanks Tony, bowing, and tells him they are going to visit the family now.

Tony looks at Rachel and asks, "Are you here because of the guest who passed away that night?"

"Yes," Rachel responds in a low tone of voice.

"What happened was an unfortunate incident . . . it really saddened all of us who worked that day." Tony seems moved.

"Was Wang the one who found him?" David asks.

"Yes. He was in shock afterward. It was a terrible scene," Tony recalls.

David expresses gratitude and bows. "We will try to discuss this matter with him at the address."

"Be careful," Tony warns, fixing David with a serious look.

"Why?" David asks.

Tony explains, "I'm familiar with these tattoos; gang members wear them in Shanghai."

David bows in gratitude, and Tony returns the gesture to both of them.

The two leave the building, heading toward the car. It's 1:20 p.m. The outside temperature is above thirty degrees Celsius.

Rachel complains about the heat and turns on the air conditioning inside the car. "Let's buy bottled water. What do you think about going to that address now? It's early yet."

"I was going to suggest that to you. The sooner we have all the information, the better for us . . . Ah! Look! It's a McDonald's, we're saved," David jokes, pointing to a restaurant sign.

Rachel's phone alerts her that a message has arrived. She reads it and announces, "It's from Tyler."

David drives and then parks the car in the parking lot. "What does he want?" he asks.

"The new investigation is interesting, but he won't go into details so as not to confuse our heads. Mozart is eating very well; he has never seen cat poop this big. Everything is in order at the office, but he misses both of us." She laughs.

"Only Tyler would write that at this hour," David comments, getting out of the car and walking toward the McDonald's.

9

"Longtang," the Mirror of Social Life

Rachel and David sit outside McDonald's discussing their accomplishments so far. Their conversation blends with the sounds of cars passing by and people talking. David has bought a disposable cellphone and is now activating it. Rachel finds nothing useful on her tablet as she searches for the address and information about Li Gubei.

"I found the address in that area. I'll describe to you what is written about this place: Qibao, an ancient city, is in the Minhang District. This is a 'park and ride' centre in Shanghai, with six bus lines and five hundred free parking spaces connecting to the city centre. Commuters can save on expensive parking fees in the city centre by leaving their cars there and then using the metro or bus lines. The project team started the plan in 2011 and made the centre operational in 2016," Rachel explains.

"So, that's the place?" he asks as they walk together toward the car.

"I'm unsure if the address is real, but the location is in the Minhang District. It's not getting accepted by the GPS. The screen shows that part, but I can't find the street. Anyway, it's about forty minutes away. Shall we go?" asks Rachel.

"Yes, let's follow the GPS as far as we can."

She agrees and sits in the passenger seat.

"Do you want to drive?" he asks, looking at her.

"You'll never have a co-pilot like me ... sit down and drive straight," Rachel responds and murmurs, "Why would I drive? You know the city, I don't."

"This traffic is crazy. It must be the heat," David huffs and starts driving.

Rachel continues reading about the neighbourhood. "The area called Minhang District was where, in the last century, there were residences called Lilong, now Longtang. It was a neighbourhood with houses known by the name of shikumens, where four or five families lived; sometimes there were six or eight in the same house. In this article, it says that a lot has changed in the neighbourhood. Some housing areas have been transformed into tourist centres, but in some residences, the renovation is still pending. Even with the new nomenclature in the remodelled areas, many of the home's residents still use their old address at the post office and GPS can't locate them."

The GPS beeps, as if responding to her skepticism, and identifies the location.

"Look! We're here," David exclaims, stopping the car at a gas station. He gets out and heads to the front door.

As he enters the store, a kind-looking gentleman, appearing to be in his sixties or seventies, greets him from behind the counter. David shows the man the paper with the address and asks if he knows this place.

The old man takes it and reads it, concentration appearing on his forehead as he thinks… he states that the address no longer exists, and that the street now has another name. He goes to the glass display case at the front of the store and points to a very narrow entrance on the other side of the avenue. He announces, "It's an alley that if no one shows you, you'll never imagine exists." David goes to the glass and looks where the old man is pointing.

The attendant explains, "Maybe this is the address you are looking for. When you enter that alley, follow it for about fifty metres until you reach the end. You will see another narrow alley on the right, and that is the old location. Only motorcycles, bicycles, or pedestrians can enter the three buildings that remain unrestored."

David asks if there are other ways out.

The elderly man says, "No," but explains that after leaving the gas station, he can park his car in the public parking lot on the next corner then cross the avenue and come back, walking until he reaches the alley.

David says, "Thank you, sir. This is invaluable help. I couldn't find this place."

The elderly man laughs, his eyes crinkling at the corners. "I've been here long enough to know the ins and outs of this place. The changes in street names and hidden alleys have fooled many people." He then tilts his head, curiosity evident in his gaze. "If you don't mind me asking, what's so special about this address?"

David hesitates for a moment, wondering if he should share the purpose of his visit. "I'm… helping a friend with some investigations into old properties," he replies.

The man nods his head, apparently satisfied with the answer. "Alright, then. Be careful walking down these alleys. There's not much light, especially at night."

David smiles. "Thanks again." He then heads back to the car, sharing his new instructions with Rachel.

She looks at him, raising an eyebrow in surprise. "That was lucky," she comments, her voice full of relief.

"We're going to walk a bit." He laughs, starting the car.

Following the instructions of the convenience store attendant, David leaves the car in the public parking lot. They return along the avenue until they find the narrow street. Upon entering, they continue walking for about fifty metres and notice those famous houses with old brick walls.

Rachel says, "These houses are old. This is pure history."

David nods and continues walking, remembering what the old man explained to him about the narrow alley.

A motorcycle with two riders wearing helmets approaches at low speed. As David and Rachel walk by, the driver stops his motorcycle next to them. The passenger asks, "Do you need help?"

David responds that they are looking for Li Gubei's family.

The motorbike driver says, "It's Duck."

The driver signals for both of them to follow him. They stop in front of an old, three-storey brick building with a heavy iron door painted black. The passenger gets off the bike and opens the iron door. The driver continues sitting on the motorcycle. After opening the gate, the passenger enters the building and gestures for David and Rachel to follow him. The three go up the stairs and stop in front of an old door. The man knocks twice.

According to David's opinion, this door was once white.

An elderly woman slowly opens the door and asks him what he wants. A strong smell of food and the sound of many people talking fill the hallway. The passenger on the motorbike speaks in "Wu," the traditional language of Shanghai, which may not be mutually intelligible to fluent Mandarin speakers. David understands a few words. The man whispers in the woman's ear and points to the two visitors.

David assumes that the man informs her they are looking for "Duck."

The woman looks very disgusted with both of them, closes her eyes, and pulls her mouth to the side. She then speaks in Mandarin to David. "How much money do you have?"

"How much do you need?" David responds.

She enters the apartment, mutters inaudible words, and begins to close the door.

"I have money," David shouts in Mandarin.

The woman, who had not yet closed the door, says, "How much?"

David carries money in a small pouch on his pants belt. After unfastening the zipper, he removes a small stack of Chinese notes and presents them to her. "Here, ninety yuan."

The man takes the money from David's hand, splits it into two halves, gives one to the woman, and puts the other in his pocket. He looks at David and says, "You're paying for my job to bring you here." Showing great agility, he runs back down the passage and disappears down the stairs.

The woman asks what they want to know because she has no time to waste.

David explains Li has a cousin named Wang and they need to talk to him.

"Are you buying drugs?" the woman inquires.

David, uncomfortable with the question and sensing the dangerous atmosphere, tries to be quick. "No, but I need to talk to Wang."

She looks disdainfully at David, taking a step back. "You a cop?"

"No," David replies in English, and adds in Mandarin, "I didn't come to buy drugs and I'm not a police officer. I want to talk to him."

She lowers her eyes and, in a whisper, repeats three times, shaking her head, showing either her insanity or genuine emotion. "Wang is not good…Wang is not a good man…Wang is not good…"

David looks at Rachel, seeking agreement.

She nods yes, and he then says, "I can help you if you need anything."

"Cigarettes," the woman requests.

David, feeling sorry for the woman and at the same time trying to get answers, promises to bring cigarettes soon.

She looks up and tells him, "Li was a good boy; I miss him so much."

David, with no remorse, asks, "Do you know where Wang lives?"

Rachel remains quiet, listening and trying to understand their conversation in a mix of Mandarin and another language she's never heard. She remains alert, careful to watch the dark hallway as there is no light and the windows are covered with what appear to be wooden logs. Rachel bends down to check her boot, where she always keeps a knife. Today she took one from the restaurant.

The woman looks at David and stops talking. With a lost look, she points to the left and says, "He lives in the building next door. There's a red stain on the iron door. His mother lives there, but she doesn't answer anyone. It's on the first floor."

"Does Wang live there?"

The woman doesn't look at David and turns her body as if to enter, but stops and says, "No, but he always brings her food." As she walks in the door, she looks up at the ceiling of her apartment and mutters some inaudible words.

David takes more money from his belt and calls the woman. "Madam."

She turns, looking at him, and says in a low, barely audible voice, "On weekends, Wang arrives very early, between five or six o'clock."

David and Rachel are quiet.

She takes the money and puts her finger to her mouth as if to say, "Be quiet." With a sad face, she enters the apartment and closes the door, saying nothing else, without giving him time to thank her.

The two leave the building and walk toward the narrow, quiet alley.

The same guy on the motorcycle stops in front of them and asks, "Did you find what you were looking for? Are you looking for drugs, problems, or solutions?"

David just thanks him for the help and continues walking, without looking back.

The men on the motorcycle follow David and Rachel with their eyes until they reach the avenue.

They hurry to the parking lot. As he climbs into the driver's seat, David admits, "I need a whiskey."

"Me too. This day is full of surprises and it's not over yet. It's only 5:30 p.m.," Rachel says.

They arrive at the hotel at almost 6:30, tired but fully awake because of the adrenaline. Navigating through the city of Shanghai in a car is a hard task because of the overwhelming traffic. What is really taxing David and Rachel is the heat. The temperature reaches thirty degrees that Friday, and tomorrow's forecast is a sweltering thirty-five. As they enter the hotel parking lot, Rachel recognizes the same car she saw at the restaurant the night before, this time without occupants.

She nudges David as they walk to the main entrance. "It was this car. Remember? I said this vehicle was at the restaurant yesterday."

"Are you sure?" David scans the area, looking to see if anyone is nearby.

"Absolutely." Upon entering the hotel, the crowd of individuals in the lobby surprises them; there are a hundred people milling around, sitting in armchairs and sofas, talking loudly.

David goes to the counter, pushing by several people, and asks one of the front desk staff if she has any messages for him or Rachel. The receptionist doesn't respond and turns to enter the office.

The number of people trying to speak to her at the same time is unbelievable, he notes.

She returns, recognizes David, and moves quickly to attend him.

Without waiting for her greeting, David asks, looking at the crowd in surprise, "What is happening?"

She explains with a laugh, "This weekend there is a big meeting in the hotel's convention hall. These guests are from Japan, Singapore, Vietnam, and South Korea, but we didn't expect them to all arrive together at the same time."

"Do you have any messages for myself or Ms. Rachel?" he asks again seriously.

"None."

As David prepares to leave, the receptionist remembers that she has something for him. She abruptly opens a drawer, takes out a piece of paper, and hands it over, saying, "Sorry, Mr. David, I forgot. You received a call from the US, but before the employee could ask for information, the line went dead. Here is the number of the caller."

David takes it, reads the number, and puts it in his pocket. "Thank you. Is the bar on the first floor?"

The receptionist confirms.

Turning, he looks for Rachel in the crowd, spotting her leaning against the wall near the elevator doors. He gestures for her to go to the upper floor.

"This is horrible," she says, laughing, and enters the first-floor bar with David. They stop and watch the turbulence. People crowd the place.

A waiter, recognizing them, advises them to go to the hotel's terrace, which also has an excellent bar just for guests. They get into the elevator and David presses the floor button for their rooms.

"I'm not giving up... I'll meet you at the rooftop bar in five minutes. If you get there first, order me one on the rocks," Rachel demands.

"And if you arrive first, order mine with two cubes."

10

Rock, Paper & Scissors—Roshambo

Rachel and David meet in the lobby at 4:45 in the morning. They rush toward the main entrance, exchanging waves with the receptionists. In the parking lot, Rachel looks for the black car she saw the night before. The two get into their rental car, and David drives down the quiet street in front of the hotel. He looks at Rachel, noticing that she redirects her attention to the street and maintains a thoughtful silence. A tired yawn escapes her lips, betraying her night's sleep.

"I didn't sleep well," she explains.

David responds empathetically, "I only slept a few hours myself."

Another yawn escapes Rachel as she expresses her concerns. "Do you think it is dangerous for us to venture into Minhang District so early? That man who guided us to Liu's family's apartment asked if we wanted drugs or trouble. Come to think of it, I'm pretty sure Wang is part of a gang, or maybe even one of the Chinese mafias."

Driving, David looks into her eyes and reassures her. "Let's talk to Li's mother. If that man is there, perfect, we can talk to him. Just follow our story; we want to meet the people who were with Ronaldo in the last few days in Shanghai."

Rachel nods but can't shake that nagging doubt. She looks at David with a frown. "I understand, but don't forget what Wang's aunt repeated: 'He's not a good man.'"

David changes the subject. "It's now 5:15 in the morning and the temperature is fine, but it's getting warm." She agrees with him and says that the temperature will reach thirty-seven degrees Celsius today.

Lost among Shanghai's towering buildings, David speaks with a sense of wonder in his voice. "Shanghai is a beautiful city. It's huge. Look around. The avenues are so wide, filled with stunning parks, countless museums, and historic landmarks. You'll fall in love with this city."

Rachel hands David a bottle of water and opens one for herself, also enjoying the view out the car window. This morning is a time of serenity, with a notable shortage of people, cars, and buses on the busy streets. There is a deep sense of peace and tranquility. David observes that many of the city's older neighbourhoods have undergone extensive renovations, but the one they are heading to remains unfinished.

Parking the car in the same place as the previous day, they get out and hurry down the narrow street. Their eyes scan their surroundings, making sure they are in the right place. In the morning, the neighbourhood's streets are devoid of pedestrians, with only a few cars and buses circulating slowly. Most of the city is still awakening from its slumber. Being Saturday, many stores open a little later to allow people to catch a few more moments of sleep.

As they reach the black iron gate adorned with the distinctive red mark, their enthusiasm subsides. They try to open it, but it remains closed, and there is no bell in sight. The alley is silent, with no sign of life. They both stand before the gate, thinking about how to summon someone from within.

David says in a low voice, "That woman, the aunt, told us that Wang would be coming today between 5:00 and 6:00 in the morning. It's 5:30 in the morning. Let's wait."

Rachel nods. "Okay."

With no place to sit, they decide to play rock, paper, scissors, known as "Roshambo." As they play, time passes, and their anticipation grows. Despite their best efforts, laughter bubbles up, escaping into giggles.

Then they hear a creak. They stop in unison, their attention drawn to the iron gate of the third building on the left. An elderly man walks out of the gate.

David approaches the man and, in Mandarin, asks, "Do you know a man named Wang who lives in this building?" He points at the building, where Rachel is standing in the doorway.

The man looks at Rachel and replies that he doesn't know anyone named Wang. Adjusting his woollen hat, he hurries toward the avenue, leaving David looking after him until he disappears into the distance.

Rachel approaches and suggests, "Should we try knocking on the gate? Maybe someone will show up?"

"At 6:00 in the morning?" David replies, rolling his eyes and ignoring her question.

Rachel gently pokes. "Why so bitter? Are you nervous?"

David groans after looking at his watch and confesses, "I'm sorry. It's 6:15 in the morning, and no one has come. I'm getting nervous. I think that woman lied to me, took my money, and even had the audacity to ask for cigarettes."

"That you didn't buy," Rachel comments.

In response, David offers no words, just a sharp look.

"Let's wait another fifteen minutes and then we'll leave. It's not a good idea to stay in one place for too long; you know it attracts attention, and that's not what we want. If you're okay with it, we can come back here after lunch. I think this might be the best solution. What do you think?" Rachel suggests, her tone laced with a desire to avoid any trouble.

"You're right," he agrees, and the two walk back to the avenue.

Suddenly, a motorcycle, with the driver wearing a black helmet, enters the street. As soon as the motorcyclist sees Rachel and David, he makes an abrupt turn, and the motorcycle roars back the way he came.

"Wang! Wang, we need to talk to you!" David shouts, his voice echoing down the street.

The man on the motorcycle revs the engine and speeds away, disappearing down the narrow street toward the avenue.

"Well, we tried… do you think it was him?" Rachel asks, but David remains silent.

She examines the surroundings, and the two walk toward the avenue.

"Maybe, but if it was him, after he saw us and heard me calling his name, I think he gave up visiting his mother. Now… why didn't he come and talk to us? Why did he run away? He doesn't know us. Let's go back after lunch and talk to his mother," David suggests, knowing that locating him again is going to be a challenge.

As they walk down the avenue toward the parking lot, David notices that the number of cars, buses, and people on the streets has increased.

Rachel looks at her partner and comments, "Staying in that alley all this time has made me hungry. I think we better go back to the hotel."

David nods, and since it is already 6:50, says, "Let's go eat."

The two get into the car, David's cellphone rings, and he answers it, his voice full of expectation. "Hey! Did you make it? Great. Send it to the London office; I'll send Tyler to pick it up."

Rachel tunes into the conversation and asks after he hangs up, "What is that?"

"Intelligence friends in Washington," David replies, matter of fact.

"Ah! An old flame?" Rachel teases, her mischievous smile dancing across her lips.

David, with a stern and serious expression, responds, "Allan left that up in the air... I thought it would be a good idea to review the entire Operation Container investigation, since we were the ones who conducted it. A friend of mine who works in Washington got a copy of the investigation. Access would have been impossible otherwise, as the court sealed the case confidential. You know, in this line of work, having the right contacts is everything. My friend will send it in the weekly diplomatic bag to the embassy in London. I'll have Tyler pick it up on Monday or Tuesday."

Rachel, surprised by her companion's secrecy regarding this investigation, adapts to the situation, nodding in approval. "That's an excellent idea. We can examine three different perspectives of the operation: ours, the FBI, and the Firm. We might discover some information that has eluded us until now."

As they discuss their review of the Operation Container investigation, a deafening boom interrupts their conversation in the car, as if an explosion engulfs them.

The car jolts violently, and David grips the steering wheel with all his might, struggling to maintain control as the vehicle spins three times, completing full 360-degree rotations on the asphalt at incredible speed. A second deafening impact hits Rachel's side of the car, bringing it to a screeching halt. The car stops when it collides with a small cement pole on the sidewalk, but the front and part of the passenger-side door are in ruins.

A heavy silence hovers between Rachel and David inside the car for what feels like minutes.

"Rachel, are you okay?" David screams, his eyes fixed on the car door attached to the small post.

"Oh, I, I'm fine..." Rachel murmurs, her voice shaking. "I'm fine, I'm fine." She repeats the words, relaxing her arms and legs to make sure they're still working. Apparently, she is unharmed.

Within minutes, a crowd of worried onlookers gathers, chatting in Chinese and gesturing toward the car and the crash site. David opens the driver's door and jumps out, pulling Rachel by the arm. Some spectators rush to help.

With desperation written all over his face, David looks into Rachel's eyes and asks, "Are you okay?"

"I'm fine; it was just the shock," Rachel replies. "When the car turned, I pulled myself to the centre, between the two seats, instinctively. It was pure luck." Rachel's face is pale, and she takes a deep breath to calm herself.

David wraps her in a comforting hug, his voice full of relief. "It was not my fault. We were very lucky that the car didn't roll over. It spun 360 degrees three times and only stopped when we hit that pole. Thank God there wasn't another car coming in the opposite direction; it would have been much worse."

"Relax, we're safe now, and it wasn't your fault," Rachel says, pressing a kiss to David's forehead, her voice soft as they both try to calm down.

Rachel takes a deep breath and walks to the car, surveying the scene. The passenger door suffered a strong impact. She bends down to collect the papers scattered on the floor and opens the glove compartment. She retrieves the iPad and checks to see if it's still working. Sinking into the driver's seat, she looks out the windshield and notices a crowd gathered around the car. Some spectators take photos, while others capture the scene on video. As she exits the vehicle, she hears a man telling someone that the truck responsible for the collision fled the scene. He's sure he saw the truck run the red light at the intersection and hit their car.

Rachel, though not fluent in Mandarin, understands what the man on the sidewalk is saying. She turns around, trying to spot the speaker in the crowd, but the Chinese voices, combined with the shock of the accident, leave her dizzy and disoriented.

David addresses the spectators, asking, "Who witnessed what happened?" Some passersby report that a truck hit the back of their car, running a red light, and did not stop.

Upon arriving at the scene of the accident, one police officer speaks to David while another reviews the details witnesses provided.

David signals to Rachel, instructing her. "Contact the hotel and car rental company. Explain the situation and ask about the possibility of sending a replacement vehicle."

She distances herself from the chaotic scene, finding a place on the sidewalk to sit. She dials the hotel number and tells the staff about the accident. Five minutes later, her cellphone rings, and someone from the rental company is on the line. Rachel recalls the events, reporting the police presence at the scene. She thanks them and hangs up. She surveys the area and notices that most of the crowd has dispersed. With a sigh of relief, she walks over to where David is talking to a police officer.

Rachel goes over the information she received, explaining that an employee at the rental company says they're not to worry. The police had already contacted and informed them to transport the vehicle to the impound yard for further investigation. The company will send a tow truck to rescue the damaged car and another vehicle so they can return to the hotel.

They continue their conversation with the police, waiting for the rental company to arrive.

A police officer states: "None of the witnesses confirmed that the truck crashed with intention, but they all testified that the truck ran a red light, hitting the back of the car."

The partners express their gratitude to the officer responsible for the information.

After a short time, the rental company arrives, providing a vehicle identical in make and colour to the one rented, as well as a tow truck to transport the damaged car. The young man from the rental store introduces himself and then seeks the police officer to discuss the matter. A few minutes later, he returns to David, handing over the car keys and asking for his signature on a new contract. David signs the papers, thanking him for his prompt help. The two then get into the replacement car and head toward the avenue.

Following a drive of a few miles, David stops in a supermarket parking lot. Nervous and sweating, he turns to Rachel. "What happened? What are these statements? Is it an accident, or was it intentional? And if it's intentional, why?"

"We'll discuss this when we get back to the hotel. Now I need to take a shower and relax," Rachel responds as she runs her hand over the back of her head.

When they arrive at the hotel, David goes straight to his room. They agree to meet again at the hotel restaurant at 10:30 a.m.

At reception, Rachel asks if there is anything for her. The attendant informs her that there is nothing. Rachel expresses her gratitude in English and heads toward the elevator. When she notices a sign stating that breakfast ends at 11:00 a.m., she heads to the restaurant.

She waits a bit and then David joins her at the table. They drink coffee and talk. A waitress approaches and informs them that the front desk has called to say that Mr. Bo from the Shanghai police is waiting for them in the lobby. David thanks her and asks the waitress to inform him that they will be down soon.

Curious, Rachel asks, "What does he want?"

"Let me talk to him," David responds.

Rachel shakes her head and mutters, "I don't know enough Mandarin for a conversation like this."

The two go to the hotel reception, seeing the superintendent, Mr. Bo, and another man sitting on the sofa in the centre of the room. They exchange polite greetings.

"Good morning, Superintendent Bo." David greets him with a smile.

Bo introduces the other man. "Good morning. This is Officer Hokkaido."

They exchange pleasantries and take their seats.

"Do you wish to speak to us?" David inquires.

The chief of police, Mr. Bo, has a curious expression as he replies, "About what happened this morning, the car accident? You were out on the streets early today."

"That's right. We woke up early trying to locate my aunt's address in Minhang District, but we discovered she had moved. We were unaware of the extensive renovations in those old neighbourhoods. The area looks fantastic now. Since we couldn't find her house, I called another uncle of mine who will send me the new address later today. As we were heading back to the hotel, the accident occurred. To be honest, I'm not sure what happened." David's gaze is unwavering as he looks into the eyes of the city police chief.

"Could you please describe how the accident unfolded?" Chief Bo asks, his gaze fixed on David.

"We had stopped at a red light. There were no cars on my side, and none approaching from the opposite direction, just a crowd crossing the street. When the light turned green, I continued down the avenue. There was a powerful impact on the back of the car, and it spun, completing at least three full 360-degree rotations. It stopped when it collided with a concrete pole on the opposite side of the car. I'm still surprised it didn't roll over; it was a miracle. We later learned, talking to some passersby on the sidewalk and with the police officers who made the report, that it was a truck that hit us. The driver fled the scene."

"I reviewed the witness statements and their accounts. I must admit, the witnesses found the accident quite unusual. Several mentioned they felt it was deliberate, as if the truck driver drove the truck toward your car." Bo then turns his attention to Rachel, who was observing the conversation.

"Do you speak Mandarin?" Bo asks Rachel.

"Just a little; I'm still learning," Rachel replies in flawed Mandarin.

Bo shows concern as he asks, "Are you two okay? Was anyone hurt?"

"We're both fine," David assures him.

"Don't worry, we will find the driver and the truck. The most important thing is that you are both not hurt. Enjoy your stay in Shanghai," the police chief assures them. The other officer, who has remained silent throughout the conversation, rises from his chair, and the two men bow to them before leaving.

Rachel and David sit back on the couch, watching the officers as they leave the hotel. Once the men are out of sight, they walk to the elevator.

Rachel asks, "My room or yours?"

"Today, your room," David replies with a laugh.

"It's a mess." Rachel joins in the humour.

"Then why did you ask?" David fakes anger, then laughs.

As the elevator doors close, Rachel notices that Superintendent Bo and the other officer are returning to reception. They hadn't seen Rachel and David inside the elevator.

"David, did you see that?" she whispers to him.

"I saw it."

As the elevator doors close, David looks at Rachel and blinks, aware of the surveillance cameras inside the elevator.

"If they want to talk to us, reception will call us," he suggests.

Rachel nods. "Let's focus on ourselves for now. I'm hungry."

"We're going to have lunch soon. I'm hungry too," David confesses, offering a warm smile.

They enter David's room and hang a "Do Not Disturb" sign on the door handle to ensure no interruptions.

11

Observant, Patient, Logical, Intuitive

David and Rachel are engaged in a discussion about the ongoing investigation. They sit across from each other, reviewing their notes. While she writes on her iPad, he scribbles on his trusty little notepad.

"Are you sure you want to do this analysis now?" David asks with concern.

"I'm fine, don't worry. Stopping is not an option right now…it's better to do what we have to do; we have little time." Rachel looks at her friend. "I can't believe it's only been a few days since we arrived in Shanghai."

"I think like you. Especially with all the information we've accumulated in three days," he says, tapping his pen against his notebook.

Rachel stops writing and looks around his room, realizing it's bigger than hers. There is a queen bed with lamps on each bedside table, a wardrobe with a safe, a counter with cups and a minibar, and a TV. The bathroom has a shower, which David likes. Although there is a large window, Shanghai's tropical climate makes it necessary to use the air conditioning.

"What scares me most is that time passes so fast. It's already Saturday," she declares while taking a bottle of water from the fridge.

"Where should we start?" he asks with his notebook in hand.

"The recording. What Alex said about Mr. Chan." She puts her phone on the table and plays the message.

They spend an hour listening and taking detailed notes on different parts of the conversation. On their fourth pass through the recording, they stop each time they detect Alex's voice or any inconsistent breathing sounds.

"You know Alex is sick, right? He is undergoing treatment. The recording shows that his breathing is laboured but strong. He has stopped a few times to think of what to say. Which is true or false," Rachel explains.

David immediately praises himself. "Working in operational intelligence analysis for years has made us experts, and Alex is aware of this."

Rachel observes David scribbling away in his notebook, jotting down every detail.

"I don't care what he thinks. The information analyst cannot increase or decrease what he knows, what he sees, or what he hears. Being successful in this field requires patience, curiosity, and the ability to distinguish the truth from the lies. To avoid premature conclusions, it's necessary to have a correct notion of what we can investigate and what we can't, connecting with the understandable and the possible."

"I agree. Let's investigate the details about Mr. Chan," he says, dismissing Alex's opinion.

Rachel nods, realizing that her partner, lost in thought, missed everything she said.

"Where do you think we should start?"

"Tomorrow is Sunday. How do you feel about going on a tourism adventure? Lianyungang is where Mr. Chan's container factory is located. Let's go there. We can try to get his home address while we're there. It's a five-hour drive," she says, rolling her eyes and rubbing her forehead.

He opens the map of Shanghai on the iPad and searches for directions to the city of Lianyungang. "Hmm... maybe..." David mutters, pointing at the path of the roads on the map.

"I don't want to ask Alex for more information. We can't tell him what we're doing here in Shanghai. I'm sure he knows about the Portuguese police operation. The matter died when he said he had no one to help us here," Rachel states.

"I will not ask the police chief either. That would raise suspicions. The superintendent thinks we came here to Shanghai to help with the Portugal operation. I wonder how he would react if he found out it relates to Ronaldo. If we inquired about a stranger who passed away in 2013 out of nowhere, that's going to stink," David says, his words punctuated by the sound of the fridge door closing. "We both know what happens when someone asks too many questions," he adds, his eyes meeting Rachel's. The sound of the bottle cap popping open fills the room.

"I understand. You're right. We can't ask for anything different from the Shanghai police. Alex has clarified the authorities have not investigated Chan's death. It even seems like a warning."

"Another thing: I can't ask intel any more questions. I don't want to draw their attention, or they're going to be suspicious. You know they work directly with the Firm. They won't give me any information." David rubs his forehead with his fingers and lowers his head in displeasure.

"How are we going to do this?" Rachel asks.

"We have information about the factory where he worked and the position he held within the company. In fact, it was a significant function in any factory here in China," he says, leafing through his notebook.

"You're right."

"Alex said that the Firm's agent who came to Shanghai talked with Mr. Chan's boss at the factory. Let's do the same thing. They hired us to investigate Mr. Chan's disappearance by his children." David tosses the empty bottle of water into the garbage can.

Rachel silently taps her fingers on the table.

"We'll look for the company's annual balance sheet on the computer. See the organization chart of the management positions in 2013. Who was who? Every company has to publish this yearly. It will take a lot of work, but we will find it," David confirms.

"Great idea."

"Once we discover the boss's name, I'll call and schedule a meeting and pay him a visit at the factory," David suggests with a smile creeping across his face.

"Alex claims that Mr. Chan travelled to Shanghai to pass on information and visit his sister. Was that true? Maybe the boss at the factory, a friend, wife, or someone who worked with him knows something different. That's just a thought, a possibility," Rachel suggests and opens a small package she picked up on top of the fridge.

"Hey! You're eating everything!" he exclaims and demands, "Give me a piece of that chocolate."

She takes another bite, looking at him, and continues with the conjectures. "Mr. Chan wasn't a fool. He was a spy and an informant, and he had to protect himself in any way he could. We don't know about his life here in Shanghai. Perhaps he came to see his sick sister. It could be it wasn't just that, but we have to find out the truth to understand what he was doing in Shanghai every month. We cannot trust anyone's word."

"Alex indirectly said that Mr. Chan was in charge of the two container operations. With emphasis, he said that he passed on more information in other operations," David says, staring at the wall.

"Now, I ask you… how many people did Mr. Chan break financially? How many organizations were affected? How many people did the police arrest? The FBI confirmed the success of their operations based on anonymous information in various media outlets." She smiles at him wickedly. "You know how it works. When we don't want to say where the data came from, we always say it was anonymous information."

David, thinking about every word she said, shakes his head and claps his hands on the table. "We will try to contact Mr. Chan's family."

"I agree." Rachel bites the corner of the right side of her mouth. "Ow, ow!"

He remains quiet and thoughtful.

"What made you so curious that you requested a copy of the second phase of Operation Container?" she asks, remembering the conversation they had.

David doesn't answer.

"I think it's great that you requested a copy of the entire investigation." She elicits a response.

"What catches my attention and makes me curious is how Alex gives up the thumb drive. When he goes to Brazil to talk to you, he doesn't complain. He says that you do the right thing by giving it to your boss."

Attentive to what David is saying, Rachel stays quiet.

"Reason with me. Alex spends a lot of money to get those documents. There are airline tickets, daily maintenance, car rental, and a hotel. Ronaldo and Chan die the same year. Do you think coincidence is possible?"

She remains silent, analyzing his words.

"Back to the tape… why does Alex agree you did the right thing by handing the thumb drive to your boss?" David completes the doubts by questioning Rachel.

"You're completely right," she admits. "I didn't see that."

"You walk into a terrible whirlwind; you couldn't analyze anything coldly back then. It's all very brutal what happens, but you can see it now, like me. Can you?" David asks.

"My God! Now I'm remembering. I see American intel agents meeting with the superintendent the same week that Alex talks to me." She walks across the room and sits down and leans over, looking at David. "Alex assures me it's okay that I didn't give him the flash drive because Mr. Chan provides other information that changes the course of the investigation."

He interrupts. "What did he say now on the phone to you? That 'after Mr. Chan hands over the thumb drive… the Firm has no further contact with him.'"

"That's right." As she sits up, Rachel's pulse quickens, and she feels a surge of adrenaline.

David continues the reasoning. "Alex lied when he goes to visit you in Brazil. Why?"

She places her hand on her head and massages her temples with her fingertips, as if experiencing a headache. She looks at him and speaks with a hint of hesitation in her voice. "How does Alex know the pen drive stays with me and not with Ronaldo? The American intelligence warns Alex that they are coming to get the information from the thumb drive in the Brazilian police HQ? Why is Alex calm? Does he know what information is on the pen drive?"

"I'm still working on finding answers to those questions," David admits.

Rachel watches her partner.

He gets up from his chair and turns and questions her. "Does anyone look for the pen drive in the hotel room when Ronaldo dies? If the documents are as crucial as Chan suggests, why doesn't Alex try to find out where they are after Ronaldo's death? Why doesn't he inform Mr. Chan about Ronaldo's death and the undelivered documents?"

Rachel gets up from her seat and begins pacing back and forth, distressed, and drinks her water in big gulps. She places a hand on her forehead, takes a deep breath, brushes back her hair, and settles back into her chair.

With the air thick with tension, they sit in silence, pondering the recent revelation. Then, as if on cue, the two turn and speak in unison.

"The thumb drive."

"That thumb drive has the answer!" David laughs.

With her eyes fixed on the wall, she doesn't respond, concentrating on calming her breathing. She turns to David and glares at him.

He continues, "Does Mr. Chan try to find out where Ronaldo is when you meet him? Does he say anything about documents other than the USB stick?"

"Do you think Mr. Chan killed Ronaldo?" Rachel gasps.

"No, that's not it. I can't explain to you how my mind is working, but I understand your question. The possibility of Mr. Chan killing Ronaldo is zero," David replies and asks again, "Did you see what the thumb drive contains?"

"Yes, I saw."

David looks at Rachel and demands, "What is on the pen drive?"

"There are many copies of export documents, as well as several reports from both Japanese and Chinese companies. I don't know what they are. There is also a list of names of people, companies, and phone numbers. I write most of what I try to identify in Chinese, although some parts are in English."

"So, is it contraband?"

She drinks more water but doesn't respond to the question. "One thing caught my attention, but I couldn't quite make it out. It looked like a blueprint for a shipping container, all outlined with measurements and specifications, like an engineering drawing. Think of the detailed plans an architect makes for a house, but this is for a shipping container, and I know nothing about them. Losing Ronaldo confused me. When looking through everything on the flash drive, nothing jumped out at me… Eventually, these documents would return to me for analysis or something, so I hand them to the head of the Department of Intelligence and then stop thinking about them."

"Does Mr. Chan tell you he will deliver other documents?"

"Oh! I remember one detail. In the elevator, I noticed he was clutching a small package, no bigger than a shoebox. The package was wrapped in plain paper and had a small plastic pouch glued to the top containing some papers. I couldn't read what was written on it, but it seemed like a mail dispatch. It all happened so fast inside the elevator," she recalls.

"I imagine the scene." David understands.

"Another thing is the way Mr. Chan throws himself into the elevator. The impression I get is that he was running away from something."

"Tell me what you think is important," David asks, sitting up on the bed.

Rachel snorts and says that even though she's tired, she'll finish. "I think a lot about why Chan has thrown himself into the elevator. The first thing he said was, 'Ronaldo'? I replied in English that Ronaldo was in the car, and I was there to get the papers. Speaking in clear English, he explained he didn't have time to make copies and hands me the pen drive. He said all the information we needed was there, but he had another document to deliver later. I said I was going to travel in the afternoon, but he could deliver it to Ronaldo at the hotel. Chan didn't answer because at that very moment the elevator stopped on the fifth floor, and about six people got on."

"Interesting, so he has more documents…" David says in a low tone of voice.

Rachel looks at the ceiling, trying to remember more facts, and continues, "In the elevator, Mr. Chan stands near the elevator exit, and I stay behind with several people in front of me. On the ground floor, he disappears, going left, in the lobby's direction. When I get off the elevator, I looked for him, but I didn't see him. I go straight through the crowd to the mall entrance. That's when I saw the two men at the exit. They are looking in all directions, as if searching for someone. I leave in the middle of the crowd, and the men follow me. That was the impression I got."

David hands her a bottle of water, smiling.

Rachel doesn't drink and says, "I felt scared because I didn't understand what was happening. I think maybe I am exaggerating. Police work, being followed… these things that go through my head. Remember the cinema story? Where did I change my clothes? So… from the cinema, I go straight to the sidewalk in front of the avenue, as I have agreed to wait for Ronaldo at the door. I stay there, looking at the traffic, the people walking. I even talk to some tourists. And I see the two men again, but now they are heading toward the cinema door."

David writes down everything that Rachel says.

She stops, as if remembering something. "They are talking on a radio they have in their hands. They are looking for someone. I think at that moment that it is indeed me they are looking for, but lucky for me, Ronaldo parks the car on the side street, and I escape."

Rachel finishes her story, and a sudden revelation comes to her. "David, they weren't following me or looking for me. They were looking for Mr. Chan."

David furrows his brow.

Rachel places her right hand over her mouth and closes her eyes, shaking her head, demonstrating her displeasure.

David asks, "Are you sure that in the lobby, you recognize those two men when you get out of the elevator?"

"I recognized them both. I saw them in the hallway on the twenty-first floor of the Konsako. The man at the elevator door, I'm sure, had a gun, and the other was standing at the emergency exit. It was them; I am positive," Rachel responds, opening the bottle of water and taking a sip.

"Now things are taking a different turn," David utters.

"Come check it out here on my iPad. Look at this. The headquarters of this Japanese company, Konsako, is in Japan. They only use the office on the twenty-first floor of the building in Shanghai for affiliate businesses. Look at this also! On the nineteenth floor is the company Mr. Chan works for, CTLG, the container company," Rachel says, pointing at the display.

David sits down next to Rachel and starts reading the screen. He stops, takes a deep breath, and concludes, "So, it isn't you they are looking for. When they go out on the street, in the same direction you go, they are trying to find Mr. Chan. Why? Why does this happen at that very moment when you are there? Maybe they are looking for Ronaldo?" David scowls and looks at Rachel. "Now I believe that what you suggested might be true."

"What did I suggest? I suggested a lot of things today," Rachel asks David as she opens a packet of cookies.

"Perhaps there are other business dealings Mr. Chan has in Shanghai that Alex is unaware of. Alex emphasized that the meeting location is new to the Firm. For five years Chan delivers documents in People's Square, but just in this delivery he changes the address."

Rachel, attentive, listens to him and continues eating her cookies.

"Now, I ask you…Why does Mr. Chan change the meeting place and prepare to meet with the Firm's envoy at that address? Why change something that has worked for so many years?" he asks, picking up a cookie.

"Because he has to go in that building anyway," she replies.

"That's right, Rachel," he agrees and continues to analyze. "Mr. Chan goes there because he has to do something else. Because of this, he is there."

"Hmm." Rachel runs this through her mind.

"Of course. He schedules an appointment at the company where he works. The place is under renovation … if anyone asks what he is doing there, he'd just say he works at that company and wouldn't have any problems."

"You're kidding me! How come we haven't seen this before?" says Rachel.

"Alex kept it a secret from you, which is why you've never seen it before." David is cold with his words, very rational, but angry.

Rachel could never imagine that Alex would lie to her.

"This entire story between you and Ronaldo in Shanghai is getting more complicated. We have serious incidents that happened that day. There is an incontestable connection between the deaths of Ronaldo and Mr. Chan! Based on everything we talked about and analyzed today, it is pretty clear these deaths aren't accidental, but there's still something missing from this puzzle that we can't see."

"Fuck Alex," Rachel blurts out. "I am shocked at what we have so far. I worked for the Firm for two years. During that period, I communicated with Alex only five times. Note that the pen drive problem never existed. Only once did he come to talk to me about Ronaldo, and he said, 'that Ronaldo is a good person, a great friend.'" Rachel makes a face, imitating Alex the day he said that. She stops talking, and her eyes fill with tears.

"I know it's shocking," David said, "but we will find the answers, I promise."

"I'm starving. Let's have lunch now! I can't do any more analysis. I'm tired." Rachel falls onto the bed and pretends to pass out.

"My God, how can you eat so much? Well, I'm hungry too. How's your body? I can't believe I didn't get hurt in the accident, but the stress was fierce; my body aches. I need to take a muscle relaxant." He rises from his chair, the sound of the wooden legs scraping against the floor echoing in the room.

Rachel gets up and walks across the room. Opening the bedroom door, she walks out into the hallway and says, "We're going to eat here at the hotel. I saw at the front desk a vending machine stocked with a variety of stuff. From what I remember, it seems to contain medicinal products. Let's go there. Perhaps it contains a muscle relaxant."

"If not, let's go to a pharmacy." David rushes toward the elevator.

12

Peek-a-Boo! I See You!

"Wow! Look at that," Rachel says and points at something on the iPad sitting on the restaurant table.

"What?" he asks without looking at her; he's playing something on his phone.

"I found the org chart of directors and such, along with the annual balance sheet of the CTLG in 2013," Rachel says, watching him celebrate a game win.

He puts down his cellphone and sits next to his partner.

She passes the iPad into his hands and gets up from the chair, warning him, "Sign the bill. I'm going upstairs. I'll be in your room in fifteen minutes."

"Okay," David says and continues reading what's on the iPad.

The server approaches the table with the lunch bill in her hand and asks David, "Please, could you sign?"

He signs, takes the receipt, and walks toward the elevator, continuing to read the information on the iPad.

Two men pass David as he leaves the restaurant, and one of them brushes his arm, nudging him. He apologizes and looks at the men, but they don't respond and disappear inside.

"Shit," David says aloud in annoyance.

Rachel doesn't go straight up to her room; she goes to the front desk. This afternoon, the hotel lobby area is empty.

"Good afternoon, Mr. Zhang. Do you have anything for me?" Rachel asks, reading the receptionist's name on his jacket.

"Yes, Ms. Rachel." Mr. Zhang picks up the flowers on the table behind him and places them on the counter.

She thanks him, opens the small envelope stapled to the bouquet, and reads, "Flowers are better than words." It does not contain the signature of the person who sent it. When she finishes reading, she looks at the attendant and says, "Please, Mr. Zhang, put these flowers in the trash."

"Yes, ma'am. Anything else?" He picks up the flowers and places them under the counter.

"No, thank you very much," she says with a smile and walks toward the elevators.

The smiling attendant hands the flowers to the receptionist.

Upon arriving at her partner's room, Rachel opens the door and overhears David talking to someone.

"Thank you, cousin. I'm will come and visit you. Don't forget to send the address." David hangs up his phone and notices her entering the room.

"Who was that?" Rachel enters the room and sits in the armchair in front of the table.

"My cousin, who lives in Hong Kong."

"Do you have an aunt who lives here in Shanghai?" she asks, surprised.

"I have. He'll send her address," he replies.

"Cool." Rachel nods, gets up, and walks toward the window. She opens the curtains, and the sun enters the room. She watches the city and the sky, predicting a beautiful day, and it makes her want to leave the hotel.

David looks at her, lost in the visuals, and clarifies, "I told Chief Bo that at the time of the accident, we were looking for my aunt's house. Assuming he asks me where she lives, who she is… you know how suspicious that is… we'll have a cover story."

She laughs and says, "You're amazing. Everything has to be perfect. As sure as the rain that falls."

Rachel continues the conversation, watching as David grabs a clean shirt from the closet and heads into the bathroom. He doesn't close the door and calls for her. She follows him, her eyes fixed on his muscular back, marked by two scars: a bullet wound and a knife cut. Helping him straighten his shirt, she understands like no one else how David's life in the FBI was difficult.

"Let's go. I need to look for a pharmacy; I'm going to buy a muscle relaxant. After all our conversation, we need to go to the hotel where Ronaldo died. We'll make up a story. Let's tell the manager that my cousin is getting married here in Shanghai and I need to see the guest rooms. Also, I want to look at the pools, restaurant, etcetera. We'll say that the guests will be in town for the weekend, Saturday and Sunday, January 25th and 26th. Thirty people. We will do an analysis of the environment where Ronaldo stayed."

"Why? What do you think this will help with? Apparently it's all described in the death investigation." Rachel shows she doesn't feel very comfortable going to the hotel.

"I need to see where he died so I can visualize everything with the information we've gotten so far. You've never been to that hotel either. You've only read the report," David says, confronting her.

"Well, if it's visualizing… It's only 3 p.m.; it's early. We can go to the Konsako building too," she suggests.

"Good idea. Let's see if we can do all that today." He leans over to put on his socks.

"David! Can you dial it back to 110 volts, please?" Rachel's laugh echoes throughout the room. David seems to run at 220 volts again. She opens the door and walks out carrying the iPad.

"Okay, okay," David says, looking in the mirror and combing his hair.

"I'll meet you in the lobby in five minutes," she warns him.

She goes straight to her room and changes the shirt she's wearing. Rachel puts on a clean white T-shirt with some graphics and trades her sneakers for a pair of mid-calf flat boots. She tucks a knife she got from the restaurant into her boot, enters the bathroom, and puts on some not-quite-red lipstick. She combs her hair and makes a mental note: *I need a manicure.*

When she arrives in the lobby, David is already waiting for her. They walk to the parking lot and get into the car, trying not to have memories of the day before.

After about twenty minutes of driving, David parks his car in the visitors' area of the Grand Kempinski Hotel's parking lot. The two enter the great hall and find that the reception area appears to be empty. They look around, trying to locate any employees. A receptionist appears and stands up from behind the counter. He lifts his head, looking at the two with a surprised expression, and then a giant smile crosses his face.

"Glad to see you, Mr. David. It's been a long time. Welcome to the Grand Kempinski Hotel."

David, with wide eyes, stands frozen and speechless.

Rachel looks at the receptionist and senses that there's more to this scene than meets the eye. She takes in what she sees and glances at the attendant's name. Finding a small badge attached to his brown suit with the name "Michael" on it, she studies the man. Young, in his early thirties, tall, with piercing eyes and curly hair, he looks like he might practice some sport or martial art. His fitted shirt fits reveals every contour of his pectoral muscles, suggesting a well-toned physique.

"Handsome man," she mutters.

Her partner remains in shock.

She looks at David, not understanding what is happening. She breaks the ice that has set in, pulling him by his right arm and saying, "This hotel is exquisite. Your family will enjoy staying here."

David wakes up after hearing her voice, looks at the receptionist, and stammers, "Hi, Michael. What are you doing here?"

"I arrived from London two months ago. I came to visit my sick mother. Her health isn't very good, and my siblings can't come to Shanghai. I stayed a little longer and now I'm working at this hotel." Michael looks David in the eye, as if trying to explain himself. He writes some numbers on a hotel card and passes them on to David. "That's my number. Call me. Tomorrow is my day off. Now, what can I do for you?" Michael asks, looking into Rachel's eyes.

David puts the card in his pocket and tells the story he and Rachel had arranged earlier.

The receptionist announces that he will call the manager to receive them. He picks up the phone at the reception and points to some couches, motioning for them to sit down.

The manager arrives and introduces herself as Mrs. Lingalyn. She is a small, very thin Asian woman in her fifties with short hair. Her eyes are almost impossible to see, but she has a wide smile on her face. Mrs. Lingalyn asks if they want to speak in English or Mandarin.

David introduces himself, introduces Rachel, and they all greet each other. He declares to the manager that she can speak in whichever language she prefers.

Mrs. Lingalyn explains to them that for the months of October, November, and December, the hotel is no longer accepting reservations as it will be closed. David informs her that he will make reservations for thirty guests on January 25th and 26th.

The manager smiles and invites the two to accompany her to the elevator. She describes the hotel's amenities, including five different suites, a games room, children's play areas, a gym with exercise equipment, three restaurants, and a bar. In conclusion, she takes them to the hotel's pools, explaining that the swimming area is a single-storey complex with four separate pools.

The two partners note that a major renovation has taken place. Wood has replaced the ceramic floors, and a kind of rubber now surrounds the entire area around the pool. They have placed cameras in every corner of the area, and a fountain separates the adults' and children's pools, all in full view of the lifeguards. It all seems to add up to a much safer environment.

Rachel and David study the entire complex and remember the photographs of the place at the time of Ronaldo's death. They come back to reality hearing the manager ask if they understood what she explained.

They hadn't listened.

Not answering the manager, and pretending she didn't understand, Rachel asks in English, "Is this place safe?"

The manager replies, "Yes, it's very safe. We have three lifeguards who rotate daily."

They all make their way back to the hotel concierge, and the manager writes an estimate of the price, handing it to David. He looks at the document and thanks her with a bow. They leave the hotel, heading toward their car.

As they leave, Rachel notices, parked a little way from the car, the same black vehicle she saw following them to the restaurant and comments this to David.

"It can't be. It's another car," he suggests. They both enter the rental, David in the driver's seat and Rachel in the passenger's.

"Maybe!" she replies, looking at the clock on the dashboard and confirming that it's 4:00 p.m.

The message he was waiting for arrives on his phone. David writes down the address and phone number and calls his aunt, explaining that he is in Shanghai with a friend and will visit her, if possible, later today, around 7:00 or 7:30 p.m.

Rachel, with the address in her hands for Konsako's lab, looks for it on the GPS.

David pulls out of the hotel parking lot and heads toward the highway. Thirty minutes later, when they arrive at the address, the first thing they see is the Cathay cinema. He parks the car on the side street, just as Ronaldo did to pick up Rachel back in 2013.

She remembers being in awe, looking at the avenue full of cars and buses. On Saturday, in that neighbourhood, there are many tourists and locals walking through the shops. It's a beautiful sunny day at thirty-three degrees Celsius.

The two get out and walk to the Konsako building. As they enter the main floor leading to the elevators, several stores on the ground floor catch their attention and they notice customers carrying various sizes of bags crowding them. They stop in front of the elevator with a group of other people.

David looks down the hall, remembering the descriptions Rachel had given him. His attention stops at the door through which they entered. Startled, David sees the same two men who passed him at the restaurant, walking slowly but not looking at any of the stores. One of them focuses on David and confirms that David is also targeting them. The man spins his head away, but the elevator door opens and people enter, carrying David inside.

Rachel and David notice inside the elevator that the mall is on the first, second, and third floors of the building. There are also dental and medical offices. The elevator is full, but by the time they reach the twenty-first floor, it's empty.

The elevator door opens, and a sign reading Konsako Enterprise Inc. Chemistry Laboratory is spelled out on a glass wall. They walk down the hall as if they are looking for something specific and no one comes to talk to them. They confirm that there are lots of people working and talking inside the lab office, but the men Rachel saw that day in 2013 are not there. The two make their way back to the elevator, this time descending to the nineteenth floor. The door opens to a company's front desk, and an attendant hails them. David reads a giant sign on the wall behind the receptionist's desk that reads CTLG.

Rachel, smiling, walks toward the receptionist. She approaches the woman and explains that they have made a mistake as they are looking for a dentist. The receptionist informs them, with a smile, that the dentists are on the fifth floor.

They re-enter the elevator and press the button for the fifth and ground floors.

Upon reaching the ground floor, the two do not head toward the main exit but leave the elevator on the left, as did Mr. Chan. Discovering a fire door, they open it and come across the stairs. Taking the stairs down, they emerge in the garage. They realize Mr. Chan used this route to escape the building after giving Rachel the flash drive. Maybe that's why the men who waited for him got lost. They return via the same staircase to the ground floor lobby and exit through the main door toward the Cathay cinema.

"Now we can see how it all happened."

"Exactly," Rachel says.

"It wasn't you who was being followed, but Mr. Chan," David reaffirms. Rachel and David walk to the car in thought.

"Did you write the name of Mr. Chan's boss from that 2013 org chart?"

"Yes, I have it here." She pulls a piece of paper out of the back pocket of her jeans. "The director's name is Chongkunli Wu. I have confirmed that Mr. Chan's name on the org chart is below his."

David turns on the windshield wipers as there was a quick downpour while they were in the building and asks her to navigate for him on the iPad.

"Look up that name and try to get a phone number or address."

David bends over, placing his hand on Rachel's head and lowering it below the dashboard.

"What are you doing?" she demands, complaining, not understanding why he put her head almost on the floor of the car.

"Rachel! Rachel, look at these two men coming into the parking lot."

She looks up and sees where David is pointing through the window. Surprised, she recognizes the car. A black Corolla is parked three parallel lines away from them, and the two men are walking toward it.

"That's the car that's been following us. It's the same guys." Rachel ducks her head again and confirms this to David.

"When we entered the elevator on the ground floor of the Konsako building, I saw them, and then again today at lunch at the hotel restaurant on my way to meet you," David says, certain they were the same people.

"Okay, come on, let's follow them," Rachel commands.

The identified car leaves toward the avenue, toward a highway that the partners do not yet know. David drives, and Rachel monitors them so as not to lose sight of them. After fifteen minutes, the two men stop in front of a house in the neighbourhood named Puxi.

David comments that this is an excellent neighbourhood in Shanghai, that many rich people and especially foreigners live there as they can still find houses of a comfortable size to live in. The two men get out of the black Corolla and enter the house. David parks a considerable distance so they can see what's going on. They decide to stay inside the vehicle, waiting to see if anyone else enters the house.

Using the iPad, Rachel looks up the address where they are parked and locates the house on Geoearth. She then accesses the Shanghai City Hall website, looking for the residence data. She finds the owner's name, phone number, and address. Rachel reads this to David, noticing that a couple approaches the car and stares at them. When David sees the situation, he improvises by hugging Rachel, and the two pretend to kiss. The couple walks down the street, smiling but not turning back.

"A couple's surveillance routine, as expected," Rachel reflects.

Rachel captures some photos with her cellphone while the men exit the house. One of them sits in the driver's seat, and the other, as if he wants nothing, takes a quick glance at the street.

"Glass eye," David says and laughs.

"As always," Rachel says, also laughing.

Following them, they drive back to the city centre.

The black Corolla stops in the parking lot of a bar/restaurant, and the two men get out and enter the place.

David turns around the block, pulls into the same parking lot, and turns off the engine. He looks at Rachel and asks, "Are we going to sort this out now?"

"Let's go," she replies, opening the door and exiting the car. Seizing the moment, Rachel takes more photos of the black Corolla and the license plate.

David opens the door of the restaurant, and they both enter. He notices the two men talking, sitting at a table almost in the centre of the room. Many people are present at the bar area, including at the counter, but it's not crowded. The stench of cigarette smoke lingers, while classic '70s rock 'n' roll provides the background music.

One man spots them as they approach the table. He tries to get out of his chair, but David moves fast, leaning over him with determination and keeping him seated.

"Aren't you going to invite us to sit down?" David asks.

The two men exchange glances, irritation clear on their faces, and one of them points to the free chairs.

Rachel sits next to the more muscular man, and David sits next to the other.

"Why are we being followed since Thursday, the day we arrived here in Shanghai?" David asks.

Rachel places her right hand next to her boot, ready to pull out the knife if necessary.

Until that moment, the two men remain silent, not making a single gesture. Their eyes look distant, and the fingers of the smaller one tap on the table as his breathing quickens, tension building in the room.

The smaller man begins. "My name is Oshiro," he says, pulling a police badge from his back pocket. His voice is firm as he adds, "I'm part of the Tokyo Police, working in the intelligence sector for organized crime." With a quick, decisive movement, he stuffs the wallet back in his pocket.

The other man does the same thing and says his name is Liwei Huang. He presents his Shanghai police badge and explains that he is also an investigator for organized crime intelligence.

David doesn't even consider their performance and states with authority, "You know all too well that I'm David Ho and this is Rachel Barnes. We don't need to make our presentations, as you must know everything about us. What we want to know is the reason for this surveillance."

"Yazuo," Oshiro replies.

David shakes his head, not agreeing with what Oshiro said. Rachel remains quiet and attentive to what they're talking about, ready to defend herself or David.

"Why Yazuo?" David asks Oshiro.

"Because of her," Oshiro replies in not-so-perfect Mandarin.

The other officer named Liwei explains, "Yazuo will try to contact Ms. Barnes."

"He gave us a phone number at the Shanghai Police Station when we talked to him," David informs.

"That number is under surveillance," Oshiro replies, staring at him.

Rachel asks Oshiro, "How are you so sure he's going to contact me?"

"Because Japanese intelligence intercepted a conversation in which he quotes you," Oshiro tells her.

"Do you think it scares me saying that? You don't know what I've lived through and the countless times I didn't die," she tells Oshiro.

"Sorry, I didn't get it. Are you trying to say you're following us to protect us?" David asks.

"No," Liwei replies to David and looks at Rachel. "We're here to arrest Yazuo."

"Oh! So, you're following us because Yazuo is going to contact us and maybe try to kill her? Are you here to arrest him? Are we your bait?" David asks with quickened breath.

A server arrives at the table and asks what David and Rachel want. Tempers are hot and no one wants to order anything, but Liwei orders two more beers. The server notes the order and leaves.

"We know what you're doing here in Shanghai. You're here trying to find out if the Yakuza killed the Brazilian federal agent," Oshiro tells David.

"Excellent! You and all the Shanghai police know this, but you are mistaken because we are here to help in Operation Portugal. Wow! You guys are amazing," David, with a sardonic sense of humour, tells Oshiro.

"Blah, blah, blah…" Liwei scoffs and says, "You should thank me for protecting you."

"I think you're the one who needs protection because you're the one who was followed to this bar." David laughs, preparing to punch Oshiro in the face.

Oshiro and Liwei get to their feet and push back their chairs, their faces set in hard lines, eyes narrowed, looking like they're ready for a fight.

Rachel and David also get up, ready to join the fight.

Liwei takes a wad of money out of his pocket and throws it on the table, looking at Rachel, and says, "He'll contact you."

"Honey, when he gets in touch, we know what to do," Rachel replies, confronting Liwei. Both men move across the floor.

Oshiro opens the door of the restaurant and they both leave the bar.

The server arrives with the two beers and pours one for David and one for Rachel. Without caring about what is happening, she takes the money from the table and heads to the next table.

David and Rachel sit down and drink their beers. They smile at each other. They clink their glasses, bursting out in laughter, drawing the attention of the other customers.

"Well, for a while, these men will disappear from our sight, but they will send others to follow us," David tells her.

She pulls out a small envelope from her pocket and starts telling her partner, "I received this today, along with a bouquet."

David picks up the paper with the message and reads.

"Bloody hell, Rachel, why didn't you tell me that?" he says, upset with her.

"Because I don't know who sent those flowers. I didn't think it was important, and I told the receptionist to throw the flowers in the trash," she continues. "So far, the flowers have said nothing. There has been no message. Maybe there will be in the future, but I can't imagine how."

"Don't worry, that's nothing," David says, analyzing the situation and understanding that this matter is best forgotten. He drinks the last sip of the beer and returns the paper to her. "What time is it?" he asks.

"6:30 p.m."

"I'm going to call my aunt. Hell! I have to find a pharmacy."

They leave the bar, heading toward the parking lot.

13

Confession Is a Double-Edged Sword—
It Brings Peace or Destroys It

"Tyler! Come on, it's too early… wait a minute," Rachel complains into her cellphone.

She looks at the clock; it is 7:00 a.m. on Sunday. Calculating the time in London to be 11:00 p.m., she turns her cellphone to speakerphone, gets up, and opens the bedroom curtains. Stretching, she climbs back into bed and covers herself with the sheet.

"Go ahead."

"Since I haven't heard from you, I'm calling," Tyler explains.

"It's fine. It's day four, and we're gathering a lot of information. Everything is going better than we thought. How are you? How is your investigation?" Rachel decides not to tell him about the accident and the intel agents following them so as not to worry him.

"The things here seem to move at a snail's pace. I can't do this alone," Tyler confesses, his voice cracking.

"I doubt it. Only those who don't know you would buy what you're saying." She laughs.

"True, but I need you and David here," he says before falling into a thoughtful silence.

"Did something happen?" Rachel asks.

"I'm missing the two of you. I can't live without being pestered." Tyler laughs.

She grumbles, wishing she could have slept for a few more hours, and pulls the blanket over her head.

"The truth is, I need your help. You have many contacts that I don't. I need some specific information from your contacts at some banks here in London. Also, do you know the management and reception team at the

Real Grand Hotel in London? The manager doesn't like me because I dated his daughter a while ago and it didn't work out. He doesn't trust me."

"I understand. They are good people. They always help whenever I need it. I'll give you a phone number and a name… get in touch with them. Now the daughter's problem, I can't solve that." Rachel laughs.

"So, you see, I've been going up to the apartment every day, right? And Mozart, that fur ball, just can't close his mouth—meowing, whimpering, or maybe he's singing Queen, who knows? I don't say 'meow,' but he's like my little fuzzy shadow, following me everywhere. It's clear he's been asking for you. I've tried to 'talk' to him, but it's like talking to a wall—a very cute and judgmental wall. If anyone hears me, they'll think I'm crazy!" Another laugh erupts from the phone.

"Miss you. We'll be back soon, next week."

"I'll call David now."

"Yes, call him. He'll be happy to hear from you. Thanks for taking such good care of Mozart." Rachel hangs up her phone.

Sitting on the bed, she watches the sun enter the room, illuminating the walls and furniture. She gets up and goes to the bathroom to take a shower. After forty-five minutes, she meets David at the restaurant for coffee. He had warned her; he doesn't want to eat anything today, just black coffee.

"Did you like my aunt?" David asks.

"Describing her unique quality is like trying to explain the plot of a David Lynch film—complex and a little mysterious," Rachel explains, choosing her words as carefully as a cat crossing a road.

"It doesn't matter. My family is all like that. Here's a surprise," David replies. "Good news. The phone number you found for Chongkunli Wu, Mr. Chan's boss—I called him."

"Oh! That is good news."

"After some persuasion, he agreed to talk to us. We have planned a meeting for Monday at 10 a.m. at the factory."

"Tomorrow, excellent," Rachel says.

The waitress brings David a cup of coffee, and he takes a sip, enjoying its powerful aroma and full taste.

"Where are we going today?" she asks.

"Let's try to find Wang," David answers.

"Did you talk to Tyler?"

"Yes, what a clown," he replies, taking another sip of coffee from the cup.

Rachel and David, after finishing breakfast, walk side by side toward the elevator.

"Let's go to Wang's house," David says.

They get out of the lobby and exit into the parking lot, making their way to the car.

Sitting in the car, Rachel looks out the window as sunlight dances across the glass. The sky couldn't be clearer, a perfect blue canvas painted with just a few wisps of white clouds. The light seems to permeate their skin. As the car passes through the avenues, she feels an unusual tranquility envelop her. For the first time in a long time, the weight of her problems seems almost insignificant, as if every kilometre travelled makes them smaller and easier to solve. The sunny day seems to reflect Rachel's new optimism; she believes things are getting better and that resolutions are on the horizon. There is a warm, reassuring voice in the back of her mind that whispers, "Everything is going to be okay." And when she looks at the endless stretch of avenue where they suffered the accident, nothing disturbs her feeling of peace.

They make it to the address in record time, thanks to the light traffic, and David parks the car in the same spot as before. Walking down the narrow street, they feel the cool breeze blowing through the nearby alleyways.

They arrive at the small three-storey building, and David pushes open the gate. Climbing the stairs, they walk down the long corridor on the first floor until they reach a blue-painted door. The sound of his two knocks echoes down the hallway. Rachel stands behind him.

A man of about thirty-five—Asian, bald, shirtless, only dressed in his underwear, and covered in tattoos—opens the door. He looks at them, moves his mouth from side to side as if he's chewing on something, and doesn't say a word.

David speaks in Mandarin. "Please, we want to talk to Wang."

As he closes the door, the sound echoes down the hallway. The two overhear a slight argument inside the apartment. A woman opens the door and looks at them.

Rachel observes that she looks very thin and pale, her skin is dull, and her long black hair seems unwashed for days.

David asks if she is Wang's mother. The woman looks disdainfully at them and questions what they want.

"I'm sorry we're bothering you." David leans his body toward the lady, introducing Rachel and saying his name.

The woman's face remains blank, showing no reaction.

He tries to explain that they are there to thank Wang.

She looks down the hall, listening to David. She gives a suspicious gaze and asks, "Thanks for what?"

The two partners hear whispers and the sounds of chairs scraping inside the apartment, but they can't make out what is being said.

Rachel approaches the door with a smile on her lips, and David explains to the woman that she is the wife of the man Wang tried to save at the hotel, distorting the history of the investigation.

The odour emanating from the apartment is a strange mixture of cheap cigarette smoke and some other smell that neither David nor Rachel can identify.

The woman looks at them with wide eyes and starts speaking in a mixture of Mandarin and a dialect that David cannot recognize.

"Do you plan on showing your gratitude with money? If you give it to me, I'll pass it on to him."

As Rachel approaches the door, she hears a faint creaking sound coming from the hinges.

In a fearful state, the woman enters the apartment and exclaims, "Wang is not here."

"Is there any way you could arrange a meeting between us and him? Pick a day and time, and we'll return," David says, his voice laced with sympathy.

With a loud slam, the woman shuts the door in their faces.

"What now?" Rachel asks.

"Wait."

A couple moments later, the old woman opens the door again, her voice almost a whisper. "This afternoon at five." She closes the door without giving them time to say anything.

The couple leaves the building and starts walking toward the avenue. Just as they are about to reach the end of the narrow street, the roar of a motorcycle engine fills the air. They look back and lean against the wall of a house under renovation. The bike passes them, just missing them as it pulls away.

David's voice rises in anger as he exclaims, "What the hell?"

"Let's get out of here," Rachel says, beginning to walk faster.

David and Rachel arrive on the avenue and walk toward the parking lot. Then, out of the blue, the two motorcycles from before hit the pavement, revving their engines. One stops right in front of David and the other stops next to Rachel, blocking her path. The tension is thick, and a sudden sense of alarm grips them both.

"What the hell do you want? Isn't it enough to almost run us over?" David turns from one man to the other as they sit on the motorcycles.

One of them, wearing a black helmet with yellow scratches, catches Rachel's attention. He's shirtless, revealing a chest full of tattoos that Rachel recognizes. Next to him, the other man has tattoos on his arms and legs and is wearing a black short-sleeved t-shirt.

"You're bothering us. A word of advice: you'd better not come back here," the black-helmeted man with yellow scratches warns David.

"What's your problem?" David asks, facing him.

Rachel holds David by the arm.

"You. I'll say it again," the man's voice is authoritarian as he repeats the words to David, "Don't come back here."

"If I come back, what's going to happen?" David retorts.

Rachel's gaze, through her sunglasses, remains fixed on the other man. Every time David speaks, he revs the engine and jumps the bike up toward them, making them flinch.

"We cannot guarantee your safety. I've warned you." The roar of the motorcycles fills the air as they speed off down the avenue.

A man who was walking behind the partners when they left the narrow street had stopped and listened to the discussion. The moment the bikes disappear, he approaches them, asking if they are okay.

David and Rachel respond "yes" but are not confident that the situation has ended.

The man informs them, "Everyone in this neighbourhood knows to steer clear of those guys; they have a reputation for being dangerous."

The two appreciate the man's information, bow to him, and hurry toward the parking lot.

"I think we have a problem," David says to Rachel, trying to control his breathing.

"All problems have solutions. Let's get out of here and talk somewhere else," Rachel says as they get into the car.

David pulls out of the parking lot and drives the car toward the same avenue where they had the accident the day before.

"I'll give you my opinion," she says, unsure of what he'll want to do.

David nods his head, a serious expression on his face.

"In London, we know we can rely on the police, but here, who do we turn to for help? Our plan involves potential risks, but will the local police provide us with protection? We don't have any rights or claims in this country. We need support. Can you imagine if something happens to you or me in a situation where we won't be able to explain how and why it happened? See what trouble we're going to have? I don't even want to imagine; it makes me upset."

David listens.

"I understand you want to come back later, but is it worth it? If he possesses any information, he won't disclose it to us. There is a connection between Wang and his family to the Triad or another gang in Shanghai, no doubt about it. Did you see those tattoos on the first man in the apartment? And the other on the motorcycle? They are images of the Yakuza. In the background, it is the same thing! The only difference is that here the Triad is in charge. They threatened us, and we'd be stupid if we didn't listen. I don't think it's good to come back here. Don't forget that we're alone in Shanghai."

"Got it, you're one hundred percent correct. Wang is involved with one of the Triad gangs, I'm sure of it," David admits. Rachel nods in agreement.

"Let's think of another way to fix this situation," David suggests and continues. "Our meeting with Mr. Chongkunli Wu at the factory is at 10 a.m. sharp tomorrow, and to make sure we're on time, we need to leave the hotel no later than 4 a.m. It's crucial that we come up with a compelling story. It's the only way we'll be able to get the answers we need. Today, we'll plan all the questions we're going to ask."

Rachel listens, seeing that he has calmed down.

"I'm on the same page as you. Shanghai can be safe for us, but it's up to us to make smart decisions and take measures. Tomorrow is very important. One thing is certain: there is a connection between Mr. Chan's and Ronaldo's deaths. Talking to Chan's boss is a strand that can now give us answers we haven't had until today."

David keeps talking; he understands she's right, and he's pulled the rope too much.

"Sorry, Rachel. You're made of iron and steel; I've always known that. It hasn't been since I worked at the agency in the States that I had so much stress and so much pressure. It's been years, and I'd forgotten what it was like to have that good adrenaline racing through my body."

"If you agree, it's almost noon. How about we do a sightseeing stop in Shanghai?" Rachel, sensing his discomfort, suggests this to calm him down.

"Let's go. It's Sunday, and it's a beautiful day. These last three days have been stressful, but it's been worth it for the amount of information we've gathered. Aside from the accident, the Triad, and the get-together with the intelligence officers, everything else is fine."

They both laugh out loud until tears stream down their faces.

"Maybe later, when we get to the hotel, you can call Michael," Rachel says, looking at him.

He turns around and replies, "You want to know the story? I know you very well…"

Rachel laughs and says, "You can share if you like, but just know that sooner or later, you'll end up giving everything away. If you decide not to tell me, I won't pester you again. But trust me, my curiosity is through the roof. Sure, I want to know."

David laughs with Rachel and stops the car at the traffic light, right where they had the accident with the truck. The two survey the avenue and the intersection of the street, trying to understand what happened.

"I've known Michael for a few years. We lived together for about six years in the States. As an architect, he secured an excellent job in bustling New York City. After, in Washington, he found another job, not in the same category as the company he worked for in New York, but he always said he didn't care that he was earning less. What mattered was that we were together."

"Was he the reason your marriage ended?" Rachel asks.

"My marriage ended before I met him, but the separation happened because I didn't want to live a lie anymore."

"Did this affect your relationship with your family and with the FBI?"

"My family didn't know what was going on, and my wife was even more in the dark. In my professional life, in my day-to-day life, everything was fine—constant phone calls, scheduled lunches at my ex-wife's house on weekends. In eastern families, divorce is just not a thing. You are married for life, no matter what the circumstances, especially when children are involved. My father was very insistent, pushing me non-stop to get back with my wife."

Rachel listens to her friend describe the past with a lot of emotion.

David is engrossed in what he's telling Rachel and continues to drive. "Our relationship got difficult until one day we broke up. He moved to London, and I moved back home with my ex-wife. She and the children received me very well. My dad threw a party for friends and family. It was an interesting celebration because my physical body was there, but my mind was elsewhere. You don't know how hard it was for me."

Rachel notices that David's hands are gripping the car's steering wheel.

"My job helped me a lot; I accepted all kinds of trips and operations that were offered. I became the 'yes' agent for everything. The family side and the relationship with my 'wife' deteriorated. I must have missed that life lesson about relationships. It's been two years since I experienced that drama."

In a crowded public parking lot, David stops the car and continues speaking, looking at Rachel. "One day I sat at the dinner table with my ex. The kids had already gone to sleep. We talked, but I didn't tell her I was gay. I was so scared; I just told her the truth about the end of my feelings toward her. She agreed to separate, imposing that we would not legalize divorce until the children are older. I said yes and agreed to all her terms."

His story catches Rachel off guard. She's moved and can't utter a single word; her eyes fill with tears for her friend.

David runs his hand through his black hair.

"In the end, I approached my father about unblocking my mother's estate from the court. Before, I never cared about it, but then I accepted it. I let my father know I was leaving the agency to start my business. He was thrilled; he never liked that I am a cop, always pushing for law school. I did law, but then in the end, the bureau was my choice. When my mother died, I didn't even think about her inheritance—I was doing well, had a solid job, good wages."

David takes a deep breath and leans back in the car seat. "The death of my mother caused me a horrible trauma from my childhood and youth. Growing up without my mother was very difficult. As you always say, everything has its time. I believe they kept the inheritance for many years in the bank to help me when I needed it. When I received this bounty, the feelings of debt, guilt, self-harm ended. In that moment, I was sure that I could follow my dreams, be who I am, and do what I want without having to ask anyone for anything."

David is sweating a lot as the car's air conditioning has stopped working.

Rachel tries to soften the heavy conversation, telling him, "When we get back from this trip or if it's possible even today still, we'll change cars."

David interrupts her and adds, "To finish the story, when I left the bureau, I called you and Tyler to be my partners in this investigation company. You accepted. When we moved to London, I didn't look for Michael at first. After three months, with my life stabilized, I decided to look for him. I found him because an old friend who lives in Washington came to London and mentioned he stayed at Michael's and his plastic artist husband's house. One night, I walked into an artist's vernissage and saw Michael there. He was excited to see me and introduced me to his 'life partner.' At that moment, he destroyed me. That's when I was sure I lost Michael forever. From that day on, I've lived with no emotional involvement with anyone. I don't want to have any."

She listens and says, "This story is very sad."

"Yesterday, when I saw him at the front desk of the hotel, I was in shock. I never imagined he could be in Shanghai, let alone working at the front desk of that hotel."

Rachel cuts off the conversation. "He gave you a phone number and said today is his day off. Call him and listen to what he has to say."

David looks at her, disbelieving.

"If he hadn't given it, I wouldn't be telling you to call him, but he gave you the number."

David seems to stare into space and doesn't respond.

"Call him now," she insists.

David takes the card with the phone number out of his pocket. He looks at Rachel, not sure if he should or shouldn't.

"Call him now," she pushes.

He calls the number written on the card, has a quick conversation without affection, and hangs up.

"What did he say?" she asks.

"He says he's going to send me an address and I'm supposed to be there by 2 p.m. I'll find him." David looks nervous.

Rachel, a big smile on her face, says, "Drop me off at the hotel. It's only 12:30. I'm going to organize the questions we're going to ask Chan's boss. Lunch in the hotel restaurant if I get hungry. Oh! Don't forget we're leaving at 4 a.m."

Crossing the avenue, David feels a whirlwind of emotions at the thought of what lies ahead. He agrees with himself: *Don't overthink it, just let things happen as they will.* When he meets with Michael, he's just going to listen to everything Michael has to say.

He parks the car underground this time. Rachel and David get out of the car next to the elevators without talking. An annoying silence predominates.

David turns to his friend and expresses his gratitude. "Thank you, Rachel."

She feels awkward. Since she doesn't like these kinds of scenes, she mentions, "Please, when you leave, bring me those documents that Chief Bo gave you."

"Two minutes, and I'll give you the papers," he confirms.

After they exit the elevator, she enters her room and starts setting up her desk for work.

When David enters her room, he places the documents on the table and asks, "Are you alright?"

"Go, go. Opportunities in this life only knock on your door once."

As he's walking out the door, David says to Rachel, "When I get back, show me the questions we're going to ask."

"Alright." Rachel pushes him out of the room and closes the door. "Bloody hell. I need to pee." She rushes to the bathroom.

14

Wang and Li's Story

"What are you going to do? They will be back at 5 p.m.," Meilin Savin shouts to Wang in the Dalian-Hua dialect, her voice tired and tinged with despair as she re-enters the apartment. The men inside the apartment struggle to decipher her meaning. This dialect proves to be a formidable barrier for those unfamiliar with it.

Wang and his three friends sit around the table, the aroma of morning soup filling the room. He remains silent, looking at his mother. Wang's friends exchange uneasy glances. Earlier, when she approached the apartment door to speak to the foreigners, Wang warned her not to reveal his presence. His face carried a stern and unyielding expression.

Wang listens to the entire conversation, keeping every word in his memory. He can't help but wonder why this couple is so insistent on looking for him now, six long years after the hotel incident. This is the third time they have looked for him. He knows they discovered his whereabouts through his aunt, and this realization torments him. His affection for Meixiu Gubei is unwavering, but he can't understand why she revealed his address.

Hui, who has stopped eating, turns to Wang, his eyes a mixture of concern and frustration. "It was your aunt who gave them the address. I'm glad I wrote their license plate number down. Do you remember? It's on that piece of paper I gave you last night."

Friday, when the partners visited his aunt, it was Hui who accompanied them to the building. Little did he know that their true intention was to meet Wang. Hui, at twenty-five, and Wang, at twenty-eight, grew up together, inseparable since childhood. They have shared their education, their work, and their lives. Their friendship is deep, and today Hui is not only a friend but also the manager of Wang's business and a trusted bodyguard.

The four of them sit at the table while the couple chats with Meilin outside the apartment. Wang gestures for Aiguo, Hui, and Mingli to shut up and pay close attention to what the man is saying to his mother. However, in their haste, Aiguo and Hui inattentively drag their chairs, creating a noise that echoes throughout the hall.

At the end of lunch, Wang rests his head on his arms, his eyes scanning his friends, the apartment, and, most importantly, his lingering mother. The visits he makes, often scheduled for Saturdays or Sundays, have become indifferent to her. He brings not only the boundless love that only a son can offer but necessities like medicine, money, and food. There are times, however, when his responsibilities make it impossible for him to come in person, and then he sends one of his friends. Together, Wang, Meixiu, and Hui pool their resources, doing everything in their power to help Meilin combat her addiction to crystal methamphetamine and her excessive consumption of *baijiu*, a potent distilled spirit similar to whiskey, the one most consumed in China.

Now, as Meilin faces the harsh reality of stage four cancer, doctors offer a grim prognosis: Her life hangs in the balance. Aiguo, the oldest of the four friends, has always taken responsibility for taking care of Meilin. The night before, he slept in the apartment, and his concern for Meilin's safety forces him to remain vigilant in case the persistent couple return.

Sunday morning arrives, and the knock on the door comes unexpectedly. Aiguo, still in his underwear, runs to answer it, thinking it's someone else. He opens the door and finds a stranger standing in front of him, asking to speak to the boss. Perplexed and taken by surprise, Aiguo hesitates, not knowing how to respond.

After David identifies the person he wants to see, Aiguo closes the door without saying a word. He warns Wang about the unexpected visitors, a Chinese man and a Western woman. Wang is sure they are the same people who have been looking for him since Friday. He calls his mother, instructing her to answer the door but to be discreet about his presence. His primary aim is to find out what this couple wants.

Meilin, sober that morning, complies with her son's request. Although weakened by her illness and the potent medications she takes daily, she walks to the door with unsteady steps. She is determined to hold her ground during the impending conversation. The moment David asked her to arrange a time to converse with Wang, Meilin, not knowing how to respond, entered the apartment to ask Wang for instructions.

Upon learning that the couple wants to arrange a meeting, Wang concludes they must have discovered his presence. He can't take any risks. He instructs his mother to tell the couple to return at 5 p.m. that same day, a calculated move to control the situation.

Wang has an incredible ability to blend into busy streets, fooling those who don't know him. His imposing height, fair skin, and well-defined muscular structure often lead people to question his Chinese heritage. His brown eyes sometimes take on a hint of green, and his straight, light brown hair further enhances his distinguished appearance. When he's shirtless, a tapestry of tattoos adorns his back, chest, and both arms. Much of what he learned about life is on the streets, alongside his cousin Li and a handful of friends, some of whom remain by his side while others have met their fate or tried to escape the neighbourhood's clutches. Wang grew up in an environment where survival often meant going it alone.

During his childhood, his aunt played a pivotal role in his life. From the age of four, she would pick him up at her sister's apartment or meet him on the street to give him food, a bath, and clean clothes. As a child, he could not understand why his mother remained bedridden, sleeping all day. His aunt explained that his mother was sick. He enjoyed the time he spent with his aunt and cousin Li because they allowed him to indulge in his favourite pastime: playing. Wang grew up in gangs in Shanghai's notorious French Concession neighbourhood, which encompasses today's Luwan and Xuhui neighbourhoods.

Wang adapted to the harsh reality of a life tainted by crime. He and his friends ventured into other neighbourhoods looking for unsuspecting victims to rob. Upon returning, they handed over their illicit gains to the gang leader, a routine that continued without encounters with the authorities. The chief shared a small portion of the day's spoils daily with Wang and the other gang members.

In the early days of his foray into robbery, Wang's cousin Li was his faithful companion. However, after accompanying Wang and his friends on several excursions, Li, at thirteen (while Wang was eight), decided that a life of shoplifting was not the path he wanted to take.

Hui fills the room with incessant chatter, a stream of words cascading without pause, while the other men lean back on the sofa, interested only in their cellphones. Wang, with his head resting in his arms, watches everything unfold. He can't help but let his mind wander, remembering a time that seems like a distant dream, a reality long lost.

Meanwhile, at his aunt Meixiu Gubei's apartment, she stands at the living room window, hidden behind the tattered curtain. She remains vigilant, her eyes fixed on the couple who visited her the day before as they leave the building next door and walk toward the avenue. They parked four motorcycles in front of the building, but she soon spots two of Wang's friends among them. She whispers to herself, "The mess is done."

Closing the window, she retreats to one of the kitchen chairs. Tears well up in her eyes, the unique pain of a mother who has lost her beloved son weighing on her heart. Amid the sounds of imaginary laughter inside the apartment, she goes back in time, as if transported to a happier time. It is as if a movie screen passes before her, and she watches the children running and playing around the kitchen, a poignant reminder of the innocence and joy that once filled their lives.

* * *

Wang and Li come from Dalian, a bustling port city on the Liaodong Peninsula in northeast China; it's a city with a rich history and was founded by Russian settlers who left a distinct cultural mark. Mandarin is the official language of Dalian, but most of the local population speaks the Dalian-Hua dialect.

Wang's family is comprised of two sisters, his mother, and his aunt, both of whom were married and lived in Dalian. Li's mother, Meixiu, was married to Boris Gubei, while Wang's mother, Meilin, was married to Vitaly Savin. Both Vitaly and Boris are descendants of Russian immigrants. Families enjoyed a comfortable quality of life. Although they did not have great wealth, they never suffered from a lack of sustenance and the need to work to earn their daily bread. Vitaly and Boris found work at the busy port, loading and unloading containers.

Life, as it always does, takes unexpected turns, and sometimes these paths lead to destruction. One fateful night, in the middle of a routine work shift, someone summoned Boris to the administration office. A stern supervisor gave Boris the devastating news that Vitaly had been involved in an accident, and the company took him to the local hospital. The situation took a darker turn when Boris arrived at the emergency room and was told that his brother-in-law had lost his life. The police, looking for clues to unravel the mystery surrounding his death, wanted to interrogate him. Fear gripped Boris as he faced this shocking turn of events. He didn't know what caused Vitaly's death or who would want him dead. He took pains to express to authorities that fifty-five-year-old Vitaly was an energetic person who was always happy and had a wide circle of friends at work. He was a dedicated husband and father, with no known enemies.

The tragic incident left everyone perplexed, and despite extensive investigations, the motive for the murder and the identity of the perpetrators remained shrouded in mystery, forever haunting those left behind.

Wang was four years old when the tragic loss of Vitaly Savin struck the family, leaving Meilin, his mother, a young widow at thirty-five. Meilin was a radiant and vivacious woman, her beauty complemented by her hair, which was always clean and well-curled. She always adorned herself with clothes made by her own hands. Despite being small, slender, and one-and-a-half metres tall, her presence captivated and enchanted everyone. However, the brightness of her life dimmed when she realized Vitaly would never return home. The nightmare that unfolded was just the start of his ordeal.

Witnessing her sister's daily descent into the abyss of alcoholism following the tragic death of her husband, Meixiu stepped in to care for the abandoned child, Wang.

As the days turned into weeks, Boris returned to work, and one afternoon, he approached his wife with a heavy heart. He confided in her. Disturbing rumours circulated at the port among co-workers. They talked about Vitaly's involvement in illicit shipments to the Russian mafia. This resulted in his life being ended by the local gang in Dalian. They warned him to be very careful because danger could be close.

When Boris finished reporting on the events at the port, his wife proposed a bold move. She suggested they leave Dalian, sell both houses, and start over in another city. Boris embraced the idea, and all five moved to Shanghai. The money from the sale of the two houses did not meet his expectations, but as Meixiu said, always consistent: "We cannot undo what we decided." In Shanghai, they used the money from the sale and some of their savings to secure two modest two-bedroom apartments. The two sisters became neighbours, living in different but close buildings in a neighbourhood famous for its dangers. Boris assured his companion that their stay in this place would be temporary and that they would soon find a safer and more promising address.

Li and Wang, just nine and four years old, began their new lives. As fate would have it, Meilin became weaker, first battling anemia and then succumbing to pneumonia. Through it all, Meixiu took on the role of caregiver, tending to the needs of her sister, Wang, and Li. Meanwhile, Boris took a job at the busy Port of Shanghai. Every day, he woke up at dawn and embarked on a gruelling hour and a half bus ride to work. In this life full of sacrifices, in the end they returned to showing signs of normality. Little did they know it was just the calm before another storm.

One fateful night, Boris came home with a fever and a persistent cough. He reassured Meixiu, attributing it to a mere flu, and insisted on returning to work the next day, despite the feverish symptoms. That same night, a concerned work friend took him home in a deteriorated condition, urging Meixiu to take him to the hospital. Boris, firm in his decision, refused to go and insisted he would recover on his own. Coughing attacks and expulsion of blood followed two days of relentless fever. In sheer desperation, Meixiu made the painful decision to call an ambulance from a pay phone. She rushed Boris to the hospital, only for him to pass away that same night.

For Meixiu, the world fell apart in those dark days. Even in suffering, she had a sick sister to care for and now two young children who depended on her. She did not hesitate, as she had always been a woman of great responsibility, of unshakable and coherent religiosity in the face of life's challenges. This indomitable spirit served her well, especially in deciding for her sister's well-being. She was forty-five when Boris succumbed to that enigmatic flu, and despite losing the love of her life, she made a firm decision not to give up.

Every day, like clockwork, Li returned from school at 11:30 a.m., following a well-established routine. He would have lunch, dedicate an hour to studying, and then take on the responsibility of looking after his cousin. Li's mother took on the role of caregiver for her sister and Wang during the morning. With this coordinated schedule and his son's invaluable help, Meixiu got a job at a toy factory, on the doll assembly line. Her shift began at 1:00 p.m., an arduous effort that stretched into the late hours of the night, sometimes ending at 11:00 p.m., leaving her to return home around midnight. Most of the time, the children were already sound asleep, unaware of the hard work she faced.

Wang and Li were the living amalgamation of their parents' DNA. The two cousins were very tall, with fair skin and blond hair, but their eyes displayed the unmistakable characteristics of their mothers, having a distinct Chinese physiognomy, although with a greenish-brown tone. During their early years, the cousins became targets of relentless bullying at school because of their unique appearance. Wang, in particular, struggled to resist taunts and often got into fights, but one day he dropped out of elementary school. Li, blessed with physical strength and resilience, persevered and completed high school. Childhood was not good for them, but despite everything, they remained inseparable. Li's mother recognized Wang's boldness and sometimes excessive impulsiveness for his age, which caused her to keep Li busy, often involving him in household chores and assigning him to help take care of her sister. However, she never allowed the two boys' bond to weaken.

At thirteen, Li became a young man, with an imposing height of 1.80 metres. Like his father, he was neither thin nor overweight, but had a robust build, with well-defined muscles and strong bones. In stark contrast to his cousin, who had an aversion to sports, Li took part in athletic activities at school, but the girls preferred his cousin. Wang's charm attracted the neighbourhood girls.

One night at dinner, when Wang wasn't home, Li told his mother about his decision to find a job, explaining that he wanted to get away from the robberies and gangs in the neighbourhood. His mother offered Li her wholehearted support. The next morning at dawn, Li ventured into the busy market street, determined to get a job. His daily responsibilities involved assisting market vendors in selling fruits and vegetables, as well as requiring the physical tasks of unloading and loading goods into trucks. He would accompany traders on their trips to different neighbourhoods. The demanding work brought a sense of accomplishment, and Li earned the respect and admiration of experienced professionals. It was tiring, but at the end of each long day, he returned home with money and food, which meant a lot to his family.

As time passed, the cousins led separate lives. Whenever their schedules were aligned, they spent time together, but trips to the cinema and leisure weekends at Parque do Povo became distant.

Wang's gradual disappearance from the neighbourhood began when he turned fifteen. At first, he would be gone for a day or two, returning with a casual explanation that he had spent the night at a friend's house. His aunt Meixiu expressed her concern and asked him not to do this, emphasizing the worry it caused her and Li. However, Wang's absences became more prolonged, extending to three days and then a week. This pattern persisted for six long years. He visited his mother and took money and food to his aunt. He never explained the origin of what he brought.

In late 2011, Meixiu witnessed Wang turning twenty-one and leaving the apartment for good. She tried to convince him to reconsider, but her efforts were in vain. Li was too busy with his work to say goodbye to his cousin that day.

Wang had a friend who took him on his motorbike whenever he visited his mother. This friend never entered the apartments but waited on the sidewalk, keeping his distance from their lives.

One rainy afternoon, when he got off the bus, tired from a long day of work, Li saw Wang on a motorcycle with his friend. It was a Saturday, around 6:00 p.m. With determination, he ran down the narrow street, hoping to catch up with Wang and talk, but the distance between them was too far. He watched his cousin dismount from the motorcycle, carrying a bag, and disappear into his mother's building. Li quickened his pace, walked around Wang's friend, and climbed the stairs to the first floor. He stood in front of the apartment door, waiting for Wang to appear.

When Wang opened the door and came out, he found Li waiting for him. "Can I come in?"

He felt disturbed by his cousin's unexpected presence. Wang replied, "I have something to do. I can't stay here for long."

Undeterred, Li persisted. "Let's talk a little."

With a touch of rudeness, Wang replied, "I don't have time."

Ignoring his cousin's attitude, Li proposed, "Let's go to the cinema tomorrow. What do you think?"

Wang, continuing to walk down the hall, looked away and replied, "We'll see."

"Cousin, I want to talk to you," Li shouted.

Wang stopped halfway, turned to Li, and revealed his bruised face. Li approached him and asked, "What happened to you?"

Wang met Li's gaze. "My life is no longer the same. That's nothing. My face is all blue and red; it's ugly. I just broke my nose and got a black eye and a cut on my forehead. It was just a fight. In two weeks, everything will be fine."

Li, carrying two heavy bags, placed them on the ground and hugged Wang, saying, "You know I'm always here to help you. I know you're in trouble, but if you need me, come home and I'll help."

Wang, returning the hug, pushed Li, using the excuse that he needed to leave. He descended the stairs, climbed onto the back of the motorcycle, and disappeared into the rainy streets, leaving Li with a mix of worry and confusion.

When Wang left Li in the building's hallway, he couldn't help but notice his cousin's tears. It was a heartbreaking moment, but life must go on, demanding that they find the normalcy to endure.

So, in the first months of 2012, amid the challenges, some positive developments were occurring in their lives. Meixiu remained dedicated to her work at the factory, while Meilin's health improved. Li, now twenty-seven, was still looking for a job at the port, still clinging to his dream.

Meixiu often reminds him of his father's years of work at the port, which resulted in substantial savings. That's what he aspired to: a stable job that would provide enough pay to get his mother and aunt out of those apartments and into a better life. He had a stable position at a temporary services company, was registered, and performed various office tasks. On occasions when an employee was absent, he replaced them, earning a little more that month. His salary was modest, but he managed to save more than half of it every month.

During the weekends, Wang would continue to visit his mother, often arriving late at night. His newfound independence with his own motorcycle eliminated the need for his friend's help to bring him home.

One night, while sharing a meal with her son Li, Meixiu broke the news to him that her sister had informed her of Wang's latest developments. He had bought a motorcycle and seemed to be on the path to bettering his life.

"I'm glad to know he's okay," exclaimed Li, a smile spreading across his face as he embraced his mother. Mother and son fell asleep that night with the feeling that Wang was okay.

Around 2:00 a.m., a faint, almost imperceptible knock echoed at the door. Awaking from sleep, Li, confused, walked to the door, being careful not to wake his mother.

"Who is it?" he asked, his voice low.

"It's me, Wang," was the reply.

Li opened the door and Wang entered; his demeanour was full of nervous energy. Worried, Li asked, "What happened?"

"I need a place to sleep. May I stay here?" Wang asked. His anxiety was evident.

"Of course, you can sleep in my bed," Li offered.

"No, no, no, I'm going to sleep here on the couch," Wang insisted.

Puzzled, Li asked, "Did you lose the key to your apartment?"

An agitated Wang replied, "I'm hiding. Sorry. I can't go to my mother's house."

Understanding the gravity of the situation, Li reassured his cousin in a calm and collected tone, "No problem. Stay here as long as you need."

Wang made himself comfortable on the couch but jumped up and ran toward the kitchen sink, where he vomited blood.

Li stood there in shock, concern written all over his face.

Wang looked into Li's eyes, trying to reassure him, and explained that he had fought and received a powerful hit to the stomach. He insisted, "Tomorrow I will be better."

Worried about his cousin's well-being, Li proposed, "Let's go to the hospital."

Wang, however, resisted. "I can't do that. Tomorrow it will pass. I need to sleep."

"I'm going to make us some tea," Li declared. He entered his mother's room, checking if she was still sleeping.

An unspoken tension hung in the air as the two sat in silence. Wang, still on the sofa, rested his head in his hands, leaning over his legs. Li brewed a steaming mug of tea and handed it to his cousin, who acknowledged the gesture with a nod before taking a sip.

Wang spoke about his situation, confessing, "I did something I shouldn't have done..."

Li, however, interrupted him, "Don't tell me anything now. Go to sleep, and tomorrow night when I get home from work, we can talk."

That night, Li struggled to rest, tormented by his worry for his cousin. He woke up early, got ready for work, and went to see Wang, who was still sleeping peacefully. Li approached his mother's room, gently waking her up without mentioning what had happened. He asked her not to tell anyone that Wang was hiding in the apartment and explained that he would go to work and return around 7:00 p.m. His mother kissed him and prepared for her day.

At 5:30 a.m., Li left his apartment, aware that the hour-long bus ride to work awaited him. Running through the narrow streets, he noticed a motorcycle parked at the end of the alley. Two men were leaning against the nearby wall. They seemed to be waiting for someone. Li's eyes recognized the distinctive design of the helmet resting on the motorcycle; it belonged to Wang's friend, the one who had taken him to visit his mother on previous occasions.

With his head down, his cap partially hiding his face, a scarf wrapped around his neck, and a long worn coat protecting him from the biting cold, Li walked past the men with great care.

He offered a wave, but only one man responded. The other asked if he had seen Wang.

"No, I haven't seen him," Li replied, continuing his way toward the bus stop on the other side of the avenue, in front of the gas station. The morning cold was biting.

Once on board the bus, Li called his mother, asking her not to leave the apartment that day. She assured him not to worry as it was her day off from work. Li also spoke to his cousin, warning him about the two men he encountered. He mentioned the motorcycle and helmet he recognized, advising Wang to remain discreet inside the apartment.

On the way back, near the bus stop on the way home, Li saw two motorcycles parked at the gas station and four men talking. He identified two of the men as those who questioned him that morning.

Li got off the bus, carrying two shopping bags, and headed toward the narrow street. The men at the gas station watched him, but he showed no reaction and continued walking down the street toward the apartment. Upon arriving home, Wang opened the door and Li placed the bags on the table. He then greeted his mother with a kiss, and she put the groceries in a cupboard.

"Cousin, they're still outside. Now there are two motorcycles and four men," reported Li, trying to gauge his cousin's reaction without knowing that Meixiu was listening.

Wang asked, "Where?"

"At the gas station," Li replied.

Wang looked at the two of them and said, "I'm sorry."

His aunt and cousin pulled up chairs and sat in front of him, eager to understand the situation.

"What's happening?" Li asked.

Wang showed his embarrassment and growing nervousness as he rubbed his hands together.

Meixiu intervened and announced that she would make tea for everyone.

"They're going to kill me, cousin," Wang whispered.

"Why?" Li asked, shocked.

"I have a debt. I went to make a delivery, and they robbed me. They stole the package, the motorcycle, and the cellphone. I don't know why they didn't kill me. That was three days ago," Wang explained, his hands still restless.

Li pressed for more information. "Who stole from you?"

"I don't know. It was a black van that hit my motorcycle. I fell, and three masked men, all armed, attacked me, beat me until I couldn't take it anymore. They took the package from my backpack, my cellphone and put my bike in the back of the van. I think it must be another gang, but not from here," said Wang, lifting his shirt to reveal his bruised body.

"I've been trying to explain it to the boss for three days, but he doesn't want to listen to my explanations. He told Hui to warn me that if I lose the cargo, I will have to pay, either with the package or with my life. I know that when they find me, they will kill me. This is not the first time something like this has happened, and whoever loses ends up dead."

Meixiu returned with mugs of tea for both of them, wished them a good night, and retired to her room.

"Where have you slept for the past three days?" Li asked, picking up his mug.

Wang looked at the floor, unable to muster the courage to look his cousin in the eyes. "I've been sleeping on the street," he admitted.

"What was in that package?"

"China White. I'm dead," Wang replied with a desperate look.

"You are crazy." Li reacted with shock upon hearing, "China White."

"I had to do this job. It's my livelihood. I'm part of the group. I never imagined this would happen to me," Wang said, his voice tinged with anguish.

"You're only twenty-two years old, and you're destroying your life. What are you going to do now?" Li asked, showing he was upset.

"I don't know," Wang admitted, his voice shaking.

"How much is the debt?"

"I only carried a hundred grams. The market value is 106,400 yuan, about fifteen thousand US dollars," Wang replied, dropping his body onto the sofa with a heavy sigh.

"What? Where are you going to get all this money? This is nonsense. Let's go to the police and report them. Maybe you won't go to prison," Li suggested.

Wang jumped up from the sofa and exclaimed, "These damn people never forgive those who cheat. They will kill me, they will kill you, they will kill my aunt and my mother if I turn them in. The police are involved in this scheme, along with many important people. I can't do this." Wang covered his face with his hands, overwhelmed by the situation.

"There has to be a solution," Li said, trying to remain calm.

"I don't know what I will do. The money I earned during all this time went to help here and buy the motorcycle. I have nothing left," Wang confessed with clear despair.

"Calm down. Let's think together. Turn off the lights in the living room and kitchen. I'll close the curtains and let's go to my room to talk," suggested Li, hoping to find a way out of this terrible situation.

The two went to the bedroom, taking extra care not to make any noise that could wake Meixiu, who had a work shift the next day.

"Did you go to see your mother today?" Li asked, his concern for his family clear.

"No, I didn't dare leave here. I can't take any risks. Aunt told me she is much better with the new medicine. She still has a few drinks now and then, but her health has improved," Wang replied, reassuring him about his mother's condition.

Li, eager to help and full of questions, said, "If you try to talk to the boss again, you can propose to continue working for him and negotiate a way to pay off the debt. Remind him of the things you did for him. And are you involved with the Triad?"

"I am Tong," Wang clarified. "The Tong is like the Triad in some ways, but it is not a secret organization. Our members are marginalized like those of the Triad, but the difference is that we have immigrants in our group, and we are not driven by political reasons... It's an important distinction, but like other gangs, we're involved in crime, but we also do some good for the community."

"Tong, what does that mean?" Li asked, trying to understand the nuances.

"This translates to 'social club,' which differentiates us from the ideals of the Triad," Wang explained, trying to clarify the distinction. "So, while it is similar in some ways, no, we are not part of the Triad."

Li nodded, processing the information and hoping they would navigate the difficult situation.

Li spoke with determination, his eyes full of sincerity. "I've been saving all these years. Since my father passed away, my mother and I save all the money we have left at the end of each month. These savings are a promise I made to myself that I will be able to get my mother and aunt out of this neighbourhood. We'll find a different place, a better city. It doesn't matter where we go, but I'll provide a decent life for these two women who raised us. It may not be much, but I'll give you what I have in the bank. I won't charge any interest or compensation; I just want the money I'm lending you back."

Wang hesitated, but replied, "No, I didn't come here to ask for money. I know how much you care about my mother, and I know you want to get away from this place, and I'm leaving today. You can't risk getting into trouble because of me."

Li, not wanting to let the matter go, continued. "The amount is five thousand US dollars, which is equivalent to 35,466.66 yuan, one-third of your debt. I can borrow that amount for you."

"They won't accept that," countered Wang.

"What do you have to lose? You're saying they're going to kill you, that you're going to die if they find you. Try it. Pay a third and negotiate the rest. Find your boss and offer to work for free. It's better having a guaranteed five thousand dollars in hand than nothing. He has always trusted you. Do you trust him?"

Wang sighed deep from within, contemplating his options. "No one trusts anyone, but there is loyalty. Everyone knows I have always been loyal to him and the Tong," he admitted.

"Then try it. The money is in the bank. You just need to let me know when, and I'll go get it," Li reassured him.

"Okay, I'll try. Tonight, I'll approach him. The moment he allows me to explain and accept, I swear I will pay in full." Wang looked into Li's eyes as he made the solemn promise.

"Okay! I'll be waiting for your message," Li replied with a gleam of hope in his eyes.

Li's eyes drooped, heavy with fatigue. He spent a long day at the office, not to mention unloading the pallets that arrived from the contracting companies. Everything was stressful.

Wang, his mind racing with escape plans, leaned over and asked, "Does your bedroom window still connect to your neighbour's roof?"

Li, half asleep in his bed, murmured, "Yes."

"Then I'll go out the window. They won't see me at the gas station. I'll escape through the back streets," Wang explained.

When they said goodbye, they hugged each other as if it were their last hug.

Wang, climbing out of the bedroom window, turned to Li and repeated, "Hey, I swear."

Three long days passed without a word from Wang, leaving Li and his mother in a state of agonizing worry. Then, at 5:00 a.m. on the third day, Wang returned.

Li ran to open the apartment door, and Wang rushed in, placing his helmet on the table. "You don't know how worried we are," Li told him.

Wang sank onto the sofa and said with relief, "My boss, Dankyno, took me in. Five thousand dollars. I promised to work on whatever they wanted so I could pay off the rest of the debt. Do you have a glass of water?" he asked.

Li went to the kitchen, filled a glass with tap water, and handed it to Wang.

"When I got to the barn... Do you know where it is?" Wang asked.

"No, I don't know," Li replied.

"Cousin, after I told him, I thought he was going to kill me right there," Wang confessed, acting as if he had narrowly escaped a fatal gunshot. "When I got to the barn, there were about five gang members waiting. They grabbed me by the arms and forced me to kneel in front of the armchair where the boss was sitting. Dankyno didn't even look at me. He sat there, smoking and fondling a girl with him. He asked me what I wanted."

Wang finished the water and handed the glass back to his cousin, who remained frozen in place, paying attention to every word.

"After I spoke, there was a long silence. The girls moved away from the chair and two of the men next to me lifted me off the floor, opening my arms into a crucifixion position. Dankyno stood up, wielding the machete he always carries. You can't imagine the terror that gripped me. I thought he was going to cut off my arms, my hands, or worse, my head. I closed my eyes tightly and prepared myself. He stood there in front of me for what seemed like an eternity and then said, 'Okay.'"

Li, gripping the glass tightly, held it to his chest in pure horror.

Wang took a deep breath and continued his narrative. "The men holding me let go, and I fell to the ground. My legs were shaking so much that I couldn't stand. The situation almost made me pee right there. I didn't know what to do or say. I just waited for him to say more."

Wide-eyed and confused, Li couldn't understand the incredible story his cousin was telling. Alarmed, he sank into his chair and absorbed every word.

"Dankyno is Chinese, but he looks more like a Japanese sumo wrestler. He has that typical straight black hair, always tied in a ponytail on top of his head. He appears to be in his forties or fifties. I know little about him, but I know he's incredibly cruel," Wang emphasized.

"I just can't understand why you chose this path," Li muttered, confused and worried.

Wang looked at his cousin, scratched his head, and continued the story. He told how Dankyno sat in the armchair and spoke. "Wang, we are like a family here. You came to us when you were a child, and you've never let me down. I'm surprised, but I couldn't expect anything less from you. Despite the risks, you had the courage to come here and tell me. You presented yourself as a trustworthy person. You have proven your loyalty to

Tong. I believe in you and accept your proposal. We will track down the people who stole our package, your motorcycle, and your cellphone. When we find the culprits, I will show that no one goes against the Tong family."

"I was speechless. All I could do was say 'thank you,'" Wang said with a sense of relief.

Li watched Wang silently.

"After thanking him, I stood up. My legs were shaking uncontrollably. Dankyno summoned four men who had been observing the entire ordeal and instructed them to find my motorcycle. He then called another man I didn't know. He told a guy to give me the keys to a motorcycle parked in the garage and a cellphone." Wang concluded his story and leaned back on the sofa, letting out a tired yawn.

"Oh my God, you did it!" Li exclaimed, a smile forming on his lips. Upon noticing Wang's sudden movement on the sofa, his expression darkened. "What's that?" The smile disappeared from Li's lips when he saw a gun under Wang's shirt.

"That's a weapon, let me finish telling you the rest of what happened. That's why I couldn't come here before," Wang said, revealing the gun and carefully placing it back in his pants under his shirt.

The cousin's expression changed from happiness to disappointment upon hearing Wang.

"This conversation happened three nights ago, and he didn't let me go get the money. I went straight to work. I had to go to the port to help load the containers. Let's get the money now," Wang suggested.

Startled, and a little confused, Li looked at his cousin as he tried to process everything he was told. He checked his watch and realized he needed to work soon. It was a lot to take in and it wasn't the life he preferred to lead. He grabbed a pen and a piece of paper from the notebook on the kitchen counter, hastily scribbling down an address and a phone number. He handed it to Wang with instructions. "Yes, we can. I work at this address. When you park in front of the store, you will see a sign above the door that says, 'Shanghai Temporary Services.' We will meet during my lunch break at 11:30. We will go to the bank together."

Wang settled down on the sofa and declared, "I'm going to sleep now. Here's my new number. Wake me up at 8:30. Then I'll go see my mother and then I'll find you."

Wang went to bed and Li went to work. Upon arriving at the company's door, he stood still, his mind racing, imagining himself experiencing everything his cousin described that morning. As if coming out of a trance, he grabbed the door handle, opened it, and concluded: "I would never do that."

Wang arrived on time and his cousin got on the back of the motorcycle. On the way to the city centre, Li explained the bank was a few blocks from the store and was called Konpang Shanghai Bank.

At the bank, they withdrew five thousand dollars in cash from the teller. The transaction took almost half an hour, and the two had to sit in front of the manager while they navigated the bureaucratic process of handling such a significant amount of money. The manager handed over the package and Li passed it to Wang, who put it in a plastic bag inside his leather jacket.

When they arrived at the door of the company where Li worked, he got off the motorcycle and gave Wang a suggestion. "When you're looking for temporary work, even if it's just for a few hours, call me. I can arrange this for you."

Wang looked confused and asked, "What do you mean?"

Li explained, "There are always vacancies in this company for temporary positions. Sometimes restaurants, bars, or hotels need extra help, whether it's washing dishes, cleaning rooms, or helping in the kitchen. Do you understand? When an employee is absent or has a day off, we fill in. You can earn good money whether during the day or at night, and you are paid according to the hours you work. What do you think?"

Wang nodded. "I think it's a great idea. You have my phone number. When you need someone, just call me and see if I'm available. It's a way to start paying back what you lent me. You saved my life; I promise I will pay you back soon."

Li nodded, saying, "Okay. As soon as a job opening opens, I'll call you."

With that, Wang sped up the motorcycle down the street. Li watched his cousin until he was out of sight and then entered the store, sighing as he realized he had a lot of work ahead of him.

* * *

Hui speaks loudly, trying to get the boss out of his thoughts. "Leave it to me. When that couple shows up at five, I'll take care of it. I'll pretend to be you and have fun with them."

Wang remains silent, lost in thought.

Mingli intervenes, seeking guidance: "What should we do?"

Aiguo says, "I followed them and warned them not to come here. I could scare them again?"

Wang slept and drifted off into a dream, a break from the harsh reality of his life. He dreamed of days when survival did not require violence. When he wakes up, he looks up and asks, "What time is it?"

Hui gives the time: "It's 12:30."

Wang gets up from the chair and walks toward the room where his mother rests. He kisses her on the forehead and says, "I'm leaving, Mom."

He closes the door behind him and faces his subordinates, giving orders: "Let's go outside."

The four leave the building and get on their motorcycles, heading toward the avenue ahead.

15

The Container Factory

Rachel admires the photographs of Lianyungang City on the computer. She looks out the window at the clear blue sky, remembering her childhood in Santos, a coastal city in the state of São Paulo, Brazil. The beaches are always full of tourists, and the iconic buildings leaning on the seafront fill her with nostalgia. Ships always enter and leave the port... but the past is a time that never returns.

She discovers Lianyungang was recognized as the land of the "Eastern Barbarians" and its name is derived from Liam Island, now known as the "Door Connecting the Clouds."

Rachel closes the computer, planning her next move. Finishing the last two bites of her sandwich, she goes to reception and leaves a note for David for when he arrives.

Upon entering the hotel lobby, she notices the clock reads 9:00 p.m. David hasn't called, and now she's concerned.

"Ms. Rachel, do you need anything?" the receptionist asks in impeccable English.

"Do you have a hotel card and an envelope?"

The attendant hands over what she asked for, and she sits on the couch. On the card, she writes: "David, go to bed early. Hope you had a great night. Lobby, 3:30 a.m. Don't be late! Kisses, Rachel." She tucks the card into the hotel envelope, gets up from the couch, and returns to the front desk.

"Do you need something, Ms. Rachel?" the attendant asks.

"Give this envelope to Mr. David when he arrives."

"Yes, anything else?"

"No, thank you very much." She walks toward the elevator.

Passing through a smoked-glass door, she spots an ATM she hadn't noticed before. After checking the symbol on her Bank of London card, she withdraws $300 US dollars—or $2,098 yuan.

She returns to her room, certain they will need money for gas, food, and so on. The day has worn on her, and she goes to sleep soon after her head hits the pillow.

The alarm wakes her up at 2:45 a.m. After a quick shower, a soft knock comes from her door as she's putting on her makeup. As soon as the door is open, David comes in and settles down in the armchair.

"Good morning, my dear partner," he says with a sweet voice.

"What time is it?"

"It's 3 a.m.," David replies, his voice hoarse from exhaustion as he watches her apply her makeup.

"How was it yesterday?" Rachel combs her hair.

Her partner peeks through the bedroom curtains and gazes at the bright full moon. He sighs. "It was good and enlightening, but I'll tell you everything later. Did you write the questions?"

"They're on the table."

David's eyes scan the open notebook, taking in the questions written on the page.

"What do you think?" Rachel asks as she walks toward him.

"Great, if it's for the answers we want. Clever, because we can put on top of these questions other questions," David replies.

She sits in the other armchair and looks at him, smiling. She gives him a wink.

"What are you looking at? Are you ready? Let's get out of here," David says, frowning.

Rising from her chair, Rachel grabs her purse, iPad, and papers from the table. She whispers, "Go ahead, tell me about yesterday."

He turns his back to her, the sound of his footsteps echoing through the room. They get into the elevator, and Rachel yawns. The hotel lobby doors open, and they head for the exit. From afar, they see the lonely and sleepy receptionist, who greets them with a smile.

"Did you get the card I left at the front desk?" Rachel inquires.

"Yes, I received it when I arrived," David replies, moving into the parking lot.

When they arrive at the hotel's upper parking lot, she notices David turning off the alarm in a car she doesn't recognize.

"Another car?" Rachel asks.

"I switched yesterday afternoon," he explains.

"Now we have good air conditioning." Rachel is happier.

Once they enter the car, David punches the factory's address into the GPS.

"Did you forget the case of water in the other car?"

"I bought another one with twenty-four bottles. Now we have thirty-six," David replies, getting out of the car and pulling four bottles of water out of the trunk. He puts two next to her.

"It's 3:45 a.m., right?" Rachel says, pointing to the clock on the vehicle's dashboard.

He puts the car in drive and heads for the avenue. "Today we will see stunning landscapes, cross bridges, and tour villages. It will be five hours of pure visual joy," declares David, with words tinged with the cadence of poetry.

"You are deep in words," Rachel declares and leans back into the passenger seat to sleep.

David drives for hours, admiring the road. He confirms on his watch that time has passed fast, and looks at his companion, saying, "Rachel! Wake up! It's 6 a.m. You've been asleep for almost three hours. Let's go get coffee," he says, shaking her shoulder before pulling into a gas station.

"Uh, I think I overslept." She looks in the mirror and tries to fix her messy hair.

"You snore."

"You could be nicer," she complains.

David gets out of the car, goes into the self-service station, and finds no coffee, just a fridge with some juices. He gets a mango juice, pays for it, and goes back to the car, informing Rachel about the lack of caffeine.

"I'm going to get some orange juice. Are you sure I snored?" she asks, getting out of the vehicle.

"Just a little," he replies with a laugh and looks around, surveying the surroundings.

Upon returning, Rachel sits in the driver's seat and suggests, "I'm going to drive, and you sleep. When we're near the factory, I'll wake you up."

"Alright," David replies, and he settles down to sleep.

The smooth highways of China bring delight to Rachel as she drives, and they impress her with the lack of traffic, maybe because of the early hour. She spots the iconic mountains she's seen in the calendars and is ecstatic about the view. After some time, David wakes up and asks for the time.

"You slept three hours. It's 9:30."

"Wow, I'm sorry. It feels like it was just a nap," David grumbles.

Rachel checks the GPS and announces, "We're only twenty minutes away from our destination."

He asks her to pull over to the side of the road and switch seats with him. He explains that at the factory gate, he will need to communicate in Mandarin to be understood.

"Okay! How did it go yesterday?"

"Damn, Rachel. Leave it for later."

"No later. We have a lot to do. Tell me, what happened yesterday?"

"Okay, before he came to Shanghai, Michael broke up with that artist in London. They have been apart for over six months." David glances at her while keeping his focus on the road.

She waits for him to continue.

"His mother is ill, a lung infection. She's in her seventies and has had pneumonia before, which is risky at her age. He stayed here in Shanghai because he hasn't seen her in a while and none of his brothers will come and take care of her," he concludes, falling silent.

"And what else?" asks Rachel after drinking some of the orange juice.

"What else do you want to know? Nothing big happened. Tonight, he's going to pick me up from the hotel, so we'll see what happens," David says with a little smile.

"Hmm…" Rachel mutters and finishes drinking the bottle of juice.

Following the GPS, David turns onto a back road off the highway and drives three kilometres before stopping at a small guard shack. The guard approaches the driver's side window.

"We have an appointment at 10 a.m. with Mr. Chongkunli Wu, Director of Construction and Planning," David informs the sentry.

The guard looks into the car, glancing at Rachel, and asks for everyone's papers. They hand over their passports. David and Rachel observe four security guards at the gate—two inside the guardhouse and two outside. While they wait, the guard reviews the documents and makes a phone call. The guard returns with their passports and two ID badges to wear around their necks, as well as a chip card to hand over upon arrival. The guard presents a clipboard for them to sign. After signing, a Baojun SUV pulls up in front of their car.

"Follow that vehicle to parking lot H," the guard instructs David with a serious expression. He nods and follows the SUV. They see many cars parked in front of unique buildings and lots of cameras on the access road.

David is quiet and very attentive. He pulls into a parking lot in front of the purple H building. Sitting there waiting, they notice a man in a grey uniform approaching. David and Rachel get out of their car.

Upon their arrival, the polite factory worker bows and introduces himself as Ken. David returns the bow and introduces Rachel. Ken asks for the chip card, which is handed over, and they follow. After going through another round of identification at the front desk of the building and navigating the building's corridors, they arrive at an iron door. Ken opens it and invites them in. The room reminds them of a restaurant, with a variety of food and drinks on a large table.

"Here we have breakfast. Feel free to help yourselves," Ken says, closing the door as he leaves.

Amazed, they look out over the room. They are hungry and help themselves to the bounty. They take their plates over and sit in two armchairs.

Rachel finishes eating first; she looks around the hall and registers that in every corner of the room there is a surveillance camera watching them. Identifying two doors showing the symbols for male and female, she concludes they are bathrooms. Rachel gets up and enters the women's. David takes the cue and heads into the other.

Finishing their business, they settle into the same armchairs, discussing the hospitality of the place. Ken reappears five minutes later. After asking them about their satisfaction, Ken guides them down a yellow hall with grey crossbars. Passing through several numbered doors, he stops at room 104 and leads them into an anteroom. "Please wait for your names to be called." In a matter of minutes, a young woman appears. "Please, can you enter the main room?"

A gentleman sitting in an armchair behind a table at the end of the room stands up, limping on his left leg, and he moves to receive them. As they approach, Mr. Wu, David, and Rachel bow in greeting. The director does the same and gestures toward two armchairs in front of the table.

Mr. Chongkunli Wu is a sixty-year-old man who walks with the aid of a cane. "You're David, and you're Rachel?" he asks, pointing with his cane.

"Yes, nice to meet you." David accompanies the director toward the armchairs.

The associates sit and observe the sumptuous decoration of the hall. There are beautiful vases with bucolic paintings about two metres high, plus some sculptures made of different colours of jade above the furniture.

"What can I do to help you? I don't receive visitors here at the factory when the matter is private. However, as explained to me over the phone, you are a London private investigation company, and Mr. Chan's sons have employed you. I've made an exception." Mr. Wu speaks to David and dismisses the secretary with a wave after she hands him a folder full of documents.

"That's right; here's our card. Rachel, I, and another associate who is in London are the owners," David explains.

Mr. Wu receives the card, reads it, and places it on the table in front of him. "I'm so happy to have you here. Mr. Chan was not only an excellent employee, but he was also a friend. They never clarified the reason for his death to us here at the factory."

"Thank you," David and Rachel say in unison.

"CTLG is a great company. What do they produce here?" David asks Mr. Wu.

"We build containers, any kind of container. Normal sizes, different sizes, refrigerated, for intercontinental travel, and for storage. It depends on what the buyer orders. If the customer, besides ordering the containers, requires loading, transportation, and shipping to any port in the world, we also do this. We have shipping offices in over thirty countries," the director explains with pride.

"So, is the company only a container manufacturing factory?" David questions.

Wu explains in a promotional tone, "No. We have over a thousand affiliates offering a variety of services, combined with this factory, covering our buyers' needs. This streamlined approach brings us greater ease and outstanding lower costs for our customers. This simplifies things, making it unnecessary for consumers to seek services from multiple companies. Our seventy-year history in container operations has brought us to this level.

CTLG is the most esteemed name in China and, in fact, the world. In addition, we have a partnership with the Chinese government."

"This company is impressive in terms of its vastness and diversity. Wonderful," David says, his tone dripping with exaggerated sincerity.

Mister Wu listens, adjusts his suit, and adjusts his position in the armchair, unquestionably thrilled with the praise.

"Did Mr. Chan have many friends?" David asks.

"Friends? Friends? I don't believe so. He always took part in the company's festive activities and was an excellent employee," Mr. Wu replies.

Rachel writes on the iPad and asks, "Was it common for him to travel to Shanghai?"

"Yes. He travelled every month," Wu replies and then glances at David.

"Did you know his children studied in the US?" David asks and glances at Rachel, raising his eyebrows.

"Yes, but no details. We have other employees who have children studying in Canada, the UK, and the US, but no one goes into detail," the director explains.

"Can you give us his last home address recorded on the official documents?" David requests.

"That's easy." Mr. Wu opens the folder the secretary brought and looks for the address. The partners watch the boss's movement and see Chan's name written on the cover of the file.

The director finds what he is looking for, writes it on a pad of paper, and hands it to David, saying, "About the trips to Shanghai, which you asked... In fact, he would let me know a week or two before he left. He was very responsible."

"On that last trip, did he also advise you in advance?" David finishes drinking the glass of water.

"I recorded this in my annual notebook," he says, picking up a small book and reading aloud. "On February 5th, 2013, Mr. Chan notifies me of his travel plans for the ninth, tenth, and eleventh of February 2013. He is supposed to resume work on the twelfth. Given the backlog of days off, he extends it for one more day." Wu pauses, takes off his glasses, and wipes them with a small cloth.

"Do you have any idea why he travels to Shanghai every month?" David asks.

"His sister became very ill. He not only visits her but also brings groceries and pays the bills for the month. He shared this at a company party a few years ago. I know his routine because during his travels, we had to intervene and fill his duties. There was a kind of competition among the officials to take his place. Whoever fills in receives a little more for those days. He also has a brother in Mongolia, although it has been years since he last visited him." Mr. Wu's affection for Mr. Chan is clear in the way he speaks.

"Sorry to ask. It seems like you liked him very much?" David observes.

"Yes, I'm sorry. He was a good man; he didn't deserve what happened." He finishes speaking and wipes his wet eyes.

David picks up the cup of tea and takes a sip, pretending not to notice the moment of sincere sadness.

Rachel asks in English and apologizes, explaining that her Mandarin is not very good. "Do you know if on this last trip he made any comments or told someone he was going to do something different?"

The director looks at Rachel, then looks back at David, lost in thought. A bell rings, and the secretary enters the office. Wu instructs her to pull a receipt from the files, from the year 2013, in February, from the ninth to the twelfth. This receipt must refer to shipping goods on behalf of Mr. Chan.

She nods and leaves the room.

He searches the folder on his desk for another sheet of paper and shows it to David. "That's a work order I gave Chan on February sixth. As he informed me on the fifth day that he was going to travel, I gave this order to go to our affiliate in the city. That way, he would earn daily wages because he would be working. Do you know our branch in Shanghai?"

"No, I don't," David lies.

"It wasn't for Mr. Chan to go to the CTLG branch office because the entire floor of the company was closed under renovation. He had to go to a lab that's in the same building," the director clarifies.

"Sorry to ask, but why did he have to go to this lab?" David asks.

"I sent him to get some merchandise that was lost, a wrong address. Someone should have forwarded that purchase to our factory here in Lianyungang. Carelessness, as they put the address of the laboratory in Shanghai on the invoice. A mistake, but we shipped on time," Mr. Wu explains.

"Who reported that this merchandise was in Shanghai?" asks Rachel.

"The call came from the management at the laboratory in Osaka, Japan. A Japanese pharmaceutical company, Konsako Enterprises Inc., prepared the container in question until the sixth day, and that's when I remembered Mr. Chan's trip to Shanghai. Fortunately, I informed the lab that I would send someone to retrieve it. Once my assistant returns, I can check all of this out for you. It took a while, but I am confident that it was indeed Chan who collected and shipped the goods." Mr. Wu, with details, has clarified Mr. Chan's actions.

The mention of the lab's name sends a shiver down Rachel's spine, as it matches the name of the details of the first container operation. Suppressing any reactions, she maintains her composure and records all responses on the iPad. Mr. Wu's office cameras are monitoring them.

"Would this kind of diversion of goods be normal?" asks a curious Rachel.

"No, it was an exceptional case. The first of its kind, to my knowledge. Upon receiving the report of the loss of the goods, I immediately requested a confirmation document from someone at the laboratory in Shanghai. On the same day, I received the confirmation call. That's when I proposed work to Mr. Chan. Considering his imminent travel and work commitments, I informed him in the evening, and he agreed. Misuse of goods is rare, but when it happens, we need to act fast for our customers." Wu finishes his cup of tea.

The secretary comes in and hands some papers to the director. He reads them one by one. He stops at a receipt, picks it up, and shows it to David, saying, "This is the dispatch of the goods at the Shanghai post office with the shipping date of February 11th, 2013. I confirmed by phone, with the lab, that he picked up the items that day."

"I apologize for the excess of questions, but for us, it's a unique opportunity to have these answers. That way we can give the family the answers for everything they asked us." David raises an eyebrow as if questioning Mr. Wu.

"You may ask. I still have time," the director declares, settling into his chair.

"In the last week, here at the factory, where did Mr. Chan work?" he asks.

Mr. Wu searches inside the file and finds a map, and a work report with the days and hours Chan entered the service, the time of departure, and the section where he was working.

"Can I take a picture of this document?" David asks and holds up his phone.

"Yes."

Once he finishes taking two pictures, David continues, "Did the family come here looking for him?"

"No, not at all. On the eleventh, he called the factory early in the morning. He informed me of his intention to mail the goods and requested two more days off to visit his brother in Mongolia. Considering his accumulated leave, I granted his request." Mr. Wu's gaze turns to the wall clock. He pauses and presses the bell under the table, calling for his secretary.

She opens the office door and announces people have arrived for the next meeting, then leaves the room.

Mr. Wu explains, upset by the situation, "I will be brief as I have a meeting. Chan did not show up for work on the fourteenth or the following days. After a week, I visited his residence, only to find the house locked and empty. A neighbour informed me that the family had moved the previous week. The news took me aback. I immediately reported the absences to my superiors. Within three days, my superiors issued an order, firing Chan and revoking his access to the factory. It's a regimental applied standard policy. We expect employees to adhere to workplace guidelines. Upon admission, individuals sign an agreement to adhere to all rules. I tried to hold back as long as possible, but there came a point where I had to abide by protocol."

The secretary enters the room again, and she motions to the director.

Mr. Wu says to David, "I only have five minutes."

"Has anyone reached out to you to talk about this matter?"

"Yes. A young man came in the first few months after Chan disappeared. He also introduced himself as being from an investigative firm and said Chan's sister hired him. It was a shock to all of us he died. Now, after all these years, you are asking me about it..." Wu motions to the secretary who is standing at the exit door of the office.

The partners get up, understanding that the interview is over. The three of them bow goodbye.

David says, "Thank you for meeting us."

"You don't have to thank me. Whatever you need from the CTLG, our company will always help," Mr. Wu states, walking toward the door.

"If we think of anything else, can I call you?" David asks, almost on the way out.

"In twenty days, I will be retired and will move to Hong Kong. You can call me on my phone." Mr. Wu pulls a card out of the inside pocket of his suit and hands it to David.

After saying goodbye, Rachel and David leave the office.

As they walk through the door, Mr. Ken instructs them, "Please come with me." He leaves them in the parking lot, and the attendant returns inside, waving goodbye. The same car that accompanied them to the building is waiting for them. The partners enter the Hyundai and follow the escort vehicle. In silence, they look at each other, and David winks at his partner. Rachel nods her head in agreement.

"Are you hungry?" he asks her.

"Yes, I am."

"Shall we eat pasta today?" he asks and stops the car at the guardhouse, waiting for security to release them. The gate opens, and David drives toward the highway. They arrive at the main road and head left into the city, opposite of the way they came. They're both quiet in the car.

"Did you bring it?" David asks.

"Yes." She pulls out of her bag the small signal detector, a spy bug, and shows him. "Here's the water," Rachel says.

David checks the signs on the side of the highway and looks many times in the rear-view mirror to make sure they're not being followed. When he sees the mall, he enters the underground garage and chooses a discreet corner to park. Getting out of the vehicle, he opens the trunk, as if looking for an item. With calculated confidence, he rearranges the objects, knowing that the cameras in the garage are capturing his every movement.

Rachel, in her meticulous way, examines the interior walls and floor, exploring all potential hiding places in search of a bug. Eventually, their quest proves fruitful. Inside the radio, she discovers a hidden miniature listening device. With deft precision, she extracts the bug without making a sound. A final check on the car reveals nothing more.

David closes the trunk, carrying a few bottles of water, and gets in. Rachel hands over the mini-listener, and he puts it into a bottle of water and shakes it. He starts the car and goes around the garage until he finds a trash can and throws the bottle in.

More relaxed, the two talk and Rachel explains, "This bug is also a wireless tracker. Soon they will try to find us here because it was the last signal they received. Let's get out of here as fast as we can."

"Glad you brought the detector," David says with a smile.

"Do you remember? I bought this at the airport the day we arrived. I had tried it in our hotel room earlier, but today it showed its worth. When I saw it in the store, I just couldn't resist buying it. It's so compact, and it cost so little, only thirty dollars—a significant find," comments Rachel, pleased with her purchase.

"I'll get one for Tyler and another for me when we return on Thursday," he tells her with a smile.

"What road is this?" She doesn't recognize the direction David is taking.

"We're going to Chan's house," David announces. "It's in town, remember?"

After a short drive, he parks the car in front of the address given by Mr. Wu. It's an unpretentious residence, the colour of unpainted cement. The front lawn is withered, completely lifeless.

Getting out of the vehicle, they approach the front door and knock. A neighbour lady approaches them, telling them the house is uninhabited. David says they are looking for Mr. Chan or his wife. The neighbour says Mr. Chan passed away many years ago and the family no longer lives there.

"Do you know where Mr. Chan's family has moved?" Rachel asks.

"No, I don't know. They were very reserved," the neighbour replies.

"What did Mr. Chan die of?" David asks, making a face like someone who knows nothing.

"The police came here a long time ago, about six or eight months after they moved in. They told neighbours they had found his body. People, filled with curiosity, began asking questions and sharing with us the news that someone had murdered Mr. Chan in Shanghai." She recounts the story with enthusiasm, typical of those who know everything about the neighbourhood.

They say thanks and go back to the car.

"Something's wrong," Rachel comments, annoyance in her voice.

"It's strange. Something like this would only happen if someone informed his wife of his death and then instructed her to vacate the property. Speaking from my experience as a police officer..." David trails off, his gaze meeting hers, heavy on the words but analytical.

"I can sense something off about this story," Rachel comments, wrinkling her nose.

They get in the car and return to the highway heading toward Shanghai.

"Fasten your seat belt. We have a five-hour ride ahead of us," David warns Rachel, a mischievous smile spreading across his face.

"After all this questioning, and they still think we're international spies? I mean, all it did was make me hungry." Rachel smiles like she's the star of her own spy comedy.

16

Sometimes, Again Means New

"Did that couple go to the apartment at 5 p.m.?" Wang asks, looking at Hui.

"No. Aiguo was there; this morning he called me before he went shopping. I checked when I got to the barn," Hui explains to the boss, standing in front of the open window in his room.

Wang shows no reaction to what he has heard and continues to admire the scenery while smoking a cigarette.

Last year, Wang bought an apartment in the Bund neighbourhood, famous for its waterfront along the Huangpu River, known as the "Mother River." The houses here blend Gothic, Art Decor, and Beaux Arts architectural styles, reflecting Shanghai's rich history. Property prices range from 25 million yuan (US$3.94 million) to 45 million yuan (US$6.5 million), signalling social and economic prestige.

"I think Mingli scared them," Hui, the manager, says, teasing him. "Boss, do you need anything?"

Wang turns, crosses the enormous room, and walks toward the piano. He sits on the stool and holds up the piece of paper handed to him on Friday, containing the license plate of the couple's car. He plays two notes and asks, "Do you remember Munvu Rent Car's owner Feng?"

"Yes," Hui confirms, his lips curling into a small smile.

"Talk to him. I need to locate this car, the name of the renter, and all the details of the lease by this afternoon. Tell him I'm the one asking." Wang hands the paper to the manager.

With a bow of respect, Hui assures him he will handle the arrangements and leaves the apartment via the private elevator.

Wang puts out his cigarette in the nearby ashtray, and his fingers glide across the piano keys.

* * *

At the hotel, Rachel is sitting in an armchair in David's room, looking over Mr. Wu's responses. She has searched her iPad many times, looking for more information, since her arrival.

David is sitting on his bed typing on his phone when it rings, breaking his concentration.

"Now you're calling daily? Give us the news," David asks Tyler.

Mindful of what she hears, Rachel stops writing.

"Tell him, if possible, to focus on the 2014 operation. Submit anything relevant about the factory and labs or any mention of the flash drive," she tells David.

He gets off the bed as he listens to Tyler; he moves across the room, opens the fridge, and grabs a bottle of water, drinks some, and continues, "I know, I know. It's never true, but we can read between the lines. One more thing... What did they seize? This is important. Can you make it quick? We leave on Thursday; we only have two more days. I'll tell her. Don't worry!"

"What's up? What happened?" Rachel's curiosity is getting the better of her.

David laughs as he hangs up the phone.

"Did he get the documents?"

"Tyler went to the consulate at 8 a.m. today and received the boxes containing the Operation Container files. He said he will look for what you asked for and sent you a kiss."

"It'll help," she says without showing much excitement.

"You don't like the idea? What's the matter?"

Rachel closes the iPad and states, "I don't think this investigation ends in two days; I mean, if we want something concrete."

"You're tired. Don't talk to me about changing the flight," he says and goes back to bed, lying down.

"I'm tired, yes, but my mind isn't, and I see something big here..." She opens the iPad again and shows the screen to him.

David approaches the table and looks.

"Mr. Wu said he got a call from the lab in Osaka, Japan. Remember?"

"Yes," he replies.

"I first asked why the local branch didn't send the package back to the Osaka lab. It's cheaper to send it to the forwarder than it is back to another country. Then I wondered why the Shanghai branch didn't send it to the shipping container factory. Maybe they wanted to save money, but because the Osaka lab makes the mistake, they want the goods to arrive on time," Rachel explains.

He listens to the analysis as he settles into the armchair across from her.

"That was before Mr. Chan goes to Shanghai," she says, getting up from her chair and pacing back and forth as she explains.

David interrupts, "Yes, but the lab doesn't know he is going to Shanghai."

Ignoring him, she says, "Read between the lines. Could it be that they indeed don't know him? Mr. Chan informs the boss about his day off on February 5th, and the boss at once notifies the replacements. On February 6th, the director speaks with the laboratory management from Osaka, confirming that the goods are in Shanghai. That same day, Mr. Wu tells Chan that he will travel on February 9th. He picks up the goods on the 11th, and that's when we met."

David can feel her excitement and connects what she's saying into a pattern in his mind.

"At the end of January 2013, Mr. Chan tells the Firm that he discovers something in the production." Her voice is full of intrigue. "The maps show he works on container coordination, construction, and planning. This is at their construction site. I think he sees something—maybe someone observes him," she goes silent, flipping through the papers on the table.

Thoughtful, David strokes his chin.

She persists. "The monthly checkup—remember that picture you took? We'll find out he works in that sector the last two weekends before he leaves for Shanghai." Her voice is imbued with certainty and mystery. "That's my opinion."

Focused on her words, David does not react.

Rachel drinks some water and reiterates, looking at him, "We're on the verge of something, I can feel it." Her voice is charged with urgency and suspense.

"I'll sort it out tomorrow. Consider Mr. Chan's sequence: find something, alert the Firm, travel, deliver the thumb drive, retrieve, and ship lab items—then he and Ronaldo die. Coincidence?"

"Are you trying to convince me that someone planned to divert this merchandise to get Mr. Chan and in the end they killed him and Ronaldo because of it?"

"It's a possibility," she replies, tossing her long hair.

The explanation surprises him. He considers the claims and tries to connect everything they have discovered in these last few days.

Rachel collects all the notes she has made in the last few hours and turns off her iPad. "I'm going to sleep."

David looks at his phone, checking the time and if he has any messages.

Opening the bedroom door, she turns and asks, "Are you going out with Michael?"

"Yes, I'll be going out soon."

"Have a great night," she says, smirking, and closes the door, walking into her room.

David grabs his car keys, wallet, and cellphone. He looks in the mirror before leaving and smiles. In the elevator, he mulls over Rachel's words, finding them plausible. Upon reaching the first floor, a group of young Western couples enters, chatting in English.

Upon reaching the ground floor, David looks for Michael. Not seeing him, he settles down on a sofa, observing the surrounding guests. A woman walks to the ATM, a young woman runs up to a couple sitting in the lobby, and two men are chatting and friendly with the hostesses. After a few minutes, Michael walks through the front door, and David gets up from his chair with gleaming eyes.

"In my car or yours?" David asks.

"We'll take mine," Michael proposes.

David smiles, and they walk side by side toward the exit of the hotel. Walking in haste, they talk about the trip. The conversation between the two is so lively that they don't notice two men sitting on motorcycles, wearing helmets, watching them.

"That's the one over there." Mingli, sitting on the first motorcycle, points to the two friends leaving the hotel.

"Are you sure?"

"The one with the light shirt," Mingli confirms to David.

"And the other?"

"I've never seen him before."

David walks over to the silver vehicle as Michael turns off the alarm. As he sits in the passenger seat, he comments in awe, "What car is this?"

"You like it?"

"I love it!" David answers, looking around.

"It's a Volkswagen Lavida. When I arrived here, I bought a car—one that's fast and has both active and passive safety features, all thanks to German engineering. The four-door I wanted wasn't available. They only had the coupe. Besides the qualities and especially the affordable price, this was my final decision," Michael explains.

"Don't you miss your Porsche?" David recalls.

"I left it in the apartment's garage in London; you can't compare," his friend says, driving toward Century Park Pudong without noticing the two motorcycles following them.

After twenty minutes, Michael enters the garage of the building where he lives.

The two motorcycles pass in front of the building, confirming the location. They return and park next to a restaurant.

David enters Michael's apartment, taking in the details: jade statues; old wooden furniture; a modern white leather sofa, a mix of classic and modern. Impressed, he comments, "I love it—beautiful and spacious. Big places like this are rare in Shanghai."

"You haven't seen *my* room yet. It is huge. I was lucky to buy this place; without a doubt a brilliant investment. The area near the park is privileged, close to the subway lines that lead to Puxi. I earned and saved a lot in New York, so I invested here. My mom found this place for sale and knew the previous owners, which helped close the deal. It's been empty for years; I never planned to use it. I had no intention of staying, but given the circumstances, I took a break," explains Michael with a big smile as he gives the tour.

David nods in amazement.

In the corner of the main wall, below the window, is a bronze serving cart filled with different drinks. Michael walks toward it and asks, "Would you like a whiskey?"

"Yes, with two ice cubes," David replies, walking around the room and admiring the sculptures displayed on an antique wooden cabinet.

"I'll get them ready." Michael looks at his friend with affection.

"Very smart to apply here, especially in real estate. You never get lost with that kind of heritage."

"I believe in that kind of capital. Stock exchange, bitcoin, and other investments are very volatile. That's not my cup of tea. I'm very conservative with what I have," Michael explains.

"Why are you working in that hotel? You're an architect, and one of the best, I might add."

"I'm fluent in five languages but working in my area of expertise here is complex. I would have to join the government program 'Work for the People' and follow all its rules—not my ideal situation. Besides the salary is too low. At the hotel, it was simple. My mom has worked in accounting there for forty years and knows everyone. She found me this job at reception, where I've been for three months," Michael says, smiling and handing his friend a glass of whiskey.

David takes the glass and reflects on how much he missed that smile.

"Let's toast to our reunion. Life is a wheel of fortune," Michael says, and raises his glass.

"Are you happy?" David asks and raises his in a toast.

"I'll answer like this… I'm in my apartment and with my mother. My salary is enough to keep me here. Yes, I took a break from the routine of my normal life, and everything is fine," explains Michael with a smile.

"Glad to hear that you're enjoying life," David observes.

"Changing the subject, who is this woman who is accompanying you?" Michael asks and sits down next to him on the couch.

"She's my partner in our company; she was a federal police agent in Brazil. I've known Rachel for about twelve years." David takes a sip of the whiskey.

"Cop too? Wow! She is beautiful."

"What about you? Any new friends?" David asks.

"No, like I said yesterday, I've been on my own for six months. I've been doing a lot of thinking, especially since I moved from London to here. Things have changed," he says, finishing his Scotch and setting the glass on the coffee table.

David is silent, looking into Michael's eyes. At that moment, they lay bare their past, present, and perhaps even future before each other.

* * *

Mingli and Hui, outside the building, relax on their motorcycles, monitoring the street and the garage. Hui calls Wang to say that they followed the man who passed by his mother's house. He adds that a second guy picked him up at the hotel and they are now holed up in an apartment building in Pudong. "What do you want us to do?"

"Find out who this man who lives in the building is and follow them when they leave," Wang orders.

Hui tells Wang that Feng has already gathered a lot of information, but he will deliver the main data later.

"Feng found out that they are staying at the Square Inn Express Shanghai Hotel in Pudong. The rental car is a guest service, but the list of who rents it is confidential. To get the data you are looking for, we will need access to the hotel computer. Feng promised. He will get this information today; says he has contacts there."

Wang hangs up his phone, recalls that he helped Feng get this job, and knows that, if needed, he always cooperates. Now he wants to know: who is this other man who has an apartment in one of the most expensive areas of Shanghai? His phone rings. On the other end of the line is Feng.

"I have all the data you asked for. I'm sending the files of the two clients through WhatsApp."

"Good," Wang says.

"There's one more thing. I think it's interesting."

"What is it?"

"The hotel worker said police officers sometimes visit the couple."

"That's it?" Wang asks.

"Yes, that's all," Feng says in low spirits. He had expected the boss to show more enthusiasm about what he had.

Wang hangs up the phone and goes back to the window. Checking out the files Feng sent him, he looks for a name in his contacts and calls a police friend on WhatsApp.

"I'm sending you two hotel records. See what you can get. It's important."

Meanwhile, in front of the building in Pudong, Hui returns to Mingli's side. "The boss wants us to find out who picked up our guy from the hotel."

"Alright, let's go. Call Wonjy and Minziu to help us. Minziu should bring a car, and Wonjy can come by motorcycle." Mingli lays out the plan.

"Good idea," agrees the manager, and then calls the two men, telling them the address they are at.

"Alright?" Mingli asks.

"They'll arrive in thirty minutes."

"I'm going to buy something to eat. Do you want anything?" Mingli asks.

"No, I don't want anything."

Mingli walks toward the entrance of the restaurant in front of their parked motorcycles.

After thirty minutes, their cronies arrive. Minziu parks his motorcycle next to Hui's and Mingli's bikes. Wonjy parks the car across the street, almost in front of the restaurant. Everyone greets each other and gets into the car.

Hui shows Wonjy and Minziu where the building is located and explains, "We're not leaving here. We'll rotate if necessary. Park the car here until they leave the building. You follow them—Mingli on the bike, Wonjy in the car. Remember, you're just following. Don't get too close."

Time passes while the four of them sleep, rotating every two hours. At 6:15 a.m., they awake and move to their positions.

Hui looks at his wristwatch and checks: Tuesday, September 10, 2019, and the temperature is twenty-five degrees Celsius. He lowers the window of the car, predicting that it will be another boiling day, and takes a deep breath.

The building's automatic garage opens, and the silver Volkswagen comes out. Hui and his partners watch. Wonjy follows with the car. Mingli stays further back with the bike, taking care not to lose sight of them.

David appreciates the city as the day starts early in Shanghai. As always, there is significant movement of people in the streets, crowded with cars and buses. Michael drives the Volkswagen, speeding along the east highway toward the hotel.

Wonjy, a sprinter, drives a black four-door Toyota Century with the windows covered in a dark film and tries to keep pace at the same speed.

Michael directs the car into the front entrance driveway and pulls up to the front door. Wonjy, following him, parks a little further away and watches David get out of the car. The Volkswagen makes a curve, accelerating toward the avenue.

In a hurry, Wonjy goes to the door, looking for David, but can't see him. He turns to his right and spots David rummaging in the trunk of a dark grey Hyundai Santa Fe in the parking lot. Wonjy enters the hotel and approaches the front desk, inquiring about room prices. The receptionist responds, while two others admire Wonjy, giggling and exchanging whispered comments. Wonjy appears to be twenty years old, although he is thirty-two, with porcelain white skin, a slim build, and average height. His presence captivates young girls.

David walks past the front desk, and one of the staff greets him. "Good morning, Mr. David."

David smiles at the attendant and walks toward the elevator.

Wonjy hears his name. After receiving the hotel information leaflets, he thanks them and heads toward the exit. As he approaches the Hyundai, he checks the time: 7:00. He pretends to take pictures of the hotel and the parking lot as well as the rental's license plate. Once inside the Toyota, he ponders his next move and calls Hui, sharing his findings and uploading the photo.

Meanwhile, Mingli follows Michael's car along the main highway heading north. Curiosity arises as to his destination and the unconventional path he is following. The Volkswagen turns off the road and onto a parallel avenue, heading toward the famous Xinjuan Road Tunnel built under the Huangpu River. As they get closer, there is a mood swing. Mingli enjoys the prospect of driving under the river and comments, "Now I know where you're going!" Surprised, he watches the Volkswagen change lanes a block from the highway exit sign for the tunnel, turning onto the right avenue.

Michael's car turns into the parking lot of the Grampay Hotel, to the back of the building where the employees' spaces are located.

Mingli almost gets lost in this lane change but keeps up. He follows the path the car takes and parks the motorcycle parallel to some other vehicles. He looks for the target and sees him closing the car door. With his cellphone, he takes photos of the subject walking toward the employees' entrance. Mingli then goes to the Volkswagen and takes more images. He checks around the building to see if there are any cameras—none that he can see. He gets on his motorcycle and returns to the front of the hotel parking.

Mingli's cellphone rings; it's Wonjy, and he answers.

"I'm done here," Wonjy informs Mingli.

"Where are you?" asks Mingli.

"I'm still here in the hotel parking lot. I got his license plate, a dark grey Hyundai Santa Fe. I'm sending you the pictures of the car and the license plate. What do you want me to do?"

Mingli looks at the photographs on his phone and is confused.

"Are you sure that's his car?" he asks, remembering the description Hui gave him.

Wonjy describes the scene to Mingli. "No doubt he was looking for something inside when I entered the hotel. His name is David in case you were wondering. I heard the receptionist say, 'Good morning, Mr. David,' and he responded."

"You did good today; I'll talk to Wang and call you back. Stay there, don't go anywhere." Mingli is smiling at the good news and doesn't notice the hotel security guards approaching him.

"Are you a guest here at the hotel?" the security guard asks, staring at him.

Startled, he almost falls off the motorcycle. He straightens himself, thinking of what to say and, smiling, answers, "No, but I will be."

Mingli gets off the motorcycle and walks to the reception.

The receptionist who attends to him admires him. Mingli is of average height, muscular and with a beautiful smile.

"Good morning, can I help you?" the attendant, Lilia, asks.

"I'd like to know the prices of the double rooms," he says, looking around.

It's 7:30 a.m., and she's alone at the front desk, detailing prices and room options. Handing out hotel brochures adorned with photos showing the pools, convention hall, playground, and exercise room, she provides a visual context for her explanations.

"If you want to book, it's best to do it today or tomorrow, on a weekday. It's crowded on the weekends," warns Lilia.

"I need to confirm before making any request. Can I sit in the lobby and make a call? I'll let the person concerned know the prices."

"Yes, would you like some coffee, tea, or water?" she asks and smiles, showing courtesy, as required by the hotel.

"Thank you, you don't have to worry." He smiles and grabs his phone from his pocket, calling Hui. He hangs up before completing the call because he sees Michael walking up to the front desk and greeting the other attendants. He returns to the reception desk and asks Lilia, "Does the hotel have an underground garage?" The attendant mentions they have two parking lots—one in front and one underground. Michael, standing at the counter, pays little attention to Lilia talking to the next guest; to him, it's just another customer. However, Mingli spots his name on his uniform badge and watches him disappear through a door behind reception.

He tells the receptionist he will confirm the reservations with the approval from his superiors. Leaving the hotel with his mission accomplished, he gets on his motorcycle. Accelerating, he disappears down the avenue. Along the way, he stops at a public park to call Hui.

"Did you call a few minutes ago?" Hui asks.

"Yes, we need to talk."

"I'm with Minziu at the port working, but you can talk," Hui replies, noticing Wang arriving on the scene.

"Wonjy is still in the hotel parking lot, waiting for orders. Check your WhatsApp. I just sent you the picture we took today. You'll find pictures of the car and the license plate. The guy that he followed was David. Here's the kicker: the owner of the Volkswagen is Michael, and he is part of the front desk staff at the Grampay Hotel," Mingli updates.

"What?" Hui, surprised by the findings, tries not to show a reaction by muttering in a low tone of voice.

"Later, I'll tell you how Wonjy and I got the names."

"Go back to base. I'll talk to Wang and then get back to you." Hui disconnects and sits in silence, contemplating his next steps. He recognizes the need for caution in how he tells this story to Wang.

Wang walks up to Hui, looking at his watch to confirm that it is 8:30 a.m. The manager passes shipping documents for containers bound for Europe to the boss. Upon receiving the stack of papers, Wang's phone rings, prompting him to answer it.

The voice of his police friend tells him he has information about David and Rachel. His hurried speech conveys a desire to end the call: "They're from London. They're here in Shanghai to help Boss Bo with some operation or investigation that led to the arrest of that Yakuza guy."

"Are they cops?" Wang asks.

"I don't have all the details. I'm not sure. What we've gathered here at the station is that they're involved in private investigations. The rumour going around is that they might be FBI—the local intelligence people knew Chief Bo before his arrival. Two days later, this pair showed up and talked to the prisoner."

"The Yakuza guy is still in jail?" Wang asks.

"No, we've already transferred him to Japan."

"Is this that Portuguese police operation?" he asks.

"Yes, that's it."

"Thank you. I owe you one. Please thank Chief Bo also," Wang instructs.

"Whatever you need." The police officer hangs up, happy to end the call.

Wang returns the heap of papers to Hui and walks down the principal port street, reflecting on what he has been told. He goes by the warehouses without seeing them, takes a deep breath, and whispers, "They're cops."

Hui, in agony, runs after the boss in a hurry and doesn't hear the whisper. Without thinking, he says out loud that he needs to communicate something urgent.

"What the heck is it now, Hui?" Wang turns and looks, his eyes centred on him.

The boss's words do not intimidate the manager because he knows that his bad mood is fleeting. What Mingli told him is much more important.

The two walk together toward Wang's car, and Hui explains with details the findings. Wang pauses and takes the cellphone out of the manager's hands. He flips through the photos of David and Michael one by one.

Wang, with his heightened senses, looks at him. "The woman? Has anyone seen her?" Wang asks.

"No."

"Send those files to my phone," the boss says.

"Do you want us to do something?" asks Hui.

"Not sure. I'll think about it, and then we'll talk." Wang doesn't get in the car; he returns to where men are loading containers.

The manager does not follow him, he only accompanies him with his gaze.

"Can you finish this soon, or will it take all day?" Wang yells at the men who are putting pallets inside a container.

Hui gives a puzzled smile as he watches the boss walk in the opposite direction. He notices Wang talking to the men handling the containers, but he can't make out what's being shouted—either by the boss or the workers. The noise of trucks pulling in and out of the harbour drowns out conversation, filling the air with the deafening sound of clanking metal.

17

Surprises Are Not Always Pleasant

David arrives at the hotel. When passing through reception, he responds to the attendant's greeting. As he enters the elevator, an advertisement for a travel agency pasted on the elevator wall catches his eye. The question in the advertisement is "What is the best in life?" He finds it almost ridiculous to think that being alive is the correct answer. When the elevator door opens, he walks to his room with his mind bothering him. Out loud, he declares, "Maybe after all the chaos and trials I've faced, being alive is what matters." Intrigued by the question, he scribbles a few words in the notebook on the table.

He opens the curtains, turns on the air conditioning, and takes a bottle of water from the fridge. Drinking, he stares into space. Sinking into the armchair, he puts his hand on his forehead and speaks to himself, lost in thought, reflecting. "Sometimes, for unknown reasons, you feel you've lost everything. Then life pushes you forward as it is the only way to bear the losses. Then, out of nowhere, the world takes a three-hundred-sixty-degree turn, and you start from scratch. So, what's best in life?"

Thinking, he gets up from his chair and declares, "I'm getting old. It's time to let go of these ideas. I'm going to take a shower."

In the shower, with his eyes closed, he lets the cold water cascade over his head. With both hands resting on the wall, he leans forward, allowing the water to run down his back. His thoughts turn to Michael. He never expected to meet him on this trip, let alone considered the possibility of a reunion. However, like an Italian song says, "What will be, will be... the possible always exists."

David steps out of the shower, wrapping a towel around himself as he looks in the mirror. Speaking in a strong, vibrant voice—as if he needs to hear his own words to believe them—he declares: "If he wants to come back, everything will have to be different."

He hears someone knocking on the door. Opening it, he sees Rachel.

"Good morning. Are we going to have coffee?" Rachel enters the room. She looks at him wrapped in the towel and gives a mischievous smile.

David turns his back on her. "I'm going to get dressed."

As he closes the bathroom door, he sees she still wears her mischievous smile. After he dresses, he comes out and asks, "How do I look?"

"Wow! That's great. I love the outfit, and your eyes are saying a lot. They're sparkling." She moves her body in a sexy movement.

"Thank you, Ms. Rachel. You are exquisite as well." David appreciates her style. He thinks she always dresses to not attract too much attention, even when the clothes are formal. She favours soft colours, and today is no exception. He notices her hair tied back in a ponytail and her makeup applied in a soft tone, except for the burgundy lipstick he knows she loves.

Rachel notes that the bed in the room isn't messy, but the curtains are open and the fragrance of Calvin Klein cologne wafts in the air. "Shall we have coffee?" she suggests.

"I'm starving." He opens the door, and the two head out toward the elevator.

"Any plans for today?"

"We have to talk. We've clarified a lot in the last five days, and now we're going to connect all the dots," David replies.

She observes her partner and notices that something has changed in him but makes no comment. Rachel just agrees, and walking together, they get into the elevator.

David and Rachel sit by the window in the hotel's restaurant, where David again finds himself lost in thought, looking up at the cloudless sky. The horizontal blinds are up, and the curtains open, letting sunlight stream in through the glass, bathing a few tables in soft, warm light.

Rachel arrives from the buffet carrying some small plates and places them on the table. "Wow, did you leave any?" he says.

Taken aback by his words, she smiles and lists all the food she's taken. "While you're lost in thought, I brought you breakfast. Feast your eyes! We've got fruit, assorted breads, cereal, eggs, yogurt, juice, cheese, ham, and cake. Hmm, looks like something's missing." Noticing her companion's distant gaze, she gets up from her chair to grab David's favourite item.

He holds her by the arm and says, smiling, "It's perfect."

"Nope! I know what you like." Rachel heads to the large table in the centre of the room, grabs two smaller containers, and returns and sits down at the table.

Seeing the cottage cheese, David smiles and starts eating.

"Now I'm going to tell you what happened last night after you went out with Michael."

"I'm listening," he says, still eating the delicacies on the table.

Rachel says, "I went to reception at 10:30 p.m. and heard an Asian man speaking in Mandarin to an employee. I waited to be attended. That's when I heard the man mention our names—Rachel and David—to the clerk. The strange thing is, I've never seen either of them before, the receptionist or the man. I was indecisive and worried. I chose not to confront them and tried to listen to their conversation."

Her partner stops eating, stares, and asks, "Are you sure?"

"David, I heard my name and yours, the way the Chinese pronounce it. Let me continue the story," she insists.

"One moment... Did they pronounce our names in Mandarin?" David asks, his face lined with concern.

"I stayed there and sat on a sofa near the counter. I had an excellent position to observe their conversation, even though I couldn't hear every word. The woman walked away and disappeared through that door behind the front desk. I could tell the guy was tense. His focus shifted back and forth to the hotel entrance. Minutes later, she returned with a piece of paper, which he put in his jacket pocket and left."

"Are you sure she's from the front desk?" David asks, taking the last sip of his coffee.

"I've never seen her. Maybe she's on the night shift?"

He finishes his coffee, showing concern on his face, and asks again, "Are you sure you heard our names?"

"I am sure because I know how the Chinese pronounce it and how difficult it is for them to enunciate. I heard him say Rachel and David."

"Let's try to figure out who she is," David suggests.

The two walk to the elevator without talking. David ponders his partner's words and wonders who could be interested in them. One thing is for sure: whoever it was doesn't know them since Rachel was right at the counter and went unnoticed. His thoughts shift to why they are in

Shanghai. He concludes they must act fast to stay ahead of whoever is tracking them, especially as they must return to London in two days.

His phone rings and he reads the name Michael.

Rachel enters the elevator; David holds the door and states, "I'm not going up. I'll wait for you in the lobby."

Fifteen minutes later, as the two meet, one of the front desk attendants walks up to them. "Ms. Rachel and Mr. David, good morning. I have a package for you." She holds out a yellow envelope.

David takes the envelope, noticing it has no return address. The attendant nods and heads back to the counter.

At that moment, the hotel is empty, so the two settle down on a large sofa in the lobby. David opens the envelope and takes out two business cards. One is from a Japanese police officer, and the other is from Chinese intel; both have cellphone numbers attached. He then looks at four photographs.

David, with caution, takes two photographs from the envelope and places them on the sofa. Analyzing them, he soon recognizes Yazuo. When taking the third photograph from the envelope, he notices two figures on motorcycles. The fourth photo makes him stop—it's of him and Michael, walking in the hotel parking lot last night. The expression on David's face hardens.

Rachel takes the picture from his hands and says, "Calm down."

"What is this? Are they monitoring us?" His tone is low, but his words tremble.

She takes the third photograph and points it out to him. "This is the only one that worries me." She shows David the image of the two men on the motorcycle.

Trying to compose himself, he picks up one last piece of paper from inside the envelope, which is written in Mandarin. Rachel listens as he translates: "Let's meet and talk. It's better to work together. Call either of the numbers."

She takes the piece of paper and reads it again.

"Holy shit! Are you serious?" he says, taking the paper back and looking at his partner hard.

"Listen … stop with that attitude, someone will notice." Rachel, firm in her words, stares at him.

He looks at the floor and says, "What the hell is going on?"

"Let's talk outside. There are a lot of cameras in this lobby, and it's getting crowded again."

The two get up and walk out the main door of the hotel. Rachel looks at him. She knows him well: when threats get close to him, he becomes flustered and loses focus on the situation. He follows her toward the parked car.

Certain that the couple is unaware they are being watched, Wonjy's car's music is blasting as his frustration grows over the heat and lack of direction from Hui or Mingli. His irritation escalates with a punch to the passenger seat. Spotting David and a woman near a Hyundai, their animated gestures signalling an argument, he takes pictures of them getting into the car.

What do I do now? There will be no time to warn Mingli, Wonjy wonders, starting the vehicle. David drives toward the avenue and passes Wonjy, who starts following them. When they stop at a red light, the stalker makes a call to the boss over the car's phone. Mingli answers and doesn't give him time to explain, ordering him to return to the barn.

"Not now. I'm following David and a woman." He speaks in a loud tone of voice, showing haste.

"Where are you?" Mingli asks, getting worried.

"I'm on Dongfeng Road. I don't know where they're going, but I'm following them."

Mingli thinks, remembering Hui's words, and since he doesn't want trouble, he says again that the manager told everyone to come back.

"Let's do it this way. Figure out where they're going, but don't do anything stupid. Don't let them see you. When you think it's alright, come back to base. I'll let Hui know."

"Okay, I won't do anything wrong. I get it." Wonjy ends the call.

David checks the car's clock; it's 8:30 a.m. His mind is preoccupied. His partner looks at him and asks, "Why are you so nervous? Don't stress about that photo, it's irrelevant."

"They're getting into my private life. What the fuck! I don't agree and I won't accept this," he says through clenched teeth.

"You seem to forget that we do the same when we investigate—surveillance, photos, wiretapping, and worse. I'm also confused why they would send this information. Maybe they want us to cooperate to arrest Yazuo.

Now, who are these other people? Bikers? And why photograph you with Michael? That part makes little sense." She tries to calm him down.

David drives toward the centre of the city, not realizing they're being followed. Wonjy continues three car lengths behind them.

"Let's pay a visit to Chief Bo," David says.

"There's something bothering me, and you could help clear it up. In the middle of your conversation, be indifferent. No third-degree interrogation or anything. Ask him if he knows Alex from the Firm, would you?"

"I thought about it the other day, and I'm going to quote these shitty cops who are following us. Leave it to me," an annoyed David agrees.

"I figured you wanted to know too," she says.

Parking a block away from the crowded police headquarters, the partners enter, identify themselves, and ask to speak with Superintendent Bo. An agent relays the request; minutes later, a young man in uniform appears. Rachel notes he can't be older than twenty-five, is athletic, very tall, and has Korean features. He introduces himself as Inspector Lu Khan and leads them down a long corridor and up two flights of stairs. In the office, a secretary greets them with a respectful bow and leads them through another door.

"What unexpected visitors this morning. Welcome, Ms. Barnes and David Ho. Please take a seat." Superintendent Bo directs their attention to two chairs against the wall.

David, calling the superintendent "Chief Bo," embraces him, and Rachel greets him with a bow. Bo asks the secretary to bring three teas and three bottles of water.

David settles into a chair. Rachel also sits down and watches the boss's exaggerated euphoria.

"Have you learned Mandarin?" The superintendent realizes she's studying him.

Surprised by the direct question, she replies in Mandarin, "I'm doing my best. What do you think of my accent?"

"I like it. Keep learning. Soon, you will speak impeccably. Let's get down to business. What brings you here this morning?" Chief Bo turns to David.

David exchanges a subtle look of complicity with his colleague, who knows these tactics. Quick focus and subject changes are classic police techniques used in multi-person conversations. One individual may ask questions or make statements directed at another to gauge reactions and attention, as well as to pick up on any subtle facial or body cues. They at once understand the game.

"Who is Wang Savin?" David asks the superintendent.

"Why? Do you want to meet him?" Bo asks as he walks to the door and questions the secretary about the tea and water.

"Remember the copy of the investigation documents you gave us on Thursday?"

"Hmm... of course." Bo speaks quietly. "What do you want to know?"

"We are looking for Wang because he is the only witness named in the depositions. It makes sense: he found Ronaldo's body," David says, feeling tension forming in the air.

"Hmm..." the boss again murmurs.

"You know, maybe he saw a Japanese guy at the hotel, and he just had a 'lapse of memory' and forgot to tell the police." David laughs at his own ridiculous idea.

"Can you imagine? If he remembers now ..." Boss Bo says, looking into David's eyes for a dramatic pause before bursting into laughter.

Rachel watches the scene and thinks, *Boss Bo's minor break left something hanging in the air, like a jokeless comedy.* She keeps her thoughts to herself.

The superintendent surprises everyone by looking at David and Rachel with an unfamiliar face. "Wang is an experienced businessman who excels in import and export. Besides being a philanthropist, he is an important donor to the less fortunate in Shanghai. The city even honoured him for his charitable contributions, but for what Yazuo told the Portuguese police ... I doubt he noticed. I can get his number for you; you might have better luck getting a response!"

Chief Bo finishes explaining. Turning his back on David, he returns to the armchair. He sits down and moves some papers on the office desk, not looking at the two of them.

"Thanks, boss. Sorry to bother you." David senses the atmosphere has turned heavy, and it's time to leave.

The partners stand up. David meets the superintendent's gaze as he takes his leave. Just before leaving the room, he turns around, feigning forgetfulness, and adds, "Alex from the Firm sends his greetings," injecting a note of mystery and suspense into the air.

"Send my greetings as well. I haven't spoken to him in a while." The superintendent smiles as he replies to David.

"Boss, one more thing. Do you know a Chinese intel officer named Liwei Huang?" David asks without bothering to leave.

"Yes. Do you know him?" Bo asks, staring at David.

"We met him the other day in a pub here in the centre and we had a little fun. We drank beer along with another Japanese intel officer." David speaks fast, not letting him ask questions.

The secretary enters the room, carrying the tray with the order. The partners bow, saying goodbye as they leave, but David still turns around and says, "I'll wait for the answer. You have my number."

Later, they arrive at the hotel, and Rachel tells her partner, "This hotel is full every day."

Looking at the elevators, David complains, "So many people waiting... I'll meet you at the restaurant on the first floor."

Rachel makes a positive sign with her hand and walks to the reception desk. "Good afternoon. Do you have anything for me or Mr. David?"

The attendant, upon seeing her, says, "No, Ms. Rachel."

On the way to the elevator, she is quiet and thoughtful.

In the hotel lobby, Wonjy, who had just sat down in an armchair, fixes his gaze on the closing elevator doors behind which Rachel disappears.

18

Imagination Can Be a Potential Reality

"Send Shu here." Boss Bo opens the office door and yells at his secretary in the hallway as she talks to a police officer.

After a few minutes, an elderly man wearing a police uniform runs up the stairs and enters the superintendent's office, out of breath. The agent is short but muscular. He has thinning hair because of age and is approaching retirement. Considered an excellent street officer in the past, today he only does special internal services.

The boss is sitting in the armchair, concentrating on some papers on the table.

The officer asks, "You need me?"

"Let Wang know the English people want to talk to him. Please motivate him to go meet the couple before they look for him anymore."

Shu nods his head and doesn't say a word. He bends his body in reverence and turns toward the door, intending to leave the room as quickly as possible.

Bo stops writing and adds, "Another thing, find Liwei Huang from intel and tell him to come here. I want to know what the hell he's doing."

"Yes, boss," the officer responds and stands still, staring at the ground.

"What are you waiting for?" the superintendent asks with a smile at the corner of his mouth.

Shu doesn't notice, as he leaves the room at a sprint.

*   *   *

At the port, Wang signs documents for waiting dispatchers. Holding the contract, he checks whether today's new containers are ready for the next ship bound for Spain. He watches from a distance as Hui speaks to agents. When his cellphone rings, he hands over the papers before answering.

Shu, on the other end of the line, catches Wang's attention.

"Chief Bo has ordered me to inform you that the English couple is looking for you. He tells you to attend to them before they ask too many questions and, he told me to tell you, he doesn't want any trouble."

Wang stops walking and contemplates the old policeman's words. He takes a deep breath and responds in a lethargic voice, "Tell Bo I'll meet the couple."

Shu hangs up the phone.

Wang walks over and tries to understand why Boss Bo put him in this situation. Near the car, he sees Hui running and waving his arms, requesting that the boss wait for him.

"Shit!" Wang says and stops walking, watching Hui run toward the car.

Wang waves back to Hui and climbs into the passenger seat of the Mercedes. The manager arrives and settles into the driver's seat, starts the vehicle, and heads toward the port exit.

"Hui," Wang shouts.

"Yes," Hui replies, startled. He looks at his boss, not understanding the reason for the yelling, and returns his attention to the avenue.

"I want information on David, Michael, and Rachel by noon, as well as the intellectual property firm in London and its clients. Also, what is the outcome of that Portuguese operation that led to the arrest of the Yakuza?" Wang is getting upset.

"No problem. I'll see to it today. Where do you want to go now?" Hui asks, trying to sound calm.

"My aunt's house," Wang replies with a distant gaze through the car window.

"Your aunt? Why?"

"I need to know what that couple talked to her about."

"I was the one who took them to the apartment. They asked about Li's family," Hui prudently narrates, worried about Wang's reaction.

"I know, I know. You just do shit and you've already explained it to me. This man offered my aunt money for information. She accepted, and you shared, but then you left. Idiot! The problem is they kept talking, and she gave my mother's address and the time I would be there. Why? What was the reason for giving them the address? And the next morning, early, they were outside the apartment again." Wang is questioning his lackey.

"I get it," Hui replies concisely, knowing it's best to agree with Wang when he's nervous.

Silent inside the car, Wang reflects on the fact that the superintendent instructed Shu to call because things have come to a head. He continues to analyze the policeman's words, and the manager's announcement brings him back to reality.

"We've arrived."

"Wait for me at the gas station." The boss gets out of the vehicle, looking up and down the avenue.

Hui doesn't answer him and takes the avenue, looking for a return route.

Wang walks in brisk steps until he reaches the small apartment building. The gate is open, and he goes up to the first floor where his aunt lives. He knocks on the door, calling her by name.

Meixiu Gubei opens it and looks at him, startled. "How long has it been? Do you need something?" she says with sarcasm, staring at him.

Her nephew walks in, his gaze sweeping the room as memories flood back. Despite his affection and gratitude toward his aunt, he almost stopped visiting her. A wave of sadness hits him; age has withered the youthful beauty he remembers playing here with Li. Since Li's death, he has only returned twice to offer support. He now helps his aunt every week with essentials, allowing her to forgo work so she can take care of her sister full-time.

She walks to the kitchen and starts preparing some tea.

He sits down in a chair at the kitchen table and, upon seeing her looking at him, confronts her. "What did that couple discuss with you over the weekend? What do they want?"

Meixiu pulls out a chair and sits down across from him. Thinking about what her nephew is asking, she says, "They're not cops. Don't worry."

"What did they say? What did you tell them?" he demands, his raised voice revealing a loss of temper.

"They came to ask about Li and you. The woman wants to meet you. As I understand it, she wants to thank you for trying to save her husband," explains Meixiu, her tone turning scathing as she adds, "as if you would help save somebody."

"Auntie! What did they say?" Wang asks again, his anger growing.

"I don't remember. They came because they knew you were Li's cousin," she says, her voice tinged with sadness as her eyes fill with tears.

He sees she's crying but doesn't react.

"It wasn't Li they were looking for; it was you," exclaims the aunt.

"And you gave my mother's address and the time I would be there…" Wang questions her in a quiet voice, trying to calm her down.

"Yes. What's the big deal? They promised cigarettes," she says as nervous tears flow.

"I'll send someone to bring you cigarettes, make a list of what you need," he says, upset because his aunt always loses control when she remembers her son.

"Why don't you come visit me more?" she asks, wiping away tears.

"I don't have time and you gain nothing from my visits." Her nephew's manner shows that he wants to cut the subject short.

"I miss my son. When I look at you, I find comfort," she says, looking into Wang's eyes, who then turns away.

"I'm going to the apartment to see my mother. Has the pharmacy been delivering the injections and other medications daily?" he asks, showing that he prefers not to discuss his cousin further.

"Yes, they've been coming daily. Thank you for everything you've done for me and my sister. Go see your mother before it's too late," Meixiu tells her nephew, her voice tinged with devastation.

Wang gets up from his chair and heads for the exit, giving up on the idea of a hug. As he opens the door, he hears laughter emanating from a room—he immediately recognizes it as Cousin Li's from days gone by.

"Bye," he says and walks out, slamming the door.

Wang walks to where Hui parked, recognizing the old man from the gas station who still serves cars. Wang takes some money out of his pocket and hands it to the man with a "thank you." Sitting in the back of the vehicle, he is lost in thought, recalling his aunt's words. Deciding not to visit his mother, he reflects on the laughter he heard or imagined. This put him off the visit but reminded him of his late cousin, his best friend. Taking a deep breath, he looks down at his trembling hands and declares aloud, "This place only brings back sad memories; I don't even know why I come here."

Hui looks at him in the mirror as he drives and understands that something didn't go right. He tries to start a conversation. "I'll have information about the couple soon."

Wang does not respond and shows no reaction. He has fallen asleep.

After a while, Hui looks again in the rear-view mirror and sees that the boss has woken up. He stays quiet and continues toward the port.

In a sleepy voice, Wang asks, "Where are we going?"

"I'm going to Port Warehouse Number One," Hui replies.

"Great, I have to make some phone calls."

Arriving at the office, Wang sits in a comfortable leather chair and surveys a pile of papers on the large, antique wooden desk. He picks up a folder labelled "Storage Number One," takes a quick look at it, and tosses it back on the table. Looking through the window, he watches the cloudless sky. The AC does its best to cool the room, but outside it's a scorching thirty-five degrees Celsius.

His secretary opens the door, a glass partition, and advises, "Chief Superintendent Bo called early. He wants to talk to you."

"I've already talked to them," he replies, and she closes the door, leaving.

He looks at a framed photo on his desk taken five years ago, when it all began. He is proud of what he has achieved since then. His company is now international, and the name Wang is influential in financial circles in Shanghai. The city's wealthy view him with disdain, despite his public reputation for philanthropy. They don't consider him one of their own, as he doesn't belong to a rich family. However, he doesn't care because he knows that in the end, money speaks louder, and he has a lot, so they have no choice but to respect him. Getting here wasn't easy, but the last three years, with growing revenues and innovative changes, have been a glorious victory.

The phone rings, and he doesn't answer, even though he can see that it's one of Tong's bosses. Since taking over as the head of Tong in Shanghai, he shakes things up. It not only decentralized power, leadership, and responsibilities but also promoted an unprecedented level of independence and subordination among affiliates. Its restructuring earns the respect of the Triad; they no longer see Tong as a lower-tier team. He even grants autonomy to conduct international business with various factions in other countries. Major Chinese Tongs such as Bing Kong Tong in California and Washington, and Suey Sing Tong in the US and British Columbia, Canada, are now aligned with him. The result? He diversifies the group's activities without getting in the way and clarifies that everyone wins.

He looks at his cellphone and says, "You're all rich. Now wait, I'll meet you when I want."

Hui knocks on the glass door of the office and enters.

Wang returns from his egocentric mental trip and demands, "What do you want?"

The manager sits in the chair in front of him. "The couple has a private detective firm, DRT, in London. They are here helping the superintendent in that Portuguese police operation—the one that arrested Yazuo, but it was a failure. They transferred the guy to Japan and now he's free. My law enforcement source says they are investigating the Yakuza. Last week, they arrived and went straight to Boss Bo to discuss something. It was about something Yazuo had said when the police arrested him regarding a police officer being killed here in Shanghai."

"What else?" Wang doesn't move.

"After you called the surveillance team this morning at 8:30, I spoke with Wonjy. They went to the police building in the centre of town. They didn't stay long. Wonjy monitored them all the way to the hotel and was back at our garage at 10:30. He's back to work now," concludes Hui.

"Hmm," Wang mutters.

"Ah yes, the couple switched cars. Check out these photos." The manager texts the photo files to the boss's phone.

Wang looks at the images and turns to Hui. "Does anyone know what you just told me?"

"No, just me, the cop, and Wonjy."

"Change the cellphones of the boys who worked on this surveillance, especially Wonjy's, and then delete all the photos," Wang orders.

"Alright," Hui says, confused but obedient.

"Who is this man, Michael?" the chief asks.

"The guys think David has a boyfriend because he stayed over in the apartment. They're sure there's some kind of vibe between them." Hui tries to keep it vague.

"Very good." Wang looks out the window again.

"Do you need anything else?"

"Put someone who won't make noise to take care of this. I want to know everything about this Michael," Wang advises.

"I'll arrange it." Hui opens the office door.

"Okay, you can go. I'll call if I need you," the boss says as the manager leaves the room.

Wang inspects the photos sent to his phone and wonders, *Why is this couple so obsessed with a six-year-old affair? They say they want to thank me, but that makes little sense. I'm sure Boss Bo must have told them I found the body, so that's the reason they want to talk to me.*

"Boss, it's the second time they've tried to call from London, but the call doesn't complete," the secretary warns him.

He ignores her, hearing her close the door. Leaning back in his chair, after five minutes, he picks up the phone and calls his secretary Mayjim in the outer office. She responds fast; two years of work for Wang have taught her he is not a man who likes to wait. At fifty-five, she spent her entire career in banking, focusing on import and export before taking on this role. Working almost ten hours a day, she takes care of all the company's export documentation. Wang sees her as his right-hand man at the company.

She enters the room and the boss instructs her, "Call the person in charge of our London affiliate. Do you have his cell number?"

"I have," she confirms and leaves.

He pulls a folder out of the drawer. The import and export branch in London has encountered some obstacles, and he is looking forward to hearing the final resolution. It took two years just to secure the paperwork to operate there, and the launch was further delayed because of conflicts with local factions of the Chinese Triad. He spent six months brokering deals to agree, allowing London to be included in his European operations. Now, with the problems resolved, they opened the branch two weeks ago. Mr. Zhang Jing Yong, the CEO, not only brings value with his contacts in the European import and export scene but also earns high respect from the Triad—a key factor in maintaining business peace.

"Wang, he's on line two," Mayjim informs him, opening the office door.

The boss picks up the phone. "Hello, my friend. I want to know if you have solved the problem of the theft of goods? Did you find out who's behind it?"

" ... "

"Did you hire an intellectual property company? What's the IP's name? I was going to suggest this to you," Wang says and lights a cigarette, listening to Mr. Zhang's explanation.

" ... "

He raises a glass of whiskey to his lips, tasting the liquid. "Oh, DRT? Are you sure?" The name paralyzes him. It's hard to believe that Zhang would hire the same investigative firm that is looking for him. Suspicious, he reflects on the irony. Zhang had warned against hiring a high-profile IP firm to avoid attention, but now here they are with DRT, a firm recommended for its expertise and stellar reputation by its own industry contacts. Wang's silence makes Zhang question whether he was being heard, which prompts him to stay quiet.

Wang resumes the conversation. "I've already tidied everything up here with the bosses in London. They won't mess us up anymore. I think it is better not to cancel the contract with the IP now, so as not to arouse suspicion. I heard the police stopped investigating when they found nothing. You did the right thing. In a few days, cancel the contract and pay all the fees. Say our company will let the local investigators handle it. What do you think?"

He can hear Mr. Zhang laughing through the earpiece, so Wang hangs up the phone.

Mayjim, upon entering the room, asks, "Are you going to need anything else? If not, I'm going out to eat."

"No, you can go," Wang replies without looking at her.

"Anything, call me on my cell." She turns and closes the door.

Wang gazes at the photo of the partners on his cellphone and again speaks out loud to himself, "Let's meet today, Mr. David and Ms. Rachel."

19

The Unforeseen Hardens or Relaxes

Lying down on the bed, David studies the container company. He answers his ringing cellphone, listens, then replies, "Are you sure? Okay. Got it, send it to my email. We still have tomorrow. Time to confirm." David hangs up the phone.

Rachel, sitting in the armchair in front of the table with her iPad, turns to David. "Is everything okay?"

After reviewing the entire case file, Tyler has concluded that the operation has connections to the fentanyl labs in Japan and China. He found records of containers seized in the US that had fake interior walls. The investigators determined the pills found there originated from Japan.

"True, I forgot that detail in the containers," she says.

"The discovery of the fake walls in the refrigerated containers left everyone amazed. It was the first bust of its kind. I told Tyler to email us anything he thought might help our investigation here. We still have a day," David says with confidence.

Rachel lowers her head in thought. Looking down at the floor, she says, "Interesting. They found Mr. Chan inside a refrigerated container."

David ignores the remark, gets up from his seat, and grabs his wallet and car keys. "Remember our first day in Shanghai, when we went to that buffet for dinner? We're going back there for lunch today."

"Sounds good. I like the price." Rachel laughs. She remembers not eating anything that night as she spent all the time talking to Alex.

She follows David, who's already out the door and into the hall, while smoothing her hair and slinging her purse over her body.

When they arrive at the lobby, the sight of suitcases scattered everywhere surprises them. People crowd into the armchairs while others stand and talk.

"Again, this mess. Today there is no bar," David proclaims.

They walk toward the main door in a hurry. As they get in the car in the parking lot, Rachel says, "We have to analyze more about this container manufacturing."

"Don't worry, I wrote everything down. We just need to confirm."

She agrees, takes a deep breath, and remains quiet.

The traffic is chaotic. David concentrates and tries to overtake a car but fails and complains. "This traffic is horrible. We're going to be late."

Rachel notices his attitude but says nothing.

"I have a surprise," David says and flashes a mischievous smile without diverting attention from the flow of traffic.

"What?" she asks, coming out of the doldrums.

"Michael is at the restaurant. You'll meet him today." He watches her, waiting for a reaction.

"Okay, and…?" Rachel returns with a cynical look.

"That's it," David replies.

She laughs.

David parks the car at the side of the restaurant and sees Michael sitting under an enormous umbrella at one of the garden tables. This place only opens their outdoor spaces on hot days for the crowds.

Michael is so involved in scanning the street that he doesn't see David and Rachel when they arrive. He also doesn't notice the motorcycle parked near the restaurant.

At that moment, a server approaches. "What can I get you?" she asks.

"A cold beer, please. I'm expecting some friends," Michael replies.

As soon as he finishes speaking, David and Rachel appear. Michael gets up to greet them, blowing kisses and giving David a heartfelt hug.

The server, waiting by the table, takes their drink orders: three beers to start.

Michael doesn't take his eyes off Rachel and comments, "You're beautiful."

"I told you…" David smiles.

"He's my best friend. Don't believe him," she says, smiling, trying to make light of the compliment.

The trio rise from their seats and enter the buffet. Loaded with traditional Shanghai dishes, the rice paste is the main star attraction. As meat is a luxury, there are a variety of vegetables, fish, and beans featured as side dishes. As David and Rachel walk down the buffet line, their eyes light up when they spot the sashimi and sushi—that's where they fill their plates the most.

All three look content as they eat and drink, toasting life itself. David starts the conversation by sharing some stories about his partnership with Rachel, setting the stage for a lively discussion. Rachel then dives with emotion into a story about an operation she was part of in Paraguay, which led to a massive bust of contraband and drugs. Throughout the meal, the conversation doesn't subside; there is constant chatter, laughter, and animated gestures on all sides.

Listening to the story, Michael finishes his meal and, showing enthusiasm, intervenes. "Wow, you've led quite a life, and that was just one mission you've told me about. I can't even imagine the other stories you have. We need to meet again; I want to hear about all your operations."

Across the street, Zao Yun, the man tasked with following Michael, takes pictures of the trio absorbed in their jovial conversation. After getting the shots he needs, he hops back on the motorcycle, anticipating his next move. He scrolls through the images on his phone, checking that each one captured the moments of the encounter. At 2:00 p.m., he sends them to Wonjy, with details of the time and place. The air thickens with silent tension as he waits for further instructions.

The three of them leave the restaurant and David informs Rachel, "I'm seeing Michael home. Do you think you can go back to the hotel without discovering a new continent?"

"I'll insert the hotel into the GPS. Don't worry, we'll talk later," she says, snatching the car keys from his hand. She gives Michael a quick kiss on the cheek. The three of them squeeze together for a group hug and take a selfie on her cellphone.

In the restaurant's parking lot, everyone gets into their cars, oblivious to any prying eyes. Rachel leaves first, on her way to the hotel. Michael and David leave for his apartment. Michael has the afternoon off and is on a mission: he's going to talk David out of going back to London.

The biker follows the two men.

Before David and Michael left the restaurant, Zao told Wonjy that he was going to follow them as well. He told him that the woman drove off alone in the other vehicle.

Upon receiving the information, Wonjy hastily heads to the hotel to wait for Rachel. He figures the restaurant is about fifty minutes away, and given today's terrible traffic, he should get there before she does. Although he doesn't trust Zao Yun—who is neither a regular nor a reliable employee—Wonjy may have problems, so he takes matters into his own hands. Needing someone to shadow Michael as quickly as possible, he hired Zao for the job, promising payment upon completion. Now he just hopes that, for once, Zao doesn't screw up.

Rachel arrives within the scheduled fifty minutes. She parks the car a little farther from the entrance because of the crowded parking lot.

Getting into a parking spot near the hotel's main entrance, Wonjy watches Rachel enter. Deciding that this is the perfect time to alert his boss that he now understands the dynamic between the trio, Wonjy calls Hui, informs him of the situation, and forwards the photos of the restaurant.

After ending the call with Wonjy, Hui immediately calls Wang to inform him of the latest developments, including that Rachel is alone in the hotel. He assures Wang that Wonjy is in place and has everything under control.

"Come and pick me up here at the office; let's go to my apartment," Wang says to Hui, implying that he doesn't care what the manager told him.

"I'm already on my way." Hui doesn't understand why the boss ignores the information, but because he knows his temperament, he doesn't push it.

After picking up Wang and arriving at their destination, they enter Wang's residence, and Hui sits in the living room waiting for another order.

"Grab a beer from the fridge and eat whatever you want," the boss tells him.

"Thank you, but I'm fine." Hui looks around and watches his friend of so many years.

Used to frequenting the apartment but never crossing borders, he sees Wang as more than a brother. Wang has always helped him over the years. Hui owns a chain of five electronics stores run by his wife's family and always expresses gratitude to his boss for his financial success. This, among other complex reasons, fuels his unwavering loyalty to Wang. He knows that sometimes he will have to get his hands dirty to keep everything running in peace.

After some time, Wang reappears from his bedroom, catching the manager's attention with his transformation. Now dressed in a navy-blue suit and a white shirt adorned with delicate light-blue stripes, he's ditched the tie but donned black shoes and a matching belt. His "One Million" cologne fills the apartment as he styles his hair.

Surprised by his boss's transformation, Hui can't believe how polished Wang looks. He's always known that Wang has a certain magnetism—women do double-takes and whisper to each other wherever he goes. However, today Wang is a step above that. With admiration, Hui exclaims, "You're looking like those international models, or rather, film stars."

"Like it?" Wang raises an eyebrow.

"I'm surprised. What's all this for?" Hui questions.

Disregarding what he said, Wang gives his orders for the late afternoon. "First, you're going to call two of our most trusted men and get them to follow this David and Michael today. Wherever they go, who they hang out with or talk to, I want to know."

"Don't worry, I'll take care of it," says the manager, jumping off the sofa and straightening his shoulders.

"Listen, tonight I'm taking the red Porsche, the new 718 Cayman, not the old one. You're in the silver Audi, following me. Bring one guy for backup, okay?"

"Are you going to drive the Porsche yourself?" Hui warns, "I don't think it's safe for you to drive the Porsche yourself."

Wang interrupts. "Listen!" the chief barks, turning.

The manager lowers his head and apologizes.

"I'm driving because sometimes I miss it. I have to. Let's go to the hotel. I want to meet this Rachel person. I need to wrap this up today, and I don't want her to see you. Got it?" Wang says, laying out his plans.

"Okay, I'm going alone too. I don't need anyone by my side." Hui pulls back at the need for added security and agrees with his boss.

The two enter the private elevator and go down to the building's underground garage. Each of them takes a car and drives to Rachel's hotel, going straight to the hotel's parking lot. Spaces are hard to find, so they end up parking far from each other in the crowded parking lot.

"I'll need to work magic to take care of him and the Porsche," Hui murmurs to himself.

Wang gets out of the car and heads toward the hotel entrance. Pulling on his jacket, he glances at his Jaeger-LeCoultre watch—it's 6:00 p.m. On point. Upon entering the lobby, he's a remarkable sight: a tall guy, imposing even by Western standards, with striking green eyes and toned muscles. He draws attention.

The women in the hotel lobby express their delight and admiration toward him. Other people there recognize him and gesture with their hands. He nods back and walks toward the reception. As he is about to reach reception, two excited young women approach him. They ask for his autograph and take a few quick selfies with him, their faces lighting up with delight.

Two hotel managers intercept him and bow in respect. With a big smile, the person in charge announces, "Mr. Wang, very honoured to have you in our hotel. What can we do for you?"

"I'd like to talk to Ms. Rachel Jane Barnes."

"Make yourself comfortable. I'll going to see if Mrs. Barnes is at the hotel," replies the manager.

"Thank you very much," he says and sits down in an armchair at the front desk. The two managers withdraw and discuss how such an important person comes to the hotel without warning.

Wang's fame in Shanghai is undeniable; he is often gracing TV screens, newspapers, and magazines for his humanitarian work in poor and immigrant neighbourhoods.

Rachel answers the phone and, in astonishment, hears the news that Mr. Wang is waiting for her at the front desk of the hotel. She is surprised by this unexpected situation, but even though David is not there, she cannot miss the opportunity to talk to the witness, and replies to the attendant, "Please let Mr. Wang know I am going down."

She notices she is still wearing the clothes she wore to lunch. A quick comb through her hair confirms that it's beyond her control for now, so she pulls it back with a rubber band. Pulling on her boots and grabbing her iPad, she hurries out of the room and into the elevator, unconcerned with her appearance. As she enters the busy lobby, her eyes scan the crowd for Wang.

A manager, Mr. Kim, approaches her and instructs, "Ms. Rachel, please accompany me."

The manager surprises her by guiding her to a secluded room behind the hotel's main lobby, as she is not aware of their destination. She realizes she had never noticed this hidden space before.

Mr. Kim leads Rachel into the room and closes the door behind them. She walks in, taking in the opulent surroundings: a tasteful living area with a private wet bar, a colossal seventy-inch TV, a conference table surrounded by six plush chairs, and a luxurious set of brown leather sofas. From an armchair, a handsome man rises to greet her and inquires, "Ms. Rachel?"

Stunned, Rachel looks at him in disbelief. A fleeting thought crosses her mind: *This very handsome man in that suit cannot be Wang.*

"Ms. Rachel?" he asks again.

"Mr. Wang." She composes herself and responds by saying his name.

The two shake each other's hands, and Wang asks if she would accept a whiskey. She realizes he expresses himself in perfect English, and that if anyone listened and didn't know him, they would think he grew up in London.

Oh my! I love this cologne, Rachel thinks to herself and replies, "Yes, I do."

"One or two ice cubes?" he asks, analyzing her.

"One cube, please," she replies, studying the man and concluding he has impeccable manners.

He doesn't understand the reaction he's witnessed and walks toward her to hand over the glass of whiskey.

Disconcerted, she takes the glass. Thanking him, Rachel says, "Sorry to be staring, but I was imagining a different person."

Wang smiles and looks into her eyes. "No problem. A toast."

"Why not?" she agrees.

"To new friendships." He raises his glass and toasts.

They sit across from each other at the conference table. Rachel's beauty captivates Wang. He fixes his eyes on her, taking in her features, gestures, hair, and the sound of her voice. A thought crosses his mind: she's perfect. He wonders how he couldn't see all of this when they visited his mother's house.

As they exchange glances, Rachel is just as smitten with him. She admires his face, his unusual green eyes, his styled hair, and the well-defined muscles that are apparent even through his tailored suit.

"Do you mind if I smoke?" he asks, resuming the conversation.

"No problem, go ahead. I smoked for eight years and quit. It doesn't bother me anymore," she explains.

"You and another person have been looking for me. Superintendent Bo has informed me today, sorry I couldn't meet you sooner." Wang explains that he came to the hotel because he has a complicated schedule.

"The superintendent advised us he was going to contact you. Let's get started. I just have a few questions," she says and opens her iPad.

"If you don't mind, I haven't eaten all day. Would you have dinner with me? I promise to answer all questions you have—anything you want to know." Wang's voice is clear and serious. He doesn't want to miss the opportunity to spend even one more moment with her.

Rachel looks at her wristwatch and sees that it's only 6:30.

"I do, but you'll have to wait for me. I need to shower and get ready. No problem?"

"Of course not. I'll be here or in the reception hall waiting for you."

She leaves the room and heads toward the elevator, fascinated by Wang's education and good looks.

Assessing the meeting, Wang stays a little longer in the reserved hall and after a while, heads out toward the lobby.

A manager addresses him: "Do you require anything else?"

"Ms. Rachel left to get her bag; I'll be waiting here for her return," explains Wang, pointing to one of the nearby armchairs.

"Feel free, sir. The reserved one is also available, and no one will bother you." The manager guides him over, bows and retreats.

Once the manager disappears, Wang makes his way through the busy lobby and exits through the main entrance. He scans the area and sees Hui, who is leaning against the Audi, smoking a cigarette.

"Everything good?" Hui asks.

"Rachel and I are going to dinner. I'm taking her to that Brazilian steakhouse. You know I can't resist good meat; I've been told the food there is top-notch." Wang's voice is tinged with enthusiasm.

"Boss, maybe you should ask someone else for security tonight," Hui suggests before being interrupted.

"Calm down, nothing is going to happen. Did you tell the boys to follow the other two?" Wang asks about the surveillance he ordered.

"They're guarding that man's apartment. Zao is on the bike. Wonjy and Bohai are in the black Toyota."

"Very well. I need to know what they understand about what happened at the hotel." Wang stares at Hui, speaking in a firm voice.

"We'll find out." Hui doesn't look away from him, understanding what his boss needs.

"I have to get back." The boss strides into the hotel entrance.

Hui drops the cigarette on the ground and stomps hard on it with his shoe. He opens the Audi door and enters.

Rachel's walk toward Wang inside the hotel captivates him. It's like she's floating, the way she walks. Her hair flows free, her makeup is subtle yet charming, and her burgundy lipstick is the perfect touch. Surrounded by this image, his eyes follow the soft swing of the salmon silk dress that reveals the waist and bust. Her shiny black high-heeled sandals and the small matching purse she carries in one hand complete the ensemble. The sight fascinates him.

The hotel staff, upon seeing her, also make comments on how beautiful Ms. Rachel is.

He composes himself, saying to himself, *What is it, Wang? Just another beautiful woman.*

As soon as she gets close to and in front of him, his heart feels like it's going to beat out of his chest, with so much emotion and desire. He says in Rachel's ear, "You look wonderful."

"Thank you, Wang. It's not that much. You're looking great, too. Did I make you wait too long?"

"No, not at all," he says, walking beside her. He can't shake the certainty that there is something more destined to happen in this encounter. It's extraordinary to experience such intense emotions in a relationship that only started half an hour ago.

Wang opens the car door for Rachel and notices the perfume she wears, Chanel No. 5.

"What would you like to eat?" he asks, steering the car toward the exit of the parking lot, believing she'll let him choose.

"Italian food," Rachel replies.

"I know a fantastic place," he agrees, a hint of disappointment in his words as he refrains from mentioning that he initially considered a steakhouse. Making the first left turn, he directs the car to the avenue, changing his intended path. It's a change of plans, but now they're going to treat themselves to a meal at one of the best Italian restaurants in Shanghai.

On the journey, a palpable tension fills the air, silencing the conversation. He breaks the silence by playing soft Chinese music. Looking out the window, she ponders her presence there. Upon arriving at the restaurant, Rachel admires the impeccable service provided by the team. People sitting nearby, and even far away, offer greetings and exchange business cards with Wang. Amid their entrance, they find little tranquility because of the constant flow of people vying for their attention. The manager intervenes and suggests a private room. As they get up from the table, she hears applause directed at Wang. Following the manager, they enter a uniquely themed room made for dining.

Sitting at the cozy table, Wang studies the menu while Rachel's perplexity persists. With her characteristic sarcasm, she can't resist joking, "So, am I with a superstar politician or a soap opera heartthrob? Or could it be a secret movie star?"

Wang laughs and explains, "I am known in the city; I was on some local television shows and the local newspapers wrote a few stories about me. They say I help Shanghai a lot. That is all."

She just smiles at him.

It is a normal dinner. They get up and sit on the reserved couch, waiting for dessert. Soon, the waiters bring it in, and Rachel decides this is the time to ask some questions. "Wang," she whispers, looking into his eyes. She lets her guard down, believing she can trust this man.

Listening, he stares at her with panting breath. He wants to kiss her, but he controls himself. "Yes, Rachel."

"I need to ask you some questions," she continues.

"Whatever you want to know," he replies and stands up.

The lounge's sliding door opens and a server enters, checking that everything is okay. Wang shakes his head, muttering that everything is perfect, and he doesn't want any interruptions. The server smiles and guarantees, "Don't worry, if you need anything, just ring the bell." She places another bottle of whiskey on the table before exiting the booth.

Refilling the glasses with a little more drink, he settles down on the couch, moving closer to her. His arm reaches out, fingers contacting her shoulder. Their gazes meet, and within her eyes, he finds a mirrored desire, an unspoken understanding. He embraces her, and to her surprise, she doesn't resist when their lips meet. This is a kiss that Wang has been looking forward to for a long time, years of anticipation coming to fruition in this moment. He surrenders to that kiss, as if the world could cease to exist. The emotions that run through him are unlike anything he has ever known.

Rachel also gives in to the kiss. A wave of desire and affection runs through her, despite knowing that this is just another magical and fleeting moment. However, amid all this, she could never have imagined that such an occurrence would take place in the heart of Shanghai.

"Let's get out of here. You can have a look at my apartment," suggests Wang, getting up from his chair and holding out his hand to help her.

He drives the Porsche fast toward his apartment.

Rachel is silent, distant, and stares out at the street.

Hui continues following the chief's car and realizes that its path leads to Wang's residence.

Upon arriving at the apartment, the wall of glass that reveals the entire city and the Huangpu River beyond captivates her. "Wow, this view is stunning," exclaims Rachel, her back to Wang, as she points out at the cityscape.

Wang's arms wrap around her in a tender embrace. When she turns to face him, her gaze finds his shirtless body, tattoos on proud display. Their lips collide in an enthusiastic kiss, a magnetic force guiding them toward the bedroom. With heat and urgency, he frees her from the confines of her dress, his eyes tracing the contours of a body sculpted through years of dedicated physical training. Once again, their lips meet, blotting out thoughts of the outside world, leaving only the heady feeling of the moment, a realm where life's complexities, mundane demands, and nagging questions fade into insignificance.

Time passes, and in the garage sitting in the car, Hui reflects. Frustrated while waiting for his boss to call, he says out loud: "This is going to be a mess. Why the hell did he bring that woman into the apartment? What was he thinking?"

The phone rings and Hui answers. Wonjy informs Hui that the targets are still at the same address and have shown no signs of activity. Hui warns his partner, emphasizing that they are ready to be there all night if necessary. Wonjy tells Hui that he considered firing Zao after the full day's work, but since Zao insisted on staying at work, he complied.

Glancing at his watch, Hui realizes it is already 9:00 p.m. He gives orders for the team to take turns eating and resting. The guideline is clear: maintain vigilance and follow the targets wherever they may be. The goal is to discover the identities of those they are interacting with.

"Boss, leave it to us. We're not going anywhere," Wonjy replies.

After ending the call, the manager dials his wife's number, her voice softening as she answers. With a sombre tone, he says he fears that the coming night will stretch on for quite some time.

20

Celebrating Love

In their sincere conversation, the two lovers delve into a past eclipsed by life's illusions and hard disappointments. During the dialogue, they address the prospect of meeting both in dreams and in reality. Despite Michael's uncertainty about dissuading his love from returning to London, he remains steadfast in making plans for tomorrow, with little concern for the present.

As David prepares two glasses of whiskey, his companion takes a shower, setting the stage for a quiet moment. Approaching the living room window of the apartment, he lets his gaze wander over the urban landscape. Amid the silent environment, he takes a sip of his drink and all of a sudden, the characteristic noise of a motorcycle fills the air, catching his attention. David watches a figure dismount from a motorcycle across the street and remove a red helmet. As darkness obscures facial details, he watches the man light a cigarette before walking down the lightless street toward the avenue. A flash of recognition surfaces; a similar bike, a familiar helmet, perhaps from elsewhere. Turning away from the window, David refills his glass, his mind captivated by the memory of that helmeted figure, muttering under his breath, "Just a trick of the mind."

Michael enters the room wearing a white silk robe and hugs his old flame.

"Do you remember a motorcycle that tried to overtake us on the highway when we were coming here this afternoon?" David asks.

"No, but I saw a motorcycle parked in front of the restaurant just as we left," Michael replies.

"Was it following us?"

"I'm not a police officer. How do I know? What's the matter?" Crossing the room, not bothered by David's questions, he asks about the whereabouts of his glass of whiskey, paying no attention to the queries.

"I suppose this is nothing, but can you remember the colour of the biker's helmet in the restaurant?"

"Red," Michael says and laughs.

David's heart sinks as the possibility of coincidence diminishes. He walks over to the window, eyes searching for the motorcycle, pinpointing its parked location. The driver remains absent. Anxious thoughts course through his body; he is worried about protecting his ex from the disturbing reality of his investigations in the city. Deciding to change the subject, he adjusts the conversation, sinking into the sofa, hiding his doubts under a mask.

Once again, the two delve into their plans, discussing details with shared fervour. Michael becomes overwhelmed with euphoria when they strike a deal. With the goal of getting married in Canada, preparations loom on the horizon. Tomorrow, Wednesday, David has a crucial meeting with Michael's mother—a conversation to convey his resolute decision. Joy is contagious, colouring their lives with shades of unbridled optimism.

Agonized, David gets up from the couch, goes to the window, and examines the scene once more.

"Are you nervous? What's going on?" Michael looks at him with reservations.

"Come here. Can you see a motorcycle across the street? Not here. On the street, over there by the restaurant, behind that white SUV," David asks Michael, guiding his gaze to the parked motorcycle.

"Too far away, I can't see. What's the matter?" Michael questions, ignoring what David shows. He walks to the bookshelf, chooses a CD, and puts it into play. The soft piano music fills the room.

David is sitting on the sofa, his gaze fixed on the floor in contemplation. Sitting next to him, Michael reflects on his posture, trying to understand the weight of the uneasiness that hangs in the air.

"Do you think this biker is following you?" Michael asks, wrapping his arm around David's shoulder.

"I think... No, I'm sure of it," David utters, struggling with his own words as he tries to articulate a notion that hovers at the edge of his comprehension—a sixth sense that defies rationality.

"Why?" Michael positions himself comfortably on the couch like a good listener.

"I'm sure it's the intelligence police officers who are following us. I'll show you something." David gets up from the couch and heads into the bedroom. He searches his jacket pocket for the photographs, finding them before he returns to the living room.

Michael follows his movements around the apartment and smiles.

David sits on the couch and tells him why they came to Shanghai. He recounts from the day they left London and how the entire investigation has gone up to this point. Michael listens, observing what's being narrated.

"I received these photos and cards at the hotel." David shows him.

He holds the photographs and sees the image of the two of them in the hotel parking lot. Michael turns to David with an expression not of concern but of irony and asks, "I understand them watching you to get the Japanese, but why would they care about us? Is anyone interested in our relationship?"

"Pressure, that's all. To put pressure on me. Idiots." David returns to the window and responds while looking down at the street.

Michael asks him to sit down next to him again.

Filled with frustration and resentment, David emphatically rejects the suggestion and heads for the bedroom. There, he collects the clothes scattered around the chair and tucks his cellphone into his pants pocket. Reemerging into the room, he fixes his gaze on the street outside, but the darkness makes it difficult to make out details. The motorcyclist has returned and is leaning against the wall of the restaurant. David realizes this man expects something. Even if the motorcyclist looked up, the apartment window would remain a hidden point of view with the lights off. He calls Michael and speaks with a mixture of apprehension and determination: "The rider of the bike returned and stopped in front of that closed restaurant. Don't you think there's something wrong?"

"What are you going to do? It's almost midnight. There's no one else on the street. It's dangerous," Michael warns David, looking outside.

"I'm going downstairs to ask a few questions. The problem isn't me; it's Rachel. I'm going to warn these bastards that this is not their territory." David's voice is laced with icy determination. He walks toward the door, ready to go down.

Michael interrupts, asking him to wait, causing David to stop in mid-motion, his hand on the doorknob. Michael runs into the bedroom.

Taking off his robe, he puts on his sweatpants and sweater from the bed. Rummaging through the wardrobe, he retrieves a small safe, revealing its contents: a pistol, which he tucks into his waistband. Upon meeting David in the living room, he presents his firearm.

"If anything happens, we're protected," Michael proclaims, agitated.

"You don't have to carry a weapon! Where did you get that?" David asks in surprise.

"Come on. I won't have to use it, but it's nice to have," Michael explains, leaving the apartment.

The street in front of the building remains empty and silent. The people in the other buildings and houses are sleeping and there are only a few cars parked outside. There aren't many streetlights on this street. With determined steps, David exits the building at a brisk pace, making his way up the street. Just a metre behind, Michael follows. Along the way, further down the street, the black Toyota that houses Wonjy and Bohai is parked to the right of the building. The car escapes the two men's attention as they leave. Leaning against the wall of the restaurant, two vehicles down from the motorcycle's previous location, Zhao lights a cigarette, oblivious to David's approach.

"Why are you following me?" David's voice erupts, catching Zhao off guard. His surprise is clear in his reaction.

Startled by David's sudden appearance, he stammers that he isn't following anyone, and a trace of fear appears in his eyes. He throws the cigarette to the ground in frustration, crushing it under his boot.

David approaches Zhao, confronting him. "You're all motherfuckers. You photograph us and then send it to me. So, what's that? Blackmail? What do you want?"

Michael, standing within four feet away, leans on a car and listens to the interrogation.

The men inside the Toyota watch the situation, trying to hear and understand what's happening.

With a quick, purposeful movement, David's arm suggests his intention to retrieve something from his back pocket, his demeanour tinged with a mixture of urgency and caution.

In a swift, chilling motion, Zhao extracts a pistol hidden inside his leather jacket, his actions fuelled by a surge of raw emotion. The sound of gunfire cracks through the air as he fires twice.

David's anguished groan fills the air as he falls to the ground, his body writhing in pain. Without delay, a pool of blood wells up beneath him, spilling onto the sidewalk.

Reacting at once, Michael draws the pistol from his belt and fires, hitting the man in the heart. A harrowing sight unfolds as the motorcyclist falls, still clutching his gun, his fate sealed. Overwhelmed by uncertainty, Michael's desperation drives him to panic, and he runs down the street, forgetting about David. He runs past the building, propelled by a mixture of fear and adrenaline.

When Michael is passing the black Toyota, Wonjy opens the car door, colliding with him, causing him to fall to the ground, disoriented. Seizing the opportunity, Wonjy pulls Michael into the car, delivering a violent blow that renders him unconscious. With deft precision, Wonjy retrieves the fallen gun from under the car, shielding it out of sight.

The street remains silent, with no lights in the buildings or houses. Even with the sound of gunfire, no one comes to see what has happened.

The Toyota remains close to the intersection of the street and the avenue, positioned on the corner devoid of buildings, dominated by houses with high walls. Holding Michael's unconscious body, Wonjy conveys to Bohai, his voice strained with urgency, "We need to go. Now!"

Keeping his foot hard on the brake and the car in neutral, Bohai steers the vehicle down the street, executing the manoeuvre without arousing suspicion. As he rounds the corner, he starts the engine and disappears into the stream of traffic ahead. Meanwhile, Wonjy calls Hui.

When the manager answers the call, Wonjy's voice shakes as he mouths his words. He reports that the surveillance sucked, went to shit, and explains every detail of the tumultuous events that unfolded.

Hui listens with care, maintaining a serene demeanour even as the weight settles in: a misunderstanding could have cost David and Zhao their lives. The unexpected inclusion of Michael, picked up and placed in the car by Wonjy, catches Hui off guard. A turning point for sure. These are events he could not have foreseen. The shit has been done. "Do you know where that big barn is that we used to store goods in the past, on that old, abandoned farm?"

"Yes, it's about three hours from here," Wonjy replies.

"That's right. Get over there and wait for my call."

"Okay. We're going," Wonjy confirms.

* * *

Wang accompanies Rachel to the hotel; she glances at her watch and confirms it is 12:15 a.m. He guarantees he will call her the next day to arrange another tour. The two can't contain their glee, their faces lighting up with the sheer delight of the fortuitous night they've shared.

Following Wang with a hint of detachment, the manager sits in his car in the parking lot, lost in thought. Wonjy's call came in. Now he has to face the daunting task of informing the boss after issuing directives. The order was plain—avoid complications, proceed with caution, everything goes sideways, as usual. Observing Wang's return from the lobby, the manager gets out of the car and, before Wang can get into the Porsche, he approaches with a hesitant stutter. "A—a—something urgent happened, and I need to talk to you somewhere else."

Wang looks at him, suspicious that something serious is coming. "Where?"

"We can go to People's Square, which should be safe," suggests Hui. His attempt to mask his nerves is overshadowed by his visible tremor. The inner turmoil is incontestable as he faces the weight of informing Wang, uncertainty coursing through every fibre of his being.

Arriving at the square, the two cross its length in companionable silence, their words suspended. The star-filled sky, adorned with a faded crescent moon, casts its enchanting spell on those who carry tranquility within and harbour love in their hearts. Which these two do not. Settling himself on a worn cement bench, Wang waits. Hui, positioned in front of his superior, takes a deep breath, mustering the courage to recount the unfolding events in meticulous detail.

Wang listens to the manager, bites his lip, and asks Hui without looking at him, "Who's this guy on the bike? Do I know him?"

Hui closes his eyes, lowers his head, and replies, "No. You don't know him."

"Does he work for us on the dock?" the boss asks.

"No. He's on the port list for sporadic jobs." The manager doesn't have the courage to look at Wang but tries to convey credibility in his words.

Wang straightens the hair that has fallen onto his forehead, stands up, and takes a few steps. He then returns and, with a troubled expression, asks Hui, "There's nothing that ties him to us? How is this possible? Did you send someone unknown to do such a job?"

"There is no link between him and us or the company. There is no traceable link to him, and Wonjy recruited him for the job. The only potential link could be between Wonjy's cellphone and his. I know Zhao, but he doesn't have my cell number," explains Hui, understanding the discomfort of witnessing an angry boss.

With resentment in his eyes, Wang speaks in a calm and composed tone. "Okay. I get it. Let's clean up this shit."

"Boss, I will take care of everything that needs to be done," Hui states with a nod, holding his head high. He spits on the ground and starts walking with a deliberate, unhurried pace, as if everything is already under control.

"Is the farm the one with a river behind it?" the boss asks.

"That's right, Yangtze River."

"It's September… hmm… is it crocodile season?"

"It is," a startled Hui replies and wipes the sweat from his hands on his pants.

"Can you make this trip in two and a half hours?"

"I believe so," the manager replies, swallowing concisely.

"Okay. Call Wonjy. He'll need to extract information from the man about the police officer's death at the hotel. I'm not kidding about this; when I'm on the scene, I want answers. Advise him to take whatever steps are necessary to make him talk," Wang instructs Hui. He then goes to the car and manoeuvres the red Porsche to a more favourable spot and leaves it right there in the square.

At the same moment, a trembling Hui picks up his cellphone and calls Wonjy. He gives orders about what needs to be done, what questions they have to ask, and how, above all, they need to get answers, whatever the cost.

After the call from Hui, the two inside the Audi don't talk, and the trip to Jiangsu is quick.

Arriving at the farm around 3:40 a.m., they park the car behind the deserted house. They advance toward the barn and enter through the back entrance. Five minutes later, a lone bulb struggles to light the weathered barn, revealing a blood-soaked Michael strapped to a chair, looking closer to death than life.

Silent and determined, Wang approaches Michael, watching him. He puts his finger under Michael's nose, confirming that there is still a shade of breath. Wonjy and Bohai pay homage with a bow to their chief before approaching, their gaze fixed on the near-dead figure.

Next to the two of them, the manager asks what they have discovered.

Wonjy reveals that the man said he doesn't live in Shanghai; instead, he lives in London but visits his sick mother here. His mother manages the place where he has worked for a few years. At one point, she told him about the incident involving a policeman's accident at the hotel—a fall into the swimming pool. Some former hotel employees, according to her, do not believe the official narrative of the incident and sometimes claim that it was a homicide. However, the man's mother provided no details, and he insists that this is the only information he knows when questioned.

Upon hearing the report, Wang steps up behind Bohai and, without delay, fires a fatal shot into Wonjy's head; blood, brains, and bone spray. In an instinctive response, Bohai tries to disarm Wang, but the chief's dominance prevails as he fires a shot into Bohai's chest. Afterwards, Wang approaches Michael and ends his life with a single shot to the side of the head.

Hui freezes, horrified by the scene unfolding before him, speechless. With the imminent course of action clear in his mind, he gathers the strength to remove the clothes from the lifeless bodies of Wonjy, Bohai, and Michael. Wonjy's eyes are open, and Hui delicately closes them, his hands shaking as he does so. He recognizes the need to address the circumstances at hand while struggling to maintain his composure. His mind runs through assessments at a rapid pace, but his own body shakes as uncertainty takes over. Torn between not knowing what to do and the fear of becoming the next target in the crosshairs, uncertainty takes over Hui.

His gaze shifts to a half-open door, where a coat and backpack lie nearby. Gathering his resolve, he gets up and runs toward the items. Opening the backpack, he discovers a cellphone, a wallet containing identification, and a change of clothes. He looks for a firearm, but he doesn't find any. As he searches the documents, he evokes an unexpected calm that surprises even himself. He then approaches Wang, presenting his findings with an attitude that belies his inner turmoil. Wang's expression remains unreadable as he looks at Hui's findings.

"Here's Zhao's cellphone and wallet. They won't find anything on him."

Watching Hui's movements with suspicion, Wang's demeanour remains even as he offers a slight, affirmative smile, nodding in approval. The gun he brought rests on his waist. His gaze lingers on Hui, then shifts to show the other weapons strewn across the floor—items the manager hadn't noticed. With a commanding gesture, Wang instructs Hui to gather not only these weapons but also any belongings associated with the three deceased.

The Yangtze River flows close behind the farm. Assisted by the chief, Hui loads the three bodies onto a wagon. Then he transports them to the riverbank before throwing them into the water. Immediately caught by the current, the bodies float, and soon a group of crocodiles appears, taking part in a frenetic show. Some crocodiles swoop over the remains with savage intent, while others take the opportunity to claim their share of the dead. The gruesome scene unfolds as nature's dark feast begins.

Wang and Hui stare for a couple of minutes as the crocodiles scramble for the three bodies disappearing into the river.

It's still night. The two of them return to the barn.

"You will pick up the Toyota and bring it back to the warehouse parking lot. Make sure you clean it with bleach, inside and out. Be thorough—inspect every detail, eliminate any traces of blood or any anomalies. Come back to the port in the morning," Wang instructs, soulless, his words flowing as if recent events have left no impact on him.

"You can leave, boss. Here are three cellphones and two pistols I found. One of them belongs to Wonjy, the other I don't know whose it is…" Hui hands Wang the cellphones and weapons in a plastic bag.

"I'm leaving. I have a lot to do today. It's 5:45 now; we'll talk after."

Hui doesn't reply, showing false tranquility and only watching the boss.

Wang grabs the bag and walks toward the Audi. He stops and puts the gun he carries on his waist inside the bag. He returns it to the manager who accompanies him and says, "Put an end to everything."

Hui picks up the bag, and his gaze follows Wang's swift exit in the Audi. Back in the barn, the pungent smell of blood has grown stronger. With care he gathers scattered items—clothes, shoes, wallets—placing them inside a large, empty fifty-gallon steel drum. The manager takes a small gallon of gasoline stored in the Toyota, pours the contents inside, and starts a fire. He picks up additional items stained with blood from the shed and throws them into the flames. Observing the moderate intensity of the fire, he deduces that the gasoline may not have been enough.

A little calmer, he looks at the flickering flame, realizing that Wonjy had been a pleasant partner; perhaps the situation did not justify such a terrible end. He claps his palms to his head, trying to change his mind, and returns his attention to the still-burning fire, ensuring complete destruction. After checking and cleaning the tin, he takes a gallon of bleach stored in the car's trunk and uses it to clean the water canister before refilling it with water.

Glimpsing his shirtless reflection, his suit consumed by fire, he remembers the suitcase that had been in the car containing extra clothes. Among them, he locates a shirt and puts it on. Thinking about the next steps, he decides to go home and see his wife and children before heading to the port, even considering a quick shower, weather and time permitting.

The sound of an airplane brings Hui back to reality. His eyes lift to the sky, recognizing the dawn. Absorbed in his actions, he mistakenly loses track of time.

He settles into the Toyota, heading down the dirt road. Travelling at a reasonable pace, his gaze shifts to either side of the path. On one side, the bamboo forest is swaying in the wind, while on the other, small bushes and low-lying plants dominate the landscape. In an instant, he slams on the brakes when a crocodile appears, crossing the dirt road. His heart races, and an image of crocodiles in fierce conflict, fighting for lifeless forms, rises before his eyes. He remembers the relentless lacerations, quick bites, and terrible tearing of the flesh of Wonjy, Bohai, and Michael.

The mysterious symphony of water returns, a chilling sound that makes Hui's breathing quicken. His eyes close to regain his composure, but his heart races, requiring deep breaths before it soon finds its rhythm. In his mind, he conjures up images of his children running to hug him and his wife leaning forward, offering a tender kiss.

The phone rings, and he answers.

"Where are you?" His wife's voice reaches his ears, leaving him speechless.

He throws his muffled voice into a low tone. "I'm going home. I'll be there in three hours."

Catching his breath and taking control of the situation, Hui drives home again. However, an undeniable realization accompanies him: today's events have left an indelible mark on his memory, a presence that time cannot erase.

21

Everything Changes

The police arrive at the scene of the shooting after receiving an anonymous phone call. It's 1:00 a.m. The first police officers on the scene find David still alive. An ambulance is called, and upon arrival, they load him and rush to the hospital's emergency room. However, the other victim is dead, covered with newspapers, lying on the sidewalk.

"The coroner's on the way," one officer announces.

Detective Chong Xi Wey scans the area for a second weapon but finds nothing. Walking around the scene, he tries to piece together the events. The discovery of only one revolver puzzles him. He positions himself three metres away to observe the corpse leaning against the wall of the restaurant. The body language suggests the bullet's impact threw the man backward. It seems the victim did not foresee the shot; it was a clean hit, clear from the way the man lies where he fell. The investigators recovered the only weapon; it was positioned next to the victim's right hand.

Detective Chong searches the body, pulling a restaurant card from the man's pocket. He confirms that the man has no cellphone, no identification document, and nothing else that could help identify him.

"Did anyone search the body?" Detective Chong asks, yelling at the surrounding officers.

Some officers shake their heads, while others just say no.

"Great, another headache for today. No papers and no cellphone," Chong announces, disappointed, rising from his crouched position on the ground.

At this moment, the Forensic Medical Institute's car arrives. Coroner Dr. Xiyang Ruixue approaches the detective. "Full night. This is already the fifth one we've collected. Did your shift start today or yesterday?"

"Today, it starts like this," he replies, yawning, handing over the restaurant card to the coroner.

Chong continues to analyze the body next to the doctor and says, "He had no cellphone, no documents."

"That'll give you work," Dr. Xiyang comments, bending down in front of the corpse and pulling off a sheet of newspaper from atop the dead man.

"Can I give my opinion?" Chong asks, getting up from the ground to address the doctor.

"Sure. Your opinions always have good ratings to me." The coroner lifts his head, looks at him, and smiles.

"The body, look ... I believe the shot was straight in the heart and there was no time to shoot or react. That's why he died holding the gun."

"We'll see ... It's been thirty seconds since I arrived. Give me a minute." Dr. Xiyang begins work on the corpse.

"You can stay there as long as you want," the detective tells the doctor and walks toward three police officers who are talking near a car.

"You guys there! Go look down the street. See if you find any more ammunition casings or anything else you think could be important." The detective points, showing the direction.

A second car arrives with three other police officers. Chong approaches them and tells them to go to the buildings and houses in the vicinity and find some witnesses.

Dr. Xiyang calls the detective over, showing the corpse's chest and saying, "It was just one shot, at most about two to three metres away. It wasn't a point-blank shot."

"Can you get an idea of the calibre of the gun?" Detective Chong asks.

"I can't tell the type based on the diameter of the wound. I have to remove the bullet from the body to confirm. Did you find the casing?" Dr. Xiyang asks.

"Not yet," he replies.

The detective walks toward his car, calling out and announcing that he is going to the hospital. All nearby officers hear him and wave. As soon as he starts the car to leave, an officer appears at the driver's window, holding a cellphone and a casing.

"Let me see those!"

The officer hands over the cartridge, and Chong looks it over.

"I found it near this phone," the officer explains.

"Okay. Give the casing and cellphone to the doctor and show me where you found them."

Chong gets out of the car, returning to the body that is still on the sidewalk. After delivering the find to the coroner, the officer informs the detective that they discovered the device under the tire of a car parked in front of the crime scene. He makes sure the phone is working and still has battery life.

The detective checks and hands the cellphone to the medical examiner, who immediately puts it inside a small plastic bag. Chong looks at the evidence and tells Dr. Xiyang, "Leave the smartphone on; let's see if anyone calls looking for the owner."

Dr. Xiyang agrees.

The detective waves goodbye to everyone once more. Driving an unmarked vehicle, he speeds to the hospital. Upon arrival, he heads to reception, and a warm smile greets him. Both doctors and nurses admire him for his professionalism, compassion, and competence in his field. He enters, greeting everyone, and approaches Lily, the receptionist on duty, saying, "Hi Lily. Do you have any updates on the guy that paramedic Chio's ambulance brought in tonight?"

Lily returns the smile, looks at the computer, and reads, "He's gone for surgery on the fourth floor."

"Can I go up there?" he asks, returning her warm smile.

"Sure, you can," she replies, going back to her files.

Detective Chong walks to the elevator at the end of the hall from the main entrance of the emergency room. He enters, presses the button for the fourth floor, and glances at his cellphone for new messages, noting that there is no signal inside the elevator. The doors open, and he heads to the nurses' station. Presenting his police badge, he asks about the young man they brought in at dawn. The attendant consults the computer while Chong looks at the enormous clock in the waiting room; it's 3:30 in the morning. His eyes scan the area, taking in the rows of empty chairs and armchairs.

The receptionist informs the detective that the surgery is still ongoing and assures him that a doctor will speak to him as soon as possible. She then suggests that he sit in one of the empty chairs.

The detective scans the seating options and chooses one from a row of four chairs. As soon as he settles down, his cellphone rings. He answers as fast as he can, earning a disapproving look and a vocal rebuke from the receptionist, who asks him to hang up the phone or turn down the volume. He offers a quick apology and retreats to the back of the room, hiding behind a pillar to continue his call.

"Detective Chong, go ahead," he says in a quiet tone of voice.

On the other end of the line, a police officer who remained at the crime scene reports that an elderly woman from a building located almost opposite the crime scene went down to the street to speak with the officers. She mentioned someone running toward the avenue. Because of the darkness, she could not determine the gender as male or female. At first, she thought the gunshots she heard were fireworks, and she glanced up at the sky, expecting to see more pyrotechnics.

"Write all the information, compile a report, and send it to me. Any other witnesses?" Detective Chong instructs and inquires in quick succession.

"No. Everyone I spoke to didn't hear a thing; they all say they went to bed early. Also, the restaurant didn't open last night because three of the employees were sick. Looks like there's a flu going around."

Chong hangs up and goes back to the chair, wondering if he's going to get another scolding from the receptionist. He makes himself comfortable in his seat, but she doesn't pay attention to him.

Detective Chong passed the police exam at twenty-one and went through several departments before becoming a detective. Now thirty-nine, he is the head of Shanghai's homicide division, a role he has always dreamed of. A hands-on leader, he prefers fieldwork to paperwork and often arrives at homicide scenes even before the day-duty team. He assists his officers by helping them see what they might be missing. He has no children, and after getting divorced, he dedicates his life to work. Charismatic and attentive, he attracts much attention from women. He is always upbeat and quick with jokes, making everyone around him feel safe.

Hours pass, and the detective feels someone tapping his shoulder and calling his name. He wakes up and tries to make an excuse, embarrassed. "I can't believe I slept; I must have been tired."

A uniformed police officer gestures with impatience, showing his inexperience. "It's 5 a.m., and the surgery is over," he informs the detective.

"Is he going to survive?" Chong asks, straightening his jacket and hair.

"Yes, sir. The doctor came in about ten minutes ago and didn't want to disturb you. He asked me to let you know that the surgery went well."

Chong looks at the officer who is holding some papers, realizing he doesn't remember seeing them before, and asks, "Do you have something for me to sign?"

"Yes, sir. It's the crime scene information." The officer hands him the documents.

Detective Chong takes the reports and starts reading.

The doctor stands at the desk talking to the nurse and signs a document. He looks over at the chairs, seeing that the detective has woken up, and calls out, "Detective Chong?"

At once, Chong goes to the doctor, greets him, bows, and calls him by name, which he reads engraved on the apron: "Dr. Junfeng."

"You were waiting all night, and I didn't want to wake you up. The surgery took a while because it was a penetrating wound. I had to confer with the team to determine if the bullet had lodged in the abdominal cavity."

"So, the projectile came out? It wasn't a fatal injury?" the detective asks.

The surgeon describes it. "The bullet went straight through. We call these penetrating injuries, which happen when an object breaks through the skin from a gunshot or stab wound. In this situation, the injury affected only the fatty tissue and muscle beneath the skin. If the bullet had entered the abdominal cavity, the damage would have been much more serious. It took us a while because we did several tests to assess the wound, but it's not too worrisome. He should recover in three or four days. We just need to watch out for infections, ruptures, and other complications. A few days in the hospital, and he should be ready to go home. He was very lucky. I'll write a report, and then you can collect it from the administration."

"Thank you very much, Dr. Jufeng. May I speak with him?" the detective asks, his anxiety showing.

"No, I expect him to wake up in about five hours. However, we will need to administer some sedatives soon after because of the pain, to get him back to sleep," replies Dr. Jufeng.

"Would it be possible to let me know before you give these painkillers?" Chong asks.

"I will inform the next doctor on duty and note this on the form. I hope they remember to allow you access; let's see what we can provide," the doctor affirms.

"Anyway, I'll be here in five hours," the detective advises him.

"Okay. My shift ended at 6 a.m. It was a pleasure." Dr. Jufeng retreats into a room.

The police officer who brought the documents accompanied Chong during the entire conversation. Detective Chong motions to him, hands back one of the signed papers, and leans back in his chair to examine the remaining documents. The officer bows with ceremony and heads for the elevator.

Chong raises his voice, causing the receptionist to give him a stern look. "I knew it! Sorry." He apologizes at once.

Reading the coroner's documents, Chong finds confirmation of his suspicions. The position of the two bodies suggests that the fatal shot did not come from the survivor; instead, the angle shows a third person at the crime scene, about five feet away. The witness's testimony supports this, as she observed someone running after the shots. His phone vibrates again. This time, he prepares himself and goes to the back of the hall, behind a pillar, to answer the call.

A police officer from the detective team for the day communicates with Chong, saying, "A woman called us on the 'found' cellphone. We briefed her on the situation, and she is on her way to the hospital. Her name is Rachel Barnes."

"Thanks," says the detective, taking the elevator to the ground floor of the hospital. He heads down to reception, intending to find this woman named Rachel who had called from the cellphone found at the crime scene.

He realizes that Lily's shift is over, and she is no longer at the front desk. Another attendant greets him. The detective asks to be informed when a woman named Rachel arrives looking for someone in the ER. He points to some chairs lined up against the wall opposite reception and informs the attendant that he will wait there.

Indifferent to the waiting patients, he sits down, aware that it has been a long time since he has been in a hospital. In the last few months, he has only dealt with dead bodies. Closing his eyes, an aseptic scent, like ether or ammonia, invades his senses, clashing with the memory of the sanitized smell of the fourth floor. Annoyed, he exhales into his hand and craves something sweet. Finding no candy in his pocket except a lone lollipop, he unwraps it. The moment it hits his tongue, comfort washes over him, allowing him to sit, eyes closed, a little more at ease.

22

The Nightmare

Rachel gets out of the taxi and runs into the hospital. At the emergency reception, she wipes away some tears and asks the attendant, "Please, do you speak English?" Rachel's voice is emotional, but the receptionist ignores her, not understanding what she is saying.

"Please, someone help me," Rachel pleads, her voice raised, mixing Mandarin with English.

The detective observes the scene at the front desk, gets up from his chair, and heads toward the woman. "I speak English. Calm down. What's the matter?"

"Please help me. This morning, a man named David Ho was admitted to this hospital. The police informed me that someone had shot him. Help me, please," Rachel continues, her speech a jumble of languages that leaves the staff struggling to understand her.

Chong shows his police ID and asks her to accompany him to the chairs in front of the reception. "I can help you. Explain to me why you are here." He remains serene, trying to calm her.

"I called my partner this morning, but he wasn't in his hotel room. We always have breakfast together. If he wasn't coming back, he would have let me know. Someone answered his phone and said they were a police officer and told me to come to this hospital. That's all I know," Rachel says, her words spilling out in English.

The detective gets up from his chair and fetches a glass of water. He hands it to her and asks, "Is he your husband, friend, Chinese, English...? Do you have a photograph of him?"

"Sorry, but why are you asking me these questions? Am I being interrogated? I need to find him, and you made me sit here. I'm wasting time." Her anxiety is growing.

"Take a deep breath. The information I'm asking for is crucial in helping me update you on his current whereabouts." The detective speaks in a low voice, his explanation flowing easily. Her words don't irritate him; he has become accustomed to consoling victims and navigating the dark terrain of homicide cases. He understands very well the deep emotional turmoil that envelop individuals in these situations.

With tears streaming down her face, Rachel reaches into her purse, her hands shaking as she reaches for her phone. Despite the tremors, she gathers the strength to display a photograph taken yesterday at the restaurant, capturing a moment shared with David. As she wipes away the tears that stain her face, she says in a shaky voice, "We have been business partners for countless years and are co-owners of a company based in London. Although he is of Chinese descent, he holds American citizenship."

Seeing that she hasn't stopped crying, the detective gets up from his chair, offers his hand, helps her to her feet, and says, "Come with me. I'm the one taking care of this case." He nods to the receptionist and points out that Rachel is with him. The attendant makes a positive sign and returns to serving the other patients.

Rachel looks at the detective, not understanding the signs but following him. She accompanies him to the hospital cafeteria, and the two sit face to face. He asks her to wait a minute before they speak. He buys himself a coffee and another for her, placing it on the table. Rachel's face still shows shock.

"What happened? How is he? What about his friend?" she asks, babbling in English.

Detective Chong, a little confused by the questions, retorts, "Let's take it easy. I speak English, but I'm not an expert."

"I'm sorry," Rachel says, dejected.

"This morning, he underwent surgery to extract a bullet lodged in his arm. The other bullet pierced his abdominal cavity at waist level, bypassing any vital organs. Fortunately, the doctor is hoping for a speedy recovery." Pausing for a moment, he continues, "Oh, what about his friend—you asked? Who's the friend?" the detective asks, watching every nuance of her expression.

"Oh my God! Shooting? Surgery? What happened?" She asks questions without bothering to answer his questions.

"We still don't know what happened," he explains, now knowing that the survivor's name is David, that one person died, and they brought the man in the photograph to the hospital alive.

"Can I see him?" Rachel asks.

"Not at the moment. He's anesthetized, resting. I'm here waiting for the doctor's call that he has woken up. I need to talk to him… By the way, what brings you to Shanghai? Are you here for a holiday?" he inquires, hoping to gain additional information relating to the case.

Though consumed with worry over her partner's predicament, Rachel's conscience remains keen for her normal routines. Recognizing the problems that lie ahead, the multiplicity of challenges that could result from this incident in an unknown land, she communicates with the police superintendent who received them the day they arrived. Turning her attention back to the detective, she asks, "Did Superintendent Bo show up? Is he aware of what happened to David?"

Chong's expression changes to one of surprise, but he remains silent, the gravity of the situation dawning on him in a way he didn't expect. The realization occurs: these individuals are not mere tourists; they associate with Boss Bo. An internal exclamation of confusion echoes inside him. He looks at her, his answer caught in the vortex of uncertainty. Reflecting on the situation, he asks her, "Do you know Boss Bo?"

Rachel doesn't respond and understands that the superintendent doesn't know what's going on. She opens her purse, takes out the card Boss Bo gave them, and calls his phone.

The detective sees her action and says nothing. "Boss Bo, it's Rachel Barnes," she whispers, her voice tinged with urgency. She recounts her current location at the hospital, revealing that David was the victim of two gunshot wounds the night before.

Taken aback by the person she is talking to, Detective Chong leans back a little in his chair, his gaze fixed as he listens to her words.

"Yes, there's a cop here. What's your name, please?" Rachel asks the detective, not remembering his name.

Chief Bo, on the other end of the line, hears Detective Chong say his name and asks Rachel to pass the phone. She hands him the phone.

Chong greets the superintendent and walks away from the table, going to the other side of the restaurant, as he doesn't want her to hear the dialogue. He talks to the boss, he looks at Rachel, and says, "…now things are different."

Agonized, she gets up from her chair and watches him, waiting for the end of their discussion.

He returns and hands over the phone. She notices his agitation. Chong looks Rachel in the eyes and asks, "Why didn't you tell me you are police?"

Rachel remains silent, acknowledging that this is not a suitable time to provide explanations, regardless of whether they are police officers or of their purpose in Shanghai. At this critical juncture, David's life takes precedence above all else.

As if expecting a reaction or word from her, the detective continues. "David shouldn't wake up before 11 a.m., according to the doctor's estimate. It's 7:30 a.m.," he informs Rachel, a pragmatic tone in his voice. "Staying here won't speed up his recovery. Perhaps we should stay away for the time being. Your help may speed up progress in resolving this case."

"Are you sure he'll wake up at 11:00? I don't want to be far away," she says.

"Yes. I had a talk with the doctor. They assured me they would notify me after he wakes up, and especially before administering any additional medication," the detective replies, walking beside her as they head toward the hospital parking lot.

"Where are we going?" asks Rachel as she sits in the passenger seat of the police car.

"Where I found David," he says, and starts the car.

"Fine," Rachel says, her words trailing off into silence. A wave of frustration washes over her as she contemplates the disturbing reality that her dear friend, a trusted partner for several years, was the victim of a shooting, and yet the circumstances of the incident remain shrouded in mystery, without explanation.

Focusing on the road ahead, with the sirens blaring at full power, the detective drives the vehicle at breakneck speed. With his peripheral vision, he observes and assesses her behaviour, hoping to glimpse any emotion. However, his observation reveals a composed exterior—not a trace of apprehension. He realizes that her years as a seasoned police officer have left her indifferent to the blare of sirens or the speed of flying cars.

"I need to call our colleague in London," she says with a hint of sadness. "We have a professional relationship, and I must inform him of the situation to alert David's father."

"Don't worry, feel free," he replies.

Tyler, surprised by Rachel's call, listens. She recounts the morning's events, starting with her unsuccessful attempt to reach her partner at 5 a.m., noting that he was with Michael. Tyler's concern is palpable, but Rachel soothes him, noting the involvement of the lead detective and Chief Bo.

"There's no need to come here. I'll update you. Cancel the return flight tomorrow, the twelfth. It's the usual agency... and check David's health insurance." She hangs up.

The detective listens to Rachel's call, impressed by her efficiency and composure. He has a fleeting thought: he contemplates how easy it would be to be with her for a lifetime, imagining everyday life and a family together. Pushing the idea away, he focuses again, looking in her direction, and asks, "Are you okay?"

"I am. Where's Michael?" Rachel asks, more aware of the situation.

"Michael? I don't know who that is," he replies, puzzled by the question, casting an inquisitive look.

"David's friend Michael. Yesterday, the three of us had lunch at the restaurant. Look at the picture... After that, they left together. I think they went to his residence," Rachel explains with a hint of nervousness, her words becoming jumbled in that moment as she processes the events. She looks at him with confusion, unable to understand the words spoken in Mandarin.

They arrive at the crime scene.

"Let's talk more because I'm not understanding this story. Please explain what happened yesterday."

Rachel explains the events of the previous day: they had lunch before David left with Michael, but she doesn't know Michael's address. She mentions going back to the hotel in the rented car and having dinner with Wang Savin, returning around 1:00 a.m. She finishes, hoping the detective will understand her account in English.

"I get it. There's a third person in this story who hasn't shown up yet," Chong says and gets out of the car.

A police officer approaches the detective and greets him.

"How many buildings are there on this street?" Chong asks the officer.

"Six residential buildings and five houses. The rest are commercial establishments," the officer responds, pointing out the buildings.

"How many of us are here now?" asks Detective Chong.

"Four."

"I want you to split up and look in each of the buildings for a resident named Michael," he instructs. The police officers walk away, and the detective accompanies Rachel to the place where they found the bodies.

Blood is still visible on the sidewalk, some parts having dried up, others not so much. Another enormous pool of blood is visible in the street. While maintaining professionalism, he describes how they found David on the street, unconscious. "Can you imagine the scene?"

Rachel watches what he's presenting calmly, her eyes taking in the details. As she studies the positions displayed, she struggles to understand what motivated David to be there so late at night. She asks, her voice subdued, a slight cough interrupting her words, her breathing revealing a subtle quickening, "Is the dead man Michael?"

"We don't know if it's this Michael you speak of or someone else, as we have found no documents or a cellphone. In that photograph you've shown me, it doesn't look like the same person," the detective replies, staring at the restaurant wall.

After about ten minutes, one officer returns, pointing at a building almost in front of the scene, and reports that the caretaker confirms a person named Michael lives there.

"Is the janitor there?" Detective Chong asks.

"Yes," the officer informs, and they walk together toward the building.

Upon arriving at the building, Chong asks Rachel for her cellphone with the photograph of the three friends.

Rachel hands over the phone, showing the image.

At the entrance, a man of about fifty welcomes them. He introduces himself as a janitor, and his bowed posture shows a sign of respect.

"Was it you who said Michael lives here in the building?" the detective asks.

"Yes, he owns the apartment and lives on the fifth floor. A wonderful person; everyone in the building is very fond of him and his mother," the caretaker offers.

"Could you tell me if the man who lives here is the same person in this photograph?"

"Yes. This is Michael and this is his friend who has been visiting him. That one is this girl by your side." The janitor points, giving a little smile to Rachel, confirming everything the detective wants to know.

"Can you take me to the apartment?" Chong asks, walking into the building without waiting for an answer.

"Sure. I also checked in the garage when the police officer asked about Michael. His car is still in the slot. I called the apartment over the intercom, but no one answered."

They walk together and get into the elevator. Arriving on the fifth floor, the janitor heads to apartment number 51 and rings the doorbell. No one answers.

Detective Chong speaks loudly as he knocks on the door, which is standard procedure. No one answers. He tries to open the door, but it's locked.

"Something's wrong," Rachel says.

"Do you have the key to the apartment?" the detective asks the janitor.

"No, but his mother does. Her phone number was on the doorway," he says, trying to help the officers.

"Could you give me the number? I'll contact her right away," the detective requests.

The janitor hands over the number.

Rachel and Detective Chong leave the building and walk up to the curb. He dials a number and, while he waits, Rachel expresses her concern for Michael's mother's fragile health. He nods, recounts the situation, and asks for the key and address of the apartment. Michael's mother agrees, and he provides his cellphone number for future contact. Ending the call, the police inform the detective of the proximity of Michael's mother's address. Chong sends a police car to the address.

Without noticing that the detective is speaking again on his cellphone, Rachel asks, "Is a warrant needed to enter the apartment?"

Talking to Chief Bo, Chong asks to forward a warrant as soon as possible. Hanging up, Chong questions, "Did you ask me something?"

As she heard the request to Chief Bo, she replies, "Nope."

After the two wait for forty minutes, the police arrive with the key. Chong then receives an email from Superintendent Bo with court authorization to enter the apartment. Detective Chong receives the key and asks a police officer and the janitor to join as witnesses. Opening the door, a cold gust of active air conditioning hits them.

The detective asks the janitor to watch the entrance and gives Rachel latex gloves for her hands and covers for her shoes. She puts them on, and they go inside. The police officers spread throughout the apartment and inspect every corner. In the living room, two glasses are on the coffee table. The kitchen is immaculate, the furniture placed in order. A green light glows on the CD player, showing that it has finished but is still on. The apartment is very tidy.

Detective Chong and Rachel go into the bedroom, discovering a messy bed with a bathrobe draped over an armchair. Their attention turns to an open safe inside the wardrobe, revealing documents, dollars, euros, and an empty pistol case.

A voice calls Detective Chong. He turns and sees that forensics has arrived. "You arrived fast. I need five more minutes," he says, smiling at one technician.

"Feel free. Let's start with the living room," the officer states.

"Search David's wallet for documents and money," Rachel says and points to the nightstand next to the bed.

The detective opens the wallet, finding cash, several credit cards, contact cards, an FBI ID card, and a personal card from both Interpol and Chief Bo.

"Are you a cop?" Chong asks, looking at David's wallet.

"We were federal police officers, me in Brazil and David in the US. Today we have a private investigation firm in London," Rachel replies, returning the same look of suspicion that he gave when he questioned her.

"Oh! Cover story…" he says with irony to Rachel.

"Think what you will. If you don't want to believe it, stay with the problem, but I'm telling you the truth." Rachel is blunt in her response.

"No need to be nervous. Chief Bo told me who you are," Detective Chong admits and puts David's wallet into a plastic bag. He walks toward a dresser in front of the bed, checking a keychain with different keys and a second wallet on top.

"You are very ignorant. If you had talked to the superintendent about who we are, you wouldn't question it," Rachel retaliates, speaking in English.

"This is Michael's wallet." He ignores what she says, opens the wallet, and examines all the cards. He confirms that a key on top of the dresser belongs to a car. He takes everything and puts it all in a plastic bag.

"You! Come here, please," Detective Chong calls the police officer who brought the key to the apartment.

Rachel goes into the bathroom and smells the perfume that David likes to use. Sadly, she looks around, trying to understand what could have happened.

In the dresser mirror, Chong watches her in the bathroom. When the police officer arrives, he instructs him to check with the garage caretaker that the keys belong to Michael's car. The officer retrieves the keys and leaves. Ten minutes later, he confirms one key is for Michael's car and the other for the front door of the residence.

Rachel, silent and thoughtful, observes all the movements of the police and the forensics.

"It's all very much in order, don't you think?" asks Detective Chong, noticing she's lost in her thoughts.

"If you don't look at that empty Glock box in the safe, everything else is fine," Rachel says with a smile at the corner of her mouth.

"What do you think happened?" Detective Chong presses her.

"I think they left the apartment to meet someone, maybe the deceased. Something serious must have happened for them to leave without their documents. But where is Michael?" Rachel responds.

"Considering the situation, two scenarios come to mind: they go to talk to the deceased, things get bad. The man shoots David. Michael shoots him back and runs away. Or Michael shoots both David and the man and then runs away. We need the ballistics results for sure." Detective Chong watches Rachel for her reaction.

"Who is this dead man?" asks Rachel.

The detective's cellphone rings, and he answers, turning his back to her. "Come with me," he tells Rachel. He announces to the officers in the apartment, "We have to go to the hospital now; you continue here."

Driving without delay, the two arrive at the hospital and hurry through the emergency entrance to the elevator. It's 11:00 a.m. Upon reaching the fourth floor, Chong introduces himself to reception, mentioning that they are waiting for him. Rachel follows at his side.

Pointing to a room, the receptionist allows them to enter.

In the doorway, the two observe a doctor and two nurses taking care of David. With a gesture, the doctor invites them to come closer and requests that they hurry.

Detective Chong sends Rachel to talk to her partner.

"David, David, can you hear me?" she pleads, her voice shaky as she speaks close to his ear.

He opens his eyes and in a very weak voice says, "Rachel."

"Oh, my dear! Thank God you're okay," she exclaims, her eyes filling with tears.

The doctor tells the detective to be quick with the interview because he has to give medication to the patient.

"David? Focus on me. I'm Detective Chong, head of homicide in Shanghai. David, can you tell me who shot you?" Detective Chong asks, repeating his question as he watches David with suspicion.

"Bike, intel, red," David mutters in English, his voice fading as a pained groan escapes his lips.

Rachel's eyes widen upon hearing David's words. She takes a moment, struggling to accept the possibility of what he's saying.

At that moment, a nurse puts the medication into the IV bag.

"He'll sleep until tomorrow. The surgery was delicate. We have to take care that he doesn't have any infections," the doctor tells the detective.

Wiping away her tears, Rachel heads for the door. Detective Chong grabs her arm, pulling her into the hallway. Surprised by his assertiveness, she stops and forces her arm out of his hands and faces him.

"What's the story?" he demands.

"Did you find some photographs with David when they brought him to the hospital?" she asks, her voice a mixture of nervousness and anger at his rude behaviour.

"The police officers who found him brought some pictures. They are with forensics for review," confirms Chong, looking at her with regret. "I apologize for my abrupt behaviour. I've never reacted like this before, but the mention of 'intelligence' unnerves me."

"We need those photos," Rachel says, not accepting his apology. Her expression reveals lingering discontent.

"Okay. Let's go to forensics, and you can tell me about this whole situation." They walk to the car in silence, each lost in their own thoughts.

Rachel's cellphone rings. She checks and recognizes Wang's name on the screen. She picks it up and stops on the sidewalk.

"Hi, gorgeous. How was the morning? Shall we have lunch?" Wang invites Rachel in a voice full of sweetness.

Glancing at her watch, Rachel realizes it's already 12:30 p.m. Detective Chong captures snippets of Wang's conversation. She signals for a moment and hesitates before getting into Chong's car.

Sitting in the driver's seat, the detective nods.

"It was a tragedy," says Rachel, not imagining she's talking to the person responsible for David's condition. She tells the whole situation to Wang. They agree to meet at 7:00 p.m. in the hotel lobby.

Rachel and the detective drive out of the hospital toward the Shanghai Police Headquarters, where the forensic laboratory is in the centre of the city.

Upon arrival at the laboratory, the police officer on duty gives the detective two photographs. He scans them, struggling to understand their meaning. Motioning for Rachel to follow, he leads her into the special ops room. Once inside, he closes the door and motions for her to sit down at the table, grabbing a bottle of water from the mini fridge next to a file cabinet.

"Would you like some coffee or water?" he asks.

"I want nothing, thank you." Rachel looks at the grey-walled room with antique furniture.

"Here are the photos. Now, explain the situation to me." Detective Chong hands Rachel the photos. She takes them and leans back in her chair, studying the images.

She starts by avoiding any mention of Ronaldo and Mr. Chan. Rachel talks about the operation in Portugal, the Yakuza leader, and interactions with Chinese and Japanese intelligence. Handing the photos back to Detective Chong, she says they are pictures given by intelligence officers wanting a meeting. They left them at the hotel reception yesterday morning.

"Are you sure this is what David was referring to at the hospital?" the detective asks her.

"That's right. You recorded the conversation. Compare," Rachel says, looking at him, sure of her words.

With a startled look, he meets her gaze, not having expected that she was aware of the recording at that moment.

The two listen to the recording.

"He talked about motorcycles," the detective says.

"I know nothing about motorcycles, just those from those photographs," Rachel replies.

"Wait! There's a motorcycle parked by the scene with a red helmet hanging from the handlebars," Detective Chong remembers, relaying this to Rachel. He dials a number on his cellphone and instructs someone to remove the motorcycle and the red helmet from the street where they found the bodies.

Rachel looks at the photographs and doesn't recognize the red on the bikers' helmets.

"This is all strange, but I can't see this case closing," Detective Chong jokes, waiting for answers.

"Why?" asks Rachel.

"The man who died at the scene was a 'docker.' We identified him by fingerprints. He did time for drug dealing, assault, and attempted murder. I'm not sure what he was doing there, or why he would meet with David and this Michael," Detective Chong shares with Rachel, relaying information from the forensics team.

Rachel emphasizes David hinted at involving intel officials.

"I'll discuss this with Boss Bo, and I'm keeping these photos. As I understand it, your partner is the victim, but where is Michael?" Chong asks aloud as the two leave the room, walking side by side down the hall.

Rachel doesn't answer but walks a few steps, stops, and volunteers, "We didn't just get these photos; I have others in my hotel room that were shipped with them. I think you should see them too."

"Okay, I will. If they are not relevant to the investigation, I will return them. If they are crucial, I will have an expert examine them," Detective Chong responds.

She agrees, and they decide to meet at 8:00 a.m. the next day at the hospital entrance.

The detective says goodbye and assigns a police officer to accompany her to the hotel. He instructs the officer to wait for her to retrieve some documents and bring them back to him.

Rachel confirms she will be there at the agreed time and asks to be informed if there are any updates on David or Michael.

Chong assures her, "Don't worry, try to get some rest; today was intense."

Back in the hotel room, Rachel, remembering David's painful explanation, glances at her wristwatch. It's 2:00 p.m. She collapses into an armchair, exhaustion taking over her. The lingering hospital smell on her shirt is suffocating. With her eyes closed, she reflects on the day, impressed by the speed of the police. Questions swirl in her mind: "Where is Michael, without documents or a phone?" Frustration boils inside her at her marginalized position in this investigation. Her stomach growls like thunder, reminding her she skipped meals. Eager to rinse off the day, she undresses and heads to the shower, lost in thought.

"I'm starving. I need to eat something."

23

"Dumplings"

"Anything scheduled for today?" Wang asks his secretary.

"No, sir," she replies. He enters his private office, takes off his coat, and hangs it on a hanger inside a large red lacquer cabinet with a gold decoration from the nineteenth-century Qing Dynasty. After a quick break, the assistant enters the office, placing a cup of coffee on the table. Catching her eye, he expresses gratitude—a surprising departure from his usual behaviour. She leaves, closing the door behind her.

Wang's cellphone rings, and he answers. "Have you arrived at the pier yet? Come to the office. I'm waiting for you."

While sitting in an armchair, Wang considers the events of last night, and his thoughts focus on cutting any threads that appear. Hui's acumen is expected to prevail, but uncertainties persist.

Wang remembers Wonjy's relationship with the manager of Warehouse #1 and the slight shudder when he saw him lifeless. A momentary sign on Hui's forehead, which Wang saw, did not go unnoticed. He reflects on their enduring partnership since their youth, recalling mischievous adventures and their unbreakable bond. Amid memories of containers and ships, he, for a moment, moves away from the world, lost in introspection.

His secretary enters the room again and advises that she is leaving for lunch. The boss remains silent, a familiar trait, and she takes her leave down the hall.

Wang recalls Rachel's approach to the hotel. He closes his eyes, smelling her perfume. It envelops him, providing a moment of calm until a voice wakes him up with a start.

Hui, without knocking on the door, enters and speaks in a low tone, "Everything's nice and tidy. I burned everything, so don't worry. No one will find out, and I've hidden the 'straps.' Maybe someday we'll need them."

Wang gets up from his chair and turns off Rachel's image. He turns to the manager and asks, "Does Wonjy's family know the guy who died?

Does anyone else in the office have his number? And what are you going to say about his disappearance?"

"This morning, Wonjy sent a message here, at the office, saying he was going to Hong Kong because a relative was sick. I sent this from his phone today. If anyone is looking for Bohai, we say they are travelling together. Bohai is a lone wolf; there is no family connection around him," explains Hui, sure of his story. He takes a few steps back, ready to leave the office.

"Did you bring the car? Stop driving for a while, forget it in the parking lot of Warehouse Number Two; so, you got it all sorted?" says Wang, his eyes fixed on the manager.

Hui, with his hands inside his pants pocket, looks at the floor, sighs, and says, "So it seems."

"I want certainty," the boss demands of him.

"Don't worry, I've got your back. Heading to Hangar Ten now, starting container loading for London today," Hui replies, a twinge of frustration under the surface. He's putting pressure on himself to act like everything is fine, even though deep down he knows things aren't fine. Worried, he avoids meeting the boss's gaze.

Wang doesn't say a word, just nods and looks at the manager as he leaves the room and closes the door.

"I'm hungry," Wang says and walks toward the closet.

The secretary enters, mentioning that she left her wallet. Even before the door is closed, he interrupts. "Hey, next time, knock before you come in. I'm starving. I'll order some dumplings; the ones at Shanghai Dumplings are top-notch. Will you get them for me?"

Building on the earlier appreciation, she musters up the courage to contribute. "Hey, chief, let me put you on another gem this place offers. It's called sheng Jian bao. Buns stuffed with pork meat and scallions, deep-fried till they are spicy inside. People go crazy for them; they're delicious." She explains the dish as if she were talking to a friend.

"Okay! Order both dishes." He accepts the suggestion because he doesn't want debates.

"I'll arrange it now." Leaving the room, she closes the door.

Wang calls Rachel on her cellphone. He doesn't remember or care about what happened to this David fellow.

"Hi, gorgeous. How was the morning? Are we going to have lunch?"

He listens as Rachel tells David's story, his gaze landing on a pencil he's fiddling with. He absorbs the hospital story, taking one look at his fingernails and thinking it would be nice to trim them. Truth be told, he doesn't care about her story. As soon as she finishes speaking, Wang offers, "Do you need help? I'll pick you up at 7 p.m. Is that good for you?" Once she agrees, he ends the call with a smile, happy that he is about to meet the goddess of his dreams again.

Wang looks down at the table. Many documents await his signature. He signs, unaware of how time is passing. The secretary, without knocking on the door, enters and places the order of food on the table, warning him that the dumplings are hot.

The boss, looking out the window at the boats, doesn't answer. When he hears the door close, he sits in the armchair, opens the package, and mumbles, "This smells great."

As he eats, a surge of emotions wash over him, igniting a cascade of memories. Moments shared with his beloved cousin flood his thoughts. Those visits to a restaurant near Li's workplace, where they enjoyed the exquisite flavours of dumplings.

Between flavours and aromas, Wang is impressed by the profound goodness that defined the character of his cousin. Gratitude grows within him as he realizes that the loan his cousin extended was nothing less than a lifeline, a thread that kept him tethered to existence.

With each bite, he goes back to the day they were on the bench. A pivotal moment. It was then that his cousin's unwavering support went beyond financial help when a generous offer materialized—an invitation to work at the temporary employment agency. The resonance of that moment still lingers, a testament to the profound impact one person can have on another's life.

With a wide smile, he speaks as if he had his cousin in front of him: "Oh, those temp jobs? Absolute gems! Who would have thought that investing a few hours could yield such lucrative earnings? I mean, my gratitude is eternal. One day I accepted your offer... Well, you were, in essence, the catalyst that transformed my life for all eternity."

Looking at the dumplings, his thoughts return to the substantial debt he owed to the leader of the Tong. Despite making progress with the payments, Dankyno kept him stuck at the port for over fifteen tiring hours.

Tasting the dumplings rekindles memories, and his expression changes. One day, after lunch, the boss called him to a meeting. Wang went to the "meeting barn" and heard "that" question.

"Do you want to pay off the debt to me and Tong?"

"Yes," Wang answered, feeling uneasy because he knew nothing came free.

Dankyno said he should go to the Grampay Hotel and send to hell a man named Ronaldo, who was staying in apartment 603.

Wang, nervous about the proposal, hid his discomfort from his boss, whose drunkenness was evident. Looking around, he confirmed they were alone, without the cautious presence of Dankyno's security, which was, as usual, made up of two or three men.

The boss urged, "Finish the task today and I'll clear your debt. Also, bring anything nearby: documents, cellphones, anything."

In conversation in the barn, Wang knew the Shanghai Tong was heavily indebted to a Japanese mafia. Some of his companions had mentioned Dankyno was still alive only because he promised the Japanese to do any work when the time came. Wang assessed the situation and realized that the moment had arrived and that he would be a part of it. That's when Wang would pay off the debts.

"To whom is the debt?" Wang asked, acting like the boss was a close friend.

The boss struggled to get up from his chair, staggering in a drunken state. Frustration got the best of him, leading to a series of curses and insults.

"What does an idiot like you get out of my business? You have no clue. Just another useless idiot, not even fit for deliveries. If you're interested in clearing your debt, follow my instructions. Don't screw up, you idiot. Hmph! You're always snooping too much."

"Tonight?" asked Wang.

"Of course," the boss replied and grabbed another bottle from the side of the chair, downing the contents.

Wang set off on his motorcycle with no direction and an uncertain task. Amid the confusion, doubts arose that left him adrift. His phone rang, and it was Cousin Li informing him that he had some job vacancies for that same night, offering a range of options: five restaurants, three hotels, two street kitchens, and a nightclub.

Intrigued, Wang asked about hotels. Li listed Holiday, Grand Kempinski, and Shanghai Inn as options.

"The Grand Kempinski, the Grampay Hotel?" Wang joked with the names, not believing the opportunity.

Li laughed and confirmed, "That's right, known by the short name, five stars. Very good. I also chose this hotel; they pay very well, and the dinner is always excellent."

Wang felt that luck was on his side and inquired about the time to be at the company.

Li advised him to arrive at 4:00 p.m. as the shift started at 6:00 p.m. and would end at 6:00 a.m.

"Okay, it's 2:30 p.m. now. I'm on my way to Mom's apartment. Do you want me to bring something for Aunt Meixiu?"

"No, thank you," his cousin replied and hung up the phone.

Perplexed, he took care while driving the motorcycle. The idea of taking a life to pay off debts to Tong and "that damn boss" never crossed his mind. He looked down at the revolver he had. Overwhelmed, he pondered how to navigate the impending night, knowing he would have to end a life to secure his freedom.

When he returned home, he saw Hui riding another motorcycle and signalled for him to follow him. They stopped in front of his mother's house. Still on the motorcycle, Wang looked at Hui and said, "I have something to tell you and I need your help."

"Whatever you want," the friend replied with express concern, as he understood Wang was not a person who would ask for help, as he always solved problems alone.

"I'll tell you at the apartment. I need to see my mother."

He pushed open the door, and they entered. Hui settled into a chair at the dining table while Wang went to the other room, calling out to his mother.

Meilin, who always slept like the dead, didn't answer. The meds she was taking had quite an effect on her, fighting the disease, sure, but also making her pass out. Without waking her, he put a sheet over her and came back, sitting next to Hui.

"You don't know what happened to me today," Wang said, rubbing his hands.

"What was it?"

"You're going to swear on your life that you'll tell no one. Swear!" Wang emphasizes.

"I swear, Wang. What's happened?"

He related the proposal Dankyno made and confirmed that he accepted. He just didn't know how to proceed.

Hui looked at Wang. "How can you trust Dank? Everyone knows he's a total son of a bitch piece of shit. I wouldn't trust him an inch. Rethink this before you end up paying the bill."

"What can I do? I said yes! If he betrays me, I will kill him later. I killed one, I can kill two," Wang stated, furious.

"Have you ever killed anyone?" Hui asked.

"Never, but I don't think it's hard. We've seen many people killed," Wang said, trying to convince himself it would be easy.

"True, but how are you going to do it?" Hui asked with a wry smile.

Wang told him about being booked at the temporary services company.

"I know this company. You told me about these sporadic jobs before."

"I got a job for tonight at the hotel that Dankyno was talking about, but I don't know how I'm going to do it." Wang pinched his nose with his fingers and then ran his hand over his face in agony.

"One shot is fastest," Hui suggested.

"It makes a lot of noise and they're going to end up catching me. I have to do it in a way that no one sees and hears anything," Wang replied.

"Hum . . . That's going to be tough. I need to cut these nails, they look like claws," Hui said, his attention on the nails of his hand.

"You're not helping me! Oh, Dankyno also told me to get the man's phone and everything else I found. He wants me to break this guy and then go to his room and look for his stuff. I'm not doing that." Wang's bad mood was clear.

"You are going to work there tonight, for sure you'll manage the opportunity you need." Hui guided his friend, giving the greatest support. "Stay smart, and everything will work out."

"Well, I better go now. It's 3:30 p.m. Come to think of it, when I'm there, I'll see how I should do it. The lucky star has always been by my side." Wang and Hui opened the door and left.

Wang pulled up on his motorcycle behind the building around 4:00 p.m. Li was already there, waiting to let him in through the back door of the store. They walked to the storage room, where Li grabbed a uniform— the kind hotel staff wear. Tossing the package to Wang, which included pants, shirt, socks, and shoes, he pointed to a nearby locker room. Inside, Wang saw a mix of people getting dressed, some temporary workers and some he assumed were new, like him. As soon as he donned the uniform, the two made their way to the auditorium to find out more details.

Xhui Ming was the station coordinator and also headed the education department. Addressing the eleven people in the auditorium, she clarified they would be working at the Grand Kempinski, or as most called it, the Grampay Hotel. She read out each name, making sure they were present, and then set the job assignments: "Three of you will be in the kitchen, one in the laundry room, one at the concierge desk, and the rest will handle cleaning." Li got the job in the kitchen, while Wang got assigned to laundry.

At 5:30 p.m., a van arrived to take them to the hotel. Wang, quiet and thoughtful, which was not normal, caught Li's attention. "Any problems? Did you go to see your mother?"

"Yes, I did," said Wang. There was something wrong. His distant, vacant gaze betrayed his discomfort.

Li kept his eyes on him. Wang, looking tormented, couldn't help but bite the corner of his mouth.

"Concentrate on something, anything. A spot on the wall, a detail on the chair, then close your eyes and wander," Li told his cousin. Little did he know he was showing Wang a way to handle the situation for the rest of his life. So, Wang did and calmed down.

They arrived at the hotel at 6:00 p.m. Then each one went to the designated sector to work.

Wang, following the department employee's tips, began putting sheets and towels in the washing machines. As his hands moved, his mind raced, trying to figure out how to locate the guy he was supposed to kill.

About half an hour later, the front desk called the laundry room, asking for a bath towel to be delivered to a poolside guest. The veteran worker nudged Wang, telling him to make the delivery and reminding him to register the extra towel for room 603. Because of his stress, he forgot the room number that Dankyno mentioned. But when registering the towel on the computer, a name caught his attention: Ronaldo Ross.

Holy shit! I swear I must have been born under some lucky star! This can't be real; no one has ever had this kind of luck. Tomorrow I'm going to play the lottery, Wang thought, trying to play it cool, but without a doubt, he was full of excitement inside.

In a hurry, he grabbed the bath towel and hurried to the service elevator at the back of the hotel. As he reached the ground floor and passed through the employee-only door, he glimpsed the pool. Hiding behind a pillar, he watched Ronaldo swim, his eyes looking for security cameras, confirming there were none. With a rush of adrenaline, he whispered to himself, "Perfect, he's alone. This is my chance."

He took a quick look at the scene. There was a lounge chair with wet towels slung over the back, right in front of the pool steps. Beside the chair, a small table caught his eye. On it was a tray with snacks, oil, salt, and an almost empty whiskey bottle with a single glass beside it.

Ronaldo kept swimming, oblivious to Wang's presence. When he paused, he noticed Wang standing there, towel in hand, waved, and nodded his thanks. Wang, showing deference, bowed his head in response. He took a few steps closer, waiting…

As Ronaldo got out of the pool, he glanced at Wang, who was a few steps away, holding his towel and watching with attention. When Ronaldo approached, intending to thank him and take the towel, his feet faltered, and he slipped and lost his balance. Wang just watched as Ronaldo's head hit the edge of the pool before he fell unconscious.

Wang rushed to Ronaldo's side, watching the blood seep across the floor from the cut on his forehead. In a swift movement, he used his foot to plunge Ronaldo's head and upper body into the water, staining it a deep, frightening red, while the rest of him remained sprawled at the edge of the pool. Assessing the scene, Wang noticed Ronaldo's body was shaking and making fleeting movements, showing that he was still alive, but only for a short time. Seizing the moment, Wang overturned the table, throwing the whiskey, glass, oil, and salt on the floor.

Glancing at the wall clock, he noticed that only a few minutes had passed since his arrival. Meticulous, he went to the lounge phone, dialling the front desk. As soon as someone answered, he let out a frantic scream about discovering a dead man in the pool. It wasn't long before three team members rushed in, taking in the horrific sight: Ronaldo floating in the bloodstained water, the chaotic mess on the floor, and Wang, pretending to be in shock, sitting near the elevator, holding a dry towel.

An employee, trying to confirm the worst, walked around the pool, avoiding stepping on the blood, and verified that Ronaldo was not breathing. The other two approached Wang, who appeared to be in shock. Unable to get a word out of him, they helped him to his feet and guided him to the elevator.

Eyes squeezed shut, a wave of laughter threatened to erupt from Wang, but he held back, clutching his stomach and muttering about feeling bad. The team, concerned about the situation, took him to the bathroom. Once inside, the door muffling any outside noise, Wang let out a triumphant, mute shout, his face breaking into a smile as he raised his fist in the air. He then fell to his knees, thanking all the deities who planned this for him.

It was almost fifteen minutes before the ambulance, firefighters, and police arrived at the hotel. Li stood beside Wang outside the building, trying to calm him down. The police officers bombarded Wang with questions, trying to piece things together, but Wang looked distant, still reeling from the shock. With visible emotion, he attempted to convey what he had witnessed, his eyes widening at the memory of horror. Another policeman approached the pair, directing his questions at them. Li provided answers about their identities, while Wang, his eyes still wide and his face pale, remained silent. The officer persisted, wanting to know what Wang had seen.

Placing both hands on his head, Wang, wanting to end the insistence, said, "I didn't know what to do."

The officer tried to calm Wang down, assuring him he was not at fault and could have done nothing differently. "It was just a tragic accident," he explained. "You just arrived at the scene and found the man's body in the pool. It's not your fault. Don't think about it anymore."

Wang tells only the end of the tragedy: when he arrived to bring the towel, a body was lying in the water with a lot of blood around it.

"That's right, cousin. A tragedy," Li said, agreeing with the officer.

"What happened?" Wang asked in an emotional voice.

"Imagine... When someone loses their balance, the imbalance can be so overwhelming that the body can't correct itself before impact. It's all about physics. The impact alone can cause unconsciousness and lead to drowning," the officer explained, patting Wang on the back. "That could be what happened."

Without expressing his happiness in words, Wang continues to act as if in shock at what he had witnessed.

At 5:00 a.m., the hotel dismissed all employees working that shift, pledging to pay everyone an extra hour of work, as per the contract.

Stressed, Wang sat with his cousin in the van and returned to the company. All the contractors who were there in the car asked questions about the guest: "What else did he see?", "What did he think when he saw the body in the pool?" Li asked them to stop because his cousin was going to vomit.

Reflecting, Wang reasoned to himself, *I did it, I got it, and I will still receive the full salary of the night of work.*

Li and his cousin arrived at the company and said goodbye, scheduling lunch the next day at 11:00 a.m. at the restaurant opposite the workplace. Wang got on his bike and headed toward the city centre. After riding a bit, he turned into a side alley and dialled Dankyno.

"The work has been done," Wang said.

"Come here," Dank replied.

"I am on my way."

At 8:45 a.m., Wang parked his motorbike in the barn's large parking lot.

The boss jumped out the door, a big smile on his face, chattering away. He put his arm around Wang as they turned and entered. From a distance, two of Dankyno's bodyguards watched the scene, their eyes following his every move.

"So, you made it? Let's celebrate. I have a table full of dumplings. Would you like some?"

"I love dumplings."

"So, what else?" asked Dankyno.

"Nothing more. He died as you asked," explained Wang, putting one of the delicious dumplings displayed on the table in his mouth.

"Cellphone, USB stick, computer. What did you get?" the boss asked with an inquisitorial look.

"Nothing. I found nothing," Wang replied and put another dumpling in his mouth.

Dank assessed him, trying to gauge whether he believed Wang's words. Wang, sensing his boss's scrutiny, remained calm and avoided eye contact, concentrating on munching on a few more dumplings.

"You understood not to tell anyone about the conversation we had yesterday, as if it never existed between you and me, right?"

"What conversation?" said Wang, returning the question, looking at his boss and smiling.

"My boy, the debt is gone. You don't have it anymore, neither with me nor with Tong. In two days, we will meet with the bosses, and I will let them know that there is no more debt." Dankyno laughed.

"I'm leaving. I need to sleep," Wang admitted.

"You can go. Take care and good job."

Wang walked out of the barn down the front street, and as he turned the first corner, he found Hui waiting for him. The two motorcycles flew together through the streets of Shanghai. At the lighthouse, when they stopped side by side, Hui asked, "Where?"

"My mother's."

When they arrive at the apartment, Wang ran to the bedroom and saw that his mother was asleep. He came over and kissed her on the forehead. He went out and closed the door.

"Are you okay?" asked Hui.

"I believe so."

"What happened?"

"I did the job. It was easier than I thought," Wang told Hui, a relaxed smile spreading across his face. He leaned back on the couch and closed his eyes, realizing he couldn't tell the true story. The image of the guest stumbling before the fall replayed in his mind, perplexing him. *Was he drunk? Did he get dizzy after swimming?* he asked himself, trying to calm his conscience with the thought. "I just poked his guardian angel, that's all."

"What about the police?" an anxious Hui asked.

"I had everything in the hotel tonight: police, firefighters, ambulance, journalists, but I handled it. No one suspected anything. Never, never, no one will find out." Wang gritted his teeth and clenched his fists.

"What now?"

"I don't know. I just know that I have no more debts to the boss or Tong," he replied, settling down on the couch. All the adrenaline left his body, and he fell asleep.

After some time, Wang woke up to the sound of Hui's cellphone ringing. He noticed Hui get up and head toward the apartment door.

"Who's that?" Wang asked, rubbing his eyes.

Hui hesitated for a moment. "It's the boss. I don't know why he's so nervous."

"You'd better leave then," suggested Wang.

"Hey, see you later," said Hui, walking to the door.

"You, me, and Li—how about lunch tomorrow at 11 a.m.?" Wang suggested with a hopeful look. "You know that place across from the temp shop? Let's meet there."

Hui only nodded in response, closing the door behind him as he left the apartment.

Wang woke up the next day at 9:00 a.m., checked on his sleeping mother and took a quick shower. When he returned, he found breakfast prepared. His aunt had arrived early to take care of her sister and prepared the food, knowing that he would wake up soon. He looked at the kitchen clock, and it said 10:20. Remembering the 11:00 a.m. meeting with Li and Hui, without making a sound, he went out, pushed the motorbike onto the avenue, and sped off to his cousin's workplace.

Together, the trio converged on the shop entrance, and Li gestured to Wang and Hui.

"Hey, keep the bikes in the alley."

"Today is on me," declared Wang, pulling them into a brief hug. "We're having shrimp and pork dumplings. Think of it as a little celebration."

With that, they crossed the street and settled into the restaurant, ordering lunch.

While eating, Hui leaned in. "You know, Dankyno was crazy last night. Something wasn't right. He was in some kind of celebratory mood, but no one could understand his ramblings." Hui took a break to eat something and continued, "Those two shady guys he's always with? They must know what all the fuss was about. Oh, and lo and behold, at one point he asked me if I'd seen you around?"

Hui took a deep breath. "I acted like an idiot; told him I hadn't seen you. Soon after that, things got wild. He took everything that was a drug and wouldn't stop drinking, saying out loud that 'you were a son of a bitch and you had escaped the debt, but you wouldn't escape the next one.'"

Wang and Li put down their forks, their appetites gone, as they absorbed the gravity of Hui's story about the previous night's chaos.

Hui said, "The two garbage men, Konguo and Sheisue, who are always next to the boss, were laughing. I believe some shit is coming. You know I don't trust them, let alone Dank."

Wang and Li looked at Hui without saying a word and swallowed another dumpling.

"In the end, the boss asked me if you were going to the barn today. I said we were going to have lunch together, and I would tell you to go later," Hui told Wang.

"Alright, that's Dankyno, always offending, but don't worry. After lunch, we'll go there together," Wang said to Hui, at the same time trying to get any worries out of his cousin's head.

Li stayed quiet, listening to the conversation. Li didn't grasp the "essence" of the conversation, but he inferred everything got resolved, and he relished the scrumptious lunch his cousin treated him to.

"I'm thinking of buying a motorcycle," Li said.

"I'll help you. Do you know how to drive one?" Wang asked.

"Did you bang your head? Don't you remember you taught me?"

"After we're done eating, you can drive my bike and I'll sit on the back. It's going to be a test," Wang instructed Li.

Hui got up from his chair and announced that he was going to the barn.

"Okay. I'll call and let you know when I'm on my way," Wang said, waving to his friend.

After lunch, the cousins went to where they had parked the motorcycle. Li suggested a quick ride around the block. Wang handed him the helmet and said, "Just go around the block and come back and get me. We need to go to the bank." Wang was going to make a pleasant surprise to the family later. He planned to pay off a significant portion of the debt he owed his cousin and aunt.

Li put on his helmet, accelerated the motorcycle, and drove off, showing his cousin that it was true: he knew how to drive. Watching his cousin ride the motorbike, Wang shook his head in amusement and disbelief, following his progress with a smile. But his smile evaporated when, in the distance, he saw a truck drive through a stop sign, crashing into something. With his heart in his throat, he wasn't sure if it was Li or another vehicle that was hit. Panic rising, he ran toward the commotion, his voice lost in the cacophony as he called out to Li.

When Wang arrived at the scene, a crowd had already gathered around the dented motorcycle. The truck was nowhere to be seen. Approaching, the world seemed to be silent. The love and support he had always relied on, the only constant in his life, now lay still on the ground. Li suffered a fatal blow to the head, the helmet rendered ineffective. Wang felt devastated. The merciless world took away his anchor.

Cradling Li's lifeless body, Wang's cruel screams echoed in the street, his despair amplified with each call of his cousin's name. In the centre of this painful scene, his phone vibrated. Upon seeing Hui's name, he hesitated for a moment and then answered.

Hui's voice, low but frantic, reached his ear. "Wang, listen! Be careful. Dankyno sent Konguo and Sheisue after you. Shoye warned me. Answer no more calls, okay? Don't trust anyone."

Paralyzed by Li's tragic death and Hui's chilling revelation, a change came over Wang. Rising from the ground, he left Li's body behind, drawing startled glances from onlookers who had just witnessed his raw pain. Each step toward the store felt heavy, but he moved with purpose. Wiping the tears from his face with jerky hand movements, he texted a friend: "I need you to pick me up from the restaurant."

Fifteen minutes felt like hours before Hui, desperate, appeared at the restaurant. Seeing Wang, whose bloodstained clothes bore grim evidence of the accident, Hui's eyes filled with worry. Without saying a word, he pulled Wang into a comforting hug and guided him to the motorcycle. Handing him a spare helmet, he muttered, "We need to get out of here." Wang, in his dazed state, nodded.

Approaching his mother's apartment, Hui circled the block several times, his eyes sharp and alert for any sign of Dankyno's men. Only when he was sure the way was clear did he guide Wang inside.

Settling his friend on the couch, Hui asked, "What happened?"

An upset Wang spoke in a low tone of voice so as not to disturb his mother and told Hui what had happened.

Hui, with wide eyes, could not express any words.

"I'm going to kill him," Wang said with shaking hands.

"I can't believe it. They must have thought Li was you on that bike. Approach Dankyno now? That's going to be difficult," Hui commented, his voice heavy.

Wang's exhaustion was clear. Rubbing his face with both hands, he tried to push away the tiredness and stress.

"It may seem impossible, but I'm making my move tonight. They'll be partying until the early hours, drinking themselves to death. And that's when I'll step in to end the celebration," Wang said with determination in his voice. He stared at the wall, remembering Li's advice about focusing on something to find calm and clarity.

Wang and Hui planned how they would enter the place that night.

Hui offered to go to the barn to hear the news, and Wang agreed, asking him to take care of himself.

When Hui arrived at the barn, he saw a group of co-workers discussing Wang's motorcycle accident. With great sadness, Hui told his partners that Wang didn't answer his phone. He mentioned having lunch with Wang earlier, waiting for him in the afternoon, but received no response to his messages. Seeing a can full of cold beer, Hui took one and poured it in honour of Wang. The others followed suit.

As dusk fell and more people arrived, conversations turned to Wang's tragic passing. Despite the pain, the impending workday caused the men to disperse as the night wore on.

Hui remained sitting outside the barn, pretending to be drunk while holding his drink. Konguo and Sheisue approached, nudging him to go home. Without blinking, Hui asked, "Did you two see Wang's accident?" The two exchanged a brief, uneasy look before admitting that they had witnessed the accident.

"How are you so sure?" asked Hui, almost falling off the bench.

"We parked the truck about four blocks down the avenue and walked back. We have no doubt it was him. The bike and the helmet were the same. We got very close to the body. The police were already there putting him in the coroner's van." Konguo and Sheisue recounted details with laughter.

At that moment, Wang appeared behind the two men and, with a swing of his machete, removed Sheisue's head. Hui, pulling out another machete, attacked and removed Konguo's head.

In silence, the two friends kicked the heads into the barn, dragged the decapitated bodies across the grounds, and entered the area in front of the barn, closing the iron gate.

Hui looked at Wang and, anticipating the next question, said, "Upstairs in the room, behind the office."

Wang entered the empty barn, went up the stairs, observing everything in front of him, walked to the study, and opened the bedroom door. He saw Dankyno was sleeping. Wang walked to the bed. Without waking the sleeping chief, he moved furiously and removed the chief's head from his body with a violent blow of his machete.

Hui entered the room, telling his friend to help put the bodies in the back of Dankyno's car.

"Where are you going to take them?" Wang asked.

"Where he always throws the dead for the crocodiles to feast." Hui smiled.

"Not the heads. Tomorrow there will be a meeting here with the Tong, and I need those three heads," Wang stated.

Once Hui had loaded the bodies, he disappeared, taking them to the farm that the chief had once shown him.

Wang cleaned the room and the chairs outside the barn. He used a truck with sand and straw, covering up the blood exposed on the dirt floor.

At 8:00 a.m., the iron gate of the barn remained closed. Hui entered, noticing some Tong members. Some were talking outside, while others were resting in their cars. Dankyno had gathered them together to announce liquidating debts, marking the beginning of a new chapter. Hui walked over and opened the gate. The participants were not Tong leaders, as Dank never worked with other leaders. They were influential overseers of various districts in Shanghai. Without hesitation, they entered the barn. About twenty of them sat on the chairs arranged in a circle.

Wang entered the office, went downstairs, and sat, self-assured, in Dankyno's chair, facing the twenty men. Meeting their eyes, he declared, "From now on, I lead the Tong."

The room buzzed with disbelief. The voices rose: "Where is Dankyno? Nobody mentioned this. Why you? You have no right."

Unperturbed and sitting where the former chief had been, Wang pulled off two sheets mounted on stilts, uncovering the severed heads of Dankyno, Konguo, and Sheisue.

"By their actions, these three made me the new leader of the Tong," said Wang, rising from his chair. He swept the men with his gaze, challenging them. "Is anyone here contesting this nomination?" Wang questioned.

Fear gripped the men, their eyes darting around the room. None of them dared to utter a single word. Everyone knew about the previous day's betrayal and how swiftly they faced retribution. They deserved it well.

Hui shouted: "Wang, head of Tong."

All twenty men got up from their chairs and shouted together,

"Wang, head of Tong."

"Wang, head of Tong."

"Wang, head of Tong."

"Wang, head of Tong."

"Wang, head of Tong."

24

Hate and Love

The investigator from the Special Operations sector opens the door to the chief's office and calls out, "Detective Chong!"

"Yes," Chong replies, his attention fixed on his computer.

"The 'experts' are calling for you in the computer lab," the police officer announces, his cellphone still in his hand.

"Thank you." Detective Chong gets up from his chair, not quite satisfied, and leaves the office, slamming the door behind him. On the way, as usual, he checks his schedule for the day on his phone. He still has two meetings to attend, an official announcement to write, and documents awaiting his signature. Upon reaching the lab, he receives the reports he requested and changes his mind and goes straight to Superintendent Bo's office.

When entering the superintendent's office, the secretary announces his arrival.

After a few seconds, he enters the main room and bows his body before the boss, saying, "Did you want to talk to me?"

"Don't disturb Rachel Barnes and David Ho. They are the victims in this situation," Chief Bo instructs.

"I only spoke with her in the morning, you know, trying to figure out the routine of David and that other guy she mentioned, Michael." Detective Chong has a touch of defensiveness in his voice. He's not a novice; he can read between the lines when superiors suggest dropping an investigation.

Boss Bo repeats the warning. "They're my guests. Don't give them any trouble."

Detective Chong tries to explain what he discovered: "It's pretty clear that David's friend Michael shot the bike guy. The bullet they pulled out matches the calibre of the box of ammo we found in the safe in his apartment. I'll have all the details and more info this afternoon."

Chief Bo signs some papers on his desk and doesn't look up at the detective.

Chong huffs in frustration, sensing they are about to tie his hands in this investigation.

"Excuse me," he mutters, his posture slumping as he leaves the room.

The superintendent continues, "Did you get any significant information from Ms. Rachel?"

"She's going to have dinner with Wang tonight," he replies, looking down at the floor, agonizing to leave the room.

"Oh, good… then Wang contacted her. By the way, what is David's condition?"

"Tomorrow I can talk to him. The surgery was a success, but the concern in the hospital was the possibility of infection. I believe now he just needs time to recover," Detective Chong replies, looking at his boss. Facing the superintendent, suspicion crosses Chong's mind.

"Hmm," murmurs the boss, his attention back on the papers he is signing.

"I don't mean to bother you, but after thinking about it… There's something you should know. I'm not sure what's going on behind the scenes in this story, and I don't want to appear clueless," the detective says in a calm tone, approaching the table.

At this moment, he gets the full attention of Chief Bo, who stares at him. "What do you mean?"

"Look at this picture and this note David received yesterday morning at the hotel concierge." Chong passes them into the boss's hands.

"What's with these images and cards?" Bo asks, holding up the photographs, waving them at the detective before looking up at him again.

The detective explains, "One card is from a Chinese intel officer and the other from a Japanese intel officer. I believe the note sent to David is to set up a meeting with them. Rachel mentioned more than once that these officers are on a mission to arrest the Yakuza Yazuo."

Chief Bo, after looking at the pictures and reading the note, stands up from his chair, scowling, and hits the table. "Is our own intel department working behind my back?" he growls.

"From what I understand over the course of the conversation I had with Rachel, yes," Chong confirms, making Chief Bo angrier.

"Clear that up," Bo demands, sitting down in the armchair and folding his hands over his stomach.

Chong continues, not even trying to calm the boss down. "This morning, I tried to get some answers out of David when he woke up, but the meds left him too confused; he couldn't form a coherent sentence. I asked who shot him but got no answer. After hearing Rachel's voice, he muttered something: 'bicycle, intel, red.' I don't know what he was trying to say because of his incoherent speech." The detective furrows his eyebrows in frustration.

The superintendent just looks at him as he continues the story.

"After that, Rachel handed over these photos and cards and told me the story. Everything is leading me to believe there are a lot of loose ends here, and that's why I'm bringing these to you."

Boss Bo, irritated and clear in his attitude, retorts, "You're dragging me into this storm, thinking I won't get wet."

Chong continues talking, with the obvious aim of irritating his boss. "Look at this photo of David and his missing friend, 'Michael,' leaving the hotel."

"What is this? Extortion or investigation?" Chief Bo asks.

"I'm not sure, but we need to figure this out fast before word gets out. Also, there are those personal cards from the intel officers, and the note about them wanting to meet David Ho," Chong replies, his eyes tracking the boss as he paces and huffs around the room.

"Call intelligence and tell them both to come here now."

"Okay, but I don't know if they'll come. They have leadership and they must know what the two are doing." The detective is adding fuel to the fire.

"Chong, did David Ho say anything accusing the two intel police officers? What's your opinion?" Chief Bo asks.

"No, I think he's trying to say something, but he's confused because of the medication. After hours of surgery, waking up with painkillers and anesthesia... That cocktail would make anyone's head spin," the detective responds, putting everything together, but without revealing all of his thoughts.

"Bring these two here. I'll talk to them," the chief says, appearing to have calmed down a little.

"We have to iron this out. There's no doubt about it. They have to explain these photographs. I'll go to intelligence myself. This is not a telephone conversation," informs Chong, ultimately offering the superintendent a solution.

"Indeed," agrees the boss, lighting a cigarette and offering one to the detective.

The detective nods his thanks but doesn't accept. Chong studies Bo's reactions. He's known the boss for years and knows that every word that comes out of Bo's mouth carries a hidden agenda. Looking at him, the detective tries to deduce his next move.

"What are these motherfuckers investigating?" The superintendent yells the questions and begins to cough non-stop.

Detective Chong, trying to contain his laughter, doesn't say a word.

"You wouldn't believe the pressure I've been under for the past two hours. The British embassy, the Americans, even American intelligence right here in Shanghai have been on my case. Can you understand how insane this is? What if these two intel officials dive into this? I don't even want to think about it," Bo vents, the weariness clear in his voice as he tells the detective everything.

"Who's this David Ho guy?" Chong asks.

"It doesn't matter who he is or isn't. Just get on the investigation, and I mean now. I want this wrapped up in twenty-four hours, and get those jerks to come see me," Chief Bo orders.

Detective Chong walks out of the room, frustration evident at every step. Just when he thinks he has control of the investigation, an order from above arrives and everything becomes a race against time, all thanks to powers and policies he will never understand. After the turbulent conversation, he doesn't know where to start, and with the clock reading 4:00 p.m., time is ticking. Shaking off his annoyance, he decides his best bet is to head to the lab one floor below, hoping to discover more useful information.

Chong barges into the forensics room, not bothering to knock.

"Holy shit, did you go to the beach or something? Your face is red like a tomato. Or maybe you're catching something?" jokes one forensic specialist, giving him a cheeky smile.

He looks at her, ignoring the smile, and asks, "Where's Wong Hu?"

"He's there in the back, in his office," she replies, turning her back without smiling.

Detective Chong quickens his pace and enters the boss's office.

Wong Hu heads the Shanghai Police Forensics Lab. With an impressive thirty-five years of experience, he has earned a reputation as one of the most respected experts in the country. Years ago, he and Chong grew closer, becoming genuine friends. Their bond deepened after a tragic car accident killed Wong Hu's wife and daughter.

In the old days, Chong could have ignored the expert analysis, but now he understands: You cannot solve a case without the support of science. He drops into a chair, not saying a word, just huffing.

Wong Hu looks up, sensing his friend's mood, and comments, "Looks like it's been one of those days, huh?"

"Sometimes I think about quitting the police and doing something else in life," the detective shares.

"Don't worry too much. You know the procedure of police work. Whatever pissed you off won't change your salary. You know the saying, 'Lead if you can, follow if you are wise,'" Wong Hu advises his friend.

"You're right," the detective agrees, showing some self-control.

"Okay, let's analyze. The bullet that killed the man was not the same one that was taken from David Ho's body. Although it is from the same ammunition box... we found in the apartment safe. No one found the gun. As for the bullet in David Ho, it came from the pistol you found next to the dead man. All this shows that a third party is involved in the crime scene. I'm about ninety percent sure this third person is our shooter," explains Wong Hu.

Chong, in silence, deduces that it was Michael who shot the man on the motorcycle but needs proof.

"Another thing—the judicial authorization to open the cellphone has not yet arrived. Would you be able to provide it as soon as you can? Your boss hasn't helped so far," Hu explains.

In agreement, the detective nods.

"A shot to the man's chest caused instant death. With full awareness of their actions, the person holding the gun was conscious of what they were doing."

"That's it?" Detective Chong asks, getting up from his chair.

"Are we going to have whiskey later?" his friend invites.

"I'm out of time, but I'll call you when I get a chance. Kiss my ass... I need to take care of some things," Chong says as he leaves the room and races down the hallway.

As he descends the stairs toward the building's exit, a fellow investigator approaches from the opposite direction. The officer hands him a document, emphasizing its importance. Chong glances at the contents, noting the deceased's previous run-ins with the law. Handing the papers back, he says with obvious impatience, "I saw this. I need details about his recent activities. Dig deeper." The officer holds the document, bends his body, and exits toward the stairs.

Detective Chong pulls the phone out of his jacket and calls Chief Bo. The boss picks up, and Chong states, "I need a court order to access David Ho's cellphone. Urgently. Also, I want permission for an unofficial meeting with intel tonight. If that cannot happen, we will need to call these officers to get their statements."

Boss Bo understands what Chong is doing and, without enthusiasm, recognizes Chong's actions for what they are: cornering manoeuvres. So there are no mistakes, he prudently responds, "I will do my best to guarantee authorization. As for intel, set the meeting, but remember, I trust you to do this."

After the call, Chong can't shake the feeling that Boss Bo might not comply with the court order and was without question not interested in the intel meeting. He heads for the exit, muttering to himself, "I'm going to take this as far as I can and as fast as I can. Whether others contribute, it's their decision."

When he is about to leave the building, another police officer intercepts him, saying, "The witness who saw a person running in the street at the shooting is here to write a statement."

"Please take it from her—the basics. Don't forget she's just a deponent," the detective orders, and the officer confirms.

Detective Chong turns around and goes back to his office instead of leaving. When he arrives, he calls for his assistant: "Biyu?" But there is no sign of his secretary.

Locating her desk calendar, he opens it and looks for a number he remembers seeing. When he finds it, he dials the landline, activating the speakerphone. The repetitive ringing fills the room, but to his growing frustration, no one answers on the other end of the line.

"Is everyone on vacation today?" he exclaims in a mixture of exasperation and playfulness. Just as he is about to hang up the call, a voice on the other end answers. Without missing a beat, Chong replies, "This is the Shanghai police homicide branch chief. I need to talk to Sung Wenghu."

Someone on the other end of the line explains that he's already gone.

"Do you have his phone number? This is urgent," Detective Chong says.

"Oh! I can't give you the number."

"Call him and say it's an order from Superintendent Bo."

About five minutes pass and the detective is still waiting on the line. When the person comes back, they say their boss's cellphone number. Without delay, the detective expresses his gratitude and dials the number of the intelligence chief in Shanghai. Detective Chong records everything.

When Sung answers, Chong cuts to the chase. In a few words, he summarizes the situation and expresses the urgency to speak with the two intel officers. "I need to assess the depth of their involvement in this case," he explains. "This is not an official conversation, but I would appreciate it if we could meet tonight, if that's possible."

Sung pauses before replying. "Give me thirty minutes, and I'll get back to you with an answer."

Chong acknowledges him. "I'll be waiting."

As soon as he hangs up, the phone rings again. Upon answering, the hospital announces that David has awakened.

"I'm going there now," the detective tells the receptionist on the other end of the phone.

He runs into the parking lot, commandeering a police vehicle before speeding off toward the hospital. When he arrives at David's hospital room, his exhaustion is evident. He hasn't eaten all day, and the countless frustrations he's faced have sapped his energy. As he exits the elevator, the cool embrace of the air conditioner revives him for a short time. It is as if he has transitioned from one realm to another. He stands still for a moment, letting the surroundings sink in. Looking around, he notices the big difference between the chaotic scenes as usually seen in emergency rooms. There are no doctors running around here; just the silence of a recovery ward. The reception area is empty except for a lone attendant busy working at a computer. Upon spotting him, she offers a gentle smile. The sterile scent of antiseptics mixed with a hint of medicinal aromas brings a strange peace. Taking a deep breath, his pulse steadies, and he heads toward David's room, taking comfort in the surrounding stillness. The weight of the day is heavy on his shoulders, but the calm atmosphere for a moment lightens it.

Opening the door without making a sound, he sees David resting.

"Mr. David," the detective calls in a low tone of voice.

David opens his eyes and turns to the detective.

"Allow me to introduce myself, Detective Chong. If you don't remember me, I was here with Ms. Rachel this morning. I need to ask you some questions."

"Yes," David replies, not moving on the bed.

"I'll turn on the recorder, okay?" the detective communicates, placing the device on the small table next to the bed.

"Yes."

"Could you tell me what happened this morning, causing you to be shot twice?"

David's voice, still weak from his ordeal, narrates the events that unfolded.

"Michael and I are in the apartment when I notice the motorcyclist outside. It's the same guy we saw earlier at the restaurant where we had lunch." He coughs before continuing. "Michael remembers him taking pictures of the place, just as any tourist would. What strikes us is his distinctive red helmet with white lettering on the side. We see this same helmet when he circles our car a few times before we get to the apartment." Taking a moment to collect his thoughts, David continues: "I thought it was a good idea to go down and confront him. You see that same morning at the hotel, the concierge handed me some photos and messages. That motorcyclist has something to do with it. So, we decide to find out."

"Are these the photographs?" Detective Chong shows the copies of the photos Rachel handed him.

"The same ones," he confirms, writhing in pain.

"Want me to call a doctor or a nurse?" the detective asks.

"Let's finish first."

"I understand why you came down to the street. What happens next?"

David's eyes are glassy, and emotion fills the room. Taking a deep, shaky breath, he begins, "Michael… in an instant he has a gun. He takes it out of his bedroom drawer. I didn't know he had one." His voice cracks a little. "I beg. I beg him to let it go. We are just going to talk to the guy, nothing more."

Hesitating for a moment, as if reliving the events, David continues, "The two of us go down the street. I take the lead and ask the man why he is following us." Tears well in David's eyes as he recounts the moments that follow: "My phone ... chooses that moment to vibrate. It's on silent, but I feel it. By instinct, I move my hand toward my pocket. But as I do," his voice cracks, "the man ... he just ... pulls out his gun and shoots me." David closes his eyes, letting out a ragged breath. "Then I hear two more shots. I think it's Michael trying to defend me ... us." He swallows hard; his voice getting weak. "After that . . . it's all a blur. The weight of my body as it hits the street, the cold sidewalk . . . and then the darkness. When I open my eyes again, I am here."

"Do you know where Michael is?" the detective asks, looking into David's eyes.

"What? Where's Michael?" David returns the question.

"We don't know. He's gone. I was hoping you could answer that question."

"How am I going to know? Where's Rachel? I need to talk to her." David, agonized and in pain, tries to move onto the bed.

"Calm down, please," the detective urges.

Tears glisten in David's eyes, the weight of the moment pressing down on him. "He fired because it was in self-defence," he whispers, emotion choking his voice. Moving with visible effort, David tries to stand up, wincing as he tries to get out of bed.

"I can't discuss this matter now because this is an ongoing investigation. Can you provide information about the man who got shot?" Detective Chong keeps asking because he needs answers.

"No. Please call the nurse," David, feeling cornered, responds, showing the pain of mind and body.

Chong, ignoring David's requests, asks more questions. "Do you think this man who shot you had anything to do with the intel cops?"

David looks upset at the detective and says, "I don't know. It could be. That's the only option I can relate to right now."

"Thank you. I hope you get better fast. I'll call the nurse." The detective leaves the room, goes to the front desk, and informs them that David has complained of pain.

The nurse gets up from her chair and runs to the bedroom.

Entering the elevator, the detective takes out his phone and notices a new message notification. It's from Sung: *Meeting at intel, 7 p.m.* Looking at the current time, he realizes he still has plenty of time. As he heads to his car, which is parked in front of the hospital, a nagging thought has him muttering to himself, "Where the hell is this Michael guy?"

Sliding into the vehicle, he starts the engine and turns on the radio. A catchy pop song fills the space. Turning up the volume a bit, he talks to himself with a chuckle: "Let's go to the meeting. And after that? Dinner. I haven't eaten all day."

The streets of Shanghai stretch out as Detective Chong makes his way through the city. From the busy city centre, you can see it giving way to quieter neighbourhoods. The trip to the intel building, about forty minutes away, offers him a moment of tranquility amid the hustle and bustle of the day. Soon, the imposing structure is before him.

Chong circles the neighbourhood before finding a parking spot in the visitors' area. His footsteps echo in the cavernous lobby as he walks toward reception. By identifying himself, he doesn't need to wait. A young woman greets him and gestures for him to follow her.

In silence, they ride the elevator up to the second floor, the soft hum of the machine filling the silent space. The doors open with a hushed sound, revealing the wide hall beyond.

She points down the hall, her voice kind but professional. "You can go in; it's the door at the end."

Grateful, Chong nods, his voice firm but tinged with the weariness of the long day. "Thank you."

He follows the shown path with measured steps and a calm attitude. Disconnecting from the issues he faced during the day, he prepares to face what awaits him in the meeting ahead.

Sung stands up as Chong enters the room, his presence demanding attention. The two men already present interrupt their discussion and turn their attention to the newcomer. Offering the customary bow of recognition, they welcome the detective.

Sung's face lights up with genuine warmth, bridging the gap between their formal roles.

"Chong!" he exclaims, moving forward to hug him. "It seems like ages since we've seen each other." Pulling away, he points to a soft armchair. "Please have a seat."

As Chong settles into the offered chair, the rest of the room follows suit, the atmosphere one of quiet anticipation. Sung, clearing his throat, asks, "So, what brings you here today, detective? Come on. What happened that's so serious?"

Chong's piercing gaze alternates between the two men, gauging their reactions before speaking. "I'd like to see some identification," he says with a tone of authority. With just a hint of hesitation, the two officers pull out their wallets and place their IDs on the table right in front of the detective.

Chong observes them: their reactions, words, and movements, comparing the details of the business cards he received from Rachel. He places the cards next to the IDs, raising an eyebrow. "Are these your personal cards?"

The two agents, with tense expressions of discomfort, look at their business cards and nod.

The tension in the room rises as Chong continues, "Now, I would like an explanation. Why these photographs? What is signifying this note to David Ho? And why the secrecy of leaving it in an envelope at the front desk?"

The intense tension in the room is thick, every pair of eyes darting around, trying to gauge reactions. Chong's relentless gaze pierces the agents, waiting for a response, while the agents themselves seem paralyzed by the unexpected confrontation.

Commander Sung's focus shifts from the incriminating photographs to the two intel officers. His curious gaze, though, isn't just a simple stare; it contains deep expectation, perhaps even disbelief.

The agents, feeling the weight of the room's collective gaze, say nothing. The atmosphere grows heavier, marked by the silence of the agents and the growing pressure to explain.

"Answer him," the boss commands.

Chong, sensing a change in the room's dynamics, leans forward a little, keeping his gaze intense. He takes a moment to collect his thoughts before speaking. "I want to understand every detail of the investigation on which you are working. Why target David Ho and Rachel Barnes, and how did those photos end up with David at the hotel?"

The first agent clears his throat. "We are watching this David and Rachel because of their association with a person of interest in our case. The photos serve as a silent signal to let them know we are watching."

His partner interrupts, "But we never meant to harm them. Someone must have exploited our surveillance."

Chong raises an eyebrow. "What about the note? The business cards?"

"The note is a means of communication to set up a discreet meeting," replies the second agent.

"We include our business cards to authenticate the message."

Commander Sung analyzes the situation and interrupts. "Why didn't you go through the proper channels and let me know about this?"

The first agent hesitates and then admits, "We thought it would be a quick, uncomplicated observation. We do not expect the situation to get this bad."

The room is silent as everyone processes the information; the weight of the situation being absorbed.

"What is this investigation?" Chong asks.

The agents shift in their seats, feeling the weight of the room's attention.

The first Chinese intel officer begins. "We have been waiting for Yazuo to return to Shanghai. Our intention is to arrest him as soon as he sets foot here."

The Japanese police officer nods in agreement. "This investigation is a collaboration between our two intelligence agencies. We got the proper clearance for wiretapping in Japan and that's where we intercept crucial information linking him to Rachel Barnes."

He leans forward, emphasizing his next words: "I'm sure Yazuo will try to contact Ms. Rachel. Our primary concern right now is determining their relationship and ensuring that Ms. Rachel remains safe."

"That I know. Continue," the detective orders.

The Chinese police officer clears his throat, looking a little uncomfortable. "We had an unintended confrontation with David and Rachel the other day in a pub downtown. The conversation, unfortunately, was tense, and tensions ran high on both sides."

He pauses, taking a deep breath. "In an effort to mend bridges and clarify our intentions, we sent these photos, thinking it would be a way to invite them into a clearer and calmer conversation. It was an oversight on our part."

Detective Chong looks sideways. "What about those men on motorcycles?"

The officer's demeanour changes. "We watched them, and it looked like they showed a keen interest in David Ho and Michael Wen Akimitsu as they left the hotel. Our instincts kicked in and we captured the moment. We forwarded it, thinking David and Rachel might recognize or have some information about these individuals. It was just to facilitate collaborative information. We did not intend to create any discomfort or alarm."

Chong studies the officers for a moment, taking in their serious expressions and the weight of their words. Feeling reassured by their sincerity, he nods to the commander, signalling his acceptance of their explanations. He stands up and bows to the police, who respond with similar gestures of respect.

Commander Sung and Detective Chong leave the room, continuing their discussion as they head to the elevator, leaving the agents to ponder the unexpected turn of events.

"I believe them," the detective tells the commander.

"You can believe it. They're excellent police officers, and they're not lying," the intel boss says with certainty about the agents.

The detective enters the elevator and turns to his friend. "Thank you, Commander Sung. We'll have a whiskey another day."

"Mark the time and place, I'll be there," the commander says, accepting the invitation and saying goodbye.

*   *   *

Rachel, in her room, observes her swollen face in the mirror. She cried so much today.

"David and Tyler are my family," she says out loud.

Preparing to have dinner with Wang, Rachel hesitates. Considering everything that has happened in these twenty-four hours, the idea of going out doesn't sound appealing. However, Wang is persistent, and she relents. With a simple appearance, she uses minimal makeup, her hair tied up in a ponytail and held on top of her head with a traditional Chinese hairpin, and a casual outfit of black pants paired with a white long-sleeved shirt. Taking one last look in the mirror, she feels toned down, but elegant.

Glancing at her wristwatch, Rachel makes her way to the front desk of the hotel. She sits down in one of the plush armchairs in the lobby, waiting for Wang.

Moments later, Wang enters the lobby. His eyes scan the lobby, and he finds Rachel. His heart skips a beat. She looks ethereal, almost dreamlike. To him, in that fleeting moment, she seems like a divine figure out of his fondest dreams.

She lifts her head from the phone, and surprised, notices Wang standing almost in front of her, staring at her.

"Oh, you're here? I didn't see you come in," she says and puts her phone in her purse.

"You're beautiful, as usual," he says, not noticing that the people around are watching them and making comments.

"Sorry, but I think you need glasses. I look horrible today. Where are we going?" Rachel says to Wang, without smiling, as she gets up from the armchair.

"We're having salmon and shrimp tonight. Sound good to you?" Wang asks, his voice tinged with enthusiasm.

"Sounds like the perfect dinner for the hunger I'm feeling today," Rachel replies, smiling.

She walks beside him as they leave the hotel.

Unlike usual, Wang is without his entourage tonight—not a bodyguard in sight. Soon, they are in his Audi, driving at a brisk pace. From time to time, he glances at her, his face breaking into a smile, unable to capture in words the happiness he feels.

As they travel, Rachel recounts the day's events and everything that has happened since dawn. She assumes he's paying attention to her every word, given his rapt gaze, but as she continues, she feels like he's not listening. To test his attention, she adds some random and disconnected words. There is no answer. She notices an ever-present but lifeless, mysterious smile. She loses her temper and confronts him.

"What the hell? Have you heard anything I've told you?" Rachel complains.

"I heard every word and understood everything," Wang replies, smiling, keeping his eyes on the road.

Rachel's intuition senses something strange about his behaviour—it's as if he's immune to the weight of her words. She hopes for compassion or agreement but wonders if the problem is emotional.

Throughout the conversation, Wang avoids any mention of David. This moment is about them—no David, no outside world, just the two of them.

Arriving at a Japanese restaurant, Wang parks the car, and a host escorts them to a reserved table. Rachel's eyes roam the room, taking in the intricate jade and coral carvings that adorn the walls. They settle into soft cushions, the table in front of them laden with seafood—an assortment of fish, shrimp, and vegetables. Two bottles made of green jade and filled with wine are ready for tasting. Wang fills a small bowl in front of him.

"These sculptures are something else," Rachel comments in awe.

Wang looks up, a playful glint in his eye.

"As do you. Let's drink," he says, raising his bowl.

The two raise their bowls, and Wang adds, "May our love be eternal."

She repeats, "Not love. May our friendship be eternal."

Wang, looking at her, takes a dark blue velvet rectangular box from inside his jacket and places it in front of Rachel. The sight of the box stuns her for a moment, making her forget about the drink in her hand. She places the bowl back on the table, her gaze fixed on the mysterious velvet case.

With curiosity and anticipation, she opens the box. Inside is a stunning pearl necklace, clasped in brilliant white gold, set with diamonds, accompanied by a pair of earrings, each with a pearl set with glittering diamonds. The elegance of the jewellery leaves her speechless.

Rachel's eyes widen at the sight of the glittering pearls nestled in the velvet case. "Holy cow! Look at these!" she gasps, surprised by the enormity of the gift.

Hesitating, her fingers touch the necklace, but do not lift it. With a stern expression, she closes the case and slides it back to Wang.

"I'm sorry, I can't accept this," she says, being gentle.

Wang's eyes narrow, disbelief apparent in his gaze. "Why not? It's a token of our friendship, reflecting the joy you've given me," he argues, the hurt clear in his tone.

Rachel meets his gaze, her eyes resolute. "I can't, Wang. Whatever happened between us last night is in the past. Today we're friends and that's all. I can't accept gifts or any other gesture of this kind."

His face darkens, an unexpected mix of anger and hurt. Slamming his hand on the table, his voice rises. "Am I not good enough for you?" The intensity of his reaction catches her off guard; it's a side of Wang she hadn't seen yet.

Rachel takes a deep breath, her calm demeanour in stark contrast to Wang's tension. She searches for the right words, hoping to calm the storm she sees brewing in his eyes.

"It's not about you being 'good enough' or not, Wang," she says, choosing her words resolutely. "I think you are every woman's dream: Handsome, endearing, intelligent… but what happened between us was just a moment in time. That's the way life is sometimes. I… earnestly apologize if I gave you any impression to the contrary."

Wang's gaze fixes on a spot on the wall; he's lost in thought. The weight of the silence is heavy, and Rachel hopes her words will help mend the distance between them.

Feeling that he isn't listening, she asks again, "Did you hear me, Wang?" Rachel laughs, getting up from the cushions.

Wang's gaze softens, moving away from the intense gaze he had cast moments earlier.

"Rachel," he begins, his voice all different, like he's giving a speech, "I'm sorry. I misunderstood, jumped to conclusions, and almost put our friendship at risk. Please forgive me."

Just as Rachel is about to respond, the sliding doors open, revealing two waiters holding trays of fresh dishes. They replace the dishes that are on the table. The aromas fill the environment.

"Could you bring us your best jug of wine, please?" Wang asks with a polite nod. The waiters exchange a brief look, smile, nodding yes, and after bowing, they leave.

Rachel resumes her seat, and the two continue their meal. The room is silent except for the clink of utensils on plates. She watches Wang as he eats, noting the serene way he now carries himself. When he pours wine into their glasses, it is with a gesture of simple companionship, devoid of any prior intentions or underlying meanings.

"Have you predicted when you will return to London? You must have a lot to do there," Wang says, putting a piece of salmon in his mouth.

"I'm still not sure," Rachel begins, taking a sip of wine. "Our associate will sort out the details. Tomorrow, after visiting David and speaking to his doctor, I will have a clearer idea of his discharge date and transfer him to a hospital in London."

Wang, absorbed, peels a shrimp, and says without making eye contact, "From what I understand, the surgery wasn't very intense. I bet he'll be ready to go in about a week."

"Wang, I'm sorry—" she starts, trying to articulate her feelings.

"Hey, no need to dwell on it," he interrupts, lifting his cup in a gesture of reconciliation. "We're still friends, right?"

"Friends," Rachel says, not joining in the toast but returning a genuine smile.

The rest of dinner is distant, the space between them filled with unspoken words and lingering tension. Wang takes her back to the hotel, the ride filled with polite but stilted conversation. The farewell is friendly but lacks warmth.

Back in her hotel room, Rachel pulls out her diary to document the night. She questions her own actions: "Was I too direct? Should I have added a little sugar to things? Is the dynamic here so different? David is always commenting on my fierce independence, joking that it will stop me from ever getting married, but why should his—or anyone else's—opinion matter?"

She puts the diary aside and goes to bed, setting her alarm for dawn. Sleep is elusive. Opening her eyes, she mutters to herself, "The real problem is Wang's sudden change in behaviour in the restaurant. That was weird. I need to be cautious around him; something about that reaction just didn't feel right."

Rachel, in her usual peace of mind, always sure of her actions, completes the analysis, closes her eyes, and sleeps.

25

Life Goes On, but with Stumbles

Taking the elevator to the DRT floor, Tyler looks at his wristwatch and realizes it's 9:00 a.m. When the partners are away, he is always late. After all, he looks after Rachel's cat Mozart, and this morning he also stopped by David's apartment to pick up the mail. Entering the office, he sees the secretary at reception.

"Any news from David and Rachel?" Tyler inquires.

Mary Lai, always one step ahead of Tyler running the office, reports her discussion with her boss.

"Rachel tried to call you last night but couldn't because the phone was busy, so she called me. She just wants to let you know that David's condition has improved, and they will see their doctor this morning about a transfer to London."

Tyler supposes he had been talking on the phone with his informant at the moment Rachel had called him. Aware of her late-night work habits, Rachel must have contacted her secretary to go over the day's events.

"Well, the morning is over because in Shanghai, it's now 4 p.m. No need to call her. Call David's dad and tell him the news," Tyler instructs Mary Lai.

With the agenda in hand, Mary Lai advises that the day has several meetings, but the main one is at 11:00 a.m. with the CEO of Sandykoni Logistics Co. Ltd.

"Is it going to be here in the office?" he asks, searching the desk for the notes he made yesterday after he talked to the informant.

"Yes, the meeting will be here," the secretary confirms.

"One thing I don't like is those security guards. I was a police officer, and I know the need to protect the CEO of a company, but those men are intimidating. I don't want complaints here in the building because of their presence," he comments without going into details.

"Do you want them to wait downstairs?"

"No. The scene could get worse, and that's not what we want. Let them act the way they want. That's what the internal cameras are for," he says, smiling at her.

Tyler reviews the informant's documents and the contract with the Sandykoni company. He recalls that DRT's task is to identify who stole the cargo bound for London. After customs clearance, the goods are ready to be picked up at the port. The organization stores them in two warehouses on the bay; however, someone redirects both shipments to another shipping company, which they have not located.

Studying each sheet of paper on the table, he tries to figure out where the error is and reads another document referring to the investigation that the local police have informed him of.

Tyler learns from the Maritime Police that the truck driver's documentation is false, with only the fingerprints of the night receptionist being found. Cameras reveal two unmarked trucks with fake license plates. The sheer volume of stolen goods suggests hidden accomplices. There are no witnesses, and that is peculiar. Most left the day before the holiday. There are only the doormen and the firm in charge of security who claim to have been in the cafeteria during the robbery, a fact corroborated by video evidence.

He acknowledges such incidents are common around the world. Despite investigations by the local police and the port, the problem is likely to remain unresolved. "Without sufficient information and reliable witnesses, the investigation will stall, but it will not be forgotten," a port agent told him.

Last night he received a crucial tip from his informants. This caused Tyler to recall his days as an RCMP officer specializing in Chinese gangs. They insinuated that the London-based Triad was behind the robbery. Although he doubted this at first, consistent information from the port made him reconsider. Containers from China, linked to London mafias like Wo Shing Wo and 14K, were likely targets—such betrayals were all too familiar.

At 11:00 a.m., Tyler meets with the company's directors about the progress of the investigation. Sipping coffee, Tyler considers information from informants and the police. Given his experience, he suspects the company may have been involved in the theft. Since signing the contract, Zhang has been eager for updates. Reflecting on the information, Tyler thinks, *They will remain in the dark today. I will use the narrative of the shipping agents, buying time, to investigate the company's ties to the London mafias.*

Listening to the CEO, Tyler smiles, reflecting on the possible links between Sandykoni and the Triad, listing illicit activities: forgery, human trafficking, prostitution, extortion, arms trafficking, contract murder, money laundering, loan sharking, illegal gambling, and predicts, *It will be wonderful to investigate this.*

* * *

In Shanghai, Rachel's taxi stops at the hospital entrance. As she leaves, a motorcycle almost runs her over. She refrains from cursing, commenting instead, "That's not common in a hospital."

The taxi driver, worried, asks, "Did it hit you?"

Still shaken, she says no and heads for the elevators. She acknowledges that David's attack has left her traumatized.

Entering David's room, Rachel sees a nurse arranging a beautiful bouquet by the window. The room is dark, sunlight peeking through the closed blinds. David spots Rachel and blows her a kiss. She smiles, approaches the nurse, and asks if the flowers are for her. The nurse smiles without answering and walks away.

David, noticing Rachel's uncertainty, reassures her. "She didn't understand your Mandarin accent. The flowers are from Mr. Wang, wishing me a speedy recovery."

"Oh! He's already forgotten about me," Rachel says, approaching and kissing him on the cheek.

"What's the story behind that?" her partner asks, interested.

"Later, but first, I want to know if you got any sleep last night?"

"No. I'm looking forward to getting out of this place and going to the hotel. Rachel, please help me find Michael," David pleads, his eyes glistening with tears.

"Calm down, my friend. It hasn't even been seventy-two hours since you underwent a delicate surgery. The doctors are monitoring you for an infection," she explains, trying to calm him down.

"I need to find Michael. This needs to be cleared up," David responds with an ensuing groan.

"I'm sure Detective Chong and his team are working the possible and the impossible to find him."

"Yesterday, that detective was quick to point the finger at Michael. Of course, Michael could have fired. I believe so, but only to defend me. By the time the gun went off, I was already on the ground. We're both cops, Rachel. We know what to do—they need someone to blame for their superiors." David defends his friend's actions, his voice strained.

"David, someone attacked you," Rachel said. "Michael disappeared— no wallet, car, nothing. There's something else you should know... They found an envelope with heroin in the safe," Rachel says, her voice crackling with sympathy, but firm in conveying the truth.

"He doesn't use it, I'm sure. That heroin was planted." David moves, uncomfortable in the bed, as the pain flares up again.

"I'm not playing devil or angel here. The detective thinks Michael seized the moment and that he recognized the man on the bike and used you to take him out," explains Rachel, conveying the police perspective to David.

"I don't believe it. Michael needs me, and he will show up when I get out of the hospital," her partner says, trying to get out of bed.

"David, please calm down. The doctors won't be discharging you soon. Do you imagine those stitches opening? Then the situation will get complicated," she says, trying to calm him down.

He cries, saying he doesn't believe what happened.

Rachel sits on the bed next to him and hugs him, crying as well.

"I don't believe what the police are saying. He's not addicted. It's not possible. We have to find out the truth. Let's find Michael." David sobs, hugging her.

"I agree. No one knows him better than you. We'll find him," Rachel says, crying, trying to comfort him.

A nurse and the doctor enter the room and notice the situation with the partners.

The doctor says, "Sir. David, if you don't calm down, you may need another surgery, and I wanted to get you home as quickly as possible." The doctor checks the display, confirming that his blood pressure and heart rate have increased.

"Let's calm down," the nurse says as she stands next to the doctor and applies a tranquilizer to the intravenous bag.

Sitting in the armchair, Rachel watches David and the doctor talking. She battles with guilt for exposing the heroin's discovery, but her determination to tell the truth prevails. After all, David would have done the same; it is essential to be prepared for both good and bad news.

Although police life has made them both pragmatic, their actions can seem callous to outsiders. Being one step ahead is crucial for them. It wasn't about guilt; it was about preparing David for any eventuality.

Rachel's attention returns to the room. David is asleep, and the doctor and nurse have left. Embracing the silence, she works on her report. Retrieving her iPad, she looks up descriptions of motorcyclists she found at Wang's mother's house. Disappointed, she realizes that neither she nor David wrote about it.

Exhausted, Rachel leans back on the couch, her eyes heavy, leafing through the report. The whirlwind of recent events has left them with a mountain of first-hand data.

"We cannot deny that Ronaldo's death connected to Mr. Chan," she murmurs. "Who knew about Ronaldo's meeting with Mr. Chan? Why did a Yakuza boss insinuate their involvement in his death?"

The phone emits a *ping*, and Rachel reads her parent's message asking to get in touch. She leaves the room and heads downstairs to the hospital cafeteria. She dials the USA.

"Hi, Daddy, are you alright?"

Rachel listens to the reason for the message; her eyes fill with tears. She tries to control herself, but the crying comes, and her breathing quickens. Trying hard not to draw people's attention, she continues listening to him and puts on her sunglasses, with tears streaming down her face. For a moment, she looks at the table, then turns off her cellphone and puts it in her jeans' pocket.

Behind the hospital restaurant, a large garden evokes the essence of a forest. A distraught Rachel weaves through the trees, tears clouding her eyes. She leans against a log, the pain weighing her down. Her father's words haunt her: "Your cousin has died in an accident in the mountains near Jasper, Alberta, Canada. Their car hit a moose, killing her and two friends." The size of these animals, measuring two metres and weighing up to seven hundred kilograms, emphasizes the tragedy. These accidents are very common in Canada, making the news even more heartbreaking.

Rachel can't stop listening to her father's voice as he was in tears...
"Claire died."

Devastated, a wave of memories and emotions crashes over her, filling
her with deep regret. Guilt consumes her—for not being there for her
cousin, for not caring enough, for not forgiving, for turning a deaf ear. She
closes her eyes, surrendering to her sadness.

A nurse touches Rachel's shoulders. "Madam, ma'am, did something happen?"

She wakes up on the lawn, realizing she has passed out or dozed off. A
woman assists her, offering help, but Rachel ignores the concern and the
grass on her jeans, attributing her condition to a low blood pressure attack.
She expresses her gratitude and walks back to the hospital.

In David's room, she retrieves her belongings, noticing that her friend is
still sleeping. Sitting in an armchair, she tries to process her next steps amid
the chaos, letting out a sigh. She freshens up in the bathroom, pulling her
hair back and applying lipstick, the mirror reflecting her tear-swollen eyes.
Back in the room, her phone lights up with a flood of messages and calls
from worried loved ones. Although tempted to respond, she waits.

As she watches David sleep, her mind races with what's next. Her travel
plans now seem pointless; her father is handling the cremation in Canada.
Meanwhile, David's imminent transfer to a London hospital depends on
her. Scheduling in her mind a visit to his mother and uncle in Toronto, her
gaze turns to the window. The sight of salmon-coloured roses provokes
new tears—a painful reminder of her cousin's affection for these flowers.

David wakes up and hears Rachel crying. "What's happened?"

"My dear, sorry if I woke you up," she says, wiping tears from her face.

"I believe I'll leave the hospital next week. That's what the doctor
said in the morning before giving me those damn painkillers. I mean,
these tranquilizers are not for sleeping, they are for killing. Did something
happen?" he asks, believing she is crying because of his situation.

"These last few days have been difficult," Rachel says with a tight smile,
choosing to keep her cousin's death a secret. She knows David must remain
stable before leaving Shanghai.

"Any news from the police?" he asks.

"No, none. Detective Chong didn't talk to me today. I'll text him."

David takes a deep breath and speaks again about Michael. "I can't understand. Why did he run away? It was self-defence. Do you know if he contacted his mother?"

"He didn't contact his family or the hotel. The detective said he left everything in the apartment but took his phone. Leaving behind documents, money, and a credit card? Doesn't that seem strange to you?" Rachel's voice is firm, hoping to divert her attention from the recent loss of her cousin.

"I think he panicked after the shooting and hid. This isn't his territory. I bet he sought shelter with someone he knows and will show up when I get out of here," says her partner.

"How can you be so sure?"

"We planned to tell his mother about our marriage. We were going to London together this week, finalizing all the paperwork. He's sensible and trustworthy. This isn't a game," David says, his voice full of emotion.

She ponders his words, feeling the truth but intrigued by Michael's disappearance. Leaving her own problems aside and supporting her partner, she says, "I trust you, but something is wrong. I'll call Detective Chong and see where these leads are."

"Did you come to any conclusions in our report?" he asks, straightening the pillows.

In a hushed tone, she moves a chair next to his bed and shares her deductions, linking Chan and Ronaldo's deaths.

He raises an eyebrow. "You have proof?"

She goes deeper. "Mr. Chan provided crucial details to American intelligence, leading to Operation Container. It connected Japan's drug industry and the Chinese mafia. Think of the losses and diplomatic problems that were caused by these seizures."

"I can see all of this," David agrees.

With a quick and analytical mind, she comments, "I'm putting the pieces together. Whoever killed Mr. Chan knew about the delivery the day I received the flash drive. Whoever killed him assumed Ronaldo received it."

"Oh, I think you got it! The dates of the deaths match Chan's disappearance… Everything closed. You escaped dying." David coughs, and the nurse enters the room.

"You woke up. How do you feel?" She looks at the altered heartbeat on the control display.

He composes himself, shows a false calm, stating that he has no pain, and jokes that he needs to eat.

Rachel, sitting down, smiles at the nurse as if everything is a thousand wonders.

The attendant looks at the two of them with suspicion. "I'll arrange something." The nurse leaves the room, closing the door.

Once she's gone, David looks at his partner. "So... tell me about Wang."

Rachel, unsure whether or not to tell him what happened between her and Wang, tells him, "You will not believe."

"You escaped another rear-naked chokehold," says David, snorting and smiling with a scared look.

Rachel laughs, covering her mouth so as not to emit the sound of laughter, and says, "Just you to make me laugh today."

"You hit the nail on the head, correct reasoning. You escaped dying that day, I believe," says her partner.

"It's only now that I realize that. I'll put it all back on paper. We're getting close..."

"What else?"

She looks at her phone, noticing the flood of messages. Silence. She pulls the blanket over her partner. "I'm going to the hotel to take a shower, eat something, and do a more in-depth analysis," she whispers.

"Bring the documents. We will study together. We have all the time we need," he murmurs.

Rachel grabs her bag and jacket and stops to look at him. Years of friendship and shared experiences have cemented their bond, demonstrating unwavering loyalty and trust. Although they were never more than friends, their constant mutual support and affection were always apparent. Within a minute, David is fast asleep.

Rachel kisses him on the cheek and says, "I'll bring the documents. Rest, my friend. In a little while, your lunch arrives."

On the way to the hotel, she recognizes the same motorcycle she saw in the hospital. The taxi stops at the sign, and the motorcycle crosses the red. She mutters, "I swear it's the same bike I saw in the hospital today. I'll start paying more attention."

251

Upon arriving at the hotel, the receptionist says, "Ms. Rachel, there are messages." He hands her five envelopes with condolences. Grateful, Rachel tucks them into her jeans and heads to her room. Upon entering, she throws her bag on the table and falls onto the bed. She goes through her phone messages, responding to each one. She decides not to return the day's calls and only calls her father.

He updates her from Vancouver. He is taking care of the cremation, as the family cannot travel there. The family is feeling very shaken. Relaying details from doctors and police, he says, "The moose was huge. The impact was quick; they didn't feel pain." He confirms Claire was not driving, and that the car was not speeding. "Animal accidents in Canada are common. You know the authorities prohibit the family from scattering the ashes in the mountains. I hope to find an alternative solution."

"When do you return to Miami? Did Milla go with you to Vancouver?" Rachel asks her father in a sad voice.

He clarifies he will soon return because he is sure that the entire procedure and documentation will be ready soon. His wife stayed at home, taking care of the twins.

She listens to her father in silence and asks, "How's Mother doing?"

"Your mother has always been the strongest person I've met in this life. She held all the emotions of the family in Toronto. If my brother didn't have her right now, he wouldn't have been able to handle it. Your cousin will arrive here today in Vancouver. He will come to collect some ashes for the ceremony for family and friends, which we will hold in two days."

"Do you think I should call Mom? She never calls me, she's always busy, but I can't imagine how devastated she must be," Rachel says.

He stops talking for a few seconds and then directs her. "Since you don't talk to each other, call her about three days after the ceremony. Enjoy talking to Henry and James. Your uncle and cousin miss you. I am so sad about her death. What happened was a stupid, unprecedented thing, but I will do what I have to do. I'm going to miss that yummy laugh and the hug that always greeted me. Right now, I'll not mix family issues in this situation. Do you understand?"

"I understand, and I'll do it. Claire was very important in my life; we grew up together, but if I were there with you, I wouldn't be okay. Here I can better reflect on a time of joy that was our youth. The art gallery and the paintings... what's going to happen now?" she asks.

"Your cousin told me they are going to prepare and exhibit all her paintings."

John's voice shakes as he speaks to his daughter; he is feeling the deep weight of sadness that weighs on his heart. "Rachel, I need you to understand that what happened was beyond anyone's control. Your cousin travelled to a place of peace—it was her time, her destiny. While that concept may be difficult to understand for many, I believe that you, with your spiritual vision, can. Cherish the beautiful memories you shared with her, ensuring that your spirit feels nothing but love. My dear, as soon as I get home, I'll call you. Now, I need to hurry. Remember, I love you."

"I love you, Daddy."

They hang up the phone.

Sitting on the bed, the stillness of the room envelops her, and Rachel's gaze strays into the distance. In that garden, she had already shed every tear she had inside her. Everything her father told her is true. He is always a brilliant guide, even though she recognizes her own imperfections. Accepting death will take time.

Her stomach growls, grounding her in reality. Rachel gets up, adjusts the pillows, and organizes the papers spread across the table. Even without David, the investigation must progress. They came with a mission, and she was determined to uncover forgotten details. Back in London, they will review everything together.

Taking a deep breath, she drinks water from the bottle next to her. She realizes that fears, conflicts, past traumas, and deep longings can resurface when least expected. It isn't the first time she hides, conceals, and postpones her emotions. Now, she must strengthen herself and continue with what needs to be done.

"Time to shower," Rachel says aloud, heading to the bathroom.

Getting out of the shower, Rachel picks out her outfit for the day, only to realize that most of her clothes are dirty. She sees a t-shirt she hasn't worn yet and puts it on. As she combs her hair, the phone in her room rings. Picking up the phone, she listens. "Miss Rachel, Detective Chong is waiting for you in the lobby." She replies that she will be right down.

Her heart races with apprehension about the detective's visit. Looking at the clock, she sees that it's almost 3:00 in the afternoon. Drawn to the window, Rachel admires the bright afternoon sun.

She gets lost in a dream, murmuring, "Oh, how I would like to be here as a tourist. It has always been one of my greatest desires to explore China's top attractions. Next time I will visit the Great Wall, the Forbidden City, the Classical Gardens of Suzhou, the Giant Buddha of Leshan. And Zhangjiajie National Forest Park—one of the most enchanting places."

Returning to the moment, Rachel leaves the room, puts the car keys in her bag, and enters the elevator. Upon arriving at the front desk, she heads up to Detective Chong, who is sitting in one armchair.

He greets her and notices her face, seeing the eyes even with the makeup, deep marks of those who cried.

"Did something happen?"

"Personal family problems," Rachel replies, trying to show indifference because he keeps staring at her.

"Oh! Can I help you?"

"There's nothing else to do," she replies with minor consideration.

"I thought you would want to know about the progress of the investigation."

"Yes, anything new?" she says, sitting down next to him.

"The intel officers are in the clear. The deceased man works at the docks and has ties to drug trafficking and contract killings. He is not innocent. Michael is still missing despite using all our informants. We analyzed David's phone and will return it soon." Chong updates her, skirting the details.

Rachel, thoughtful, analyzes everything she heard.

He explains that they recreated the crime at the scene and in the apartment, suggesting that someone framed David. The friend's act of taking the gun outside showed intent on killing. The important fact is that David's statement at the hospital revealed that Michael saw a man on a motorcycle photographing them in the restaurant where the three of them had lunch.

"That's interesting, he didn't tell me that," Rachel says, but thinks she hasn't gone into detail with her partner about what happened the night of the shooting.

"Were you talking to David today?"

"I was with him; he's in pain, but the medical team is taking good care of him. Now, I need to have a talk with the surgeon before we go back to London," she replies.

"Why did you come here to Shanghai? Don't fool me because I know it was for work. Did you finish what you came here to do?" he asks, still trying to understand what the partners came to town to do.

"More or less. In the end, it will be impossible to finish, but we'll come back another time." Rachel blurts out an answer, without a definitive explanation, but doesn't satisfy the detective.

"Do you need any help?" he asks, curious.

"Thank you for the offer; I'll let you know." Detective Chong notices the sadness etched on her face, feeling the loss of the vibrancy he once admired.

"That's not the Rachel I remember... I'm sorry. Is there any way I can help you?"

She takes a deep breath, looks at the detective, and admits, "My cousin, who was my friend and sister, passed away."

"Oh, I'm sorry, my condolences," Detective Chong says, shocked at the confession.

Getting up from the armchair, Rachel staggers but composes herself by saying, "Don't worry, I've already improved. During the day, it was tough."

"Can I do something?" he asks, standing next to her.

With a smile, she reveals she has eaten nothing all day. "Some food that is light, warm, but also substantial," she said.

"Allow me to find the perfect location. Simple, only police frequent this place," he says and laughs.

Rachel agrees, saying it sounds like the perfect spot. The two leave together, and in the parking lot, a man sitting on a motorcycle positioned behind a van uses his cellphone to take photographs of her and the detective.

"Did you come in a police car?" she asks.

"I have an unmarked official vehicle," he replies and points to the vehicle.

"Let's go in my car so we don't set up private police car use," Rachel says, pulling the keys out of her purse. She turns off the alarm in her car and hands the keys to him.

"You're very correct," he says and starts laughing.

"Isn't it meant to be?"

"You must have been an exceptional police officer," the detective says, getting into the car.

"Rules are rules. Why break them and then have to answer for such small things?" she retorts.

"I agree with you, and I'm starving too," he says, changing the subject, and starts driving, pulling out of the hotel parking lot toward the avenue.

She smiles at the detective, and he says, "I like you."

"I'm starting to like you too," Rachel responds and laughs.

The motorcycle follows them. After a while, Detective Chong parks the car behind a restaurant. As they enter through the back door, a chorus of greetings greets the pair. Detective Chong responds, hugging some, patting others on the back, smiling at the women, and nodding to the rest. Finding an empty table near the wall in front of the counter, he directs Rachel to sit down.

A waitress approaches. "Good evening, Detective, what's going on today?" the waitress asks, speaking in difficult-to-understand Mandarin.

"Two beers and *xiaolongbao*," he replies.

"I'm already bringing the beers," she notes, walking toward the kitchen.

"Rachel, do you understand what she said?" Chong asks.

"I understood something, but it was fast, and the music and the people talking… hard," she replies, and winks with her left eye.

"Where did you learn Mandarin?" he asks, taking the beers from the hand of the returning waitress.

"I've been studying for years, although not consistently. When I was in London, David was my go-to for language help, especially with the accent, but being here in Shanghai has been transformative for me. I have been immersing myself in Mandarin over the past few days—reading, writing, speaking, and listening all the time. There is no better way to learn a language," she explains.

"That's excellent. Okay, let's talk in Mandarin. If you don't understand something, ask me, and I'll explain it to you," he says with a smile.

Rachel laughs. "I'm still a little afraid to speak, but I understand well, and I can read. Shall we train you in English?"

"Not today," he replies.

"What are we going to eat? I'm starving." Rachel takes a sip of beer and looks toward the kitchen.

"Xiaolongbao or dumpling soup, this dish is traditional here in Shanghai. You can eat it in the morning, afternoon, and evening. Imagine little dumplings stuffed with pork, shrimp, vegetables, or crab and a delicious hot syrup over them," Chong tells her, running his tongue over his lips.

"Bloody hell! I'm starving, and you're giving me that description," Rachel says, smiling at the detective.

The waitress approaches, serving dinner along with two more cold beers.

"Eat," he suggests, offering her a portion.

Rachel watches Detective Chong, imitating how he eats each dish.

Noticing her joy, he can't help but smile, pleased with his choice of dinner.

Outside the restaurant, a motorcyclist watches from a distance. As dusk falls and the neighbourhood calms down, a Mercedes pulls up alongside him. Wang is visible smoking a cigarette through the rolled-down rear window. Leaning over, the motorcyclist sticks his head inside the car. The boss directs his gaze toward the man and inquires, "Are they still in the restaurant?"

"Yes, boss."

"Go home; you've worked hard today." Wang hands him an envelope.

"Yes, sir. Thank you very much, sir." The boy returns to the bike, turns it on, and drives down the street in silence.

The car window closes, and the Mercedes driven by Hui pulls away in the opposite direction of the restaurant.

26

Bye, Shanghai

Rachel's phone rings. She reaches over and picks it up.

"Good morning, beautiful," Wang says.

Rachel listens, stretches, but doesn't respond.

"Let's go for a walk. I want to show you the Huangpu River, the history of my country," he suggests.

"I think it's a wonderful idea, but I have to go to the hospital first," she replies.

Wang doesn't say a word.

"Why don't you come with me? You can meet my partner. He wants to thank you for the flowers, and then we can go for our walk."

He remains muted in thought, then responds, "It would be an honour to meet David."

"It's 7 a.m. and my friends don't call me at this time for sightseeing, especially on a Friday," Rachel says with a laugh.

Again, he doesn't answer.

"Come pick me up at 8:30. Will that work?" she asks.

"Great, I'll be there," he agrees.

She hangs up and checks incoming messages and emails. Many people have still written, comforting her through grief. She decides to call her father. "Dad, are you okay?" Rachel's voice shows her concern for her father.

He replies, his voice heavy with exhaustion, "I'm hanging in there, sweetheart."

He shares that the cremation took place the night before. Unfortunately, his nephew couldn't make it to Vancouver in time and had to spend the night in a hotel room. However, amid the sadness, family friends emerged as a positive aspect and resolved all the paperwork. The unforeseen delays caused him to extend his stay in the city. Today, his grim task is to collect the ashes and deliver them to James. The weight of this responsibility weighs on his shoulders, but he knows it's something he needs to do. Through it all, he remains hopeful that he can return home soon.

"Glad everything went well," Rachel offers.

"This afternoon I am going to Miami. We can talk later," he informs her.

"Okay, love you so much," Rachel responds before hanging up.

Looking at her phone, she reads 7:30 a.m. She looks out her bedroom window and remembers the forecast of thirty degrees Celsius. Gratitude fills her for being alive and for her father's efforts in keeping the family together. Amid her sadness, she remembers her responsibilities and resolves not to succumb to despair. Opening her wardrobe, she realizes she has worn everything she brought from London. Today she decides, "I'm going to buy clothes in Shanghai." She takes a quick shower and heads to the restaurant.

After breakfast, Rachel arrives at the hotel reception at 8:20 a.m. and the staff greets her.

Hearing a commotion, Rachel spots Wang in the lobby, surrounded by selfie-takers and fans. Laughing, she approaches and asks in English, "Can I get your autograph?"

Wang responds, "For you, the world," and taking her hand, they walk out of the hotel toward the parking lot.

As they get in his car, she says, "I'm glad you came; you're going to love David."

Looking calm, Wang steers the car toward the city centre, nodding every time she mentions something.

At the hospital, they pass through corridors and the reception. Despite the surrounding people's warm greetings and waves to Wang, Rachel remains composed, walking toward the elevators. They enter and Rachel presses the floor button. The ascent is silent. Upon arrival, she approaches the reception and receives immediate access, all thanks to the detective's prior authorization. Entering the room, they find two doctors and a nurse talking to David.

David's face breaks into a wide smile when he spots Rachel, and he announces, "You can rent the jet; the doctors say they will release me on Sunday."

She looks at him and returns the big smile.

One doctor turns to Rachel. "If everything continues as we predicted, following the correct medication and not encountering any more stress, maybe on Sunday, if not... I will release him only on Wednesday."

"Thank you for the good news, Doctor," Rachel says, bowing.

The doctors and the nurse leave the room, talking to each other about the patient.

"David, I want to introduce you to Wang," Rachel says.

Her partner on the bed looks at the man next to Rachel and says, "Rachel has spoken well of you. Please take care of her and also, thanks for the flowers."

"I'll do my best," Wang replies.

She sits on the bed next to her friend, and Wang sits in the armchair, staring at David.

"How are you?" Rachel asks David.

"I'm fine, waiting for Detective Chong. We're supposed to meet at 10 a.m.," David responds, glancing at Wang.

"Wang invited me to learn about the history of the Huangpu River this morning on a boat trip. I accepted; I need to turn everything off," Rachel says, rotating her finger at her temple.

"Okay. Then I'll tell you what happens with the detective," David advises.

She gives David a tender kiss on the cheek before getting up and heading toward the exit.

The bedroom door opens, and to everyone's surprise, the detective arrives earlier than expected.

"Are we having a party today?" David's face explodes into a grin with enthusiasm.

In a warm manner, Rachel greets the detective, introduces Wang, and says goodbye with a friendly wave.

Wang, captivated by their genuine affection, doesn't realize he's being introduced to Detective Chong.

Detective Chong extends his hand in a friendly greeting, and Wang, surprised, gets up from his chair, almost falling over.

Without waiting for Wang to catch up, Rachel walks out the door, leaving behind a warm atmosphere in the room.

"It was a pleasure. We'll see each other," Wang says, waving goodbye to David and following Rachel.

In the hallway, Rachel waits for him.

Detective Chong, seeing the confusion, asks David, "Do you know Wang?"

"No, I just met him today," David replies.

The quick detective shakes his head and continues, "Let's get down to business."

David, surprised by Detective Chong's strange reaction, watches and says nothing.

Walking down the hallway with Wang toward the elevator, Rachel asks, "What did you think of David?"

"You seem to be very close," Wang comments, walking and showing no emotion.

"We're like a family," Rachel retorts, trying to gauge his attitude this morning.

In silence, they stand in front of the elevator. A silent crowd occupies the chairs and armchairs in the area. The doors open and three masked nurses pushing an empty hospital bed exit, followed by about ten people, signalling the start of visiting hours for hospitalized patients.

Being right at the elevator entrance when it opens, Rachel and Wang don't have time to back away as the crowd invades the lobby.

Rachel's initial thought is shock. "Holy shit!"

When two visitors rush out of the elevator, they trip over Rachel and Wang, causing the four of them to fall to the floor. A brief commotion ensues as some try to help the fallen, while others laugh at the accident, trying not to make any noise.

Detective Chong, coming running from the room, approaches the crowd, looks, and doesn't understand what happened, but at a glance, he sees Rachel and Wang entering the elevator.

"What happened?" Rachel asks Wang inside the elevator, laughing and wiping off her jeans.

He doesn't respond, his face showing repulsion.

Rachel stays silent, watching and thinking, *He looks like someone who ate something and didn't like it.*

As she finishes cleaning herself, Rachel feels a weight in the right pocket of her blazer. She puts her hand in her pocket and feels a cellphone. She refrains from taking it out, to avoid attracting attention, and looks at Wang, who continues to clean his suit.

"Are you okay?" he asks.

"I fell in the chaos, but I'm okay." She laughs, showing no concern. Rachel tells him she needs to go to the bathroom on the ground floor and asks him to wait for her in the car.

When they arrive on the ground floor, he walks to the exit of the hospital as Rachel enters the restroom. After taking the strange cellphone out of her blazer pocket in the bathroom, she confirms it's turned off. She puts it into her bag, deciding that she will only turn it on and call when she arrives at the hotel. As she leaves the hospital, she tries to remember which people came to her when she fell and helped her up. She concludes, however, that she can't remember.

On the way to the tourist port area, Wang stays quiet as he drives.

"Where are we going? Is the port far from the hospital?" Rachel asks.

"No, why the rush?" Wang, still nervous about what happened in the hospital, looks at her and answers with a hint of harshness.

Baffled by his response, Rachel tries to smooth over the situation. "I'm not in a hurry; I just wanted to know the way," she replies and turns her face to the window, looking at the shops on the avenue.

He remains silent, his attention on the traffic.

Rachel ignores Wang. She remembers the doctor's words. He mentioned Wednesday, which implies that David may not leave the hospital on Sunday. She calculates the preparations she'll have to make. Will Superintendent Bo allow them to travel? Do they need court approval?

Showing no emotion, she decides it needs immediate attention.

Wang drives in silence, sometimes casting a glance at Rachel. Embarrassed by his fall in the hospital, he can't believe he let this happen. Furious, he blames the hospital staff, ignoring the fact that he and Rachel blocked the elevator entrance. He parks the car in the private area of the port after entering through the employee gate. Catching Rachel's attention, Wang announces, "We're here."

* * *

At the hospital, Detective Chong, upon hearing the confusion in the hallway, leaves the room to see what happened. People talking is not normal, as the hospital is usually a place of silence.

David, without caring about the situation, watches the detective leave the room. He knows there will be more questions when he returns. Today, he feels clearer and ready to face any uncertainties. The doctor assured him that the surgery on his arm was minor and would only leave a slight scar. Although his stomach surgery was more complex, recovery should be quick. The risk of infection persists, but he shows no signs of a fever. David sees it all as just another life experience. However, Michael's absence is consuming his mind, and he is worried that the detective won't talk to him.

Troubled by the doubts surrounding his friend, David asks himself, *Why did Michael run away instead of helping and calling an ambulance?* He knows the police will scrutinize Michael's actions. Reflecting, he cannot understand Michael's decisions. Where is he now? Even his mother had no news. Who is helping him hide?

The detective re-enters the room, approaching the bed.

"Good morning, David. How are you feeling today?" he asks, and with a smile on the corner of his mouth, he repeats the same questions as when he entered the room. He takes the chair in the corner and sits down next to the bed.

"Much better than yesterday, detective. What's the news?" David inquires, staring at Chong.

Chong takes a deep breath, hands David his cellphone, wallet, documents, and money. He looks back toward the door and says, "Nothing much."

David purses his lips, pulls out his phone, and sees that it still has a charge. Then he opens his wallet and checks the documents. He turns to the detective. "How is it possible for someone to disappear like this? Family and friends being monitored, without money and documents... How can you not find him?"

"Someone must be helping him hide," replies the detective, making notes on a pad of paper and returning the same look to David.

"Did you come here because you think I know something?" David questions.

"We are monitoring his mother and the hotel staff with whom he was closest. We could track the last cellphone signal north of Shanghai by crossing several towers, but all connections disappeared after that. The battery must be dead," the detective explains.

David ponders this, as he didn't realize his friend was carrying his phone.

"The doctor will discharge me on Wednesday at the latest and I'm going to the hotel with Rachel. Maybe I'll stay here in Shanghai a few more days because you're going to need me," David states.

"No. I believe... the police no longer need you. What we have will solve the case. The criminal case and investigation will not stop. Right now, we just need to find Michael. However, because of this, I doubt you will travel soon. You will need judicial authorization, but because you will have to stay here a while longer..." The detective suggests, "I believe that you and Rachel will need my help in the investigation you are doing." His suspicions have not decreased.

"We came here because of Operation Portugal, to help Chief Bo," David says without looking at the detective, shifting his body to get more comfortable on the bed.

"Blah, blah, blah, David. Only Chief Bo can turn a blind eye, leaving you free to investigate the story of a police officer killed by the Yakuza, which... because we don't know why... is the same hotel where your friend works. Go ahead, tell me the true story." The detective provokes David.

"You're confusing everything. Michael works at this hotel, but he didn't even know about the police officer who died there. I don't know what you're trying to invent; you're imagining things that aren't happening. He's innocent in this story; he just defended me, and what happened was self-defence. I'm not lying. I don't understand why he ran away." David shakes his head, looking at the sheet, unfazed by the detective's ease in summing up an entire situation in a single sentence.

Chong, staying silent, observes his reactions and decides to threaten him. "David, you can continue with this story, but I'm going to dig deep into all the answers; I want to hear the truth. If you're hiding anything from me about Michael, I'll find out."

"I don't know what you're talking about," reiterates David, speaking in a higher-than-normal tone of voice.

At this moment, the nurse enters the room and mutters to the patient, "Time for your medicine."

Chong stands up, picks up the chair, and puts it in place. "Thank you, David. I'll contact you."

"What the hell was that?" David mutters, frustrated, and looks at the detective with hatred as Chong leaves the room.

The nurse stands in front of him with his pills in a small cup.

"Please excuse me," he says to the attendant, positioning himself on the bed to receive the medicine.

She doesn't understand what David said to the detective, but she keeps smiling and hands him the three pills to swallow.

After she leaves the room, he pulls out his phone and writes a message to Rachel: *I need you here. Come as fast as you can. I'm fine. It's about our reason to be here.*

Lying in bed, he remembers Michael from the few happy days they spent together. A chilly wind enters the room, making David cover himself with the blanket on the bed. He relaxes and sleeps.

* * *

Wang bought this tour from a specific company due to its shorter duration. September, with the city's pleasant temperature, is the ideal month for this trip. The fifty-minute route covers the Bund, the Huangpu Bridge, and then returns along the opposite bank of the river.

Rachel enjoys the guide explaining and showing them the curiosities, as she skims the message that arrived on her cellphone. Sitting next to Rachel, Wang tells stories of places he has visited and tells her the rich history of the river, showing her the places that have transformed over the years. He mentions that night tours offer an unparalleled experience with dinner, music, and dancing. Although Rachel listens, her focus remains on her phone and the message she received, masking her distress.

As the tour draws to a close, Wang's behaviour shows his hope for a romantic rekindling, although Rachel has clarified that they are just friends and nothing more will happen. He remembers a moment in a restaurant when he struggled to control his emotions. Watching Rachel, he reflects on self-sufficiency and independence, watching her interact with others on the boat and taking photos. Wang struggles with feelings of envy, longing for the same self-confidence. When she sees him looking at her, she nods, smiling. Wang approaches her, expecting an intimate hug. Rachel, always independent, returns to looking at the Pudong neighbourhood and continues to capture images on her cellphone.

Wang pulls back, then again approaches, saying, "I overheard the conversation you had with David, and I can help you. I can have my jet take you to London. What do you think?"

Surprised, Rachel turns to him, trying to understand why he is offering the private plane. "Thank you, but this decision isn't only mine. David is the one who will decide. I'll talk about your offer and then I'll let you know," Rachel replies with a smile.

All confident, he tells her that after the boat ride, they will have lunch in a typical Vietnamese restaurant.

"Sorry, Wang, but I can't have lunch with you today. I committed myself to other tasks. Can we do this another day?"

Perplexed by her "No," he smiles, giving her a sharp look, and says, "I understand."

At that moment, the boat anchors at the pier of the Bund, and the two hold onto the bow beams because of the swing and the approaching beat on the dock.

Wang helps her out of the boat, and they walk to the parking lot in silence. As they approach the vehicle, a slender oriental woman with long hair runs toward them.

Holding a child's hand, she screams, saying, "Wonjy, where is Wonjy?"

Rachel witnesses the commotion and concludes, from the woman's pleas in Mandarin, that a man named Wonjy has disappeared. The desperate woman claims to be the child's mother and Wonjy's wife and insists that Wang knows his location. Wang responds with a firm denial, urging her to leave. The tears of the woman and child flow. Trying to calm her down, Wang offers money. Receiving no response, he whispers something close to her, throws a stack of bills to the kneeling woman and, saying nothing else, returns to the car with a frightening expression on his face.

The scene shocks some passengers who also got off the tour boat and are walking nearby.

The two get into the car, and he drives at high speed out of the harbour.

"Who is Wonjy?" Rachel asks Wang, who is staring at the avenue in front of him.

"I don't know who Wonjy is," he replies, muttering in Mandarin.

"Poor woman, she's looking for her husband. She seemed so desperate." Rachel looks at him, trying to see some reaction.

Wang doesn't answer.

"Where do you want to go?" he asks in a harsh voice, convinced that the woman destroyed the day.

"To the hotel, please," she responds, analyzing the situation and his attitude.

After arriving at the hotel, Wang doesn't get out of the car. He looks at her and informs her he will call tomorrow.

She opens the door of the vehicle, looks at him with a smile on her face, and says, "It was a glorious morning, very educational. I'll wait for your call."

Upon arriving in her room, she remembers David's message. Taking her cellphone from her bag, she writes she will be at the hospital in an hour.

Sitting in the armchair, gathering her reports and iPad, she orders a taxi from reception. After sniffing her blouse, she swaps it for a fresher one. Checking her phone, she notices that the temperature has risen to thirty-three degrees Celsius. Reception calls to let her know the taxi has arrived. Before leaving, she turns on the air conditioning.

Upon getting into the taxi, she instructs the driver, "Central Hospital, please."

* * *

Wang, unhappy with the situation he experienced on the tourist pier, drives to the apartment. On the way, he calls Hui, demanding to know where he is. Hui informs Wang that he went to take groceries and money to his mother and aunt.

The boss orders him to come to his residence; they need to talk without wasting time.

While at Wang's mother's house, Hui enjoys coffee and freshly baked snacks prepared by Meixiu Gubei. Even though he senses something wrong in the boss's tone, he still finishes his snacks. He then hands Meixiu a bundle of money for medicine and emergencies. After a sincere thank you and hug from her, he kisses the women goodbye and leaves, closing the door behind him.

Hui reflects on Wang's strained voice and approaches his car parked at the gas station. Knowing that Wang was going for a walk with the woman from the hotel, he wonders what is going on… often thoughtless actions frustrate him. Some shit went down. Hui knows he is the one who has to solve the problems that Wang creates. Analyzing, the friend understands that Wang's forced sociability contradicts his inherent anti-social nature. In everyday life, this attitude leads to erratic behaviour, leaving those close to him confused.

The boss uses the act of charity as a facade to get involved with society. Fortunately, people don't notice and don't examine his lack of genuine emotion because having intimate relationships is sporadic. Hui recognizes Wang understands his own cruel behaviour. However, Wang's continued disrespect and violation of the rights of others, especially those closest to him, angers Hui. He recognizes that in public, Wang can be persuasive when necessary.

Driving the car, Hui wonders aloud, "What did Wang see in that woman? He was always anti-social. Now this…" He is not agreeing with Wang's attitude. "I always thought women would make him uncomfortable. She doesn't know how destructive he is."

Hui struggles to understand his boss's actions, reflecting on the years they spent together, filled with a mix of pity, fear, favour, and understanding. Despite enduring Wang's aggression, Hui finds the events of Wang's youth traumatic. His mother, sick from drugs and drinking, is on the verge of death because of cancer, and there is the unresolved trauma of his father's murder when he was just a child. This succession of tragedies forces Wang to harden and build a wall against any emotions, transforming him into an internalized and inflexible monster.

"Now he's in love," Hui says to himself and laughs.

Stopping the car at the traffic light, he watches people crossing the avenue. Thoughtful, he affirms to himself, "This will not end well."

He enters the building's garage and parks the car next to the Mercedes. He doesn't get out of the vehicle just yet and remembers what happened four days ago, lamenting, "Poor Wonjy."

After a few minutes, Hui exits the car and heads toward the private elevator.

* * *

At the fast-paced hospital, Rachel enters David's room.

"You took your time," he says, distressed.

"Oh, bloody hell, what's going on, David?" she asks, startled, not understanding what happened.

"You can't imagine what that detective told me. Well, he suggested this…" Moving around in bed, he tries to sit in a more comfortable position.

"What was this?" she asks in a stern voice, looking at David's face.

"He insinuates Michael is involved in the Yakuza boss's story and that we are investigating Ronaldo's death at the hotel. The connection between our supposed investigation, the death, and the attempt to kill me was suggested by him. Also, he proposed I am keeping Michael hidden. It's all nonsense." David is talking at high speed about Detective Chong's assumptions, his words confusing due to his anxiety.

"Okay. I understand nothing. Start all over again. Let's go in parts."

"He mentions it is strange that Chief Bo would let us reopen the case of the death of that former officer linked to the Yakuza. Michael works at the same hotel was too much of a coincidence approaching a breaking point."

"He's not right. I may not like to admit it, but coincidences can happen. This detective is mistaken," she says, echoing David's stress and worry.

David stares at her without trusting the words.

"Why did he bring this up?" she asks and opens the window shutter, letting the sun into the room.

"I asked him if he was going to need me because I'm going to be discharged on Sunday or Wednesday. He was very adamant when he said no but said that he believed we would need him for our investigation here in Shanghai. I had already lost my temper and kept insisting that we came to help in Operation Portugal." He sinks down on the bed as if exhausted, the fatigue showing in his voice.

"He didn't believe what you said?" she asks.

"He didn't believe me and then told that story." David gestures to Rachel and makes a circle with his hands to suggest she check the room.

Rachel nods and although she doesn't have the proper equipment in her bag, she inspects the area for wiretaps and cameras. She checks under the bed, behind the furniture, examining the flowers in the vase, the painting, and the walls. When she finishes her search, she gives David a thumbs-up, showing that the room appears free of any devices.

"The detective is the head of the Shanghai homicide department; he knows his job well. Trust him to find Michael and sort out this mess. We need to get back to London, treat you, and reconnect with your family. They're worried too. We have our own matters to attend to. Chief Bo is aware of our mission and has given us leave. Whatever we can't resolve now, we will find a way later. If we need to come back, we will," Rachel assures David as she continues wandering around the furniture, checking light fixtures in the room.

He nods. "As soon as I leave the hospital, I will try to find Michael."

"You're going to go back to London and go to an excellent hospital. We have to go home, and everything will clear up," Rachel says, struggling to calm him down.

"Okay. Let's go home and then see what to do," he agrees, although not convincingly.

"Wang offered his jet. What do you think?"

"Wow, rich friends," David says in surprise.

"He's interested in something else, but I've clarified that we're just friends now. What happened, happened, and it's over." She sits in the armchair.

"Oh! So, it happened?" her partner says with a smile.

"David!" Rachel looks stern, but with a sly smile on her lips.

"I get it, but I guarantee he's in love."

"Forget it," she says.

"Nope. Don't forget. I accept the jet; it will save a lot of money. Thank him for me."

"Okay. I'll let him know to have it ready for Wednesday afternoon. Okay?"

"Great," he confirms.

Rachel brings a chair closer to him, stating that she needs to discuss something serious. Her cousin's death and the funeral arranged by her father in Canada are the topics of her conversation. While she acknowledges receiving calls and messages, she admits she hasn't contacted her mother or uncle yet. When she finishes telling the news, the tears don't come, but a deep sadness surrounds her.

David reflects on the emotional turmoil Rachel must have felt upon learning of the death of someone she considered as close as a sister. Years earlier, she had told him how her parents separated. John, her father, remarried and built a new life. Her mother, looking for a fresh start, moved to Toronto, drawn by her deep friendship with her ex-husband's brother's wife. Her mother's friend succumbed to cancer, leading her mother to marry Rachel's uncle. Family tensions and career plans drove a wedge between Rachel and her cousin as they grew up, following the unexpected union with her uncle. The relationship with her mother became distant.

"Can you acknowledge the fact?" David asks.

"I am fine. Despite the losses…" Rachel hides her struggle as she smiles and mentions that today she woke up feeling much better and tomorrow she will be excellent.

"Okay, anything you need, I'm here to help," David says. He understands that no words can bring her comfort in a situation like this. He understands the difficulty that suffering individuals have with letting go when they're alone every day.

Rachel hugs her friend and puts her head in his lap. "Wang doesn't inspire trust, even though it seems instinctual. His look, he's distance from everything… something is amiss." She grimaces, moving her nose and turning her mouth to the right.

"If you think it's better not to take the jet," he suggests.

Rachel looks at him. "No… that's not it… I don't know. The jet will help. It's me… I know myself. Sometimes I feel it with certain people, but let it go. I have a lot to prepare for our trip."

"Decide how you think it should be done," he advises.

"I'll think about it," she replies.

"He seems like a nice guy," her partner comments and starts laughing.

Rachel looks at him, pulling the phone someone put there that morning from her pocket.

"What is this? A new phone?" he inquires.

She explains what happened at the elevator door when they were leaving the floor. She describes feeling a weight in her blazer pocket and that was when she discovered the cellphone. "I haven't called yet."

"Call! You're killing me with curiosity. I don't know how you can stay so calm about some things," David says, shifting in bed and groaning in pain.

She calls and confirms that she has no missed calls, just a written message: *We need to meet. Y.*

David and Rachel say together, "Yazuo."

27

Surprise!

The elevator door opens, and Wang enters the living room of his apartment. A white silk curtain sways as the wind blows through the open windows. The sun illuminates the room. He walks without the normal rush of everyday life toward the breeze and takes a deep breath. Still furious, he picks up a small sculpture on the coffee table and throws it at the kitchen wall, smashing it into countless pieces.

"That woman ruined my day!" he yells, looking into the large mirror in the living room.

"Did you see Rachel's face? She heard the conversation. She tried to understand what that bitch was saying in Mandarin and watched my reactions," he vents to someone imaginary.

He picks up the ashtray on the table and throws it at the mirror, missing and hitting the nearby wall.

"Who does that woman think she is? How did she know I went to the port? It can't be a coincidence!" Wang shouts, questioning himself until he stops in front of the window and fixes his gaze on the boats on the Huangpu River. He closes his eyes for a few minutes and feels the warmth of the sun on his body, calming him down.

He grabs his phone from the back pocket of his jeans and calls Hui again.

"I need you now! Come to the apartment," he orders and hangs up before the manager can give any answer.

As he lies on the couch, confused thoughts flood his mind. How will he face Rachel? Memories flood in. Hui mentioned visiting his mother's house, delivering groceries, medicine, and money over the years. After Li's death, he distanced himself from his mother and aunt—because of their accusatory looks and because of his increasing commitments to the Tong. "Success requires sacrifices," he says out loud in a raised voice.

With no regrets, he accomplished his goals, but he acknowledges he cannot heal his mother, and his aunt no longer has affection for him. She preaches Buddhism but doesn't follow it, often quoting Buddha to make him feel responsible for past actions. Dismissing her attempts to blame him, he entrusted the deliveries to Hui.

Hui valued both women, delivering provisions every weekend, savouring the family bond he never had. He was raised by a woman who claimed to be his grandmother. His days revolved around arduous work in the fields and selling vegetables in the city. But one day he disappeared. Alone, Hui turned to life in the city, resorting to theft and deceit, and in the end joined a gang where he met Wang. Years later, he searched for his "grandmother" but found the place abandoned and she was nowhere to be found. He never went back.

* * *

In the city centre, at the hospital, David sleeps in the bed and Rachel naps in the armchair.

She wakes up, lowers the blinds, grabs her belongings, and leaves in silence, closing the door behind her. Heading toward the elevator, she sees the receptionist focused on the computer and starts a conversation in broken Mandarin.

"Thank you for helping me out this morning when I fell," Rachel says. The attendant looks serious.

"Oh, were you one of the people who fell?" the nurse asks, getting up from her chair and pointing toward the elevator. "I'm sorry, it wasn't me who helped you. I'm not allowed to leave my post. I can't get out of here and help lift anyone up." She sits back down and watches Rachel.

"Oh, I got the impression that two nurses helped us," Rachel says with a sweet look, trying to keep the conversation going.

"Let me remember… hmm…" The receptionist thinks, looking toward the elevators, and says, "There were two nurses sitting in the room. They were expecting some patient. The uniforms were for private nurses, and they were the ones who helped you. I didn't see them after the confusion."

Rachel thanks her and enters the empty elevator, speculating about the possibility that one of those individuals placed the cellphone in her jacket pocket.

Upon leaving the hospital, she hails a taxi and directs the driver to the hotel. Resting her head against the back seat, she gazes at the car's roof and realizes her hand is shaking and her stomach is rumbling with hunger. She takes a deep breath, aware that she is tired and stressed.

Upon arrival, she glances at the reception clock and gets startled. It's 4:00 p.m. and time has passed quickly. She asks the receptionist, "Anything?"

"No, Ms. Rachel," the attendant replies, looking underneath and in the drawers of the counter to ensure there's nothing for the guest.

She thanks him and heads toward the elevator.

*   *   *

At Wang's residence, Hui enters the private elevator. Upon entering, he notices that one of the glass windows is open. He gets curious when he sees the curtains swaying with the breeze and the sun spreading throughout the room. He murmurs, "That's a miracle, without air conditioning."

Wang stands with his back to the room, watching the river and ignoring the manager's arrival.

"Boss, are you okay?"

"You said you were in control of everything and that no one would look for those men."

"Guaranteed, why? Did something happen?" the manager asks.

Wang turns and watches him for a few seconds that seem to stretch out. He sits on the couch and informs Hui about what happened at the tourist pier that morning.

"I didn't know Wonjy had a wife and child. We've known him for years, and he never talked about it. What do you want me to do?" Hui continues talking, trying to show no nervousness.

"Make that woman shut up. From the way she spoke, she seemed to know Wonjy's steps. See what she knows and put an end to this problem, anticipate what to do," Wang says with blood in his eyes.

"I'll find out what happened," the manager replies, patting the hems of his pants with his hands, as if cleaning them. He looks at the shards of glass from the ashtray scattered across the wooden floor, predicting problems.

"Hui, I don't want trouble," the boss says without taking his eyes off him.

"There won't be any problems. I'll solve it, easy."

Wang gets up from the couch, ignoring the manager, walks toward the open window, and lights a cigarette.

"That's it? I'm already going. Oh, your mother and aunt have received the provisions, and they are fine. Anything, I'll have my phone," Hui says, walking toward the elevator.

When the door to the elevator opens, Wang commands, "Do a complete maintenance check on the jet; I might need it."

The manager remains silent, entering the elevator, allowing the door to close behind him. Looking in the mirror, he sees strands of white hair framing his face. He ponders, feeling like he's turning grey, which is very early for his age. Tiredness often overwhelms him, and he has no enthusiasm for talking to his old friend. Gathering himself together, he says out loud in a resolute voice, "I can't think of it that way. It's just another day of stress." The elevator door opens, and he heads to the car.

Wang admires the scene through the window, but he has noticed something different in Hui's attitude. "He's not as efficient as he was in the past; soon I'll need to replace him."

*　*　*

At the hotel, Rachel enters her room and examines the reports spread out on the table. Full of hope, she believes that in these pages lies the key to Ronaldo's mysterious death. Settling into the armchair, she looks at her iPad and starts writing her next tasks:

1) Secure an apartment or house for a month (discuss with David because of the delay in judicial release)

2) Discharge from hospital; consider hiring a physical therapist (check with doctor first)

3) Coordinate with Chief Bo on the investigation and verify when the partner testifies (Do I need a lawyer present?)

4) Schedule a meeting with Michael's mother

5) Cancel the jet with Wang

6) Y (decide the next step of the device)

7) Contact Detective Chong

She pauses, reviews her list, and mutters out loud, "I feel like I'm forgetting something, but I can't put my finger on it right now." Reviewing the list, she pauses at the mention of Detective Chong, muttering, "Could he pose a problem? Would Michael lie to David? Does David want to stay in Shanghai because he knows Michael's secret hideout? Was Michael part of

Ronaldo's death? His presence in that hotel seems too coincidental." She frowns, inhaling with concern. "Did I miss anything in my investigation?"

She fiddles with the papers on the table and wonders, *What connects Michael's disappearance and Ronaldo's death?*

Lost in the questions and with the phone on silent, she doesn't hear it ring six times. After a while, she gets up from the chair, yawning, and picks up the device from the bed. She looks at the screen and sees Alex's name appearing. Rachel answers. "Sorry I didn't answer sooner."

Alex says he learned of her cousin's death and asks if she needs any help in Canada.

Rachel explains her father took care of everything.

Alex wants to know about David because he has spoken to Superintendent Bo. He asks when the two will return to London.

"David leaves the hospital next week, and we'll be back soon to London," she informs, showing no emotion at all.

He stays silent.

Rachel doesn't desire to be distant like last time and asks if his health has improved.

The head of the Firm explains everything is going as God wants, and he left the hospital a week ago. The doctors have warned him he doesn't have long to live, but he wants to get everything in order.

She doesn't go into details. Disguising what she heard, she says that he will have a long life and miss the times she worked at the Firm.

Alex feels no enthusiasm in her voice. He thanks her, they say goodbye, and each hangs up the phone.

Rachel has always admired her former boss; their bond was always professional, never matching the depth Ronaldo shared with him. Their relationship went from work to a genuine connection full of confidences. Alex supported Rachel when she needed it, but they were never real friends.

Now, she doubts Operation Container #2, the story of the flash drive, and the unsolved mystery surrounding Mr. Chan's death. With the recent death of her cousin and David's accident, she becomes suspicious and wonders, *Why did he call now? And even asked when we'll return to London? Why did he need to talk to Boss Bo? Nosey man.*

She goes to the fridge, grabs a bottle of water, and continues talking to herself. "Okay, none of this is suspicious, but I don't like inquisitions, especially when the person already knows everything and keeps asking questions. It looks like he lost something and is trying to get information.

"Oh, bloody hell." She remembers she needs to get the signal tracker.

She doesn't recall where she stored it and searches for the device. After contemplating for a few seconds, she heads to the closet and peeks inside the suitcase. Opening it, she finds the spy bug detector. She tracks the main room and bathroom, checks the telephone, sockets, chandelier, and lamp. Fatigued, she confirms the lack of anything suspicious in her room. Taking a deep breath, she puts the device inside her bag. Rachel decides that tomorrow she will inspect David's hospital room again.

* * *

On the other side of the city, Hui is upset when he departs from Wang's apartment. For a long time, he knew Wonjy had a woman he lived with. Knowing his boss would complain, he chose not to tell him, but he also didn't expect Wonjy's wife to come looking for him. To ensure that no one notices, he must take responsibility for cleaning up this mess.

Driving and thinking about what the boss told him, Hui goes to the old warehouse, a place where port workers relax by having a beer and chatting after a day of work. Along the way, he hopes an idea might come.

Wang's company offers free drinks to its registered port employees. Tables, chairs, and a bar are available at the barn for the port workers to enjoy their drinks and chat. The company offers two free beers to employees who show their identification. This gesture, designed by the boss, not only earned him his employees' praise but also allowed him to monitor general conversations and gossip. Drinks are free, conversations are lively, and the atmosphere is light. While some employees make it a daily ritual, others go straight home. Although Wang designed this meeting place, he does not visit it. However, the manager is a regular, and his words and actions carry weight among the employees.

Hui parks the car outside the barn and walks in, greeting and hugging the employees. At the counter, he asks for a beer. Three men sitting at a table call him over. He walks up to them, greets them, and settles into his chair. He fills the glass with beer and makes a wordless toast. They raise their glasses, not knowing what the greeting was, and drink.

Wei is one man at the table and has been working with Hui for a few years. He says that the day at the port was heavy and complains that the company needs more employees in the loading of goods. He explains that today the ship had a delayed departure, which caused the transport of the products to be paralyzed.

"Hmm." Hui sighs and takes another sip of beer.

Another man named Feng, sitting next to Wei, comments: "It's been a while since Wonjy, Young, and Jie came to collaborate with us. Are they still active?"

"Wonjy went to Hong Kong to visit family. Young and Jie help with the cranes on the other side of the pier," Hui informs the men and finishes drinking what's left in his glass.

"Anyway, it's good for you to know you're missing people there," Wei says again, and the manager pours another glass of beer.

"That's easy, I can fix that. See you tomorrow," Hui says, getting up from his chair and putting the empty bottle on the counter.

"Hui, did you say that Wonjy is in Hong Kong?" Wei asks.

"That's what he said Tuesday. Why?" the manager asks from the counter and stares at him.

"Weird… yesterday his wife was at the gate of the boarding pier. I don't know what she was doing there," Wei says.

"I'm going… tomorrow we'll talk. Goodnight to those who stay." Hui pretends to ignore what Wei said about Wonjy's wife and walks out of the warehouse, waving to those who stayed.

On the way home, the manager thinks about Wei's words, seeing problems ahead, and changes his plans. Upon reaching home, he observes the street devoid of any streetlights. Only inside the houses is there light. As he passes in front of his house, he sees several vehicles taking up all the spaces.

Hui expresses frustration about the crowded street as he parks the car five houses away from his. "Shit, this street is always crowded."

He enters his garage, picks up the motorcycle, and pushes out without making a noise. A block away, he climbs onto the motorcycle and disappears into the darkness. After a thirty-minute drive north of Shanghai, he finds himself in an agricultural neighbourhood. The dense forest, combined with the surrounding darkness, can disorient anyone.

The bike jolts on the unpaved road, but the firm, dry clay ensures a smoother ride. He observes that the houses are at considerable distances from each other. Parking his motorcycle against a tree off the road, he goes in search of Wonjy's farm. The silence is engulfing, allowing him to sneak closer to the house. By hiding near the front door, he finds protection in the darkness within and outside the house. He throws a rock into a can, causing a distant dog to bark. However, it soon calms down, restoring silence.

The door opens, revealing a slender woman with her hair falling freely down her back. When she leaves the house, Hui, from the shadows, recognizes her. His actions are quick. In one swift motion, he grabs her neck and tilts her head. A chilling crack cuts through the air, and she falls, lifeless, into his arms. Without making a sound, he carries her back inside, placing her on the cold kitchen floor. As his eyes adjust to the dim light, a soft glow coming from a half-open door catches his attention. From the back of that room, the voice of a child trembles, the weight of innocence and loss intertwined in the call: "Mom, Mom..."

Hui moves toward the kitchen and hides behind the door. The little girl enters the room calling for her mother, and he attacks the same way he did with the woman. Without mercy, he breaks the child's neck and lays her next to the other body on the ground.

Inside the house, he searches each room, driven by a purpose that not even he understands. When he sees a broom leaning against the wall of the room, he sweeps up the dirt tracks left by his shoes. He notices the house's simple but immaculate decor, with no clutter. His gaze turns to the photographs of Wonjy with his wife and child hanging on the walls of the house and on the bedroom furniture.

Returning to the kitchen, he positions the woman and child near the gas cylinder. Knowing what he is doing, he turns on the four burners on the stove, letting the gas flow. A memory nudges him; he remembers a faint glow from the couple's bedroom. Upon re-entering the room, he confirms his memory: a solitary candle still burning. He takes the candle and places it under the window curtain, watching the flames spread. He calculates and estimates that the entire house will be on fire in a few minutes. After closing the bedroom door, he leaves the impending hell behind.

Timing the explosion, he steps only on bushes and grass to obscure his tracks. He climbs on the motorcycle and speeds up along the dirt road. A few minutes after leaving, an explosion echoes in the distance, but he remains focused, without looking back. Upon reaching the avenue, Hui slows down, making a peaceful journey back to his house. Forty minutes later, he enters the garage with the motorcycle. He takes a black trash bag that he always keeps under the tool bench, takes off his clothes, and places them in the bag, including the shoes he is wearing.

Leaving the garage, a noise coming from the back door of the house catches his attention. He pauses in the garden, looking at the vast expanse of the sky, where the stars shine without a care. The serenity of the night seduces. He thinks about lying down on the grass and enjoying the profound silence that surrounds the neighbourhood. Planning to do it after dinner, he looks at the time—it's 8:30 p.m. Everything seems calm, suggesting that his family may already be asleep.

As he opens the door, an unexpected burst of light floods his senses. The silence disappears when a chorus of "Happy Birthday!" bursts through from about twenty people with their loud voices. Taken by surprise, Hui's knees buckle, and he sits, perplexed, on the cold kitchen floor. This was the last thing he expected: a room full of familiar faces: brothers-in-law, sisters-in-law, neighbours, and appearing amid the jubilant crowd, his wife and children rushing to his aid with open gestures, hugs, and faces lit up with joy.

Speechless, a wave of emotions washes over him. Gratitude. Love. Surprise. Hugging everyone, his shocked expression turns into a sincere smile, reflecting the warmth of the unexpected celebration around him. Hui forgot that today was his birthday.

At this moment, he remembers he is naked.

28

Recklessness

Rachel returns from her breakfast in the hotel restaurant. She has lived alone for years, but today she remembers she has David and Tyler. Her cellphone rings as she opens the door and enters the room. Happily, she responds to her DRT partner: "Is Mozart's nanny still going strong?"

"Good evening. Is everything okay?" Tyler speaks in an apprehensive tone.

"Okay. Tell me some good news." Rachel coughs.

"Are you sick?" her partner asks.

"That cough is nothing, just carpet dust. A little stressed, maybe, and tired," she responds, coughing again.

"I can't imagine what you are going through these days. Please, take care of yourself."

"What's new?" Rachel asks again, composing herself.

Tyler says the company that hired them before the trip has a bit of a strange history. On the day of the meeting, the CEO informed them that someone had stolen the cargo in the containers at the Port of London that they had brought from Shanghai.

"Okay, I remember. Did something happen?" Rachel asks with a hint of concern in her voice.

Her companion reveals, in a serious tone, another layer of the situation. "My informants discovered that the company is Triad-owned in Shanghai, with connections to London. I can guarantee that if it's not the Triad, it will be another gang working together, and I'm sure of the information."

Rachel knows most of her partner's informants, especially those at the port. Her partner has cultivated a network of trusted sources over the years through friendships and occasional "gifts." This network includes police officers, warehouse workers, and directors' secretaries, many of whom Rachel knows.

Tyler reports, "My people informed me that the company is a shell and does not have a registered physical headquarters in London. They have three rented loading and unloading warehouses and a contract at the port. I asked the CEO, and the excuse he gave was that they would soon rent a HQ. I am waiting…"

"Did you confirm this data?" Rachel asks.

Tyler reports that the contract phone number became inactive after a week, and during the last meeting with the CEO, there were concerns about this issue. The CEO offered no explanation, only asserting the presence of inaccurate information in the contract. However, after persistent questioning, he eventually provided him with his personal cellphone number.

"Rachel, I've been a cop my whole life," he says. "This company is not legal in London. I believe we lost something along the way in this story."

"What else did you get?" Rachel asks, processing Tyler's information as she writes it down.

Tyler warns Rachel that more serious matters are to come, as he has begun consultations with contacts in Canada. He adds, "Informants have assured us that the proper company and owner are in Shanghai. The individual who presented himself to the DRT is not the owner. We understand the CEO does not need to own the business. The curious thing is that this company belongs to one of the biggest gangs in Shanghai and works in collaboration with the Triad. The boss is a millionaire playboy named Wang, who also has a reputation for helping the city's less fortunate—like a Robin Hood of the Chinese mafia."

Rachel sits stunned, trying to absorb the startling revelation.

"Did you hear me?"

"Yes," Rachel replies, confused, seeing scenes with Wang at the hotel gatehouse, in the restaurants, in the apartment, on the boat… At that moment, her eyes fill with tears of anger.

Unable to see her reaction, Tyler continues with his report. "The story of this man, Wang, or so he calls himself, is that his business grew so much that he began trading outside of China, including places like British Columbia in Canada, Barcelona, Spain, and here in London. I'll contact my agency today or tomorrow to obtain and gather more information. Another thing to note is that a Triad gang here in London led the assault on the port. It's a battle between big players… the local mafia didn't agree to be part of the deal Wang struck with the Triad in Shanghai. This robbery was a struggle for power and dominance in the area. Do you understand?"

"I got it," Rachel says, almost whispering, disappointed in herself.

"Did you hear me?" Tyler asks again in a loud voice, agitated at not hearing Rachel's voice.

She composes herself and says, "I heard. We met a Wang here in Shanghai. It could be the same person, I don't know... Could you get the name of the company in China that did this export?"

"Of course. I have yet to receive the port clearance document from the police investigators; it will contain the name of the company. Come to think of it... with David's problem and the investigation, how will you know if this company that hired us here in London is part of the Chinese mafia?" Tyler asks, worried about so many things happening at once.

Rachel remembers the possibility of her phone being tapped by the police. Therefore, she must be careful with what she says. She says, "Don't worry, there's an excellent detective who is taking care of David's case. He is a friend, and I'll ask for his help."

"Okay. I'm at ease knowing that you have the support of excellent local police. Anything important, I'll let you know. Kisses, *minha bonita Brasileira*." Tyler hangs up the phone.

Rachel, stunned, stares at the ceiling, thinking, *My God, what the heck did I do? It can't be the same Wang.*

Even after the call, Rachel knows that her duty must come first. She gets out of bed, pushing herself, aware of how serious the situation could be, and carries out the tasks she had set out to do that day. Her demeanour is imperturbable, almost clinical, when she goes to the hospital to examine her partner's room. She makes a mental note to look for a real estate agent on her cellphone. If David agrees, she will rent an apartment as soon as possible to save on high hotel fees.

Besides all these responsibilities, she also visits the mall. She has been putting off buying new clothes, but today she is determined to go shopping. As she contemplates Tyler's revelations, she closes her eyes for a moment and mumbles, "Oh my God."

With a sense of urgency, she finishes getting dressed, picks up the phone in the room, and calls the front desk to order a taxi.

* * *

Forty minutes later, in the hospital, David wakes up. With the help of the nurses, he gathers the strength to get out of bed. Walking supported, but with determination, he crosses the room alone and walks down the corridor twice. The previous night he had received his painkiller, and now he just needs to take the prescribed medicine for infection and treatment. During his first walks, doctors suggest he be careful and remember to take the recommended precautions and not exert himself too much.

When Rachel enters the room and sees him standing, her face lights up with joy. "Wow, look at you. How do you feel?" she asks with happiness in her eyes.

"Look, I'm almost dancing," David replies, cracking a smile as he tries out some cautious, swaying dance moves.

"Careful," exclaims his companion, alarmed, moving toward him.

The two hug, celebrating yet another victory in life, the simple but profound achievement of surviving.

She closes the bedroom door, hands over four sheets from her notepad, and shows the sign of silence with her index finger to her mouth.

David understands and picks up the notes, sitting down on the bed. He looks at the first paper that says she will scan the room and asks him to speak something out loud.

Rachel pulls the device out of her purse, shows it, and her partner nods.

David talks about how much he misses Michael, about the disappearance and what may have happened. He says he remembers when he met him in Washington and the bars they frequented.

Rachel, scanning the entire room, finds a listening mechanism inside a socket, below the window just behind the curtain. She shows it to David and puts the device back in the same place. She gives a wink to David and says out loud, "Don't worry, Detective Chong will find Michael."

With a troubled face, David looks at her because of the discovery and, frowning, reads the second note: "Would you rather rent an apartment or a house?"

He answers aloud with a misleading question: "Did you go back to Michael's apartment with Detective Chong?"

Rachel responds that she didn't go back and only went there the day the tragedy happened. David smiles and nods, making a thumbs-up sign with his right hand.

While reading the third page, David understands that Rachel is asking him to talk to the doctors about his health and the certainty of being able to leave the hospital as soon as possible. He agrees with the message and nods his head.

Sitting in the armchair, she talks about the trip along the Huangpu River. She explains the historical significance to the people of Shanghai and how, for centuries, the city evolved because of the trade carried out by boat. The natural beauty she witnessed on the vessel amazed her.

As she tells her story, David examines the fourth message in his hand, his expression showing confusion. "I would love to go on that trip," he says.

Rachel laughs and continues, "Unbelievable. Even I didn't think it was possible to get up in the morning in this situation and go on a historical tour. I'll take you; I promise."

David writes on the paper.

She reads what he wrote: *Let's get out of this hospital.* She nods her head in agreement.

"Are you planning to have lunch nearby? The doctor's rounds should be soon."

"Yes, I'll be leaving soon. I need to buy some clothes and personal items. It seems like the days are getting colder." She gives him a soft kiss on the cheek, heading toward the exit.

"Where are you going?" he questions.

"I found a mall nearby that has the same stores I frequent in London. I checked it out this morning," Rachel clarifies as she leaves.

"Alright, call me later or just come back. I look forward to seeing what you purchase."

* * *

At the police station, Detective Chong is on the phone talking to intelligence agents monitoring the cellphones linked to Michael's disappearance. He asks about any new leads. The agent responds, "The conversations are ordinary. There is some gossip but nothing concrete."

"Thanks. Keep me updated," Chong says before ending the call, looking at the pile of papers on his desk.

He approaches, looking at the documents he couldn't pay attention to. Meticulously, he separates the interconnected cases of David's attempted murder and Michael's disappearance. He is determined to solve them, believing this will reveal the true reason for the partners' visit to Shanghai. Chong focuses on a green folder on the table. He is certain it wasn't there the day before, and he analyzes the contents.

When he finishes reading the content, he leaves the room, taking long strides, heading toward the superintendent's office. When he arrives at the office door, he faces several journalists and a crowd of police officers. Realizing he can't get past to the superintendent, he heads back to the stairs, muttering to himself., "I don't like to waste time, even if it costs a scolding."

He thinks about the documents in the folder that show the fingerprints of the dead man who shot David. The Criminalistics Institute identified the fingerprints. They belong to Zhao Bai, who uses the code name Zao Yun, a former prisoner with an extensive criminal record. An important fact catches Chong's attention. At the time of his last arrest, Bai claimed to be a dockworker and gave his work address as the Shanghai port administration. These documents, along with two more photographs, are now official for the investigation. Analyzing, he concludes that this data is a drop in the ocean. If he can find where Zhao worked at the port and one worker recognizes the photo, he will discover the reason for his death. Detective Chong takes his car from the police parking lot and heads alone to the port administration.

* * *

Meanwhile, Rachel has fun at the city centre mall, sometimes remembering Tyler's words and trying not to get discouraged. She finds the stores she was looking for and buys what she needs. The main thing that fascinates her is the prices because everything she buys is three times less than what she pays in London, although the task takes twice the planned time. Carrying several bags, she leaves the mall and jumps into a taxi. Rachel tells the driver to head straight to the hotel and murmurs, "Sorry, David, I'll be back here next week, and you'll come with me. Then you'll see what I'm going to buy. I'll need three suitcases."

Upon arriving at the hotel, one of the receptionists assists Rachel. He advises her that he will take the bags and packages to her room.

Rachel is worried about David leaving the hospital. She takes his key and enters the room, checking that everything is in order. Her phone vibrates, and she sees that David has sent a message: *Excellent! I leave the hospital tomorrow at 8:00 a.m. The doctors agreed.*

She returns to her room and writes that she will be at the hospital in half an hour. Looking at the shopping bags on the table, she decides she'll put the clothes away later that night. She takes a deep breath and remembers what her partner said that morning about how much he misses Michael. Feeling sadness invade her, she thinks, *Michael, we will find you.*

Rachel calls reception and orders a taxi.

* * *

Detective Chong arrives at the port and heads to the administrative building. At reception, he shows his badge and asks to speak to someone from human resources.

"Is there a specific person you'd like to see?" the receptionist asks.

"Anyone available?" he replies.

She contacts the HR department, and soon Mr. Chen Wye, Director of HR Registration, comes over to meet him.

Chong gets straight to the point: "I need to check if a man named Zhao Bai works at the port."

Chen Wye, a man in his late forties, had a rapid rise through the administrative ranks. People know Chen Wye because of his uncle, who was once a port superintendent. No one disputes the nature of Chen's rise.

As the HR director searches his computer for the name provided by Detective Chong, he explains the intricacies of employment at the port. "We have around three thousand registered employees who work at the port, separate from private companies. Each of these companies, totalling around two thousand, has its own HR department supervising its workers. We cannot access details about these employees."

Chen continues, "Our records monitor the movements of our personnel within port terminals daily." Since he can't locate Zhao Bai's name, he adds, "Companies take care of their own people and provide a list of contractors present at the port every day. Terminal gatekeepers ensure security by monitoring the listings sent by companies and also checking day labourers who are not in the system."

"Is there no other way to confirm the name?" the detective insists.

"You said that this person works as a stevedore, so it is best to go to the labour management body, which manages the supply of this type of freelance worker in the port operations. They have the daily records of the terminals."

Detective Chong listens to the explanation and acknowledges his lack of knowledge of the port's procedures. He knows a special police team takes care of problems at the terminals. As he comes alone without informing the local team, accessing useful data could be difficult. Following his initial plan, he asks Mr. Chen for permission to visit the terminals. He hopes to show Zhao Bai's photograph to the workers, thinking someone might recognize him and offer valuable information.

The director approves Detective Chong's request and arranges for a car and driver to take him to the terminals to speak with ground staff, but not on board the vessels.

"There are terminals in different areas. It could take at least a week," advises the director, suggesting that Chong bring official documentation to gain access to restricted areas.

"I'll arrange that," Chong responds, thanking him and leaving with his designated driver.

In the car, Chong reflects on the information he gained, noting the slowness of the vehicle, which is respecting the speed limit of 15 km/h. Impatient, he comments on the slowness without receiving a response from the driver. He looks at the huge cranes and containers, then looks at the document in his hand, absorbed in its details.

The driver informs Detective Chong that he will take him to the nearest terminal, given the long distances to the others. Chong nods in acknowledgement.

They arrive at the cruise terminal's administrative building. Chong observes the boats docked in the distance before heading toward the passenger reception. Showing Zhao Bai's photograph to the receptionists, he asks if anyone recognizes the man. Several employees examine the image, but they all deny knowing him. Chong leaves the venue and sees a lively crowd of multilingual tourists approaching the girls from the reception. As he watches them, he realizes he made a mistake. Zhao Bai, a dockworker, would not be associated with a cruise, and this terminal focused on tourism. He takes a deep breath and heads back to the car, berating himself for the misstep.

Inside the car, the driver, a gentleman in his mid-sixties, watches Detective Chong lean back in the seat and asks, "Can I see the picture?"

The detective hands him the picture and says nothing.

The driver of the van asks, "Where does this man work?" Chong explains that the man worked at the port. He lacks knowledge of whether he worked as a dockworker at the Port of Shanghai in the past or present.

The old employee returns the photo. "My name is Yong. Nice to meet you."

The detective apologizes for the lack of manners and bows his head in respect.

Yong speaks with the firm voice of one who understands the subject. "We have to go to Yangshan Port because it is a deep-water port that accepts container ships. It is in Hangzhou Bay, south of Shanghai. If this man worked as a longshoreman, that's where you'll find others who know him."

Detective Chong, surprised, says, "It could be."

"I worked at the Port of Shanghai for thirty-five years in different terminals and you do not find that type of employee in this area. Another thing: go to the labour management building and not the administration building where you were. Do you know the blue-tiled building on Guanguinan Street? This is the place that records the labour supply of self-employed workers in port operations." Yong looks over and sees Chong has his eyes closed. As he does not get an immediate answer, he shrugs and starts the car.

The phone rings and Chong answers it. On the other end of the line, Boss Bo asks why he didn't respond sooner. The detective tries to explain himself but it's impossible.

"Go to the address I sent on your phone. Check out an explosion that happened last night. You are the best one to know if it was an accident or something else. The victims' bodies are at the chief medical examiner's office," Bo says quickly.

"Leave it to me. I'll let you know as soon as I have any information."

When Chong hangs up, he remembers what the driver told him. He recognizes that Yong was very convincing in his explanations, and it is the correct decision to make. Annoyed, he bites the corner of his mouth, wondering what he is going to say.

"I agree with the idea. First, I need to provide a few things. Please, park at the administration door."

The driver stops, and the detective thanks him as he gets out of the vehicle. The old employee watches him walk away and says to himself: "He still has a lot to learn about the port."

*   *   *

Rachel, in the taxi, makes several phone calls to real estate agents who display ads in English. She discovers that most of them do not speak English; only those at two real estate agencies do. She gets the information she wants. In the end, she arranges visits to two apartments in the Bund neighbourhood. The taxi leaves her at the hospital door, and she goes up to David's room. As soon as she enters, she asks, "What did the doctors say?"

David mentions that Dr. Han Zheng wants to talk to her.

Without wasting time, she goes to the floor's reception desk and asks to speak to Dr. Han, explaining that this is for the discharge of patient David Ho. The nurse tells her that Dr. Han is seeing other patients but will visit David's room when he returns.

Rachel returns to the room, and advises David, "The doctor will be here in a little while."

"So, did you buy the entire mall?" her partner asks with a smile.

"Almost. I'll buy more stuff next week."

"Are you worried about me, or something else?" David can see something is off.

"A little distressed with other things that I have to arrange," Rachel replies and notes David gesturing her over. She approaches, and he whispers in her ear, asking for paper and pen.

Rachel delivers the goods and says, "I'm a little stressed. Tired. I woke up early today."

"Did you buy beautiful things?" David asks Rachel as he writes in the small notebook.

"I bought a lot and I'm going to fill two more suitcases," she replies and laughs loud enough that they hear her in the hospital corridor.

He laughs, returns the notebook and comments, "That's the partner I know."

Rachel leans back in the armchair and tells him, "I'm going to sleep. Wake me up when the doctor comes." She opens the notepad, reading the message, and her eyes widen.

The door opens, and the doctor, accompanied by a nurse, enters and confirms, "Mr. David is leaving."

"Without question," David replies with a wide smile on his face.

Dr. Han Zheng meets Rachel's gaze. She stands up, the weight of concern clear in her posture, and he nods in acknowledgement. He informs her in clear English that she can pay the hospital bills now, which are waiting at reception on the second floor.

"Rachel," he assures, "we will give you the guidelines for David's physical therapy and medication list in English." He pauses, allowing the information to sink in, before adding, "The hospital board decided this, considering David's intention to return to London. This ensures continuity of his care, helping the next doctor to understand his needs for recovery."

Seeing the hint of anxiety in Rachel's eyes, he adds, "As for the medicines, you don't need to worry. They are available at our hospital's pharmacy. We have organized everything for you; you just need to pick them up."

"Doctor, we are going to stay here in Shanghai for about two weeks. Would it be possible to do physiotherapy here at the hospital?" she asks Dr. Han, who watches as she closes her eyes and takes a deep breath, noticing how tired she is.

"When closing the bill, explain to the receptionists who assist you what we discussed here. Take advantage of the moment and schedule physio-therapy. Choose the days and times that suit you best. Any problems, call me. Leave a message and I will get back to you as soon as possible." The doctor hands her a card.

Rachel accepts the card and bows. "Thank you."

Looking at David, who looks ready to jump out of bed and run away, the doctor says, "I'll discharge you today."

"Do you want to leave today?" asks Rachel.

"Sure. I want to leave now!"

"Okay, I'll arrange it," Dr. Han communicates.

"Thank you, doctor. Thank you for everything," David says with emotion in his voice, looking at the doctor and the nurse.

"You don't have to say thank you, David; we just did our job. You're an excellent patient," the doctor finishes and heads for the exit door of the room. Dr. Han stops and turns his gaze to Rachel, saying, "Take care of yourself. You look exhausted. Take advantage at the reception and meet with me next week." She agrees, and the doctor and the nurse leave the room.

Rachel runs over and hugs David. They are both so relieved and happy.

A nurse enters the room with lunch on a tray. She leaves it on the little table and retreats, watching the partners hug each other.

With her eyes filled with tears, Rachel grabs her purse and says she's going to have lunch at the hospital restaurant. Her partner gets out of bed and walks with a little difficulty. He hugs her again, saying, "Thank you, Rachel. Thank you for being my sister and my friend." The two hug each other and feel the emotion of the moment.

"Let me go eat something. I have a million problems. I must get you out of this hospital," she proclaims and leaves the room, heading toward the elevator, wiping away the tears that, thankfully, this time, are of happiness.

*   *   *

On another side of the city, Detective Chong arrives at the small site and notes that the fire has destroyed everything. Flames devastated the house, the crops, the barn, and the surrounding trees within a radius of two hundred metres of the explosion. The police officer who stayed at the scene waiting for him gives a salute and fills him in.

They confirmed two bodies in the area: one adult, another believed to be a child, and a dog. They took these bodies to the Legal Medical Institute. A document exists where the expert confirmed the absence of fuel.

The detective agrees and lights a cigarette. He walks toward the house, observing details he knows from years of experience. The police officer accompanying the detective explains that the fire occurred last night, and neighbours stated they heard an enormous explosion nearby.

"Was it suicide?" asks Chong without looking at him.

"It is hard to know if it was suicide or an accident," the officer says and tells him about finding destroyed bodies.

"Hmm," the detective murmurs, smoking his cigarette as he walks through the rubble of what remains. "Did any neighbours testify? Who lived in this house? Did you get people's names?"

"The names are in the report of the officers who were here in the early hours of the morning. They interviewed several people."

The detective notices a small group of individuals standing in front of the site's entrance gate. Chong sees a lady crying and a man hugging her and moves to talk with them.

"Did you know the residents here?" Detective Chong, at random, asks those watching the tragedy.

A man approaches and says, "Yes." He informs them that a wonderful family lives there. The husband works at the port, and the wife and their daughter stayed at home. Very emotional, he covers his face and starts crying, saying that they were excellent neighbours and caused no problems.

"Hmm..." Detective Chong thanks him. Analyzing the neighbour's words, Chong walks toward the car, wondering, *Where is the third body?*

* * *

Rachel is having lunch in the hospital cafeteria. Her cellphone rings, and she hears Tyler's voice, saying, "I have great news."

"Tell me." She wipes her mouth with a napkin.

"I'm boarding this afternoon; can you come and pick me up? I will arrive at Shanghai Pudong airport tomorrow at 9:25 a.m.," he says with a fast-paced voice.

"Oh my God! What a wonderful surprise! Of course, of course I'll come get you," Rachel says, expressing joy.

Tyler admits he hasn't taken a break in a long time and has always dreamed of exploring Shanghai. He assures Rachel not to worry, emphasizing that the company is in excellent hands and that all ongoing investigations are under control. With a hint of enthusiasm, he shares that he delegated opportunities for two potential clients to Tom.

Rachel, not understanding, asks, "Who is Tom?"

Listening to his partner, Tyler tries to jog her memory. "Remember the queen's police officer? The one who transitioned from personal security because he wanted to open his own investigation firm?" With a voice full of emotion, Tyler explains how elated his friend was, and even promised a thank-you dinner in London when they return.

"Oh, yes, I know who he is. Good people. I didn't know his company was already up and running."

"Do you want me to bring you something from the apartment? Don't worry, Mary Lai will take care of Mozart."

"No, I need nothing. Thank you for convincing Mary."

"Three heads think better than two. I'm out of the situation you're in. That way, my vision will be a second opinion once I'm up to speed on everything," Tyler explains.

"Okay, send the flight number and the airline to my phone. Tomorrow at 9 a.m., I'll be at the airport," Rachel confirms.

29

Bar Gossip

Moving trucks and people going in and out make Warehouse #2 one of the most requested by single employees today. This warehouse, like two others in the same area, is part of Mr. Wang's export and import company.

Since dawn, the owner, the manager, and countless contract and fixed employees work hard in the warehouses. Goods are being shipped to Europe, so everyone has to be careful with this cargo. These particular warehouses are within the port, far from the container loading and unloading terminals. Most of the deposits in the area are on the access roads to the cove. Wang got lucky at an auction a few years ago and bought three warehouses there for an excellent price. This facilitates business in loading and dispatching of goods. The export process has many details, and there can be no mistakes, as any delay by the exporting company incurs exorbitant fines.

Wang, reading some papers from the customs clearance, asks Hui, who is standing three metres away from him, about the number of rented containers. The manager checks the number and shouts, "Eighteen containers."

"How many hired men work on this shipment today?" the boss asks. He walks away from the front door of the warehouse as yet another crowded truck is leaving.

The movement in and out of the warehouses is enormous. Trucks with containers of different sizes are stocked with boxes, pallets, etc. When the loading finishes, workers close the trucks and drive them to an adjacent area near the warehouse. Upon arrival at the bay, workers guide them to a courtyard designated to inspect documents and goods. Once the inspection is complete, the government inspection body will seal the container and place it on the ship heading to the destination. The work extends for one to three days or more, concluding when all the containers are aboard the cargo ships.

"Forty men," Hui shouts on his way inside the warehouse.

Not hearing Hui's response, Wang moves fast toward the manager. The noise here is deafening. Not only are there warehouses loading, but five or six warehouses from other companies are doing the same thing today at the same time. Men shout, trucks and cars honk, wheels grind in the gravel, chains clang, brakes squeal, and the loading of items in the containers adds to the symphony. All conversations, responses, and questions need to be shouted.

Wang gets close to a few pallets behind where the manager is and stops. He hears one employee ask if Hui knows where Wonjy is.

Hui, alert, seeing Wang hiding behind the boxes, looks at the man and asks, "Why?"

"Oh, this morning when we went to have coffee at the cafeteria, we heard that his wife and daughter died in a fire on Friday night," the employee says.

"I can't imagine where Wonjy is. What a tragedy. Who told you that horror…?" Hui looks around, trying to see where Wang is, not seeing him hidden behind some pallets.

"The police went to the bar today to ask about Wonjy," one of the warehouse loaders tells the manager. Someone inside the warehouse shouts his name. The employee turns and runs into the warehouse without finishing the story. Seeing the worker enter the warehouse, Hui tries to analyze what he said. His cellphone rings, and he answers it.

Wang, who overheard the entire conversation, deduces what he should do and leaves. He doesn't say goodbye to the manager or give any guidance. He just walks toward the car parked about a hundred metres away from the warehouse.

When Hui notices, he watches the boss head toward the vehicle. Hui shows no outward reaction and tries to continue reading the documents, but his head is worse than the chaos that surrounds him. Fixed on the papers, he can't read what is written on them. What he sees is the scene where Wang shot the three men. He remembers Wonjy falling to his right side with his eyes open, trying to say something, and after a few seconds, he was dead. The sound of the gunshot and the memory of the crocodiles chewing and biting the three bodies is frightening. The noise of the explosion on the farm, which returns to his memory, completes the vivid sounds, making Hui's body and spirit shake. He hears someone calling him and comes back to reality. His mouth is dry, and he runs his hand across his forehead, wiping away the sweat. His heart beats so hard that his chest hurts. He looks again and sees Wang's car driving away down the avenue of warehouses.

"All that's left now is for that son of a bitch to dump all the blame on me!" Hui spits, his fists clenched. His voice rings with unmistakable anger. It's fortunate that no one is around to hear it.

The manager enters the warehouse and starts looking for the employee who told him what happened at the bar, but he can't find him. His phone vibrates, and he recognizes the sender of the message. *Let's have lunch. We need to talk,* Wang texts.

Hui doesn't answer. After over twenty minutes, the boss writes the same message again. When he reads it again, he looks at the time and sees it's almost 10:00 a.m. He writes back to Wang: *Yangen Fried Dumpling, 12 p.m.* Wang replies: *Okay.*

Hui no longer trusts the one who claims to be his friend. He suggested the busy Yangen restaurant as a meeting point, knowing that Wang would hold back in public, wanting to maintain his image. Hui is guarding himself against Wang's potential violence, aware of his past reactions. Although Hui is not afraid, knowing the secrets he keeps about Wang's life, he recognizes he is only postponing an inevitable confrontation, but he remains resolute.

Wang arrives at the dock office, enters the room, and concentrates, with his gaze fixed on the wall. His secretary looks inside the room and turns around. She understands it's not the right time to talk. In complete silence, she withdraws. A second after the door is closed, Wang opens it and asks, "Do you need anything?"

Frightened and tense from the situation, she responds by stuttering, "No, no, sir. I was just going to let you know I'm leaving. It's my lunch hour."

"Don't forget to lock the glass door of the office," Wang says across the room toward the exit, a stern expression on his face.

* * *

Hui arrives early at the restaurant and books a private room. He selects their meal and drinks, instructing the waiter to have everything ready by the time Wang arrives, anticipating that they will need to eat during their conversation. He requests additional cushions and places his phone under one of them, prepared to record the discussion. This is a departure from his usual behaviour, driven by a strange sense of guilt and fear. Over the years of their friendship, Hui has encountered disagreements, frictions, and arguments with Wang, but they always navigated these situations. However, Hui has noticed a change in Wang. Rude and sarcastic attitudes in his words have become routine, lacking calmness, and he is raising his voice during discussions. Hui believes a woman named Rachel has played a role in this shift.

Hui looks at his watch, certain that Wang's arrival is imminent. He warns himself not to mention Wonjy's name. As he reflects on the events at the warehouse, he struggles to reconcile them with Wang's decisions regarding Wonjy's family. He believes Wang lost control because of feeling humiliated by Wonjy's wife and daughter, and he questions whether it was a shame for a wife to know the truth about her husband. Hui wonders if Wang's ruthlessness, even targeting Wonjy's family, is a grave mistake. He remembers he informed Wang about Wonjy's wife, who sought him out in other places, and how Wang instructed him to deal with it without remorse. He questions whether he can still reason with Wang and whether their relationship will continue as it has in the past.

Hui takes another sip of his drink, anxious and vigilant. He believes Wang is unbalanced and needs to protect himself.

A little late, Wang enters the restaurant, and a waiter takes him to a private room. Wang, without a greeting, sits down and questions why they are at this restaurant. Hui responds, explaining that the food is affordable and of excellent quality, and that he will cover the bill. Wang seems dissatisfied but doesn't protest further. Hui pours beer for both of them and says he has already ordered dumplings.

Wang, with a hint of frustration, questions Hui about the employee at the warehouse, questioning him about Wonjy's whereabouts. Hui dismisses this as employee curiosity and bar gossip, assuring Wang that everything is under control. However, Wang says the police are investigating. Hui records their tense conversation. Hui maintains his composure, reminding Wang that the last information they received from Wonjy was his notification to Wang's secretary about his trip to Hong Kong. Wang looks surprised and then laughs. Hui, sensing that Wang might be unstable, yawns, reminding Wang of his idea to resolve the situation.

In the windowless room, the manager's words are a whisper, but Wang, catching every syllable, moves his head, looking him in the eyes. He understands the depth of what Hui just said. Raising his face, Wang looks at him, his eyes filled with frightening amusement.

At that moment, the boss's cellphone signals a new message. Wang reads it.

The sliding door of the private room opens, and two waitresses enter, carrying trays with a variety of dishes. They place the small portions on the table in front of the two of them and add one bottle of beer to Hui's right. Before the waitresses ask if they want anything else, Wang stands up, knocking one girl over, and retreats from the room toward the restaurant exit. The women, baffled by the situation, ask if everything is okay. The manager, smiling, replies that an urgent phone call from work has required him to leave.

"Ahh..." she grumbles and smiles.

"Don't worry, I'll eat all these treats you brought."

The waitresses retreat, closing the door to the private room.

Hui's expression changes to one of seriousness and concern.

Wang leaves in a hurry. His heart is heavy because of the suspicion that Hui may have recorded the conversation. He takes a deep breath, trying to calm his racing heart, and walks to the restaurant's parking lot. The cacophony of the street shakes him: the shrill sound of a drill from a nearby construction site, distant horns, and sirens. He pauses, looks around, clenches his fists and mutters, "I hate noise and crowds."

He stands still, watching the commotion. The sidewalk is full of people: some carrying bags, others leaving stores, well-dressed professionals on the phone, and groups chatting on benches. The sun shines, its heat contrasting with the cold wind. Wang, wearing sunglasses, jeans, a shirt, and a layered sweater, blends into the crowd, unrecognizable. He walks again, with firm steps. Such is his inner turmoil that if anyone had spoken to him now, he might have attacked.

Arriving at the parking lot, he gets into the car with his voice full of anger. "How dare you? Who do you think you are? He'll try to blame me for this. Do you think you have control over me? Just wait and see. You'll regret this." With a determined movement, he starts the Mercedes and speeds away.

Wang arrives at the pier, stomping hard, and doesn't even look at the secretary as he passes by. When he opens the door to his office, he notices a man sitting in the reception chair drinking coffee.

Just before he can enter the office, the secretary informs him, "Detective Chong has been waiting for you for half an hour."

Looking at her, his gaze turns cold—cold enough to freeze the most powerful fire—as he remembers her previous message, which only mentioned a police officer, and not Detective Chong's name. Taking a deep breath to compose himself, he instructs, "Please bring two coffees and two waters to my office."

Wang walks toward the detective and, smiling, greets him. He apologizes for making him wait so long.

Chong stands up, smiles, and says, "Ahh, you were quick. I didn't even notice the time go by."

The chief, pointing to his room, asks the detective to settle in. The secretary comes in with two coffees and two waters, placing them on the table, and then withdraws.

"We met at the hospital. Am I right?" Wang asks and holds up one of the water bottles.

"That's right. It was at the hospital, in David Ho's room. You went there with Rachel Barnes," Detective Chong observes the manner of the owner of Warehouses One and Two on the pier.

"Well, how can I help you, Detective?" Wang asks as he sits in the armchair without looking at the detective.

Detective Chong takes two photographs from an envelope and places them in front of Wang.

Without touching them, Wang's eyes scan the images. His face remains impassive, but there's a flash of recognition when he spots Wonjy. The second photograph is of an unknown man he doesn't recognize.

The detective, noticing Wang's scrutiny, touches Wonjy's photo and identifies him, then does the same to the unknown man, calling him Zhao.

Wang's gaze lingers on Wonjy's photograph. "I've seen him near the pier," he admits, then looks at Zhao's image, "but I don't know this man." Handing back the photographs, Wang asks, "Why would you think I know them?"

Detective Chong, with an unflappable demeanour, puts the photos back in the envelope. Meeting Wang's gaze, he states, "Because they are employees of your company."

Wang tries to hide his surprise. Having no interest, his index finger goes to his bottom lip, scratching it as he looks down, thinking about his next words.

"I'm not the one who hires the employees who work there. Maybe, as I told you, I saw them. There are so many employees. Now, my manager, who hires the men who work here, knows who is who is in here. You can confirm; the name of the manager is Hui." Wang, without taking his hand off his chin, with a satisfied smile, has told the detective the name of his old friend.

"Can I talk to this Mr. Hui?" Chong asks.

Wang calls the secretary and asks her to contact the manager, requesting him to come to the office, now.

She leaves the room and calls.

The boss again offers coffee and water to the detective. He refuses.

"Are you keeping very busy, detective?" Wang asks, removing the coffee tray and glasses of water from the table, placing them over the file.

"Nothing more than normal," Detective Chong replies.

"I imagine it's difficult for you, day and night dealing with violence," the owner says as he sits back down in the armchair.

"An occupational hazard for the benefit of society," the detective points out.

"Hmm…" Wang mutters and nods his head.

The secretary comes in and says that Hui can't come to the office this afternoon as he's on his way to the departure terminals in Hangzhou Bay, scheduled for tomorrow at 8:00 a.m.

Detective Chong gets up from his chair, bows, and thanks Wang, saying that he will return tomorrow.

The two say goodbye.

Seeing Chong leave the room, Wang calls the secretary and orders, "Call the…" He stops.

Wang was going to say "son of a bitch" but restrains himself and starts again: "Please call Hui again. I need to talk to him."

Standing in front of the office window, the boss bathes himself in the warm sun. He looks out at the distant cranes in the harbour, and a sudden calm invades his mind.

"Boss, Hui doesn't answer his phone."

"No problem. I'll get in touch later."

"Do you need anything else?"

"No. I'm going out. I need to have lunch. I'll have my phone," Wang informs his secretary.

After a while, Wang walks down the stairs of the deserted warehouse toward the parking lot. For no reason, a wave of dizziness comes over him. Looking down, he notices his hands shaking. He stops and leans against a stack of boxes. His body tenses, his heart races. An inner voice, or perhaps instinct, encourages him to go to the car.

Gathering his composure, he quickens his pace and soon slides into the driver's seat. A coughing fit takes over him, and he grabs a bottle of water from the passenger seat, taking several gulps. After a few moments, he sees his reflection in the rear-view mirror, and a slow smile appears on his face. Resolute in his next steps, a new calm envelops Wang.

The cellphone signals a new message: *Take care of the merchandise sent today. It's all set to be stolen tonight or tomorrow before shipping.*

Wang's network of informants spreads throughout the port, always providing him with information about allies, adversaries, and competitors. Today's information, however, disturbs him—an imminent theft that is sure to affect his finances, a move he cannot afford to ignore. Weighing his options, given the severity and urgency of the information, he calls to meet with the Tong chiefs. His source is a trusted spy embedded in the Shanghai Triad.

He composes a message to Kang Wu, the chief of North Tong, instructing him to meet that night and bring with him the other three chiefs: those of the south, east, and west.

Driving the car at high speed, he remembers that when he took over the organization, he was a young man with no experience but with ideas. Most of the men admire him and say he is smart and intelligent about the new proposals. Kang Wu is one of the few from the past era who stands one hundred-percent by his side and helps him implement the concepts he suggests to the new Tong.

Everyone knew the power and danger that Tong was before the changes, but in Wang's hands, it became the most important outside the Triad in Shanghai. In the beginning, there were over sixty small affiliates that worked with Tong and countless others without a real coalition. Wang restructured the order's organizational chart and chose Kang Wu, Huan Zhang, Guozhi Zhou, and Changpu Liu as heads of the north, south, east, and west regions of Shanghai.

Wang and Kang handpick their men from the most ferocious, unrelenting, and esteemed factions. These are leaders who had their own formidable organizations, for the relentless drive overshadows who is to ascend. However, the foot soldiers under these chiefs are a contrast, bound by unwavering loyalty and dedication. Wang respects these men; they are shrewd and have aspirations like his own: to carve a place within Shanghai's political echelons. The synergy is instantaneous; he has chosen his allies well. To an outsider peering into their gatherings, it would be challenging to discern who among them is the sociopath, the narcissist, or the psychopath.

Upon taking their positions, each chief selects three sub-chiefs to oversee various illicit operations: drug and human trafficking, arms deals, migrant smuggling, counterfeit trade, money laundering, illegal gambling, extortion, and cybercrime.

Implementing TOC—the Theory of Constraints, spearheaded by Wang, was a game-changer. It streamlines their operations, especially in exports, ensuring unparalleled success. By prioritizing areas demanding immediate enhancement, TOC's main agenda is trimming the excess to maximize profit. This strategic move bolsters Wang's standing within the Triad, culminating in a unique business alliance.

Factions that failed to adapt to the new Tong structure faced eradication. Over a six-month period, Shanghai witnessed over two hundred mysterious deaths declared accidental. Now that the landscape of the underworld demarcates, whoever is part of it has to choose between the Tong or the Triad. Any other faction ceases to exist.

Kang Wu reads the message in surprise and agrees to tonight's dinner. He returns, saying he will advise the other bosses.

Wang enters the underground garage of the building where he lives and parks the vehicle in his private parking space. Upon arriving at the apartment, he calls his secretary and asks her to provide a new card for the private entrances, as well as the parking lots of the building where he lives. He adds he lost the key access. As for the password, she shouldn't worry because he will change the password on his cellphone.

She asks if she should make other security cards.

Wang says "No," ending the matter. He then orders her to reserve a table for five at The Ritz in Pudong tonight.

"Anything else, boss?"

"I need a private driver. Hire one I know. Send me the name and file before confirming."

She agrees and says she will return the information in a moment.

After hanging up, he remembers he has eaten nothing today, and his stomach growls. Wang opens the refrigerator, and seeing it empty, gives up on eating. He lays his body down on the couch, closes his eyes, and tries to rest, but the glare of the sun entering through the window doesn't leave him alone. He sits, stretching his legs on the cushions.

"Today I will chart your destiny, Hui. Do you think you can play with me?"

A new message signals on his phone. He reads the message from his secretary and writes to Kang Wu: *Jin Xuan—The Ritz-Carlton—Shanghai, Pudong/ Private Room Perola—7 p.m.*

As he's about to set down the phone, it rings again—a call this time. Recognizing the caller ID, Wang answers with playful joy. "Well, if it's not the most beautiful woman on the planet."

Rachel's laughter echoes from the other end. "Some things never change with you, always the charmer."

"Always at your service," Wang replies, his voice dripping with genuine happiness. "Anything you need."

Rachel, her voice bubbling with enthusiasm, shares, "Tyler, my other partner, just landed in Shanghai. He's here for a vacation and to support David's recovery. How about the four of us grab a meal? You came to mind since you're the only close friend I have here."

Wang, eager but trying to mask his excitement, offers, "Sure, how about tomorrow? I will pick you up at the hotel at 5 p.m. Does this work?"

Rachel's gratitude shines through. "Perfect. We'll meet you at the hotel lobby then. I appreciate this, Wang. I know how busy your schedule is but given that you're my go-to for local expertise, I thought I'd reach out."

Wang, ever the gracious host, assures her, "Leave it to me. I'll ensure Tyler has an unforgettable time in Shanghai."

He recognizes the need for subtlety, sensing an opportunity to reconnect with Rachel. Each word, each action, needs careful consideration. "Until tomorrow then," he adds.

"See you later," she replies, ending the call with a wicked smile on her lips, feeling David and Tyler's eyes on her.

*   *   *

Detective Chong leaves Wang's office convinced that something in their conversation wasn't right. The information he got doesn't match what several other people told him that day.

Before going to Wang's office in Warehouse #1, Detective Chong stops by the Legal Medical Institute. He needs to confirm details of the recent explosion: there are only two fatalities—would it be possible to verify that the victims are a woman, a child, and a dog? After verifying these details, he goes to the investigation department to analyze the witness statements from the neighbours around the destroyed house.

A witness who testified piques his interest. He states that the deceased woman's husband, Wonjy, works at the pier and is a humble person who smiles through everything. A neighbour who runs a small snack bar close to the port warehouses made this statement. This neighbour claims Wonjy works in one of those same warehouses. Chong flips through the other statements, but nothing else stands out.

Since Superintendent Bo is not yet at the police station, Chong decides that his next step would be to visit the diner owner to get more details. He takes Zhao Bai's photograph, thinking that perhaps the witness will recognize him. It's a long shot, but it's worth a try.

Parking his unmarked car a block away, Chong approaches the diner, taking in the scene. Ten men lounge at tables outside, drinking coffee, while inside, three customers enjoy snacks and beers at the counter. The interior is so small that customers have to stay outside, as it cannot accommodate the counter and its owner.

Chong introduces himself to the man behind the counter, referring to the tragic explosion. In response, the owner, being considerate, opens a section of the counter, inviting the detective to come in and sit on a stool next to the sink. As Chong sits down, the man expresses his sadness over the incident. "It's devastating. What happened last Friday… is inexplicable, a true tragedy."

All the men eating snacks and sitting outside hear the owner talk about the fatality and one asks, "Liao, what happened? What tragedy is that?"

Detective Chong analyzes the reactions of the people present when Liao says that Wonjy's wife and daughter died in an explosion at their property.

The news shocks the individuals there. Some ask about Wonjy, others say it's not possible, and one of them shouts, "Has anyone seen Wonjy today?"

No one answers.

Liao moves his disgruntled head and comments, "Wonjy is a well-liked person among everyone who works here."

Detective Chong, coming out from behind the counter, repeats the same question aloud: "Has anyone seen Wonjy today?"

The men, afraid to answer because there is a policeman asking, stay muted, shake their heads, and leave the cafeteria to go toward the warehouses.

The only worker left is still sitting, eating and drinking. Without paying attention to anyone, he says, "Maybe Wonjy doesn't even know what happened to his family. He's always drunk."

The detective, attentive, sees that this man could give him some other information and continues the conversation: "I'm here for just that, to meet Wonjy and communicate the passing of his family."

The man watches the detective and informs him, "He works in Warehouse Number Two. Look for Hui, he's the manager."

"Have you seen Wonjy these past few days?" Detective Chong asks the bar owner, who, standing next to the table, overhears the conversation.

"It's been a few days since he's been here to eat," Liao replies.

The detective asks the other man who finished eating: "Wonjy only works in this warehouse?"

"I think only in this warehouse, maybe number one as well… he's an old friend of the owner of the company and Hui, he's a childhood friend," the man replies and pays Liao for the coffee and food.

Detective Chong puts a photograph on the table and asks, "Do you know this person?"

The worker and the owner of the cafeteria both look at the photograph and say that they've seen this man walking around. They report he is quiet, without friends, but they don't know his name or where he works.

Aware that he is now getting answers, the detective insists, "When was he here?"

The man next to Liao holds the photograph and confirms, "I've seen this guy here in the area. He's that screwed-up guy who only shows up looking for work when he needs money."

"Do you remember where you saw him working?" Detective Chong, elated by the discovery, continues.

The worker explains that the man in the photograph only seems to loiter there. He never saw him talking to anyone; he is always alone. He says that he hasn't been in the area looking for a job in a long time and, of course, he has worked in the warehouses.

The owner of the snack bar agrees with what is being said.

"Maybe if I go now to Warehouse Number Two, I'll find Wonjy there," the detective says.

"I didn't see Wonjy today," the two men say, repeating what they have already said.

The worker walks toward the warehouses and says aloud: "It could be. I think you'd better go straight to the warehouse and talk to them there." He waves goodbye.

The detective thanks Liao, who hands Chong a piece of paper, which he pockets without looking at it when they say goodbye.

Detective Chong returns to the police station and finds that his secretary has not yet arrived. He calls the identification institute and asks for a photograph of the man named Wonjy by fax: "by yesterday, if possible."

* * *

Hui, feeling the weight of the situation pressing down on him, checks the seals on each container that will ship out today. The men who helped him with the containers return to the dock, leaving him isolated among the huge piles of metal. His solitude gives him no comfort; instead, the urgency of his next conversation with the detective consumes him, turning his stomach and tensing his muscles.

Leaning against the cold exterior of a container, he takes a deep breath, trying to calm the storm inside him. The events of that morning replay in his mind, further intensifying the emotional turmoil he feels.

Inside and outside the warehouse, Hui and Wang are supervising the loading process when a buzz of conversation spreads among the workers. An employee who had just arrived from the snack bar leans over to Hui and says, "The police are asking about Wonjy."

With his keen hearing, Wang, outside the warehouse, catches a snippet of the conversation, observing that Hui, dexterously diverts the topic, but the discomfort remains present.

Hui's focus shifts from overseeing pallets and boxes to the implications of the workers' news. The atmosphere is thick with tension. Hui's instincts go on high alert when an unexpected lunch invitation from Wang appears on his phone.

As Hui drives toward Warehouse #1, he can't shake the memory of Wang listening in on their conversation. His phone rings, bringing him back to the present. An urgent voice informs him, "A police officer was asking about Wonjy at the cafe. Someone mentioned that he works with you at Warehouse Number Two. The police will most likely come after you."

Taking a moment to process, Hui stops, weighing his options. Before he can complete the plan, another message from Wang appears on his screen, reiterating the invitation to lunch. Hui reads it and writes: *Yangen Fried Dumpling, 12 p.m.*

He gets an answer: *Okay.*

Noting that all employees have left, with the shipping documents in their hands and security already on site, Hui returns to reality and walks to the parking lot and gets into his car. His thoughts are still confused.

Since the police visit, Hui's anxiety has increased. Aware that he would face consequences if exposed, he feels the weight of Wonjy's tragedy pressing down on him. Meanwhile, Wang, oblivious to the details and assured that Hui will handle the entire matter, knows he has escaped blame. Blinded by rage and betrayal, Hui pounds his fists on the steering wheel, his scream echoing within the confines of his car. Stopping to steady himself, he looks through the tinted windows, grateful that no one has seen his collapse.

"I need to know what the police are looking for and what they know."

Hui, determined, drives toward Warehouse #1.

30

Mature

Rachel runs out of the taxi and enters the airport's international arrivals area. "Even the airport smells different," she notes. To her left, passengers carry tickets and passports, while others drag suitcases to the check-in counters. The staff tags the luggage. Flight announcements mix with the murmur of cheerful conversations and heartfelt goodbyes. The environment reignites her desire to travel. Her recent trip to Shanghai weighs on her. Taking a deep breath, she thinks *I need to rest. When I'm in London, I'm going to disconnect for a while.*

The flight information screen confirms a fifteen-minute delay for Tyler's plane. She sinks into the nearest seat, placing a hand on her racing heart, feeling an overwhelming exhaustion. The memory of scheduling David's doctor's appointment concurrent with his physical therapy next Friday floods back. "Am I getting sick?" she ponders, doubting it's anything serious. A loud growl in her stomach reminds her of the meal lost in the morning rush. *I need coffee and something to eat,* she thinks. Spotting a snack bar, she orders a coffee and a cheese croissant. She settles down at a table; although many are available, she finds herself among a noisy group nearby.

As Rachel takes a bite, she reflects on how her life has changed in just two weeks. Losing her cousin, David's near-death experience, Michael's mysterious disappearance, and Ronaldo's haunting memories. "Oh, hell! What else could go wrong?" she contemplates. She hopes Tyler can shed some light on Michael's situation and perhaps uncover details about Ronaldo's passing. Resting her forehead on her hand, she wonders if the values she once held close have disappeared. Age seems to weigh on her. Startled back to the present by the scalding sip of her coffee, she exclaims, "Oh my God."

Scratching her head, Rachel remembers the need to close the hotel bill and go to the supermarket. The day before was a whirlwind. She rented an apartment with three bedrooms, a living room, a kitchen, two bathrooms, a full laundry room, a garage, and most importantly, a stunning view of the Huangpu River and the city skyline—all for a price that seemed like a bargain compared to London rates. That night, she picked David up from the hospital and brought him to the hotel. Earlier today, she asked the real estate agent about retrieving the apartment keys, only to find out they will only be available at night. If everything goes according to plan, they will move in tomorrow.

David, as always, believed the price was too expensive. She explained the pros and cons, and in the end, because of the neighbourhood, he felt encouraged and said it was worth it. Rachel paid in advance for three months with the possibility of extending the contract. She didn't want to rent it for that long, but David insisted.

After Michael's disappearance, Rachel understands the need for a change of plans. Resolving the police and legal issues will allow them to return to London within three weeks. However, if they do not find Michael, David intends to stay in Shanghai to get answers. Although Rachel empathizes with the situation, she recognizes her duty to the business and the customers they share. Her intention is to return to London as soon as David's health stabilizes. Emphasizing the need for his arm to recover, she is sure that he will soon want to rent a car. Once confident in his health, she is prepared to continue her normal life. *How I'd like to be on a beach right now.* Rachel closes her eyes, shakes her hair, and smiles as if she imagines the sea breeze.

Checking the flight screen, Rachel sees that Tyler's flight has landed. She walks fast to the arrivals gate, surrounded by families awaiting their loved ones. The joy, the hugs, and the happy exclamations warm her heart. Soon, she spots Tyler.

"Tyler!" Rachel calls; her enthusiasm abounds. He reciprocates the gesture, and she runs toward him, hugging him. It's a long hug, full of affection.

"How's my favourite partner?" Tyler asks, smiling, a heavy backpack slung across his shoulders. "Glad you're here. You've lost weight. How come? You aren't taking care of yourself?" Tyler says, looking at her with concern.

"Don't stress about it. There were a lot of minor problems and with the setbacks, I wasn't hungry. Now you're here and everything will get better," she says, smiling.

The two walk, arms around each other, toward the airport taxi section. In the taxi to the hotel, Tyler asks, "How's David? Is he better?"

She explains David is sleeping at the hotel. Giving him an update on everything that has happened since he got shot, she includes details about the surgery, recovery, and upcoming physiotherapy. According to her, he is healthy, and the current challenge is finding Michael.

"I'm at peace knowing that David is okay."

In the taxi, her partner looks outside, observing the buildings, streets, and busy life of Shanghai. Now and then he points out tourist attractions to Rachel. His fascination is evident.

"You're going to love this city," she declares, laughing.

"Rachel," he responds, "you don't know how much I've wanted to visit here, whether for work or pleasure. I'm sure I'll make the most of my time."

She winks and asks, "Did you get the company information you cited yesterday morning?"

"Yes, I brought everything."

Rachel's lips press together as she falls into a reflective silence, choosing not to comment. Watching Tyler, she discerns his joy more deeply than most could just by the radiant smile and bright eyes on his sun-kissed face and his lively conversation.

Upon arriving at the hotel, they go up to the reception desk. Unnoticed, David approaches and wraps Tyler in a surprise hug from behind, eliciting smiles from onlookers at their warm reunion.

The receptionist addresses Tyler in English, handing him his room key and hotel information. Expressing gratitude, Tyler walks with the group, taking in the hotel's vintage charm.

Entering the elevator, Rachel says, "Don't worry about the language. David and I are doing better than we expected."

Tyler seems surprised by Rachel. "Are you telling me you under-stand Mandarin?"

"Not when I got here. Today I can maintain a simple conversation, and I understand well what people are saying," she responds, a little embarrassed.

David interrupts the conversation. "Now her Mandarin sounds great; two weeks of total immersion, reading, speaking, listening, and writing. It's difficult, especially with the dilemmas she had to face here alone. She transformed herself into three people and did very well."

"That's wonderful, congratulations." Tyler nods at Rachel.

When they reach their floor, she shows him their respective rooms, and then they enter Tyler's. "You thought of everything," Tyler says, opening the door.

In the room again, Tyler hugs David. Rachel sits in an armchair and watches them.

"If it wasn't for her and the doctors, I don't know what would have happened," David confesses to his partner, exhaling deeply.

Tyler opens his suitcase, pulls out two files full of documents, and places them on the table. He informs them he has already purchased his return ticket, with the date open. He sits in the armchair across from Rachel and, laughing, asks, "Do you have enemies here?"

Standing up and reacting, Rachel closes the curtain. She asks for silence with her index finger raised and says, "Enemies? How could David and I be in this situation we live in? No, we've only made friends in Shanghai." Rachel's eyes turn to Tyler. She then points to a socket below the window. Rachel removes the outer cover and reveals a hidden bug.

Tyler's eyes widen in shock, and he stays speechless.

"Are we going to have lunch soon? I know a fantastic restaurant," David asks, getting up from the bed.

"Okay. I'm going to take a shower. We'll meet in David's room. It's 11:15. Give me twenty minutes," Tyler suggests.

The partners leave the room. His face changes from neutral to one of deep concern and surprise. He takes back the two files, puts them in the knapsack, and puts the clothes in the closet. Pausing, he sinks into an armchair, contemplating the gravity of the situation facing his partners in Shanghai. Rachel's changes, especially her weight loss, now make sense. He feels an urgent need to help.

After a refreshing shower, as soon as he leaves the room, his cellphone rings. Mary Lai, from the office, checks in, making sure everything is okay and asking about Rachel and David. "They're okay, sweetie. I predict we'll all be back in a few weeks," he assures her. After a little more conversation, he hangs up.

In David's room, the two partners delve into the revelation that Tyler shared the other day with Rachel—the possibility that Wang is a mafia leader in Shanghai. David absorbs every word, enraptured by the unfolding of the narrative.

A soft knock interrupts them; it's Tyler. David rises from his seat to let him in. As Tyler grasps the end of the conversation, he asks with genuine curiosity, "Is this the same Wang we're talking about?"

Rachel ponders. "Wang runs an import and export business on the pier. He is also a city celebrity, portrayed by the media as a philanthropist. Wherever he goes, people surround him, eager for a chat or a photo."

David's gaze meets Tyler's. "Now that you're here, let's piece together what we know. Let's find out if this is the same Wang." Both Tyler and Rachel nod.

"Are we going to have lunch?" David asks.

"Of course! Today is a celebration. You left the hospital, and Tyler arrived. Tonight, I'm going to drink till I fall down, but not at lunch." Rachel smiles, picking up the room phone and asking the front desk for a taxi.

"I'm starving," Tyler exclaims, opening the door.

They enter the elevator, and David again tells Rachel that it's time to rent a car. She listens to her partner and realizes that she shouldn't have returned the car to the rental company. The car was useful. One night she used the vehicle, which Detective Chong drove, but believing they would travel to London soon, she thought it best to seal the deal. Not wanting to argue, Rachel nods in agreement.

A manager and the reception staff approach the partners as they pass toward the hotel door. "Mr. David, we are happy about your recovery. Everyone here at the hotel was worried."

"Thanks for your words. I'm brand new," David replies, smiling and hunching his body in thanks as he holds on to Tyler.

The partners leave the hotel and get into a taxi parked in front. Inside the car, they make jokes about each other, having fun. At that moment, obstacles do not exist. The three of them are together for whatever comes and goes. On the way to the restaurant, Tyler comments, fascinated by the city, "This city is beautiful."

"I also fell in love with Shanghai," Rachel confesses.

"I want to visit Yu Garden, Jade Buddha Temple, Historic Longhua Temple, and Pagoda, and if it's possible, I want to go to the Walls and Beijing," Tyler instructs while David and Rachel watch, surprised by the demand.

"Why are you making those faces? These are my dreams. I want to see these places."

"I want to see these places too," says David, laughing.

"Me too," Rachel adds.

The three of them laugh together.

When they arrive at the restaurant, they decide to sit on the patio. David's sadness is apparent, remembering Michael. The waiter comes over and they order three beers. As the place is self-service, the trio walks together to the table of delicacies, choosing what they will eat. Returning to the table, Tyler asks, "What's this about having a bug in my room?"

"In the first few days here, we felt someone watching us, evaluating our purpose. I was sure, at that moment, that it was the police or the government. I believe whoever did this just wanted to make sure our intentions were pure. But things changed," Rachel says, taking a moderate sip of her drink.

"I believe Detective Chong installed these wiretaps, thinking, especially regarding David, that it might implicate us in Michael's disappearance."

David's face contorts in frustration. "This detective even insinuated that Michael, and I played a role in Ronaldo's death. It's absurd!" Tyler notices the genuine anguish in David's expression.

Rachel, deep in thought, absorbs David's revelation.

"Another thing: I need access to the investigation into who shot me and why Michael disappeared. I need to be informed about what happened and what the investigation has uncovered. If we don't have the slightest bit of information, we won't be able to figure anything out," David pleads as Rachel devours a chicken thigh. She nods and continues eating.

Tyler laughs at Rachel's response while devouring the chicken. She understands Tyler's gaze and starts laughing too. David, as always, looks at the two of them, not understanding the situation. Everything is back to normal.

Rachel finishes lunch and assures David that they would be better off talking to Chief Bo, as he can be more persuadable than Detective Chong. This time, it's David who nods and shoves a mouthful of pasta into his mouth.

"Sure, I agree, but who is this Boss Bo?" Tyler questions.

Rachel reminds Tyler that she mentioned Boss Bo before and clarifies that since the first day they arrived in Shanghai, he has been helping them.

She talks about the interview they did with Yazuo, the head of the Yakuza, and how the superintendent was impeccable. She remembers the case of the intelligence agents and Chief Bo pushing them away. Tyler, concentrating on her words, also takes a bite of spaghetti and nods his head.

David cuts a chicken breast and doesn't hear what she says, his attention on the plate in front of him.

Rachel summarizes the death of Mr. Chan. She reports the trip to the container factory, the truck accident, and highlights the investigation at the home of Wang's mother and cousin.

"Interesting. What connects this Wang?" Tyler replies.

Rachel clarifies Wang is the only documented witness in the investigative process, as he was the one who found Ronaldo's body. Soon after the investigations, David's accident occurred, which is why she ends by stating that they don't have all the explanations for the little time they had. Even if she doesn't believe in the word, she maintains the confirmed facts appear to be coincidences.

"I'm gobsmacked," Tyler says aloud. "You could write a book with only two weeks here. My God!"

David pays for lunch, and the three of them head toward the exit of the restaurant.

"Rachel, we'll rent a car today," David insists.

"Are you sure you can drive?" she asks, annoyed by his insistence.

"Of course I can. Let's rent because I know the city and we can stop this taxi expense," David points out, looking toward the taxi that waited for them at the door of the restaurant.

Inside the car, David explains the destination to the driver: "Shanghai's Promenade, the Bund."

The taxi driver nods his head and drives off.

"Why didn't you mention the name of the hotel? Where are we going?" Tyler asks.

"Today you're in for a surprise. We are heading to the crown jewel of Shanghai, a place rich in architectural diversity, with hallmarks of French and English influence. The iconic Huangpujiang River flows through it, taking us to Huangpu Park, the oldest in Shanghai. The park itself whispers stories of clandestine spy meetings, shady assassinations, and strained alliances during the Japanese invasion. Later, if you're up for it, we can embark on a cruise to witness where the Huangpujiang and Yangtze rivers meet. I've secured our tickets for the cruise. It will be an opportunity for us to talk, away from prying ears," David says with an air of mystery.

Tyler looks at David with a raised eyebrow. "You're well versed in Chinese culture, aren't you? Ever thought of being a tour guide?"

David offers a wistful smile. "Not as much as you might think. I grew up in California. My parents moved there when I was just a baby. My upbringing was all-American. In fact, it was very difficult to learn Mandarin at home. My parents chose not to teach me; they didn't want interference in my 'American education.' Everything I know about my roots, I learned on my own."

"I've already taken that boat ride. You'll love it," Rachel, enthusiastic, informs Tyler.

"Wow! I didn't expect this today. Let's go, I want to enjoy every moment here in Shanghai," Tyler exclaims, ecstatic with what David prepared.

The taxi stops at one of the most picturesque locations along the west bank of the Huangpu River—the Bund. Getting out of the car, the three are stunned by the image of the river.

Walking along the boardwalk, the architectural symphony of Western-style buildings enchants them, reminiscent of the late nineteenth and twentieth centuries. Each structure tells its own story, featuring diverse architectural styles: neoclassical meets Beaux-Arts. Gothic shadows sit alongside radiant baroque buildings.

The vibe at the Bund is palpable. Locals and tourists flood the area, adding to its electric atmosphere. People of all nationalities take photos against the backdrop of the river, filling the air with a multitude of languages, and children's laughter resounds. There's an undeniable spirit of joy and wonder that permeates the air.

"This is a wonderful place. I needed a place like this. I want to relax," Tyler says, looking at Rachel with a smile on his lips.

She approaches her partners, who talk, gesture, and laugh. The sensation she feels is one of enormous peace.

After walking for a long time, they reach the end of the boardwalk and read a sign: "Bund Historical Museum."

"We've arrived at the park," David announces.

The view from where the three sit is the Monument to the People's Heroes, a concrete structure commemorating the martyrs of the revolution. Several people are sitting on the benches, talking, while others eat. Some sit on the grass enjoying picnics, and couples walk hand in hand. They find an empty table with cement benches and sit down.

Tyler stares at David and Rachel, his expression solemn. "It's time we addressed the issue at hand," he says. He opens his leather bag, revealing two packed folders full of documents. He hands one to David and one to Rachel, and they delve into the pages, eager to uncover their contents.

Clearing his throat, Tyler details his findings: "In our investigation, the dots connected very well." He recounts a crucial meeting he had with the CEO of the company that hired them. "I clarified that the robbery at the pier was not just a random diversion—it was gang-related." Tyler remembers the CEO's reaction, noting the man's skepticism and abruptness. "He didn't digest the explanation, nor did he have the patience to listen to me. He just got up, with no formality, and left."

The next day, Tyler found an unexpected document. "They cancelled our contract with DRT," he says, holding up the paperwork. "However, true to their word, they have enclosed a cheque for the full contract in case of any breach on their part."

Rachel and David remain silent, attentive to his report.

He fixes his gaze on Rachel and says that the one who brought the document breaking the contract was a lawyer and a secretary to the CEO.

"Were these women Chinese?" Rachel asks.

Tyler responds, "They were lawyers with offices in London, and I did not discuss the cancellation; I just signed the breach of contract receipt and received the cheque. In the end, when delivering the signed document, the lawyer was adamant that there would be no further investigation. As they left, I voiced loud and clear, 'Your opinion, not mine.'"

David and Rachel examine the termination papers and the duplicate cheque credited to the DRT account.

Tyler's brow furrows in contemplation when Rachel asks, "Did the CEO's behaviour lead you to suspect the company?"

Tyler takes a deep breath before responding, "The findings of my investigation suggested deeper underlying issues. The director's irrational response, followed by the sudden termination the next day, all confirmed my reservations. It was as if the pieces of the puzzle had fallen into place. My suspicions were not just unfounded doubts; there was more obstruction to the narrative than what they informed us."

Rachel's gaze sharpens with concern. "Were you threatened or intimidated in any way?"

Shaking his head, Tyler, in a firm voice, replies, "No," proceeding to unravel the complex story.

The weight of Tyler's words is heavy in the park filled with a mysterious past. "My sources confirmed that one of the Triad factions in London orchestrated the robbery. The shipment, sent by a non-Triad associate from Shanghai, was an attempt to infiltrate the London market. Another thing is that the stolen goods included narcotics—heroin, fentanyl, and other potent synthetic products. The London gang only imported these substances."

Rachel, her face pale with realization, interrupts. "It's a blessing that you dropped this investigation when you did. That revelation could have tarnished DRT's reputation, putting our business at risk."

Tyler's voice shakes as he continues, "What devastated me, however, was the fate of my two main informants. After sharing this information with me, they both died in a car accident. They were leaving work together when the 'so-called' tragedy struck."

"What?" David exclaims in surprise.

Some people in the park turn to watch them, but the partners don't pay attention.

"Unbelievable, but it was an accident. I confirmed with the traffic agents who responded to what happened. The police officers who investigated confirmed to me it was a tragedy." Tyler shows his sadness about the event.

"This smells to me like the same fatality as Ronaldo. First accident and then homicide," Rachel notes, stunning the two of them with what she says.

Rachel continues to look at her partners and completes her thought. "Sorry, I don't believe any police reports anymore if I don't verify it myself."

"Well, back to the subject," Tyler says.

"Are you sure it was an accident?" David asks.

The partner reveals that, after the deaths of the informants, he almost gave up continuing the investigation. In the end, he dug deeper and discovered the name Tong, a gang based in Shanghai. He says he contacted some police associates in the United States and Canada, who informed him that a group called Tong currently exports Chinese products and narcotics. One surprising fact that intel reported was that they entered the American, Canadian, and Spanish markets, and this was their first attempt in the London market.

"So, it's not a small gang, it could be the Triad itself," Rachel comments.

Tyler states, "I couldn't locate the buyer of the goods that were exported. Luckily, I knew who exported. The company is called Savingu International Logistics Co. Ltd. and the owner, known as the head of Tong, is called Wang Savin Wei."

Tyler searches inside the bag for some papers and shows them to the members of the DRT.

Rachel's eyes widen with surprise at the complete name.

"I received these copies of documents from Canadian, American, and London intelligence officers. You can see that the information is just the same." Tyler shows his partners the evidence.

David and Rachel look over the documents, and a simultaneous understanding washes over them. "Wang," they murmur almost in unison.

Tyler's eyebrows furrow in confusion. "Do you know him?"

For a moment, David is silent, his gaze rising, lost in thought, but then his eyes fall on Rachel with a knowing look. She swallows hard, her voice shaking as she begins, "Yes, I know him. I … let's just say I know him."

Tyler's perplexity deepens, and he looks from Rachel to David for clarification.

David, trying to lighten the mood, laughs and shakes his head, full of fun. "Oh, man, here we go."

Rachel takes a deep breath, looking regretful. "I admit it. It was a vulnerable moment. A mental and physical breakdown. I don't know what happened that night, but I needed someone, and I turned to Wang."

Her eyes glisten with tears, struggling to maintain her composure. Standing up brusquely, she says, "I'm sorry," before running toward the park bathroom, leaving David and Tyler in sombre silence.

Tyler follows her with his gaze and turns to David. "Did they have an affair?"

"No. It was just one night, and she dumped him," David responds to Tyler.

"Are you sure it's the same person?" Tyler, eager to learn more, asks.

"She's a hundred percent positive. She knows what she's talking about," David replies to his partner and looks at the path Rachel has taken, worried.

After a few minutes, Rachel returns to the table, looks her two best friends in the eyes, and says, "I'm embarrassed. What else am I going to say? I can assure you both that it was only one night."

"I know, Rachel. You told me." David tries to calm his partner, agreeing with what she says, and hands her a bottle of water he removed from his backpack.

After drinking some water, calmer and more confident, she looks at Tyler, who stares at her. She says, "Wang is engaging, but something is amiss about him. He shows signs of being possessive and has a varied sense of humour. He pressured me, and I didn't like it, so I sent him walking."

Tyler's face tightens, the crease between his eyebrows deepening as he asks without hesitation, "Did he ever make you uncomfortable? Did he cross the line?"

Rachel takes a deep breath. "No, it was just the opposite. He was extravagant and generous. Charismatic, rich, always in the spotlight, signing autographs. Everywhere we went, a diverse crowd approached him, paying their respects or handing him their cards. "But Tyler…" she hesitates, choosing her words with care. "From his look, his mannerisms, and certain things he said… he didn't seem so ordinary. When words weren't enough, he resorted to gestures. He tried to give me lavish jewellery and even offered to let me use his private jet." She laughs, a hint of disbelief in her voice. "He even proposed marriage."

"I'll be honest with you. First, if I were in your shoes, I might have done the same and dated Wang. And believe me, I've made my fair share of questionable decisions, especially after one or two drinks," Tyler says. David and Rachel exchange amused glances, their laughter bubbling up again, easing the tension in the air.

Rachel's expression darkens as she recalls a disturbing incident at the port. "After our boat ride, as we were heading to the parking lot, a distressed woman with her daughter approached us. She pleaded with Wang, asking about her husband. Although my Mandarin is not fluent, I could feel her desperation. What horrified me was Wang's cold and dismissive response. The poor woman was so distraught that she knelt down, sobbing.

In the end, he threw a wad of money at her. His insensitivity," Rachel continues, her voice full of disapproval, "surprised me."

Tyler's jaw clenches, his eyes narrowing. "I need to see this Wang face to face. I lost two of my key informants in what they call an 'accident.' Deep down, I too am convinced they were silenced." The gravity in his voice underscores the seriousness of the situation.

Rachel pulls out her phone and calls Wang's number from memory, saying, "How's this for no hesitation?" David and Tyler watch in surprise. Wang answers the phone, and Rachel, artificial, reciprocates his charm, making him believe she's interested. She invites him to dinner to introduce her partner who has arrived in Shanghai.

"I'll do whatever you want. Are we going out tomorrow? I'll pick you up at the hotel at 5 p.m., okay?" Wang asks. Rachel agrees and suggests that he help her make a sightseeing itinerary in Shanghai. Wang concurs and hangs up.

Rachel's talent for manipulating the situation leaves David and Tyler in awe. She announces, "Okay, all set. Tomorrow at 5 p.m. at the hotel, he'll come to pick us up, and the four of us will have dinner."

"We'll have to move from the hotel to the apartment tomorrow," David reminds her.

Rachel, frowning, sends a message to the real estate agent to arrange moving into the apartment. Moments later, she receives a confirming message and announces, "Good news. We can pick up the apartment keys tomorrow at 11 a.m. We're ready to move in!"

"Then it's decided. Now, let's take this boat ride," David says.

The three of them head to the pier at Shiliupu Wharf near the Bund to board their cruise. At the port, they observe a diverse crowd waiting to board. As it gets darker and the weather changes, they put on their coats and admire the star-filled sky and the enchanting moon.

"I'm super excited about this cruise," Tyler comments as they get in line.

David explains his choice of tickets for the shorter cruise without dinner, leading to a playful debate about dinner plans, with Tyler insisting on Shanghai's famous dumplings.

The cruise begins by revealing the stunning night view of the Huangpu River, with its illuminated buildings on both sides. "Oh my God! That's beautiful," Rachel exclaims.

During the cruise, Rachel and David share with Tyler the details of their investigation over the past eleven days. Tyler, absorbed, loses interest in the ride as he listens to their stories.

After the cruise, Tyler suggests reviewing the report on the computer when they get back to the hotel. As they enjoy the light show, Tyler brings up a crucial point about the connections between Wang, the Tong gang, and the suspicious accidents. "Let's be objective, this story that Wang was the only witness in Ronaldo's case, plus the possibility that he is the head of Tong in Shanghai and the drug exports that are being made, perhaps, by his company... it's all connected," Tyler concludes.

David and Rachel listen, agreeing with Tyler's assessment. They resolve to rethink their investigation strategy with the new information Tyler has brought.

"I agree, but I also need to find out where Michael is. I have to find him," David adds with full conviction.

"Don't worry, I'll be the first to help you," Rachel reassures him.

"At no point did I rule that out. We're going to investigate Michael and cover our footsteps with the excuse of Operation Portugal," Tyler adds.

The three of them, united in their determination, disembark from the boat. They hail a taxi and head back to the hotel, captivated by the beauty of Shanghai's vibrant streets.

Back at the hotel, they disperse to their respective rooms to freshen up and meet back at the lobby in thirty minutes. "Don't forget to take the meds. I'm going to take a quick shower and meet you guys in the lobby," Rachel reminds David, who assures Tyler he's feeling much better and looking forward to starting physical therapy.

"Let's go find Michael," Tyler says with confidence as they part ways.

31

"It May Not Be What It Seems."

Detective Chong walks down the stairs of Warehouse #1, head lowered, a weight of worry etching lines across his face. He can't shake the feeling that something remains unsaid, something hidden beneath the owner's peculiar behaviour. Stopping on the top step, he reanalyzes the recent interaction in his mind. Wang is almost certain when he says he doesn't know the man in the photograph. The people at the other warehouses, the ones he talked to over coffee this morning, tell a different story—a story where Wonjy is not a stranger but a childhood friend of Wang and Hui, the manager.

With unanswered questions in his thoughts, Chong leaves the warehouse, putting the puzzle together as he walks down the street toward the port. He looks at the endless expanse of warehouses painted with huge letters and numbers spread across the side walls. Observing the harsh routine of the place, he discovers a new world that never interested him. Trucks loaded with stacked containers roam the busy streets. Workers perform a chaotic dance, with carts moving from one location to another amid a symphony of marches, slow-moving traffic, and shrill screams. The uproar surrounds him, almost swallowing him.

With his eyes on the warehouses, the sight of the number four sets him in motion. He remembers when Liao, the owner of the snack bar, put a paper in his hand. He takes it out of his pants pocket and reads the name.

"Come on. Maybe today I'll find out where Zhao works," Detective Chong says to himself, walking toward Warehouse #4.

Chong arrives in front of Warehouse #4, his mind so confused that he doesn't notice the heavy truck coming toward him and almost hitting him. He staggers back, scared, his heart almost coming out of his mouth, watching the vehicle pass him, avoiding what could have been a horrible accident. Unbalanced, he falls to the dirt and pebble ground. A cloud of dust forms around him. One loader runs out of the warehouse toward him, shouting, extending his hand to help him up.

"Hey, are you okay?" the worker asks with genuine concern. "Be careful here. We all want to go home."

Chong, catching his breath, says, "I didn't see the truck. I don't know the port very well," and a blush of embarrassment warms his cheeks. He pats his pants and shirt clean, trying to get the dirt from the street off his clothes, and stabilizes himself, still recovering from the shock.

The employee squints at him, noticing the detective's persistent gaze at the warehouse. "Looking for someone there?"

"I'm looking for Boss Dong," Chong replies, his voice firmer, the name hanging in the air between them.

"Oh no, Dong is not here. He is in the office. Go down this street," the employee points out, "and turn right at the next corner near the parking lot. You will see a staircase next to the wall of the building. The office is at the top." The employee walks away from the detective and enters the dark interior of Warehouse #4.

"Thanks!" Chong shouts, but his gratitude dissolves into the clamour of the port, unheard.

Arriving at the office, the detective knocks on the door and opens it. He sees a scene of controlled chaos before him: a metal table buried under a massive pile of documents, notebooks, and maps. Behind it sits a man.

"What do you want?" A burly man raises his head, peering from behind the mountain of papers, his features marked by a mixture of annoyance and fatigue. His voice is an echo in the cluttered space, a silent barrier against unsolicited disturbances, but undeterred, Chong enters.

Boss Dong was a longshoreman for over thirty years. Upon his retirement, they offered Boss Dong the opportunity to run Warehouse #4. He gained a reputation for his actions rather than his words. Few people dominate the port like him, and those he serves admire him for his simplicity, humility, and ability to coordinate the men into their positions.

"Boss Dong?" the detective asks, showing his police badge.

The man motions to come in and points to a chair.

Detective Chong settles down and introduces himself. "Chief Dong, I'm Detective Chong, head of homicide in Shanghai."

"What can I help you with, Detective?" the chief asks, getting up from his chair and leaning against the table, facing the visitor.

Chong takes the photos from inside the envelope he carries and shows them. He observes the reaction of the head of the warehouse upon receiving the images.

Dong takes the two photos and stares at them. It shows on his face that he tries to remember. He returns Wonjy's photo, saying: "This one has been an employee of Warehouse Number Two and One for years. If you go there, look for Hui or Wang, and they can introduce you to Wonjy."

"Hui or Wang?" repeats Detective Chong and writes on the notepad as if he doesn't know.

"That's right, Hui, the general manager, and Wang, the owner of the warehouses. Wonjy, in this photograph, has been working there for years. It looks like he's a childhood friend of Wang and Hui's." Chief Dong explains what he knows with no concern.

Detective Chong notes the sentence "They're childhood friends."

Boss Dong looks at Zhao's photo again and says he remembers this man but isn't sure what to say about him. He pauses for a moment and calls two names over the intercom: "Dhanzy or Hujhi, come to the office."

While waiting, the detective places the picture of Wonjy on the table and writes in the notebook what Chief Dong narrated. In a minute, the office door opens, and two men appear, gasping for breath from the rush from the warehouse to the office.

"What's going on, boss?" Dhanzy says.

"Dhanzy and Hujhi, look at this photograph," Chief Dong orders.

The two of them look at Zhao's picture.

"Who is this man?" Chief Dong asks, staring at them.

Hujhi speaks: "His name is Zhao. Sometimes he shows up around here or in the other warehouses, trying to get a job. He's not a 'permanent' in any of the warehouses."

"Is he working here today?" Boss Dong asks Dhanzy, the general manager of Warehouse #4.

"Nope. I haven't seen him in a while. The last time he tried to work here was about two or three weeks ago, I'm not sure. I filled the vacancies early, and I couldn't hire him," Dhanzy, getting suspicious with all the questions, replies to the boss.

"I remember," Hujhi good-naturedly confirms to Chief Dong.

"What do you remember, Hujhi?" the boss asks.

Detective Chong, sitting in front of the three men, observes each one's facial and body reactions. From experience in interrogations, he can assure that Dhanzy and Hujhi are not lying about Zhao.

"I saw when he came here and Dhanzy said there were no more vacancies. I didn't pay attention and left the warehouse. That's when I saw Hui walking down the avenue, and I told Zhao that I was leaving and to go talk to Hui at Warehouse Number Two. It looks like he got a job," explains Hujhi to the boss.

Chief Dong looks at the two men. "You two always get me in trouble," he says.

Detective Chong introduces himself to the two employees. He greets the two workers before fixing his gaze on Hujhi.

"How do you know he got a job at Warehouse Number Two?" Chong's words are blunt but show a subtle curiosity and suspicion with gentle but unyielding firmness. His eyes, attentive and probing, seek more than just the verbal answer; he looks for subtle signs hidden in Hujhi's response.

"The next day, early in the morning, myself and some employees here at number four, when we came to work, saw him arriving on a motorcycle. He left the motorcycle in the parking lot of Warehouse Number Two and went straight in," Hujhi replies.

"Is there a problem with Zhao?" Dhanzy questions.

Detective Chong's mind races, pondering whether to publicize Zhao's death. After a moment, he decides to keep the information hidden. He doesn't know if there might be more important data, so he doesn't want to scare whoever is pulling strings in the shadows. That's why he keeps everything simple, even distant, masking the turbulence of his thoughts with a casual attitude.

"No. I just need to talk to him, that's all." His words hang in the air as he maintains a steady gaze, ensuring his expression reveals no urgency.

"Hey, you need to talk to Hui, the manager, about Zhao," Hujhi tells the detective. "Sure enough… he knows where to find it."

Dhanzy and Hujhi look at Boss Dong. "Can we get back to work now?"

Detective Chong, pushing back his chair, says, "Hang on, one last thing. Do you guys know Wonjy?"

Dhanzy interrupts, "Yeah, the guy's been here a long time. Everyone knows him. He works at warehouses number one and number two with Hui and Wang."

Chong narrows his eyes a little. "Did you see him around these last few days?"

"No," both men respond in unison.

"Thank you." He leans forward in a quick bow.

Boss Dong, a little curious, asks, "How did you end up at Warehouse Number Four? Did someone tip you off or something?"

"I heard some conversations at the snack bar this morning. I thought maybe one of those guys worked for you."

Boss Dong nods. "Alright, then. If you need anything, just shout. I'll be here." He returns the bow to Chong.

Chong puts a card in Dong's hand and leaves. The other two nod, leaning their bodies forward. Dhanzy and Hujhi glance over at Chief Dong. "Can we get back to the grind now?"

Leaving the office, Chong goes downstairs. At the base of the stairs, he stops, takes out a small, worn notebook, and scribbles down some quick, concise notes, his brow furrowed in contemplation. Upon returning to the place where he left the unmarked police vehicle, near Warehouse #1, he sees Wang walking on the sidewalk and then stopping next to a car. Something about Wang's posture sparks concern in Chong. A disturbing intuition tells him that Wang is not well.

Increasing his pace, Chong tries to close the distance between them, but as soon as he gets closer, Wang, without noticing him, gets into the car and disappears down the street in the opposite direction. Chong can only stand there watching Wang disappear from view, a tight knot of discomfort forming in his stomach.

The detective takes his car and returns to the police station in the city centre.

Upon arriving at the superintendence, he enters his office and analyzes all the information he collected that day. Fortunately, he can now locate where Zhao worked. People who knew him had commented on the motorcycle.

He thinks, *Why does Wang say he doesn't know him if Hui hired him two or three weeks ago?*

Writing in a notebook on the table, he says out loud, "That will have to be answered. Despite his wife and daughter being killed in an accident and no one having seen him for a few days. Wonjy hasn't shown up yet."

Detective Chong scratches his head and remembers that Chief Bo is Wang's friend. *Is this going to be a problem?* he thinks.

The secretary comes to his door, and deep in thought, he doesn't notice her. She knocks on the door and says that Boss Bo has called several times asking for him. "Boss Bo ordered you to go to his office when you arrive."

"Okay, I'm on my way," Detective Chong says. "This is not a coincidence…"

Sighing, he gets up from his chair and walks toward the hallway, runs up the stairs, two at a time, and enters the superintendent's office. He passes the super-intendent's secretary, who smiles, pointing for him to enter the boss's office.

"Did you want to talk to me?" Chong asks and bows in respect.

"Where have you been all day?" Boss Bo asks.

"Looking for the relationships and connections of this guy, Zhao. I'm also investigating the explosion at the farmhouse. It's difficult, but I'm moving fast… I want this investigation to end as soon as possible." The detective yawns, showing his tiredness.

"Have you found anything yet?" the superintendent asks.

"I'm just getting started," Chong hesitantly responds.

Boss Bo continues to engage in the paperwork in front of him, his pen moving with precision over the papers he signs. Chong looks at him, on guard, evaluating his response, as he's unsure if he should reveal more. With everything still open, he prefers to keep it a secret for now.

The superintendent sighs. "Alright, keep me posted."

Aware that he needs to get out of there, Chong admits, "I have a lot of things to do. Just call me if necessary." He almost runs out of the room.

Back in his office, Chong instructs his secretary, "Call Dr. Gonjgin at the identification institute and get someone from the homicide division on the line as well."

Before long, he's talking to the IIS doctor. In a firm tone, he demands, "I need an update on who the husband of the woman who died in the explosion is." He masks his growing tension with professional sharpness. Then, when talking to one of the operation officers, he gets straight to the point: "Find all the records—criminal, procedural—whatever, from the husband of the woman who died in the explosion."

After hanging up, Chong pauses, rubbing his temple. An uncomfort-able thought invades him; he had forgotten to get Hui's full name from

Wang's office. A fleeting expression of annoyance appears on his face, and he mutters to himself, rummaging through his pockets, "Where the hell did I put that card? I forgot to ask about Hui's surname." He continues to try to regain his thoughts.

Ignoring the oversight, he mutters, "That's no big deal. I'll talk to Hui tomorrow."

Detective Chong sinks into the worn leather armchair. Through the slight creaks of the armchair, he calms down. His right hand strums an impatient rhythm on the table and his gaze fixes on nothing. He mutters to himself with a low voice and a sense of frustration. "I can't understand why Wang would say he doesn't know Wonjy. The dockworkers I spoke to today said that Wonjy, Hui, and Wang have known each other since childhood."

His hand slips into his pants pocket again, and his fingers touch the business card Wang handed him earlier. When he removes it, he looks at the text.

He calls his secretary, and she answers, "Yes, boss."

"Call this number and find out the full name of the general manager known as Hui."

She leaves the room and, after a few minutes, comes back, saying, "Hui Chowei is the manager's name."

Detective Chong, satisfied with the information, asks her to call IIS and provide Hui's full name. He also asks her to call the operational department and request a search for that name this morning.

*   *   *

At that same moment in the Pudong neighbourhood. Wang dresses as if he's going to a party and not a professional meeting. He looks in the mirror, blinks at himself, and admires his silver-grey tie. He finishes his whiskey, and his cellphone rings. The name written on the display is Hui.

"Where are you?" Wang's voice cuts through the line.

Hui picks up the distant echo, suggesting a speakerphone. Without knowing who might be next to the boss, he responds with caution: "Heading home. I'm done with all the loading. I gave your secretary the shipping and inspection papers. At 8 a.m., I'll be at the office to meet Detective Chong. Anything else?"

Wang's tone is hushed, almost a whisper. "I have urgent things to do now. Come to my apartment later. We'll talk tonight, okay?"

Hui's exhaustion is clear. "Look, not tonight. I'm exhausted. We'll talk tomorrow."

Wang's frustration grows, his voice tense. "That's not a request, Hui."

Hui's own temper rises. His words are harsh: "I don't care if it's an order. I've been on my feet for over fifteen hours, dealing with crap, and I've sorted it all out. You understand me?"

Wang tries to contain his anger, but there is a hint of panic in his voice. "Listen, Hui, I'm serious. Detective Chong will arrive at 8 a.m. sharp and is eager to talk to you. We need to be on the same page tonight."

"Everything is in order, and we know nothing about Wonjy's family. We have all of his work documentation from all these years in order, such as salaries, extras, bonuses, union, and vacations. He wrote he went to Hong Kong to visit family on the company cellphone. What more do you want?" Hui explains, his voice changing as he loses his patience.

"Well, if you guarantee and take responsibility, I'll believe it. Tomorrow we'll see." The boss hangs up the phone without letting Hui say anything else.

Wang winces, furious at the way the manager debated. He fills his glass and downs another shot of whiskey. As the meeting is important and he will have to decide many things, he tries to calm down. He recalls Rachel and envisions her in the living room of the apartment with him. A moment of joy surrounds him. Tomorrow he will go out to have dinner with her.

He thinks again about what he has to do in the meeting and confirms, "The decisions made tonight could change reality. I have to be careful."

Driving at high speed on the way home, Hui stops at a red light and punches the steering wheel of the car a few times, exclaiming, "Who does he think he is? It's been years since he spoke to me in that tone. He's a vile son of a bitch."

Taking a quick breath, he glances to the left out the car window and realizes a police car has pulled up beside him. Frightened, he pulls himself together, puts both hands on the steering wheel, and looks ahead, as if frozen in time, waiting for the signal. He knows the police officer is watching him. The green light appears, and Hui drives the car with double the attention down the avenue. He looks in the rear-view mirror and sees the police car disappear around the first corner he had passed.

"Shit, why do I care?" he asks himself, trying to calm down.

At that moment, Hui recalls what Wang said: "Well, if you guarantee and take responsibility..."

"Now I understand; this son of a bitch is going to put all the blame on me. Let's see what the detective wants to know. No one is going to put this on my ass..." Hui says, irritated.

* * *

Wang arrives at the hotel, and in the lobby, Kang Wu's head of security is waiting for him.

"Hey, boss," greets Guowei, lowering his head in respect.

"Evening, Guowei. Has everyone arrived yet?" Wang asks, walking beside him toward the elevator.

"Everyone is present. Where is Hui?" Guowei's voice carries a hint of surprise, missing his usual companion.

"Just me tonight," Wang replies, his words brief.

Wang, standing in front of the elevator, scans the hotel lobby with an experienced eye. He locates the surveillance cameras and counts the two reception employees. His attention turns to the hotel's main entrance, noticing the staff: an attendant, a doorman, and a valet, each playing their role with ease. Remembering the beauty of the hotel on the upper level, the meeting spaces, receptions, and conference areas on the top five floors cross his mind, not to mention the opulent array of international restaurants on the rooftop.

His memory reminds him of the last time he was there, his eyes taking in the familiar light-beige marble, his ears attentive but registering the gentle current of the ambient music, while the soft, discreet lighting and the fresh scent of nearby foliage fill the space. Upon reaching the ground floor, the two men enter the elevator, and, in that brief space of time, they disconnect from the complexities of the outside world.

Upon arriving on the fifty-fifth floor, Kang Wu welcomes him and hugs him. The opulence of the hall is incomparable. Everything is in a contemporary style but elegant and rich in decoration.

The other three bosses are sitting in comfortable armchairs, awaiting his arrival. Hearing Wang's voice entering the hall, they get up and head toward him. Wang embraces them one by one, like a son or father who respects his family members.

Guozhi goes to the bar and chooses one of the best whiskies. He lifts the bottle, showing it to Wang, who nods his head in approval. He fills a glass with two ice cubes and hands it to the boss.

"Today is a day of decisions and celebration. It has been five years since we have been together," Wang says and raises the glass in a toast with the men.

"Salute to our union," Kang Wu toasts.

Those present repeat the phrase and salute: "To our union."

Wang asks Kang Wu to have the escorts of the chiefs leave the hall. The security guards and the number two or three of each leader's hierarchy withdraw. The bosses sit around the round wooden table.

"Turn off your phones; we can't risk someone recording our conversation," Wang instructs as he places his phone on a side table, and the other chiefs do the same.

"Why this urgent meeting?" asks Changpu.

"Don't you miss me?" Wang jokes, eliciting laughter from the bosses. He settles into the armchair, takes another sip of his whiskey, and announces, "I put an informant inside the Triad some time ago. I will not specify who he is, nor the place where he acts or anything else that could put the person's life at risk."

The four leaders look at each other in surprise and remain focused on what the boss has informed them.

Wang's voice fills the room with tension as he informs everyone: "He called me this afternoon and warned me that the Triad is planning to steal our merchandise that leaves early tomorrow morning." His eyes, steady and penetrating, examine each of the bosses, assessing every muscle of their reactions.

"Impossible," Kang Wu retorts, his voice a fragmented mix of disbelief and anger, his demeanour filled with raw indignation.

"Why impossible?" Huan Zhang, fighting back his own anger, responds.

Guozhi, the man who directs Tong's activities and finances with unwavering command, speaks, trying to control the charged atmosphere. "It's possible, and we all know it. The Triad would fight wars here, there, anywhere, without batting an eye, all in the name of maintaining their power and reputation. Now, I'm saying this is possible because of the Tong's obvious envy. Look at us. In five years, we have built an empire right here in Shanghai. They see our advanced technology and innovative intelligence as threatening assets, realizing that our capabilities affect their daily profits. The Triad, of course, doesn't just want ten percent of our daily profit. They want much more."

"You are overreacting, as always," says Changpu, pouring the rest of the bottle of whiskey into his own glass.

Wang leans in, a touch of urgency in his voice. "Hui just called. He called to inform us they loaded our cargo and took care of the paperwork—inspections, permits. So how the hell do they plan to attack us?"

The room stays tense, everyone thinking.

Kang Wu breaks the silence. "When does the boat leave?"

Wang says, "We should finish loading and configuring the material from other companies between 4:00 and 5:00 in the morning."

"We need our men on that boat. Now," says Changpu, looking at the leaders.

Guozhi's voice shakes, a mixture of frustration and anxiety. "Look, any robbery they're planning will be on the boat before departure. On the open sea, it would be too risky."

Wang nods, absorbing the information. "I'll get another call around 10 p.m. We should have more information then."

Changpu swallows hard, eyes fixed on Wang. "This will bring me to the end of the line, Wang. We are talking about over a million yuan here."

"We've all invested a lot in this," Wang retorts, his gaze unwavering.

Kang Wu, as always, does not display any signs of being disturbed; he is just absorbing the reactions, threats, and vociferous outbursts of those around him. His fist hits the table, making the room shake.

"Shut up! Nothing will happen!" His voice is uneven, strained, and furious.

Wang, about to leave, stops, turning to take in the cacophony, the absolute chaos that envelops the table.

Recovering from the tension, Wang's voice mixes with the uproar, an accusatory arrow aimed at Kang Wu. "You always protect them!" His eyes are fixed and full of meaning.

"I know that you, as a friend of the Triad leaders, questioned this action… Now to say that it is impossible for this to happen…" argues Guozhi and sits down in the armchair.

Kang Wu's gaze sweeps over the men, his breathing rapid and uneven as beads of sweat run down his furrowed brow.

With strength, Wang picks up his glass of whiskey and drinks it in one defiant gulp. "Alright, everyone shut up. Let's give Kang Wu the floor," Wang, now recalibrated, shouts the order, leaning back in his chair. He fills his glass from an extra bottle of whiskey and focuses his attention on the unfolding scene.

"Wang, I am Tong's voice, its negotiator with the Triad. Remember, you are the one who appointed me five years ago." His voice evens out, a deliberate calm amid the storm. "Understand that being the liaison, working out agreements, keeping the peace—that does not protect me from dissent. We have been in a peace treaty with the old guard of the Triad for years. But now, with the new leadership, even though they respect our financial influence, the relationship is not what it used to be. A year has passed since our last meeting and things cannot continue on this path." Kang Wu lays out the situation with unwavering eyes, meeting each man's gaze with genuine sincerity.

"Should *you* have already scheduled a new meeting?" shouts Huan Zhang.

"I proposed twice, and you guys turned it away. No one explained to me why you didn't want to get together," Kang Wu returns, looking at the bosses.

"You can try to pass the blame for the situation. Now, if someone from the Triad is going to rob us tonight, I don't care if it was the new boss or the old boss who gave the order, I will defend what is ours," Huan Zhang says, filled with indignation.

"Wang, talking about this won't solve it anymore—we're past that point." Changpu's voice cuts through the tension, hard and assertive. "First, if we expose the informant, he will be as good as dead, and we will trigger a war, confirming our suspicion and providing proof of it. If we consider the information to be credible, it also shakes our trust in it. We are at an impasse. So, what's our game here? Whether we choose to set up a new meeting or prepare for war, our position is defensive," he states, outlining a way out of the situation, saying each word with firm determination.

The leaders talk, and Wang watches Kang Wu in silence.

"We will have to send some men to protect the boat and bring others in as quickly as possible. Only then will we be able to defend our exports," advises Changpu.

Wang's voice cuts them off, letting out a hint of controlled anger. "You all know that someone stole last month's export at the Port of London. Someone planned it well; they emptied the warehouses of all legitimate documentation." Wang's eyes roam the bosses, probing, searching for any glimmer of guilt or prescience in their expressions.

"Yes, I am aware," Huan Zhang admits, his fingers preoccupied with his scalp.

Guozhi's voice is sharp and accusatory. "You said you had everything under control," he says, pointing at Wang.

Kang Wu's words hit the room with a strong, chilling force. "Don't even try to tell me it was the Triad who stole our products." His gaze is unyielding, fixed on the boss.

Changpu's eyes lock onto Kang Wu, his voice seething with pent-up frustration. "That's all we need right now." His gaze doesn't waver, the words hanging in the tense air.

Wang's voice scrapes through the thick tension, each word weighing with a mixture of frustration and suppressed anger. "We called the local police. We looked for every clue and still no evidence, no names, nothing! I even included a company of private detectives in the search. And what did they find out from the informants at the docks? That one of the Triad gangs stole our merchandise in London Harbour." Wang slams his fist on the table, the impact echoing in the charged air.

"The bastards say we didn't have the right to enter the London market. Yes, we had agreed with the Triad here in Shanghai, but they are acting like idiots. So, tell me, Kang Wu, how the hell do you explain this?" Wang's eyes, shining with a scorching and unyielding gaze, fix on Kang Wu.

A thick tension envelops the room, each man sitting, eyes wide, bodies rigid, hostage to a mix of terror and expectation. Everyone knows Wang's notorious explosive temper, especially in situations like this. All the chiefs' eyes turn to Kang Wu, each asking, fearing, begging him to say something, anything, in response to the fury unleashed before them.

Kang Wu's voice cuts through the tension, a sharp mix of defiance and menace. "Look, we made the deal with the Triad when our focus was on importers—the United States, Canada, the Americas, Europe. Everything was going well until someone stole the products in London. In all these years, we have never had this problem. So don't you dare blame me or cast a shadow of suspicion in my direction." Kang Wu returns to Wang with intimidation, standing firm under Wang's scorching gaze, shielding himself from the unspoken accusation that hangs in the air.

"I did what I could—I quashed a lawful police investigation, I shelled out a small fortune on police officers, detectives, and whistleblowers…I closed the matter before it could destroy our operations." Wang's voice remains steady, his gaze fixed on Kang Wu. "Now I ask you, how will you ship to London again and try to establish a connection in that city?"

Changpu's voice fills the room. "Look, we have two gigantic problems on our hands," he declares, his fists clenched. "There's no point discussing London here right now; it won't change anything that happened. Tonight, right now, we have to protect the containers that are going to be shipped!" His words ripple through the room in a flash of desperate urgency.

Wang takes the floor. "Huan Zhang, you are the best connected with the administration, captains, and superiors of these ships, aren't you?" Wang's voice trembles, a rare note of anxiety appearing. "Go over there, talk to them, get your hands dirty, and put about twenty of our men on that ship. Spend whatever it takes. These goods need to get where they are going. Otherwise, our debt will increase to three times the London fiasco. This shipment is coming from the Golden Triangle. Can you imagine the fires of hell burning our bodies if that happens? If the cargo disappears?" The words from Wang hang in the air, and dread continues to envelop the room.

"Okay, boss," Huan agrees and gets up from his chair.

"Guozhi, Changpu, I need fifty of our smartest guys on that dock right now." Wang's voice is low but permeated with tension, his gaze flickering between the two men. "Choose the best ones you have. Put them where they will be most useful—handling cargo, working on the docks, managing shipments, tariff rates, and anywhere else you think they might need a watchful eye. That way, no one will escape our control and they won't have the courage to steal our containers tonight." Determination takes over his features. "And listen, this is crucial. I don't want any shots fired. I want them subdued, trapped, and stored in one, two, or three containers. No fatalities. We can't afford to turn the spotlight on us." Wang's order, unequivocal and final, resonates in the expectant silence of the room.

"Don't worry, we'll take it one by one," Guozhi assures him.

"I'm going. There won't be any guns. My men don't need that," Changpu agrees as well.

On the side table, Wang's cell rings, as it sits together with the other bosses phones. He stands up and answers. Silence prevails in the room. Wang only murmurs, agreeing, and after almost a minute of listening, hangs up. He gazes at the anxious bosses and declares, "All confirmed, they're going to steal this tonight."

The men look at each other, murmuring.

"Alright, go there and sort everything out. Kang Wu, you stay. We need to talk." Wang's voice is level, stone-cold but underpinned by coiled tension. "Huan, Guozhi, Changpu, be careful there. Call me if anything happens. I'll be here, waiting. Come back here at 5:30, or whenever you're sure the coast is clear," he adds, stitching each word together.

The three chiefs mutter a unified "okay," bowing together. They each pick up their cellphones and leave the room with silent, shared understanding.

Kang Wu does not move at all during the moments of agitation and indignation of the leaders. He sits with his hands folded on the table, looking at the empty glass of whiskey in front of him.

When the footsteps in the hallway disappear and silence takes over the room, Wang drags a chair, placing himself in front of Kang Wu, his eyes fixed, unblinking, on the man in front of him.

"Can you imagine how much money we lost in this operation in London?" Wang asks.

Kang Wu takes the empty glass, gets up, and moves the armchair away. He goes to the bar, pours more whiskey, and drinks it all. Kang gives Wang a disdainful look and says, "Do you want to find fault in these two situations? It won't be me." He leans back in the armchair and looks out the window into the darkness.

The boss, without emotion, looks at his partner of years, saying nothing as Kang Wu continues.

"After tonight, only two things can happen. One, there will be a war between the Tong and the Triad and the other, a meeting, if they accept. I hope it's just the meeting where we can wash the dishes and adjust the agreements again."

Wang takes a deep breath, drinks, and doesn't respond.

"If they declare war on us…You will be responsible for us losing everything we have built. We discuss everything in this life; none of us can be intransigent with things that are easy to resolve. We do not have the strength to overcome them. Why don't we call our Triad friends and set up a meeting?" Kang Wu's voice explains with wisdom and calm what is going to happen. However, he sees in Wang's eyes the inflexibility he has been showing for some time and becomes nervous.

"Why would you want to do that if they're the ones who are cheating us?" Wang asks.

Kang Wu doesn't respond to Wang and continues talking. "If we get everything straightened out before 5 a.m., there will be no blood running down the docks and no other problems…

"By handing over the informant, we can ensure that the Triad higher-ups will be negotiable as we highlight their error. You will demand the London market, the ship will sail, and everything will be peaceful again," says Kang Wu.

"You seem confident that this will happen. Are you part of the Triad now?" Wang notices the sweat running down Kang's face and, impatient with the criticism, confronts him.

"I will not argue with you. I don't want and don't need confusion with you or others, and we can't have problems with the Triad. For years we have lived in peace, made a great deal of money, and stabilized Tong in Shanghai and in the international market. We can resolve it with a peaceful solution. We kill two birds with one stone," an annoyed Kang Wu insists to the boss.

"Well, I bet you we will capture the Triad men who go to the port tonight, and not a drop of blood will fall. So, let's see who will give the orders… it will be me," Wang expounds with his ego, saying what he wants to do, not looking at Kang Wu.

After his declaration, the boss gets up from the armchair and goes to the bar in the meeting's corner room. He grabs a bottle of whiskey, fills two glasses, and puts in some ice cubes.

"What makes you think you can give the orders? It doesn't matter if you capture them or not; understand that the shit thrown on the fan will return," Kang Wu says, twisting his head to the left and snorting.

Wang hands over the glass of whiskey as if nothing is happening and says to his companion, "Let's eat and wait for the answer."

Kang Wu gets up from the armchair, walks toward the bathroom, and stops, looking for the cellphone he can't find.

"Are you looking for this?" Wang asks.

Kang Wu stares at him.

"It's here on the table with mine." Wang returns his gaze, pointing to the phones at the edge of the table.

Kang Wu doesn't respond; he just goes straight to the bathroom. He is sweating and is aware that his breathing is anything but regular. When he enters, his blood pressure plummets; clinging to the sink, he feels his body trapped, his clothes stuck to him, soaked with sweat. An agonizing need to use the bathroom takes over, and unexpected diarrhea leaves him stuck there for what seems like an eternity. His head falls between his knees, fingers pressing hard into the back of his neck as he tries to compose himself.

Before he leaves the bathroom, he has a clear idea; he can't let Wang see him unbalanced like this. Appearing to recover, he takes off his shirt and dries it with the hand dryer. He looks in the mirror, recognizing the cruel truth. Age is no longer on his side. He is old, inside and out, but he is not yet ready to die. His eyes catch sight of a small hotel bag on the black marble sink. Hidden within are a comb, cologne, and cream. A lifeline. He cleans himself up, pulls himself together, finding stability. Now he just needs to find some salt or eat something. This should help his blood pressure recover.

Wang notices Kang Wu's prolonged absence from the bathroom but doesn't worry about it. Instead, he calls the hotel reception, asking about the dinner they ordered with the booking and explaining that for now, there will only be two people dining. The rest of the team will return at dawn.

When Kang Wu exits the bathroom, his eyes follow two waiters who are exiting the room with an empty cart in tow. His gaze lands on the table where the food was served, and he sees Wang sitting in a chair pouring wine into two glasses. Kang Wu moves to the table, sinking into his chair, eyes scanning the array of tempting dishes. His fingers search for the saltshaker, finding it positioned next to the pepper in front of his plate.

"I'm hungry," he declares, picking up a plate of dumplings.

"Let's make a toast first." Wang raises his glass.

Kang Wu, looking at him, takes the wine glass and together they toast.

In the corridor, some of Kang Wu's security guards are still waiting for him. Guowei is his head of security and was the one who received Wang at the entrance. As the two bosses are still having dinner, he goes underground and checks if the vehicles are in order. In the elevator, he remembers Hui didn't accompany Wang to the hotel and calls to check.

The manager answers and doesn't say a word. He hears Guowei say, "Hui, why didn't you come with the boss?"

Hui, returning home, recognizes the voice of his friend and says, "Hello, Guowei. Haven't spoken to you in a while."

"An important meeting like this with the five Tong chiefs and you're not here. Did something happen?" he asks.

Hui, at the same moment, understands that something important has happened. He is convinced that there's something in the air but can't identify it, especially given the abnormal meeting with the Tong's bosses. He knows Wang… always premeditating both the possible and the impossible. He suspects Wang had to hold this meeting, intending to assert himself with the leaders. If something unexpected happens, he will need their support in the actions he must undertake. "Insurance died of old age!" He remembers the saying and the reasons. *I'll have to be careful with my words.*

"Guowei, I worked on the ship all day. You can't imagine how tiring today was, and I just got out of there now. Since I'm dirty and need a shower, there's no way I can keep up with the boss. We talked, and he sent me home. I'm exhausted. Today was difficult…" Hui replies to his friend.

"Oh, okay, I got it. I called because you're always glued to him. We're here in Pudong, and it's not a normal thing for him to arrive alone. Especially here at The Ritz," Guowei says.

Upon thinking, the manager identifies the hotel and realizes its proximity to Wang's apartment, just a five-minute walk away. Recalling Guowei's self-centred nature, he begins with, "You're familiar with the boss's quirks. You know how he loves to wander the streets alone, mingling with ordinary people and giving interviews. The public always had a strong connection with him. But today, I have peace of mind knowing he is under your watchful eye. I'm sure his entire security team is with him. I'll tell you a little secret: his apartment is just five minutes from the hotel. That's why we didn't have reservations; we knew he would be under the best care with you."

Guowei accepts the compliment: "Understood, Hui. Don't worry, this place is safer than you think. Leave everything to us and thank you for your trust." The manager couldn't help but notice he had further inflated Kang Wu's security chief's already inflated ego.

"Let's arrange lunch or dinner. It's been a while since we've met," Hui invites.

"I accept. It's been a while since we went out for lunch." Guowei, with his ego on the rise, embraces the invitation.

"I'll call you this week," Hui advises.

"Okay, I'll wait." Guowei hangs up the phone, floating in the air about the high morale of the team under boss Wang.

Hui arrives home and parks the car at the garage door. As always, the street is unlit. It's a starry night, but the chilly wind comes through the car window, and he shivers. He remembers that heat from last week and thinks, *Wow, I'm glad that's gone.*

He ambles toward the back door, his mind filled with Guowei's words. Although he knows there remains no trust left in his relationship with Wang, he struggles to accept that his boss would plot something against him. He considers tomorrow to be essential because of the detective's questions and the need to grasp Wang's statement.

Hui looks at the sky, sees the stars, and says to himself, "Maybe this lunch with Guowei will help my future. It all depends on what happens tomorrow."

The second he walks into the house, his wife wraps him in a warm hug. He looks into her eyes, full of deep affection, and hugs her back.

32

Friends, Business Aside

After dinner, Rachel, David, and Tyler decide to stay in the hotel. They search the three rooms and find no hidden surveillance.

"What happened? Are they all gone?" David says with a laugh.

"I believe with Tyler's arrival, someone has taken it off," she comments and continues searching the furniture in David's room.

"It's obvious they're scared of me," Tyler jokes with a smile.

Rachel calls Tyler and places the open iPad on the table. She puts a pencil and paper next to the iPad, and Tyler reads the report. David settles into another armchair next to him. The two read together, discussing what's written.

"The important thing is that you experience this complete report; it is easy to ask questions and have the answers right away," Tyler says.

"As you say, if you don't understand something, just ask," David replies.

Rachel lays down on the bed, watching her two partners. Tired, she closes her eyes and yawns. "Any questions? Write them down, and then we'll talk."

"What's the night like in Shanghai? Interesting? Can we go somewhere I might like?"

Rachel gives a full laugh, saying, "Night, what night? We've been working twenty-four hours for over ten days. I want to take a few days off and enjoy the city. Everyone I talk to tells me that the nightlife here is wonderful."

She opens her cellphone, reads the news, and keeps laughing.

The partners look at her, understanding how stressful the investigation is and all that happens. She doesn't notice them watching her and returns to reading the report. After an hour of reading and taking notes, the two stare at Rachel, who now sits across from them waiting for the questions.

"I have five questions," Tyler says.

"Only one," David adds.

Rachel, looking at David, says, "Alright, let's start with Tyler's questions. You can chime in too."

David rolls his eyes. "It's okay, I always get the spotlight last."

Rachel laughs. "Last in is first out, remember?" She blinks.

Ignoring the banter, Tyler interrupts, focused and intense: "Enough joking. I need to know. Did Yazuo ever mention Ronaldo's death to you? Also, was Mr. Chan's death at the same time as Ronaldo's? This guy Wang who had something to do with Rachel, is he the same Wang from the case, the witness? Did he discover the body in the hotel? Doesn't it seem suspicious to you how he got so close to Rachel?"

Rachel raises her hand, overwhelmed. "Wow. Slow down. Let me understand what you just asked."

Tyler, undeterred, continues: "There's more. Michael's mother ran that hotel for approximately two decades. The report mentioned that Michael and David crossed paths in Washington, then again in London, but after that, nothing. Then again, during the investigation, Michael shows up working at the same hotel we're investigating. That's... weird, right? Why was this mentioned in the report?"

David's voice, full of frustration, asks, "Rachel, did you write the story of how Michael and I met in that report?"

She replies, a little embarrassed, "No, that wasn't supposed to be in the report. This note is because of what Detective Chong mentioned, but I didn't relate it to our investigation. I shouldn't have mixed that personal information with what we discovered. Sorry."

Tyler furrows his eyebrows, noticing the details. He exchanges looks with both of them but remains silent.

A surprised David prepares to speak but thinks better of it, leaving his words hanging in the air.

Rachel, sensing the rising tension, interjects, "Okay, guys, take a deep breath. Things are spiralling a bit, and we need to stay focused and balanced." She gives David a pointed look, sensing his growing discomfort. "David, relax."

Tyler, trying to defuse the situation, says, "Why is everyone nervous? They're just direct questions."

Exhaling, Rachel says, "Look, based on our conversations with Yazuo and what we've seen in the investigation files, we believe the Yakuza has no hand in Ronaldo's death. According to the documents, there is no link with the organization."

Tyler scoffs. "Hmm."

Rachel continues in a serious tone. "Yazuo learns about the Brazilian Federal Police officer's story from some source. He has established himself, and his operations are in Portugal. His arrest here? It is just bad luck on his part—he shows up to see one of his lovers at the wrong time. My guess is that with the language barrier and everything that happened with the Portuguese police, I believe Yazuo spread this rumour as a diversion, perhaps even to intimidate the police."

David, interrupting, says, "Without that, we can't say for sure they were involved. End of story."

Rachel gets up from her chair and goes to the fridge to get three bottles of water. She hands one to each of them before settling into her seat. "Remember that meeting with Allan? He presents this idea about Yakuza involvement, something we hadn't discovered. So, we dig deeper. Especially after finding out about Mr. Chan's death. Everything—the dates, the events—everything points to the possibility that Ronaldo's death is not an accident, especially with that flash drive coming into the picture."

Tyler nods to Rachel, then looks at David, saying, "Your reasoning is based on the evidence and your own investigations?"

David, looking irritated, stands up out of the blue. "Tyler, I can't accept your suggestions."

Tyler, smiling, defending himself, responds, "Hey, I was gathering information from the report. I'm playing devil's advocate."

Rachel, eager to get the conversation back on track, interjects, "Can we move on?"

Both men mutter, "Yes, continue."

Rachel continues. "Now, about Wang... My opinion is . . . I think there should have been a more in-depth investigation when Ronaldo died. However, that didn't happen. David and I talked to a guy called Tony who works with Wang at that employment agency at the time of Ronaldo's death. Tony is already suspicious of Wang, something about tattoos that are typical of members of the Triad. There is also the matter of the death of his cousin—the same cousin who introduced him to the work at the agency.

On paper, it seems simple, sure, no crime. I can't shake the feeling that there's more to this than meets the eye."

David, patting Tyler for emphasis, adds, "See, it could just be an ordinary incident, the kind that could happen to anyone, anywhere but Rachel. She doesn't trust anyone and questions everything. She's always prepared to go deeper."

Rachel, with a hint of exasperation in her voice, retorts, "We discussed this, remember?"

David, avoiding Rachel's gaze, mutters, "Maybe I misinterpreted the report."

Rachel, trying to clarify, says, "Look, if you read the dossier that Chief Bo gave us, you'll see that Wang just gives a quick statement at the time of the incident, and the authorities release him." She looks at the two men before continuing. "They didn't have any formal interviews at the police station. Why? This is a key question. The authorities did not question some employees at the temporary employment agency as well. They should have questioned Wang, but they focused the investigation on the hotel reception, the CCTV footage, and the guests. A huge oversight."

David, softening, says, "You're right. My bad. I think I just crossed wires—mixing personal anecdotes with what Detective Chong shared."

Rachel, a little excited, clarifies, "Everything I wrote is how events unfolded, just like that. It's all there in black and white. The last part of these notes was what we said at the hospital."

"Alright, guys, let's stop here. We met to analyze and figure things out, not to throw accusations," Tyler intervenes, trying to reduce some of the tension in the room.

Rachel says, "As for Chan... God, where do I start?" She holds her hair up with the pen, showing tiredness.

Seeing his friend sweating, David interrupts. "Do you want another water?"

She nods. "Yes, thank you." She takes a deep drink from the bottle he offers before settling into her seat. "We were shocked when Alex from the Firm told us about Chan's murder. I called him, saying we need to get a contact in Shanghai, and 'boom,' he tells me the news of his death. He says he didn't mention it before because of everything that involves Ronaldo's death. I'm speechless."

Pausing, she notices David, disengaged from the conversation, doodling on a piece of paper. A little irritated, she says, "David, can we concentrate? We need to understand this."

He looks up, nodding.

Rachel comes back with, "When we decide to investigate Mr. Chan's death, the details get murkier. They find his body almost eight months after he disappears, stuffed inside a refrigerated container, left in some random parking lot full of those metal storage boxes. An important piece of information. The same week he doesn't show up for work, his family moves away. This isn't just a rumour, his boss confirms it to us, and so does a neighbour."

David, interrupting Rachel's narrative, states, "This is crucial, so pay attention."

Tyler, absorbed in the details, just nods and continues taking notes.

Returning to the subject, Rachel continues, "There have been a lot of coincidences in this timeline. Mr. Chan disappears right around the time we're in Shanghai. I can't pinpoint the exact date of his death, but our travel dates, 'by coincidence that you well know doesn't exist,' line up very well. The family's sudden move after his disappearance is another enigma."

Tyler looks up, curious.

Rachel continues: "David and I thought a lot about reaching out to Boss Bo and asking about Chan's death. We chose not to question him, aware that we would be in a difficult situation if he asked about our knowledge of him. We don't know about Chan's dealings in China and the real reason behind his murder. Our mission is Operation Portugal." She stops talking and becomes thoughtful, ensuring she's covered all the details.

"This investigation has been a roller coaster, but we haven't fallen off," Tyler comments, feeling the drama. "I can't even imagine the pressure you two were under."

With a deep sigh, Rachel admits, "Michael is the next question and, honestly, I'm lost." She closes her eyes.

Tyler writes every scrap of information while David looks down.

Rachel resumes: "If we're talking about the Michael that David introduced me to, I remember him at our lunch. He is charming, optimistic, and radiates positivity. However, when we visit Michael's apartment with the forensic team, Rachel sums it up: Detective Chong paints a strange picture of him."

Tyler mutters, "Chong is smart, changing the narrative like that."

Rachel, gathering her thoughts, lays out her argument. "We need to get straight to the facts. It's illegal for anyone to own a firearm in this country, but Michael has one hidden in his room. The law is clear on this. In addition, he removes it from the apartment the moment he notices someone following David. Why resort to such an extreme measure for what should just be a discussion about a motorcyclist following them? Does he know this man? Does he only pick up the gun in self-defence, or is he worried about David? Also, about the gun... is it because he's an undercover cop, a criminal, or someone who would be under threat?"

Tyler, trying to remain neutral, adds, "I think you've nailed it."

Rachel, sensing David's discomfort, tries to reassure him. "Look, David, I don't want to sound accusatory. We're all here trying to find the missing answers, right?" She pats David's arm in a gesture of comfort, but he remains impassive. She purses her lips. "Detective Chong has his reservations about David and Michael. This case attracted attention, and the police formed a special team. Think about it, a foreigner shot in this country. It's a nightmare in international relations. No wonder Boss Bo wanted to end this yesterday and sweep it under the rug."

David, interrupting for the first time, reveals, "I talked to my contacts in Hong Kong a few days ago. They'll have something for me tomorrow."

This is news to Rachel and Tyler.

Rachel, choosing to address the larger issue at hand, continues: "One glaring anomaly that Chong pointed out was Michael's conspicuous absence. Since the incident, he hasn't used his credit cards or accessed his bank account and has made no calls from his phone. He leaves the house with just the clothes on his back. So how is he living? Who's helping him? My gut tells me that more happened that night. David gets injured and can't witness everything. Tyler, I may have exaggerated in my speculation, but I believe that if anyone can provide information about Michael, it's David." Rachel, exhausted, leans back in her chair and closes her eyes for a moment, trying to compose herself.

Tyler, sensing the rising tension, turns to David, saying, "David, please understand. We do not intend to upset you. We're just trying to make sense of everything. Tomorrow, they're going to interrogate you with questions about Michael, and you need to be ready. This isn't our territory, and if they try to blame you for something, we need to know the 'why' behind it. I mean, I don't think we'll get to that point, but you know how investigations go. Everyone is under the microscope. The only ones who know what happened that day are you and Michael. I'm here to offer a new perspective, and you know I'm always looking at everything from a different angle, but I'm responsible and I mean what I say."

David, who had remained silent throughout Tyler's monologue, finally breaks his silence. "I'm not trying to offend you or Rachel. Believe me when I say this, I would be the last person to hold a grudge. I've known you both for years. We've gone through good and bad times together. You two are more than colleagues; you are my family. My faith in you both is unshakable."

David continues, his gaze unwavering. "Your insights today make me consider aspects I have never thought about—dates, places, incidents, everything that revolves around Michael and me. I love him, and deep down, I believe he still cares about me. Tyler, you and Detective Chong— you two are echoing the same words. It's not a coincidence but a pattern, a series of events that we have yet to piece together. The realization hit me hard today. Seeing everything from a detective's point of view…is destroying my previous notions."

Tyler feels moved by the depth of David's words. He listens, concentrating as David, his voice thick with emotion, says, "Why would anyone attack me? Could Michael be behind this? If I consider Detective Chong's words… or your doubts, Tyler… or even Rachel's arguments… am I supposed to believe Michael had such thoughts? Isn't that going too far?"

Rachel, empathetic, gives a small nod of agreement.

Taking a deep breath, David wipes the fresh trail of tears from his face and continues, "There was something I mentioned in passing to Rachel yesterday… something I wrote she couldn't understand. I should have been more honest about it, but I just… couldn't muster the strength."

Rachel, feeling the gravity of what is about to be revealed, gets up and closes the curtains, ensuring a more private environment. "What were you hiding?" she asks.

As Tyler watches, David, with hesitation, shares, "Detective Chong mentioned Michael had a 'close friend' here. He was careful not to label him a lover. This guy, Andrew, shares an apartment with Michael here in Shanghai. The same apartment that Rachel and I were in."

Rachel asks, "The same apartment I visited with Chong?"

"That's it," says David.

Rachel's brow furrows. "But that makes little sense. The apartment had no signs of anyone else living there—no clothes, no photos, no personal effects. Everything we found, everything we analyzed, was from Michael."

David, looking even more defeated, explains, "Chong told me this at the hospital. He mentioned that when he spoke to Michael's mother, she insisted that Michael's loved one was not me, but Andrew. Apparently, Andrew is in London at work and should be back any day. The narrative is hazy because Chong was sparse on details. The building's doorman corroborated Andrew's story, even providing a contact number that the police used."

David's composure crumbles when he finishes. "Honestly, I brushed it aside because I thought it was another one of Chong's mind games, a tactic to shake me down. Michael and I had plans and dreams of moving to Canada and building a life together. We were going to get married!"

Tyler intercedes. "Hey David, take it easy." He hands him a bottle of cold water to calm him down.

Rachel, her eyebrows furrowed in concentration, recalls the events of the day she was at the apartment: "I remember talking to that doorman during the forensic scan. He mentioned no one else who lived there, let alone this Andrew."

Tyler, with a hint of skepticism in his voice, asks, "Are you sure about this, Rachel?"

"As you say," she responds, her eyes still closed as she tries to replay that day in her mind. "I was the one who showed him David's picture on my phone, and Detective Chong was there with me."

David, looking more serene than before, states, "I need to meet this Andrew. Somehow, I feel like talking to him will fill in a lot of the gaps."

Tyler, checking his wristwatch and feeling the exhaustion in the room, says, "It's getting late. Maybe we should get some rest. Tomorrow, with a clearer head, we can analyze everything we discussed tonight."

Rachel, however, gives him a playful smile. "Wait. David is still owed a question." She turns to David, her smile softening the intensity of the night.

Tyler slumps a little in his seat, giving David a tired but expectant look. "Okay, David, please ask the question."

David, trying to keep a straight face, asks, "How long has Wang been the head of the Tong?"

Rachel, laughing, says, "As for Wang and his supposed leadership of the Tong. Well… when I was at his apartment, I didn't focus my attention on that… but I guarantee I didn't see any Tong flags or fridge magnets, if that's what you were imagining… and I didn't get any business cards, member of Tong VIP Club. Oh, and about his tattoos… I didn't do a full inspection of his lower half," she says with a wink.

Tyler, bursting into laughter, interjects, "Alright, alright! Let's not get too deep into *those* details."

David raises an eyebrow. "I'll try with American intelligence? I'm not sure they'd be eager to help with that, but I can try." He smiles: "At the very least, they owe me for that disaster in Iraq."

Tyler, flipping through the pages of notes, mutters, "To be honest… sometimes I think people leave out important information just to see us running around like headless chickens. I'm going to have a little 'talk' with my source in Canada. As for Allan," he pauses, looking at Rachel, "not a word. It's like he disappeared off the face of the earth."

Rachel's gaze hardens. "If Allan has information, we need it. You know what's most disconcerting? This whole Wang thing. It's as if there was an intention for some things to stay hidden in the shadows."

Tyler stretches, his yawn exaggerated. "You know, for a mission that's supposed to be simple, this thing has more twists and turns than an Alfred Hitchcock movie."

Rachel gives a sad smile, her gaze turning soft as she turns to David. "Hey." Approaching him, she says, "Let's work this out, okay? We always do." She wraps him in a comforting hug, a moment of silence amid the turbulent questions.

Tyler also stands up. "I'm tired and I need to sleep. David, what did Detective Chong say that upset you?"

"He told me, looking in my eyes, that he would find out what the reason for our investigation here is and that he doesn't believe we came to help Chief Bo. He said he is sure it is because of Ronaldo's death, implying that Michael was involved. I saw it written on his face that he was pleased to tell me about Andrew; a real asshole," David says indignantly.

"I get it. He's behaving as we would. Try to understand his position as well, which can't be easy. I know this hurts you. We have to stay cool and try to see the whole situation," says Tyler, watching David get up from the chair with difficulty.

"Let's go to sleep. I'm tired too. It's almost midnight. Good night, everyone," Rachel finishes as she opens the door and leaves the room.

"Okay, let's rest. Tomorrow is another day, and we'll have other ideas," David responds.

Each of the partners goes to their rooms, and the silence at the end of the conversation between the three clarifies that something else needs to be investigated.

Tyler falls onto the bed and passes out.

Rachel, lying down, tries to sleep, but the conversation they had doesn't let her relax. *How did I meet David?* she asks herself, trying to remember.

Hmm ... it was in that border operation, in the south of Brazil, with Paraguay. David was with an American operational team, Ronaldo, myself, and five other Brazilian police officers, waiting for a boat smuggling cocaine and marijuana. I remember a shootout taking place, and no police officers getting injured while we arrested two drug dealers. It was exciting, one of my first operations involving shooting, seizure, and arrests, recalls Rachel with a smile. *If I'm not mistaken, it was Alex, from the Firm, who gave the tip to American and Brazilian federal intelligence. I was new to the police.*

She remembers David and Ronaldo's laughter, celebrating the success of the operation... and how Ronaldo praised the American agent, always talking about his friend's outstanding qualities...

Rachel falls asleep.

David, lying in his room, finishes taking the medicine that the hospital supplied him. Feeling annoyed, he gets out of bed and lies down on the bedroom floor. He tries doing exercises with his legs to see how his abdomen reacts and is relieved he doesn't feel any pain. He moves his arm and feels a little tiredness in his muscles. His arm shakes. Most importantly, there's no pain.

"I have to do more exercises with that arm," David says to himself.

The image of Michael comes to mind. He gets up from the floor, takes a bottle of water from the fridge, and sits on the bed, remembering how they met. He thinks it must have been about seven or eight years ago. They were only together for a year, hidden from friends and family. David could no longer handle his marriage and the pressure from his father. He wanted a divorce. All this stress led to the end of the relationship with Michael. After two years, they met again in London, but do not reconcile. Now in Shanghai, paths crossed again. He speaks out loud: "This is destiny. Is there anything more perfect?"

David grabs the remote, glances at the TV, switches it on, and then switches it off.

He returns to bed and keeps analyzing the words of Tyler and Detective Chong. He lies down and remembers the few but intense days they spent together. His face shows concern. "I remember asking Michael if he knew a federal police officer who had died in that hotel. He tried to avoid the topic, as if he wasn't interested in talking about it."

Sitting on the bed, David writes what he remembers. His eyes settle on the table next to him, the dim lamp illuminating the hotel's pad of paper. He has a memory of Ronaldo arriving at the Washington airport. That day, Michael went with him to receive his Brazilian friend. They went to have coffee at the airport, and everything was quick, conversations and laughter. Yes, Michael knew Ronaldo.

The scenes of the night they went down from the apartment together to the street come back to mind, and he remembers when he warned his friend that he didn't need to take the gun. Michael insisted it was best to protect himself. Now calm, he remembers the questions Rachel asked and the reasons it wasn't right for Michael to take the gun. He tries to remember some emotion or word that might relate the man on the motorcycle to him or Michael. He gives up; he doesn't remember, his memory getting confused. David looks at the clock on his cellphone and sees that it's one o'clock in the morning.

He goes to the bathroom and washes his face with cold water, trying to calm the anxiety that has taken over his body. David goes back to bed and says to himself, "None of this is tangible. Bringing up the distant past, it seems like I've left reality. I'm going to sleep, and tomorrow I'll start again on the investigation."

David turns off the lamp and sleeps.

33

Sometimes It's Better to Lose Than to Get Lost

Hui's hands shake. Frustrated, he looks for the flash drive. He remembers hiding it in his home office last week. His heart races, panic rises as he searches through drawers, cabinets, and piles of documents and can't remember where he put them. Anger makes him remember fragments of conversations and fleeting images from the day. He can't shake the guilt of sending Wonjy to take Michael to the farm. Who could have imagined what would happen? The weight of this feeling destroys him daily.

Consistent in his reasoning, Hui concludes Wang did not expect nor imagine that he took photos and recorded the events of that macabre day. What a surprise... everything was recorded: the barn soaked in blood, discarded clothes, wallets, and cellphones of the now dead men. As Wang left the farm, he recalls taking photos of the back of the car. He is trying to find excuses because he doesn't understand why he did this. Maybe it was the horror of the scene, or maybe it was the echoes of his boss's constant reminders to document everything in all these years of common work.

Deep down, Hui believes perhaps Wang desires information about the items destroyed in the fire. It's his way of being thorough, but now, stopping in his frantic search, a sigh escapes him. "My innocence... I'm just trying to protect the boss."

As Hui continues his search, memories come flooding back. He didn't dispose of the weapons by throwing them into the river, as many might have done. Instead, he buried them. He mentioned this to Wang but never revealed the location because the boss didn't ask. The clothes, documents, and other items? They're all reduced to ashes.

He can feel the weight of the air around him, and his heart races in his chest. Pausing for a moment, he halts his search for the flash drive and runs a shaky hand across his forehead. All wet. On the bar shelf in the office, he grabs a glass and pours himself a generous portion of the whiskey Wang gave him as a gift last Christmas. Taking it all in with one gulp, he grimaces at the bitterness and then takes a deep breath, attempting to concentrate.

Trying to remember where he put the flash drive, he tells himself that these photos can save him. Wang is not a naive person to forget or forgive. He holds calculated, rooted grudges that are almost Machiavellian. If Wang feels slighted or wronged, that resentment will only deepen… and he will be the one who pays the price.

Shaking his head to rid himself of these disturbing thoughts, Hui mutters, "I can't keep obsessing over Wang."

Hui's determination revives, and he continues his search, his mind swirling with thoughts and fears. His heart is already racing. He feels a pain in his chest from it beating so much as he imagines all the scenarios that could happen. The investigation has just begun, and he can't help but ponder what might be next.

Taking a deep breath, he mutters, "Tomorrow, I need to face Detective Chong with my answers ready. I will answer all questions. I will be precise, calm, and very polite."

His voice becomes more intense: "The detective's visit shook Wang today. I know him better than anyone."

While lost in thought, he makes a noise in the office without realizing it. Rummaging through the desk drawers, he exclaims, "Why is the detective so interested in talking to me? Just because I manage the warehouses? That must be it. Tomorrow, I'll be sharp on all the questions."

With a mix of confidence and paranoia, Hui realizes that dealing with the police is difficult. One slip, one overheard conversation, and everything could fall apart. He suspects that Wang, cornered, could say or do anything, especially if he thinks he has a way to escape the situation. The weight of the consequences presses on Hui's chest, and he feels paralyzed for a moment. However, he also knows he has something explosive, something that will protect him but destroy Wang.

Pouring himself another whiskey, he looks out the window, his mind heavy with the implications for his family. The effect would be disastrous. These photos, if discovered, could put not only him in danger but everyone he loves.

Brought back to reality by a sound, he rushes to close the office door and tries to hear what is happening on the other side. It's late at night, and his wife and children are sleeping. However, footsteps are coming down the stairs.

The door opens, and his wife emerges with confusion on her face as she asks him, "Who were you talking to at this time? Aren't you planning on waking up early tomorrow?"

Quick to divert attention, Hui responds, pointing to a book on the table, "Just lost in thought while reading. How about some tea?"

She nods.

"Okay, I'll make some. Go to bed, and I'll bring it to you." She leaves the office, leaving Hui awash in a sea of worries.

Enjoying the moment alone, Hui searches the closet drawers with intense agitation. The weight of his importance causes his mind to return to a special box where he holds cherished memories. Opening a closet door, he examines old documents and books and discovers the box. The wave of relief washing over him when he sees the flash drive inside is unimaginable. He holds it, deep in thought, undecided about what to do. He considers postponing his decision and puts it back in the box. Tomorrow, he promises himself, he will find a safer hiding place. It's perilous to keep it at home.

Leaving the office, he climbs the stairs, feeling the weight of a ton on each leg, fatigue pulling at each step. The hustle and bustle of the day has taken its toll, and he longs to sleep in the arms of his beloved wife.

His wife enters, placing the tea on the bedside table. The two share a brief, silent moment of affection before darkness envelops the room.

Screams emanate from the street.

"Fire! Fire! Fire!"

Rushing to the window, Hui and his wife encounter a scene of total chaos: terrified neighbours, the shrill screams of sirens, and the blinding lights of fire engines coming to an abrupt stop in front of their house.

"Get the kids!" Hui shouts, not waiting for a response as he runs out of the room.

As he runs down the hallway, his heart stops when he sees his youngest son frozen on the top step, tears streaming down his face. Without hesitation, Hui picks him up and heads straight to the office. Cradling his son with one arm, he opens the closet with the other. In a hurry, he grabs the box, takes the flash drive, and puts it in his pyjama pocket.

Leaving the office, he sees his wife leading the other children to the front door. A familiar face from the house next door enters, calling for Hui, but when he sees his wife with the children, he helps her out of the house.

With his son's sobs echoing in his ear, Hui runs out, grabbing his wallet and car keys from the marble sideboard on the way. In the garden in front of the house, he realizes the full scale of the disaster. Flames consume the neighbouring house, while Hui's house, still untouched by the fire, presents a grim situation. Firefighters are fighting a fierce battle against the fire.

A sudden thunderous explosion shakes the street; something exploded in the kitchen of the neighbouring house. The flames shoot upwards, dominating the sky. As fear and disbelief grip him, Hui's gaze finds his wife and children across the street. Neighbours who offer comforting arms surround them.

One neighbour, recognizing Hui's stunned expression, approaches him with concern. "Are you okay?"

Hui acknowledges his neighbour with a nod.

"It looks like the family isn't home," comments the neighbour, with his eyes on the raging flames.

"What did the firefighters say? Any idea how it all started?" Hui's voice is desperate.

"They say it started in the back, near the kitchen entrance, which is similar to yours," offers the neighbour.

Another neighbour, her voice shaking with fear, interjects, "You're lucky! Those firefighters... did wonders."

Hui's gaze passes over her, settling on a shadowy figure across the street: a man in a cap trying to hide his face. There's something unusual yet familiar about him... Hui's thoughts become confused, his vision blurs, and his trembling hand rises to his forehead. His nervousness increases, but he struggles to maintain his composure.

"We... were lucky," he murmurs, his voice choked to a whisper, his breathing ragged. He looks back at the man in the hat; he had disappeared.

The flames disappear, and the feeling that something is wrong asserts itself. Going to the fire engine, Hui looks for the person in charge of the rescue team. Amid the chaos, a police officer confronts him, and he identifies himself as the owner of the neighbouring property.

The fire chief, his face stained with soot and exhaustion, approaches Hui. "Is everything okay with your family?"

"We are okay," Hui says, his voice stuttering. "We're just shaken."

The fire chief fixes Hui with a piercing gaze. "Wait, aren't you Hui? From the port?"

Hui is in a storm of emotions that are all working together to create a mix of anguish, tiredness, and anxiety in his head. He can't register the fire chief's words. He asks an apprehensive question: "Can we go back to our house?"

Seeing this daily, the fire chief recognizes the troubled expression in Hui's eyes. "Yes, you can. Luckily, your neighbours were travelling, and thanks to the spacious layout of the land and wind direction, your house escaped major damage. You may need to repaint the side where it got a little charred, but it's superficial damage."

Offering Hui a reassuring pat on the back, he turns to join his team, already in the truck and ready to leave. Gratitude wells up in Hui, and he bows, although he is oblivious to the fact that the fire chief is already walking away, unaware of his gesture of thanks.

Hui, his shoulders heavy from the night's events, lifts one of his sons, while his wife and other children follow him into the house. He looks through the curtain and confirms that most of the onlookers and neighbours have dispersed, but the flash of cameras and the buzz of the live television broadcast tell him that reporters are still milling around. He looks at the kitchen clock: it's 5:30.

"I need a shower. Then I'm going to the port," he declares, climbing the stairs. Each step feels like climbing a mountain.

His wife, always attentive, notices his wear and tear. "Hui!" she calls.

He pauses, looking at her, his eyes empty. The paleness of his face, without colour and vigour, worries her.

"Can we talk?" she pleads.

He takes a deep, tired breath. "Not now."

Entering the room, he throws himself on the bed, but the weight of his suspicions threatens to consume him. Taking the flash drive out of his pocket, he squeezes it between his fingers.

"If my instinct is right..." he murmurs, "I'll end this before they know it." With that heavy thought, he gets up and goes to the bathroom.

After his shower, Hui falls back into bed, trying to piece together the chaotic night. Visions of the frantic escape, the firefighters, and especially the mysterious man in the cap spin through his mind. Sitting up, he realizes the face is familiar. He recognizes it as someone he had seen at the port years before. Without wasting time, Hui runs to the wardrobe without paying attention to put on the first outfit he finds. Speechless, he takes the motorcycle keys and drives off at high speed.

When the clock strikes 8:00 a.m., Hui enters the Warehouse #1 office, waving at the secretary. He sinks into his chair, trying to mask his exhaustion, but the shadows under his eyes betray him.

"Hard night?" she jokes with a smile.

"It was, but it wasn't the fun kind," he retorts with a tired but warm smile.

Just then, Detective Chong intervenes, entering the office. The detective's presence changes the atmosphere.

Hui stands up, extending his hand in greeting.

"Do you have a moment to talk? I need a private place," Chong says, his gaze steady and questioning.

The secretary interrupts: "I'm going to have a coffee. You two can use the room."

Grateful, the two men settle into armchairs, facing each other, ready to start the conversation.

Detective Chong, in one motion, pulls out a notepad from his leather briefcase with a casual yet professional demeanour. With a brief smile, he asks, "Your ID, please?"

Hui, obeying, takes it out of his wallet and hands it over.

Chong takes a quick photo with his cellphone and returns the document.

"I have a series of questions for you. Wang pointed me in this direction, mentioning that, as the manager and person responsible for hiring, you would be the best person to answer them. The individual I'm investigating works at the warehouse." He then takes a small recorder out of his briefcase, placing it between them. Meeting Hui's gaze, he asks, "Mind if I use this?"

Hui nods in acceptance, his thoughts going to Wang with a mixture of frustration and resentment. Detective Chong takes a photograph from a yellow envelope and hands it to Hui. The familiar face he sees sends a shock through his mind. Recognizing the man in the photo, Hui's heart rate quickens, but he remains calm. Chong, with his pen resting on his notepad, asks without rushing or even looking up, "Do you know this individual?"

Hui studies Detective Chong, detecting a certain negligence in his behaviour. It's not what he expected from a police officer, and it catches him off guard. He muses that maybe now he can relax a little. Feeling a hint of security, he shifts in his chair, assuming a more comfortable posture, and the weight of the situation lessens.

"Yes, he works here," Hui replies, returning the photo.

Chong, suppressing a yawn, continues, "Uh, how long has he been working here at the warehouses?"

Based on his memory, Hui responds, "I don't know the exact time, but he has been part of the company for years. You can check the details with our secretary's records." Almost imitating the detective, Hui suppresses a yawn, his eyelids heavy.

Chong, quick to realize the contagious nature of yawning, quips, "Late-night party?"

Recovering his composure, Hui says a few words about the previous night's commotion at his residence.

Detective Chong, still pretending to be drowsy, reassures him, "Don't stress. Just a few routine questions."

Hui leans back in the armchair; his eyes follow Detective Chong, who is flipping through some papers he took out of his leather brief-case. Given Chong's indifferent attitude, Hui reflects on himself, arguing that these issues may just be bureaucratic formalities. Maybe everything is under control.

With his attention still fixed on the papers, Chong asks, "How long have you known Wonjy?"

"We grew up together," Hui responds, the ease in his voice revealing the bond.

"Can you call him for me?" Chong's gaze now remains on Hui, studying him.

"From what we know, Wonjy is in Hong Kong visiting his family," Hui says with a hint of amusement on his lips, as he expected this line of investigation.

"Ah! Do you have any documents for this leave? Is he on vacation?" Chong persists, eyes unwavering.

"When the secretary comes back, you can ask her. All our employees use the company's cellphone number to report any changes to the work schedule, such as when they are late, are sick, need to take time off, are travelling, and so on. It's a practical solution, as the warehouse area is very noisy, making telephone conversations impossible," Hui explains with a smile.

Chong, without missing a beat, asks, "Did Wonjy send a message through this system?"

Hui maintains his demeanour as he confirms mentioning his trip to Hong Kong to visit family, feeling that he has answered all the questions.

In conclusion, Detective Chong revisits the subject, appearing nonchalant, treating it as a casual conversation. "So, just to be clear… you, Wang, and Wonjy, have you been tight since you were teenagers?" He gathers the papers scattered on the sofa.

"Yes, we have been friends for a long time, since childhood. We've been through a lot together," Hui responds with a laugh, oblivious to the fact that his response may have exposed a discrepancy in Wang's story.

Chong's eyes sparkle with a mix of amusement and intrigue. "It's encouraging to know that these friendships still exist; where people grow side by side, supporting each other," he says, with an ever-widening smile.

Hui just nods, reinforcing the sentiment.

Leaning his body forward, Chong ventures into more delicate territory. "Did you know Wonjy's family?" he asks.

Chong observes Hui's silent reaction.

"I heard about it yesterday. A regrettable fact. The company, as is customary, sent a floral tribute for the funeral," he responds with a neutral tone, almost devoid of emotion.

Detective Chong's keen observation detects an almost imperceptible deviation in Hui's behaviour. It's one thing to claim a lifelong bond and another to react without emotion to news of such magnitude about someone linked to that bond.

Hui, after speaking, feels the change in the room and no longer feels comfortable in the chair. His eyes don't stop moving toward the door, hoping the questions are behind him.

However, Chong, with slow movements, holds out a second photograph to Hui: "Here's another aspect of the investigation that you can clarify."

Hui's heart pounds as he stands up to see the image. The moment his eyes land on the face in the photo, a wave of memories comes flooding back. Confused, the manager returns the photograph.

Chong's sharp gaze focuses on the manager's reaction.

"I don't recognize this man," Hui says, trying to regain his composure while planning how to get out of there.

The detective is insistent. "Take another look. Someone informed me he works here at this company."

Hui is obviously nervous and resists looking again.

As Chong puts away the photograph, he can't help but notice Hui's growing desire to vacate the office.

For Hui, every second seems like an eternity. Regretful for letting his guard down, he can't shake the feeling that Detective Chong is several steps ahead.

Just as the tension in the room becomes unbearable, the secretary enters, breaking the silence. "Are you finished, gentlemen?" she asks, her tone offering slight relief.

Eager to divert the detective's attention, Hui confirms, "Yes, please show him Wonjy's latest message."

She searches her desk, picking up a cellphone from her desk drawer. As she scrolls, Hui's nervousness becomes clear; he didn't expect the detective to show him Zhao's photograph.

Chong, always the observer, scans the room, following the dynamics between Hui and the secretary, who are both eager to locate the message.

"Here it is." After what feels like an endless amount of time for Hui, the secretary announces, showing the date, "September eleventh, 7 a.m."

The detective takes her cellphone and reads the message. "Wonjy mentioned the need to resolve a family matter in Hong Kong, stating that he would be in touch when he returns."

Taking advantage of the opportunity, Chong asks for a photo with a printout of the text and writes Wonjy's phone number.

Hui's anxiety is notable; he moves back and forth, tries to stand still in the doorway, and his foot taps the floor in an anxious rhythm. Upon hearing the secretary's explanation and seeing the detective absorbed in the details of the message, relief washes over him.

"It looks like we have resolved Wonjy's matter," Hui says out loud, a hint of smug satisfaction curling his lips.

Returning the cellphone details to Chong, the secretary waits for a nod of approval.

Chong, deep in thought, doesn't address Hui's comment.

The restless manager tries to change the energy in the room, and asks, "So, Detective, can I go back to my job?"

The unspoken tension remains heavy, but the next step is in Chong's hands.

Detective Chong tilts his head. "Alright," he begins, his tone deliberate. "You can go back to your work. However, you will need to come to the police station to give an official statement. It's just a formality. It shouldn't take over thirty minutes. I'll call the office to schedule an appointment."

Hui, breathing a sigh of relief, nods his head. Appearing as a routine procedure seems to strengthen his sense of security. "Understood," he replies.

They exchange brief goodbyes, and Hui leaves the office almost at a run.

After Hui's quick departure, Detective Chong sits in the armchair, his eyes watching the secretary as she prints out the information. Writing the last details, she places the document in an envelope and hands it over.

Detective Chong, always playing with words, concludes that he needs to evaluate his impression of the manager.

"Mr. Hui seems like a competent professional, doesn't he?" he muses aloud.

She sits down in the chair and replies, "Very professional."

Chong raises an eyebrow, surprised. "It's interesting. When Hui mentioned that he, Wang, and Wonjy have been close since childhood, it surprised me because friendships like that are so solid."

She nods, confirming. "From what I've heard here from other employees, they shared a lot of memories. They always have stories to tell about the times they spent together."

The detective purses his lips and says, "So, do they maintain a regular habit of communicating?"

"Yes," she replies. "They talk daily. Although I haven't seen Wonjy at the warehouse in a few days because of his trip."

Chong pauses, casting a playful glance her way, a departure from his professional demeanour. "You know, if I may be so bold, you are exquisite. How about we have lunch sometime?"

The unexpected compliment catches her off guard, and her face turns red. "I'd like that," she says, a smile lighting up her face.

"Good," Chong says, holding out his card with his phone number to her. "Put your number here." She hands him her cellphone.

He punches in the numbers, and when she takes the phone back, he gives her a wink. "I'll call you as soon as I have time off," he promises.

Still smiling, she responds, "I'll be looking forward to that."

He knows he's caught a big fish; he wants more information. He thanks her, bowing, and leaves the room, heading toward the stairs of the warehouse.

Detective Chong walks and observes the closed rooms in the hallway. When he reaches the top of the stairs, he sees Hui talking to Wang at the entrance to the warehouse. He slows his descent by taking two steps back and returns to the office.

When he opens the door, the surprised secretary looks at him and asks, "Any problems?"

"I think I've lost my pen," the detective explains, looking at the floor.

Together, they search the hardwood floor.

"I don't see it... what colour is it?" she asks, looking under the couch.

"Black," he replies, pretending to look for it. He touches her hand, then apologizes.

Without her seeing, Chong pulls out a pen from his jacket pocket and says, "I found it. Thank you for helping me search."

Wang, standing outside in the hallway, not letting them see him, over-hears their conversation.

"Always at your command," she replies with a smile.

At that moment, Wang enters and faces the two of them on their knees on the floor. "Is everything in order?"

The secretary stands up, wiping her skirt and nodding. "Yes."

Detective Chong stands up and bows, saying, "Good morning, Wang. I talked to the manager today. He was thoughtful and helped me understand the value of having childhood friends."

"Did you get the information you needed?" Wang asks, not realizing what the detective said.

"Of course. He was enlightening and helped me in the investigation," Detective Chong says with a sarcastic smile on his lips and a piercing look on Wang's back.

The boss listens as he walks toward the office and, before closing the door, says, "Good."

With the door still ajar, the detective asks sarcastically, "You're going to come to the police station to give an official statement, okay?"

Wang turns around and presents a confrontational posture, predicting that something isn't right. "No problem. Send me the day and time; I'll be there," Wang replies and closes the office door without saying goodbye.

The detective nods, looks at the secretary, and whispers in her ear, "Is he always this uneducated?"

She replies, laughing, "Always."

Chong returns the smile and says, "I'll call you. We'll have lunch."

She agrees and begins arranging some papers on the table.

Detective Chong leaves the room, walks down the hallway, and pulls out a second address from his pants pocket.

After a few minutes, Wang opens the door and asks, "Any important appointments today? Has anyone called me?"

"No. Today you have nothing on your agenda; only Superintendent Bo called early in the morning," she says and confirms, flipping through her notebook on the desk.

He doesn't answer; he just observes.

The secretary turns her gaze back to her boss and has the distinct impression that he is not there. His dead eyes are not blinking, and there is no movement in his face. A chill runs down her spine, and she asks if he needs anything else.

Wang unexpectedly shows agitation, as if awakening, because he now realizes the detective's insinuation. Agitated, he replies, "I'm going out, and I don't know what time I'll be back. Call Hui and tell him to call for anything. I'll have my phone."

"Yes," she replies, still frightened. She realizes that she no longer recognizes this man.

Wang leaves the office with worry lines on his forehead. Reflecting, he analyzes the detective's words, wanting to know what he asked Hui and what the answers were.

He stops at the top of the stairs and remembers Chong smiling, confronting him in the office. He compares what he talked about and the manager's attitude when they met at the door of the warehouse before seeing the detective.

"Ah! You're here! I've been trying to talk to you. Why don't you answer me?" Wang had said.

"Didn't you tell me to be here at 8 a.m. sharp?"

"Yes, how was the interview?" Wang continued, staring at him as he walked toward him.

On the street crowded with cars and trucks, the noise was hellish. He remembers that employees from different warehouses greeted them and went toward their respective work warehouses.

Wang, standing in front of Hui, looked at him and asked, "Did you say shit?"

The manager didn't answer either question. He just stared at his boss.

"What's wrong with you, Hui? Have you gone deaf?" Wang yelled at him.

"Everything is in order. I answered what he asked me and handed him the message that Wonjy sent to the secretary. No need to worry." Hui finished speaking, turned his back on Wang, and walked toward Warehouse #2, hearing the boss shout.

"Very nice not to have to worry about you... now you... take care of yourself."

After the conversation, Wang entered the warehouse. Some employees who arrived early greeted him. He reciprocated and went upstairs to the office. In the hallway next to the room, he heard the detective's voice and listened to the conversation.

"Black... found. Thank you for helping me search."

The secretary replied, "Always at your command."

At this moment, the boss entered the room, surprised to still find the detective on the premises.

The noise of employees going up the stairs and others talking brings Wang back to reality, and he concludes that there must have been a problem in the interview. Again, he remembers the detective speaking with a smile on his lips, which cannot be normal. Also, that one answer Hui gave helped him understand the value of having childhood friends. In the end, he spoke of the need to go to the police station to make a statement.

He starts down the stairs and mutters to himself, "I need to talk to Hui."

The secretary calls, and Wang answers.

"Boss, Hui doesn't answer his cellphone. I left a message that when it's possible, please contact you."

Wang hangs up and lets out an angry roar. Some workers hear him. "Where's that idiot? What is he doing?"

He walks with firm steps out of the warehouse and into the parking lot.

* * *

After leaving Warehouse #1, Hui returns to his residence, and on the way, his cellphone rings. He doesn't answer, just letting it ring. After it stops, he identifies the message from Warehouse #1 and hears the secretary informing him that Wang needs to speak to him. Tired from staying up all night, besides the stress of the fire, the interview with the detective, and the conversation at the warehouse door with Wang, he chooses not to call back.

"Maybe I'll call later, but not now," he says to himself.

Driving, he remembers the face of Ishiro, the Japanese man, in that confusion of reporters, police officers, and firefighters. When paying attention to what the neighbour was saying, he didn't notice his features and now understands why he didn't recognize him. All the people he talked to were residents of the region. Only when he fixed his gaze on the man with the cap and saw that he looked away did he realize he was not from the neighbourhood. He understands the need to be quick and careful in his next steps because of the unforeseen war with Wang. He thinks about his wife and children. Hui concludes that the best thing to do is send them to her family in the countryside for a while.

The radio warns him that in the afternoon it's going to rain. A pop song plays, and he turns it off.

Stopping the car at a red light, he sees the detective's face demanding that he look at Zhao's photograph again. He remembers the insistence and questions, sentence by sentence, of their discussion. Distressed, he understands everything was an act, and the police must have more information because they showed him Zhao's photo. The confidence that took hold of him the moment he left the office disappears. He closes his eyes, passes his hand over his forehead, and takes a deep breath. He concludes the bomb will explode in his hand. Horns sound behind the vehicle and he speeds up and drives away.

He arrives home and goes inside. He looks at his children running toward him and remembers Wang's words: "It's great not to have to worry about you, now you ... take care of yourself."

Hui kisses the boys and his wife. He looks at them, worried and appre-hensive. He says he's going to work, walks into the office, and thinks to himself, *I need to do something. I will not let this wave get me wet. If it comes close, I'll take everybody down with me.* He sits in the armchair and remembers this morning in the barn.

It was 6:45 a.m. when he parked his bike at the gate. The sight of the number of vehicles outside and inside the parking lot surprised him before getting off the bike. Upon entering, he discovered that several of the men who work in Warehouses #1 and #2 were there drinking beer while others drank coffee. He recognized some who worked with the Tong bosses and, curious and smiling, approached them and waved to everyone.

"Hey boss, I missed you. Let's celebrate. The drinks are free," one man, who appeared to be drunk, said, inviting Hui to sit at a table with two other employees near the bar.

"How was the night?" the manager asked, smiling. Approaching the counter, he grabbed a cup of coffee and sat down at another table with the employees of Warehouse #2.

"We locked about sixty men in two containers," another man, drinking coffee, told the manager.

Hui took a sip of coffee, and a third man spoke up: "They received a beating despite not stealing anything. Some people got injured, but we followed Changpu's instructions and didn't use a gun. We used a knife, club, and stick."

"Good to hear. You're the best in Shanghai." Hui was inflating the egos of everyone there.

An inebriated man with staggering steps leaned against the table and asked the manager, "Is it true that they are from the Triad and were going to steal a boat?"

Hui, calmly turned his gaze to the man and the others who stopped and put their attention on the question. "Think of it this way: I'd better do as I'm told and not ask questions. The boss wouldn't like to hear that you're questioning orders."

Silence settled around the table and some men sitting at other tables got up, said goodbye, and left. Others waved goodbye and got into their cars. The noise of vehicles leaving the barn made Hui feel calmer. He didn't want to answer questions because he didn't know what happened last night.

Most of the tables were empty, and others only had one or two workers left.

Yuze and Lixin sat at the table with Hui. The two workers showed they had drunk a lot but could still articulate.

Yuze commented in a slurred voice, "You didn't say, but everyone knows they were men of the Triad. There's no point in hiding it."

Hui warned, "Sometimes it's better not to speak your mind."

Lixin spoke, landing a punch on the table. "Some of those we trapped in the containers said that now there will be war between the gangs. I'm ready for any fight, just call me. I'm with you, Hui."

The manager, in the short time since he had arrived at the barn and with the few words he heard, understood everything that had happened last night. The important thing was to find out what he wanted to know, so he threw the question out: "Where's Ishiro, the Japanese?"

Yuze, with a slurred voice, unable to hold his glass straight, replied, "Last night, before the party, Wang called him on his cellphone. The big mouth, as always, said he was going to do some work for the boss and left smiling, making a money sign with his fingers. Early in the morning, he returned, said he was going on board and went on the boat."

"I asked too, and he said he was going to take a vacation," Lixin confirmed.

Hui laughed. Now he knew who ordered Ishiro to set his house on fire, but his powerful guardian spirit animal helped him, and the neighbour was the one who received the gift. He said goodbye to the boys, who had laid their heads on the table, almost asleep, and told them to go home.

The two men got up and staggered toward the parking lot. The manager watched as they walked away.

At his home office, after remembering everything that happened in the morning at the warehouse and at the barn, he decides what he needs to do. In silence, he looks at the blue sky filling with black clouds through the window.

"That's not a good sign."

His wife comes into the office, bringing tea. "Did you eat anything today?"

He looks at her, hesitating to respond. He looks into her eyes and says, "Pack your suitcase and the children's. I'm going to do some renovation on the house's wall, and maybe it will affect our room and the boys' room.

I want you to travel to your mother's house today. It's been a long time since you've been there. She'll be happy to see you all."

Seeing that he doesn't smile, falsifying words with a worried face, she asks, "Did something happen?"

"Not yet, but it could happen," he says, taking a deep breath and staring at her with a grave expression on his face.

She gets the message. Without waiting, a child runs into the office, hugging Hui. Hugging her son as well, Hui's wife smiles and says, "Let's go visit Grandma."

The other children near the door hear what she said and run to hug their mother. She looks at Hui, and he nods his head. The wife and children leave the office, heading for their bedrooms.

Hui wipes his hand over his face and goes to the closet, taking the flash drive from the box. He puts it in his pants pocket and looks at the cellphone in his hands. He opens it and searches for the name Guowei, then calls him. His friend answers.

"Shall we have lunch today?"

Chief Kung's security replies, "You can't imagine the confusion left over from last night, you know?"

"That's why we need to relax. Let's eat dumplings. I'll pay," Hui says, showing no anxiety.

"Pick me up here at the office in half an hour."

"On my way."

Minutes later, driving the Toyota, Hui remembers Wang told him to leave the car in Warehouse #2's parking lot for a week, and he did . . . almost. He left it for five days, and now, in the morning, he put the motorcycle in its place.

After a while, the two friends are sitting at Yangen Fried Dumpling, having lunch. They like this restaurant because the food is excellent and cheap.

"These dumplings are delicious," Hui says, shoving a whole one into his mouth.

Guowei stops eating and says to his friend, "Because of last night, the Triad council set up a meeting with Kung. This is going to suck."

"Boss Kung can take it," Hui replies, chewing.

"I don't know, it's gotten ugly. Wang pulled the rope too tight," Guowei explains and stares at him.

"Why do you say that?" Hui asks and stops eating.

Guowei, with a suspicious look, says, "The boss told me this morning. I don't even know if I should tell you because you're Wang's best man. Are you here to probe information from me?"

"No, I'm here as a friend, and I've seen Wang cross the line of common sense and start leading Tong to disaster for a while," Hui comments, looking at him, putting his hand to his forehead, and rubbing his eyes in annoyance.

Guowei knows Hui well; feeling something more in these words, he trusts him. Guowei recounts his boss's conversation to him that morning.

"Yesterday, he informed me that Wang was behaving unusually, making unfounded accusations against him and attempting to persuade the other bosses against his work. In the end, Kung strove to dissuade him from attacking the Triad because it was just a matter of making a phone call; they would talk, stop the attack on the port, and understand each other. Your boss didn't accept and preferred to confront them."

"Wang doesn't take advice anymore. Whatever he decides is done, and consequences no longer exist," Hui says, completing his friend's words.

"Your boss's actions yesterday could cause a new war between the organizations, and we will be on the losing side. Even though they know we have made progress in our business, they will not allow what happened. The new generation is not as tolerant as the past. Conversations are rare today, and problems get resolved overnight."

"We are rich; Tong makes money like water coming out of the tap," says Hui.

"Don't forget that the Triad is a crime syndicate, Chinese transnational organized crime, and has operations in many countries. They have survived two thousand years; do you believe we can take them down?" Guowei wipes the sweat from his forehead and laughs out of the corner of his mouth.

"It's just drug control that's the problem," Hui says.

"Well, my friend, you've said everything; you touched on the most important subject. Your boss is smuggling heroin and fentanyl without their consent. The reason for everything is there... Whoever is in charge did not make this agreement." Guowei wipes his mouth with his hand as he finishes his glass of baijiu.

"I know that, and there's no point talking to him at this moment; he's out of control," Hui agrees, pouring more baijiu into his friend's glass.

"Kung said that if he organizes this mess, your boss will have to give up drugs. Control of heroin distribution in the world is not in Wang's hands. Why do you think the Golden Triangle exists? You can—"

Hui interrupts Guowei mid-sentence. "He will never give up, especially now, because someone has stolen all the merchandise in London," he says and pours another glass of baijiu. "He's counting on the full boat that left this morning."

"That ship is dead. My boss will try to negotiate peace by handing over the ship to them. Kung is the man who connects Tong to the Triad. Respect for him comes first. Everything he does is done," Guowei reveals to Hui.

"Wang and the other bosses are going to kill him." Hui stares at him, rubbing his hands with his napkin.

"There is no other way for peace to return. The meeting will be this afternoon at 2 p.m.; then we will invite Wang, Zhang, Changpu, and Guozhi to dinner. Let's see what's going to happen."

Guowei pours more baijiu into the glasses, and they toast each other, pronouncing nothing.

Hui analyzes the situation, sees a way out of his problem with Wang, and says, "I have an important piece of information. After meeting the Triad and before you call the leaders, I need to talk to Chief Kung." Hui looks at his friend.

Guowei analyzes his friend's face and nods. He looks at his watch. "It's only 12:45 p.m.; what do you think about going together now and talking to him?"

"Done."

The two leave the restaurant and head toward the city centre. On the way, Guowei talks to Kung, and he agrees to meet with Hui before going to meet the Triad bosses.

Hui's cellphone rings while he's driving, and he answers it.

"I'm glad you answered because I need to talk to you."

"I'm sorry, who's talking?" Hui asks, not understanding.

"Detective Chong. Could you come here to the police station downtown? I'll be waiting for you today at 2 p.m."

Hui reflects, looks at Guowei, and says on his cellphone, "One moment, I'm going to park the car."

The detective doesn't respond.

Hui stops, covers the mouthpiece of the device, and says, "I have to go to the police station. I will give my statement. Would it be possible for Chief Kung to reschedule our conversation?"

Guowei sends a message to his boss explaining the situation.

Boss Kung comes back and says he will see Hui at 8 a.m. for breakfast the next day.

Guowei shows the message to Hui, who reads it and agrees.

The manager returns to the conversation on the phone and assures the detective that he will be at the police station at 2 p.m.

Detective Chong responds, "At the entrance, when you identify yourself, ask them to call me."

"Alright, see you then." Hui takes a deep breath and, with a stagnant look, says goodbye to his friend.

"What is this statement that you have to make?" Guowei asks.

Hui sighs, closes his eyes, and says, "Some crap Wang did, and I'm trying to clean it up."

Guowei mutters meaningless words, opens the car door, gets out, and says he's going to take a taxi. "See you tomorrow," he says and, like a soldier, salutes his friend.

Hui starts the car and drives toward the city centre, his head full of conflicting ideas.

34

Changes Bring Truths

It's 9:00 a.m., and Wang didn't sleep at all last night. His cellphone rings as he drives to the office at the port. He answers, "Good morning, Bo."

"Can you help me here?" asks the Shanghai police chief, his voice full of concern.

"Anything for you," Wang says, parking the car in the nearest space. The boss rubs his temples.

"This morning, we received a report about major chaos at the port. A fight broke out at sunrise over some shipments bound for Europe. The informant also mentioned that around twenty guys went missing after the fight."

Wang raises an eyebrow. "Now that's something."

The chief continues, "I asked some of my men to scout the area. Everything seems calm. No signs of trouble. No one in the port offices or on the docks knows of any fighting."

"What's the problem if everything is okay?" Wang asks, sensing Chief Bo's discomfort.

"It's just… our informant. He's always been right. He's never given us any wrong information," admits the superintendent, his voice full of concern.

Wang leans back and raises an eyebrow.

"Look, my ship went out last night. Everything went according to plan. No problems, no drama. My boys would have let me know if there was any problem."

"The thing is… it wasn't last night. It was early this morning," Superintendent Bo corrects him, frustration showing in his voice.

Wang laughs, realizing his mistake. "Oh, that's too bad. Look, I'm going to have a look; I'll see if I can hear any information about some late-night or early morning drama down at the docks. As for your trusted informant, call him again. There must be a misunderstanding."

Superintendent Bo runs his hand through his hair. "He's already called me three times this morning. He swears it's all true."

"I'm going to ask around; see if any of the locals heard anything," Wang says, eager to change the subject.

The boss admits, "You were the first person I thought of. We have been together for years, and we have always considered you our interlocutor at the port."

Wang reassures him. "If I find out anything, you'll be the first to know. You can leave it with me, okay?" he suggests, signalling that he wants to hang up.

"Be careful."

Wang heads straight to the port. Looking in the rear-view mirror, a mischievous smile appears on his lips. He feels confident that he has covered all angles and believes that no one will find out. Now for the real enigma: who is passing information on to the police? Wang laughs at the idea as he spots Hui's motorcycle inside Warehouse #2.

He turns off the car and settles back in the seat, thinking out loud, "Who's talking?" He closes his eyes, trying to imagine the faces. Without knowing it, he massages his eyes and stifles a yawn. "I think I'm going to bring out the big guns on this one." He takes out his cellphone and texts Changpu, Huan Zhang, and Guozhi: *Lunch. Mengzi Road. 12 p.m. sharp. Remember our year-end party there?*

One by one, they return the message, confirming that they will be present.

* * *

Meanwhile, at the hotel, the real estate agent informs Rachel that she can collect the apartment keys whenever she wants. The cleaning staff cleaned the apartment, and the real estate agent informed the landlord of the change. Now she just needs to meet the janitor.

After breakfast, the partners decide to get the keys and see the apartment. Upon arrival at the building, the caretaker welcomes the three of them at the entrance. He shows them where the elevators are, as well as the stairs that go down to the underground parking lot. He gives Rachel a document that says what the condominium's rules are, and she signs it. The three take the elevator to the ninth floor, apartment number ninety-one.

David comments that he likes the entrance to the building, the glass door with iron hardware, and the calm street. Tyler and Rachel notice the camera inside the elevator.

When they stop at the floor, the door opens, releasing them. Each floor has only two apartments. The caretaker informed them that a family from the countryside bought number ninety-two, but their move-in date is unknown.

Rachel opens the door, and David jokes, "Ninety-one, huh? A decent feng shui number, that."

Tyler smiles, pushing David. "Since when have you become an expert in feng shui?"

Rachel laughs, gesturing toward the inside. "Come in."

David gives Tyler a mock-annoyed look, turning away. Rachel's eyes sparkle as she looks around. "Isn't this room wonderful?"

Together, they step inside, amazed at the large space. Their eyes roam over plush white leather sofas, an enormous rug adorned with abstract patterns, and walls painted in calming shades of white and blue.

As Rachel closes the door behind them, the apartment's crown jewel, a panoramic glass wall, reveals a mesmerizing view of the Huangpu River, and a swath of the city's skyline captivates their attention.

When she visited this place, she fell in love. The floor-to-ceiling glass wall is reminiscent of Wang's apartment; this same architecture left her impressed as well. Wang's flat was twice as big as this one, but that didn't matter to her. The view is breathtaking.

David, unable to look away from the cityscape, mutters, "This view is unreal." He turns to Rachel, who is glowing with pride.

Tyler's eyes widen in surprise. "How much does this cost you every month?"

"One thousand and one hundred American dollars," Rachel says, walking toward the kitchen. "We paid for three months. If we return it early, I get a refund."

Tyler raises an eyebrow. "That's it, like fourteen hundred Canadian?"

Rachel nods. "More or less," she responds as Tyler peers into the kitchen cabinets, checking how clean they are.

"Damn," Tyler marvels, approaching the window. "Back home in Canada, a place like this would cost twice as much. How did you get such a great deal?"

David takes a quick tour of the rooms. Returning to the living room, he comments, "The rooms are a little cozy. There is a suite with a king-size bed. That's mine," he declares, looking up as if daring someone to challenge him.

Tyler smiles. "So, you've taken possession?"

David waves his hand. "There's another bathroom for you guys. Rachel, this one is cool. Much better than I thought." He goes to the living room window, taking in the view.

Rachel bows, grinning. "Thanks."

Tyler nods. "I approve."

Rachel smiles. "Much better than staying in a hotel, right? Oh, and we have a dedicated parking space."

David takes a deep breath, feeling the breeze, and says, "Speaking of parking, how about we rent a car today? Tomorrow we can move in and do some shopping. Is there air conditioning?"

Rachel coughs a little, avoiding David's question. "Let's go back to the hotel first. We need to write the things we'll need: sheets, towels, groceries, cleaning supplies, all of it."

The trio leaves the apartment. As they wait for a taxi, Rachel squints at the clock. "It's only ten o'clock? Maybe we should stop by the police station downtown, see Chief Bo."

David and Tyler exchange looks and nod. "Sounds good."

Rachel calls Chief Bo. He answers, not expecting her call.

"Rachel? What happened?"

"Hey, Boss Bo. We're in town, and we'd love to stop by and introduce Tyler. He's our partner in London; he's here on vacation."

Boss Bo feels intrigued. "Sure, come this morning. I'll be waiting."

Their taxi arrives, and they get in. After touring the city for a good forty minutes, they stop in front of the imposing stairway entrance of the police building.

Inside, Boss Bo is having a rough morning. Analyzing the reports and trying to understand the confidential documents received by his secretary, he concludes he must have received some dubious information. As he reflects on the information, something fresh crosses his mind: Rachel's surprise visit.

The DRT trio enters the police headquarters. A police officer was already waiting for them and takes them to the superintendent's office.

Upon seeing him, Rachel approaches and bows in respect, followed by David, who gives Bo a warm pat on the back, asking if everything is okay. Tyler, following local etiquette, bows, earning a nod of thanks from Chief Bo.

"Why the unexpected visit this Monday morning?" Boss Bo asks in his shaky but understandable English.

Rachel smiles. "Boss, your English is improving!"

Bo laughs. "Thank you, thank you. You're very kind."

David takes a deep breath. "You know, you're the first person I'm visiting since I got out of the hospital. Just... thank you for everything you did during that hellish week." David rises from his chair and bows with respect.

Boss Bo's eyes soften. "David, come on. I'm just doing my job."

David, with no embarrassment, says, "Sorry to ask you, but is there any update on my case? How is the search for Michael going?"

Boss Bo gestures to his secretary, who is standing at the office door. "Call Detective Chong and the chief of operations." Returning to David, he explains, "Just give me a second, David. I'll give you the latest news."

Meanwhile, Tyler's eyes wander around the room, taking in the pictures on the wall, the framed diplomas, various awards, and the decorated office showing power and respect.

Catching Tyler's curious look, Chief Bo asks, "What do you like best?"

Tyler smiles timidly. "Sorry for being curious. This is quite an office. Can I call you Boss Bo also?"

"Of course," replies the superintendent, lighting a cigarette. He looks at Tyler and offers one, which Tyler accepts with a nod of thanks.

Tyler looks at the walls again. "Impressive collection of accolades you have there. A lifetime of achievements and fantastic memories." He lights the cigarette and takes a drag.

Boss Bo also takes a drag, and a cloud of smoke surrounds him. With precision, he looks at Tyler. "Are you a police officer, also?"

Tyler nods in confirmation. "Yes, I retired from the RCMP. Now I'm taking a break from life and came to explore Shanghai."

Boss Bo laughs. "Well, this town has a way of attracting people and doesn't have concerns if you find it difficult because you don't want to leave."

Tyler smiles. "I bet."

As David and Rachel watch Boss Bo and Tyler conversing despite language difficulties, the secretary enters, serving water, tea, and coffee to everyone, then leaves.

"I must say," begins Tyler, full of enthusiasm and jabbering in English, "the little I've seen of Shanghai? I'm amazed. Plus, meeting the Shanghai police chief! This day has turned out better than I expected."

David conveys Tyler's feelings to Chief Bo in more fluent terms.

Chief Bo's eyes turn to Rachel, concern showing in them. "Rachel, you look thinner. Are you eating well?"

She offers a shy smile. "It's been a turbulent week, boss. I promise I'll get back on track. Better meals, regular hours."

Just then, the secretary returns and reports that Detective Chong was outside the building and had turned off his phone. Moments later, Detective München, chief of operations, enters, bowing. "Good morning."

Boss Bo's expression twitches. "München, any idea where Chong is?"

München, sensing the tension and eager to protect his colleague, responds, "He's working down the street. He called me about fifteen minutes ago, asking for some data. He should be back soon."

Boss Bo nods, taking a deep breath and stubbing out his cigarette. "Alright, tell me how the investigation into Michael's disappearance is going."

Detective München explains, "The investigation is going well, and with the latest surveys, Detective Chong needs to go to the port." He notices his boss is not attentive and continues, "Detective Chong went to the pier to look into the case of this Zhao, the guy with the motorcycle who died. The last known place he worked is at the port. Chong feels he is on the right path. Just yesterday, we talked about the explosion on that farm. He said he had a lead: The husband of the woman who died on the farm and Zhao worked in the same warehouse. That is the information that he gave me."

Boss Bo's impatience presents itself. "What about Michael? Any updates on his disappearance?" He walks away from the table, frustration clear in every line of his face.

München hesitates for a moment, hearing the nervousness in his boss's voice. "Nothing. All the informants have nothing, no trace of him. His phone is off, no bank transactions, nothing to tell us where he might be."

David, Rachel, and Tyler exchange uneasy glances.

Boss Bo, trying to regain his composure, nods to München. "Thank you. If anything comes up, let me know." He motions for München to leave.

The tension in the room grows worse. Breaking the silence, Chief Bo looks into David's eyes, his expression a mixture of frustration and concern. "David, we're working hard. We're turning over every stone. I even have informants on the street looking for information. I'm sure we'll get a clue soon."

David runs a hand through his hair, nervousness clear on his face. "I can't understand this disappearance," he says, agitation in his voice.

Seeing David's distress, Chief Bo responds, "I can imagine your pain. The moment I know anything, you will be the first to know. You can be sure."

Turning his attention to Rachel, Boss Bo speaks to her in Mandarin. "Besides the current problems you have been experiencing, how is the Operation Portugal investigation going?"

Rachel meets Chief Bo's gaze and chooses her words with care. "After David's accident, everything had to be put on hold. Investigating the city alone is impossible. My limited Mandarin left me without the ability to navigate. Dealing with matters related to the accident and then with the death of my cousin, it was not possible for me to dedicate myself to the investigation."

Boss Bo says, "I heard about your cousin's passing. My deepest condolences. I have committed to helping Interpol and will ensure you receive all the help you need. Is there anything urgent I should know?" He leans toward her, hinting that he knows something and is waiting to hear from her.

Rachel hesitates, unsure of what he wants to know. Boss Bo's aim hides in his choice of words. "Give me a few days," she responds. "David just got out of the hospital, and now we're starting physical therapy. I haven't reviewed the data we've collected. I think in about two days I'll be able to give you some insight into what we've collected, and I hope you'll help me create a list of names to cross-check." Boss Bo looks at her.

"Also, we're moving from the hotel to an apartment for the next three months. As soon as I have the exact address, I'll pass it on to you."

David can't help but give Rachel an impressed look. She has a knack for reading between the lines. Sensing that Boss Bo might have more information than he was letting on, she played along and left the cards in his hands. By offering some of her information, she encouraged the chief to trust them even more. David appreciates her smart approach to discuss moving home without hesitation.

Chief Bo holds Rachel's gaze for a long moment. "You three make quite a team. I hope you are enjoying Shanghai?"

The superintendent stands up, signalling the end of the meeting. David, Rachel, and Tyler follow suit, bowing in a respectful gesture of thanks before leaving.

As they leave, Chief Bo's secretary enters the room, placing a fresh cup of coffee on the superintendent's desk and informing him that someone is on the line waiting to speak to him. The chief gives a wave, watching the trio leave before picking up the telephone.

Listening on the phone and not responding, his face turns to consternation. He sits in the armchair, absorbing the news on the other end of the line. As soon as the call ends, he takes his cellphone out of his pocket and calls a number. He speaks in a low voice, expressing a mixture of disbelief and frustration. "How did they let this happen? Now it's going to get out of control!"

He listens, head down.

The secretary, at her desk, looks at him and senses the tension in the room. She gets up from her chair and, without disturbing him, closes the door, but she still hears some words.

"My fault? Look, I'm doing my best here, and they just left my office."

Boss Bo's fingers trace an unknown song on the table. His movements reveal agitation in his breathing. He shakes his head, disbelief clear in his voice. "So, the embassies are now in negotiations with the leader of the nation! This will be out of our hands. If things get tough, I don't want to know. I'll throw him to the wolves."

He stands up, still holding the phone, exhaling a tired sigh. He hangs up the phone and tries to walk, but he staggers, leaning on the edge of the table.

* * *

As they head down the hallway toward the building's exit, David, Rachel, and Tyler spot Detective Chong running through the reception area, heading straight for the stairs that lead to Chief Bo's office.

Going down the stairs, the trio can hear loud voices speaking in Mandarin. The scene at the reception is hilarious: the police officers on duty mock and joke at the breathless detective as he runs past them.

Capturing snippets of the conversation, David explains to Rachel and Tyler, "They're saying that Boss Bo is going to execute Chong today because he hasn't known his whereabouts since this morning."

Chong stops walking in front of them after listening to David's translation. With a brief bow of respect, he says, "I need to speak to you."

David's eyebrows rise. "What's going on? Any news?"

Chong's voice is full of apprehension. "I think so. Can we meet?"

"Tonight?" David asks.

Rachel interjects, "We have that dinner with Wang at 5 p.m., remember?"

Unfazed by Rachel's reminder, Chong presses, "How about later? Somewhere private?"

Without hesitation, David responds, "Sounds good. As soon as we get back to the hotel, Rachel will call you."

"Done," Chong agrees, already turning to run up the stairs to Boss Bo's office.

The trio laughs at how Chong is desperate to report to Boss Bo. They leave the building and head toward the street in search of a taxi.

"I'm thinking about lunch," David tells his partners.

"Me too," Tyler agrees, already feeling the first pangs of hunger.

Looking at her watch, Rachel announces, "It's only 11:20. There's an avenue nearby with several shopping malls and restaurants. Just two blocks from here. We could go for a walk, and maybe buy some essential items to take back to the apartment. Then we'll have lunch. That way, tomorrow, we can just focus on the move."

Both David and Tyler nod, disappointed that they have to wait to eat.

* * *

Boss Bo's frustration peaks when he hangs up the phone. Losing control, he throws the coffee cup on the floor, which breaks into countless pieces.

His secretary, alarmed by the noise, enters the room. Bo waves her away.

Detective Chong rushes into the superintendent's office, out of breath and wet with sweat. "My apologies. I should have informed you about my departure today."

Boss Bo's gaze is distant, not acknowledging Chong's presence. The broken cup catches Chong's attention, signalling that he may be in trouble. He tries to find a plausible explanation.

Still seething, Boss Bo breaks the tension. "Sit down."

"I'm fine standing," Chong responds, trying to make himself comfortable.

Boss Bo approaches him, narrowing his eyes. "If you're about to tell me a story, think long and hard about what you're going to say."

Chong swallows hard. "Is all this distress about David Ho's investigation?"

"I heard from München. He mentioned you found a link between Zhao and the farm explosion," Chief Bo reveals, his words filled with frustration.

Chong's face pales, and he curses München for passing on information.

"Look, I still don't have solid evidence and I can't guarantee anything," he stammers, trying to show that he is right to not give unsubstantiated information.

"So, they work in the same warehouse? Did you go there today? What did you discover? Why didn't you inform me? What has changed? Why these secrets now?" Chief Bo's voice rises, reaching the detectives in the hallway, who can't help but hear and gather at the front door.

Surprised, Chong realizes he underestimated the situation. Not updating his boss was an oversight, but sharing his suspicions with München was the mistake that could crucify him.

"Boss Bo, please just listen to me," Chong says with desperation in his voice. "I should have told you. My goal was to make sure our information was rock solid without compromising the department's reputation. Let me take the evidence I've collected so far, and I'll lay it all out for you."

He takes a step back, hoping to leave the room.

The superintendent's eyes are cold and glued to him, preventing Chong from leaving. "Do you think I'm a fool? Do you think you can trick me? You'll not get out of this without problems."

Chong's determination makes him retort, "I've always been straight with you, boss. My silence wasn't deceit, it was caution. I'm one-hundred-percent dedicated to solving this case, and I give you my word. I'll see this through to the end and find out everything."

Boss Bo's gaze is relentless. "You're off this case. Hand over everything you have to München. From now on, I don't want to hear a single update from you on any investigation. One more slip-up and I'll suspend you. No deceptions, no more games, no more excuses. You think you can string me along?"

The stress of the call had already frayed Boss Bo's nerves, and Chong's actions only fanned the flames. His frustration is boiling over.

Chong, feeling trapped and desperate, falls to his knees. "Boss, please understand. This is much bigger than I think. The information became very compromising, and I feared the implications if the two cases became intertwined."

Chief Bo looks at Chong. The detective's words make him hesitate. The superintendent walks to the office door and shouts to the police officers who are trying to listen to the conversation: "Enough gossip! Go back to your posts!" The police officers walk away, but the whispers and smiles continue.

As soon as the hallway is empty, Boss Bo returns to the room, closing the glass door with a thud. His gaze now fixes on Chong with a mix of curiosity and anger. "Okay, Chong, now tell me. What did you find out?"

Chong, eager to justify his actions, reports his findings. He explains the connection between the husband of the woman who died in the explosion and Zhao's workplace.

"I visited Warehouse Number Four, spoke to the manager and some workers. They recognized the photos I presented to them. The manager and workers confirmed that the two men work in the port area. They planned to come here and provide a statement." Chong, careful about what he can and cannot say, omits any mention of the names Wonjy and Wang.

Boss Bo raises an eyebrow, skepticism written all over his face. "You're not making all this up, are you?"

"No," Chong counters. "I have already arranged for these individuals to come and corroborate what they have told me."

The boss's anger dissipates. "Why didn't you inform me? Why didn't you inform me of this yesterday when I pressed you?"

Chong watches as Boss Bo goes to his desk and takes a cigarette from the pack. He lights it with the gold lighter that has his name etched on it, reflected in the glow.

Taking a deep breath, Chong replies, "Yesterday, I talked to some employees at the warehouses. I needed to verify the clues before presenting them. I verify everything I heard before revealing my whereabouts to you today." Chong, cautious with his words, provides enough details to appease the boss's anger at that moment.

"Hmm…" Boss Bo mutters, narrowing his eyes as he looks at Chong with a mixture of suspicion and curiosity.

Chong, feeling the need to be transparent but with restrictions, continues: "I'm telling you the truth. This morning, I visited an old barn on the outskirts that was renovated as a bar for the enjoyment of the port employees, dockers even. When I arrived, the place was buzzing like they were in the middle of a celebration. Someone mentioned it was a birthday party, and they were also honouring the port's night shift crew for some kind of work on site, something about dispatching a ship that would not leave."

Boss Bo's posture remains rigid, his eyes unblinking. "Are you hiding any details?"

Chong, eager to assuage any lingering doubts, replies, "No way. The only solid information I got was from three people at the scene who recognized the men I'm looking for from the photos and confirmed the place they work. That was the reason I went there today."

Boss Bo's tone becomes sharper. "Do you have this documented? I need to see everything."

Chong straightens up, regaining some confidence. "I haven't finished the report yet. I need to gather some more data, but I promise that before nightfall, you will have the complete report."

Boss Bo exhales, showing calm. "Alright then. Inform me later today." He waves his hands for Chong to leave, showing that the discussion is over.

As soon as Chong leaves the office, the secretary hurries in and reminds the chief of the next meeting at noon.

Absorbed in his thoughts and not yet connecting the dots between Chong's discoveries and previous information about a disturbance at the port, Chief Bo observes Chong's retreating figure and muses, "Let's see what he finds. It might shed some light on what's coming."

* * *

On the outskirts of the city, Wang sits down to have lunch with Guozhi, Changpu, and Huan Zhang. Today, thanks to Guozhi, who's happy to spend a little more, they set aside their usual frugality for meals. He orders a bottle of "Kweichow Moutai," a renowned Chinese liquor.

Raising his tiny glass, Guozhi proposes, "A toast!" With a firm nod, he declares, "Ganbei!"

The others echo in unison, "Ganbei!" and they all drink together.

Placing the cup back on the table, Changpu interrupts the brief pause. "Any news about Kang Wu?"

Wang, refilling his glass, replies, "I expect a call from him soon."

Huan Zhang, anxious, presses his boss. "Do you think the negotiations will proceed as we want?"

Wang meets Huan Zhang's gaze. "He assured me that everything was in order, but if things go wrong, we will need to prepare. We have invested much more in this export deal than projected. As of yesterday, we have the green light to broker deals anywhere in the world. Kang Wu attested to this, and there is no turning back now."

The chief's words carry weight, but the gravity of the situation seems to be ignored by the others, who are more engrossed in their meal than the urgent matter at hand.

Wang's ringing phone interrupts the conversation. He excuses himself and goes to the balcony to answer the call. When he returns, his expression is unreadable, and he remains silent.

The atmosphere between the chiefs changes, becoming more celebratory as waiters arrive bearing full trays, placing an array of sumptuous dishes on the table.

Changpu, unable to contain his admiration, comments, "Wang, you have impeccable taste in restaurants. It's been a long time since I've witnessed a banquet like this, both in terms of quantity and quality."

The leaders pick up the delicacies displayed there. The tempting aroma fills the air. However, Wang's plate remains empty, in stark contrast to the others. After a contemplative pause, observing the bosses, he breaks the silence. "I just discovered that one of our people informed the police of details about the morning's events at the port. Has anyone heard about this?"

The table is silent. Guozhi, Changpu, and Huan Zhang exchange glances, realizing the gravity of Wang's words. In unison, they protest, defending the loyalty of their subordinates, pointing out that no rival gang member escaped the previous night.

Wang's tone hardens. "The informant is someone of ours, and this was not the first report. According to the call, a fight over a shipment on a boat that left early in the morning took place. The informant detailed that about twenty men disappeared in the chaos. Don't you find the level of detail alarming?"

The chiefs lose their appetites. Wang's revelation carries a heavy weight, making the dishes appear nonexistent. The festive ambience faded, leaving behind an atmosphere of tension and suspicion.

"I'll look into it," Changpu declares.

Guozhi chimes in, frowning, "I'll dive into it this afternoon."

Huan Zhang, ever the voice of reason, insists, "Let's stay calm and think through how we're going to approach this. Just as we have our informants infiltrating our rivals, they have also placed one or more among us. Now that we are aware, our priority must be to unmask these traitors."

With mutual nods of understanding and agreement, they return to eating.

Changpu turns to Huan Zhang, musing, "We must act with caution and avoid any mistakes."

Wang adds, "If we discover more than one, we must identify them all."

Chewing a mouthful of fish and rice, Guozhi suggests, "How about putting out some bait? Feed some false information and see who bites."

Huan Zhang scolds his friend: "Guozhi, swallow your food before sharing your ideas."

Wang jokes, "He never mastered the art of eating without talking. I think it's challenging."

Huan Zhang laughs. "It's simple. The brain doesn't work on an empty stomach."

A wave of laughter spreads around the table, the tension eased by their camaraderie.

However, Wang's cellphone rings again, interrupting the atmosphere. He looks at the caller ID and answers, keeping silent while listening. The call is brief, but when he ends it, everyone at the table sees Wang gazing into the distance, his eyes fixed on some invisible point.

The chiefs, without understanding, stop their meal and wait for Wang to speak.

Wang notices the worried looks exchanged between the leaders and says, "Kang told me he delivered the two containers with the men today.

He will try to arrange a dinner with us and the new board members. Kang also clarified that he would do his best to ensure that Tong remains intact."

Huan Zhang raises an eyebrow. "Are you buying what he's selling?"

Wang pauses and responds with a firm tone, "We will postpone judgments until my contact informs us what is happening inside. After that, we will decide our next steps."

The chiefs agree and raise their glasses in a silent toast before returning to their meal.

35

"We Are All Interconnected"

As Detective Chong leaves the office, he wonders how to resolve this situation without putting Wang's name on the report. His recent conversation with the superintendent leaves him uneasy. Relief evades him, yet he is grateful for having calmed the situation with a guarantee to deliver his report later today.

As he enters his office, he says to his secretary, "Don't let anyone into my office for a while." She nods in agreement.

Inside, Chong slumps into his worn armchair. Trying to settle into the old chair, he looks around, noticing that the mountain of paper on his desk has diminished, thanks to his diligent secretary. He digs through his leather briefcase and takes out some papers. Fatigue weighs on him like a heavy cloud.

He rubs his face, yawns, and murmurs, "The pieces of this puzzle are now going to come together. Now it's time to figure out how they fit." The morning was full of information he could never have imagined. After the interview with the warehouse manager, he visited the barn, the meeting point for workers from Warehouses One and Two. He thought it would be a place of fun and camaraderie. Instead, he discovered that the place was full of gossip and allowed drinking. His instinct tells him that this case is turning into something much bigger. The dots are connecting, suggesting a potential link between the two incidents he is investigating.

He flips through his notes, his fingers searching for that specific set of scribbles. He needs to remember every word of what those men told him. His gaze darts upward, eyes roaming the ceiling as he turns his head, trying to ease the tension. A throbbing headache arrives, a common companion during intense investigations. Analyzing all the possibilities for why the pain has returned, he concludes that maybe it's because his stomach is empty.

Picking up the intercom, he asks the secretary, "Could you get me some soy milk and fried dough sticks from that diner on the corner?"

With a hint of enthusiasm in her voice, the secretary replies, "Of course!" She enters the room, and Chong reaches into his pocket and hands her some money. She leaves with agility and quickness in her steps.

"Rachel and David... I need to check this out," he mutters, staring at a paper in his hands, thoughts swirling.

Taking a deep breath, Chong turns his attention to the scribbles on the papers he took out of his briefcase. Vivid memories come back. He had parked the car in front of the warehouse, and two motorcycles were parked against the rustic wall. His lack of familiarity with the place made him act with caution, his eyes alert, observing everything.

He was unaware that this inconspicuous barn was a favourite location for employees of Warehouses #1 and #2, as well as other contract employees. They gathered there, relaxing from their daily routine, indulging in gossip and a beer before returning to their homes.

He hesitated before entering the place. Detective Chong's gaze fell on an almost empty dirt-floor indoor parking lot to his right. He looked down at his feet, frowning as he noticed the reddish-brown dirt staining his polished black shoes. Walking forward, relief washed over him as he stepped onto the solid, cement entrance of the barn. Without wasting a moment, he took a handkerchief from his pocket and brushed off the dust.

He surveyed his surroundings, seeing several dirty tables, each surrounded by four empty chairs, a few scattered on the floor. It was obvious that a party had filled the space: crumpled cups, discarded napkins, and some cans were left over, disposable plates and cups awaiting collection on the floor and on the tables. To his left stretched a large terrace, complete with cemented benches and a sturdy wooden counter that seemed to barricade the exterior, signalling a no-entry zone for outsiders.

Advancing further, Chong saw two men unloading crates of beer from a truck, while another was busy inside the warehouse, arranging glasses and other kitchen utensils on metal shelves. At the end of the barn, which only had a naked light bulb on the ceiling, he saw another figure, who appeared to be cooking, judging by the noise of rattling pans and by the flame that appeared above a piece of furniture.

His gaze shifted to a nearby table, where three uniformed dockworkers were chatting. As he passed by them, he felt the collective gaze. Chong stood firm, acknowledging that his attire alerted them to his status as an outsider.

When he arrived at the counter, the man arranging the kitchen utensils came up to him with an apologetic tone. "Sorry, sir, we only serve the people from Warehouses One and Two."

With a practised move, Detective Chong reached into his jacket pocket, pulled out his ID, and presented it.

The man behind the counter leaned forward with a respectful nod and said, "My name is Xiaobo. How may I help you, sir?"

"Has there been any kind of meeting or party here?" Chong asked, his voice firm.

Xiaobo hesitated for a moment, eyes darting around as if assessing how much he should share. The slight tremor in his voice betrayed his nervousness. "Yes, there was. It was a birthday celebration. Some dockworkers were also celebrating the successful dispatch of a ship. Anything specific you would like to know?"

Chong nodded, acknowledging the explanation, and then said, "An espresso, please."

In the blink of an eye, a waiter approached, placing a steaming mug of coffee in front of him. Chong nodded in thanks, reaching into his pocket. He took out some coins for payment and, with discretion, placed a photograph of Zhao next to the money.

Xiaobo studied the photo, his face registering recognition.

"I haven't seen this man here for some time. You see, the administration has tightened access policies. Now only permanent employees with warehouse identification can enter."

Without missing a beat, Chong presented another photograph, this time of Wonjy. Xiaobo took a deep breath as he held the photograph. "Wonjy is a regular customer; he always comes here at night, but I haven't seen him in a week. Funny, his wife was here looking for him a few days ago. If you want to know, maybe the people at that table can help."

Detective Chong followed Xiaobo's lead, his eyes landing on a table a few metres away.

Turning sharply, Xiaobo shouted, "Zi Han! This gentleman needs your help!"

Zi Han, a sturdy figure with a sun-lined face, stood up with his eyes fixed on Chong. Instead of approaching, he gestured for Chong to come closer. Chong obeyed, and without wasting time, approached.

Without uttering a word, Zi Han pointed to an empty chair. Chong took out his ID, showed it, and sat down. The tension was evident. The other men seated assessed Chong with a mixture of curiosity and caution, their faces remaining impassive.

Removing Wonjy's photograph, Chong placed it on the table, his voice thick with urgency: "Do any of you recognize this man?"

One employee reached out, lifting the photograph for a closer look. "That's Wonjy," he confirmed.

Nodding, Chong said, "I need to locate him. Could you help me?"

Zi Han, always cautious, looked at Chong with a hint of suspicion. Holding the photograph between his thumb and forefinger, he asked, "What's your deal with him?"

Taking a deep breath, Chong responded, the weight of the news marking his voice, "I'm not sure if you're aware there's been a tragic accident. His wife and daughter... they didn't survive. There was a gas explosion in their house." Chong stayed quiet as he took the photo back.

A guttural exclamation of disbelief erupted from one man. "That can't be true!" he declared, horrified.

From the counter, Xiaobo, having caught snippets of the conversation, approached the table, his face in shock. Without waiting for an invitation, he pulled up a chair, settling in the middle of the group, waiting for more details.

"Do any of you know the family?" Chong asked, stopping to take a sip of his still-warm coffee.

Almost in unison, three of the men shrugged, their voices overlapping. "Not really."

However, Xiaobo, with a tremor in his voice betraying his shock, asked, "When did this happen?"

"Friday night," Detective Chong replied, noting the mix of emotions that manifested among the group. Zi Han's reaction stood out. The man seemed to collapse, his gaze dropping to the ground, his lips pressed into a tense line.

"Now I remember," Xiaobo muttered, more to himself than anyone else. "She came here on Friday morning looking for Wonjy. It's heartbreaking."

With sudden attitude and showing uneasiness, Zi Han pushed his chair back. With a hoarse voice, he announced, "I need to leave. The entire night was just work, and I'm tired." With a nod to the others, he left the place with his head down.

Though the remaining two men at the table offered Chong an overview of Wonjy's connections to Warehouses #1 and #2, he was not interested in the information because it was the same as what he had heard. The trio, Wonjy, Hui, and Wang were always together.

Detective Chong sensed there was more to it but recognized the men's hesitation in speaking. He made a quick decision, taking Zhao's photograph again and presenting it to the pair. They took a cursory look, confirming that Zhao hadn't been around in a while. They were also quick to clarify their own positions: "We are indirectly associated with Warehouses One and Two. We work for the port company moving ship cargo." The statement had a purpose, signalling to Chong that it was time to end the conversation.

Chong thanked everyone, bowing, and hurried out of the gate. He went toward the car and noticed Zi Han smoking, leaning against the side of a motorcycle. He approached him and asked with command, "Do you have anything else to tell me?"

Zi Han looked at him and scratched the side of his left eye and took a deep breath. "Friday morning, I took my son on a boat trip to the Huangpu touring boat. Me and some other people walked to the parking lot on the way back from the tour. We all saw a woman on her knees crying with a child in front of parked cars. The people who were accompanying us ignored the situation and went straight to their vehicles, paying no attention to what was happening."

Detective Chong analyzed and listened to Zi Han, asking for him to continue.

"I recognized her because I know Wonjy's family. It was his wife and daughter. They were asking Wang about Wonjy. Do you know the owner of Warehouses One and Two? It was him with a Western woman... an ugly scene because he was screaming, and Wonjy's wife looked desperate. I took my children and my wife away because I didn't want them to pay attention to what was going on there and put them in the car. When I looked back, I saw Wang throwing money at her and then getting into a vehicle with the woman accompanying him. Then he sped off."

"What time did that happen?"

"I don't remember, but I believe it was 11:00 or 11:30 in the morning. It was my day off. I haven't seen Wonjy in days. He doesn't work with us on a day-to-day basis, but he always comes here to drink and chat. He's a person who helps everyone. His job is with Wang. He's the jack-of-all-trades, like Hui."

Seizing the moment, Chong presented Zao's photograph to Zi Han. Zi's response was immediate, a laugh filled with mockery. With a pointed finger hovering over the photo, he commented, "This guy? He's nothing but bad news. He shows up at every warehouse whenever he needs money. Many of the local contractors would never hire him because he can't do any job right, only engage in 'questionable activities.' I can't understand why others tolerate it. The last time we saw him at Warehouse Number Two was last week while he was talking to Hui. We were busy with some containers, and there he was, lurking. The next day, I saw him and Wonjy leaving together."

Chong's eyebrows furrowed. "What car does Wonjy drive?"

Zi's response was immediate: "A black Toyota, but it's one car in the warehouse fleet. He doesn't have a personal car."

Glancing at his watch, Chong saw he was late for work. He took out a business card from his pocket and handed it to Zi Han. "If you have more information, please get in touch. And when I say, 'I would appreciate it,' I mean it."

Zi's eyes softened for a moment, his voice betraying emotion. "You know, Wonjy is a decent guy. He lives with his family. The idea of him doing any harm to his wife and daughter is impossible." As he accepted Chong's card, anguish was clear on his face.

"If something, anything, comes to mind, call me. Make sure you do," Chong reiterated, urgency in his tone. Without further delay, he took off and left the scene.

Startled from his reverie by the sound of a knock, Chong's gaze darts to the door where his secretary stands. His expression remains distant, lost in Zi's words and the enormous case he may have uncovered.

Placing a bag full of the ordered food on his desk, the secretary looks at Detective Chong, a hint of expectation in her eyes. "I'm going out for lunch. Do you need anything else before I leave?"

Chong fixes his eyes on her with a contemplative look. "That number I gave you yesterday, the warehouse manager's…?"

She sighs, shoulders slumping, a flash of annoyance passing across her face. "Yes?" She was looking forward to the break, and the possibility of leaving late discourages her.

"Call him now. I need to talk to him. Once that's done, you can go to lunch."

A small smile forms on her lips. She makes the call and passes the phone to Chong, stating that Hui is on the line.

Maintaining a calm demeanour, Detective Chong's voice shows a hint of urgency as he instructs Hui to be at the police station at 2:00 p.m. today. When he hangs up, his gaze lands on a stack of papers on his secretary's desk.

His fingers drum on the table, as if playing music. "I need solid proof," he mutters, more to himself than anyone else. "Today is the day I'll have it."

A quick glance at the imposing clock on the wall shows 12:45 p.m. Feeling hungry, Chong turns his attention to the food in front of him. While picking up some snacks, his other hand rummages through the accumulated files, examining those from the last four days. Forensic reports, identification documents, notarial records, SCSI findings, and transcripts from multiple wiretaps detail the interconnected events surrounding Zhao's death, David's shooting, and the farm explosion. An unexplored white folder catches his eye, but he sets it aside.

Halfway through the meal, Chong picks up the intercom, forgetting that his secretary is on her lunch break. Hearing no response, he chuckles. "Guess I'll have to eat faster then."

After a while, the door opens, and his assistant returns. "I'm back from lunch. Let me know if you need anything else."

Upon seeing her at the door, Chong gestures for her to come closer. Stopping to wipe the remains of his meal from his lips, he stares at an unfamiliar white paste.

"Where did that come from?" He points at the table.

Handling the folder and leafing through its pages, she clarifies, "I placed it here yesterday afternoon. It contains photographs and an analysis of the transit company's CCTV."

Surprised and wide-eyed, Chong shakes her hand. "Thanks." With a renewed sense of purpose, he walks over to the couch, placing his laptop on the coffee table in front of him.

As he examines the report and accompanying photos, a familiar sight catches his eye: Zhao's unmistakable motorcycle. With a rush of anticipation, he rips open the plastic bag stapled to the briefcase and holds out the flash drive, plugging it into his laptop.

The footage and analysis of the report outline a clear timeline, showing that at 9:00 p.m. on that fateful Tuesday night, Zhao's motorcycle entered the street. What's most intriguing is that it doesn't come out. Before Zhao arrives, three cars enter the same address. They identified two of the cars, along with their owners' details and addresses. The third, a black Toyota, remains a mystery, as the license plate details do not exist in the traffic administration database.

Absorbed, Chong reviews the footage, focusing on the black car. Detailed analysis suggests that any occupants inside are indiscernible because of the film on the windows. However, there is a peculiar detail: a white spot on the right rear of the car. It looks like it could be a sticker, but the image is not conclusive. The last information in the report is that this Toyota captured in the images left the street toward the primary avenue at around 00:30 on Wednesday.

A triumphant exclamation erupts from Chong. "Yes, this is it!"

His sudden outburst causes the secretary to rush back into the room. Taking advantage, he gives her instructions: "Put Detective München on the line now. Find him as soon as possible."

Without missing a beat, she nods. "Right away, boss," she says and leaves, closing the door behind her.

Detective München, with sixteen years of service, is an experienced officer. He and Detective Chong share a friendship that goes beyond the professional sphere; they have been partners in countless cases over the years. München began his police career in traffic enforcement, which gave him an unparalleled knowledge of the city's intricate network of streets. After passing the detective exam a decade ago, he solves cases with unique intelligence. Outside his duty, München is a family man with a wife and three children, exuding an aura of calm and firmness that contrasts with his professional personality. What makes him stand out is his voice, which sounds comical, like a sports announcer during a heated football match. Jokes from colleagues in the police department abound, but München remains unfazed. When he speaks, it's fast, leaving no room for interpretation. If you lose track, too bad… it won't be said again. Chong has always admired München, especially for his unwavering desire to help and his inability to say the word "no."

In the office, Chong organizes the huge amount of documents in front of him after reading the report. He spreads them out on the couch, each categorized by a label of investigation and names, spreading them out further across the carpet. From his leather bag, he takes the small recorder, adding it to the handwritten notes, photographs, and summaries accumulated over the last few days.

Talking to himself, a habit he finds useful, he mutters, "I need to go over all this again." His gaze darts between the papers on the floor, and for a moment he looks overwhelmed, pressing his hands to his temples, trying to control his thoughts.

In a louder voice, as if seeking an epiphany from the universe, he ponders, "Why did I assume a connection exists between these two cases?"

A bright moment hits him as he examines the names listed in the investigation documents. Pressing "send" on the intercom, he instructs his secretary, "Please get all available records about Wang Savin Wei, Hui Chowei, and Wonjy Deng from the registry office in the underground archives." He emphasizes the urgency of obtaining cellphone records from the past three weeks.

She disconnects the intercom and enters the room.

Chong scribbles down the phone numbers associated with the names, passing them to her. "Send the request to the court, talk to someone there… We have to achieve this today or tomorrow at the latest." He asks her to dial Wonjy Deng's number, and if someone answers, transfer the call to him.

The secretary takes the paper and says that first she will make the call, then she will go to the underground office, and she will arrange for the request for the numbers.

Chong agrees, calming down. He concludes he is on the right track, and the restlessness dissipates.

The office door opens as Detective München walks in, showing determination with a mix of amusement and exasperation in his voice. "What have you done now, Chong? Thanks to you, I felt like a lobster thrown into a boiling pot this morning. You owe me a lot for that."

Chong, full of enthusiasm, replies, "You bet I'll pay you back, but wait until you see what I found." He motions for München to come closer, displaying some images on his computer.

München leans over and looks at the screen. As the video plays, showing several vehicles entering a certain street, München's eyes widen. "Where the hell did you get that?"

Chong smiles. "SCCTV. Everything is happening so fast that we forget. Look at this. That's our answer."

München's mind races, trying to connect the dots, reading the report and seeing the images.

"Here... this is where we will find the answer to the Michael question. This car! It's all coming together. The car entry and exit times, the incident, everything. Do we have any information about this Toyota? Owner or address?"

Chong's face turns serious. "Here's the problem. The license plate is fake. We don't know about the car's owner or history. Also, the car's windows have this tint or something, making it impossible to see the driver, but look at that." Chong points to a different white mark on the back of the car. "This could be our ticket. It could be a sticker or some kind of marking; it's difficult to identify."

München sinks into an armchair. "This is going to be like looking for a needle in a haystack."

Chong doesn't feel intimidated. "We're going to have all our street informants looking for this car. This car can't stay hidden forever."

München agrees. "Alright. I'll get the operations team in right away. You take care of the traffic guys; their boss... you know he can be a little... complicated."

With a confident smile, Chong concludes, "I'm going to go there and ask the traffic chief to give authorization for a citywide search. Let's impound this car."

München leaves the room, his rapid footsteps echoing down the hall. The slamming of the door punctuates his hasty exit, emphasizing the urgency of the situation.

Left to his thoughts, Detective Chong sits on the floor amid a sea of documents. He mutters to himself because he needs to listen to his own voice, a habit he's found in moments of overwhelming information. "This case … is morphing, taking on a life of its own, but where have I heard of that black Toyota before?"

Leafing through his notes, he stops at one made during his visit to David in the hospital. "David appears to be a victim here, but there is a deep connection. He and Michael have known each other for a long time. Michael's mother was the manager of that hotel during the police officer case, and now David and Rachel were revisiting the issue after all these years. It's strange that Michael works at the same hotel now, just when David and Rachel are in Shanghai. Is this just a coincidence?" Shaking his head, he mutters, "This is going to get me in trouble. I will pay attention to this matter later. I need to stick to the present."

Standing up, Chong walks around the room, trying to solve the puzzle. "Let's figure this out. Michael's shot killed Zhao. Zhao injured David. Michael flees the crime scene, but most importantly, there is a car ready to take him away. If anyone says this sequence was accidental, I will…"

His voice trails off as his frustration grows. He grabs a nearby bottle of water and takes a big drink, hoping to control the thoughts and emotions that don't dissipate, making him more agitated.

Chong continues connecting the dots, moving his hands and trying to see the intertwined threads of this narrative.

"So, one moment we have a tragic domestic accident that takes two lives. The husband of one victim, named Wonjy, disappears, leaving a vague message at work. Interestingly, Wonjy and Zhao shared the same workplace."

He pauses again to concentrate. Chong takes a deep breath, his mind racing to put the pieces of everything together.

"Then we have this second topic: the mysterious death of a police officer in a hotel, and the element of surprise, Wang, as a witness. The same Wang involved in our present investigation."

His hands scribble on the whiteboard on the wall, trying to map out the relationships and coincidences. Documenting each name and event, he sees a network of connections emerging. "So, Officer Ronaldo's death brings in Michael because of the hotel connection, and Wang, who was the one who discovered the deceased officer. Wang's close childhood friendship with Hui and Wonjy is also relevant to our current situation. He is the head of the same company where our two main characters work: Wonjy and Zhao."

He pauses again, steps back, analyzing the information written in front of him.

"Then the moment has come. Wonjy travelled and Zhao met his end. It's like a well-orchestrated symphony, but who is the conductor?"

Chong fills the room with tension as he racks his brains over the complexities of the case. One thing is certain to him—the events intertwine in a way that is not mere coincidence, and each piece of evidence leads to more questions.

The detective stops his writing and remembers the partners.

"In the third position, we have David and Rachel investigating the death of the police officer at the hotel, and they find Michael working there. Michael murders Zhao, and David gets injured by Zhao. I am sure the one connecting these two investigations is Wang!"

The detective takes a folder from the armchair, opens it, reads it, and adds it to the board.

"Time. That's it! Hours and days have seen these two investigations intertwining. I need those phone records."

"Where are the notes from Warehouse number four?" Detective Chong asks himself, searching the pile of papers on the carpet.

The door opens inches away, the secretary's eyes filled with urgency. "Detective, Boss Bo wants to see you."

"Thank you," he says in a low voice. The weight of the situation, he is seeing, has become dangerous.

She steps back, leaving the door open for him.

Looking back, Chong notices the hands of the clock pointing to 1:00 p.m. He feels his stomach tighten, anxiety gnawing at him as he climbs the stairs.

Arriving in the hallway, two uniformed police officers pass him, saluting. Lost in the storm of his thoughts, Chong doesn't reciprocate and heads to Chief Bo's office. Stopping in front of the office, Chong hesitates, moves his hand to cover his mouth, thinks about going back, but goes inside.

"How can I explain this?" he whispers to himself. "I can't reveal what I discovered... not yet."

He goes to the anteroom, where the secretary points to a soft armchair. "Sit down," she advises, her eyes suggesting caution. "Boss Bo has company."

Chong sinks into his chair, his mind racing. *What did I get myself into? I don't know why, but I think I got my hand in a jar full of shit*, he ponders, feeling a tightening sensation in his gut.

Boss Bo's robust laugh resonates through the room, causing the secretary to stand at attention. Chong does the same, standing up as the door to the main office opens. What he sees next is breathtaking. Wang Savin Wei and Boss Bo engage in an intimate and informal farewell, the two hugging each other, far removed from their professional personas.

Chong feels a wave of despair. He bows in respect as the pair walk toward the hallway, nearly touching his knees. Caught up in the moment, Wang doesn't even look in Chong's direction.

As soon as they are out of sight, Chong falls back into the armchair, disbelief clouding his face. He massages his knees, trying to calm the whirlwind of emotions. His breathing becomes ragged. The magnitude of what he witnessed hits him hard. The secretary, unfazed, is busy preparing tea.

Chong feels a sudden pain in the back of his head.

"Water, please," he murmurs. She points to a nearby jug without saying a word. He takes several sips, trying to regain his composure.

Detective Chong, trying to figure out what's going on, turns to the secretary. "Why did Wang come here?" he questions, his voice full of suspicion.

She looks up, surprise clear in her eyes. "Ah, do you know Wang? He is so charming! He always brings me chocolates when he comes to visit Chief Bo." She points to a wrapped box on her desk.

Chong, forcing a smile, responds, "Wow, I guess I'll have to up my game. Next time I will bring you chocolates."

Her smile turns to teasing as she responds, "Well, you're not Wang."

His patience thinning, Chong continues, "Okay. Not that I'm curious, but why was he here?"

She lowers her voice. "Earlier today, the boss got a call about some incident at the port. I think Wang was here because of it." She doesn't lose concentration on her computer screen while informing him.

Just then, Superintendent Bo enters the room with a stern demeanour. His gaze settles on Chong, and, with a nod, he signals for the detective to follow him. The weight of the moment hangs in the air.

Once inside the office, Bo's tone remains professional. "Do you have the materials I asked for? Everything I need?"

Chong's mind races, considering how to frame his response without implicating Wang, Hui, and Wonjy. "Yes, boss," he assures. "I have everything and will update you on what is still in progress."

Bo rummages through his desk. "Alright then, sit down. Tell me."

Detective Chong leans forward, the weight of his discoveries pressing down on him. "Here's what I found out," he begins. "I went to the port, Zhao's place of work since he is a longshoreman. But the same day I put all this together, you sent me to that farmhouse... the one that exploded. A woman and child died in the explosion, but there was no sign of her husband. My investigations reveal he travelled to Hong Kong just two days earlier."

Chief Bo, furrowing his eyebrows, says, "It seems to me like two separate incidents."

Chong is still speaking with a sparkle in his eyes. "It would seem so, except for the fact that this missing husband works with Zhao at the port."

Boss Bo examines a document on his desk and then looks down with disdain. "Seems like a mere coincidence to me."

Chong's frustration boils over, his voice full of irritation, but he maintains the appearance of calm. "Coincidences like this don't just happen."

Bo responds with indifference, paying attention to what he was signing. "Continue."

Chong shifts in his seat, choosing his words. "Speaking of weird things, did you know that Michael's mother was a manager at the same hotel he worked at? She dedicated over two decades of her life to this place."

Boss Bo raises a glance at the detective that is capable of cutting into Chong's soul. "What did you just say?"

Chong doesn't hesitate. "This Michael's mother worked at that hotel for over twenty years. I only found out about this because David and Rachel from Operation Portugal were there asking questions."

Boss Bo's brow furrows even more. "Where are you going with these two in your investigation?"

Chong feels he is treading on delicate ground. The superintendent's intense scrutiny makes him feel like he's involved in something more complex.

"It is just a passing mention," Chong backtracks. "I bring it up given the strange coincidences, but it has no bearing on the main point."

Boss Bo's gaze remains intense, locking onto Chong.

"Still, it's an interesting fact."

Feeling cornered by the unexpected attention, Chong moves, intending to leave the office.

"Anyway," he continues, trying to regain his balance by changing and redirecting the attention. "I have already received the CCTV footage, showing vehicles and Zhao's motorcycle entering the street where the crime occurred. In the early hours of the morning, a car reappears and leaves the street, confirming that the vehicles that entered at night belonged to residents of the same street. An important fact. This car that comes back has a cold license plate. Here's the twist in the story: this car leaving the street in the footage coincides with Zhao's estimated time of death and David's statements. I'm sure, boss, that we found the car that took Michael from the crime scene." Chong's voice is steady. A hint of pride appears as he concludes his findings.

"Very well! We need to track this car," acknowledges Superintendent Bo, a smile appearing on his face.

Chong, looking tired, responds, "München is taking care of it. Later, I plan to stop by the traffic administration to talk to the boss in person."

Bo's gaze sharpens, his concern clear. "You look exhausted. Is it the stress, lack of sleep, or both?"

Chong rubs his eyes, tiredness showing. "A little of both. It's okay; I'll handle it. Give me seventy-two hours, boss. I believe I can get to the end of this mystery. After that, we can issue the warrants and make the arrests. That's my self-imposed deadline." He stifles a yawn mid-sentence.

Bo nods in thanks but adds a note of caution. "Good, but remember, in seventy-two hours come back and update me, and for your sake, Chong, don't trip over your own feet."

Chong bows and leaves the room. Outside the office, he lets out a sigh of mixed emotions and, with a mischievous smile, thinks, *What have I gotten myself into?*

While he is deep in thought, a fellow officer approaches. "Detective, a man named Hui is waiting for you at the reception."

Acknowledging him with a nod, Chong mutters to himself, "There is no time for breaks now. Whatever it is, I'm going to find out what's going on."

36

Even without Meaning, One Lives in Reality

"Good afternoon, Detective." Hui tries to ease the tension he feels with a wide smile.

Chong, showing his exhaustion, raises an eyebrow. "How's the traffic? Terrible?"

Hui shrugs. "A little... I had to leave my car in the police building parking lot. I couldn't find a vacant space nearby. The street had too much traffic. Ah yes, the guard gave me this note. He said you will need to sign it for when I leave. Does that sound right?"

Chong sighs. "I better sign now before I forget." Without even looking at the paper, he scribbles his signature and hands it back.

Motioning for Hui to follow him, Chong leads the way down a hallway. At the end, he opens a door, revealing a dark and austere room. A metal table with two chairs occupies the centre and, in one corner, a camera is mounted on a tripod. A single overhead light is off. Turning it on, Chong gestures for Hui to sit down. "Get comfortable," he murmurs. "I need to get some things and then I'll be right back." He leaves the room. Hui remains alone.

Hui looks in every corner, the setup reminiscent of an interrogation room. He tries to stay calm, certain that someone is watching behind the mirror. Picking up his cellphone, he tries to distract himself, scrolling through messages and notifications.

Chong enters his office, calling his secretary. "Ask München to go to the room number two observatory. Tell him that's where I am."

Without missing a beat, she calls the head of operations to convey the message. Meanwhile, Chong gathers some essential folders and puts them, along with a notebook, in his leather briefcase. As he leaves, he coughs and puts some coins on the assistant's desk, saying, "Get us three coffees from the cafeteria. Take them to room two and aquarium two." She gives a quick thumbs-up in acknowledgement.

As Chong walks down the hallway, he rehearses the line of questioning, putting together the mental map he has created. A missing link remains, a crucial detail that he needs to uncover.

Chong and München arrive together at the "aquarium," the glass-walled observation room they have used countless times. They exchange a knowing look; a mutual understanding passes between them. With a smile, München opens the first door, while Chong opens the second.

Hui raises an eyebrow when he sees Chong. "I thought you forgot me."

Chong, playing the pleasant host, offers a smile. "Do you mind if I record our conversation?" he asks, pointing to the camera.

Hui, exuding confidence, shrugs his shoulders. "I have no problem."

Chong begins: "I will refer to some statements you made to me earlier; I hope you can shed some light on them." He turns on the video camera.

Hui sits back, feigning indifference. "Should I have a lawyer for this?"

Chong pauses, weighing his words. "If you prefer, of course. You were very cooperative this morning; I'm just trying to clarify a few things. Everything will be on record for our sake. We can reschedule this interview if you prefer. However, make sure you are prepared. Later this week, I'll need you and Wang for formal statements. How about we have this conversation now instead of later?"

Hui considers for a moment. Given his previous discussion with Chong and his confidence in covering his tracks, he agrees. "Let's go ahead."

Chong wastes no time. "Do you know the employees of the warehouses next to numbers one and two?"

"Yes," confirms Hui.

Chong intensifies his gaze. "An employee at one of these warehouses stated Zhao began working at Warehouse Number Two. This employee stated Zhao mentioned this to him, and several others confirmed seeing him at the warehouse. He states that one morning, Zhao parked his motorcycle in the parking lot of Warehouse Number One, entered, and left after with Wonjy. True or false?" In a dramatic move, Chong shows some photographs of Zhao, placing them on the table for Hui to see.

Hui hesitates, his fingers brushing the photograph. There's a brief pause where the only sound is his laboured breathing, the weight of the trap pressing down on him. He laughs, moving his eyes to the side, toward the door.

"You're right," he admits, running a hand through his hair. "This morning, I was exhausted, and coherence was not part of my words. A fire almost consumed my house last night. It... shook me, to say the least. I didn't remember this is Zhao. I hired him as a temp. He needed money, and I helped. He and Wonjy went out together to do some work at the port, but after that, I haven't seen him."

Chong, seizing the moment, places more photos on the table: clear images of Zhao's lifeless body, and a single photo highlighting a gunshot wound.

"Zhao is no longer with us," says Chong in a deep tone, examining Hui's reaction.

A visible shiver runs down Hui's spine; surprise takes him from the brutality of the images. His eyes go from the photos to Chong's penetrating gaze. Panic sets in. His mind races, trying to figure out how much knowledge the police already have.

"That's... horrible," Hui manages, his voice shaking.

Chong continues, without slowing down. "Someone killed Zhao last Wednesday. Did you know that?"

Hui, desperate to maintain some semblance of control, responds in few words. "No, I didn't."

Chong leans in, his voice full of suspicion. "So, Wonjy never mentioned it? They go out to work together every day, right? Wasn't that also the same date when Wonjy texted he was going to Hong Kong?" Without giving Hui a moment to collect his thoughts, Chong continues.

Hui's eyes turn to his wristwatch, anxiety showing on his face. He stands up, walking away from the table without warning. "Detective, you mentioned I could leave if necessary. I guess I'll have to come back another time."

Chong, calm and unyielding, spreads out six harrowing photographs of charred remains and the burned wreckage of Wonjy's house. "I was hoping you'd stay a little longer. I have doubts about the explosion at Wonjy's house, where his family died."

Hui's heart races, his gaze darting between the photographs and Chong. Although he tries to mask it, his alarm is unmistakable. "I need to leave. Work commitments," he stammers.

Chong puts the photos together. Looking up, he meets Hui's gaze, staring at his movements. "Very well. We can resolve this another time."

Just as the tension rises, the door opens, revealing the secretary balancing two cups of coffee. She puts the plastic cups on the table.

"Thanks, just leave it," Chong murmurs with a fleeting smile.

The atmosphere remains thick with tension as Hui and Chong make their way down the hallway. Arriving at the building's exit, Hui desperately searches his pockets for the parking receipt, becoming more nervous when he doesn't find it in his jacket.

With irony in his voice, Chong brings up the suggestion he made earlier about signing the ticket. "Just in case something happens?" He raises an eyebrow. "It seems like this is a sign. Don't worry. I will accompany you to get your car."

Offering a grateful, if shaky, nod, Hui bows a little in thanks.

As they walk, Chong, trying to ease the tension, makes a casual comment about the day's traffic congestion. Hui, still stunned by the questions and the photographs, just listens to him, lost in his own thoughts.

Detective Chong stops walking and looks around, catching Hui's attention. With suspicion in his voice, he reveals, "In the same place where Zhao died, another injured person had to be taken to the hospital."

The brief break from walking down the street has strengthened his nerves a little, and Hui feigns fake surprise. "Oh, really?"

Chong narrows his eyes but senses Hui's discomfort. "Yes. An American FBI agent was the victim. Sounds like something out of a Hollywood script, doesn't it?"

Hui's eyes widen in shock. "An FBI agent? How did this happen?"

Feeling that he now has the upper hand, Chong leans closer to Hui's ear, his voice full of implications. "What they are saying here in the building is that we may soon have some foreign officials collaborating in the investigation."

A sudden wave of nausea threatens to overwhelm Hui. He swallows hard, trying to maintain his composure, but his face reveals his growing panic.

They soon arrive at the parking lot. Chong, with an air of determination, clears Hui's ticket at the exit with the doorman. Showing signs of being shaken, Hui says goodbye. He almost runs into the car and leaves at high speed. He leaves the parking lot without looking back.

As Chong watches the car drive away, something catches his attention: a white mark on the back of Hui's car. His brow furrows in disbelief. With his heart racing, he turns to the parking attendant, asking for the registry of the car that had just left. Looking at the information, he notices the description: a black Toyota. He tries to remember the license plate number from previous surveillance footage but can't. Without wasting a second, he takes a photo of the registration card with his phone and instructs, "I need the parking footage from today. Send it to my office now."

The attendant, sensing the gravity, responds, "Yes, sir. I will send it now."

Meanwhile, München, who has been watching from a distance on the stairs, approaches Chong as he returns to the building. "I've interrogated a lot of suspects…" muses München, "but that guy? His reactions were obvious. It's as if all the questions struck home. Do we have anything concrete on him?"

Chong, his face tight, responds, "Before? Not really, but now… we're on the right path." Without slowing down, he returns to his office, ready to put together the diagram on the board on the wall.

*　*　*

The digital clock on the dashboard of Hui's car reads 3:30 p.m. He is gripping the steering wheel so hard that his fingers have turned white. No matter how hard he tries, he can't calm his mind. The frightening images Detective Chong has shown him, combined with the imminent threat of international involvement, make his pulse quicken. He tries to remove the disturbing images, but the horrible photos intrude on his thoughts.

A sudden desire takes hold of him: he wants to hug his wife and his children, feel their warmth before they leave. However, as the reality of his situation with the police sinks in, he can't shake the fear that everything will soon fall apart, and the consequences will be dire.

Arriving at home, he doesn't find the familiar mess and rush of children; instead, there is an unprecedented silence. As he climbs the stairs, he notices the missing toys on the floor and the lack of clothes scattered around. He feels himself sinking into emptiness. Entering the master bedroom, he checks his wife's empty closet, confirming that they have already left.

Collapsing on the bed, with sad resignation in his voice, he murmurs, "Maybe it's for the best. Things are about to get worse."

Taking out his cellphone, he scrolls through his contacts and selects "Guowei." The call goes through and, without wasting a moment, he says,

"Can you schedule that meeting with the boss today? If he asks why, tell him that there are serious and imminent problems that could affect the structure of the Tong."

There's a pause on the other end of the line before Guowei responds, his voice uncertain, "I'll try."

*   *   *

At the hotel, Rachel, Tyler, and David meander through the busy lobby, settling on a spacious four-seater sofa. It's almost 5:00. As they chat, their laughs sound genuine and contagious, eliciting envious glances from other guests.

Rachel, radiating elegance in her newly purchased outfit, looks like she stepped straight out of a fashion magazine. She adorned herself in a soft yellow pantsuit paired with a ruffled white blouse that accentuates her cleavage. Her long, flowing hair draws attention. Meanwhile, David wears a casual blazer, and Tyler, ever the rebel, wears his signature black leather jacket.

The sweltering heat of the day wanes, bringing much-appreciated respite. As the trio swap stories about their shopping adventures for the apartment and the pleasant change in weather, Rachel's ears pick up the lively conversation of two women nearby.

Following their gaze to the hotel entrance, she sees several guests surrounding Wang, who has just arrived. Some emotional young women approach him, requesting a selfie. Wang, always kind, responds with a broad smile. Upon seeing Rachel, he raises his hand in a wave, to which she responds.

Sensing the change in atmosphere, Tyler jokes, "What's the commotion? A flash mob?" His eyes dart around, trying to make sense of the sudden excitement.

David, pointing in the general direction of the entrance without focusing on it, jokes, "Must be some K-pop sensation. Look at those women almost fainting with their hands over their hearts."

Rachel laughs. "K-pop is from Korea. We're in China."

David and Tyler burst into laughter at the confusion. Still amused, Rachel adds, "It's just Wang entering." She rolls her eyes like this can't be serious.

The pair stand up, craning their necks to locate the man causing all the commotion.

"Is this Wang?" David squints, trying to remember their brief introduction in the hospital.

Tyler, impressed, comments, "The guy has the charisma of a movie star." Smiling, he enjoys the spectacle.

The lobby is buzzing with whispers and laughter.

"Women are all over him; I mean, the guy is handsome," Rachel jokes as she gets up from the couch.

Tyler, ever the tease, quips, "Oh, look what you're missing."

She smiles, walking toward Wang.

"Handsome men are magnets for trouble, Tyler. I don't want trouble." As she approaches, the sparkle in Wang's eyes is unmistakable. He smiles at Rachel with his heart.

David and Tyler are not far behind. Meeting them halfway, Wang laughs, scratching the back of his head. "Sorry for the confusion, it's always like this. I can't seem to elude it."

David, still trying to assess the situation, assures him, "Don't worry." He can't help but look at the eager spectators, some of whom are taking photos.

There's a brief pause, then Wang's gaze lands on Rachel. "We should leave. My car's in front of the hotel."

As they head for the exit, two wide-eyed girls approach, begging for a photo with Wang. With a conspiratorial wink at Rachel, he says, "Take the keys, please? It's the white Mercedes out front."

With the keys in Rachel's hand, the trio steps out into the cool night, spotting the elegant vehicle. They pause, waiting for Wang.

When Wang appears, he straightens his suit, combs his hair with his fingers, and, in an exaggerated and playful English accent, orders, "Everyone in the car."

The scene is so unexpected that the partners can't contain their laughter. Tyler, ever curious, asks, "Is he always... like this?"

Wang's eyes meet Tyler's in the rear-view mirror. "Tyler, right?" When Tyler nods with a smirk, Wang continues, "Public outings with me are always a spectacle, but they're positive publicity. Nice to meet you."

Rachel, seated, steals a glance at Wang, processing the charm offensive she just witnessed. She reflects on his behaviour.

Tyler smiles and returns the greeting. "The same."

The energy in the car is a mix of anticipation and curiosity as Rachel asks, "So, where are you taking us?"

Wang's eyes shine with excitement. "I can take you to a fancy restaurant, but I want them to experience the real taste of Shanghai. We are heading to the ancient Chenghuangmiao Street. Very well known... it is one of Shanghai's main culinary paradises. Sounds good?" He glances over his shoulder, eager to see David and Tyler's reaction.

Rachel scolds, "Eyes on the road, Wang!"

Wang laughs. "Alright, alright." His excitement remains unchanged.

David joins the conversation. "I heard about this place. It's well known. All the tourists go there."

Wang agrees. "They call it the Snack Kingdom. Believe me, it's an essential stop for anyone visiting Shanghai."

The unanimous feeling in the car promises a culinary adventure ahead.

Wang continues, "Have you ever heard of the famous Yuyuan Garden? There is no place like it on Earth." Without warning, he reaches out, takes Rachel's hand, and presses a soft kiss to it. She blinks at him in surprise.

David and Tyler exchange confused looks in the backseat, not sure how to respond.

Trying to cut through the sudden tension, Tyler interjects, "That garden is on my must-visit list."

Wang's voice softens. "The street we're going to is near the garden, but it's closed at night. We can plan another day if you like."

Stopping in a busy alley, the four continue on foot, with Wang guiding, sharing information about each delicacy they find at the stalls. The time flies by in a whirlwind of flavours, aromas, and laughter.

After two hours, they arrive back at the car. The conversation is about shared experiences of authentic Chinese cuisine.

Courtesy of the Tong mafia, Tyler thinks to himself.

"I never tire of eating *Shengjiaobao*, those fried buns stuffed with pork," remembers Rachel, her eyes shining.

David, overcome by a wave of nostalgia, says, "For me, it has to be the *guotie*, the ones in the pan. What about the *xiaolongbao*, those delicate steamed buns? My mother used to make them. Brings back memories."

Wang's eyes meet David's in the rear-view mirror. A soft, understanding smile plays on his lips. "That's cool," he says with interest.

David nods, a hint of melancholy in his eyes.

Tyler stretches and adds, "The highlight for me was the crab with rice cake. Absolute perfection. I've had something similar in Canada, they call it crab shell cake. And let's not forget the tapioca pudding."

Arriving at the hotel, Tyler pats his stomach. "Honestly, I doubt I'll be eating for another two or three days. Tonight was a culinary roller coaster. Thanks, Wang."

David, ever the professional, adds, "We're in for a long day tomorrow. Thanks again, Wang, and good night."

Rachel tries to get out of the car, but Wang stops her. "Can you stay a few more minutes?"

She agrees, watching Tyler and David disappear into the hotel elevator.

Sitting side by side in the car, Wang's voice trembles. "Rachel, if I ever hurt you or overreacted, I'm sorry. I didn't want to ruin what we have."

Surprised, Rachel reassures him, "Wang, there's nothing to forgive. We're friends, and that will not change."

Eyes shining, Wang murmurs, "I was afraid I'd lost you, that you'd push me out of your life."

Rachel, wanting to lighten the mood, says, "Don't be dramatic. We're fine." As she gets out of the car, she gives him one last comforting smile. "Good evening, Wang."

Wang sits there, watching her silhouette disappear into the hotel entrance. His cellphone rings. Picking it up, he hears a groggy voice on the other end of the line: "Wang? It's Hui. I just woke up. Did you want to talk?"

* * *

Rachel gets out of the car and heads toward the hotel lobby. Upon arriving at David's room, she's greeted by the sight of David and Tyler talking, their laughter filling the room. Rachel says, "Am I interrupting a joke I shouldn't hear?"

David looks at his watch, a hint of concern in his eyes. "He should have called already," he mutters.

Tyler, checking his watch, nods. "It's only 8:30."

At the same moment, Rachel's phone vibrates. It's a message from Detective Chong: *Arriving in fifteen minutes.*

The trio exchange a look, reaching a silent agreement. David announces, "I'm going to freshen up" and heads to the bathroom.

Tyler stretches, getting up from his chair. "I'll wait for you guys in the hallway."

Rachel jokes, "Wait a second. I need my lipstick."

Minutes later, the three meet again in the hotel lobby, sitting on the soft sofa.

Detective Chong arrives. As he enters the hotel, a change in the atmosphere is noticeable. His piercing gaze finds the trio, and with a curt nod and a deep, respectful bow, he greets them in the traditional manner.

As a sign of mutual respect, everyone stands up and returns the bow. Rachel, acting as a bridge, introduces Tyler, making Chong bow once again.

Breaking formality, Chong asks, playing with words: "Bar or nightclub?"

Smiles spread across David and Tyler's faces as they respond in unison, "Nightclub."

Rachel, looking somewhat confused, gives the detective a stern look, insisting, "Bar."

A wave of laughter runs through the group. Chong also laughs.

"Looks like the majority wins. To the bar." He casts a teasing look in Rachel's direction.

Heading to the parking lot, Chong leads them to a sleek blue Tiggo SUV.

"Is this your personal car?" Rachel asks, raising an eyebrow.

Chong smiles back. "All mine."

Settling into the spacious interior, Chong turns to David and Tyler. "How about exploring Shanghai's nightlife sometime?"

Tyler, ever enthusiastic, responds, "Anytime you want."

David, however, adopts a more measured tone. "Of course, but only after the case is closed."

"Done," Chong replies, starting the engine and driving the vehicle onto the main road.

Rachel asks, "Where are we going?"

Chong responds with an enigmatic voice. "Speak more Loudly."

Rachel's eyebrows furrow in confusion and she responds, "What did you say?" Her tone borders on indignation.

The tension in the car is thick.

David and Tyler exchange uneasy glances.

412

But Chong just smiles, clarifying: "Relax! That's the name of the bar."

The trio experiences a sudden understanding, and laughter fills the car. Rachel, a little red in the face, joins in the fun. As they continue to laugh, they take out their cellphones to search for Speak more Loudly, discovering that it is a famous spot in the city. They continue to crack jokes about the bar's unique name for the rest of the trip.

The boom of music vibrates in the air as they park behind a building. As they get out of the car, the rhythm intensifies, but they can't identify the source. Once out of the car, they understand the music is coming from another bar, the entrance full of exuberant young people, the boisterous atmosphere spreading through the streets. Laughter and conversations dance in the air, mixing with the melodies.

The valet, recognizing Chong, approaches with a nod. Without saying a word, Chong tosses him the keys, a silent understanding between the two. They notice the swarm of cars parked around; this is a very popular place.

Entering through the back door, a sea of faces greets them. Flags of various countries hang overhead, providing a touch of global style to the establishment. Customers chat around a large bar with drinks in hand. The ambience is further enhanced by the soft sound of background music, giving a warm and intimate feel.

Guided by the waiter, they make their way through the busy crowd toward a small elevator at the back of the hall. The journey feels like a transition to another world. When the doors open on the third floor, an exquisite display of Japanese decor greets them. Elegant and understated, it contrasts with the lively bar below. The waiter leads them to a glass-enclosed balcony, where everyone sits and enjoys the panoramic view of the vibrant city.

David, observing the serene interior, turns to Chong. "Why are we here?"

With sincerity in his eyes, Chong responds, "I needed a private place to talk and apologize to all of you."

David's eyes scan the place, noticing that they are the only ones sitting on the balcony, creating a bubble of privacy amid the urban cacophony. His gaze turns to Chong, staring at him.

Breaking the brief silence, Chong asks, "What will it be? Whiskey, beer, or a cocktail?"

Almost in unison, they respond, "Whiskey."

Chong points to the menu, showing it to the waiter and selecting a bottle. "A bottle of this whiskey and this complete variety of starters," he instructs.

Their night is just beginning.

Looking at Chong, David, Rachel, and Tyler appear to be agonizing over an explanation. The tension and silence in the air are visible, a stark contrast to the hustle and bustle of the bar they had left behind.

Chong takes a folded piece of paper from his pocket. Placing it on the table, he pauses, taking a moment to collect his thoughts. His eyes contain a solemn sincerity as he begins, "First, David, I owe you an apology. You got caught up in a storm. I recognize you were a victim. While I'm still investigating, I want you to know this. What I've found so far, it's not about you."

The trio remains silent, the weight of the detective's words sinking in.

The waiter realizes the seriousness of the conversation. Showing practised skill, he places a platter with various appetizers and a bottle of Japanese whiskey on the table. Chong, grateful for the brief interruption, dismisses him with a nod.

Pouring the amber liquid into the glasses, Chong makes a toast. Without waiting for the others, he drinks in one quick motion. Looking at David, he asks, "Have you ever heard of or met a man named Zhao?"

David, following Chong's example, drains his glass before responding, "No, I've never come across anyone with that name."

As Rachel and Tyler try the appetizers, Chong continues, exposing some parts of the complex web of connections he discovered. "Let me explain: Zhao was associated with Wang, who was a witness to the death of police officer Ronaldo. Ronaldo stayed at a hotel run by Michael's mother, and it was Michael's gun that killed Zhao."

The table becomes enveloped in stunned silence for a moment. The complexity and interconnectedness of it all seems almost impossible.

David, his voice shaking, asks, "How did this happen?"

Chong spreads his hands across the table, emphasizing his point. "Think about this sequence, and there's more."

Rachel's face loses its colour. Swallowing hard, she asks, "So you're saying that Zhao worked with Wang?"

Chong nods. "Yes."

The realization hits Rachel hard, causing her to down all the whiskey in her glass in one go.

The atmosphere at the table grows heavy when David, trying to process the perplexing connections, asks, "Are you saying that all these ties, which in your interpretation would be random, go back to Ronaldo's death?"

Chong pauses for a moment, nodding his head. "Yes, but consider this: Michael's mother, like you, is just a pawn in this game. You being on that street at that moment was an accident; the fight was between Michael and Zhao."

"But… Michael disappeared without a trace," David stammers, trying to make sense of the revelations unfolding in the detective's words.

Chong leans across the table and, his voice low, says, "Michael isn't the only one. Zhao had a colleague, Wonjy. The two left work together the day of the shooting. With Zhao dead, Wonjy disappeared. All we have is a message left at work saying he was leaving for Hong Kong."

Rachel's face turns pale. "Wait, what was that name again?"

"Wonjy," Chong repeats, refilling the cups for the four of them.

Her eyes widen. "I heard that name the other day."

Tyler, alert, questions, "Where, Rachel? Are you sure?"

The detective and David wait with bated breath.

Chong interjects, "Before we continue, Rachel, it's essential to note that Wonjy has been a close associate and friend of Wang's for years. With this revelation, there is an even deeper connection between Wonjy and Zhao."

Rachel takes a deep breath, organizing her thoughts. She recounts the chilling scene she witnessed at the port. The unsettling picture of the distressed woman and child, imploring Wang for answers and the heartless cash thrown at them, repeats in her mind.

A stunned silence falls over the table. The revelations have taken an unexpected turn, weaving together a complex tapestry of intrigue and mystery.

Tyler fills Rachel's glass, only for her to gulp it down. The whiskey bottle empties and the detective, sensing the atmosphere, signals the waiter by pointing to the bottle.

David's voice, looking at Rachel, breaks the sombre silence. "When did all this happen?"

The memory seems to flash through Rachel, making her voice tremble. "It was the day I went to visit you with Wang. I said I would visit the Huangpu River. Before the appointed time, the detective arrived. Yes, it was Friday."

In the middle of the conversation, the waiter arrives and puts another bottle on the table. The detective doesn't hesitate; he refills each glass, the liquid glistening in the dim lights. Chong looks up and meets the gaze of each of them. "I'm going to the end of this investigation. I will remove one stone from another."

The partners exchange glances without understanding what he means.

Chong sighs, continuing, "Your memory, Rachel. Stay calm. Your statement matches the same one I received today. Another witness was present with his family and told me the same story. He also remembered a foreign woman with Wang: you."

Rachel agrees. "Yes, there were other people. They saw everything."

David's eyebrows furrow, irritation in his tone. "But what does this horrible story have to do with Michael's sudden absence?"

The detective, keeping a close eye on their reactions, directs the conversation. "That Friday night, another tragedy happened. That same woman and her daughter who were at the port died in a gas explosion in their home."

Rachel chokes. The memory of the woman and her daughter hits her like a train slamming into her chest, triggering empathetic sobs. Tyler wraps a comforting arm around her, whispering calming words.

Chong takes out a second piece of paper, drawing as he speaks. "Imagine this circle. Inside, we have Wonjy and Zhao, both linked to Wang. So far, we have two deaths, one injured, and two missing people, all pointing to Wang. Add the wife and daughter, and we have four deaths. Circle back and everything points to Ronaldo and, by extension, both of you." As they look at the connections, a dense fog falls over the table.

David swallows hard and closes his eyes. When he opens them, they can see the tears, and he asks, "Do you have any evidence that Michael's dead?"

The detective looks at him with pity and says, "No, but I can prove he left in a car that morning."

David's tears fall down his face. He tries to accept the maze of pain and mystery that the detective has exposed. He struggles to form words.

Detective Chong, with a steady, unreadable gaze, voices the question that remains in everyone's mind: "These threads point to Wang's involvement. Do we have tangible evidence to implicate him and bring him to justice?"

Tyler shakes his head, his voice dark. "I don't believe you have proof yet."

Chong looks at him and confirms. "We are close. Don't worry, I'll wrap this up." The detective pauses, letting the gravity of his next words make the partners think. "We only have a seventy-two-hour window to close this case. I ask everyone to keep their distance from Wang for now. Let's continue our lives as usual, but with caution. I have confidence in our ability to handle situations like this with wisdom. I assure you we will find our answers. However, before I leave, I have a question."

David, snapping out of his daze, nods. "Go ahead."

Chong takes a deep breath. "Were you all brought here because of the untimely death of the federal police officer at the hotel?"

Rachel, regaining her composure, responds, "Yes, you are correct. We needed to check whether it was a mere accident or a premeditated death."

Chong raises his hand. "I believe the complexities of this incident will prompt another investigation. For now, I want to validate my suspicions, to know if I'm heading in the right direction." With a sigh, he pours the rest of the whiskey into his glass.

The weight of the night hangs over them, and each person is lost in thought, making words rare.

Detective Chong waves his right hand, grabbing a nearby waiter. He passes a card to the young man, who processes the payment.

As everyone stands up, the atmosphere of the bar settles around them. Tyler gives Chong a sharp slap on the back, breaking the tension. "The next round is on me, right?"

Detective Chong, surprised by the sudden camaraderie, lets out a laugh. "Done," he responds with a nod, a moment of joy amid the heavy atmosphere.

37

The Monsters Expose Themselves

Wang's car engine breaks the morning silence as he arrives at police headquarters. The driver, always alert, gets out and opens the door for the boss. Wang gets out of the car and looks around. Today, to his relief, the paparazzi with a thousand flashes aren't around, nor are the reporters. As he examines the environment, his eyes settle on a serene sight: a group in the square practices Tai Chi with synchronized movements, giving an image of tranquility.

Standing on the steps of the police headquarters, Wang's mind shifts to the conversation he had with Hui last night. He had to bite his tongue in the desire to attack, to launch accusations, which became very strong during the conversation. In the afternoon meeting with Boss Bo, he didn't mention the office interrogation and now... an official questioning?

Shaking the thoughts away, he recalls his own actions after leaving the superintendent's office at lunchtime yesterday. He went straight to the port, and a surprise awaited him, a subpoena, to testify. Fearing something he doesn't expect, he called the company's lawyer.

He remembers Hui's voice on the call—calm—perhaps too calm last night. Although Hui had detailed the meeting with Chong, what disturbed Wang was not the questions or the photographs; it was the mention of a task force arriving in Shanghai. This would complicate things.

A blue BMW interrupts his reverie in front of the stairs. It stops and two men get out of the back seat and greet Wang. The car moves away as if wanting to distance itself from the police building. Together, the trio heads toward the entrance, completing the reception formalities.

As they head to the waiting benches, Chief Bo enters the building. With a raised eyebrow and a brief nod, he registers their presence. The atmosphere thickens. "What brings you here so soon?"

"I'm here to meet Detective Chong at 8:00," Wang replies, looking at Bo.

Boss Bo's surprise is obvious. "I don't know about this," he mutters, but before anyone can say anything else a policewoman beckons Wang and his lawyers, showing them to follow her.

Wang smiles, gives one last wave to the superintendent, turns on his heel, and with his lawyers in tow, follows the police officer. The game, it seems, has begun.

The sound of Boss Bo's shoes echoes as he climbs with surprising vigour, given his age and stocky build. Bursting through the doors of his office, his temper explodes. "Call Detective Chong now!" he screams.

His secretary, startled by the sudden outburst, fumbles with her phone, trying to locate Chong. Her voice shakes. "He's in the middle of an interrogation, sir, in aquarium number two."

Boss Bo sinks into his chair, his face red and his breathing laboured. Anger clouds his thoughts. "How dare he interrogate Wang without my knowledge?" he roars, letting his frustration boil over.

Searching for the schedule on his desk, his eyes land on one document: a subpoena and the schedule for today's interrogation. The realization hits him like a ton of bricks.

"Who left this here?!" he shouts, waving the paper in the air.

His secretary rushes into the office, looks at the document, and responds, "Detective Chong left it late yesterday afternoon. After you left. See the date and time stamp? 5:30 p.m. It's all registered in the system and in the cabinet book."

Boss Bo's anger increases as he feels more and more deceived. He can't interrupt the interrogation because it's all official. Desperate to regain his composure, he coughs, choking on his own saliva. His stomach boils...

"Bring me chamomile tea," he says.

When the assistant leaves, she can't help but give her boss a worried look. His jacket and tie are wet, and beads of sweat glisten on his forehead. The murmur of his voice, speaking on his cellphone, reaches her ears, but she can't decipher the words. She speeds up her steps to get the calming drink, leaving the distraught boss alone.

* * *

When the first light of dawn filters through the curtains, Hui is lying in bed, staring at the ceiling. The silent house seems to echo memories;

memories of a life that changed without warning in less than twenty-four hours. He feels as if someone has thrown him to the wolves, but he's determined in his choice, being sure that this was the right path for his family's safety.

Dragging himself out of bed, he steps into the shower, letting the warm water wash over him, though it doesn't do much to ease the weight on his heart. When going down the stairs, he observes his surroundings, noticing every intricate detail of the house where he lives. He had never paid much attention to it before. The works of art chosen by his wife, the fragrant flowers, the transparent curtains that let the world peek into their lives, all there with no one to appreciate them now. Tears blur his vision.

When he enters the kitchen, he feels a pang of nostalgia when he sees the children's small, colourful dishes. Everything has changed, but amid this turmoil, he remembers what Kung Wu told him yesterday: "Face what lies ahead, and I will be by your side."

Sitting on one of the kitchen chairs, he remembers the day before. His meeting with Chief Kung was a beacon of hope. Guowei, his faithful friend, brought the final issue to the decision he made. In the building's garage, before they went up to the office, Guowei's concern in the question was decisive: "Are you ready to talk?"

With unwavering determination, Hui replied, "I am."

Seeing the gravity in his friend's eyes, Guowei probed, "Are you sure about this?"

Meeting his gaze, Hui declared, "It's what I have to do."

Understanding dawned on Guowei's face, realizing the magnitude of what must have happened. Together, they went up to Chief Kung Wu's office, united by trust and friendship.

They arrived on the twenty-fifth floor and entered the boss's office. He welcomed them and asked Hui to sit on the sofa on the right side of the room. Guowei sat on the left side and the chief was in the centre.

"Do you want a drink?" asked Kung Wu.

"No, boss. I'm okay." Hui showed a little nervousness and rubbed his hands together.

"Let's get down to business," the boss said, addressing the manager.

Hui took a deep breath, his voice shaking.

"Do you remember that story about a man called Ronaldo? The guy who had a fatal accident at the hotel in 2013?" Hui began. "It turns out he's not just anyone. He was a Brazilian Federal Police officer." He paused, running a hand through his hair. "It's a complicated story, Kung. Dankyno set everything up because Tong owed money to the Yakuza. He forced Wang to believe that he would either kill the man or he would die."

Hui's eyes seemed distant for a moment, as if revisiting a frightening memory.

"But Dankyno, the traitor that he was, turned against Wang even after Wang killed the man. He wanted to get rid of Wang, but fate was harsher, and Wang's cousin died in his place. That was the last straw for Wang, pushing him to overthrow Dankyno and claim Tong's empire."

Kung leaned in; his eyebrows furrowed. "The Yakuza? Are you saying they're involved in all that mess?"

Hui's gaze was heavy with history. "It's deeper than you think, Kung. The claws of the Yakuza are everywhere in Dankyno's dark stories."

Kung lowered his head in thought, trying to put the pieces together. "But you mentioned something to Guowei… about current problems in Tong?"

Hui's throat tightened, and he nodded at the boss, his voice only a whisper. "Water, please." Guowei, sensing the tension, handed over a glass.

Hui took the glass, and the boss watched him. Trembling, he drank the water in one gulp, trying to calm his nerves.

Regaining some composure, Hui met Kung Wu's eyes. "There's more, Kung. It's related to some tourists named Rachel Barnes and her partner David Ho." He sighed. "They tried to track down Wang, digging up old stories, especially about that Brazilian police officer. Wang… didn't like it." His voice shook with emotion.

"Wang ordered the boys to follow them and find out what they knew, and this led to a bloodbath. Zhao, Wonjy, this guy named Michael, and Bohai all died in a single day." He paused, taking a deep breath. "The problem is that no one knew about this man, David Ho, who is an FBI agent. It turns out that someone tortured Michael, his boyfriend, before he died. He stated until he died he lived in London and did not know about the death of the Brazilian officer."

Chief Kung's eyes widened, disbelief showing in his voice. "Wang did this? He killed Wonjy and Bohai?"

Hui nodded, using a handkerchief to wipe away the sweat running down his temples. "Yes, but that's just the tip of the iceberg," he murmured.

Chief Kung's eyebrows knitted together. "Is there more to this? Continue." Kung got up and poured three glasses of whiskey on the coffee table and looked into Hui's eyes. He sat down to listen to Hui.

However, Hui's hands shook as he picked up the cup, causing some of the amber liquid to spill out. Taking a deep breath, he said, "Wang... he is having an affair with a Western woman, a tourist, but she told him to go for a walk, which irritated him a lot, making him lose control. What drove him crazy happened last Friday. Wonjy's wife confronted him on the tourist pier."

Hui's voice cracked. "After that, he decided Wonjy's family was a liability. His wife, his daughter... he had me eliminate them." The manager admitted to having executed Wang's orders.

The room seemed to close in as the boss processed the information. His face contorted into a mixture of fury and sadness. "Are you crazy, Hui?! You don't lay hands, ever, on our families!"

Tears filled Hui's eyes as he experienced devastation. "It was a choice between my family or Wonjy's. I tried, boss, I tried to talk to him, but Wang... he lost control. Wonjy was my friend, my dear friend." Sobbing and trying to explain himself, his voice didn't come out, choked with emotion.

Guowei, who had been silent until now, tried to say something but controlled himself by looking at Hui with disdain and horror. The manager turned to his friend and saw his expression that said it all.

Throughout the room, everyone could hear the soft sound of the recording device as it continued to capture each word.

"It's over," whispered the boss, his voice full of anguish.

Tears streamed down the manager's face. The two men in the room looked at him with a mixture of disdain and pity, between anger and genuine pain from the manager's words.

Hui, trying to balance himself, continued to talk about the police from earlier in the day. "I had to go to the police station," he began, his voice shaking. "The detective bombarded me with questions and showed me photos. As I was leaving, the detective said something that alarmed me.

He let slip that a US task force is arriving to help with this investigation. I've thought a lot, and if this is true, other international agencies may join, especially from England, given Michael's connection. Something will happen. We have two foreign police officers in this story, one dead and one injured, and the whereabouts of Michael are unknown. A storm is brewing."

Chief Kung's weariness was etched across his features. He responded, "You didn't come here to give me a news update. What do you believe is about to happen, Hui?"

Swallowing hard, Hui responded, "If multiple agencies get involved, a media frenzy will be inevitable, which could draw unwanted attention to Tong. It will only be a matter of time before they track Wang's involvement in the murder of the Brazilian officer and that Englishman. The spotlight on us would be catastrophic, and the Triad's activities would make headlines because it would connect us to the union. We have been operating under their permission. However, a problem of this magnitude involves them… they will not cover us when it explodes." Hui's voice trembled, betraying his fear. "I'm sure of what I'm telling you, boss. I called Guowei right after I left the police department."

"Why are you telling me all this?" demanded Chief Kung, his posture tense.

Hui mustered up his courage and explained to the boss: "Wang didn't just betray you. He is playing a dangerous game, pitting leaders against each other, and I could no longer stand by his decisions, and now my family and I are in his crosshairs."

Chief Kung, trying to process everything, paced the room, stopping for a moment to light a cigarette. He recalled Wang's audacious attempt to fool the bosses at the last meeting. Recognizing that he did not receive favourable feedback from the Triad in relation to the recent proposal he made, he felt he was sitting on a powder keg. How would the Triad react if they knew an international task force was arriving because of Wang's recklessness? This would endanger not just Tong, but all leaders, including himself.

Chief Kung's eyes narrowed, fixing on Hui, who was now drinking another glass of whiskey that Guowei provided. "If we want to have any chance, Hui, we have to expose the police officer's death at the hotel or the murders at the farm. How do we do that?"

Hui straightened up in his seat, feeling the gravity of the moment. His voice, unwavering, replied, "I hid the weapons. They have fingerprints. I also took photographs of all the belongings of those killed that day, even of the car that Wang drives to the farm. I took photographs as he left the place. I've got it all."

The boss sighed and ran his hand through his hair. "Proof is one thing, but we need a confession. A genuine admission of guilt. Wang has a positive reputation here in Shanghai: the philanthropist, the hero. We cannot ignore the huge number of people he has helped, least of all the politicians and officers who are in his pocket." He looked at the recording device, noting how much time had passed.

"We could try recording it," Hui suggested.

Guowei, who had been silent until that moment, interrupted with a tone of authority. "Just one recording will not be enough in a case of this magnitude."

Hui, seizing the moment, laid out his perspective. "His concern is public perception. Consider this: if Triad leaders understand the full magnitude of what is happening and what is yet to come... You see, no task force will intervene without the government's blessing, and they will get it. You don't believe the Triad will consider this trivial... They will feel the threat to their business because this will happen in trade, in exports, in smuggling routes. The syndicate will have to act. They control the entire drug production and pharmaceutical sectors. What do you think will happen to global exports when news comes out about a dead and injured official involving their name? It will be a shock to the market, harming even the government. Once this situation arises, public sentiment, welfare projects, and humanitarian efforts all take a backseat. In the end, it will hit where it hurts most: in our wallets, in our pockets." Hui looked into the eyes of the two men, noticing their obvious astonishment. He had rehearsed this monologue for Chief Kung countless times in his head, and it seemed like his words had the desired impact.

"Boss," Guowei said, his eyes fixed on Kung's, "I believe Hui's words." The weight of the situation was clear in his voice.

Kung Wu's footsteps echoed as he walked around the room, settling into an armchair at the shiny marble table. He picked up a gold pen and a notebook, pausing for a moment, his gaze passing between the two men. "We need an urgent meeting," he declared.

Hui watched, his voice steady despite the underlying tension. "I'm with you, boss. Whatever you need, just say it."

Kung Wu stared at Hui. "Do you realize that the risks you will face are now enormous? It will be Wang or the police who come after you. Prepare yourself because the danger is imminent. Be discreet and, for the love of your family, don't say a word about our conversation. Play your cards right if you want to get out of this alive."

Hui swallowed, slouching his head. "I'm ready."

Kung Wu got up from his seat, showing calm but speaking bitter words. "Stay alert, and I'll have your back. Just face the storm that's coming, and I promise I'll be there to support you."

Hui stood up, giving a gesture of deep respect as he bowed.

"When you are dealing with Wang, try to be normal. Don't let him feel any changes in your words or behaviour," advised Kung, moving his head in an affirmative gesture.

Their farewell was brief but full of understanding. When Hui left the office, the weight of the world seemed to rest on his shoulders. Upon entering the car, a whirlwind of emotions consumed him. He believed in his heart and mind that he made the right decision, especially for his children's future. They were too young to understand the depth of what was going to happen, and perhaps, in time, after they knew the truth, they would one day forgive him and forget the trials and tribulations they would suffer in the years to come.

Lost in thought, he hesitated before starting the car. Taking a deep, calming breath, preparing himself for the next phase of this dangerous journey, he called Wang's number on his cellphone. When the familiar voice answered, he feigned tiredness. "Wang? It's Hui. I just woke up. Did you want to talk?"

* * *

In the city's heart, tensions rise inside the interrogation room of the central police building, often referred to as "the aquarium" because of its glass walls. Detective Chong and Wang get into a heated argument.

Wang's lawyers urge him to remain silent, but he ignores them, responding, "I'm not the manager. How do I know who he hires? I have to trust him, don't I?"

"You expect me to believe that Wonjy and Hui aren't close? Everyone knows that the three of you are long-time friends," presses the detective, leafing through a stack of documents containing witness statements corroborating their relationship. "Hui assured me how close you have always been. Both Wonjy and Zhao work in Warehouses One and Two as registered employees."

Wang's frustration increases, and his gestures become more nervous. "The photo you showed me? An old one. I didn't recognize him at that moment. That's why I said I didn't know him. But yes, I've known Wonjy since we were kids, and yes, he works with us."

Detective Chong transforms, maintaining a calm demeanour as he tries to defuse the escalating situation. "Look, Wang. Hui provided evidence that Wonjy sent messages to your company about a trip to Hong Kong. We have already received the copy and attached it to the investigation file. Regarding the incident at the pier, Rachel gave us preliminary testimony that the disagreement you had with Wonjy's wife was not very serious."

Wang is nervous and can't hear Chong's words. Every other word out of the detective's mouth seems to be "Hui": "Hui said this," "Hui arranged this," "Hui confirmed…" In a bold move and with a firm resolute voice, Wang muddies the waters even further: "This whole thing about Wonjy's wife and daughter—I know nothing about this. This Zhao you keep asking about, the name doesn't ring any bells for me. These photos mean nothing to me. As for the company cars, my lawyers have already given you a list of the vehicles I own."

Wang's two lawyers lean in, whispering in his ear and begging him to remain calm. Detective Chong, unfazed by Wang's outbursts, examines the papers on the desk, searching for something specific. Meanwhile, the police officer in charge of transcribing the interrogation on the computer avoids making eye contact with Wang, focusing on the laptop in front of her.

Detective Chong's piercing gaze lands on Wang. "Is there anything else you would like to say?"

At that moment, one lawyer signals Wang to get up and leave. Wang gets up from his chair and wipes his suit with his hands, saying, "Only the company manager, Hui, takes care of the employees' affairs, like hiring this Zhao you mentioned. When I ask about this man, why did you question me in the office? Hui vouched for his character. About the black Toyota, if my memory serves me right, only Wonjy and Hui drive that vehicle. The name Michael? I've never heard of him." Facing the detective, Wang continues: "I want to be very clear here … these questions you are asking me, ask Hui. He oversees the hiring and manages the daily activities of the warehouse workers. Oh, and about that incident at the tourist dock? I mentioned it to Hui, and he assured me he would take care of it."

Detective Chong stands up from his chair, nodding his head. "Thank you for your time," he says, bowing in a gesture of respect.

Wang, accompanied by his lawyers, leaves the room, with the weight of the interrogation hanging in the air.

The detective turns to the policewoman, who displays a mischievous smile. "Ready for the next round?" she jokes.

He laughs. "The party is about to start."

She arches an eyebrow, her smile widening into a sarcastic grin. "Going to see the superintendent? He tried to contact you three times."

He nods, gathering the papers scattered on the table and placing them in his briefcase. "Now things are going my way."

Wang exits through the imposing doors of the police building. After a brief goodbye to his lawyers, he calls Boss Bo's number on his cellphone. When the call goes unanswered, Wang's frustration increases.

The car stops in front of him, the engine purring quietly. Wang, maintaining an air of composure, sits in the back seat. "Take me to the port office," he instructs the driver.

As the cityscape passes by, Wang's mind returns to the interrogation. Every question, every subtle implication, and the incriminating photographs that were thrown under his face all replay in his mind, but it didn't scare him. He closes his eyes tightly; a grimace crosses his face. "There is going to be shit," he whispers.

Taking his cellphone from his suit pocket, he calls Hui, but it goes straight to voicemail.

Meanwhile, at the port, Hui's busy working in Warehouse #2. The soft buzz of his phone vibrates in his jacket pocket, and he stops working. Looking at the screen, he confirms the missed call, but ignores it. He waves to the boy who's helping him check some boxes, and hands over the clip-board full of papers. "Inspect those pallets, sign for them, and then hand them over to the secretary."

The employee agrees, taking the clipboard.

Hui walks from the warehouse toward the parking lot. He gets into the Toyota and heads toward the deep-water port for another load. Kung Wu's advice rings in his ears, urging him to maintain a facade of nor-malcy. He looks at his phone once again, noticing another missed call from Wang. With a sigh, he puts away the phone, deciding not to return the call for now.

*   *   *

Detective Chong walks with confidence toward the superintendent's office. He feels a surge of determination, prepared to convince his superior that he has enough evidence to detain the manager of Warehouses #1 and #2, thus avoiding the premature arrest of Wang. This tactical measure will allow him to build a stronger case for Wang's eventual arrest. As he rehearses his speech, his phone rings.

When he picks it up, he hears Rachel's urgent voice. "Detective, it's Rachel. Can we talk over lunch? I have something to give you that could change the game."

He replies, "Rachel, there is a place near the police building, in one corner of the park, called Noodles House. Meet me there at 11:00."

As he puts his phone in his pocket, he finds himself at the entrance to Boss Bo's office. The secretary, upon seeing him, raises her eyebrows in a mix of recognition and expectation. Understanding that confusion would prevail in the environment, she leaves the room without saying a word.

Chong takes a deep breath and knocks on the door. The quick reply of "Come in," echoes from the office.

Upon entering, he notices the boss staring at him. Chong waits a moment and then ventures the question: "Did you want to see me, sir?"

The big clock on the wall reads 10:00 a.m., and at that moment, Chong's stomach makes a frightening noise, echoing in the room's silence, expressing his hunger out loud.

Boss Bo's gaze shifts to the sound but remains fixed on the detective. "Update me. What progress have we made?"

Detective Chong pauses for an instant to collect his thoughts. "Sir, during the interrogation, Wang confirmed what I already suspected about the warehouse manager named Hui. Without knowing it, he helped us with information about Zhao's murder, Michael's disappearance, and the tragic deaths of Wonjy's family. I have gathered evidence and believe it is crucial that you review it before we decide on our next steps."

Surprised by Chong's words, Boss Bo motions for Chong to sit on the soft couch. "Show me," he says, understanding that Wang was the person 'helping' the investigation.

Detective Chong takes another deep breath, anxiety tightening his chest as he settles into the seat across from Chief Bo. In a systematic order, he reports the statements of Hui, the warehouse manager. He details the number of testimonies collected in the last twenty-four hours without mentioning Wang's name. In going over the details of Wang's interrogation, he avoids any information that might implicate the principal actor in the intricate web of events.

Presenting a series of court-stamped documents, Chong explains, "These documents describe telephone exchanges between Hui and Wonjy last week. They were in close contact throughout the night of the crime." He pauses, letting the gravity of the statement sink in. "We are awaiting further records, but the evidence significantly points to Hui as the linchpin of both investigations. Our interaction with Wang has only solidified our suspicions."

Chong, pausing for a moment to meet Boss Bo's inscrutable gaze, continues, "Boss, I'd like to call Hui in for a formal interrogation. With your approval, I would also like to request a temporary arrest warrant to be issued after the interrogation."

Boss Bo remains static, his face revealing nothing. He examines the documents, noting with approval the obvious absence of Wang's name. "Give me some time to think," he says. "I will review this and get back to you." Signalling the end of the conversation, he gestures for Chong to leave.

The boss's composure takes the detective aback; he expected a fight or argument. When Chong leaves the office, the secretary gives him a thumbs-up, impressed.

Chong responds with a slight nod, his face revealing no emotion.

Picking up the folder Chong left behind, Boss Bo straightens his suit and notifies his secretary that he is going out for lunch.

She nods and looks at her watch. It's only 10:30 a.m.

* * *

After Hui left, Kung Wu became lost in a whirlwind of thoughts throughout the night. Each one was scarier than the last. With Guowei by his side, they delved deeper into the information conveyed by Hui and searched the computer for any trace of the incidents mentioned by Hui in the news. Newspaper archives, social media buzz, and official reports painted a grim picture that was difficult to refute. The more they dug, the scarier reality became.

Every incident, every victim, felt like a needle in Kung Wu's body. While he may have tolerated Wang's transgressions in the past, the gravity of recent events weighed on him. He realized that although he had the means and contacts to protect, cover up, and facilitate Wang once again, this was a path he no longer wanted to take. Not just because Wang might never recognize or appreciate the gesture, but because Kung Wu predicted a cascade of worse problems if he continued to allow Wang's recklessness.

Thinking, he called an old friend, one of the Triad bosses, someone he had known and trusted for over three decades. After a few minutes, his assistant entered the room, holding a tray of steaming mugs of coffee. Kung Wu ended the call, declaring, "Pack your bags. We're travelling."

Guowei, surprised, looked at his wristwatch. "It's 7 a.m., boss. Can I at least drink the coffee?"

"We will buy some during the trip. Our schedule is tight. We have to be there at 10:00. I'll tell you on the way." Kung Wu's urgency was real. He grabbed his suit from the hanger and headed straight for the door.

38

Decisions Are Always Sentences or Judgments

The weight of the day sits heavily on Chief Bo as he exits the central police building. He dismisses his driver, opting instead to take the wheel himself. Today is not just another day. It's his wife's birthday, and tonight's party is not just a celebration but also a planned meeting with some of Shanghai's most influential figures.

He enters the flower shop near his workplace, a store he has visited countless times. This morning, he orders three dozen red roses divided into three bouquets. He hands the cards for the bouquets to the young attendant, and he sees her face light up when she recognizes the names. "The usual address?" she asks with a bow.

When Boss Bo, with a smile on his lips, leaves the store, the vibration in his pocket brings him back to the moment. Picking up the phone, he reads the message: *Confirmed and allowed. Team arrives in twenty-four hours. Delivered. Don't worry.* The weight in his chest deepens. The day before, news broke that a special team from the US and UK is being sent to help in the search for Michael. He's sure David must have pulled some strings, but Detective Chong's slow progress makes this intervention inevitable. Six agonizing days have already passed.

His fingers tighten around the phone. Frustration grows inside him, and he takes a moment to breathe and compose himself before getting into the car.

He drives to his residence at full speed. The laughter and familiar chatter of his wife and her sisters greet him as he enters the house. "Aren't you going back to work today?" one of his sisters-in-law jokes, wrapping an arm around his waist. The warmth of the hug contrasts with the cold reality of his work.

He laughs and responds, "No. I'm staying here with you."

His wife, beaming, replies, "Very good. I need you to help me with several decisions for the party." She leads the sisters into the house, and he looks at them with affection.

He enters his home office and locks the door behind him. Boss Bo pulls out the guest list for the night: politicians, association directors, bankers, and dear friends are all invited, people from around the world. One name stands out: Wang Savin Wei. Sinking into his chair, he presses a hand to his face. The weight of the situation falls on him, and in a whisper, he admits, "I can't do anything; it's going to be goodbye for him."

He puts the small notebook back in the drawer and picks up the landline from the desk. Opening the address book, he dials a number. When it's answered, he says, "How long has it been, Judge Hu Haoyu?"

*   *   *

At the busy port, Wang enters his office and checks his watch. It's 10:20 a.m. Having received no news, he sends a message to Kung Wu, who doesn't respond. Becoming restless and searching for answers, he tries calling Guowei, who also doesn't respond. Both of their phones are off. The minutes feel like hours, and as it approaches 10:30, Wang feels a surge of anxiety. "Why aren't they responding?" he says, punching the table.

His secretary, startled by the sudden noise, peers through the door. He looks toward the door and asks, "Did anyone contact me this morning?"

She opens the door, feeling the tenseness in the room. "No, sir," she responds, watching him.

Wang looks out the window, lost in a sea of thoughts. He breaks the silence and asks, "What's on today's schedule?"

The assistant returns to the table and looks at the diary. "Well, there's Boss Bo's wife's birthday party at their residence at 5 p.m. In addition, employees are loading containers at the port south of Shanghai. I believe Hui is overseeing this."

"Put Hui on the line for me," Wang instructs.

She leaves the room, returning with a worried look. "He doesn't answer his cellphone."

Wang ponders for a moment but decides not to stress. *Hui turns off his cellphone when he's busy.* Taking a jacket off the hanger, Wang puts it on. "If there is any update, call my cellphone. If you need me later, I'll be at Boss Bo's house."

She agrees and returns to her desk, feeling that the day has already started with problems.

* * *

The morning sun illuminates the highway in a soft golden hue as Kung Wu and Guowei head toward Hangzhou, the tourist capital of Zhejiang Province. The journey is smooth and quick, thanks to the impeccable roads on this side of China. Departing from the busy centre of Shanghai, they reach their destination in just over two hours.

Behind the wheel, Guowei drives with ease, breaking the silence in the car with a reflective statement. "You know, I never could understand the Wu Chinese dialect. Despite my parents' efforts to make me learn it, I never did."

Kung Wu, absorbed in reading his morning emails, looks up. "But can you speak the basics, the 'everyday' language? How to express gratitude or ask a simple question?"

Guowei smiles. "Sure, I can handle that, but if things get complicated, I go back to Mandarin."

Kung Wu raises an eyebrow. "Speaking Mandarin in Hangzhou can be tricky. Many Wu speakers won't understand you unless they have learned Mandarin."

Guowei laughs, muttering something that doesn't belong to the Wu dialect.

Kung Wu looks out the car window with a hint of impatience on his face. "Are we close to the hotel yet?" he asks, looking at the clock and seeing that it's 9:30.

Guowei looks at the rear-view mirror, a playful smile forming on his lips. "Just five more minutes and… ah, here we are." He pulls in and parks the car and turns to Kung with a laugh, satisfied with the accuracy of the arrival time.

Kung looks out. "Impressive place. What's it called?"

"Shanghai Ancient Hotel Hangzhou," Guowei replies as he jumps out, moving to open the door for Kung, then takes the bags out of the trunk.

As they walk toward the grand staircase leading to the hotel entrance, Guowei notices two approaching men. He recognizes them. He remembers them as security guards associated with some Triad bigwigs. They help with the luggage in Guowei's hands, and the group enters the opulent reception hall.

Guowei discusses reservations with one receptionist at the desk. He notices his boss is not by his side, seeing the other security guard who received them lead Kung toward the elevators. Guowei then turns to the young security guard next to him, who helped him with his luggage, and asks, "Have we met before?"

The security guard reminds him, "Yes, I met you at that art exhibition earlier this year in Beijing."

Guowei's face lights up in remembrance. "Ah yes! Those beautiful paintings and sculptures!" With a warm smile, he follows the young man to the elevators.

After leaving their belongings in their respective rooms, Guowei turns to the security guard accompanying him. "By the way, my name is Guowei."

The guard bows in respect. "I am Haitao."

"Can you take me to where my boss is?"

"Sure, this way."

Guowei follows him down the hallway, counting the doors until they reach suite 804. After a quick knock, a man who exudes an air of authority opens the door. Three familiar faces, Cao, Jiang, and Meng, all who envelop him in friendly hugs, greet Guowei. The other five men in the suite, more reserved, offer polite waves and handshakes.

The environment feels warm and welcoming. Guowei knows he must follow certain protocols. As they settle into the lounge bar, Haitao asks, "What can I get you to drink?"

"Just water, thank you," Guowei replies, appreciating the hospitality.

Cao motions for Guowei to come to the window. With a mix of curiosity and apprehension, Guowei approaches and looks, following Cao's pointing finger. He comes across the sight of a traditional roof-covered wooden boat on the river. The boatman, dressed in a suit, wields a long pole to steer and pushes the vessel forward.

"Your boss is on that boat," Cao, in a matter-of-fact manner, states.

Guowei's eyes widen, and he looks at Cao in disbelief.

"Don't worry; they're just talking," Cao assures him.

Cao returns to the bar stools. After remaining at the window for a moment longer, Guowei returns to the group, starting a light conversation and sharing in laughter.

Kung Wu, on board the boat, did not expect today's events. He didn't imagine talking in a place like this. The rower, as expected, is the security guard for Shanghai's deputy chief mountain master, Mr. Zeng, a man Kung has known for over three decades. The other two occupants of the boat, Mr. Xie and Mr. Peng, are important people in charge of the Beijing Triad. Although their presence is intimidating, Kung Wu is determined to carry out his mission.

The two Beijing chefs sip their drinks in contemplative silence. Zeng breaks the silence and addresses Kung, informing him the Triad rejected his proposal. "It's simple … betrayal is not something that is in our vocabulary. Any of our men, they act with our permission, they act according to our directives… but we don't fool anyone. Now… unauthorized trading? Attempting to bribe us? The number of transgressions is too long."

Kung Wu swallows hard, feeling the weight of the words. Now he realizes the terrible implications of this encounter. War is on the horizon and, with no need to say a word, he feels that his fate is sealed, perhaps in this river. Overwhelmed by the gravity of the situation, he falls to his knees. "That's the reason I'm here. Please listen to me before you judge."

The three leaders exchange glances, feeling Kung's call.

"Speak," orders Mr. Peng.

Desperation and urgency are clear in his eyes, and Kung places the recorder on the table. As the previous night's conversation between Hui and him unfolds, the leaders listen. Once he finishes, Kung details his concerns about Wang, emphasizing his increasing unpredictability.

The atmosphere on the boat becomes even more tense as Kung Wu waits for a single word from the three men, which is not spoken.

The three men exchange glances.

Xie nods, causing Mr. Zheng to instruct the boatman, "Back to the hotel."

Upon noticing the return of the boat, the bosses' security guards take action. Guowei, sensing the urgency but unaware of the situation, follows behind them. They arrive at the dock, and the men help their respective bosses off the boat, with Guowei helping Kung last.

As they head toward the hotel entrance, Mr. Peng signals to one of his men to take Kung to his suite. The designated security guard approaches them with a stern expression.

Kung's discomfort is apparent, and he is almost unable to walk. Guowei, sensing his boss's anguish, asks, "Boss, what happened?"

Dragging his feet, weighed down by the weight of events on the boat, Kung ponders the emotions he has endured. He takes comfort in believing that he did right by the organization, hoping that if anyone had to contain what was coming, it would be Wang, and not the entire Tong. Leaning on Guowei to walk, he whispers, "Let's find out now."

Inside the opulent Diamond Suite, the Triad bosses sit on plush couches, engrossed in hushed phone conversations. Kung Wu and Guowei, to the left on the suite's balcony, admire the serene view of the lake. The interior of the suite is a hub of activity, with security guards tending to the chiefs' every need, refreshing drinks, replacing ashtrays, and ensuring nothing is missing.

With body aches and stress overwhelming him, Kung mutters, "I need to sit down." With Guowei's help, they enter the suite. Xie, observing their approach, signals Kung to sit in the armchair in front of him, while gesturing with his hand for Guowei to move away.

In a moment, Mr. Xie leans over, whispering something into Kung's ear. The room's occupants cannot understand a word, but the tension has become real. After this movement, time does not pass; it seems like an eternity. Mr. Xie leans back in his chair, looking into Kung's eyes. Without saying a word, Kung kneels before him, offering a gesture of submission and respect in a slow and deliberate bow.

Guowei, flanked by two bodyguards of the Triad chiefs, can only watch, stunned by the scene unfolding. Kung's old friend, although belonging to the rival faction, steps forward and extends his hand to help him up. The room remains filled with tension, awaiting the Triad bosses' next move.

Rising from the couch, Mr. Feng stretches and announces, "I'm hungry. Let's have lunch." Without waiting for a response, he walks out the door accompanied by his security guards toward one of the hotel's renowned restaurants.

Everyone follows him without question.

As Kung shares a meal with the other leaders, Guowei feels like a fish out of water. He was told to pack his belongings and prepare the car to leave the hotel after lunch. To his surprise, someone had already paid the bill.

As Guowei puts the bags back in the car's trunk, Cao approaches him, hinting with a little mischief, "I think we'll meet in Shanghai soon."

Feeling nervous and unsure about what might have happened to his boss, Guowei manages a forced smile. "We will meet more often, I believe."

The bosses descend the hotel steps, and a line of elegant cars awaits them, engines purring and security personnel on standby. After a series of goodbyes and embraces, each leader heads to their respective vehicles.

Kung Wu, looking exhausted, gets into their car, settling into the soft seat without uttering a single word. Sensing the urgency of the moment, Guowei does not hesitate. The car leaves the place at high speed, heading toward the city centre. A heavy silence fills the interior of the car.

Trying to understand what is happening, Guowei asks, "Boss, would you like some water?"

Kung Wu takes the bottle, not bothering to nod in thanks. His gaze is distant, his mind is racing, trying to process and predict the consequences of the day's events.

Guowei can feel the tension every time he glances at his boss. Kung Wu's fingers massage his temples, and the deep lines of anguish on his face are a testament to the gravity of what happened.

Unable to bear the oppressive silence, Guowei blurts out, "Come on, boss. What happened?"

Taking a deep breath, Kung Wu responds, his eyes full of emotion: "They believe in us, Guowei. If they hadn't… we wouldn't be here now. We would both be dead. That was the original order."

The weight of the revelation almost makes Guowei cross the car into the oncoming lane. He brakes and parks on the side of the road, struggling to process the information, and stammers, "What do you mean?"

Kung Wu's voice cracks as he tries to explain. "They had orders, Guowei. Orders to execute us and the entire Tong leadership. Today."

As he recounts all the horror he experienced, Kung Wu's face turns pale, and he opens the car door, leaning over to vomit.

Panicked, Guowei struggles to offer a bottle of water. "Here, boss, drink this one too."

Seeing Kung Wu's state, Guowei's instincts kick in. He starts the car, heading to the highway, trying to offer some comfort. "Look, let's go home. You're going to rest. We'll arrive around 4 p.m."

Kung Wu, gathering his composure, insists, "No, Guowei. Take me to the office. There are things we need to put into action. Now!"

Feeling a surge of determination, Guowei agrees and continues on.

* * *

Rachel and her partners are sitting at a table outside their chosen restaurant without other customers, the noise from the street masking their conversation. They have arrived earlier than the agreed-upon time because they want a moment to collect their thoughts.

Detective Chong appears soon after, sounding agitated and speaking rapidly. Without pleasantries, he says, "I'm in a hurry today. Why did you want to meet me?"

David slides two thick yellow envelopes across the table. Chong flips through the contents, furrowing his eyebrows. He looks at the three partners. "Can I have these?"

"Those are for you," David replies. "Tyler got this data from American and Canadian intelligence."

Chong's gaze shifts to Rachel, his attempt to smile at her looking strained. "Is there anything else you need?"

Rachel, noticing the tiredness on Chong's face, responds, "We would like to contact the intel agents who confronted us."

"I'll take care of it and let you know," Chong says. "Look, I'm out of time today. How about we meet again tomorrow night? I'll call Rachel, and we can work something out."

She nods, and her partners imitate her. After Chong leaves, Rachel comments, "Anyone else notice? He's wearing the same clothes as yesterday. And those dark circles—"

Tyler interrupts. "Yeah, I saw it."

David remains thoughtful, absorbing his observations.

A waiter approaches with a tray full of steaming bowls of noodles. The trio's eyes follow Chong, watching him disappear into the busy square.

* * *

Inside the busy police headquarters, Detective Chong moves with urgency. He combs through official testimonies and documents, hoping to uncover other evidence that points to Hui's involvement in the recent series of mysterious disappearances and deaths. His secretary, efficient and focused, processes incoming reports, categorizing them before delivering them to Chong.

Chong's cellphone interrupts the frenetic atmosphere. He responds, and as he listens, a rare smile appears on his face. He hangs up with a joyful expression and tells the secretary: "I'm going to court. If anyone asks for me, I'm with Judge Hu Haoyu."

Running to his desk, he looks for the "Hui Chowei" folder. Once he finds it, he double-checks its contents, ensuring that all evidence is in place. A quick glance at the clock on the wall tells him it's half-past twelve. Organized as always, he puts the folder in his leather briefcase.

"That's it. I think we got it. Tell München to prepare two operational teams. We'll serve an arrest warrant, and remember, with absolute discretion—no one can know about this. I'll be back in an hour."

She nods, picking up the phone as Chong leaves.

When Chong returns an hour and a half later, he enters the office and doesn't even notice the director of operations lying on the couch, waiting for him. Chong's secretary follows close behind. Reasoning at a speed above normal, he emits the right words amid impatience. Chong turns to the secretary. "Have someone check Hui's whereabouts at Warehouse Number Two, confirm where he is…"

"I'll do that," the secretary says, dialling the number.

München gets up and enters the scene at that moment, catching Chong's immediate attention. Speechless, Chong hands him two documents, and the two men concentrate on the papers.

Silence settles in the room as the secretary asks questions during the phone conversation. The two men go to the door, interested, their attention fixed on her voice, trying to read her expressions.

Ending the call, she looks up, meeting Detective Chong's gaze. "She says no one knows where he is, and his phone appears to be off."

Acknowledging the news with a firm nod, Chong enters his office, München following behind, closing the door. Inside, the two exchange a series of ideas about the documents. Chong says, "We'll watch the residence and the port entrances to Warehouses One and Two. Our target will arrive at one of them and keep an eye out for the black Toyota with the distinctive white marking on the back. We also need to seize that."

München replies, "I distributed his photograph to the entire team. Don't worry. We'll arrest him today."

The two head to the operations room, where the respective teams that will take part in the operation await instructions. Chong takes command: "I will lead team one; München, team two is yours. How many cars are at our disposal, including mine?"

München does the math. "We have four from the operations sector, two cars for each team."

Chong agrees and instructs the teams: "Keep your radios on. We will do nothing in a hurry, but with perfection, and above all, our safety is fundamental. Good luck and let's bring it."

The energy in the room is visible as the twelve agents prepare for the task at hand. In the underground garage, the unidentified vehicles are prepared for departure.

39

Tears Wash the Soul

It's 1:30 p.m. when Rachel enters David's room. "Are your bags ready? I called reception and asked for a luggage cart." Her voice shows a sense of urgency.

David nods as he walks past her. "All ready," he murmurs, his voice distant as he steps out and closes the door behind him.

"Tyler is at the front desk paying the bill. Can you believe he only brought a backpack? He says when he needs clothes, he just buys new clothes and discards the old ones." Rachel lets out a small laugh.

David, stopping near the elevator, looks at her. "You know Tyler." His voice monotone, not sharing the humour.

Rachel watches him, feeling something strange. Their usual warm smiles are absent, replaced by a terse demeanour and short answers.

The sound of the elevator arriving interrupts them. One of the hotel attendants comes out manoeuvring a cart. David returns and opens the bedroom door, allowing the young man to get his luggage.

When they arrive at the hotel's large reception, a group of hotel employees approach the trio, bowing. Grateful, David and Rachel nod and smile back.

The attendant hands Rachel the daily bill, and she looks over at Tyler. "Did you use your company card?"

Tyler nods, walking beside her. "Everything's fine," he confirms, guiding her toward the parking lot.

Earlier that day, David rented a car. They met with their favourite detective at 11:00 and, despite his injury, David could drive with no noticeable difficulties. Now back behind the wheel, he steers the vehicle out of the parking lot and onto the busy avenue.

Rachel speaks up. "Your arm looks better. But don't forget physical therapy on Friday."

David looks at her, a smile forming. "Let's see if I still need it."

Tyler, with concern on his face, adds, "That's right, make sure none of those tendons get worse."

Rachel looks out the window, losing herself in the picturesque scenery. "Such a beautiful day," she comments.

"That's right," Tyler agrees, also enjoying the moment.

David, sensing the atmosphere, also smiles after a while.

Tyler's voice wavers. He doesn't know how to break the news. "Ah, while I was paying the bill, the hotel received a call for Rachel. As you didn't answer, I answered. It was Rose, from the Firm."

Rachel's face turns thoughtful. "It must have been when we were going down in the elevator," she murmurs, her gaze fixed on Tyler.

In the rear-view mirror, David notices Tyler's tense expression. "What's up? Is something wrong?"

Tyler swallows hard. "I'll just break the news. Alex… he's back in the hospital and… it looks like he's in pretty terrible shape." Without waiting for answers, he looks out the window to protect himself from their reactions.

Rachel's face drains of colour, but she remains silent, processing the news.

David's voice hardens. "Is this any way to break news like this?"

Tyler's voice cuts like a knife. "What do you want me to say? You're his friends. I'm not."

Rachel, blinking back tears, murmurs, "We'll contact Rose later."

David, looking shaken but trying to concentrate on the road, mutters something under his breath and continues driving.

The trio enter the apartment building's garage, trying to leave the heavy news behind for a while. There is a fleeting feeling of joy, a brief escape from reality, as they ride the elevator up to their new apartment.

Once inside, Rachel, with a subtle show of strength, carries her two heavy suitcases to the bedroom, while David and Tyler unpack their few belongings in their own spaces.

Tyler, still carrying the weight of the previous conversation, sinks onto the couch, turning on the TV to distract himself.

From the kitchen, Rachel calls out in a gentle voice, "Does anyone want a drink?"

Both men refuse, each lost in their thoughts.

David arranges his clothes on hangers, taking a moment to survey the tidy bathroom. Everything is in its place. He reflects that no one can accuse him of being messy. His organization is impeccable. Feeling hungry, he goes to the kitchen and examines the contents of the refrigerator. "I'm starving," he admits.

Rachel gives him an amused look. "You only ate four hours ago. Keep it up and you're going to need bigger pants."

Ignoring her words, David replies, "There's a fantastic restaurant near here."

Tyler perks up, turning off the TV. Those noodles from before had little effect. "I'm going with you."

Rachel rolls her eyes. "Okay, okay. Let's go to lunch." Grabbing her purse, she leads the way.

As David drives and Rachel and Tyler enjoy the view of the city, the shrill sound of sirens pierces the air. All the cars on the avenue pull alongside other vehicles, stopping, allowing five unidentified cars with sirens and flashing headlights to pass by at high speed.

Rachel, following the disappearing cars, comments, "This is intense. Unmarked cars with sirens running like that."

David, focused on the road, comments, "It's unusual to see the police being so open about an operation here."

Tyler, squinting at the receding vehicles, thinks, "It must be something big."

Rachel, restless, looks at her wristwatch. "How long will it take to get to this restaurant? It's already 3:30."

David works their way through traffic. "Almost there. Ten minutes."

Tyler laughs. "Glad you said it was close to the apartment."

"Do you want to drive next time?" David retorts, half joking.

Rachel and Tyler both chuckle out loud. "Oh, no. We're fine," they chorus, smiling.

* * *

Close to the neighbourhood where the partners rent the apartment is the renowned St. Paul Riviera Garden condominium in the Jinqiao neighbourhood. Although seen as middle-class, it has properties ranging from modest homes to large mansions.

Hoping to arrest Hui at his residence in the Jinqiao neighbourhood, a team of plainclothes police officers takes up positions near the house, going unnoticed by the neighbours.

As Hui returns home, memories flood his mind. The residence he bought when he got married is itself a debt settlement, a deal made between one of Wang's contractors and Warehouse #1. Combined with his life savings and his wife's wedding dowry, he sealed the deal with Wang's help. To keep things clean, after a year, he transferred the property into his wife's name.

Upon entering Riviera Garden, he sees the side wall of the house scarred by the fire in the neighbouring house. At first, he thinks a fresh coat of paint will repair the damage, but remembering how it looked after the fire, he concludes that a more extensive renovation may be necessary. Ignoring this thought, he opens his garage with a click on the remote control. Used to the silence of his neighbours and the locality, he pays no attention to parked cars. The Toyota slides into its usual position.

Leaving the car, he heads through the back entrance, toward the side gate that leads to the garden. Just then, two men approach from the shadows and show their police badges. Hui stops. One of them says in a calm voice, "Let's have a chat inside, okay?"

As if he expected this moment to come, Hui calmly nods. As they enter the garden, Detective München, accompanied by three other police officers, enters as well. The small group comes together. The conversation is brief and simple, ensuring that the street remains unaware of the police's presence.

München breaks the silence. "Do you prefer to talk here or inside?"

Hui responds, "Inside would be better."

München's gaze sharpens. "Is there anyone else at home?"

Hui shakes his head. "No, they are all outside the city."

Detective München, with a solemn expression, ensuring that Hui understands what he is going to say, reads aloud the provisional arrest and search and seizure warrants while unfolding the papers in his hands.

"You can do whatever you want," Hui murmurs, resignation clear in his voice. He lowers his head, watching as München places the cuffs on his wrists.

The police, with notorious experience, begin searching the office. In a few minutes, they collect a computer, a laptop, two boxes full of documents, and several notebooks.

The chief of operations signals one officer with precise gestures. The officer approaches, standing right in front of Hui. In an unwavering voice, he informs Hui of his rights, emphasizing his right to a phone call and a lawyer.

Hui just watches, numb. His gaze follows the officers as they continue their search, and when some go up the stairs, a shadow crosses his face, but he remains calm.

While loading evidence into police vehicles, München assesses Hui, trying to gauge his emotions. "Do you understand the reasons behind your arrest?"

Looking up from the floor, Hui meets the detective's eyes, his voice shaky but clear. "Yes."

The head of operations, noticing a jacket thrown on an armchair, places it over Hui's cuffed hands in a slight gesture of consideration. They lead Hui out of the residence and into one of the waiting vehicles.

Another police officer, following München's previous instructions, goes into the garage, starts Hui's Toyota, and leaves, heading to the police department. The forensic team will examine it later that day.

Inside the police car, Hui, without showing his nervousness or even sweating, remains silent. However, beneath his serene exterior, his world is falling apart. Clinging to hope, he remembers Kung Wu's words and, with a deliberate effort, relaxes his tense shoulders, hoping there is a way out of this.

As the clock strikes 6:00 p.m., München contacts Detective Chong, updating him on the arrest. Wasting no time, Chong contacts Chief Bo and informs his command superior of the news.

In police operations, the twists and turns can be distressing because the unexpected always happens. Despite their best efforts at discretion, the news leaked out to newspapers, radio, and TV, all swarming for the news.

Detective Chong's phone rings. His secretary is tense with stress. "Detective, the media is invading the police station. You should turn on your cellphone to the news," she explains. "The media are linking the manager of Warehouses One and Two in the Port of Shanghai to the terrible explosion on a farm that resulted in the death of a woman and her child. The authorities have arrested him. This is the news in focus."

Chong feels a surge of anger. Someone opened their mouth. Taking a deep breath to calm down, he returns to talking to his secretary. "Don't allow the press in," he retorts, "and tell the man on duty at the desk to let them know we'll be holding a press conference later." He hangs up and picks up the radio, informing Detective München and his team about what is happening. "Use the basement entrance, no sirens, and put Hui in a cell as discreetly as possible."

München understands the directive and soon faces a live report on his phone. He watches a reporter speaking, with the station building's staircase in the background, detailing the arrest and the painful consequences of the explosion at the farm, which killed a woman and a child. Shaking his head, he instructs his convoy to take a more discreet approach. Vehicles move through the streets to the back entrance of the police building. As Hui's world crumbles around him, they take him to an underground cell.

Inside, Chong makes his way to the chief of operations office. Watching München take off his bulletproof vest, he ventures, "What was it like? Did he resist?"

München sighs and puts on his jacket. "No, very passive, almost as if he knew what was coming."

Chong's eyes harden. "I need your report by the end of the day."

Exhaustion clear in every line of his face, München responds, "It's being put together by the boys. It should be ready soon. I... I need to get out. Let's get in touch tomorrow." With a nod, he leaves Chong alone.

Left in the day's tumultuous aftermath, Chong returns to his office, which presents a mess, with papers scattered everywhere. His secretary had left, but not without leaving behind a mountain of unfinished work. Picking up a file from his desk, Chong whispers to himself, "It looks like it's going to be a long night."

* * *

Boss Bo's house is full of thrilled people. The rhythm of a live band fills the air, punctuated by laughter and clinking glasses. Rows of tables feature a tempting array of dishes, and a makeshift bar sits by the pool. A bartender mixes drinks and serves a never-ending stream of guests. The crowd is a mix of dignitaries, close friends, and family, all mingling in celebration.

Wang, always punctual, comes in with a bouquet of roses for the birthday girl and a nice bottle of whiskey for the superintendent. Many of those present have crossed paths before, whether through business, social events, or casual meetings, but tonight, all interactions reignite again.

Across the room, the police department superintendent, gathered with a group of partygoers, observes Wang, who is the centre of another crowd. Wang's magnetic charm is on full display, with men wanting to chat and women drawn to his charisma. Chief Bo watches as his wife and sisters-in-law keep Wang close, making sure he knows everyone present, leading him from group to group around the sparkling pool and into the expansive hall.

Amid the joyous chaos, Boss Bo's phone vibrates. Apologizing, he takes it out of his pocket and reads the message. His expression falters on his face. He smiles again and walks through the crowd of supporters, heading toward Wang. "Do you believe it? My wife left me for you," he says. "On her birthday, no less."

The birthday girl and her sisters-in-law, standing next to Wang, wrap him in a hug, offering assurances he is the only one in their lives.

"You're the actual star tonight," the women comment.

Boss Bo, with his eyes fixed on Wang, responds, "No, it's him," and adds, "you were looking for the bathroom, right? Come with me. You wouldn't want the women waiting for you outside. That's not ideal."

Wang caught the underlying tone and without hesitation follows Boss Bo. As they make their way through the crowd, guests reach out, touching Wang's arm, sharing greetings and laughter. Just before they reach the bathroom, Boss Bo, who walks in front with Wang following him, enters the kitchen storage room, the door closing behind them.

Wang hesitates to enter the room, seeing that the place has poor lighting, with shelves full of various supplies. His brow furrows in confusion. "What's all this? You've been avoiding me all day. First that interrogation this morning and now this?" he demands, his voice carrying a trace of anger and frustration.

Bo's face is dark. "They have taken Hui into custody. I suggest you take your legal team to the police station," he says, concentration in his words. Seeing the shock on Wang's face, he walks toward the exit door.

When Bo closes the door behind him, Wang is stunned, the weight of the revelation making his knees weak. He stops for a moment, taking a deep breath, trying to calm his racing heart. He takes out his cellphone and calls a familiar number from his contact list. Once the line connects, he says, "Go to the police building in the city centre. Take care of Hui Chowei. I mean now!"

Hanging up, Wang's mind races. Thoughts tangle with emotions, creating a storm of confusion. He has to get away from here. Get some fresh air. Get some clarity. As he opens the door, he almost collides with a young waiter who looks scared, apologizing.

"Can I help you with anything, sir?" the waiter asks with suspicion.

"A bathroom," Wang responds, his voice sounding more strained than he intended.

The waiter, noticing Wang's urgency, takes him to the bathroom close to the kitchen.

Upon entering, the light casts eerie shadows, and Wang's reflection in the mirror appears, almost as if he is looking at a doppelgänger. The deafening music irritates his senses. He turns on a faucet, splashing ice-cold water on his face. However, his reflection doesn't ripple or distort, it just stares at him, cold and unsettling.

Wang, emotionless, stares at the being in the mirror. He takes the towel and dries his face, but the evil smile of his reflection cuts through the darkness in which he finds himself. Wang hears his own voice full of malevolence: "Isn't that what you wanted?"

Wang, looking at the image, steadies himself and raises an eyebrow as he responds, "Maybe."

In a quick moment, the reflection punches the air in celebration, then sobs whisper with unexpected joy: "Isn't this your master plan? Someone has to 'pay the price.'"

Wang clenches his fingers, holding back a tremor. He holds the reflection's gaze, his mind racing. The sinister doppelgänger rejoices again before warning, "Don't forget that Hui has damning information."

Wang recovers and turns on the tap, talking to the mirror. "Think again. He wouldn't dare risk his family."

The reflection leans in, almost touching the mirror with its face, and asks, "But if you don't take action, who will remain in this story?"

Wang's eyes shine with defiance. "Your games won't sway me," he retorts, turning his back on the mirror and heading toward the door. However, the voice of the reflection continues. "Mark my words, if you ignore the signs and don't take action, you'll be next."

Wang doesn't look back and calls his lawyer on his cellphone. "Don't let him testify. Whatever it takes. Silence him."

On the other side, the urgency of Wang's words makes the lawyer explain himself. "I'm careful. Things are getting out of control here in front of the building. Leave it to me."

Once ending the call, Bo's sister-in-law tries to seduce him with an insinuating smile, interrupting Wang's quick steps. He smiles, allowing her to follow him. The party goes on. The pool area is full of light, music, and fortunate people. Chef Bo is in the centre, surrounded by guests.

The sun sets, and the blood-red horizon emits a chilly wind.

From the mansion's kitchen, four waiters appear, pushing a cart with a luxurious three-tier cake. The music starts, "Happy Birthday to you..." while the sky, already black, explodes in a cascade of fireworks.

However, Wang feels a storm brewing and knows it's time to leave.

Music plays in the background, with couples dancing and laughing on the poolside dance floor. On the large balcony, groups of guests relax on luxurious sofas, engaged in conversation and laughter. In the middle of this scene, Wang approaches the birthday girl, takes her hand, and gives her a kiss, saying that he is leaving. Boss Bo's wife's eyes shine with joy at his gesture. Without letting go of him, she runs to where her husband is, telling him about Wang's departure.

Boss Bo stands up, looking at Wang. Smiles that don't identify as fake or real grace their faces as they close their hands in a firm grip with respect.

Upon leaving the mansion, Wang can't shake the feeling that something is amiss. Once in the parking lot, he pulls out his phone and types to his lawyer: *Any updates?*

The lawyer's call comes almost immediately. "He's isolated for now. He seemed pretty calm. I told them he's off limits until tomorrow. The cops are looking at the evidence they've collected. I'm still waiting for official charges. Do you want to talk to him?"

Wang exhales and then nods his head, even though he knows the lawyer can't see him. "Pass him the phone!"

Hui's voice is firm on the other end, but Wang can sense the underlying tension.

"Boss?" Hui requests.

"What's the charge?" Wang's voice remains calm, not betraying any emotion.

"It's not clear yet."

Wang's instructions are explicit. "Remember, silence is your best defence. They can't have anything concrete, right?"

Hui's response is instantaneous. "Understood, boss."

Wang adds, with a hint of menace in his tone, "Remember, you have a lovely family waiting for you."

The tension in Hui's voice is unmistakable. "I won't forget."

Wang can almost hear him biting his lip in anxiety.

"Give the phone to the lawyer."

The lawyer's voice, professional and reassuring, shines through. "I'll take care of it. I'll call you with any updates."

Wang ends the call, leaning back in his chair, lost in thought. The reflection in the mirror, the anxiety in Hui's voice, the lawyer's determination—everything swirls in his mind.

Without noticing someone approaching, he hears a knock on the window, interrupting his reverie. A young parking attendant looks at him.

"Leaving, sir?"

With a curt nod, Wang responds, "Yes." Without wasting another moment, Wang starts the engine and speeds off into the night.

*   *   *

The night air is a little chilly. Rachel and her partners return home after dinner. Settling into the cozy atmosphere of the living room, the trio relaxes.

"Dinner was amazing," Rachel sighs, sinking into the plush sofa, stretching her legs with a satisfied groan.

"I agree," Tyler says, nodding.

David, however, goes straight to the bedroom. After a while, he reappears with a mischievous smile on his lips. "I think the traffic was worth it after all," he comments with a hint of sarcasm in his tone.

Rachel and Tyler exchange amused looks, smiling in agreement.

Without missing a beat, David grabs the remote and turns the TV on. He then walks to the kitchen and grabs a small bottle of water.

Tyler, trying to understand the unfamiliar channels and languages, fumbles with the remote control, pressing it in sequence, looking for something in English.

Rachel, half-watching, exclaims, "Wait! Go back!"

Tyler returns to the previous channel where a horde of journalists are outside a police building—the same one they visited that morning.

"David! Can you understand what they're saying?" Rachel screams. The quick speech doesn't let her understand.

Joining them, David focuses on the report. As the gravity of the situation becomes apparent, his expression becomes serious.

Seeing the transformation on David's face, Rachel and Tyler press him: "What did they say? Tell us."

David hesitates, then takes a deep breath, sets the bottle down, and drops to his knees on the carpet. He struggles to find the right words. "Do you remember Detective Chong mentioning that the house explosion, the one where the woman and child died, could be involved in Michael's disappearance?"

Rachel nods, remembering. "Yes, the husband worked with Wang, disappeared, and was friends with the man who shot you."

Tyler, perplexed, asks, "So, what's the connection now?"

David's voice shakes with a mix of shock and excitement. "They've arrested someone associated with the fire and deaths at the farm."

Rachel's eyes widen. She keeps her eyes fixed on the screen, trying to understand what they are saying.

David's urgency breaks the stunned silence. "We need to call the detective now!"

Tyler's voice tries to bring some semblance of calm. "Listen, he told us he would call us. We should trust him. We have to stay calm."

David, still kneeling on the carpet, eyes glued to the TV, whispers, "Whoever they arrested might have answers about Michael."

Rachel, her voice tight with worry, presses, "What else are they saying?"

David's voice shakes. "They're holding a press conference tomorrow." He hangs his head, fighting the wave of emotions. Tears fall down his face.

Rachel's heart breaks at the sight. She approaches him, wrapping him in a comforting hug.

Tyler, not knowing how to help, runs into the kitchen. He mixes sugar and water in a glass, thinking that the ancient medicine might help with David's anguish.

When Tyler returns, David has got up from the rug and is heading to his room. Rachel follows, wrapping him in another comforting hug, whispering words of comfort and hope.

Wiping away tears, David's voice is full of emotion. "I'm sorry."

Tyler, joining them, says, "David, you need this release. Cry, let it all out... there's no point holding back emotion. I don't know how you guys managed this for so long."

Rachel declares, "I'm going to call the detective." She calls the number, waiting for the familiar voice on the other end.

Detective Chong's voice comes in a rush. "Rachel, it's absolute chaos here. I believe... I will talk to you tomorrow night. Don't worry, I will update you as soon as I can."

Nodding, even though he can't see her, Rachel replies, "Understood. Thank you." She hangs up, turning to face her partner's expectant eyes. "He said he'll call as soon as he can."

A moment of silent understanding passes between them. They have been through countless operations together and know that in times like these, patience, although impossible, is key.

* * *

In one of the main buildings in the city centre, Guowei manoeuvres the car into the parking lot in the building's basement that houses Kung Wu's office. After parking, he and his boss climb into the empty elevator. The moment they enter the room, Kung Wu goes straight to the table, opening his diary, looking for a specific name.

Guowei, familiar with the layout of the room, takes a key from the drawer of a piece of furniture next to the large sofa. With the key in his hand, he heads to the bathroom in the hallway outside the office.

Kung Wu's cellphone comes to life as he punches in some numbers. "We need to meet," he states with an assertive tone. "It has to be a very discreet place for this conversation." Upon hearing the answer, he instructs, "I'm in the office. Hurry, but make sure no one knows you're coming here." Once that's done, he puts the phone back into his pocket.

His attention changes when Guowei re-enters the room.

"I'm much better now. I need to make some phone calls," Kung Wu explains with a hint of gratitude in his voice. "Go home, freshen up, and then come back and take me home. I'm not going anywhere now."

Guowei nods, putting the key back in the drawer. "Thank you, I won't be long. I'll be back soon," he replies before leaving the room.

Alone now, Kung Wu's demeanour calms down. He sits in his armchair by the window, looking through the glass at the moonless night, watching the sky get darker and darker. Lost in thought, he walks over to the drink cart, pouring himself a double shot of whiskey. When drinking, he feels that life still pulses in his body.

40

Follow the Rules

Detective Chong wakes up, his body aching from the office couch. His eyelids feel heavy. Blinking against the dim light, he sees the clock on the wall: it reads 5 a.m. As he stands up, he tries to remember the last piece of evidence amid the scattered papers he was examining before exhaustion had overtaken him. He can't remember. The weight of stress and exhaustion has left him confused.

He goes to the file cabinet and takes out the bag with emergency clothes that he always keeps ready in one drawer. In a small plastic bag, there is a toothbrush and toothpaste, and in another, the essentials: towel, black jeans, underwear, socks, and a presentable shirt. Without hesitating, he leaves the office and goes down the stairs to the lower level. After entering the elevator, he presses the button for basement one.

When the door opens, the police gym's empty spaces greet him. Laughing, he confirms that even for the usual fanatics it's too early. About to enter the bathroom, a sudden memory hits him. He forgot the soap. Searching the showers, he finds a small, discarded piece.

"That's enough," he murmurs with a half-smile.

After a revitalizing shower, he puts on his clean clothes. He takes a brief look in the mirror as he combs his hair back to its usual state. Leaving the bathroom, his gaze roams the gym equipment, half expecting to see someone early in the morning exercising, but still, there's no one.

"Very lazy, these people." He laughs to himself. "Nobody's ready to train this early."

Upon returning to the elevator, he faces the eerie silence of the building in the morning, which is unusual, as many people are in the building. Once in his office, he begins the laborious task of gathering and organizing the avalanche of papers on the floor, placing them one by one on the table.

As he works, his stomach growls, demanding attention. He goes down to the reception desk, finding two police officers on duty.

One of them looks at him, surprised. "Do you need something, Detective Chong?"

"Do you know if the bakery is open?" he asks, hope clear in his voice.

The officer looks at the clock. "It's only 6:30, Detective. They open at 7:00." Shrugging, the police officer returns to talking to his colleague, both of them absorbed in a small TV screen.

Resigned to search, Detective Chong leaves the building, taking in the fresh morning air. He feels serenity as he walks toward the city centre's historic square. Along the way, he comes across a group practising Tai Chi, offering them a friendly wave. The coolness of the morning is a pleasant surprise, showing the remnants of the previous night's rain. There is something comforting about the lack of the city's usual clamour and the crowds that pass by daily. For a moment, Chong finds solace in the peaceful start to what he knows will be another heavy day.

Arriving at the bakery, he comes across a locked door. He waits on a nearby cement bench, sitting in a puddle caused by the previous night's rain. The cold water soaking through his jeans makes him jump up, a slight annoyance crossing his face. As he tries to remove the moisture, the faint buzzing of mosquitoes near his ear sends another wave of irritation through him. He shrugs. It's just water, after all... but then a soft noise catches his attention.

When he turns around, he sees an elderly man struggling with the heavy iron door at the entrance to the bakery. Detective Chong doesn't think twice and hurries over and lends a hand. As soon as they open the door together, the detective, catching his breath, asks, "Do you have coffee?"

"Of course, I made it fresh twenty minutes ago," the old man replies with a grateful smile, leading Chong inside.

Detective Chong sits down at a clean table, noticing the wet sheen still on its surface. Moments later, someone places a steaming cup of coffee in front of him. The inviting aroma draws a sigh of satisfaction. On impulse, he orders a ham and cheese sandwich, eager for something hot and filling. The elderly man nods and disappears, only to return with the requested meal.

As he savours each bite, Chong's mind turns to the challenges ahead. Today, he depends on Hui's testimony. If everything goes according to plan, he might have enough to arrest Wang. A thrill of anticipation runs through his body as he finishes his coffee with a satisfied smile. He pays for the meal, thanking the old man, and returns to the police station.

However, as he approaches the police building, an unusual commotion catches his attention. A frenzy has replaced the normal activity of people entering the building's steps. There are parked vans with satellite dishes on display at random, reporters holding microphones, and cameramen jostling each other in search of the best angles. The police are already present, placing yellow tape to prohibit entry. A crowd gathers in the right corner, some holding signs, but their voices rise in passionate cries for justice for a tragedy involving a mother and daughter. Uniformed officers approach to maintain order. Taking a deep breath, Chong knows the day's challenges have only just begun.

Detective Chong mutters under his breath, "News travels fast."

Chong dexterously makes his way through the sea of reporters and onlookers, and enters the police building. The atmosphere inside is thick with expectation. He notices two female police officers have replaced the familiar faces of the officers on duty this morning.

Climbing the stairs, he finds his ever-reliable secretary already at his desk, arranging the papers scattered around.

He arches an eyebrow. "Couldn't wait for the sun to come up?"

She smiles, not missing a beat. "I thought you'd need me earlier today."

München enters, stretching and yawning. "Good morning, everyone. I slept like an elephant last night."

Chong, looking confused as he picks up folders from the floor, jokes, "Are elephants light or heavy sleepers?"

Unfazed by the remark, München gets straight to the point. "When are we going to start?"

"Between 8 a.m. and 8:30 a.m.," Chong responds. "I'm waiting for the reception team to notify me of the lawyers' arrival."

"Don't worry, I'll prepare aquarium number two," München says, looking up from some papers on Chong's desk. "By the way, forensics hasn't finished the work on the car yet. After some… persuasion, they promise a report this afternoon."

Without hesitation, Chong snatches the papers from München's hands, responding, "Good."

When the chief of operations leaves, Chong organizes the classified documents, storing them in a white folder. He then approaches his secretary, hands her another stack of papers, and says, "I need two copies of each, please."

She nods and gets up to take the order when the loud ringing of the phone on her desk interrupts her. Chong watches her as she has a brief conversation and then hangs up. She turns to Chong. "The police officers on duty are alerting you. Boss Bo arrived and went to his office."

"What about the lawyers?" he asks.

"They also arrived and went straight underground to see the prisoner."

"Lawyers, now?" Chong raises an eyebrow.

She confirms, "That's right."

Moving as if the world has stopped, Chong shakes his head and says, "Make these copies. We have a long day ahead of us."

In the basement cell, the atmosphere becomes tense when Hui and the two lawyers enter the room known as the "lawyer's aquarium." Encased in glass, the room offers auditory privacy. The police have visual control of the exterior, but its design ensures that the detainee can talk in peace. Lawyers always place prisoners with their backs to the observation corridor.

The lawyer who met with Hui the day before casts an appraising glance at the prisoner, noting the radical change in his behaviour. Hui looks to have withered overnight, appearing to have lost weight in a few hours.

Sitting with his hands cuffed to the table, Hui avoids the lawyers' eyes.

"Are you okay? Did you eat?" the lawyer asks, worried.

"Yes, I'm fine. They gave me coffee this morning," Hui murmurs, raising his eyes to meet those of his defenders. "What's my next move?"

"Remain silent. Don't answer questions," advises the lawyer. "If they ask something basic, like about your family or identity, whisper it to me first. I will guide you on whether to respond. You understand?"

Hui nods, his voice inaudible. "Yes, I do."

"It's almost 8:00," continues the lawyer. "They will come and get you soon. I'll be by your side. Don't worry."

The other silent lawyer continues to quietly observe and take notes on the conversation.

Gathering his courage, Hui lifts his chin and stares at the lawyer, seeking answers. "What's next?"

The lawyer says, "They'll try to extend your pretrial detention. Especially since you'll be answering their questions this time."

Hui's eyes close in anxiety. "Am I staying here?"

The lawyer shakes his head. "No. Regardless of your cooperation today, they are going to transfer you to one prison around the city. Expect another round of interrogations in the next forty-eight to seventy-two hours. They are racing to gather more evidence."

"Hmm..." Hui's voice trails off, reflecting his inner turmoil.

The lawyer approaches with urgency in his voice. "Look, Hui, it's simple. Are you innocent or not?"

Surprised by the question, Hui's eyes dart between the two lawyers, uncertainty clouding his expression.

The lawyer softens the issue, placing his hand on the table for emphasis. "You don't need to tell me. My job is to defend you, not seek the truth." The other lawyer nods, reinforcing the sentiment.

The unmistakable sound of police boots interrupts the conversation. Two uniformed police officers knock on the glass door, signalling to Hui that the time to leave has arrived. The officers remove Hui's handcuffs from the table and handcuff him again, this time with his hands behind his back. He stands up, his face showing defeat. The lawyers follow the trio to the elevator. The only sound in the hallway is the non-stop noise of fluorescent lights. Upon reaching the ground floor, the elevator door opens, leading them to aquarium two.

Detective Chong and the clerk are already inside preparing for the interrogation. As the others enter, he recognizes the same lawyers who represented Wang. The chief lawyer and Hui take their places while the second lawyer stands behind Hui. The clerk is ready in front of the computer and waits for the questions to begin.

As Chong adjusts in his seat, he gestures for credentials. The lawyers hand over their IDs, their eyes scanning the room, settling on the small camera on a tripod in the room's corner. The red light flashes, signalling that the recording has started.

Detective Chong fixes his gaze on Hui, his voice firm. "Let's begin. State your full name, social identification, occupation, and current address."

* * *

Across town, Wang's footsteps echo as he enters the office at 7:30 in the morning. The memory of the interrogation presses hard on him, but his lawyer's reassuring voice still repeats in his ears: "Don't worry."

Inside the office, he tries to release his frustration, but he holds back. On the surface, he maintains an image of calm. With measured movements, he takes out his cellphone and dials Kung Wu, who answers after a few rings.

"Kung, where have you been? Why haven't you returned my calls?"

In a calm voice, Kung Wu explains, "I took a day off yesterday. I took the family to Jinshan City Sand Beach."

Wang's voice becomes cold. "You were to inform me about the outcome of the meeting."

Kung Wu hesitates. "I didn't call you because no decision has been made."

Wang's frustration bubbles. "Waiting won't help, Kung. I have to send an order tomorrow. Everything is okay, documented, sealed, and ready to be loaded," declares Wang.

Kung Wu's response is quick: "That's risky. It'll only make things more complicated."

Wang retorts, "Nobody tells me what I can or can't do. It seems like you've forgotten your place."

Trying to act without provocation, Kung Wu warns, "Consider the current situation, especially with your manager now in custody. Are you aware of the allegations?"

The weight of Kung Wu's words does nothing to quell Wang's resolve. "This shipment is crucial, Kung. There is a significant amount at stake."

Kung Wu persists. "Wait until we hear from the Triad. If something happens to the cargo again, the spotlight will be on us, and we won't be able to manage it."

"We'll see about that." Wang's icy voice tries to intimidate Kung Wu. "Meeting tonight at 7 p.m. Same hotel, same hall. Make sure all the leaders are there." He cuts off the call.

Wang's secretary enters the room. "Good morning, boss. You're here early. Just so you know, there are no meetings scheduled for today."

Wang's response is a sharp look, so piercing it might as well have been a dagger thrown at her. Feeling the storm brewing, she retreats, muttering, "If you need anything, just let me know." She closes the door behind her.

After a moment of contemplation, Wang opens the door and instructs her with a clipped tone in his voice, "Reserve the room for 7 p.m. in the same place we used last time. We need seats for five people. Once confirmed, send a message to me with the details. I need to leave now."

She nods, her voice steady despite the tension. "Understood, sir."

Wang leaves Warehouse #1 and heads toward the parking lot. Several employees greet him, smiling. When they no longer see him, they gossip. The topic of the day is Hui's arrest. One of them says he would confirm if the boss went to get the car.

The employee leaves the warehouse and, on the sidewalk, sees Wang entering the parking lot. He returns to the warehouse and informs the other employees that he has already left. The concentration on speculation becomes greater. One of them goes up to the secretary's room and opens the door, demanding, "Why was Hui arrested?"

Surprised by the question, she doesn't understand and asks him to repeat it.

The employee asks again, and the secretary, who was standing, falls back into her chair gasping, "You're kidding."

"Don't you watch television?"

"Yesterday I went out drinking with some friends, and when I got home, I fell into bed."

"Did the boss say anything?" he asks.

"The same as always. Are you sure about that?" The secretary is in total disbelief.

"Of course, it's on television; they didn't give his name, but they said it's the manager of Warehouses One and Two. There will be a press conference and they will broadcast it on television."

"Why was he arrested?" she asks.

"They're saying he killed Wonjy's wife and daughter."

She almost faints, and the Warehouse #1 employee rushes to help.

"You know nothing? If it's true, the police will soon come here to take our statements," he says as he hands her a glass of water.

After a few minutes, feeling a little better, she pulls herself together and tells him to stop gossiping and go back to work. She says that the boss will be back soon.

The employee closes the door and runs downstairs and tells the other employees that Wang is returning.

The secretary pauses, lost in thought. Her co-worker's words resonate with her. She remembers that about a week ago, she witnessed a strange fight between Hui and Wang. They didn't notice her when she heard snippets of the conversation. Wang's voice was unmistakable, demanding: "Is everything clear? Did you bring the car?"

Reflecting on these words, the other voice echoes in her memory, with a reassuring response from Hui: "Everything is in order, boss. I kept the 'straps' because we might need them someday." And then Wang, pressing even harder, "Is it all clean?"

She did not understand what they were saying, but thinking it wasn't for her ears, she grabbed her belongings and left, feeling that she had intruded on a confidential matter. Trying to ignore this, she spent time with the warehouse workers, laughing and talking. When she returned to the office, she greeted Wang and Hui, acting as if nothing had happened.

Remembering what Wang asked of her, she takes a deep breath and begins searching her notebook for the details of her latest hotel reservation. After reserving it again, she sends the confirmation message to Wang's cellphone. Thinking about everything that was said to her today, she writes, *I have a throbbing headache. I won't be able to work today.* She takes her bag, locks the office, and leaves.

On the way to the bus stop, the word "straps" keeps tormenting her. Where had she heard that expression before? Determined to find out what is happening, she decides to ask her friends about it as soon as she arrives at her apartment.

* * *

In the new apartment, the smell of perfect coffee fills the air, all thanks to Rachel. She outdid herself by preparing fried eggs, crispy bacon, fried steaks, buttery boiled potatoes with chives, and toasted bread, which all now sit perfectly on the table. It's hard to believe she did all this herself.

"I've been wanting a breakfast like this for a long time! Rachel, you've made my day," David exclaims as he takes another bite of bacon.

Tyler raises an eyebrow, sipping his black coffee. "When did you go to culinary school, Chef Rachel?"

Rachel laughs, her eyes bright. "Thanks, Tyler."

The mood changes when Tyler asks the two friends, "So, what's the plan for today?"

"I was thinking about going to visit Boss Bo," David suggests.

Tyler takes another sip of coffee and looks at Rachel.

"You know…" Rachel says, pulling her phone closer to her, "I read the news this morning. There will be a police force press conference. Since we are involved in Michael's disappearance and David's attempted murder, I believe we'll get an answer soon. We shouldn't contact them. I'm sorry we have to wait, but in our line of work, patience is key."

David's expression hardens. "Isn't there something we can do?"

Tyler looks at him. "Of course not, David. We don't have all the information. Remember what Chong said that night at the bar? He asked us to stay out of this and trust him."

David's voice rises in frustration. "So what? Am I supposed to just sit here and do nothing and let strangers take care of this?"

Rachel's voice softens. "He told us yesterday to stay calm. He promised to keep us informed."

David explodes. "I don't know if I can trust someone I don't know. Let him take care of everything?" Without waiting for a response from his companions, he gets up from the table, leaving breakfast, and disappears into his room, closing the door.

A tense silence follows. The situation is delicate and weighs on the two friends who remain at the table.

Rachel sighs, pushing her plate away for a moment, and looks at Tyler. "Honestly, I wish I could turn into a little ant and sneak into that interrogation room." She smiles, but sadness is in her eyes. She goes back to having her breakfast.

Tyler just nods and puts a forkful of potatoes in his mouth.

41

The Balance in the Right Slaughter

Detective Chong hears his own loud voice, making him try harder to control himself. His face is a mix of frustration and anger. "You're pushing me to the limit!" he explodes at the manager. Hui looks defeated, with his head down, trying to find solace within himself. He takes a deep, shaky breath, exhaling, wondering how to escape the one in this room.

Next to Hui is his lawyer, who stands up. "This is not right!" he screams. "You are trying to intimidate my client. You know very well that he doesn't have to answer if he doesn't want to!"

Chong, frustrated, ignores the lawyer's protests. "Write this down," he instructs the clerk. "The prisoner refuses to cooperate."

The lawyer's voice now has a disapproving tone. "You're overstepping your bounds, Detective. I'm going to make sure this interrogation isn't valid. You can't just force a prisoner to talk. I'm going to have this reviewed by the end of the day."

München enters the room, calling his partner. "Chong," he says as if nothing is happening, "a word?"

In a flurry of chaos, Chong knocks over a chair as he stands up. Without bothering to pick it up, he leaves with one last furious pound on the door. The clerk sighs and puts the chair back in place.

Once in the hallway, Chong vents to München. "He won't talk! The lawyers guiding him well. He answers all questions with silence or 'no comment.'"

München places a reassuring hand on Chong's shoulder. "Take a deep breath. Calm down. I'll take care of it from here. Now it's my turn."

Chong, although still upset, agrees and walks away. As he enters the observatory #2, he gives München a half-smile, thanking him for his help.

München enters the interrogation room, looking around, and introduces himself. Hui doesn't meet his gaze, but the lawyers introduce themselves. München's eyes stop on Hui, studying the collapsed body of a broken man.

The lawyers take advantage of the break in the interrogation and start talking to each other. One of them makes notes with codes on a pad of paper and shows it to the other.

München looks at the clock. The hands confirm it's almost 11:00 in the morning. A silence settles in the room when he realizes Chong spent two-and-a-half hours in exhaustive interrogation and got zero answers.

Taking a deep breath, he begins. "Hui, when I put those handcuffs on you in your house, you told me you knew why. This, now, is your chance. Your lawyer's job is to defend you, of course, but I'm here seeking the same thing—the truth. If you're innocent, help us find out who isn't. And if someone is pressuring you to stay silent, let me know. We'll keep you safe, I guarantee."

Hui raises his head as if looking for something and fixes his gaze on München. For the first time in hours, there's a flicker of emotion in his eyes, a hint of something other than turmoil and despair.

München understands the look. Those eyes, moist and restless, betray a storm of internal thoughts. Something has changed in Hui.

The lawyer, experienced and always attentive, intervenes. "Detective, you're trying to plant ideas in my client's head," he snaps. "He is silent because he had no part in any of this. Without a shred of evidence, you've arrested and brought him here. As soon as you have something concrete, perhaps you can bring him back, but today I will work to get him out of this unfounded preventive detention."

However, München's gaze does not move away from Hui's. Behind those eyes, he sees a plea, a silent cry for help. He wants to speak, but something, or someone, is stopping him.

Detective Chong presses his face against the glass of the observatory, narrowing his eyes when he hears the lawyers will try to get Hui bail. Frustration bubbles inside him; he hates seeing people gaming the system, especially when it means the guilty go free. The idea of standing still, defenceless against a rigged system, sickens him. He rushes to Boss Bo's office with this new urgency, not giving Bo's secretary a chance to announce him.

As he enters, he pleads, "Boss, I need your help."

Boss Bo looks up, a serene contrast to Chong's frantic demeanour. "I did what I could, Chong. Now is not the right time. I am waiting for the representative from the Ministry of Justice, together with the US and UK authorities."

Chong's eyes move in confusion. "Wait, what? Why?"

Bo sighs. "You wasted a lot of time, Chong. A task force is being created, with the help of intel, to investigate Michael Wen Akimitsu's disappearance."

Chong's voice is full of disbelief. "Did you agree to this?"

Bo's answer is sharp. "It wasn't a request. The directive came from above." He points his finger at the sky and his voice takes on a mocking tone. "We have no other way. *Order who can, obeys who has a sense.*"

The weight of the situation seems to hit Bo. He sinks into his chair, closes his eyes, and pinches the bridge of his nose, as he was once taught to make the stress go away. Chong understands the signal and knows that this movement shows that the person is full of information and tries to prevent it from penetrating his mind as well.

Witnessing the tension in the room, the secretary takes a glass of water, places it in front of Boss Bo, and leaves, closing the door.

Chong's voice shakes with anger. "I will not give up on this investigation," he says, shaking his head.

Boss Bo meets Chong's gaze with a sad expression. "We have no choice. The story has spread across the international media. It is beyond our control."

Chong's face reveals suspicion. "Did David Ho cause this?"

Bo responds, "Yes," as he looks through the papers on his desk. He selects one and hands it to Chong. As Chong reads the document, he sits in the chair across from Bo, handing it back.

After a silence, Chong speaks: "I understand, but before we hand over the investigation to them, I have one last request."

Bo raises an eyebrow. "Continue."

"We are requesting to extend the temporary detention for another five days," says Chong. "This will prevent their access to the prisoner. They will need to justify their actions to a judge to gain full custody of Hui. Even with intel's influence, this will take a few days."

Bo agrees. "It's a shrewd move. I will contact the judge. Stick around."

Chong gets up. "There's no way around it. I'm going to go to court now. Call me, and I'll get the provisional warrant from the judge. We cannot allow delays." With a curt nod of gratitude, he rushes out of the office.

Meanwhile, in the interrogation room, debates continue over Hui's right to remain silent. München adopts the assertive tone of a sports commentator, addressing the defence team. "Anyway, we are going to transfer you to the penitentiary today. We will inform you about scheduling a new interrogation session in two days."

The chief defence lawyer stands up while his colleague puts his belongings in a folder.

Two police officers who were at the observatory arrive in the room to escort Hui. One of them informs München, "We're taking him back to the cell in the basement."

"Just a moment," the lead defence lawyer interrupts as he watches the officers take Hui away. "I insist on conducting a forensic examination of his body before sending him to the penitentiary," he declares.

München, already on his way out, says over his shoulder, "I will follow all standard procedures."

Hui appears panicked, looking around as if looking for an escape. Noticing this, one of his lawyers approaches, trying to comfort him. "It's okay. Just remember, you're going to the waiting area now. Stay calm."

With those words, Hui seems to find some calm and shakes his head as he continues on his way, showing no resistance.

Walking alongside the other defence lawyer, München expresses his concerns. "If he remains silent, it will not end well, as the guilt becomes greater."

The lawyer shrugs. "It's his choice." Diverting the path, he joins his colleague.

München says goodbye, bowing in acknowledgement, and goes up the stairs toward Detective Chong's office.

The lawyers enter the elevator, the hum of the machines filling the brief silence between them. When the doors to the third sub-level basement open, they find themselves in a hallway with countless LED lights. On this floor, along the corridor, are three rooms with walls prepared in glass. The so-called "private aquariums" are closed spaces where no whisper escapes. Inside one of them, they see Hui, his eyes fixed on theirs. Entering the room, the lawyers calm Hui down. "You did well. Just stay strong and stay still," says one of the lawyers.

Hui gives a weak nod in agreement.

"It will be today or tomorrow that they will transfer you. As soon as I resolve everything with a judge friend of ours, we will come by again and discuss our next steps," says the other lawyer.

Gratitude is in his eyes, and Hui bows in thanks. With parting words, the lawyers leave the room, and the guards guide Hui to his temporary cell.

* * *

München runs toward Detective Chong's office, his footsteps echoing in the silent hallway. As he approaches the entrance, the secretary intercepts him. "He's not here," she says, her voice full of urgency. "Detective Chong went to see the superintendent."

Taking a deep breath to alleviate his racing heart, München heads straight to the superintendent's office, trying to maintain an air of calm. Once there, he approaches the boss's secretary with a questioning look. Without waiting for München to ask, she tells him, "Chong went to court."

As he processes the information, a variety of conversations catch his attention. The Beijing delegation, led by an adviser to the Minister of Justice, enters the superintendent's office. Bo's secretary then enters with the rest of the guests. Then the personal security guards and secretaries of the respective authorities close the glass door behind them.

München, with his instincts on alert, steps back, pressing himself against the files, hoping to blend into the shadows. He can't help but take in the sight before him. Two tall, blond men in US Army uniforms dominate the scene, while two others, a man and a redheaded woman, chat with two Shanghai intel police officers. In the hallway, three well-dressed men and two women in smart business attire await orders, their presence adding to the cramped feeling of the space.

Holding back a laugh, München can't help but find the scene before him a little amusing. The room, already small, now seems almost packed with the six sizable men. At that moment, the secretary, with a grace that contrasts with the scene, gets up from her chair and offers in a gentle tone: "Would anyone like a drink?" Polite refusals and soft murmurs of gratitude fill the room.

Looking around, München feels like he is being watched. Turning to the files in the room, one of the intel officers' gazes becomes more intense. A moment of recognition in the officer's eyes appears before he breaks away from the group and heads toward München. With a friendly smile, he pulls München into a heartfelt hug.

Matching the officer's warm demeanour, München smiles and jokes in Mandarin, "Who are the foreigners?"

The words scare the foreigners, who look in their direction. Surprise also overtakes München. He hears the guests speaking perfect Mandarin.

Feeling a hint of embarrassment, the officer next to München rushes to defuse the situation, introducing the newcomer as the head of operations for the Shanghai police. Nods and greetings echo around the room as everyone acknowledges the introduction.

München, with an awkward smile, pulls the intel officer into the corridor, far away from the curious eyes and ears of the entourage. The joy disappears when he asks, "What's going on?"

The officer raises an eyebrow. "Don't you know?"

München's heart races, sensing something is wrong. "No. What happened?" he asks, nervousness in his voice.

The intelligence officer's voice drops. His expression is serious. "A task force from the US and England is here because of Michael Wen Akimitsu's disappearance and David Ho being shot."

It feels like someone slapped München in the face. "What?" His voice escapes, showing his discomfort.

"Yes," the officer continues, nodding to a figure in the distance. "That man over there with Chief Bo is an adviser to the Minister of Justice. The governments made a deal."

Feeling as if he is out of breath, München staggers, resting his hand on the wall for support. "This isn't right. We're close … so close to ending this."

The agent claps a reassuring hand on München's shoulder. "Whether it's right or wrong for your team, we have to come together now." With that, he returns to the room, switching to fluent English as he talks to the officers.

München, head of operations, wavers a bit, disappointment weighing on him. He sends a quick message to Detective Chong: *Call me ASAP.*

A quick response emerges, the detective's urgency clear: *Take Hui to prison. Now!*

Looking at his watch, München notes the time: twelve o'clock sharp. He rushes to the operations centre. Upon arrival, two police officers greet him. Without hesitation, he summons them: "Call everyone back, whether they're out for lunch or on street duty. We've got work to do."

* * *

At the apartment, Wang gets out of the shower. The smell of a musky cologne fills the air as he applies it to damp skin. His mind races, anticipating the next meeting with the leaders tonight.

The soft ring of his phone breaks the silence. Searching, he finds a message from his secretary: *All booked.* He gives a brief nod and a fleeting smile.

As Wang examines the expensive collection of hanging suits, he debates which one will exude power and control for tonight's meeting. Another cellphone alert catches his attention. He scans the text, narrowing his eyes. In a slow, deliberate voice, he murmurs, "So he chose silence. Perfect."

Seeking reassurance, he types back, *Any other problems?* No response. The discomfort affects him. He sends another message, and nothing is returned.

Restlessness overcomes him. Wang walks to the window and lets the sight of the beautiful Huangpu River calm his heart. He turns to the dining room, looking in the full-length mirror. In his chosen attire, he sees his reflection as the powerful figure he presents, until something strange happens. The reflection moves. The earlier scene of Wang looking at the river replaces the confident image.

As the boundaries between reality and illusion fade, Wang interrogates the character in the eerie silence of the room.

Wang's gaze pierces the mirror. A malevolent smile plays across his mouth. "See how simple it was to sort things out?" he teases.

But his reflection isn't imitating him. Instead, he remains rigid, captivated by the haunting allure of the river image.

"You are a fool if you believe I would dance to your tune," Wang sneers, his eyes cold and unyielding, defying the image.

The reflection, still and separate from him, responds without turning. "Do you think we resolved everything? You are blind to the obvious."

A hint of panic invades Wang's composure. He runs his agitated fingers through his hair. The figure in the mirror remains calm. "Do you think I wouldn't know how to handle the situation?"

The image smiles. "Don't forget that he has an ace up his sleeve," he warns, turning his back to Wang in a show of disdain.

"He is silenced and will remain so," Wang says, his voice full of menace. The reflection, with a smile, turns to look at Wang. "For how long?"

With a wry laugh, Wang growls, "You'd do anything to be in my shoes. But you're just a shadow." He finishes and walks away toward the bedroom.

A ring from his cellphone makes him stop. The message says, *No problem. Authorities will transfer him to prison. I believe tomorrow, don't worry.*

Wang closes his cellphone and puts it in his suit pocket. He massages his sore neck, letting out a tired yawn. Taking the lighter from his suit's inner pocket, he lights a cigarette, smoke swirling around him.

He returns to the dining room, standing in front of the mirror that now shows no reflection. Smirking, Wang scoffs. "I've said it before, and I'll say it again, no problem."

From the depths of the mirror, a voice murmurs, "Do you think it's over yet?"

Wang, unfazed, retorts, "I do and undo whatever I want. And now I have a more serious matter to attend to. Tonight's meeting will put an end to Hui's affairs for the last time. You were no help at all."

Wang's reflection, with its sinister gaze, is back, but Wang doesn't let that intimidate him. He turns around, his shoes clicking as he heads for the private elevator.

Upon entering the underground garage, Wang's eyes fall on the driver standing next to the car, a patient figure. "Let's go to the port administration," Wang orders, his voice full of authority.

As the car glides through the city, Wang's thoughts turn to Rachel. On impulse, he dials her number. The phone rings, and then her voice, a slight contrast to the weight of the day, makes him forget his problems.

"Shall we have dinner tomorrow? It's going to be an important day for me."

A brief hesitation on the other end, then Rachel responds without gusto, "I would like to go, but the hospital scheduled David for an appointment and physiotherapy. We don't know what time it will end." An intelligent answer, created on the spot, especially since today is only Wednesday and the appointment is on Friday.

Wang's disappointment is overwhelming, but he hides it well. "Okay. Just call me when you're free," he replies, trying to keep his tone calm.

"Sure," Rachel murmurs, the relief clear, before ending the call.

*   *   *

Detective Chong opens the door to his office in the police building, the weight of the morning lying heavy on his shoulders. The clock strikes 2:00 p.m., and the air carries a whisper of victory. The judge responds and grants the provisional arrest warrant extended for another five days.

Then, just as he processes this, his secretary approaches, warning him, "Don't forget that you must be at the intelligence building at 5 p.m. Direct orders from the superintendent."

He gives her a tired look, a half-sigh escaping his lips, but says nothing. Handing her a crumpled white envelope, he instructs, "Three copies of the warrant are here. Take them to Chief Bo's office and make sure they're sent to the proper authorities by the end of the day."

She nods her head, grabbing the envelope and leaving the room as quickly as she came.

Sitting on the old armchair, Chong tries to accommodate himself on the worn cushion, a mischievous smile appearing on his lips. *We've got five more days,* he thinks, *that's all I'll need.*

The door opens, and München stumbles in, panting. "We achieve it?" His voice is choking.

"Five more days," Chong repeats.

Relief and anxiety appear in equal measure on München's face. "I sent him to the prison with twice the usual guards," he says with pride in his voice.

Chong leans back, closes his eyes for a second, and lets out a deep, tired sigh. "Nice job."

München swallows hard and asks, "Did you know about the task force that arrived here today?"

Chong takes a deep breath, showing his tiredness. "I only heard about them when I met with Bo about the warrant."

München's expression exposes his frustration. "I'm… I'm tired of these betrayals," he confesses.

Chong fixes him with a piercing gaze, his tone firm but comforting. "Five days, München. He's locked up. Trust me, these guys will get down on their knees for us at the end of this."

München's face breaks into a wide smile. "Ah! I remembered. Something big happened. You should watch the video of the interrogation."

Chong's attention is immediate.

"Hui was silent with you for two and a half hours, but when I spoke to him, the look he gave me … it was like he was trying to tell me something. Then the lawyers intervened, and he fell silent again."

"What did you say to him?"

"I told him he would only be safe with us. If anyone is after him, we will protect him."

Chong's interest piques. "What time did you transfer him? Which prison did you send him to?"

Looking at the wall clock, München reports, "He must have arrived by now. It was around 1:30 p.m. when the van left for Qingpu Municipal Prison in Shanghai. After your message, I made things happen as quickly as possible."

"Half an hour trip," Chong mutters, thinking aloud. "Yeah, that sounds about right. They are processing him right now. Introduction, shower, change of clothes, paperwork. All of that will take another hour and a half. I think I'll go over there. Try to talk to him."

"Wait a minute, let's go a little later," suggests München, approaching the exit.

Chong raises an eyebrow. "Why?"

"We have that meeting at 5 p.m. in the intelligence building. There's no way around it," München retorts, opening the door.

Frustration clear, Chong slams his hand on the table. "Okay, but will you come with me later?"

Detective Chong's phone vibrates. He checks the message, and it's from Rachel: *Do you have any updates? Wang called early for dinner tomorrow. I declined.*

Chong's gaze follows München, who is already halfway across the room.

Typing, Chong replies, *We can talk tonight, weather permitting. Otherwise, tomorrow. I'll keep you posted.*

*　*　*

The trio leaves the apartment to take a walk along the Bund, where the mighty Huangpu River stretches before them. The place has a stunning view, but David seems lost in his own world. Meanwhile, Tyler is in full "tourist mode," taking photos with strangers, Rachel, or even just himself.

Tyler looks at David and asks, "Do you feel any better?"

With a sigh, David responds, "Yes, but it's the constant anxiety and fear that are consuming me. I feel like in the last few days I've aged decades." His gaze turns to the river's flow.

Taking a break from walking, they stop to enjoy the view.

"Do you remember the London police, the ones from the warehouse case I told you about? They might reopen the case, and it looks like things might move forward." Tyler shares the important news and takes a selfie.

"That's great news!" Rachel exclaims.

"As soon as this mess is over, we're going home," Tyler states, looking at the two of them.

David counters, stating that he just needs to discover Michael's whereabouts.

"What I meant was that we should wait until he sorts everything out, causing no problems," Tyler emphasizes.

Rachel agrees. "That's fine with me."

The trio sits on one of the river benches. Staying silent, they look at the sights and sounds of the busy promenade.

Breaking the silence, Rachel says, "I should call Detective Chong."

David, ever perceptive, suggests, "Just send a message."

As if on cue, Rachel's phone rings. It's Wang, suggesting dinner the next night. She comes up with an excuse and he understands.

David's face turns red with anger. "If he laid a hand on Michael, I swear I'll finish him."

"Take a deep breath," Rachel says. "Things may not be as they seem. We should wait for the detective to explain."

David's mind races. His thoughts are a whirlwind, making him oblivious to Rachel's words.

Tyler exchanges a knowing look with Rachel, and she shakes her head. She picks up her phone and types a message to the detective, who responds.

Tyler leans in. "What did he say?"

"There might be some updates tonight," she relays, shooting a worried look at David.

The trio soon return to the car, with David at the wheel. As they drive through the streets toward the apartment, Rachel's phone vibrates. She answers, listening. After a moment, she hangs up, tears glistening in her eyes.

David feels the change. "Rachel, what happened?"

She takes a shuddering breath. "Alex… he's gone."

David leans over, giving her arm a reassuring squeeze. "I'm sorry. The final stages of the disease are relentless."

Tyler, lost in thought, mutters, "I hope he's at peace, even though part of me believes he's in hell."

Wiping away tears, Rachel adds, "No matter what, he was there when I needed help."

David's voice is firm, echoing a protective instinct: "You have a big heart, Rachel. Just… be careful who you let in."

As David manoeuvres the car into the building's garage, a silence surrounds them, each absorbed in their own thoughts.

42

"Confession Is What You Believe or What You Know"

There's chaos at the intelligence nerve centre in Shanghai, and extra police are being deployed that night. Journalists and reporters spread the news of the arrival of the Minister of Justice's advisers. Speculations are running rampant in the media because of the mysterious purpose of the visit.

Superintendent Bo, along with other high-ranking officials, has received instructions to organize a press conference that day or the next in order to dispel rumours and maintain calm in the city.

At the huge table in the meeting room are twelve chairs, occupied by four foreign police officers, the representative of the Ministry of Justice, two intel agents, Superintendent Bo, the intel deputy, Detectives Chong, and München, and in the final chair is the director general of Shanghai intelligence, Mr. Sung Wenghu.

The detectives stop talking and examine the scene at the table. Conversations flow and foreign officials seem almost fluent in Mandarin. Eyebrows raised; the detectives exchange a quick glance.

Chong, leaning toward München, whispers, "Do you speak English?"

München smiles. "A little. You?"

"About the same."

A suppressed laugh escapes them both.

When Superintendent Bo stands up, the room falls silent. His presence draws everyone's attention. He greets the participants, announcing each one's name. According to protocol, upon being introduced by Chief Bo, each individual will stand up and bow, regarding the others.

The American and British officers play their roles, expressing themselves in near-perfect Mandarin.

Under his breath, Chong comments to München, "They have good manners."

München kicks Chong in the foot, urging him to restrain his comments.

At the centre of attention, the representative of the Ministry of Justice begins a detailed speech. He outlines the collaboration agreement reached to investigate the mysterious disappearance of the British citizen Michael Wen Akimitsu. They intentionally leave out David's name. The speech emphasizes sympathizing nations and the urgency of a quick resolution of the matter.

When the ministry representative finishes speaking, the room explodes into applause. Superintendent Bo, taking advantage of the moment, stands up again and greets Detectives Chong and München by name. As the two detectives stand up, Bo praises them, noting their incomparable dedication and readiness to help in any situation. He reports on changes in the intelligence unit in Shanghai to facilitate the new investigation.

The room resounds with another round of applause. Both Chief Bo and the minister's representative then arise and move to an adjacent room to talk. Director Sung, following suit, encourages attendees to join them, mentioning a modest offering of tea, juices, and light drinks awaiting them in the next room.

In a low voice, München tells Chong, "Go away now; I'm sure I can handle the situation."

Chong checks his wristwatch and notes the time: 6:15 p.m. He nods to München. "I plan to be back by 10 p.m. Keep your phone nearby; I might need your help."

"Understood," München replies, watching Chong leave unnoticed through another door.

The participants, absorbed in their conversations and drinks, don't notice Chong's departure. München integrates with the foreign officials, informing them of recent updates on the investigation.

Upon noticing Chong's absence, Boss Bo approaches München with a questioning look. "Where did Chong go?"

München replies, "He had an urgent matter to attend to, but he said he would be back soon."

Boss Bo's eyes narrow. Maintaining his composure, he then adds, "Tell him to call me."

"I'll let him know, boss," München guarantees.

Chong leaves the intelligence building, driving at high speed. His thoughts turn to the interrogation room and Hui's evasive gaze. The detective believes he knows a lot but cannot speak and concludes the lawyers instructed the man to be silent.

As he concentrates on his analysis, his cellphone rings, interrupting his thoughts. He parks the car on the side of the highway and checks the message: *Forensic examination completed. Traces of blood found in the back seat.*

A rush of adrenaline runs through Chong. With fists clenched, he pounds the steering wheel in triumph, exclaiming, "This is it! This is what I've been waiting for!"

Reinvigorated by the news, he returns to the highway, driving his car at a higher-than-normal speed, and arrives at his destination five minutes before his estimate.

Upon arriving at the penitentiary, Chong passes through the layers of security. His badge helps him pass the rigorous protocols.

Inside, the authorities have placed Hui in a protective cell, sharing the space with two other inmates awaiting trial. The trio exchanges stories, but Hui is not talkative. However, just as Hui is coming to terms with his new reality, the metallic jingling of a guard's keys echoes through the hallway.

A guard stops in front of the cell with his eyes fixed on Hui.

"You have a visitor."

Hui gets up, his eyes shining with anticipation of getting out of there. The cold steel door opens, and the manager enters the bright hallway. He obeys the prison guard and turns away, pressing his face against the icy wall, his hands finding their way behind his back. Everyone hears the familiar click of handcuffs.

The agent, confident that everything is in order, locks the cell. In the corridor where they are located, five inmates accompanied by two police officers walk in a line. It's dinner time, and the guards are taking the inmates to the cafeteria.

Hui, with his back turned, does not see the prisoners passing by him. The guard finishes locking the cell, and when he turns around, he sees one prisoner in line throw himself at the manager, burying a knife in his back. With no momentary action, he witnesses Hui being stabbed again.

The prison officer attacks the prisoner, throwing his body at him. The prisoner continues stabbing Hui until the officer overpowers him, but it's too late.

Hui is on his back on the ground, totally covered in blood.

The other two guards, threatening the four inmates with clubs, dominate the situation. Screams and more screams call other prison officers, who activate the prison sirens.

The overpowered prisoner shouts to Hui, "That's what you deserve for killing women and children."

Hui breathes hard, expelling blood from his mouth.

Several correction officers arrive in the hallway and take him away to the infirmary. Hui screams in pain.

Someone informs Detective Chong about the incident and explains they will place the inmate in an ambulance. Agitated, he shouts, "The prisoner is mine!" The guards hear the detective and direct him to the vehicle, allowing him to enter the ambulance.

Inside, the ambulance has a cold, sterile light. Hui, bloodied and weak, recognizes Detective Chong when he enters. His voice, hoarse with pain, makes a desperate plea: "I don't want to die."

Chong's eyes are wide. "Stay with me! Don't you dare close your eyes!" The ambulance speeds up, the sirens ringing at maximum volume.

A paramedic, with a syringe in his hand, tries to approach Hui, but Chong stops him just as Hui whispers. Leaning over with his cellphone on, Chong strains to hear every word.

"Go to my house," Hui chokes out, pain lacing every word, "My room… under the bed, at my feet." A chilling cough interrupts his speech, with blood staining his lips and splattering onto Chong's face. Chong's heart skips a beat when Hui mumbles, "Pen drive."

Each word seems to come from the depths of Hui's last moments, causing him immeasurable pain.

Once again, the paramedic, desperate, tries to intervene. "Please let me administer the intravenous!"

Chong, his voice filled with a mixture of fury and urgency, retorts, "You are witnessing a confession to a crime! Don't interfere!" He brandishes his phone, which is recording everything.

The paramedic's eyes widen in a mixture of disbelief and horror.

Gathering the last of his strength, Hui continues, his voice hoarse, in a more aggressive tone. "It's all there… Michael, Wonjy, Bohai… dead… thrown into the river… crocodiles… I killed… Wonjy's wife and daughter…" His voice trails off, his breath falters, and his eyes close.

Chong, with his phone still recording, stands frozen, almost in shock. The revelations are devastating. The paramedic, reeling from what he had just heard, sits down, scared, on the floor of the ambulance under the weight of the confession he heard.

In front of the two, Hui's condition worsens minute by minute. His half-closed eyes roll back, and his body convulses, the unmistakable sign of a stroke starting. Amid the growing crisis, Detective Chong, displaying an unnerving calm, leans close to Hui's ear. "Who is behind this, Hui? Give me a name."

In his sitting position, the paramedic cannot hear the detective's whispers, but panic takes over him. Losing control, he crashes into the glass partition, urging the driver to go faster. They are losing Hui.

Panting, Hui whispers back, each word a struggle: "The weapons... on the farm... Wang's fingerprints."

"Where, Hui? Tell me where."

"Yangtze... River... behind the farm... north." With that, Hui's strength diminishes, his eyes close, and his voice is silenced.

Chong straightens and gives a troubled look to the paramedic, who, without warning, moves to Hui's side to check his vitals. Minutes later, the ambulance stops in front of the hospital's emergency entrance, where a team of doctors is already waiting for them.

The back doors open, and the medical team springs into action, transferring Hui to a stretcher. Before the paramedic can get out of the car, Chong stops him, demanding his identification and instructing him to report to the city centre police station the next morning to tell him everything he heard. The nervous paramedic takes the identification necklace off his neck and throws it in Chong's direction, rushing into the hospital.

Leaning against the ambulance, Chong notices Hui's lawyers entering the hospital. He takes a deep breath and enters too, exchanging nods with the lawyers.

A familiar nurse informs him, "We have rushed the patient into surgery."

Grateful, Chong hands her the paramedic's identification, asking her to return it. She takes it and disappears down the hallway.

Leaving the hospital, Chong sees a police car nearby. He approaches and the officers salute. Without saying a word, he settles into the back seat of the police car, lost in Hui's words. After a few moments of reflection, he calls München, informing him of the events. He instructs him to meet him at the downtown hospital now. The detective also asks München to get the keys to Hui's house from the seizure department. Concluding the call, he leans back against the seat and closes his eyes.

"I'll be there in fifteen minutes," responds München, calculating the time from the police department to the hospital.

Inside the police cruiser, Detective Chong has a clear view of the hospital's entrance and the frantic activity of the emergency department. His professional colleagues are nearby, immersed in a silent conversation.

Chong listens to the recording on his phone: "Go home… my room… at the foot of the bed… flash drive." The situation has now changed and requires all of his ability because the case has become more complex.

He notices the hospital entrance swelling with vehicles and people. As he watches, local media vans continue to arrive, reporters spreading out, cameras trained on the entrance, faces eager for a story. Hospital security staff and some police officers struggle to contain the sudden influx, trying to maintain order. He observes two more police cars pulling up, and the hospital security staff push back the press into the garden, creating some breathing space for the hospital.

Chong rolls down the window, gesturing for the two officers next to the squad car to join the others, reinforcing the ranks against the media onslaught.

As he gets out of the car, Chong sees the nurse approaching the crowd of reporters.

"The doctors will hold a press conference as soon as they have updates on the patient's condition," she says in a steady but firm tone.

Mumbling to himself, Chong comments, "I'd love to know who tipped those reporters off."

München arrives, parking his car behind the police car. A quick call about his arrival alerts Chong, who was paying attention to the nurse. The detective hurries and gets into the vehicle.

Surveying the scene, München exclaims, "What the hell happened here?"

"It's crazy." Chong recounts the events at the penitentiary.

München, with raised eyebrows, asks, "And in the ambulance? Did he say anything?"

Chong delivers the chilling confession, his voice firm but filled with the weight of implications.

München, impressed by the revelations, tries to understand what Chong revealed to him. In shock, he sits still, without starting the car.

* * *

Outside the hospital, the atmosphere is full of expectation. Reporters, perched on the garden walls and huddled in their vehicles, await any news.

A reporter confides in a colleague from the same network: "I need to find a bathroom." Walking alone, she heads toward the ambulance parking lot. When she sees a young paramedic cleaning an ambulance, she approaches him. "Excuse me, do you know where the bathroom is?"

He points in the direction and then returns to cleaning.

Her reporter instincts kick in. Observing the environment, she notices that no other ambulances in the vicinity are being cleaned.

"Was this the ambulance that transported the prisoner from the penitentiary?" she probes.

The young man pauses, captivated by her striking appearance. "I can't say anything," he says with a hint of hesitation in his voice.

She smiles with all the charm possible for a woman, her eyes shining with purpose. "Was it you who helped him when he arrived?"

He remains silent. Having finished his cleaning, he closes the back door of the ambulance.

In a last desperate move, she pleads with an angelic face, "Listen, this is my first big story. If I don't get a convincing story for my editor, they won't let me work anymore. I have a mother to take care of."

He seems to falter, and his expression softens. "Look," he says, "I'm a witness. I can't talk until I give my statement to the police."

Seizing the moment, she replies, "Let's make a deal… how about this? We talk now, you give me an exclusive. Tomorrow, you testify. When you leave the deposition, postpone any further interviews for at least two hours. Call me when you're ready to go public, then you can talk to whoever you want."

Without waiting for an answer, she takes out her phone and turns it on.

He looks into her eyes, weighing the risks and rewards of the situation.

She sees that he's going to give in and offers, "I'll pay whatever you want." The desperation in her voice, combined with the allure of money, makes the conflict more interesting.

She continues, "I'll make it worth it. Today or tomorrow, I'll pay you, however much you need."

After a moment that feels like an eternity to her, he asks, "How much?"

She opens her purse, revealing a wad of cash. "I have two thousand with me now. I'll give you three thousand more tomorrow. Is that enough?"

"You promise you won't publish anything until tomorrow?" His voice contains skepticism.

"I promise," she assures.

With a deep exhale, he says, "Okay, I'll take it."

She hands over the two thousand and turns on her cellphone recorder. He tells the harrowing story, detailing every moment, from the prisoner being loaded into the ambulance to the chaotic arrival at the hospital. His voice trembles as he recounts the inmate's chilling confessions about the heinous crimes he committed.

Her heart races with each revelation. Unable to contain herself, she continues, "Did he mention any accomplices? Any other names?"

"No," he replies, shaking his head. "From the way he said it, it sounded like he acted alone, but the genuine shock was when he talked about feeding the bodies to crocodiles."

Her face drains of colour. "How horrible... Are you sure you can't remember the names of the men he mentioned?"

Sitting on the steps of the ambulance, the young paramedic hesitates over his words, trying to remember the details. She watches him, willing him to remember the names.

"Right... I think one name was foreign. Maybe... Wonjy? Yes, and another name, Michael, also sounds foreign. But the third... I can't remember," he admits with frustration in his voice. "The detective recorded everything."

She gives him a triumphant smile and takes a photo of him with her phone. "You just made history. You're going to be famous," she says, her voice full of enthusiasm.

He frowns, a little surprised. "He whispered other things to the detective that I couldn't understand."

With a reassuring pat on his arm, she responds, "It's okay. You gave me a lot of important information." Taking a card out of her shoulder bag, she hands it to him. "Call me when you're ready." Without another word, she runs away.

"Hey! Remember, post nothing until tomorrow!" he calls out to her, chuckling as he watches her figure moving away.

Near the hospital entrance, chaos reigns. Reporters jockey for position, each trying to secure the best point of view. A doctor, looking tired but calm, approaches a set of microphones.

"The surgery, despite being challenging, is a success. We believe that the patient will survive," declares the doctor in a firm voice. "Given the delicate nature of the procedure, I ask everyone's patience. I will provide another update in four hours."

As reporters shout at each other and try to get the scoop, they ask questions. Rushing in, the doctor, accompanied by his team and guarded by police officers, leaves the sounds of reporters' screams behind. Soon realizing that the frenzy has subsided and that they won't get any more information, many journalists abandon the place.

* * *

Whether it's the silence of dawn or the gentle embrace of dusk, the glow of Shanghai's city lights always maintains the energy of Shanghai All Day Post. Day or night, the fast pace remains uninterrupted. Journalists from different shifts, with their eyes reflecting the city's stories, write without noticing the time or the latest news. While an insatiable hunger for stories fuels some, others survive the night by drawing on some invisible reserve. However, among all of them, Zhang Mei Zhi stands out.

Mei Zhi's uncle, the newspaper's driving force, is a visionary man.

"Mei Zhi?" he shouts from his office, calling out to her.

She dreams of one day being editor-in-chief. No task given to her is too big or small, as she sees each one as a stepping stone, an opportunity to learn and grow. Today was no different. While others did not accept that lacklustre assignment at the hospital, the information they received was that a prisoner had been stabbed in the municipal prison, and, almost dead, they took him to the city centre hospital. She dived in headfirst and accepted the request to check it out, and now she has a story that could make headlines in the coming days.

On the warm reddish wood furniture in the meeting room, she sits in front of her uncle, her eyes shining, believing that she has now won the promotion she dreams of. He leans over the papers on the table. He is intrigued by her interview; the witness's account is unbelievable. It sends shivers down his spine. Doubt clouds the director's face as he reads the names that Mei Zhi claims to have uncovered. He believes the story is a total fabrication.

"It's a lie," he insists, questioning the veracity of her explosive story.

Mei Zhi, with the fire of conviction in her eyes, knows better than anyone that everything the paramedic told her is true.

"Alright, you don't believe me? I'm going to take this straight to a TV network. Let's see if they don't buy it and hire me on the spot." Her voice is full of defiance.

He looks at her with a serious glare and orders, "Play me the recording. I only read the description. Please."

She lifts her chin, challenging him. "Sign this first, and I will be the editor-in-chief of this newspaper. After that, you can hear it."

He exhales and coughs. "I can't just do this right now, but listen, if your story is like you say… I promise to think about the next journalism manager position for you. We have three serving in that position; you would be the fourth rounding off the board, and at the first opportunity, I will give you the position you so desire."

With a triumphant smile, she unlocks her phone on the table and presses play. The weight of the words on the recording shows on his face as he listens with attention and amazement. When he sees the paramedic's photograph, his voice shakes with disbelief. "You will win the prize of the year with this report."

Smiling, she puts the phone back in her pocket. "I made a promise to him. We will only publish it after he gives his statement to the police tomorrow morning."

With an ironic smile, he stands up. "You did the right thing. That's what we say."

With panic in her eyes, she stares at her uncle. "Are you going to make me look like a liar? I need to pay him another three thousand for what he told me."

"We need to get the story out now." He moves toward the glass door of his office, his hand resting on the handle.

She interrupts, her voice tinged with panic: "I can't break my word!"

His footsteps echo as he walks toward his desk, determination on his features. "This is front-page material for tomorrow." He picks up his phone, ready to set things in motion.

In desperation, she moves forward, trying to intercept the call, holding her hands over the phone. "Hang on!"

He stares at her, a challenge in his eyes.

"The choice is yours," her uncle's voice challenges. "Become a journalism manager or break your promise."

She hesitates, a storm of emotion welling in her eyes. Seconds pass, and she is unable to understand why her uncle is blackmailing her. She murmurs, "Okay. Write the story," her voice slurring by the decision.

* * *

Wang's footsteps echo in the luxurious hotel lobby, catching the attention of Guowei, who is waiting for him. Kung Wu's security chief bows in a gesture of respect and greets him. "Good evening."

Wang's eyebrows arch, a shadow of discontent crossing his face. "Have you lost your manners? The correct phrase is, 'Good evening, boss,'" he says, his tone exuding authority. "Did you forget your place?"

Guowei, surprised, tries to recalibrate himself, remembering Chief Kung's advice to treat Wang as he always has. "Is something wrong, boss?"

Wang's eyes lock with Guowei's. Deciding he doesn't have the time or patience for a confrontation, Wang walks toward the elevator, giving Guowei a clear signal to stay back, and he does.

Upon exiting the elevator, several security guards in the hallway stand at attention. Each bows to Wang as he passes, their faces etched with silent respect.

Wang enters the hall and is greeted with a colder welcome than usual from the bosses. Something has changed.

Without a preamble, Changpu snaps, "What happened to Hui?"

Guozhi demands, "Why was he arrested?"

Under pressure, Wang sits, noticing that none of the other bosses offer him a drink. Kung Wu steps forward and places a glass of whiskey in front of Wang, then sits down next to him. The gesture does not go unnoticed.

Wang takes a moderate sip and begins. "I have top-notch lawyers for Hui, but they say the situation doesn't look good. He's being implicated in the deaths of Wonjy's wife and daughter."

A collective sigh fills the room, the weight of the revelation clear.

Wang continues, his voice firm, "The lead detective talked to Hui in my office. Hui insisted Wonjy was in Hong Kong, but the detective didn't believe him. I don't know what evidence he could have, if any."

Tense, Huan Zhang's eyes narrow, his voice low. "Are you implicated in this?"

Wang's reaction is immediate, his gaze piercing and cold. "Implicated? Are you insinuating that this bloodshed is on my hands?"

Huan Zhang does not back down, moving forward with raw intensity. "It's not about direct blame, Wang. Think about it. Our guards, our partners, they move under our orders. Everyone here knows that your bond with Hui goes back to childhood times. Hui wouldn't lift a finger unless you wanted it. He has proven his loyalty to you countless times."

Kung Wu's eyes dart from face to face, gauging reactions, reading tension.

Wang's voice brims with incredulity: "So now every action, every decision any of you make, falls on my shoulders?"

Huan Zhang does not back down. "As leader of the Tong, yes. It is your obligation and duty to have this control."

The air becomes thicker with tension. The other bosses realize the volatility of the situation, understanding Zhang's logic but wary of provoking Wang. Changpu, trying to mediate, rubs his forehead.

"Look, Wang, you got him excellent lawyers. That's what matters now. We know the nuances of the system; Hui will be out soon."

Nodding, Guozhi glances at Changpu for solidarity. "Yes, I'm with Changpu on this."

Huan Zhang, however, remains defiant. Looking at Wang, the silent defiance is real.

Wang's voice takes on a chilling calm, his words a veiled threat. "Life becomes short, I don't know if by destiny or fate, for those who choose to be blind to the truth." His eyes fix on Huan Zhang.

A heavy silence covers the room.

Turning to Kung Wu, Wang prods, "What about you? Any accusations to level at me?"

Kung Wu meets Wang's gaze; his mind goes back to the silent conversations with the Triad leaders and one in particular with Huan Zhang after his arrival in Shanghai. Right now, angering Wang is not in his best interest. He believes Wang can eliminate Hui in prison because of the manager's possession of crucial evidence. Redirecting the conversation, he asks, "Why did you call this meeting?"

Wang, ever the strategist, responds, "I would like to hear your opinion, as I will send the new shipment tomorrow."

Kung Wu interrupts him, looking to the chiefs. "The bosses here are not stupid. Everyone at this meeting understands that we are not the decision-makers for the entire Tong. Wang is the representative of our organization and, as we have survival rules in this world, we cannot allow any harm to happen to the affiliates who trust and believe in the structure we have built over these years. Ask your security guards in the hall if they would put the entire Tong organization at risk just to satisfy our desires. Some, afraid of dying, would agree without qualms. The people closest to us would try to talk to us and understand the reason for our attitude."

Guozhi asks, filling his glass with more whiskey, "Why are you giving this speech?"

Wang, huffing in his chair, swallows all the whiskey in his glass.

"Because you forget that a few days ago, we faced the Triad. Do you think they forgot about that?" Kung Wu asks Guozhi, who doesn't respond.

"You were the one who meet them. It's all solved?" Wang again tries to turn the bosses against Kung.

"Yes, and like I told you, I still don't have any answers. They can accept the deal, but they can also disagree and attack us. Think about it, if Triad comes after us, they *will* kill us, and every Tong in Shanghai will disappear. Will you assume this responsibility?" Kung Wu, his face burning with anger, addresses the bosses and gives Wang a withering look.

Silence reigns again at the table.

"They would never attack us. What they gain from us, they don't want to lose," says Wang and drinks, finishing the last drops of whiskey in his glass.

"You don't look the same … that's why they would exterminate us and take over everything. Can't you see that too? Do you confront them and think there will be no response?" shouts Kung Wu to Wang.

"What do you suggest?" Wang asks, staring at Kung. He bites his lips and squeezes his hand, breaking the empty glass.

"Wait for the answer." Kung Wu completes his message, not bothered by the blood running down Wang's hands.

The table bosses, shocked by the scene of Kung Wu screaming and Wang breaking the glass with his hands, see the blood flow and spread across the table. Everyone is quiet, too shocked to move.

Guozhi runs to the bathroom, grabs a towel, and hands it to Wang, who wraps his hand.

Wang's hateful look at Kung Wu is frightening. He gets up from his chair and leaves the room, saying, "Let's do what Kung suggested."

The bosses, surprised by Wang's erratic behaviour, exchange glances but remain silent.

As soon as the door closes behind Wang, Huan Zhang moves fast to lock it. Turning to Kung Wu, his eyes serious, he suggests, "We should get together again somewhere else, just the four of us."

The leaders nod, their mumbled whispers filling the room.

Outside, Wang, with his thoughts in a chaotic whirlwind, heads toward his car parked just outside the hotel door. Slamming the door, he yells to the driver, "Take me to the apartment, now!"

As the city passes by the window, he thinks, *Why don't they trust me? What's going on here?*

Distracted by looking in the rear-view mirror at the expression on Wang's face, the driver misses a signal change and runs a red light, causing Wang to slide forward as the driver applies the brakes.

"Are you trying to kill me? Don't you know how to drive?"

"I'm sorry, sir," the driver murmurs, casting a nervous glance at Wang in the rear-view mirror.

Wang continues, his voice full of disdain, "That idiot Changpu, always competing with me. He's just a damn dog." The driver gives another worried look, feeling the storm brewing in the backseat.

Lost in his own world, Wang murmurs, almost inaudibly, as if he is conversing with some unseen presence.

The sharp ring of his cellphone breaks the tense atmosphere. Looking at the screen, he reads a message from his lawyer and, with a frustrated sigh, mutters, "Just what I needed. Shit like that."

* * *

Detective Chong and Detective München open the door to the manager's residence and head upstairs to the master bedroom. Together, they lift the mattress and, using their combined strength, turn the bed upside down.

"Do you have a screwdriver?" Chong asks, inspecting the construction of the bed.

München fumbles in his pockets and then remembers. "I have this multi-tool wrench on my keychain. It should do the trick." He takes out the tool and hands it over.

Analyzing where the item they are looking for could be, the two detectives unscrew the six legs of the bed. Each leg has a rubber cap at the end, which protects the laminate floor. Once removed, Chong detects something unusual. Inside one leg, there is a hidden flash drive. He holds it up for München to see and then tucks it into the inside pocket of his jacket. München takes photos of the altered leg that hid the USB.

The detectives put the bed back together, ensuring it appears intact. As they leave, Chong locks the front door.

Settling into the driver's seat, Detective München turns the key in the ignition. "And now?"

"Let's go to my office," Chong replies, his face thoughtful.

Chong's phone ringing interrupts the car ride. An emergency room nurse's voice fills the line, updating him on the recent surgery. "Despite its complexity, the operation seems to have been successful. We are optimistic. The next six hours are crucial."

Chong hangs up the call and tells München the news. His hands grip the steering wheel tighter as he speeds up.

Detective Chong and Detective München enter the police station and don't waste a moment as they run up the stairs to their office; they greet their colleagues at their passing with only a nod. The urgency is real. The head of homicide and the director of operations run to the work desk and turn on the computer. Chong hands over the found pen drive and inserts it.

A low growl from Chong's stomach breaks the silence. "Man, I'm starving," he mutters.

"We're going to eat something soon. Let's see what's on this thing first," München says as he accesses the contents of the USB.

They look through the files, and a series of photographs catches their eye. As they scroll through the photos, they piece together the dark story of what happened on the farm, a narrative reinforced by Hui's chilling confession.

The images reveal the interior and exterior of a once-red warehouse. Its interior is a mess: bloodstained clothes discarded on straw on the floor; various documents scattered around, perhaps recoverable with some zooming; some cellphones; and a blood-covered chair. Of all the images, one stands out: three revolvers, the metal of which shines under the camera's flash. Another disturbing image, with no sign of what it could be, is that of a green can with flames. Moving the photos around, they notice a car on a dirt track, recognizing the Audi that Wang drives. München writes down the license plate number to confirm later. Next are photos of the farm's lush green landscape and a dilapidated wooden house next to the road.

Finishing the analysis of the photos, the two detectives sit in heavy silence. The horror that unfolded in that place was notorious and shocked them both.

"Three lives lost there: Michael, Wonjy, and Bohai," Detective Chong whispers, his voice cracking with emotion.

München, with his eyes still fixed on the screen, asks, "Do you know who this Bohai is?"

Shaking his head, Chong replies, "No, but we'll find out."

"The problem is the address of this place. Without knowing, how are we going to get there?"

Chong, deep in thought, looks at the photos, his hunger forgotten. "I'm working on it," he murmurs. His cellphone breaks the contemplative silence.

Boss Bo's voice sounds. "Where are you?"

In a torrent of words, Chong details the visit to the penitentiary, the attempted murder of Hui, and the subsequent events at the hospital.

The Superintendent of the Shanghai Police already has information about what happened when he called Chong. The detective, upon hearing the boss's voice, summarizes that Bo is drunk, a mixture of professional detachment and confused concern.

"I give authorization to Hui's lawyers to take Wang to the hospital. After all, Hui considers him family."

Detective Chong, surprised by this revelation, disappointed and angry, falls silent and a sudden dryness in his throat makes him cough. "Thank you for letting me know," he manages. "I will ensure that we document and deliver our findings and actions to you tomorrow." Chong hangs up the call, his mind racing. He passes his hand over his forehead and eyes, feeling the tension.

After overhearing the conversation, Detective München turns to Chong, his eyebrows furrowed in concern. "What's the next step? You haven't told him everything. This could cause serious problems."

Chong, trying to convey a confidence he no longer feels at that moment, says, "I'm going to write a full report. He'll be in for a surprise when it arrives on his desk tomorrow."

At his desk, Chong examines the discovered images. München, peering over his shoulder, taps the monitor, directing Chong's attention to a specific photograph.

"See that? The can was on fire in an earlier scene, but now? The glow suggests it's full of water."

Chong, ever the investigator, frowns, trying to decipher the subtle details. "Every image has a narrative. What is the message behind this one?"

München is confused. He shakes his head and doesn't respond.

Chong goes back to the task at hand, categorizing the images. He pauses again at the can of water, eyes fixed on the image, trying to understand. "Why this photo? Every image captured has a reason. What's missing here?"

München, eyes still glued to the screen, shrugs.

Chong stands up, breaking the trance state the two detectives had fallen into. "We can't afford to waste any more time," he declares. "Who are your two best men on surveillance?"

München doesn't hesitate. "Xuesong and Yuze," he replies.

"Do they drive motorcycles?"

"Yes, they can drive any vehicle."

"Instruct them to follow Wang starting from 5 a.m. tomorrow," instructs Chong.

"I will inform them."

Chong, ever the careful planner, adds, "Work out the mission order. Keep it discreet, with no names and explicit mention of surveillance. Think you can handle it?"

München nods, smiling. "Consider it done."

Chong's eyes narrow, and his instincts kick in. "I have a hunch we'll find that address. Bo will let Wang visit Hui in the hospital."

München smiles. "There's more to this than meets the eye, isn't there?"

Chong nods. "There always is. Let's find out."

43

Pull the Rope and Watch the Clock Go "Tick-Tock, Tick-Tock"

Dawn breaks, and many have not slept. The vans deliver the newspapers all over the city of Shanghai before the newsboys open for business. One newspaper features the headline "The Truth That Is Being Hidden" alongside a photograph of the paramedic who gave the interview. The newsstands begin to open and put the exposed periodicals up for sale. Passersby stop; some shop, and others read. The article and comments shock several men who are reading the headlines among themselves. Others call friends and family about the news. It doesn't take even half an hour; by 7:00 a.m., the morning news on television announces the story. Reporters and journalists create a frenzy in front of the police headquarters and the hospital where Hui is being treated.

Detective Chong exits the elevator and heads to the cafeteria. Having arrived at the hospital at 6:00 a.m. and getting only four hours of sleep the previous night, coffee is the most important thing on his mind right now. As he crosses the corridor on the ground floor, he recognizes the two lawyers who were at the interrogation yesterday. He looks at his watch, noting that it's now 6:45, and wonders, *Don't these guys ever sleep?*

Watching the lawyers from afar, he sees Wang identifying himself to the reception nurse. The detective gives up going for coffee and positions himself facing the elevator door, as he saw they are walking toward him. The lawyers and the owner of Warehouses #1 and #2 stop behind him as the elevator door opens. Everyone enters, greeting each other to begin their day.

"Looks like we all arrived together. Everyone going upstairs?" The detective smiles as he presses the button for the eighth floor.

"Yes, we're going to visit our client," one lawyer says with authority.

"Superintendent Bo told me last night that you would be coming. I didn't think it would be so early, though."

Everyone is silent.

They arrive on the floor, the door opens, and the hallway is empty except for two policemen on sentry duty. Together, the three visitors make their way to the room. Halting his path, the detective engages in a discussion with the nurses at the station.

Preventing the three men from entering, the cops incite a minor argument. Detective Chong, far down the hall, gives a thumbs-up to the guards, authorizing the three to pass.

As soon as they enter, one locks the door, and the other lawyer comments, "The stress has already started."

Wang, standing away, looks at Hui on the bed.

The lawyer who locked the door tells the other to go out and check what the detective is doing at the nurse's desk. Muttering and complaining again, the junior lawyer leaves the room.

Wang and the lawyer sit on the small sofa and talk about the future case that the court will take against the defendant. Hui is sleeping.

The boss yawns, showing his fatigue, and the lawyer asks, "Did you have coffee today?"

"I didn't sleep well last night and forgot to have one this morning."

Without delay, the defender offers to pick it up from the hospital cafeteria. Wang accepts. The lawyer leaves the room and closes the door.

Wang approaches Hui and says, "I could kill you now, but it would be a waste, don't you think?"

Hui opens his eyes and grimaces in pain, moaning.

Wang asks, pulling and shaking the handcuffed-to-the-bed Hui, "Where are the weapons?"

Hui, with his eyes wide open, stares at him, startled.

Close to his ear, the chief whispers, "There's no point in hiding your family. I'll find them one by one."

When Hui tries to speak, a strange sound comes out of the manager's mouth.

Wang doesn't mind the stench he gives off when Hui tries to explain. He puts his ear to the manager's mouth and hears the hoarse voice without precision. "Underneath the gallon of water. I buried it."

The chief walks away and says, his teeth bared, "I'll get you out of jail, and then we'll talk."

The long-time friend moves his head to the side and closes his eyes, as if losing his senses.

A doctor and two nurses open the door to the patient's room. The detective and junior defender follow them. They enter the room and see Wang on the couch. He puts his finger to his mouth and says, "He's sleeping."

The doctor, in a low voice, demands, "The patient is going to undergo an examination, and everyone must leave, except the nurses."

Wang, the detective, and the defender leave the room.

"Too bad you couldn't talk to him," Detective Chong says.

"No problem, I'll be back this afternoon," Wang assures him and walks down the hallway, watching as the smiling nurses recognize him and point. He smiles back and nods without approaching them.

At that moment, the lawyer who went to get the coffee walks toward the two, almost spilling the coffee on the detective, but recovering in time. He hands the hot liquid to Wang. The lawyer, with a changed attitude, speaking in a loud voice, addresses Chong: "Did you receive Hui's statement in the ambulance? I'm going to report you to the public prosecutor's office today. I will end you, this investigation, and all these trumped-up charges."

The detective, surprised by the discovery, utters, "Are you crazy?"

"Crazy? Look at this newspaper. Watch this interview."

Wang stands aside, watching the discussion. He cranes his neck and reads the headline on the paper the lawyer is showing.

Detective Chong takes the newspaper from him and reads the report. He pushes the newspaper back into the hands of the lawyer and walks away, muttering, "Son of a bitch!"

This news catches Chong by surprise, causing him to enter the first door he finds, the stairwell of the hospital. He runs down a few steps and looks up to see if anyone has followed him. No one. He takes his cellphone out of his pocket and calls Chief Bo, who is arriving at the office just now.

The first thing Bo hears is, "Did you give the lawyers the information in my report?"

Without understanding the reason for the question, he answers, "The report was excellent. I'll forward it to intel in a moment. Did something happen?"

"Haven't you read the newspapers yet?" Chong asks.

Boss Bo picks up the three newspapers that the secretary leaves on the table every morning and looks at the headlines on each until he reads "The Truth That Is Being Hidden." He keeps running his eyes through the article as he talks on the phone. "Who did it?"

Chong thinks fast, reflecting on the words the lawyer threatened, and says, "The ambulance paramedic. He's arriving at the building at 8 a.m. to give his statement. Everything is ready at the registry office. Besides being a witness to the manager's confession, ask him to explain this account."

"Leave it to me." Chief Bo hangs up his phone. He passes by the secretary and asks her to notify the notary that he is on his way.

"Yes, sir." She makes the call as Superintendent Bo passes through the door.

Wang, standing with the lawyer in the hallway, reads the interview in the newspaper. He shows no reaction. "Now what?"

"Now I don't know. According to the report, Hui confessed to these five deaths. I need to read the files, then I will send them to the courts today."

Wang nods his head and bends it back with a hunched posture, doing some weird stretches. He opens his mouth and yawns, saying, "Do what you can. Stay there and try to talk to him after the doctor leaves. Let's see what he has to say."

The lawyer, concerned about the strain in his voice, agrees.

Wang says, "I have a lot of work to do today, and I'll be back later in the afternoon." With no enthusiasm, he walks down the hall toward the elevator.

Detective Chong, after finishing his conversation with Chief Bo, runs down to the ground floor of the hospital. He sees the crowd of journalists at the hospital door. Not seeing his partner's car, he calls München over the radio and asks, "Where did you park?"

München explains that he has pulled into the parking lot near the front of the hospital. He instructs Chong to leave through the back door.

A minute later, the partner parks the unmarked vehicle and Chong gets into the passenger seat.

München, with a suspicious look, asks, "Did you get it?"

"Oh, yeah, I got it! Hui came through. North Shanghai, Jiangsu, maximum three hours."

"You're terrible," München says, smiling as he positions the car away from the hospital.

Another officer in one of the staked-out vehicles confirms over the radio that Wang has not yet left.

"What else?" the chief of operations asks Detective Chong.

"Remember the water can in the picture? He's buried every-thing underneath."

"I knew there was something strange about that image."

A police officer standing in front of the hospital, among the journalists, calls Detective München on the radio. "Wang just left and looks like he's going to talk to reporters."

The journalists, bumping into each other, try to approach Wang, who walks toward a vehicle that has stopped in front of the hospital.

The security guards, pushing the reporters, try to make way for the boss, but one of them next to the car shouts, "Mr. Wang, he is your employee. Do you have any statements?"

"I believe in justice," Wang says and smiles as he gets into the car.

The driver, making his way out of that confusion, drives the Audi fast toward the port.

Stuck in traffic, Wang asks the driver to drop him off at the apartment.

After a while, he arrives at the building's garage. The boss thanks him and dismisses him, saying, "I won't need you anymore today." The driver picks up a second vehicle next to the parked Audi and leaves.

Wang pretends to walk toward the private elevator. When he sees the driver leaving the building, he turns and gets into the Audi and directs it toward the avenue.

Agent Yuze, on the motorcycle parked next to the garage of Wang's building, begins "the tail."

The other police officers, along with the detectives, get stuck in traffic and are late in getting to Wang's apartment building.

Over the radio, the agent on the motorcycle informs Chief München that the target is heading toward National Highway 204.

"That's it, on the way to Jiangsu," Detective Chong verifies to his partner.

"Where are you?" München asks Agent Yuze.

"Leaving the city on the way to the highway. I need a car here to cover me."

"I'm five minutes away from you," Xuesong replies over the radio to his partner.

"Okay, I'll take it slow and let you know," Yuze communicates.

"Xuesong, didn't you take the motorbike?" Detective München asks.

"No, I needed to charge the drone."

"Got it," the boss replies.

München follows, heading toward the highway. He estimates he is about ten to fifteen minutes behind the officers.

"Don't worry. The boys are doing a fantastic job," Chong says, trying to calm him down.

In the car, Wang doesn't realize he's being followed. Calm and confident that he will recover the weapons, he drives at the maximum speed the highway allows. He talks out loud to himself. "There's no way. Only I can do it. The news is going to blow up during the day, and by the time they realize what they have to do, I will have already destroyed everything."

Today, the highway is tranquil, with few cars or trucks. He looks in the rear-view mirror and the road is clear. Only two cars coming from far away pass him at high speed.

Wang reflects again on what he read in the newspaper. *He did very well in taking everything on board. In the end, things will come to a head, and I will rest easy. I owe Boss Bo one, and when I get back, I'll send him a gift.*

He takes a deep breath and remembers last night when he called and talked to Bo after his lawyers informed him about Hui's attempted murder. The superintendent, without realizing his words, revealed that he had just returned from a meeting, but his voice showed that he had drunk a fair amount. In addition, he also mentioned that a task force arrived in the city to investigate the disappearance of Michael Wen Akimitsu, stating that they had a tiring meeting and that today there would be a second one to structure the investigation.

"Chief Bo, won't this affect our business?" asked Wang as if he were worried about the transactions at the port.

"No, it has nothing to do with the port. Come on, Wang. What do you need?"

"I'd like to visit my manager. I can't believe what they're accusing him of. He would never do those things."

"Of course, I'll allow it, but I'll let you know that something bigger is going on. Everything alright with you?" Chief Bo questioned.

Wang recalled arguing with the leaders and tried to remain calm when talking to the Shanghai police superintendent. "Of course, everything is in order. I just got out of a meeting. I spoke a lot with the minister's adviser, and the Englishman's disappearance took on unimaginable proportions. He told me he had permission, if the man was located, by an informant or by any other means, to strike a plea deal. This way, we'll finish this investigation as quickly as possible. What worries me most here is that you never know what they are going to report," revealed Chief Bo, an important piece of information for Wang.

Wang did not respond. Reflecting, he remembers Kung Wu's words. He concluded that the men up at the top were moving and it wasn't the Tong but the Triad who were there.

"I'm going to visit Hui tomorrow, okay?"

"Have one lawyer call me, and I'll give you the go-ahead." Chief Bo hung up his phone.

Driving fast, Wang looks at the signs at the entrance to the city and confirms with the car's clock that in no later than twenty minutes, he'll arrive at the farm.

He remembers what the newspaper published and what Chief Bo told him, and he murmurs, "This is going to suck. I've got to get there fast."

Speeding up the vehicle, he flies down the road.

Xuesong in the car and Yuze on the motorcycle continue to follow.

Yuze, parking on the road, informs his boss over the radio that they have arrived in Jiangsu and asks how long until the other teams arrive.

München confirms within a maximum of ten minutes.

The agent starts the motorcycle and continues on the road but is already far from the target. Following, he maintains a certain distance because of the excess of curves in this area. This way, he can control Wang's car, as the motorcycle is always in a corner behind the vehicle. After a while, he stops the motorbike on the road and waits for his partner, Xuesong, to overtake him. The car now follows the boss.

Yuze distances himself as far as he can, as per München's order. The motorcycle, at that moment, would draw a lot more attention to that location.

Xuesong, following, sees Wang's vehicle enter a side road. He slows down and tries to track the target, giving up because he is certain he will lose it. He enters the same dirt road on the way to the farm.

Scanning the area, Wang seeks to locate the once-red barn and finds it. His vehicle stops in front of the double wooden gate. Exiting the vehicle, he swings it open. Past the old house, he drives the car and parks it at the back of the barn. In his observation, this approach guarantees it won't be visible to anyone on the road.

The agent following the vehicle did not see Wang when he entered the location but locates the red barn and notifies the chief. Observing the entire area, he drives unassuming down the road. Xuesong stops in front of the red-barn farm. He confirms tire tracks in the wet mud, understanding that a car has just passed through that gate. As he cannot stay stopped there because it is a very open area, he calls his boss and explains what is happening, asking permission to activate the drone.

München follows, heading toward the highway. He estimates he was about ten to fifteen minutes behind the officers. After hearing the entire report, he understands Xuesong is alone, and everyone knows how dangerous Wang is. He orders, "Get out of there now, and once you're a safe distance away, you can activate it. We're coming."

The policeman continues driving down the dirt road until he finds a shortcut in the bamboo forest on the side of the highway and parks the car. Xuesong prepares the drone and activates it for aerial imagery. Happy to have given the boss the idea of bringing this device, he launches it into the skies.

Beneath the water can, Wang digs in agony as the murmur of the wind-blown vegetation echoes like music, but it makes a dry sound in his ear.

In silence, the drone covers the barn area, showing Wang digging. Without him noticing, the device flies overhead, taking photos as the recording starts. Apprehensive about whether Hui told the truth, Wang digs with a shovel and finds the plastic bag. Wang removes the bag from the bottom of the hole, opens it, and checks its contents. He looks up at the skies, smiling in gratitude, and notices the drone above his head.

At first, he is confused, then he realizes what he is seeing. Fear grips him. He doesn't understand what is happening. Wang runs toward the sound of water hitting rocks and logs. It has been raining a lot in this region, and the violent river has rapids flowing through the land. Running, his shoes try to get stuck in the mud. He knows it's not far; it's another fifty metres. He continues running and looking over his shoulder, seeing three cars speeding past the barn, following him.

Within a minute, the vehicles activate their sirens and lights, and Wang, desperate, continues running toward the river without stopping. Reaching the edge, he takes the revolver from his waist, holding it in his right hand and the bag in his left. Detective Chong and Detective München, along with six other officers, run up to him, observing him holding the plastic bag.

At the riverbank, Wang stares at the officers.

"It's over," Detective Chong shouts.

Wang stretches out his arm, bag in hand, over the rushing water. The drone keeps flying overhead.

"You can play. We'll get to you in the end. We will not lose," Detective Chong shouts.

A few policemen with ropes move down the stream, away from where Wang is standing, following the rapids.

"You want the bag? Come and get it," Wang taunts.

Detective Chong walks toward him. München tries to hold onto his partner's arm and fails.

"Give me the bag," Chong shouts from about ten feet away.

Wang is no longer nervous, and he knows that this is the end point. He raises his right hand, points at the detective, and fires two times.

Chong falls, and the policemen, together, shoot Tong's boss several times, causing him to topple into the water. The bag and the body fall into the riverbank, and a policeman throws himself in, tied to a rope. Three other officers holding the rope pull him, Wang's body, and the bag in, detaching them from a bunch of logs.

Detective Chong gets up from the dirt and wipes away the mud that has stuck to his pants. He unbuttons his shirt, exposing the two dents in his bulletproof vest.

"You fooled us," München exclaims, hugging his partner.

"Nope. I threw myself to the ground because I knew you would defend me." Chong smiles.

Officers pull Wang's still-breathing body out of the water.

"Bad things don't die without causing problems," München says, looking at the scene.

The drone filmed everything and has taken off in the direction where Agent Xuesong is controlling it.

One officer approaches the detectives and tells them he has already called for an ambulance.

The other, who took the bag, hands it to the chief of operations, who opens it and checks that there were three revolvers inside.

Chong ignores Wang's body lying on the dirt. He runs to the car and grabs the printed photos from the USB stick. He calls München and orders him to ask for help from the local police and call forensics to come to the farm.

After a while, an ambulance, accompanied by several other local police cars, arrives. Officers from München's team help paramedics take Wang into a waiting ambulance.

Chong instructs two police officers from the operations section to accompany Wang to the hospital in Jiangsu city in one car. They will remain there until someone replaces them.

München finishes talking on the phone and announces that forensics is on the way; he looks at the time and confirms it's noon.

The two chiefs analyze the photographs, trying to find evidence that the three men who Hui mentioned died at this location.

*   *   *

Rachel always wakes up early, but David and Tyler prefer to sleep in. It's 8:00 a.m., and she's in the kitchen, trying her best not to make too much noise as she prepares coffee for everyone. However, despite her efforts, the tap gushes water, the frying pan hisses, and the plates and cutlery clank on the table, waking Tyler from his sleep. He stumbles over to her and murmurs, "Can you make me three eggs?"

"Good morning." She greets him with a smile as he plops down on the couch and turns on the television.

The TV plays loudly in Mandarin. He switches between channels, looking for someone speaking English. Tyler gets up, moving toward the bathroom and tells Rachel, "Today I want to go for a walk. We're going to visit a Buddhist temple and, if possible, I'd like to take a train."

Rachel laughs as she cracks the eggs into the frying pan, but then, as she listens to the news from the channel Tyler had left the TV on, she freezes. She runs to the TV, reading the text and listening, trying to understand the reporter's sombre voice.

"... he said the names of the dead were Michael and Wonjy, and he didn't remember the third name. He claims that someone threw the bodies as food for crocodiles, horrifying me the most."

Rachel hears the second journalist ask if she believes the statement. The journalist responds that the paramedic is at the police station right now. This reporter insists that the news must be true.

Expressing their gratitude to viewers for watching the morning news, the two reporters promise to return with more updates as soon as they have more information.

This news disrupted Rachel's morning. Advertisements appear on the TV, but she remains frozen, unable to utter a word. The acrid smell of burned eggs wafts through the apartment.

Tyler runs out of the bathroom and throws the steaming frying pan into the sink.

Rachel, seemingly without control, changes the television channels. Her frozen gaze fixed on the screen catches Tyler's attention. Seeing that something has happened to her, he removes the remote control from her shaking hand. "What happened?"

Rachel can't speak. She stutters, with her eyes still fixed on the screen.

Tyler grabs a glass of water from the kitchen and hands it to her. "What's going on, Rachel?" he asks again.

She tries to speak, her voice shaking with disbelief. "The news, the reporter."

The confusion shows on Tyler's face, and he asks again, "What happened?"

Rachel lowers her head, looking at the ground, her voice shaking in disbelief. "Where is David?"

"He's still sleeping," Tyler replies, the worry in his eyes growing.

Rachel takes a deep breath, her voice shaking, and tells him what she heard the reporter say.

Tyler's face contorts, and he intervenes. "You must be misinterpreting the words in Mandarin."

"No," she insists, her voice resolute. "I'm not. The reporter mentioned Michael and Wonjy's names and disclosed the location where he dumped the bodies."

"This is surreal," Tyler mutters, shaking his head in disbelief. He grabs the remote and flips channels, hoping to find another source of the morning news.

Meanwhile, Rachel takes her cellphone from the kitchen and sinks onto the living room couch. She reads the day's news, and one report provides a detailed account of what a local newspaper had published.

> *According to the information we got, another prisoner attacked the prisoner we mentioned yesterday. He received many stab wounds to his body, almost losing his life. He then confessed to the police and ambulance attendant about the deaths of five people and the horrible fate they suffered.*

Tyler listens as Rachel tells every frightening detail of the news. The news leaves Tyler and Rachel in a state of profound shock as they struggle to accept the harsh reality of what they have just learned.

Rachel relays the disturbing information to her partner, explaining that the paramedic is testifying to the police now.

Her concerned partner asks, "Why didn't Detective Chong call?"

"I don't know," she responds, her voice low and full of worry.

Without hesitation, she dials Detective Chong's cellphone, but receives no answer. She sends him a message, but there's no sign he has read it.

She tries calling Boss Bo next, but he doesn't answer either.

The two exchange worried looks and Rachel swallows hard before saying, "Wake up David, we need to do something."

Tyler turns off the television and goes to the bedroom to call David. David, still half asleep, staggers into the living room and flops down on the couch. "Why did you wake me up?"

Rachel and Tyler stand in front of him, just looking at him. Little by little, he notices the abnormal attitude of the two in front of him.

"Something's wrong?" David asks, sitting up on the couch.

Rachel, holding the remote control in her hands, seems distant and turns the television back on. She flips through several channels and comes across a news program where four journalists are involved in a heated discussion about the same disturbing topic.

David listens to the narrative of yesterday's attempted murder and the journalists talk about the investigation in a local newspaper's headline today. During their discussion, they mention the names of the deceased and describe the horrible fate of the bodies. They conclude with the statement that the prisoner confessed to the murder of the mother and daughter on the farm. A silence takes over the room.

David's world crumbles around him as he covers his face with both hands, falling to his knees on the carpet. He screams in despair, "No, no, no."

Rachel and Tyler rush to his side, hugging him, sharing his anguish.

Through his sobs, David finds the strength to say, his voice shaking, "We can't just sit here and do nothing."

Tyler offers a suggestion: "Call your friend at intel in Shanghai."

David runs to his room and calls the number. His former FBI partner responds, explaining that the task force had arrived the day before. Their plan was to meet again at 10:00 a.m. with local police and Chief Bo to better understand the unfolding situation. He admits he has seen the news, but no one was sure what was going on.

"You're late," David mutters.

The intel official tries to explain himself, but David hangs up the phone.

Tyler takes charge. "Let's talk to the superintendent. We need to go there. There's no point sitting here."

Rachel agrees, and together they decide to act.

David, feeling overwhelmed, announces, "Okay, I'm going to take a shower," and heads to the bathroom.

Rachel and Tyler, in the living room, hear David's muffled sobs coming from the bathroom, heartbreaking proof that nothing is okay.

* * *

The entrance to the Shanghai Police Headquarters building buzzes with journalists and reporters, representing various national television networks, all expecting the departure of the paramedic.

The testimony was tiring, and the witness had to explain the reason for the morning publication of the distressing facts in the local newspaper. At 9:30 a.m., he walks out the front door, only to be met with a growing crowd of people running toward him. Fear takes over him. He cannot move, standing on the stairs, unsure of how to respond, while a growing

crowd of people rush toward him, bombarding him with questions, clicking cameras and countless microphones. He feels unable to determine how
to proceed or to whom to respond. With bulging eyes, he doesn't say a
word. Escaping the chaos seems impossible.

A strong hand grabs his arm, pulling him down the stairs. Reporters
continue to bombard him with an incessant stream of questions. Shocked
and with an accompanying hand on his arm, the journalists' words become
an indistinct noise in his ears.

Someone opens a car door and pushes him into the back seat. A young
man sits next to him, while the paramedic notices the same woman behind
the wheel from the previous night.

"I'm sorry, it wasn't supposed to be like this," she apologizes, speeding
the car away from the chaotic scene.

He remains frozen, silent, his eyes fixed on her, unable to find the words
to respond.

She speeds through the streets, manoeuvring to outrun any cars, following them through the winding alleys of the city centre.

Sitting, his breathing still rapid, he wipes his nose and snorts with a mix
of emotions. His voice, full of resentment, says, "You promised me."

"I'm sorry," she replies, her voice full of regret. "My boss made me do
it, and I couldn't stop it."

After apologizing, the journalist continues to drive with one hand on
the steering wheel while the other reaches into her coat pocket, taking out
an envelope and handing it to him.

"Here is the three thousand I promised you," she says. He accepts, stuff-
ing the envelope inside his jacket without bothering to check the contents.
His gaze remains fixed on her.

"You're safe now," she assures him.

The paramedic looks at the young man who rescued him from the
frantic crowd and nods his head in thanks.

With immediate danger behind them, she parks the car in front of a
restaurant and turns to him, asking, "Should we get something to eat?"

The paramedic agrees, a sense of relief washing over them both as they
prepare to leave the day's chaos behind, if only for a brief time.

44

"The End, for Some, Is the Beginning"

Detective München searches the trunk of his squad car and pulls out two rolls of yellow tape with the words "Crime Scene, No Trespassing" emblazoned on them. He hands one roll to a police officer on his team, instructing him to place it around the farm gate and around the nearby fence. The police officer hurries to comply, doubling his caution because of reporters. Besides what the head of operations requests, he also isolates the barn. This will prevent anyone from entering until the forensic team arrives, as any possible DNA evidence could be crucial to building the case.

Dr. Xiyang Ruixue contacts Detective Chong, informing him of his arrival at 2:30 p.m. He requests that Chong do his utmost to preserve the crime scene until then.

Superintendent Bo also contacts the detective, confirming receipt of the message in the morning. However, because of meetings with the minister's adviser, with intel, and with foreign police officers, he can only respond now, at 12:30 p.m., concerned.

"How are you? I was anxious, Chong. What about the other officers? Was anyone hurt?"

Chong assures him that he and everyone else have no injuries and mentions that Wang got injured and is receiving treatment at Jiangsu Municipal Hospital. He explains two police officers from the operations sector are monitoring and maintaining security at the site. They need to be replaced by the local police, as the situation remains volatile.

Cutting to the chase, he asks, "I need you to send a team or two to the hospital to monitor the prisoner."

Boss Bo agrees and expresses his joy. "You can't imagine how happy I am with concluding this investigation. This is a significant achievement for us," he adds. The conclusion is a moment of relief amid the chaos.

The detective pays little attention to the superintendent's words and informs him that he will not return to Shanghai today because forensics will require his help. He emphasizes, "We need to find the DNA of the men murdered at that location."

Interestingly, Boss Bo asks, "Did Wang react?"

"Yes. He reacted, and the drone filmed everything. I'm glad we brought it; without it, we wouldn't have been able to prove anything," Chong responds.

"The press here still doesn't know. No one has called me yet," Bo reports.

Chong adds a hint of irony when he alerts the boss, "Don't worry, it will soon be full of reporters trying to talk to you. I don't know how they get information so fast."

"Another thing, Rachel Barnes called my cellphone; I didn't answer. I'm sure they'll be knocking on the door soon," adds Bo.

"They will understand when they hear the explanation. David Ho will be upset, but they are also police officers, and they will know that we are doing our best to clarify everything," advises Chong, trying to reassure the superintendent.

Nodding, Boss Bo says, "You're right. I also have to report on the truck accident; the report was ready last night. Don't worry, leave it to me. One more thing, Wang's secretary came here in the morning looking for you. The head of the registry office spoke to her, and she's given a testimony. She made an official statement, and I'm sure it will surprise you."

"I'd believe anything," Chong responds before hanging up.

With his eyes alert and his mind absorbed, Detective Chong walks across the uneven terrain of the farm, looking for something, anything, that went unnoticed before. Upon seeing unknown Jiangsu officials in the restricted zone, his voice is immediate and firm: "Please go out and wait outside the compound." Responses that range from reluctant compliance to murmurs of apology hang in the air, but they leave.

One of München's agents rushes toward Chong, the words coming out of his mouth in a rushed mess. "Detective, a prosecutor just ran past the tape. He's giving orders to the Jiangsu city authorities."

Chong, staying calm, locates and addresses the prosecutor. He recognizes him from the Shanghai courts, reflecting that those in the echelons of power orchestrated the visit. He tilts his body, a small smile playing at the corners of his mouth.

The prosecutor's words cut through the air, laced with a mixture of irritation and bewilderment. "What is happening here? We have received no information, and no notifications of operations in this area have reached our desks."

Walking shoulder to shoulder with the prosecutor, Chong ventures into an explanation, his words measured. "We arranged everything at the last minute, and if we hadn't done it that way, we would never have been able to get the material evidence."

The prosecutor's eyes, wide and bright with a mixture of shock and intrigue, fix on Chong. "Material evidence? Did you find something?"

There is a nod, saturated with subtle confidence from Chong. "Yes, it's all tied up."

"Wang Wei is dead?" The prosecutor's voice cuts through the farm's surroundings. His eyes roam the land as if trying to evoke a hidden figure.

Detective Chong, eyes narrowed, decodes the precise intent behind that inquisition. It's the crux of the prosecutor's unexpected visit, isn't it?

He responds, with a steady calm in his voice, "I don't know. The ambulance brought him to the city hospital. I believe he may be in surgery, or he may be under a sheet. No update has reached me yet."

The prosecutor, unfazed, states, "I'm done here. I'm going to the hospital. What about you? Why are your boots still trotting in this red mud?"

Chong responds, "Oh, boss, waiting for the forensic team. Still involved in this, you know... duty demands that we hold out until the end."

In a whirlwind of dust and mud, a car door opens. Without a parting glance or a casual farewell, the prosecutor, cellphone pressed to his ear, walks away from Chong. His voice returns as he enters the vehicle: "Yes, boss, heading to the hospital."

Detective Chong watches the scene unfold, a murmur escaping through parted lips, more to himself than to anyone nearby: "He came to get information and left the same way he arrived: empty-handed."

München, standing on the opposite side of the barn, overhears Chong's conversation with the lap dog of a prosecutor. Moving up to his partner's side, he inquires, "Do you think that the poor excuse of a prosecutor will cause us a problem?"

"I refuse to succumb to worry. Do yourself, all of us, a favour. Split the team into three and let's find a place to eat. This will last through the night, and the forensics team will be here soon," Chong instructs, his voice firm but tired as he walks toward the squad car.

München frowns. "How long do we have?"

"They'll be here in an hour, maybe less," replies Chong with unshakable certainty.

München returns to the team, his voice carrying authority as he divides them into three groups. The agents, looking somewhat exhausted, express a preference to remain in place, asking their boss to bring sandwiches, soft drinks, and water rather than venturing into the city. With a nod, he agrees.

"Alright, let's eat and I'll get what they need." Chong sits down, sliding into the driver's seat with surprising speed that belies his fatigue.

München, sitting in the passenger seat, asks, "Are you going to drive, Chong?"

"Why? Do you have a problem?" Chong retorts, starting the engine. His voice is just above a whisper as he focuses on the dirt road before them.

"I hope you're okay. What did you feel when he shot you? Tell me, I'm your best friend." The director of operations, worried about his partner, tries to get him to vent.

Driving at high speed, Chong stops the car and looks toward his friend, who has a scared expression and doesn't understand what's with his companion.

München sees him punching the air and banging his fists on the steering wheel, applauding and shouting, "We did it! We did it!"

München screams in celebration with him.

In a minute, Detective Chong becomes serious, puts the car in drive, and heads back toward the city as if nothing had happened.

* * *

Rachel, Tyler, and David arrive in the city centre. The congestion of vehicles near the police building prevents any attempt to park nearby. Finding a place around the square, a little way away, they hurry toward the police building. The raucous jumble of journalists at the main entrance forms a barrier, and the collective buzz is a frenetic symphony of curiosity and impatience.

Looking for a strategic entrance, the trio walk through the building, entering through a subtle side door, presenting themselves at reception.

The hands of the clock do not yet show 1:00 p.m., and the officer on duty, after a brief but polite recognition of their personal documents, informs them that Chief Bo will assist them, but they will have to wait. Guided by a subtle gesture, they sink into the hard reception chairs, their eyes absorbing the architectural eloquence of the well-known police palace that surrounds them.

As Rachel's gaze travels across the hand-painted windows, her eyes lock on two men speaking while walking toward the exit, and a flash of recognition sparks in her eyes. *They're the intel cops from that argument at the bar.* Driven by urgency, she jumps out of her chair and walks toward them.

David and Tyler follow her with raised eyebrows as she addresses the officers. David recognizes them. Rachel returns with the agents and makes introductions. Tyler, with his ever-present manners, bows to the two officers while David waves a more subdued salute.

Rachel says, "We've been trying to contact you. Given how busy Detective Chong is with this investigation, I believe he hasn't had time to convey our message yet."

"What do you need?" Oshiro asks.

"Is intel still investigating Yazuo?" asks Rachel.

David ignores the conversation, isolated in his own thoughts.

Tyler, amazed that Rachel is holding a conversation in Mandarin, watches them.

"Any problems?" Oshiro asks.

"Someone put a cellphone in my pocket last Friday. It without a doubt belongs to him, but I haven't tried to get in touch," Rachel informs him, taking the object from the bag and handing it to Oshiro.

David gets up from his chair and looks uncomfortable. He meanders from one side of the lobby to the other.

"Is there a problem?" Liwei, looking at David, asks Rachel.

"No, no problem."

"What are you doing here in the building?" Oshiro asks her, looking at Tyler.

"Are you with the task force that arrived yesterday?" asks Liwei next.

Surprised by the information, Rachel thinks fast and responds by explaining the look that Oshiro gave Tyler: "He doesn't speak Mandarin. We came to talk to Chief Bo."

Oshiro holds the cellphone Rachel gave him and asks, "Are you sure?"

"There's a message from him. I just turned it on once. I read it and hung up right away."

"Why did you decide to hand it over to us now?" Liwei inquires.

"I should have delivered it before now. That would have been the right thing... All good now. It's as it should be."

"Come tomorrow to intel. Here's my card. Call me, and we'll meet. I need official statements to go with this," Liwei notifies her.

"No problem. I'll call." Rachel thanks them, smiling.

The two agents stand up, bow in respect, and almost run out of the building. The partners return to their chairs and wait.

It's now 2:00 p.m., and a police officer on duty approaches the members and tells them to go upstairs. Chief Bo is awaiting them.

* * *

The two detectives, after eating and buying meals and supplies for the agents, return from the city. As they approach the entrance to the farm, they identify news vans and several journalists in front of the gate. As München gets out of the car, reporters surround him and bombard him with questions. Ignoring them and not giving any answers, he opens the police barricade tape on the gate. Chong speeds up and enters the property. München replaces the tape and re-shuts the gate. Feeling bothered by the number of questions, he turns to journalists and clarifies that he doesn't have any information to announce, maybe later.

The police officer who operated the drone, along with his colleagues, waits for the detectives. München and Chong, after distributing the snacks, join the operator in the back of the van and watch the film. The footage shows from the moment Wang dug and found the plastic bag to the removal of his body from the river.

"I like it. It's excellent, there will be no doubt," München praises, slapping the agent on the back.

Chong approves and says, "I should have parted my hair to the left. I don't look good in those pictures."

The three of them laugh.

At that very moment, two Shanghai forensic vehicles arrive at the scene and park behind the van in which they are talking.

Chong greets the doctor and informs him of what happened on the farm. He hands over the photographs from the USB stick, the bag with the weapons, and Wang's wet cellphone. He explains that the only thing they didn't find was the gun he was carrying when he fell into the river.

Dr. Xiyang Ruixue thanks him for all the information. Looking serious, he orders, "Chong, I'm going to ask you and everyone here present, without exception, to leave us alone in the area for at least an hour. I'll call you on your cellphone if I have questions; I'm going to need your help."

"Alright, doctor, let's get the cars and wait out front."

"No! Leave the cars where they are. You can see that there is a lot of movement in this area, and it will get worse if you remove them now. The mud... you can see it is soaked, and of course... Hmm, it could be... that something got lost."

"Let's go to the gate," Chong shouts and waves to the officers to follow him.

*　*　*

At that same moment in Shanghai, Superintendent Bo receives the three members of DRT and asks them to sit. He tells his secretary that he doesn't want to be disturbed and asks her to bring tea, coffee, and water. She nods.

The three of them bow as a sign of respect. They settle down on the sofas and wait for him to speak.

Chief Bo takes some papers from the table and sits in an armchair next to Rachel. He says, "I was hoping you guys would come sooner, but I'm glad that you came now."

"I'm sorry to ask, where is Detective Chong?" Rachel asks.

"Is it true that Michael is dead?" David can't stand it and asks the fatal question.

Chief Bo looks at Tyler, waiting for him to question something as well, but remembers he doesn't speak Mandarin. He returns his gaze to the other two and answers, "Let's break it down."

"Please, boss, I need to know the truth," David insists.

"I ask you to calm down; you're not giving me a chance to explain," the boss says, adjusting himself in his chair and looking at David.

Tyler notices that the expression on the superintendent's face has changed; he's sure that it was in response to something David said.

The superintendent turns his gaze to Rachel and explains, "Rachel, Detective Chong has been working out of town since yesterday and will not return until this investigation is complete."

"I understand, boss, we're cops," she replies.

David, dismayed, falls silent.

The secretary enters the private room and places tea, coffee, and water on the coffee table, then leaves.

Boss Bo's fingers wrap around the glass of water, his steady gaze fixed on David. His voice, a gentle flow of calm amid the obvious tension, resonates throughout the room. "David, the information we are getting during the day is as ambiguous to us as the news is to you. Whether Michael is alive or dead, we are also still in the dark. Chong is working to shed light on this as we speak. Do you understand me?"

David, pain etching his features, struggles with a hoarse voice. "We saw on television that there is a witness who heard the confession about the deaths of three men. One of them was called Michael. Is there any truth to that?"

Chief Bo nods, sincerity written all over his face. "It's true, David. The witness came forward this morning. We have obtained a confession from the prisoner who is now lying in a hospital bed with his life hanging in the balance after an attack." The boss reveals as much as he can without taking his eyes off David.

David opens his mouth to speak, whispering, "Boss..."

Rachel steps forward and interferes by drowning out his words.

Chief Bo's attention shifts from David to Rachel, an acknowledgement of her intervention.

Rachel, her voice a calming balm, says, "Your dedication to solving this case is obvious, boss. The detective's dedication to clarifying and closing this case, despite the risks involved, is also obvious to us. Sorry for the interruption and thank you for your commitment to addressing our concerns. We will wait for any news at the apartment."

David, silent, offers no words, but his eyes, which scream a silent plea of despair and hope, remain glued to the floor.

Tyler, after finishing his coffee, observes each person, reading the discomfort on the faces of the people sitting there.

Chief Bo informs: "Yesterday, I received the conclusive report from the truck accident investigation. The driver confessed to being drunk that fateful morning." He places the report in Rachel's hands, his eyes conveying silent sympathy.

Rachel examines the document, her eyes turning to David. His gaze is still anchored on the ground. Prior to returning the report, she says, "Thank you" in a low voice for the update.

The superintendent, inserting an additional note of seriousness, continues. "This may interest you, David. Representatives of the American and British police landed here yesterday. I incorporated the agents into our Shanghai intelligence team. We have already met in two very interesting meetings; all that's left now is for them to dive into the task at hand. However, one certainty hangs over us: if everything unfolds as Detective Chong predicts today, we will disband the team and send them back." His eyes fall on David, who remains a motionless statue amid the hustle and bustle of words.

Rachel, surprised but poised, looks at Boss Bo and then at David, deciphering the unspoken trouble her partner has gotten himself into. Not wanting to delve deeper into the subject, she sees it's time to leave. Without hesitation, she gets up from the couch, Tyler imitating her movements a second later. David also recovers, and together, they bow in gratitude, a silent acknowledgement of the boss's unwavering support. They exit the room, leaving behind an atmosphere tinged with unspoken words and unanswered questions.

A tense David moves beside Rachel, his voice a harsh whisper cutting through the hallway: "You shouldn't have interrupted me."

Rachel, unyielding, responds with an equal measure of sternness. "How could I not? Besides the mess you've created by involving intelligence channels about Michael, you've been defying Boss Bo, who has been our strongest ally in all of this. It's hard to believe that you were once an intelligence officer."

Amid the harsh exchange of words in the hallway, an uncomfortable Tyler surveys their surroundings before intervening. "Let's not argue here."

David, his frustration boiling, throws a dissatisfied question in his direction: "When are we going to get some actual information?"

Rachel, trying to calm him down, advises as she moves toward the stairs leading to the lobby, "Take a deep breath, David. Get a grip."

David stops, looking straight ahead. Tyler puts an arm around him, and together, they follow Rachel.

David suggests to Tyler, "Let's find out which hospital the prisoner is in."

Tyler, next to Rachel, addresses David: "First, let's get something to eat because I'm starving."

Rachel suggests the same place they had gone with Detective Chong. "There's that restaurant right around the corner."

David, with a contradictory firmness in his voice, counters, "No. Let's go to the one we visited with Michael."

Rachel, amazement shining in her eyes, asks, "Are you sure you want to revisit that place?"

"Yes. If he is dead, I will have to accept that. I choose to keep the wonderful memories we created here in Shanghai," David declares, his voice firm, and his eyes reflecting a surprising resolve. His friends look at him, surprised by this sudden change in behaviour.

Together, they walk in silence through a sea of reporters clustered in front of the building, crossing the park toward their vehicle.

Upon arriving at the car, Tyler, scratching his head, comments, "Rachel showed me the photos you took there… some advice, don't allow yourself to be overcome, but be prepared for the worst. We'll soon have a definitive answer."

Nobody answers. They get into the car, with David once again taking on the role of driver.

* * *

Doctor Xiyang radios in, ordering Detectives Chong and München to come to the barn.

Chong summons two police officers to accompany him. München asks the other agents not to allow anyone to enter the farm. One last look at the road makes him happy with the various local traffic officers there, helping with road closures and setting up detours.

Approaching the barn, the detectives continue their walk.

Detective München was called by the police officer who escorted the ambulance into town. According to the chief officer's report, the surgery is still ongoing, and Wang's body contains five bullets. Doctors are doing their best to remove them, allowing him to survive. He adds that a prosecutor, accompanied by Jiangsu politicians, arrived at the hospital and discovered the incident, staying there for a short time before leaving. The police officer takes advantage of communication with the team leader to ask for reinforcements, as reporters and mainstream media have already camped at the hospital.

Chong and München, with disciplined patience, avoid entering the barn. They stand in the doorway, watching Dr. Xiyang and two other experts work inside, collecting samples with focused diligence. A deafening noise makes them pay attention to the sky. The distant pulse of the helicopter blades permeates the tranquility of the place. Three helicopters surround the farm area.

Chong, his voice a hushed, urgent whisper, instructs München, "Alert Chief Bo of what is happening and have him exercise control over the television networks flying overhead."

München, acting, leaves the area to begin the call.

Dr. Xiyang gets Chong's attention, calling him over. Chong approaches and absorbs every detail the doctor tells him. "We discovered blood on the chair and isolated it."

Chong, with a subtle wrinkle marking his forehead, asks, "Is there a possibility of DNA identification?"

Doctor Xiyang states, "Yes. We found blood on the ceiling beams. From previous analysis… this suggests that someone shot a person in the head. We found many drops of blood on these wooden beams. This deserves in-depth analysis. I ask that your men help me remove these beams and place them with the utmost care in a van or truck."

Chong, his handwriting on the specialist's requests on a notepad, nods.

The doctor continues: "After removing the straw and the floor covering the floor, we identified blood in three different places. We extracted the boards where you can see the blood stains, as well as the ones next to them. We wrapped them in plastic. They are there in the corner. I need a considerable vehicle to transport these beams and these parts of the floor. We are isolating the area with the material we have, considering the ever-present risk of contamination. It is essential that all this material reaches the laboratory today."

"I'll organize this now," Detective Chong states.

Dr. Xiyang, pausing, meets Chong's gaze with a seriousness that encompasses them both. "Chong, something vile happened here," he mutters.

The detective, with his hand resting on his forehead, nods his head in agreement.

Doctor Xiyang continues, his voice firm, "We will also take the water container for examination. The firearms are in perfect condition, which should make fingerprinting easier."

As the doctor approaches the door, Chong's gaze remains anchored on the barn, as if trying to stitch together the fragments of the horrific scene that took place inside. His focus is on each section of harvested wood.

"In the location where the tin was, we unearthed something promising. A little deeper in the hole, we recovered some burned clothes and fragments of paper."

Chong, out of a trance, declares with renewed vigour, "I'll get everything you requested now."

Doctor Xiyang, trying to still appear calm in the tense atmosphere, reassures him. "Do it and don't worry. We'll send everything to the lab today, and by tomorrow night at the latest, we should have some preliminary answers."

Chong, with an undercurrent of urgency permeating his words, emphasizes, "I need those DNA tests and fingerprint analyzes to be sped up."

"We will proceed with the utmost care, ensuring that we carry out everything with precision. Be sure—we'll discover what is to be found. Do you have access to samples from the individuals who may have died here?" the expert asks.

Chong is sure that everything will work out. "We can arrange for sample collection today. The mother of one victim lives in Shanghai; getting samples from the other two may present a challenge, but I'll manage."

Dr. Xiyang nods his head, and a single word is uttered: "Great."

"I'm going to see to all of this now," the detective reiterates.

"Just a warning: the forensics will stay here for a few more days because there has to be a sweep of the terrain. We have to perform the full service. I'm going to talk to Chief Bo and ask for help from the military. This work will require at least twenty people."

"Okay," the detective agrees, walking out of the barn with heavy steps. He picks up his phone and dials.

Boss Bo's voice emanates from the other end of the call. Chong, showing fatigue but remaining firm, passes on the details shared by the forensic specialist, along with an urgent request for a police medical team to visit Michael's mother in order to collect DNA.

Bo, always a constant force, informs him, "I have already given the order for the helicopters to vacate the area, and you don't need to worry about the truck; I will arrange one in the city of Jiangsu. They'll get there in an hour at most."

Looking up at the sky, Chong confirms, "Two of the helicopters have left, but one remains; it's easy to identify, it has a red stripe."

Bo's voice has a soft, authoritative assurance: "He'll be leaving soon as well."

Chong hesitates before adding, "Boss, another aspect requires your attention: the prosecutors. One was here a few moments ago; I recognized him from Shanghai. He asked about Wang."

In a calm and firm response, Bo instructs, "Calm your mind and focus on your tasks, Chong. The Attorney General's Office received a document from me this morning detailing the emerging operation and subsequent events that you relayed to me. They received the information but elicited no reaction. If just one problem existed, my office would already be involved in bureaucratic chaos. Regarding Wang's situation in the hospital, I contacted the local police; they will oversee security there. I already sent the boys back here. Detective, your work has been impeccable, and you are to be congratulated."

Chong remains motionless, phone in hand, and ends the call. The events of the day may have instilled a sense of pride in people, and everyone will remember everything. However, his gaze remains on the barn. On the other hand, remembering the five deceased and the horrible scene of the merciless murder of three individuals in that place, confessed by Hui, eliminates any desire for celebration. This evidence, which the experts seized, presents a macabre testimony of exterminated lives and the current loss of bodies, leaving no chance for their return to the desolate arms of their families.

Back to reality. The abrasive sound of a car horn jolts him. His eyes flicker toward the arriving vehicle. When the door opens and Chong enters, he notes München has taken command and, saying nothing, they decide together: the way forward leads back to Shanghai.

Kung Wu, isolated in the tranquility of his home, stares at the television. He shows no display of emotion and is just absorbing the news. His wife is out with friends, and his adult children no longer bother him with their nocturnal adventures and thoughts. The 'house help,' silent and efficient, hands him a glass filled to the brim with whiskey, which he drains in a gulp. The ringing of his cellphone alerts the silent environment, and without a flicker of emotion, he responds, absorbing the information. A pad on the sofa side table receives his scribble: an address, followed by the words 7 *p.m. Have Dinner.*

Guowei enters the room and receives the note. Kung's voice is firm. "Check where that address is; we need to be there at 7 p.m." Guowei, with a submissive nod, takes the paper. Kung's fingers turn off the television. He appears calm, but an undercurrent of concern furrows his brow. After climbing the stairs toward the master suite, he takes a shower.

After an hour dedicated to preparation, Kung descends into the living room, summoning the hired help in a voice that carries a layer of unspoken weight. "Inform my wife that I am not sure about my return time." Bowing, the woman shows an embodiment of respect, as Kung exits through the garage. Guowei, with the door ajar, stands ready while Kung gets into the car, each lost in their thoughts as the vehicle comes to life on the bright streets of Shanghai. "Do you know where this hotel is?" Kung Wu's voice suggests a mix of anxiety and determination.

Guowei, furrowing his eyebrows, replies, "Yes, I know. It's at 'the mouth of the trash.' Are you sure you want to go there?" Kung Wu takes a deep breath before exhaling a single thoughtful response: "I need to." The oppressive silence that envelops the car's interior eats away at Guowei. While driving, Guowei sees his boss's figure in the rear-view mirror and realizes that he is watching the winding streets of Shanghai with concern.

Upon arriving at their destination, they stop in front, remaining seated in the car. Two men, dressed in suits, leave the hotel. Guowei rolls down the window, and one of them addresses the boss in a formal but demanding tone.

"Boss Kung, please accompany us." Getting out of the car, the boss waves to his security guard. The other man directs Guowei to a parking space at the back of the hotel.

Inside, they escort Kung to a private room. Several tables are empty, with chairs placed on top. However, six men occupy a table arranged in the centre of the room. All are expecting his arrival. When Kung approaches, they stand, extending reserved greetings. The Triad command in Shanghai is meeting there for deliberations.

Recognizing each man, and with a respectful bow, Kung's eyes fleetingly meet those of his long-time friend, whose smile, although moderate, offers a fragment of familiarity amid all the formality on display.

As he sits down, a young waitress who moves around the room in a practised choreography serves dinner. To Kung Wu's latent surprise, the dialogue taking place at the table deviates from the immediate turbulence engulfing the city. No reference to television news has found its way into the conversation, and neither the names Wang nor Hui interrupt the lively conversation between the men. Instead, the words revolve around family stories, memories of children, wives' trips, and social gatherings between friends—a somewhat surreal oasis amid the storm raging beyond the confines of the room.

Kung Wu, although surprised, observing everything, joins the unexpected behaviour of the assembly. He reflects, *When in Rome, act like the Romans,* and partakes of the meal before him.

After dinner is complete, the Big Boss makes a subtle gesture with his hands, prompting everyone to stand up and walk toward an organized area in the right corner of the room. Seven chairs surrounding an intimate space await them, each accompanied by a side table with an ashtray, a glass, and a bottle of whiskey. While the chiefs settle into their seats, the waitresses return to the room, distributing and lighting cigars. The men, adopting a casual demeanour that masks the seriousness of the meeting, sip their whiskey and smoke cigars, chatting. Their conversations are light-hearted, without probing questions or direct addresses to Kung Wu, who, amid his indifferent surroundings, feels a growing discomfort taking over.

After the young women leave the room, there is a pause, and one boss asks Kung a direct question, breaking the careful veneer of the casual conversation that surrounded them. "What do you think of a new generation taking care of Tong?"

Kung Wu, mid-sip, chokes on his whiskey, surprised by the abrupt change in dialogue he was hearing. His mind, agile despite the gravity of the situation, plans a response.

"The new generation is the fruit of the old. The new generation cannot manage what the old generation has built without their instruction and wisdom. However, when the old generation guides and makes the new generation aware, their potential becomes limitless."

A round of applause reverberates through the room, with some bosses nodding in approval and raising their glasses in a resounding toast to Kung's words. Then, from the middle of the semicircle, the oldest one, with a sober attitude and penetrating gaze, asks another question.

"Who would you appoint to command the Tong today?"

Kung Wu, looking at him, feels an undercurrent of conspiracy against him. He responds with an outward calm that belies thoughts that his life could be at stake at this very moment. A subtle wave of tension permeates the room as Kung Wu analyzes the minefield of the conversation, uttering with a tone of respectful humility: "Excuse my ignorance, but I wouldn't dare presume to know whom to nominate. The Triad chiefs in Shanghai have the unparalleled acumen to orchestrate any transition that may occur."

Even when Kung Wu cedes the responsibility of the future appointment to the hands of the Triad, his inner resolve brings no glimmer of hope for what he feels is to come. His longtime ally, whose gaze is now fixed on him, declares, "Wang and Hui are relics of the past. Now, a new chapter is about to be written in the Tong."

"I agree," Kung Wu responds, pausing before continuing, "and I would very much like the other three Tong chiefs to be present here." The Tong's unwavering loyalty to the proposal displays Kung Wu's character among those who run all the organizations in Shanghai.

As his words fade into the silence of the room, the door through which the waitresses had exited moments before opens. To Kung Wu's surprise, the other three bosses he had just mentioned, Huan Zhang, Changpu, and Guozhi, enter the room, their arms wrapped around the young waitresses and their hands holding glasses full of whiskey.

A visible wave of surprise hardens Kung Wu's stance. He looks at them with care and gets up from the chair. The dread in his mind grows, anticipating the machinations that may unfold in this clandestine meeting.

A trio of chairs, added to the narrow circle, provide seats for the arriving chiefs while the young women leave. In a room now filled with anticipation and wary glances, the top boss of the Triad in Shanghai stands up, attracting the collective attention of everyone present.

He speaks. "The affairs of Wang and Hui have reached their resolution. Ahead of us lie new times, new ventures, and new businesses. Our hands remain unsullied by involvement in this matter, but the future of the Tong will be a matter for the four of you to decide. However, I will offer a name to command the new era of the Tong. I recommend Kung Wu."

Kung Wu's eyes, once stoic and cautious, now shine. Dry saliva runs down his throat, betraying a storm of emotions that shake his experienced exterior. After almost fifty years intertwined in the Tong organization, he did not expect this moment in his life, a commitment he never dared to imagine.

Huan Zhang, Changpu, and Guozhi exchange scared, brief, uneasy glances, unexpressed feelings coming to the surface. In a synchronized movement, they rise from their chairs and bow to everyone present, their bodies forming an arc of tacit acceptance and respect for the new head of the Tong, Kung Wu.

The silence that follows is dense, punctuated only by the faintest breaths and the restrained creaking of the leather of the chair Kung Wu is sitting on. His gaze, though fearful, transforms, fusing apprehension with a rekindled flame of a dormant dream and a hint of the allure of power.

* * *

Detective Chong, his shoulders hunched from the weight of the day, enters his office, his gaze drawn to the clock on the wall that shows 7:00 p.m. already. The secretary's empty desk catches his eye. There is a sheet of paper, the message scrawled in large, hasty letters reading: *Detective, call Liwei at intel.*

He sinks into the old armchair, his muscles aching with a fatigue that has seeped into his bones. He dials the number and Liwei responds, informing Chong that Rachel gave them a cellphone and now intel will operate to capture Yazuo. He listens, offering tacit agreement to the detailed action before ending the call. He sits there for a moment, lost in the spiral of reflections provoked by Liwei's words.

Duty, persistent and unyielding, keeps fatigue at bay, propelling him forward without thought of rest or sustenance yet. He takes out his cellphone and calls a familiar number. When he hears Rachel's voice, he detects a tone of surprise concealed by professional cordiality.

Chong cuts through all formalities. "We need to talk. Send me your address. I'm on my way."

His voice contains a tone of stern determination, an effort against tired muscles and attracting paused reflection, a testament to the tireless quest to get everything in order. Despite the air of urgency in his statement to Rachel, he proceeds with deliberate actions afterward, preparing himself for the unexpected continuation of the trajectory's end.

Each step he takes across the room echoes with the weight he feels. He opens the refrigerator and, with unsteady hands that cause drops of condensation to fall everywhere, takes out a bottle of water. He either doesn't notice or doesn't care. As he rummages through the file cabinet, he comes across a pair of folded jeans and a clean shirt. Without hesitation, he changes right there.

Donning his jacket, he moves down the hallway toward the building's parking lot. The tangible vibration of his cellphone catches his attention. He looks at the screen, reading the address Rachel has sent. In the car, he enters the data into the GPS, allowing it to guide him to his destination.

As he drives, his fingers flex against the steering wheel, a distracted action brought on by fatigue. His body, devoid of its usual vigour, protests against his every movement. He realizes he needs a shower to wash away the day, a healthy meal to fill the void in his stomach, and sleep to calm the storm in his mind.

Parking the unmarked vehicle in front of the building, he stops for a moment, his eyes finding his own reflection in the rear-view mirror. His face shows many signs of tiredness. His voice, just above a whisper but charged with real urgency, murmurs, "What am I going to do? I need to finish this."

At the building, the doorman greets him and directs him to the elevator, letting him know that Ms. Rachel is waiting for him.

At the apartment door, she greets him and he enters. "Do you want a beer or water?" asks Rachel.

"Nothing, thank you."

Tyler approaches him. "Tired?"

"You can't imagine."

Tyler slaps the detective on the back and returns to the couch. "I know how that feels."

David gets up from his chair and looks at him in total despair, wanting an answer.

Detective Chong explains himself and thanks them all for having him over tonight.

Rachel points to an armchair, and he settles down.

"I've just arrived from Jiangsu. I don't even know how to tell you, but I came here to have an honest conversation, and you deserve to know everything that's happened."

Everyone sits down and listens to him narrate what has transpired in the last two days.

After thirty minutes, the detective gets up from his chair and walks toward the door.

Rachel, with tears streaming down her face, opens the door to the apartment. "Thank you for coming here to tell us the news."

"It's going to be okay. The crucial thing is that it passes," he says in an attempt to comfort her.

"I know. I've been there. It's difficult."

Before leaving the apartment, the detective looks toward the couch and sees Tyler hugging a crying David. Seeing them in a vulnerable moment where they've lost hope, he tells Rachel, "As soon as I have more information, I'll call you. I'll have to see you later this week."

"I'll be waiting," Rachel says and closes the door.

Deep in thought, Detective Chong enters the elevator, reconciling himself with the emotional turmoil he has just left behind. He whispers to himself, "Michael, you're lucky. I'm not sure there's anyone who would cry for me like that."

Leaving the building, he waves to the doorman, stepping into the emptiness of the night outside.

45

Chance Can Be a Great Friend and an Enemy

In the modern urban area of Shanghai, a taxi stops in front of the steps of Jing'an Temple. Rachel and Tyler get out of the car, and soon after, Detective Chong arrives and parks his car in a space reserved for guests' vehicles inside the monastery grounds. He crosses the immense square in front of the temple and greets them with a bow. The partners do the same.

"How are you doing?" the detective asks them, noting that Rachel has indeed lost weight.

"Accepting and living life in the best way I can." Her voice shows sadness.

"Where's David?" Chong asks in English.

Tyler replies with a friendly smile, "At the temple. He came early in the morning."

At that moment, a black Bentley Mulsanne stops in front of them. The driver gets out and opens the back door. A small, elegant lady, dressed in black with a short veil, descends and walks toward the more-than-a-hundred-years-old staircase. As she passes Detective Chong, she bows her head in greeting, and he does the same. The driver, after leaving the vehicle in the reserved area, runs to her and helps her climb the stairs.

"The wake is empty!" says Rachel, looking around and then looking at her wristwatch, checking the time, which says 8:00 a.m.

"This lady is Michael's mother. I don't even know why she's here," said the detective. Chong explains that there will be no ceremony, and they will remember his name on a plaque placed with the families who helped the temple.

"We came today because David recommended it. He explained to us that the ceremony took place over seven days at Michael's residence with only family members. Different from our culture," she says.

"David is correct. That's our tradition. I'm upset because he couldn't go to the ceremony at the residence," the detective says, exposing what he thinks.

"You're right. David suffered in silence, thinking that someone would invite him. He arrived here early today after finding out that the family would hold this ceremony. In the end, his ceremony was within his heart," Rachel tells the detective without discretion.

"How is he facing all that's happened? It's been nine days."

Tyler offers a reply. "Chong, it wasn't easy after you broke the news to us. It was three days of desperation with sleeping pills and tranquilizers. He didn't go to the scheduled physical therapy, and there were days when he didn't take the antibiotics. Sometimes I thought he just wanted to die."

Chong, upset, acknowledges Tyler's words, nodding in understanding.

"Last Sunday, when you told Rachel that the DNA tests came back positive, she and I didn't know how to tell him. You confirmed all the information you reported and presented to us. He was in his room that day when we received your confirmation. Upon hearing Rachel's words, David looked at us with no reaction. He just turned his back and went to the bathroom. We heard him turn on the shower. We're certain he cried, but when he got out of the shower, he was another man. What he needed was confirmation, and that's what you gave him."

"He's better now?" asks Chong.

"Another man. I will not say he's back one hundred percent—that's impossible—but I think the worst is over," Tyler says, completing his explanation.

Together, they talk and climb the steps to the temple.

The detective asks if they handed over the keys to the apartment.

Rachel explains they returned them to the real estate office yesterday and went back to the hotel. They paid a small termination fee and received the advance payment for the remaining months. They donated everything they purchased to the real estate agency and received a discount on the fee.

"What about you, Tyler? I imagine it wasn't a dream vacation," Chong asks.

"It's okay, no problems. I'll come back another time and bother you more," Tyler replies, smiling at the detective.

When they reach the top of the stairs, they realize the temple is empty. Some monks clean the fallen leaves from the trees that have blown through the door, others sit on the ground praying, and some talk among themselves, getting ready to leave. The three continue their conversation outside the sanctuary.

"David told me there are very few people Michael knew here in town. His social circle was all within the hotel staff. I believe that's why there are no people visiting this ceremony," Rachel, sad and upset, evaluates.

"It's a shame that your story here in Shanghai ended like this. You were only going to stay for a week and completed twenty-five days. I have an idea… why not extend it for a month? Things never go as fast as we would like them to go. We could walk around and relax without stress."

"We need to go back, and you're invited to visit us in London. I guarantee you'll have unforgettable days." Tyler smiles.

The DRT partners and the detective see several monks praying and entering the temple, but they can't see David.

"When are you leaving?" Chong asks.

"Tomorrow night," Rachel replies, looking him in the eye.

"I'll take you to the airport. I'll call tomorrow at lunchtime, and we'll meet," Chong decides.

"You don't have to."

"I want to."

"Look, David!" she says, pointing, seeing him talking to Michael's mother inside the temple.

"Let's take a break before we jump in," Tyler suggests.

"Detective, do you know anything about the intel operation that was tasked to arrest Yazuo?" she asks.

"I wouldn't tell you, but since you asked, it's better you find out from me."

The day is beautiful, with a scorching sun, causing everyone to look for the shade of the trees. The partners and the detective settle on one of the cement benches.

Tyler jumps up and shouts, "I burned my ass!"

Rachel puts her hand to her mouth and starts laughing.

Embarrassed, Tyler says, "Sorry. It came out. I had no intention."

The detective ignores the rivalry and continues talking. "They operated two days ago with no success. They planned everything… Yazuo was supposed to arrive on a jet here at Shanghai airport, but he didn't show. Authorities arrested the pilot and another man as they found drugs on the plane."

"Not a total loss," she says.

"Seems he fled Tokyo because the police there received a notification about the arrest of the pilot and his partner, as well as the seizure of drugs, and when they went to apprehend him, he was gone. According to the detainees, Yazuo asked to transport the merchandise. Now Interpol is searching for him for drug trafficking. They'll soon apprehend him."

She contemplates this news but says nothing.

"Is there any danger to Rachel?" asks Tyler, a hint of worry in his voice.

"I can't say yes or no. We have to stay alert."

She nods her head, disappointment on her face. She doesn't like it and it shows.

"Don't worry, they're going to arrest him," the detective says.

David comes out of the temple and sees them sitting on the bench. He walks up to them, smiling, and when he gets close to the detective, offers his greetings. "Thank you for everything. Without you, we would still walk in darkness. You were exemplary."

"This was a team effort. All police officers dedicated themselves day and night to this investigation. You can't imagine how happy we were that we didn't have to use the task force," says Detective Chong with a laugh.

David, half-smiling, then explains, "I spoke to Boss Bo yesterday and apologized. The superintendent said he understood my desperation."

"Well, you've got your lives back and mine has more work. I have to make two enquiries today for a new investigation, and tomorrow I'll take you to the airport." Chong bows in respect and walks toward the steps. His cellphone rings, and of course he answers.

In a state of agitation, David shares with his partners that Michael's mother has invited him to the family residence at noon that day.

"Did you accept?" Rachel smiles.

Detective Chong's voice cuts across the sky toward them. "I'll call tomorrow," he reiterates to the three friends. They look at him in surprise as he descends the stairs, almost skipping every second step.

The three of them wave goodbye.

David returns to his partners and replies, "Yes, of course I will."

"I agree. It doesn't matter what happened in the past. You were an important part of Michael's life, and he was important in yours. She can't erase that. Maybe that's the thing she wants to talk about with you," Tyler suggests to his partner.

"Shall we go in?" invites David.

The three walk together and enter the ancient temple. They find themselves enveloped in an aura of timeless beauty and historical splendour. The delicate aroma of sandalwood incense wafts through the air, creating a feeling of tranquility and reverence. Sunlight filters through the colourful stained-glass windows, casting vibrant patterns onto the polished white marble floors. The walls are adorned with intricate golden dragons. The ceiling has painted frescoes depicting ancient legends in rich and deep tones of red, gold, and jade. A serene and majestic image of the Buddha stands at the centre of it all, radiating a sense of peace and enlightenment for all who behold it. Then the three partners together perform ceremonies in memory of Michael.

As they leave and return to the car, David says he's hungry, as always.

Rachel agrees and states that she will accept any place with an excellent breakfast.

"We're going to the hotel. The breakfast service goes until 11 a.m. and it's not 10 a.m." David starts the car and drives toward the hotel.

Tyler observes his partner, noticing that he is more talkative and healthier in his attitudes. Happily, he hugs him, even though David is driving. "We will always be together, brother."

At the hotel, after eating breakfast, the partners head up to David's room to discuss their plans.

David informs his partners, "I'm going to return the car tomorrow and I've already told the front desk to close the bill early."

Rachel and Tyler can't hear him because they're focused on their cellphones.

With his suitcase on the table, he arranges it for the third time, complaining that he has no place to store his things. "Rachel, do you have room in one of your bags?"

"Nope. There's no room. My three suitcases are full."

"What did you buy that crammed three suitcases full?"

She doesn't answer and laughs at something she is looking at on her cellphone.

David keeps trying to close his bag.

"What else did Boss Bo tell you?" Tyler asks, without looking away from his phone.

He stops fighting with the suitcase and looks at Tyler, who is lying on the bed fixated on something on his phone. He also glances at Rachel, leaning against her pillow, doing the same.

"Yesterday, he didn't go into details. He explained that Wang died in the hospital and Hui was sent to the prison hospital. I didn't push him further because I believe our scene in this play is over. He was polite, showed that he understood my desperation for the investigation, and accepted my apology. Oh, he also said that he will soon go on vacation to Washington. Then, if he can, he'll visit us in London."

"In the end, everything became clear," Rachel says, interrupting the conversation to look at her phone.

"Looks like he knows someone there. He emphasized the city of Washington and didn't explain whether it was for tourism or something else." David returns his gaze to the still-open suitcase.

"Hmm… it must be work," Rachel murmurs, glancing at her phone again.

"Can someone help me pack this suitcase?" he asks, looking at the two of them on the bed, but no one answers. They just ignore him. "Oh, it's impossible to talk to you two."

"Are you leaving now?" Rachel looks at David as he grabs the car keys and his wallet.

He takes a deep breath and looks at her. "Do you want to come with me?"

"Yes, but wouldn't that be rude? She didn't invite me," she replies, looking at the jeans and boots she's wearing.

"I don't want to go alone, okay? Let's go."

"Okay, but I'm not changing my clothes."

With a childlike smile on his face, David opens the bedroom door.

While Tyler is playing, Rachel informs him they won't be long. He blows her a kiss.

David and Rachel go down to the hotel lobby. Rachel goes to the front desk and asks if there is anything under her name. The receptionist informs her that there is not. She thanks him and walks to the hotel's exit.

David waits for her next to the car, and when he sees Rachel, he waves. She runs up and hugs him, saying, "No flowers."

The two laugh together and get into the vehicle.

He drives toward the avenue.

"Do you know where the address is?"

"Yes, I know. It's a fancy neighbourhood here in Shanghai. It's on the outskirts. Only rich people live there." David pays attention to the GPS along the way.

"I didn't know Michael was so rich," she admits, her voice full of surprise.

"Not him. His mother is rich. She gained many assets after her husband's death," he explains, as if it means nothing.

After thirty minutes of driving, they arrive at a luxurious condominium. As they get closer, David slows down, guiding the car through the alleys covered in leaves and flowers that wind past the elegant residences. Each house they pass looks more beautiful than the last, all built in the timeless Tudor style. Some of them resemble English mansions, each possessing its own unique qualities of refinement.

The sloping roofs adorned with several chimneys, and windows with Gothic arches and diamond-shaped panels draw attention. Red bricks adorn most of these exquisite homes, fitting into a special frame made of thin boards or stones that fill the spaces. They seem to have taken the utmost care to preserve the serene atmosphere of this place and maintain its timeless beauty.

"This place is beautiful." Rachel's voice is full of wonder as she looks around.

David nods and begins a meticulous search of the residences.

"Have you been here before?" Rachel asks.

"No. Michael describes this place. He liked it here, especially in the area dedicated to environmental protection. Behind these houses is a government-protected ecological park. It's a well-maintained area," David responds as he guides his car toward a house, stopping and facing the door.

As the two exit the vehicle, a man approaches and inquires about their purpose.

Rachel recognizes him as the driver who took Michael's mother to the Buddhist temple.

David explains he was called for a visit, and, at that moment, the front door of the residence opens. A woman in a white uniform addresses the man, saying, "Leave it, he's a guest."

Bowing, the man retreats to the back of the house.

Leading David and Rachel inside, the woman takes them to a reception room.

Ms. Mei's secretary introduces herself and invites them to make themselves comfortable, assuring that the owner will soon be with them.

David and Rachel settle into the soft blue armchairs, reminiscent of the Louis XV style. They take in their surroundings and notice the watercolour paintings adorning the walls, which appear to be of significant age. They note a photograph of Michael embracing his mother, next to a beautiful vase of wildflowers on a small table near an open window. A gentle breeze causes the white voile curtain to sway.

David fixes his gaze on the photograph as the memories it evokes awaken his emotions.

Michael's mother enters the room, looking surprised to see the two guests sitting there. "David, did you bring guests?" she asks, her tone carrying a hint of curiosity.

Rachel, feeling uncomfortable with the situation, gets up from her chair, trying to correct her embarrassment. "I'm leaving," she says. "I only accompanied him here."

David intervenes, his posture hunched, and speaks in response to Mrs. Mei's unexpected arrival. "I'm sorry, I invited her, and I didn't think it would be a bother," he explains.

Michael's mother acknowledges David's response and tries to defuse the situation. Her look is cold toward Rachel. "No, it's not a nuisance. David! What I have to discuss with you is private." She points at Rachel. "You can stay here, and it won't be a problem. If you like books, we have an extensive library across the room."

Grateful for the sort-of kind response and still feeling a pang of embarrassment at having accompanied her partner, Rachel bows.

At that moment, Michael's mother's assistant enters the room carrying a tray with a jug of water and a kettle of tea, accompanied by two cups.

David turns to Rachel and suggests, "Make yourself comfortable. I'll go outside for a chat."

Feeling a little embarrassed about the situation, Rachel responds in a low voice, "It's okay."

When David and Ms. Mei leave the room, Rachel takes a moment to quench her thirst, drinking water from a glass. She looks at her wristwatch and realizes that it's now 12:20 p.m. Grabbing her phone from the small bag tucked away in the chair, she texts Tyler.

I knew I shouldn't have come. I'll be back soon. After finishing the message, she turns off her cellphone and puts it back inside her bag.

Standing up, Rachel looks out the window, where the radiant day bathes the entire space behind the house. She watches David and Ms. Mei walk along the stone path. She admires the well-arranged geometric patterns formed by the play of stones of various sizes and different colours in a sober style.

With her curiosity aroused, Rachel decides to explore the books and opens the door that leads to the hallway, heading toward the one shown by the owner. Upon entering the adjacent room, the grandeur of the library displayed on the shelves surprises her. In the centre of the room, she sees a comfortable green two-seater sofa accompanied by a small table. The room has no windows, just a French door that gives access to the outside of the house.

Intrigued, Rachel approaches the door and peers through the glass, revealing a beautiful garden adorned with herbs and English lavender. Upon leaving, the colourful tulips that snake across the stone floor captivate Rachel. Large trees provide cover in the back of the yard, the same area where David and Ms. Mei had ventured earlier.

As she explores the space a little further away, she sees David walking next to the owner and hears Michael's mother's voice mentioning her rose garden on the other side. A light drizzle falls, and Rachel becomes absorbed in the distant voices. She ventures deeper into the reserve, past several bushes of varying sizes, and sees the two figures ahead, facing each other, engaged in what appears to be a heated argument.

Curiosity wins, and she approaches, hiding among the trees and small bushes. The rain intensifies a little, but it is a passing cloud as the sky remains blue, with a partial sun trying to appear. Rachel strains to listen to the conversation.

"You are to blame for his death. Never forget that we had your back." Ms. Mei's voice carries a harsh tone, offending David.

"Don't tell me this, with you trying to act like a saint, because you didn't help me at all. You had a debt with Alex and paid it off. I was just a courier for Alex and you. I gave you the pills, and that was it. That was all," David retorts in an aggressive tone.

Rachel overhears the conversation but remains confused as to what the argument is about. Hiding behind a tree, she can't see them and crouches near a bush, continuing to listen to their conversation.

"I lost my son because of that whore you brought into my house. I should have killed her along with that Ronaldo. Then none of this would have happened, and Michael wouldn't have died." Ms. Mei's words brim with venomous hatred.

"We leave tomorrow," David replies.

Shocked by what she heard, Rachel, after so long looking for answers, understands that it wasn't just Wang who was involved in Ronaldo's death. Fear courses through her, and her breathing quickens. She doesn't know how to proceed, uncomfortable in the crouched position she is in. A wave of nausea takes over her, making her cover her mouth with both hands and, in an unexpected movement, she rustles the branches of the bush.

David hears the noise and runs toward her, discovering Rachel.

She lifts her head and sees her partner in front of her. The rain stops. He pulls her by the arm, and she kicks him. The two fight, and Michael's mother, with a log in her hand, appears from behind and hits Rachel on the head.

Unconscious, Rachel falls onto logs and rocks, a trickle of blood running through her hair.

David checks to see if she is alive, picks her up, and carries her in his arms. He looks at Ms. Mei, who is cleaning her hands. "What are we going to do?"

"We're going to kill her and make her body disappear," she responds as she walks toward the residence.

David continues carrying his partner into the house.

It's much later when Rachel wakes up and realizes that someone has tied her to a chair. The headache she feels is nauseating. Trying to see in the darkness, she blinks twice. Near the top of the wall is a small window that doesn't provide enough light into the space. A moon hides behind the clouds, trying to release its shine. She assesses her location and concludes she's in a basement. Trying to free herself from the ropes that restrain her, the chair's feet make noise on the cement floor. The tight ropes do not allow her to move, and her body aches. Rachel, aware of what she heard, remembers David's words to Michael's mother and tries to calm down.

She hears a door open in front of her, reflecting a light, but the darkness continues to block her vision. Alert, she hears someone approaching and recognizes David.

He looks at her, takes the tape off her mouth, and asks, "Why? Why didn't you stay in the room?"

With a weak voice, concluding that at that moment she doesn't have much else to say, she asks, "You going to kill me?"

David turns his back to her, and she continues.

"How are you going to explain my disappearance? Let me live, no one will ever know this story," Rachel begs her partner in a desperate, murmuring voice.

He looks at her again, noticing that her head is on her chest and blood has soaked through her hair. He doesn't respond.

Rachel asks, crying, "Why did you kill Ronaldo?"

"I was just the courier; I didn't kill him."

Tears stream down her face, and she lifts her head, looking at him.

David returns her gaze with a stern expression and a coldness that she has only seen during operations.

"Out of consideration for our years of friendship, and before you go, I'll tell you. Remember Operation Yakuza? The man you arrested in the Yakuza operation was Alex's brother's son. When they deported him to Japan, someone showed no forgiveness and murdered him. Only with this can you get an idea of what's coming."

Rachel nods and looks around at the darkness. She tries to compose herself and pretends to pay attention to what David explains but, in reality, she is looking for a way out of this situation.

"I had access to the sleeping pills that Ronaldo took when he was in Washington, when he stayed at my house. Do you remember? This was a week before you went on vacation to Shanghai. He lost the box with the medicine; that's what he thought. After that, the two of you travelled to Shanghai, and since everything was in order for Mr. Chan to hand over the flash drive to him... it was unexpected to know that you were the one who took it."

Rachel shifts in her chair, and David approaches, checking the ropes that hold her. He moves away from her and continues his story. "Michael's mother was the manager of that hotel and owed Alex a debt. Her husband was Japanese, also a courier for the Firm, but he lost a package that ended up in the hands of the Chinese government. Mr. Chan should have received and delivered the documents, shipping them in a container to the United States."

He stops talking and returns to the chair with Rachel, checking that the ropes are tight around her body.

Rachel lets out a tired groan, prompting David to continue his disturbing narrative.

"The Chinese government had been monitoring Chan since 2010, three years before you met him. The risks of placing the new packaging in one of these containers became dangerous. Thus, Alex convinced Ronaldo to take the 'documents' under the pretext of a routine task, without knowing that they would end up in his possession. The urgency was to secure these documents before the government approached Mr. Chan. Then his unexpected trip arrived on the scene, like a bolt from the blue. It was the perfect scenario. Ronaldo would take the flash drive and succumb to a fatal overdose of pills. Mr. Chan, who was under government surveillance, was also supposed to be killed. Two birds with one stone. However, we didn't know that you would be the one taking the flash drive."

"I can't believe you were part of this conspiracy," Rachel murmurs, her voice shaking.

David, showing no regret, continues explaining: "Yes, I have my reasons. I stole his medicine and gave it to Alex. We knew he had a nighttime swimming routine, making it simple to slip the pills into the whiskey he always ordered. We have been planning this operation for a long time. Wang, the idiot, took steps to guarantee Ronaldo's death. Alex orchestrated this with Tong. If Michael's mother's operation failed, the Yakuza would succeed in Wang's hands. Things may have taken a different turn than expected, but in the end, everything fell into place. Chan also met his fate, although that may be none of your business."

Rachel, with feigned anguish, claims that she isn't feeling well and begs to use the bathroom.

David observes her. He lifts her head by her blood-soaked hair and checks her moaning appearance. Knowing how she acts; he unties her and walks away from her. Rachel tries to get up from the chair. An overwhelming wave of dizziness takes over her, causing her to lose her balance and fall onto the cement. Despite witnessing her struggle, David pays no attention to her plight, ignoring her as he turns toward the door.

In the total darkness of the room, kneeling, her eyes adjust, and she discerns the shape of his body and the tones of the clothes he wears. In an instant, a wave of memories floods Rachel's mind: a shared history, friendship, love, and tender moments, all now meaningless. Without thinking twice, feeling the burning blood running down her face, she focuses on his back and jumps up just as he moves away from her. With a precise jump and a strength that surprizes even her, she buries the knife from her boot in the vulnerable spot on the back of his neck. He falls to the ground, dead, with his brain disconnected from his spine.

Dizzy with adrenaline and shock, Rachel clings to the wall for support, her fingers shaking as she wipes away the blood running from her head and nose. Her eyes, now more accustomed to the shadows, find the exit, which she opens with the utmost care, revealing a steep staircase to an upper floor. Her gaze lands on another closed door at the top. She steps over David's lifeless body, which is blocking access to the basement, and pushes him inside with her foot, as if kicking a piece of trash out of the way. After closing the door, Rachel climbs up.

She reaches the top and discovers what appears to be a kitchen. The night peers through the windows. Rachel squints in the dim light, trying to see better, and opens the first drawer she finds. She locates knives and selects one of the largest with a resolute attitude.

Voices coming from the other end of a hallway put her senses on predator alert. She approaches one of the kitchen doors and identifies the voice as Michael's mother, giving orders to someone in Mandarin. She hears her say the name "Andrew," and he responds with the words, "Yes, the car is ready." Stunned, she sees the two walking in her direction.

Made of marble, the island in the centre of the kitchen is wide and tall. Rachel runs and hides behind it, crouching down. The man, upon entering, turns on the light, and Ms. Mei orders him to turn it off, explaining that the light would wake up the house staff. Remembering that their room was in an area behind the kitchen, he turns off the light and opens the cellar door. Michael's mother wraps her arm around him and leans on him, asking him to help her down the stairs.

"The basement door is closed," he says, looking down.

"David is down there with that bitch."

The man places Ms. Mei in front of him, and he holds her arm with one hand while leaning on the railing with the other. They begin the descent down the stairs.

Still hiding behind the island, Rachel sees the opportunity, gets up, and sticks the huge knife in the man's back. He lurches forward, falling on Michael's mother and sending them both rolling headfirst down the stairs.

She runs into the living room and grabs her bag, which is still in the same place where she left it. Rachel opens it, takes out her cellphone, and sees that the battery is low. The first number that appears is that of Chief Bo, who answers. In overwhelming agony, she tells him everything that happened.

The superintendent's voice, firm but reassuring, tells her to remain calm. He guarantees that a police car will arrive within minutes to help her. With a quick goodbye, he hangs up the phone, and his expression changes. The words she spoke and the chilling account of David's revelation about Mr. Chan's death weigh heavily on his mind.

Perplexed by this turn of events, Boss Bo walks to the desk in his home office. Reaching into a drawer beneath a pile of folders, he retrieves a pistol and tucks it into his waistband. Reflecting on the past, he sits in his armchair.

He remembers the day Mr. Chan walked down the stairs of the Konsako building's garage. He followed and greeted him, saying, "Hi, Chan," in a friendly manner. "What are you doing here? Shall we have some lunch?"

Mr. Chan accepted the offer and climbed into his friend's car, certain they would return later so he could retrieve his own vehicle. They chatted about the weather as Bo pulled the car out of the garage and headed to the avenue. Mr. Chan, still holding a package, revealed his urgent need to mail it to the container factory.

Bo agreed, taking him to the nearest post office to send the shipment. While waiting in the car for his friend to return, Bo shook up a bottle of water and placed it next to the passenger seat. When Mr. Chan finished at the post office and returned to his car, wiping the sweat from his forehead, Bo presented the bottle of water, which Mr. Chan accepted. It didn't take long for the poison to take effect, and Bo confirmed Mr. Chan's lifeless body in the post office garage.

Driving toward the port, Bo arrived at the abandoned container park, which housed countless idle containers awaiting recycling. Making sure no one was watching, he entered through the gate and double-checked the area to confirm there were no security cameras. He secured the place to abandon the body. Satisfied that there were no witnesses, he deposited Mr. Chan's body inside a non-functional old refrigerated container. Without delay, he returned to the police station to continue his work.

Reflecting on the tumultuous events unfolding before him, Chief Bo's mind returns to the pivotal moment that set all of this in motion. Years ago, he was a mere uniformed police officer, without titles or distinctions. At that time, he received an extraordinary summons from a superior in the intelligence sector. Their mission: investigate Chan for possible espionage. Little did he know that this opportunity was the one he had longed for, a path to an orchestrated destiny.

Nothing in this world happens by chance. The intelligence operation handpicked him because of a hidden connection: his brother worked in the same factory as Chan. Armed with the orders he had, Bo frequented his brother's house in Lianyungang, studying the spy's routine. Their paths crossed several times in the busy city, and, over the course of a year, they shared common places, thanks to Bo's brother. Despite being aware of Bo's dead-end position as an administrative police officer in Shanghai, Chan had genuine affection for him. Shared drunken nights brought tears over lost loves and complaints against inept superiors, and this vulnerability brought them closer together.

Then one day, Alex came to Shanghai. The opportunity arose, and the person responsible for the Firm met Bo. Over the course of a year of meetings, dinners, and joint outings, Alex evolved from a mere contact to a dear friend. His return visits to the city always coincided with shared dinners with Bo and Chan.

During one of these meetings, the head of the Firm broached the subject of Bo's career progression. After years of unwavering dedication, he stated Bo had to climb the career ladder. He offered to leverage his government connections and guaranteed Bo a more prestigious position. Boss Bo accepted without hesitation. In a brief period, he rose from administrative chief to chief of staff to the executive director of the Shanghai superintendent. The intelligence agency did not make any complaints, as such promotions were common and they never had strict expectations regarding espionage investigation. They accepted the promotion. However, the deep-rooted friendship between Bo and Chan endured.

Months passed, and one fateful afternoon, Alex called Boss Bo, catching him off guard with a disconcerting revelation about the dangers of maintaining a friendship with someone who could be a foreign spy on his turf. This would destroy his career, his name, and perhaps worst of all… it would lead him to eternal prison or, even worse, death. Unwavering in his determination, Alex painted a bleak picture, articulating that if Mr. Chan met an untimely death, Bo would rise to the coveted position of Shanghai police superintendent, ridding his homeland of the enigmatic spy and cementing his career in law enforcement.

Bo weighed the gravity of the situation, realizing that it went far beyond his initial expectations. Contemplating the broader implications, he agreed to Alex's proposal, taking on the arduous task alone, involving no one else. It remained a secret known to no one.

Boss Bo's eyes shoot open, his palm damp against his forehead as he takes a deep breath and shakes his head. He looks out the window and observes the dark sky. He grabs his car keys and leaves the house without saying a word to anyone, the weight of his past actions pressing down on him.

Rachel ends her call with Chief Bo and dials Detective Chong's number. When he answers, she speaks in a low voice, almost a whisper, unaware of the potential dangers around her. She recounts the harrowing events, her voice shaking with despair and tears streaming down her face. Detective Chong instructs her to remain hidden and assures her he is nearby, promising to arrive within minutes.

Trying not to make noise, Rachel moves around the house. She leaves through the main door, seeking refuge among the bushes in front of the house. In that position, she can check the police cars entering the scene. She thinks about calling Tyler, but her cellphone's dead battery stops her.

Before long, Detective Chong arrives, and Rachel runs to him, seeking comfort in his embrace. He questions her: "Is there anyone else in the house?"

"I don't know," she replies, her voice shaking with uncertainty.

Chong returns to the car, unlocks the trunk, and takes a revolver from a secure box. "Show me where they are," he instructs, leading the way as Rachel follows behind.

When they reach the kitchen, Chong turns on the lights. The sudden light wakes up an employee who runs toward the kitchen, confronting them.

Detective Chong identifies himself, ordering the perplexed employee to return to the staff house and await other police officers who will pick her up for further interrogation. Stunned and without saying a word, she obeys.

Rachel guides Detective Chong to the basement entrance, her heart pounding for a quick resolution.

Detective Chong walks down the basement stairs, hiding the gun behind his back, tucked into his waistband. Using a small flashlight, he scans the lit space, revealing two individuals huddled together at the bottom of the steps. He approaches, squinting into the darkness. When trying to step over the pair to get to the basement door, the groaning man clings to the detective's leg. With a quick kick to the face, Chong forces the man to let go. He then identifies Michael's mother, her faint moans confirming her survival. He opens the basement door and discovers David's lifeless body, with blood staining his back. Upon closer examination, Chong confirms the man's death.

He calls Rachel, his voice echoing through the basement as he instructs her to call 911 and request an ambulance. Rachel remains silent, leaving him perplexed. In a frantic run, he climbs the stairs. As he approaches the kitchen entrance, he freezes, looking at Boss Bo, who has Rachel in his hands and a gun pointed at her head. Chong freezes, unable to reach the gun holstered at his waist.

"Don't move, Chong. You've already caused me enough trouble," Boss Bo warns.

"We can resolve our differences without involving Rachel," Chong pleads.

"She's more involved than you think. Are they all dead?" Bo asks.

"Yes, they are," confirms Chong.

Bo presses the barrel of the gun against Rachel's head, causing pain. She moans. Weakened but determined, Rachel calculates the ideal judo manoeuvre to disarm Chief Bo, a considerable opponent. Twisting her face, she signals her intentions to the detective, fixing her gaze to the right, and Chong understands her unspoken message. In one quick move, he throws his body back down the stairs toward the basement. In response,

Chief Bo fires a shot at him, causing Rachel to seize the opportunity. With precision, she performs the "Tricksy" Ippon Seoi Nage judo move. Rachel, in a quick movement, holds Boss Bo's arm and kneels, tipping his body over hers, unbalancing him, and in a quick transition she throws his body. Then she knocks the gun out of the dazed chief's hands.

"That took a long time…" comments Detective Chong upon returning to the kitchen.

Rachel, leaning against the kitchen island, hands the gun to the detective, a trickle of blood emerging from her nose once again.

The detective handcuffs Chief Bo, injured in the fall, and calls an ambulance, the police, and München.

When he finishes talking on the phone, he turns his gaze to Rachel, noticing she is lying on the floor.

* * *

Tyler, full of concern, paces the hotel room. It's dawn, and to his growing discomfort, neither Rachel nor David have returned. He dials David's and Rachel's cellphones many times, anxiety increasing with each missed call and message. Distressed, he runs down to the hotel reception, requesting that they contact Detective Chong at the city centre police station. He remembers giving the detective his own cellphone number but realizes he forgot to get Chong's in return.

While talking to the receptionist, a car stops at the hotel entrance, and two police officers enter, asking about him. Tyler identifies himself in English, while the counter attendant translates for the officers in Mandarin. The receptionist tells them that Tyler will accompany them.

Tyler's heart races as he fights the growing sense of dread, fearing the worst has happened. The car speeds up, sirens blaring, intensifying his anxiety. Alone in a foreign country, without any existing friends or familiar faces, he feels lost. The vehicle stops in front of an unknown building. He gets out of the car and follows the officers as they lead him down a hallway.

Passing through a series of open doors, he continues walking, his destination unknown. A distinctive odour permeates the air, making him realize he must be in the morgue. Frightened by the uncertainty of what awaits him, he accompanies the police to a safe room, where a covered body lies on an iron table.

They remove the sheet, and Tyler recognizes David's lifeless form. His body shakes as if he's going to faint. A nurse and a police officer rush to support him. In a panic, with tears streaming down his face, he asks about Rachel in English to the doctor. The doctor tries to offer reassurance in broken English, but Tyler remains inconsolable.

The officers escort him out of the shadowy scene, guiding him into the hallway. Overwhelmed and unsure of what to do next, he turns toward the exit of the building. Then, to his astonishment and immense relief, he sees Rachel entering the front doors of the building, accompanied by Detective Chong. Without hesitation, he runs to her, and the two hug.

Detective Chong, standing at the hospital entrance, exhales in relief, nodding as he watches the emotional reunion unfold.

* * *

After five tiring days of testimonies in the central police building and ongoing investigations, the court releases the partners. They will answer all remaining questions from consulates and embassies later. Shaken, Rachel and Tyler say it's time to go home.

"Thank you for bringing us to the airport," Rachel says, her voice tinged with fatigue, but she manages a small smile aimed at the detective.

"I told you, you were supposed to stay for thirty days, didn't I?" Chong comments, exchanging a smile.

"It may not have been the last five days we thought it would be," Tyler adds with a laugh, addressing the detective, "but it's been quite a ride."

Detective Chong looks at Rachel and tells her some surprising news. "I have a surprise for you two. They arrested Yazuo this morning in Berlin."

Tyler exclaims, excitement lighting up his face, though he notices that Rachel's behaviour is far from enthusiastic. "You assured us that you would arrest him."

"There is more," continues Chong, "we have reopened the investigation into Ronaldo's death."

"That is fantastic news," Rachel murmurs, her voice tired but grateful, as she hugs the detective.

Chong himself is moved by the moment, and the three share a heartfelt embrace, their bodies uniting in a strong bond of camaraderie.

As they make their way through the airport lobby, they look back and discover that the detective has disappeared from sight.

After a while, sitting on the plane, settled in their seats, a comfortable silence envelops Rachel and Tyler. Watching Rachel's closed eyes, Tyler says in a low voice, "Are you okay?"

Her eyes open and she meets his gaze. "Yes, I am. Now let's start again. Are you ready?"

"I'm with you…" Tyler responds. "I've never been one to give up, and together we will make this company the best it can be." His confidence in the future shines through his words and offers a glimpse of the journey the two will have ahead.

Rachel shares news with Tyler, her voice tinged with a mix of relief and curiosity. "Allan responded to us about our message."

Tyler leans in, intrigued. "How did he respond?"

With a calm demeanour, Rachel reports Allan's message. "According to Allan, they cannot investigate the Firm because it is an institution, a proper organization, almost like a government in itself, and run by those at the top. We shouldn't worry because Alex is dead and no longer a threat, but they continued to monitor Rose."

Tyler nods. "It seems like it's for the best. Making trouble with them would only lead to more trouble, like trying to cover up a shit smell with perfume."

A genuine laugh escapes Rachel's lips, and she comments, "Working with you is a joy. You bring a smile to my face every day."

Tyler reclines in his first-class seat, which doubles as a bed. "I think I'll sleep the entire trip."

"Sounds like a plan," Rachel agrees, settling into her seat. With a shared understanding, both prepare to rest, knowing that their future endeavours await them, marked by a renewed sense of purpose and determination.

46

The World Goes Round, and We Dance to the Music

"Did you buy a new Christmas tree?" Rachel complains, her voice tinged with annoyance as she listens to the phone conversation. The secretary opens the door and stops, showing a sheet of paper dangling in her trembling hands. Unperturbed, the boss continues speaking with an unwavering tone.

"I'm busy right now. Here's what we'll do: take it to the office this afternoon, and we'll decorate it together. It's only a week until Christmas." With a quick click, she hangs up and turns her attention to her assistant.

"Ms. Rachel, the driver is waiting in the garage. You're late. It's already 8:30 a.m., and we scheduled the meeting for 9:00."

"Thank you, Amelia," Rachel responds, her gaze fixed on her desk. "Are you leaving early?" she asks, concern softening her tone.

"I have some chores to do. If that's okay, I'd like to leave at three. It's my last chance to tie up loose ends for the year."

"I know you have a test at college today. Don't worry, I know you can do it," Rachel encourages her with a warm smile.

With a nod, the secretary leaves the room, only to return moments later carrying a large open box. "The new cards have arrived. Where should I put them?" she asks, eager to complete her tasks.

"Leave it here on my desk," Rachel instructs, closing her laptop and placing it in her briefcase. Her assistant puts the box in the designated location and, once placed, leaves the room.

Rachel gets up from her chair with calm movements. She takes her bag and jacket from a nearby hanger. She pauses, looking at the package on her desk. Her curiosity gets the better of her, and she pulls the flaps apart, revealing several packages of varying sizes, all with her and Tyler's names on them. She selects one and opens it, revealing the new cards with the company name "RT—International Investigations Ltd."

Contemplating the company's new business cards with a thoughtful expression, her mind wanders. "It's difficult to predict the mind of a human being," she reflects.

She takes out one of the small packages and puts it inside her bag. In a hurry, she heads to the elevator and tells Amelia, at the reception desk, "Call Tyler and tell him I'm on my way."

Amelia, still adjusting to her new role, digs through her address book to find Tyler's cellphone number, as she hadn't memorized it yet.

The elevator doors close, and Rachel takes a moment to adjust her appearance in the mirror. She reaches the garage and steps out of the elevator, the click of her high heels echoing on the cement floor.

The driver, noticing her approach, trying to be discreet, covers his discarded cigarette with his well-shined black shoe. However, the lingering smell of mint hangs in the air.

"Good morning," the driver greets, his smile radiating warmth as he opens the back door of the car.

"Good morning, Hassan. Sorry I'm late," Rachel responds to the driver's smile as she enters the vehicle.

"No problem." Hassan closes the door.

Rachel notices the faint smell of lavender inside the vehicle and admires the radiant and clean interior. She glances at Hassan, who meets her eyes in the rear-view mirror.

He asks if she wants to listen to some music. Rachel declines, saying, "No, thanks. I'm not in the mood today," as she takes her phone out of her purse.

Hassan looks in the mirror again and murmurs, "I'm sorry. You're always late."

She laughs and murmurs, "That's a conversation we've had before."

Her phone rings, and Rachel answers. Before she can speak, an accented voice asks, "Rachel Barnes? How is your Russian? ..."

Acknowledgements

In my almost thirty years as a federal police agent, the challenges and camaraderie experienced have profoundly shaped my career, thanks to the remarkable people who have been by my side. This recognition is dedicated to my colleagues, who have been instrumental in both our successes and our shared difficulties. I express my sincere gratitude and respect for everyone, including those no longer with us, whose sacrifices, bravery, and dedication to justice have left a lasting impact on me. Our bonds, forged in adversity and triumph, go beyond the ordinary, connecting us to a purpose greater than ourselves. Your support, resilience, wisdom, and spirit have been crucial to our collective journey, creating a narrative understood only by those in this unique life of law enforcement. To my brothers and sisters in arms, present and remembered, I offer my deepest thanks for your companionship, guidance, and sacrifice, which have indelibly shaped who I am and our shared legacy.

I also greatly appreciate the assistance of Vilto Reis on the Brazilian Portuguese version and Soraia Pestana for her unwavering support.

— L. McEwen

www.ingramcontent.com/pod-product-compliance
Lightning Source LLC
Jackson TN
JSHW020927181224
75608JS00002B/2/J